Jane Austen's Sanditon

A Village by the Sea

ARTHUR M. AXELRAD

authorHOUSE®

AuthorHouse™
1663 Liberty Drive
Bloomington, IN 47403
www.authorhouse.com
Phone: 1-800-839-8640

This book is a work of fiction. People, places, events, and situations are the product of the author's imagination. Any resemblance to actual persons, living or dead, or historical events, is purely coincidental.

First published by AuthorHouse 6/20/2010

ISBN: 978-1-4520-0180-7 (e)
ISBN: 978-1-4520-0178-4 (sc)
ISBN: 978-1-4520-0179-1 (hc)

Library of Congress Control Number: 2010905619

Printed in the United States of America
Bloomington, Indiana

This book is printed on acid-free paper.

Contents

Introduction and Acknowledgments

Although Jane Austen's final manuscript has never received its due attention, in recent years it has been recognized as worthy of being discussed along with the completed novels. This book is meant to stimulate interest in what a close reading of the work will reveal it to be, Jane Austen's potential masterpiece. Like all such studies, it is a work-in-progress and invites corrections and additional thoughts. I have deliberately created an ambiguity in my title by not italicizing the name of the village by the sea that serves as the backdrop to this story.

I have again used for my cover illustration Hugh Thomson's frontispiece to the edition of *Pride and Prejudice* published in London by George Allen in 1894 (supplied by Chris Viveash) to show that this work is a continuation of *Jane Austen Caught in the Act of Greatness*. This new book is best used in conjunction with my earlier publication, which contains a diplomatic transcription of the *Sanditon* manuscript as well as a detailed analysis of every correction. In turn, *Jane Austen Caught in the Act of Greatness* should be used in conjunction with *Jane Austen: The Manuscript of Sanditon* (a facsimile of the original manuscript, edited by Brian C. Southam).

This work-in-progress would not have been possible without the efforts of everyone listed in my bibliography, with particular thanks to R.W. Chapman, David Gilson, Deirdre Le Faye, Luanne Bethke Redmond, Teran Lee Sacco, Brian C. Southam, and Chris Viveash.

Even more than to anyone else, however, I must express special gratitude to the true author of this story, Mrs. Ashton Dennis.

"But then you know, madam, muslin always turns to some account or other; Miss Morland will get enough out of it for a handkerchief, or a cap, or a cloak.—Muslin can never be said to be wasted. I have heard my sister say so forty times, when she has been extravagant in buying more than she wanted, or careless in cutting it to pieces."

I. A New Novel:
New Cloth from Old

"Susan" > "Catherine" > "Charlotte"

Emboldened by her recent completion of a manuscript with a revised climactic scene—of tenderness unparalleled in any earlier efforts—leading to the reconciliation and subsequent marriage of Miss Anne Elliot and her Captain Frederick Wentworth, in early 1817 Jane Austen set in motion her next major project. Unlike her preceding novels probably created in their entirety at Chawton Cottage—*Mansfield Park*, *Emma*, and *Persuasion* (although Queenie Dorothy Leavis has suggested that the first two of these were based on earlier work)—this effort represented a return to her earlier practice of revising previously written material. *Sense and Sensibility* and *Pride and Prejudice* had been remarkably successful redactions of books originally composed in the late years of the preceding century. This time, however, she was about to attempt a rewrite of a rewrite. It was to be an ambitious project, one that she would be unlikely to engage in if Irene Taylor is correct in conjecturing that "when Austen undertook the last novel, *Sanditon*, she was suffering from Addison's disease and knew she was dying" (428).

We have long known that in 1803 Jane Austen through an intermediary, William Seymour, sold for £10 to Crosby & Co. of London a manuscript (possibly anonymous) entitled "Susan," advertised by Benjamin Crosby in his periodical miscellany, *Flowers of Literature for 1801 & 1802* (1803), as "Susan; a Novel, in 2 vols." but never published (Axelrad, 1993). "A new discovery, previously undocumented, reveals that the *Flowers of Literature* advertisement is not unique and that *Susan* was announced elsewhere, not simply in Crosby and Co.'s own publications. An announcement in *The Dorchester and Sherborne Journal* for 26 August 1803 provides a list of 11 novels published by Crosby and Co., and emphasises the provincial network characterising his business practice. A full transcription of the list is given below:... In the Press—Susan, 2 vols." (Mandal: 519).

And we know that on April 5, 1809, Jane Austen (initially signing her own name—"J. Austen"—but adopting the pseudonym "Mrs. Ashton Dennis" when she re-wrote the palimpsest in ink over the original pencil) wrote to Crosby & Co. asking about the fate of her manuscript (*Letters*: 174–175; Notes 400; Axelrad, 1994; Modert; F-197–F-198; British Library Add. MSS 41253B, folio 12), only to be haughtily informed by Mr. Richard Crosby that he had no plans to publish it but was prepared to return it for the original price of £10 (British Library Add. MSS 41253B, folio 13; facsimile in Axelrad, 1994: 37). We next leap to informed conjecture that in 1816, through the agency of her brother, Henry, Jane Austen regained rights to the manuscript, which she in part reworked. How extensively she rewrote the original material has been vigorously debated, with Brian Southam presenting perhaps the most extreme argument in one direction: "Although nothing has survived to show us the exact nature of the changes made at this time, we can be fairly certain that as far as the style was concerned, the 1816 revision was very thorough indeed" (1976: 3), and William Deresiewicz with equal vigor taking the opposite view: "The critical consensus, however—which in this case I see no reason to question—is that neither in 1803 nor in 1816–1817 was the earlier work ["Susan"] significantly altered" (12). The only indisputable change is the short prefatory note observing that the original, set in an earlier historic period, no longer reflects current society.

ADVERTISEMENT,

BY THE AUTHORESS,

TO

NORTHANGER ABBEY.

THIS little work was finished in the year 1803, and intended for immediate publication. It was disposed of to a bookseller, it was even advertised, and why the business proceeded no farther, the author has never been able to learn. That any bookseller should think it worth while to purchase what he did not think it worth while to publish seems extraordinary. But with this, neither the author nor the public have any other concern than as some observation is necessary upon those parts of the work which thirteen years have made comparatively obsolete. The public are entreated to bear in mind that thirteen years have passed since it was finished, many more since it was begun, and that during that period, places, manners, books, and opinions have undergone considerable changes. (Facsimile: xxiii–xxiv)

For someone who prided herself on creating contemporary stories, this thirteen-year-plus gap strongly argued against publication of the novel in its present state. Despite the investment of £10 to buy back the manuscript rights, some revisions, and the prefatory paragraph (of which the text may be by Jane Austen but not the stated title, *Northanger Abbey*, which she never assigned to the manuscript), there were many good reasons not to pursue this old project. Its being issued posthumously in December 1817—the inappropriate and deliberately misleading title, *Northanger Abbey*, was of course not the author's, being attached to the work when it was published along with *Persuasion* (likewise not the author's title)—did not reflect the author's intention. Writing to her niece Fanny Knight on March 13, 1817 (five days before discontinuing work on the new manuscript eventually published as *Sanditon*), "Miss Catherine is put upon the Shelve for the present, and I do not know that she will ever come out" (*Letters*: 333; Modert: F-433), the author implies that the book once called "Susan" has been renamed after the newly rebaptized eponymous heroine. What is uncertain but attractive enough to be of interest is the argument that the manuscript currently in progress was an updated version of the story recently retrieved from Richard Crosby.

A minor digression: It is generally assumed that Jane Austen wrote this advertisement. For example, James R. Keller asserts, "The late publication [of *Northanger Abbey*] seems to have been anticipated by the author before her death: the initial volume contains an authorial preface in which she apologizes for those elements of the novel that, to the contemporary reader, must seem dated" (131–132). However, in view of how unlikely it is that Jane Austen intended publishing "Susan"/"Catherine" despite buying back the rights, I think it doubtful that she composed this paragraph. Her confiding to her niece that "Miss Catherine" has been put upon a shelf makes clear that the old manuscript is no longer being considered for publication. There is a bizarre illogic in announcing at the outset that the novel is hopelessly outdated—by thirteen years, no less—and yet expecting a potential reader to purchase it. The spurious title, "Northanger Abbey," alone argues against her being the author of the passage. In addition, use of the third-person voice—"the authoress" (as she identifies herself in the famous letter to Mr. Richard Crosby) or "the author"—creates uncertainty that the writer herself is speaking. Even more convincing, as I hope to prove, is her decision to use the new manuscript in place of the older one as more current and a better representation of her fully developed skills as a novelist.

Another compelling argument against Jane Austen's having written this advertisement is that if she is literal about the book's appearing thirteen years after first submission, she was planning to publish the manuscript in 1816, in the same year that she was hard at work on the far more sophisticated novel posthumously appearing as *Persuasion*. Very little time would have been available to rewrite the earlier effort to bring it up to date, and publication of this charming but immature tale of Catherine Morland along with the remarkable story of Anne Elliot seems unlikely. That *Northanger Abbey* and *Persuasion* were published together in December 1817 was no more than a slightly crass way on the part of her literary executors to make some money out of their sister's reputation aside from making her work available to her readers. The books were advertised so as to attract the widest range of readers, with *Persuasion* identified as a "novel" and *Northanger Abbey* identified as a "romance" (with a misleading title meant to suggest that it is part of the tradition of *The Castle of Otranto* and *The Mysteries of Udolpho*). No one seeing this title in December 1817 or the following months would have imagined that the estate called Northanger Abbey, which is anything but medieval in appearance, plays a minor role in the story, or that the novel is if anything a parody and denunciation (certainly a renunciation) of a short-lived and unfortunate literary genre.

However, putting "Catherine" on a shelf in no way meant that the material was to be discarded. This new project in early 1817 was to be no less than a complete revision of "Susan"/"Catherine," with a plot that bore some basic similarities to its predecessor and characters who represented mature versions of those who had peopled the earlier story.

Her completed novels had already established a dependable albeit predictable formula: a young heroine meets a young hero; they fall in love; they marry. Everything in the fragment leads to the conclusion that in its essential elements the new work will be much like the rejected older work but with a wider range of characters in a more contemporary setting. There would be the various literary references that set the story of Catherine and Henry apart from the other novels, and this time the reader would see the important contrast between reading for commendable pleasure and profit, and reading to indulge passions and idleness. Charlotte and Sidney are drawn together through a chain of events not of their making, and their budding romance will make up the core of this new novel.

It is always reassuring upon proposing a theory of this sort to find support in the work of scholars who have read these materials with great care. Probably no one has paid as much attention to this final manuscript as Brian Southam, and so he speaks with authority in positing what I have arrived at independently.

> *Sanditon* can be regarded as a recasting of *Northanger Abbey*. Jane Austen marks the connection jokingly by returning again to the archaic Fanny Burney device which she had employed to launch the earlier novel—getting the comedy of manners under way by tracing the experiences of an innocent and marriageable young woman on her first entry into society, with all the conventional pitfalls of fashionable behaviour and the embarrassments of dealing with unwelcome suitors. The burlesque parallels are intentional. Catherine Morland comes fresh from her Wiltshire village, the eldest daughter in a family of ten children, Charlotte Heywood from the remoteness of Willingden, the eldest daughter still at home out of fourteen children. (1976: 7–8)

Further corroboration of this theory is found in a letter (recently brought to my attention by Deirdre Le Faye) dated August 8, 1862, from Anna Austen Lefroy to her half-brother, James Edward Austen-Leigh:

> "Now for the characters, so far as they are sketched—premising that I give up Sir Edwd. Denham—& don't mean to say a word for him—but you are not just to the Heywoods. They stand in

the place of the Morlands. In the last named family the Wife is the more prominent character—the talker in short; in Sanditon it is the Husband, & I think Mr. Heywood talks as much to the purpose as Mrs. Morland. Perhaps we were to have seen very little more of the Heywoods; in which case they are made enough of— On the other hand, in Northhanger [sic] Abbey Mrs. Allen stands out before her Husband but in Sanditon the Lady is kept back. I do not mean to deny Mrs. Allen's being more cleverly imagined than Mr. Parker—at least it may be so—but I think she would have been much the most tiresome in real life." (Le Faye, 1987: 58)

Anna Austen Lefroy's finding parallels between some minor figures in *Northanger Abbey* and this manuscript is just one step away from suggesting that the unfinished work is a rewrite, eventually finding its way into print, of the shelved novel.

Although he does not commit himself to this theory, by linking "Susan"/"Catherine" to the story of Charlotte, Alistair Duckworth lends additional support: "Like the Morland family at Fullerton, the Heywoods live in a kind of prelapsarian setting" (213). In observing that "the novel was put 'upon the shelve for the present' early in March 1817[,] indicat[ing] that she was not wholly satisfied with *Northanger Abbey* as we have it today" (22), Frank B. Pinion moves in the direction of this theory but never quite reaches it. Without in any way suggesting that the unfinished manuscript was to be a replacement for the rejected "*Susan*"/"Catherine," John Mullen pulls them together as similarly "literary" in noting that "just before she died, the new novel on which she was working was invigorated by the follies of novel readers just as *Northanger Abbey* had been" (2007: 377). Marvin Mudrick does not focus on *Sanditon* as an updated "Susan"/"Catherine," but in observing that "topography, the Romantic poets, and sex as comedy are... the three new ingredients of *Sanditon*" (256), he cites three of the major changes that took place.

The author herself may not have recognized the problem in the "Susan"/"Catherine" manuscript, but it was staring at her in the person of the heroine. As much as we adore Catherine, lively and engaging at seventeen, we have no assurance that she will develop into a young woman worthy of Henry Tilney. Far worse, because of her present immaturity, she cannot possibly serve as the author's mouthpiece, nor can her perspective ever be regarded as that of her creator. As the product of a budding author in her early twenties, she is a marvel of lights and shadows, but as the central character of a work by an experienced and published novelist beginning the fourth decade of her life, Catherine is a hindrance that must be discarded. Hence, the precious "Susan"/"Catherine" manuscript, however important it may have been in the author's development of a distinctive voice, must be set aside, not only temporarily but for all time. From its ashes, so to speak, arose an old concept with a new leading lady.

Charlotte Heywood—at twenty-two about halfway between the young Elizabeth Bennet and the close-to-spinsterhood Anne Elliot—significantly older than the unformed seventeen-year-old Catherine Morland but like her raised in the simplicity of the country amidst a large and loving family, is so clearly the heroine of this novel that it is difficult to understand some critical hesitation at assigning her this distinction: for example, the noncommittal, oblique "protagonist of *Sanditon*" (Bok: 442) or "The only reason we know Charlotte Heywood is the heroine is that the narrator tells us so" (Spence: 231). Far more in harmony with the text is Brian Southam's assertive claim in her behalf, "And what of the heroine? Charlotte Heywood seems cast for the role" (1986: 370). Elaine Jordan confidently settles the matter in declaring that "the focalized, sensible, heroine is Charlotte Heywood" (44), as does John Halperin in discussing "*Sanditon*'s heroine, Charlotte Heywood" (1983: 184). If we are to take Jane Austen at her word (even if given lightly), she had plans at least as early as 1813 to create a heroine with this name: "I admire the Sagacity & Taste of Charlotte Williams. Those large dark eyes always judge well.—I will compliment her, by naming a Heroine after her" (letter to Cassandra Austen dated October 11/12, 1813) (*Letters*: 235; Modert: F-275).

Like her younger predecessor, Susan/Catherine, Charlotte is offered an unexpected opportunity to see the great world, and so she proceeds to the sea coast, now the "in" place—where it is as requisite to be gazed upon as to gaze upon others while seeking health and a marriageable partner—instead of the now déclassé watering spa in Somerset to which Catherine had been conveyed. Again like her earlier avatar, Charlotte is fond of reading, but unlike the impressionable bride of Henry Tilney she distinguishes from the start between reality and the fantasy of romantic fiction. Like the discarded manuscript, this is a very "literary" work in that there are frequent references to published poems and novels. Charlotte's reading a great deal in her enforced isolation in Willingden is to be expected, and the text goes so far as to indicate that she has read some poetry and some romantic novels.

Her initial perception of Clara Brereton as *a complete heroine* is the clearest possible evidence that she herself is the heroine of this novel. By fabricating a fantasy world around the beautiful but impoverished dependent in Lady Denham's home, Charlotte creates for us her own reality, very much like when a modern fictional detective refers to Sherlock Holmes (who in turn dismisses C. Auguste Dupin as "a very inferior fellow"), forcing us into an aesthetic uncertainty about actuality vs. invention. More akin to Elizabeth Bennet than to any other of Jane Austen's creations, Charlotte judges her surroundings with eyes that are perhaps less fine but serve her better in forming first impressions. Further and even more importantly, Charlotte represents to a greater extent than any preceding heroine the voice of measured reason of Jane Austen herself, "implicitly present[ing] to us our author's point of view" (Moody, 1998), and almost every episode in the narrative is seen through her eyes or takes place in her presence.

In his recent publication, Joe Bray has given us much food for thought about Jane Austen's narrative style (with special emphasis on *Emma*, *Mansfield Park*, and *Persuasion* along with *Northanger Abbey*), asserting that "the popular conception of Catherine Morland as a foolish reader of Gothic novels does not capture the complexities of her reading in the novel. Rather than 'identifying' fully with her favourite heroines, Catherine is able to keep one foot in the 'real' world of her immediate surroundings even as she is most immersed in the fictional worlds of her reading" (144). Mr. Bray could as well have been describing Charlotte, still young although the eldest of the children still at home, who at 22 as an updated version of Catherine has had more time to read novels. Miss Heywood would for practical reasons be inclined to absorb the marriage theme because as the next eligible maiden in the family she must seek a suitable mate, and even more than Catherine she recognizes the importance of distinguishing between romance—however it may entice and entertain—and reality. In this most literary of all of Jane Austen's works, two of the characters—Clara Brereton and Sir Edward Denham—are not only drawn from romantic fiction but they are perhaps aware of their indeterminate existence and are playing out their assigned roles. We have dialog in excess with Sir Edward, but so far we have not heard the voice of Clara Brereton and therefore have no idea of who she really is. Both characters make an enormous impression on the impressionable visitor to Sanditon, and her fondness for reading novels has colored her view of her new acquaintances. Mr. Bray would have had a more interesting subject for this line of discussion if he had bypassed Catherine for Charlotte.

In the same way that Jane Austen blends her narrative voices by mixing third person reporting with direct quotations and indirect reported speech, she moves in and out of Charlotte's mind, sometimes speaking as the author and sometimes speaking through her lead character. Hence many passages remain ambiguous as real or imaginary. For example, Sir Edward's desire to emulate the scoundrels of popular fiction of the late 18th century, and in particular his determination to seduce Clara Brereton, could as well be how Charlotte interprets his intentions as how Jane Austen intends developing his character. It is no accident that once the opening scene on the rough road has passed, Charlotte is on stage in every episode, always participating or viewing, often judging.

Despite their acknowledgment that Thomas Parker is an inexperienced entrepreneur and therefore may be risking his family fortune as well as being an incurable gossip who prates on about people whose worst qualities he generally praises, critics take him at his word in his adverse commentary on Sidney, his younger brother.

In the unfinished manuscript, as in the work published as *Northanger Abbey*, we encounter a young man of wit and manners, no longer an unlikely clergyman but reportedly a sophisticated denizen of the beau monde. Through Thomas Parker's slanted characterization and his own brief but telling scene in Chapter 12, Sidney Parker—our newly transformed Henry Tilney—is presented as the catch of the season, replete with both personality and wealth. The sparkling male lead, woefully miscast in the rejected novel as a young cleric but now finally given his true calling, has been brought up to date to match the contemporary setting. As Jon Spence observes, "he is not like Austen's other heroes—he lives too much in the world" (232), but neither is Charlotte quite like any of Jane Austen's other heroines, nor is the setting in any way parallel to that of any of her earlier novels. In what would have been her masterpiece, she has gone far beyond anything that preceded it in breadth of subject-matter and sophistication of characters.

With the bar set so high—Henry Tilney is, after all, Jane Austen's most accomplished portrait of a young man—we can only lament our loss at not having the opportunity to see how much our author would have improved upon a character who was already unique among her creations. Despite the obvious trademarks of a fictional hero, Sidney Parker has failed to be uniformly seen as occupying this critical role, with even Brian Southam wondering at how his character will be developed: "Is Sidney Parker to be a Frank Churchill, a Henry Crawford, or a Bingley/Darcy?" (1986: 371). The answer, of course, is none of the above: a Henry Tilney!

That Sidney Parker is the destined hero of the novel has by no means received unanimous agreement. David Bell concedes that "of all Austen's heroes, Henry Tilney is the only one who at all resembles Sidney Parker," but he tempers this assessment by warning that "even that resemblance is fairly superficial" (162). Aside from questioning the character's indebtedness to Henry Tilney, David Bell suggests that "what most clearly connects Sidney with the would-be heroes is his unsettled way of living" (163–164). That Sidney has an unsettled way of living is reported by his brother, Thomas, mingling affection with severity and impatient like any older brother acting as a surrogate father with his younger sibling (and perhaps even mildly envious of his freedom from the constraints of a family and business commitments), the same man who advises Charlotte during their ride to Sanditon that "those who tell their own Story you know must be listened to with Caution." He might well have added that those who tell stories about family members with unlimited personal freedom and money to burn must be listened to with even more caution. David Bell, lacking confidence in Jane Austen's hints, asserts that "almost all of the admittedly limited evidence suggests that Sidney Parker is not hero material.... If in her seventh novel Austen were to decide that her heroine can do no better than Sidney Parker, that would be a new direction indeed" (166).

If it is so that the manuscript published as *Sanditon* represents Jane Austen's revised and updated "Susan"/"Catherine," then just as the heroine is at least loosely based on her predecessor, Catherine Morland, so the hero is based on his original, Henry Tilney. A new version of Henry Tilney will have all of that remarkable young gentleman's best qualities, such as wit, courtesy, and enough gravitas to indicate that despite his youth he is mature and ready to enter the state of matrimony.

But, one will hear immediately, this is not the Sidney Parker who emerges from the pages of the manuscript. Rather, he is footloose, irreverent, and clearly not contemplating that long and serious walk down the aisle with a young lady with whom he will spend the rest of his life.

We clearly have two different pictures of Sidney Parker and must select the correct one. First of all, the prevalent view of this character is based on what Thomas Parker says about him, in part stemming from disappointment at not receiving an expected letter from him. It is worth noting that Jane Austen heavily emends Thomas's initial passage about Sidney, with each level of correction making the junior brother more unsteady and clearly not someone that Charlotte could consider husband material. As the text shows, Thomas becomes increasingly verbose as he expands on his displeasure with Sidney's behavior, moving from mild disapprobation to charges of serious lightheadedness.

"What is it, your Brother Sidney says about its' being a Hospital?"

"Oh! my dear Mary, merely a Joke of his. Sidney says any thing you know.
>
"Oh! my dear Mary, merely a Joke of his. He pretends to advise me to make a Hospital of it. He pretends to laugh at my Improvements. Sidney says any thing you know.

He has always said what he chose of his eldest B^r— & to his Eldest B^r &
>
He has always said what he chose of & to us, all.

A young Man of Abilities & Address, & general ease of manner Miss H. — who says anything
>
Most Families have such a member among them I beleive Miss Heywood. — There is a someone in most families who is privileged to say anything.
>
Most Families have such a member among them I beleive Miss Heywood. — There is a someone in most families privileged by superior abilities or spirits to say anything.

Sidney is very clever
>
In ours, it is Sidney; who is a very clever Young Man, — very lively, very pleasant — living very much in the World & liked by everybody. I should
>
In ours, it is Sidney; who is a very clever Young Man, — and with great powers of pleasing. — He lives too much in the World to be settled; that is his only fault. — I wish we may

>

In ours, it is Sidney; who is a very clever Young Man, — and with great powers of pleasing. — He lives too much in the World to be settled; that is his only fault. — He is here & there & every where. I wish we may get him to Sanditon.

I should like to have you acquainted with him. —

And it would be a credit to the Place! —

>

And it would be a fine thing for the Place! —

Such a young Man as Sidney, with his neat equipage & fashionable air, — You & I Mary, know what effect it might have:" Many a respectable Family, many a careful Mother, many a pretty Daughter, might it secure us, to the prejudice of E. Bourne & Hastings." —

The same disparaging tone is seen in a later passage when Thomas condemns his younger brother for not writing as hoped. Grudgingly, however, he admits that Sidney's not writing could well mean that he is on his way in person (which we soon see to be the case).

When they met before dinner, M^r. P. was looking over Letters. — "Not a Line from Sidney! — said he. — He is an idle fellow. —

I sent him an account of my accident from Willingden, & thought he would have vouchsafed me an Answer. — perhaps it implies that he is coming himself. — Not unlikely. —

>

I sent him an account of my accident from Willingden, & thought he would have vouchsafed me an Answer. — But perhaps it implies that he is coming himself. — I trust it may. —

The issue now is the reliability of Thomas Parker in speaking about his brother—or any other topic. The text implies that he married a woman with little to offer in the way of commonsense companionship. We also learn from the text that he has invested what may be a large part of his patrimony in a business venture with a woman in whom he places little trust and whom he clearly does not understand well, praising her in terms that Charlotte soon learns are seriously in error. He has moved from his comfortable family estate to a new home, with on the whole far fewer comforts and security. Upon leaving London to return home, without much thought (and without having consulted with his business partner) he has rashly taken a detour to find a surgeon to bring back to Sanditon. Reading the advertisements inaccurately, he has gone to the wrong Willingden, where despite common sense and the mutterings of his driver, he has attempted to negotiate a pathway never meant for a horse-drawn carriage. Upon extricating himself from the overturned carriage, he has clumsily injured himself. He has then proceeded to regale his unresponsive hosts with hyperbolic praise of the salutary effects of the air and water of Sanditon. On the return journey with Charlotte as guest, he has warned her not to take at face-value what people tell about themselves, serving also as the author's warning to us not to believe what her characters say without subjecting their dialog to careful scrutiny. In the course of discoursing on Lady Denham, whom he finds considerably more sympathetic than Charlotte learns to be the truth, Thomas has praised the virtues of Clara Brereton, who we later find has a secretive side unknown to her circle of acquaintances. In the process of discrediting his brother, he has also extolled the qualities of his sisters, particularly Diana, a lady who Charlotte soon learns is generous but foolishly intrusive as well as garrulous. Only an older brother speaking of his younger sibling within a family unit could with mixed feelings admire and jokingly condemn as "a saucy fellow" a gentleman in Sidney Parker's position, which may not command the wealth of a Rushworth or a Darcy but might very well rival that of a Bingley. The question is now obvious: How reliable is Thomas Parker as a reporter about Sidney Parker (or anyone/anything else)? The equally obvious answer is: not very.

In contrast to Thomas's prejudiced account of Sidney, we read what Charlotte sees and hears upon their brief encounter near the end of the manuscript:

> It was a close, misty morn^g, & when they reached the brow of the Hill, they could not for some time make out what sort of Carriage it was, which they saw coming up. It appeared at different moments to be every thing from the Gig to the Pheaton, — from one horse to 4; & just as they were concluding in favour of a Tandem, little Mary's young eyes distinguished the Coachman & she eagerly called out, "T'is Uncle Sidney Mama, it is indeed." And so it proved. — M^r. Sidney Parker driving his Servant in a very neat Carriage was soon opposite to them, & they all stopped for a few minutes. The manners of the Parkers were always pleasant among themselves — & it was a very friendly meeting between Sidney & his sister in law,

who was most kindly taking it for granted that he was on his way to Trafalgar House.

This he declined however. "He was just come from Eastbourne, proposing to spend two or three days, as it might happen, at Sanditon — but the Hotel must be his Quarters — He was expecting to be joined there by a friend or two." — The rest was common enquiries & remarks, with kind notice of little Mary, & a very well-bred Bow & proper address to Miss Heywood on her being named to him — and they parted, to meet again within a few hours. —

There is almost no resemblance between the Sidney of his brother's pronouncements and the Sidney of this short passage. Charlotte's view as well as ours of people described by Thomas Parker—Lady Denham, Clara Brereton, Sir Edward Denham, and Diana Parker—is considerably altered upon a personal encounter. I believe that the text clearly proves that Sidney is not as his brother reports, and thus we can safely take him for the hero of the novel and Charlotte's future husband.

The text, furthermore, makes clear that Sidney is a welcome guest in his brother's house, as evidenced by Mr. Parker's expressing great disappointment that he rarely visits and Mrs. Parker's warm greeting and invitation to stay with them (not what we might expect if either feared a bad influence on their minor children) and even more by little Mary's gleeful discovery that the approaching driver is none other than her beloved Uncle Sidney. Charlotte will count herself fortunate to snare Sidney by the end of the novel.

Some commentators have suggested that the character of Henry Tilney is modeled on the writer and Anglican clergyman, Sydney Smith (1771-1845). "In the winter of that year [1797], there was staying at Bath a young clergyman called Sydney Smith, tall, pleasant-looking and extraordinarily amusing in a vein of humour peculiarly his own. He was employed by a family called Hicks Beach as tutor to their son; the Hicks Beaches knew the Austens. A year later Jane began to write a novel later to appear as *Northanger Abbey*, in which the heroine visiting Bath meets a tall, pleasant-looking young clergyman called Henry Tilney, extraordinarily amusing and in a vein of humour very like that of Sydney Smith" (Cecil: 79). However, Lord David Cecil concedes, "[There is] no record that the two ever met" (79). Chris Viveash likewise remains skeptical about a meeting between the most interesting conversationalist and the most talented young novelist of the time: "The notion that Jane Austen once met Sydney Smith in the Rooms at Bath when they were both visiting the spa during November of December 1797 is a most beguiling conceit. There is no evidence to substantiate this theory; however, it has to be admitted that Henry Tilney is as delightful a creature as any fictional character, and it must surely be highly flattering to Sydney Smith to be thought his prototype" (255). If there is any validity in the unfounded belief that Henry is based on Sydney, we have a logical next step: that Sidney is based on Sydney.

Around Charlotte and Sidney, Jane Austen has assembled a group of complementary figures, some original and some reminiscent of characters already met in earlier novels, all designed for the sole purpose of creating the kind of novel that she had been writing from the start of her career: an amusing or touching account of a young woman's search for an eligible single man.

Among the male characters, only Thomas Parker is sufficiently developed for us to form a complete picture. As a happily married man—with a rapidly growing family and a less astute business sense than is perhaps healthy for him—he cannot fully participate in the social scene in Sanditon. Addicted to talking, he reveals more about himself and his family than Charlotte or the reader would expect upon such a short acquaintance. The first four chapters are taken up almost completely with his dialog, and he has plenty to say in later passages. But he is not merely a mindless prattler like Mr. Collins, making up for modest mental acuity in directness of purpose and uttering the most penetrating line in the extant manuscript, "Those who tell their own Story you know must be listened to with Caution." Despite some amusing passages, he is essentially a serious character and therefore not central to the burlesque comedy that marks this work.

His youngest brother, however, is an entirely different matter. The breakfast scene with poor Arthur Parker is delightful comedy since his youth assures us that despite his aversion to air he is a sufficiently healthy specimen who only needs the encouragement of a young woman to abandon his slothful life. Nowhere else in her novels has Jane Austen indulged in such detail about food preparation, fears of illness, and the workings of stomach linings. Relating these things with full sobriety to a young woman to whom he has just been introduced tells us how naïve this young man is, but his interest in the Beaufort beauties—he actually takes a few extra steps out of his way to behold them—is a promising sign.

And then there is Sir Edward Denham, who should be allowed to speak for himself (something that he does at great length if not to much effect). If he were not so amusing we might fear that another Henry Crawford has come upon the scene, but no one can doubt that Sir Edward will be unsuccessful in his planned seduction. As a matter of fact, he is likely to end up as the seduced. Brian Southam has brilliantly delineated this entertaining character.

> Sanditon is too young to have won Brighton's notoriety as a favoured spot for assignation and elopement. But it already has its statutory seducer, one of those wicked baronets that Mrs. Morland was supposed to warn her daughter against, who "delight in forcing young ladies away to some remote farm-house" (*NA*, p. 18). The joke is now modernised and pushed further. The baronet in *Sanditon* is too poor to indulge in the "masterly style" of seduction in "some solitary House" in "the Neighbourhood of Tombuctoo" but is still ready to plot "the quietest sort of ruin & disgrace" near at hand. The joke about Sir Edward is not just that he is remarkably adaptable; he is also slightly old-fashioned and out of touch with the geography of dissipation. (1976: 8)

William Deresiewicz has perfectly hit on the comic side of Sir Edward in summarizing him as "that Don Quixote of Don Juans" (5), but the young would-be Lothario lacks any of the tragic implications of the early seventeenth-century Spanish epic hero. Nor can he claim even one of the 2,065 successful conquests accounted for in Leporello's famous aria. Oddly, Sir Edward—"one of Jane Austen's most brilliant creations" (Halperin, 1983: 186)—is often classified with John Willoughby and Henry Crawford as villainous seducers and threats to the happiness of the heroine. Nothing could be further from the truth, as he is clearly meant to be a comic character who would not know how to follow through with a successful seduction even in the unlikely event that such a possibility presented itself. Jane Austen does, however, attribute to him one positive trait that dubiously sets him apart from other young men of his class, who devote all of their time to hunting and fishing. "In a manner reminiscent of [the heroine of] Austen's much earlier novel *Northanger Abbey*, [Sir Edward] has read so many Gothic novels that he has convinced himself 'that he was formed to be a dangerous Man'" ("Sanditon." *Wikipedia*).

The text is evasive about his age, but I suspect that he is rather younger than generally assumed, perhaps junior even to poor Arthur, who has barely reached his majority. In the sole representation that I have seen of the Baronet (by Maximilien Vox, *The Works of Jane Austen. Sanditon and Other Miscellanea.* Ed. R. Brimley Johnson: facing page 49), we see a very stylish, wasp-waisted (a corset?) gallant of the period. With such a lively creature on the scene, I do not understand why anyone would think that this novel was meant to be about hypochondriacs, who play only a minor role. Lady Denham may feel some faint, lingering solicitude for her nephew-through-marriage because although he has inherited the title and perhaps Denham Park, with the legacy came no serious money. And because of his youth and inexperience he has no means of increasing his meager fortune other than what sounds like an ill-conceived plan to build a cottage on some forsaken land in the hope of leasing it to some vacationing gentleman. If his silliness and misguided notions of vanquishing and then abandoning Clara Brereton are placed in the right perspective, he turns out to be somewhat pitiable or at the very least non-threatening and therefore pure comedy. He has read about the dastardly acts by men of much greater prowess than himself, and his fate must be to live through their doubtful achievements. As for other characters in the novel, the library and its contents become a metaphor for his life.

David Selwyn identifies the lending library as of special importance to the story, but he sees it in a very dark light: "The only shop that Jane Austen created to exist, as it were, in its own right, to play its part in expressing the meaning of the work, is the library in Sanditon.... it embodies the hollow commercialism that lies at the heart of both the resort and the text" (2005: 223–224). Perhaps closer to what Jane Austen had in mind is illustrated in Thomas Rowlandson's lively drawing, "The Lending Library, Scarborough, 1813" (Marsden: facing page 8). Mrs. Whitby's emporium is both a necessary feature of the seaside community and a symbol of a literary world in which reading is simultaneously a pastime and a delusion.

As part of Charlotte's fantasizing about Lady Denham's young companion, Clara Brereton must—like all proper heroines—be at risk. And who is more qualified to threaten her than Sir Edward, to Charlotte the very personification of the fictional heroes/villains of the novels that she (as well as he) has been reading? That Charlotte is nonplussed at viewing the tryst in the garden is no surprise although the perceptive reader will understand that it is not the first and will certainly not be the last such meeting. Clara has on occasion, and without much conviction, been compared to Jane Fairfax, who is a much simpler creature, ready for a life of domestic servitude if that is to be her fate. Clara, in contrast, has determined to seize the opportunity to secure for herself the former family fortune by ingratiating herself with Lady Denham, with becoming her heiress her goal. Although Sir Edward is somewhat foolish and ordinarily below her observations, his propinquity—not to mention his title—makes him the most eligible bachelor in the immediate foreground. Her intention is clearly to become the wealthy wife of a young man with a title. Behold the next Lady Denham.

As expected, women are the dominant figures in this work. Even in the truncated state of the manuscript we can see that Sanditon serves as the accidental converging point of five young women—Charlotte Heywood, Clara Brereton, Esther Denham, and the two Misses Beaufort—in search of husbands. The timid Miss Lambe may well be a sixth of this group, since it is unlikely that her father has sent her to England, where there must be some titled young blade around to take her to wife and her money to the gambling table, merely for an education. All other aspects of the novel—valetudinarianism, exploitation and speculation, gluttony—are secondary to this central romantic plot, which as in Jane Austen's preceding novels will conclude with the marriage of the heroine and the pairing-off of some other lads and lasses.

Although Sir Edward is both too poor and too self-absorbed to appeal to one of these women despite his title, Clara Brereton, having established herself as his superior and fully cognizant of his bizarre plans to seduce her (either locally or in some faraway place using funds that he does not possess), has taken the upper hand and permits the occasional rendezvous, during which he makes his protestations of love. Her scheme is certainly to win as much as she can of the Brereton money by ingratiating herself with Lady Denham to the extent that the dowager leaves her estate to her younger cousin in such a way that it cannot be revoked (in the same manner as Mrs. Ferrars favored Robert). Precisely how she phrases her blandishments must remain a matter of conjecture since in the extant text she never utters a single syllable.

At the same time, Clara will inveigle Sir Edward into a secret engagement, to which he is bound but which she can break if he becomes noisome. She is the serpent taken to Lady Denham's bosom, a far cry from the charming and totally sympathetic Jane Fairfax. Having the enormous disadvantage of poverty—in contrast to the earlier "Miss Brereton"—Clara Brereton plans to take a page out of her wealthy cousin's history by marrying advantageously in terms of money and title. A union with Sir Edward would convert her into a new Lady Denham, and with whatever the present dowager gives him and her own expected inheritance from her protectress, she will be able to fulfill her ambitions. Nothing in the text suggests that Miss Clara Brereton, clever and plotting under the nose of her hostess, is "powerless" (Sales: 214). Rather, she possesses "a density, an unsettling mysteriousness not found in characters in Austen's earlier work" (Spence: 231–232), personal traits that along with her disconcerting beauty make her a power to be reckoned with. Her secondary role, however, is clear despite the assertion by William Deresiewicz that she is "*Sanditon's* presumptive heroine" (35).

Taking a page out of *12th Night*, Jane Austen has given us from *Sense and Sensibility* on a series of primary and secondary heroines: Elinor/Marianne, Elizabeth/Jane, Fanny/Mary, Emma/Jane, and Catherine/Isabella. In *Persuasion* alone, planned to be a shorter and therefore more compact work, do we find a single heroine. The first of each pair is clearly the central character of the novel as far as the reader is concerned, but to a great extent the second of each pair is the expected heroine in this kind of story. Hence Jane Austen balances precariously between the "real" world of how we read the story and the "fictional" world of the characters who come to life within that story. That Charlotte consciously recognizes Clara as the heroine of a romantic novel—such as what we are now reading—is a very self-conscious display by the author of her skill in blending not so much reality and illusion as illusion and illusion. Like Sir Edward, Clara Brereton is drawn from literature, making the library and its exotic contents a metaphor for her identity.

Elaine Jordan suggests, "Clara Brereton might have become a replay of Jane Fairfax" (44). If that had happened, we could agree with some short-sighted critics that this manuscript reflects Jane Austen's waning powers as she succumbs to her fatal illness. But the text tells us something entirely different—that despite her deteriorating medical condition she is at the peak of her form, consciously inventing not merely a new world of fiction but remarkable new people to populate it.

It is Miss Esther who is perhaps in the worst plight of the young women. She is too highborn to seek a spouse among the lower classes but too poor to aspire to a husband of the same or higher rank. What could Lady

Denham be thinking in insisting to Charlotte that "Miss Esther must marry somebody of fortune too—She must get a rich Husband" despite lack of a suitable dowry? Unlike her social inferiors Jane Fairfax and Clara Brereton, she cannot consider becoming a governess or a nursery maid. However, she has insufficiently won the sympathy of critics to receive any consoling commentary, with about the only mention being Jon Spence's offhand remark that the worldly Sidney Parker "maybe... will fall in love with Charlotte, or maybe with Clara or even Esther Denham" (232). This third-place ranking is not a cause for much optimism. Her hopes can only lie in her brother's making an advantageous marriage so that he can provide a dowry. Clara Brereton, an unanticipated interloper, has become a rival for Lady Denham's attention, conditional affection (something normally outside the dowager's narrow range of feelings), and financial benevolence. A toadying sycophant who is assigned no dialog in the extant text but can be assumed to alternate between begging from her superiors and contemning everyone of a lower station, Miss Denham is torn between hoping that her aunt-by-marriage continues to enjoy a healthy life so that she can sponge off her and praying that the elderly dowager joins her two departed husbands after perhaps leaving some kind of pleasant surprise for her *young folks* in her will. I would not count on it, Miss Esther. In the meantime she has to suffer enforced humility at being seen in the modest equipage that her titled but moneyless brother can provide.

We never learn Miss Esther Denham's age, but the possibility exists that she is older than Sir Edward, perhaps even approaching early spinsterhood. Her aunt-through-marriage is either excessively obtuse or truly insensitive in not understanding that one of the reasons that the young woman wants to stay for part of the summer in Sanditon (aside from the dampness of Denham Park) is that unless she is here for the vacation season she has no opportunity to compete for a husband.

The Misses Beaufort—the musically inclined elder sister, unnamed since she enjoys a special distinction, and the artistic Miss Letitia— having extended themselves to their utmost in fashionable couture, must sit patiently—and silently in the extant text—for someone of wealth to pay his suit. Jane Austen is unusually severe in her strictures upon the siblings, who are neither more nor less frivolous than any of their contemporaries. If they have learned that Arthur Parker, young, affable, and gluttonously lazy, but possessed of an independent income, has against all expectations made it a practice to walk a few steps more than required so that he can go past their window in the hope of catching a glimpse of one of the beauties, perhaps their efforts at sketching and music-making will not have been in vain.

Miss Lambe remains the unknown factor in the incomplete puzzle since she may have been intended as the future bride of one of the eligible bachelors on the scene in Sanditon. For us, however, she must remain a fragile and enigmatic figure hovering in the background. Lady Denham has her very much in mind in the immediate future as an imbiber of her asses' milk and in the longer run as a short-lived spouse for Sir Edward, but we hope for a better future for her. Jane Austen probably knew no one personally who could serve as a model for this character. "Austen's deployment of the term 'half mulatto' is idiosyncratic, and biographical evidence suggests that her engagement with contemporary debates over 'race' and slavery was relatively slight" (Salih: 351). Recognizing that Miss Lambe is "uncharacteristic in *her* fictional world perhaps, but by no means an altogether extraordinary figure in the period under discussion" (Salih: 332), she may have planned to keep the young woman offstage, never appearing in person and uttering no dialog. Our author would have been hard pressed to create a convincing idiolect for someone of such an origin. "If she *had* spoken, it seems unlikely that Austen would have deployed the 'negro dialect' that instantly and insistently marks" women of similar origin in contemporary novels (Salih: 353). Nevertheless, Sara Salih suggests that "Austen's only 'brown' character—so briefly invoked and so tantalizingly incomplete" (330) plays an important role in the story in hinting at "the social history of England [that] is central to Jane Austen's last, unfinished text" (329). Although Sara Salih writes very persuasively about the character's literary/historic background, her title, "The Silence of Miss Lambe," may not indeed describe the young lady accurately, since Diana Parker's report that upon her first immersion "she [was] so frightened, poor Thing" suggests a clamorous scream characteristic of the other females subjected to this form of health cure.

Women dominate the less romantic side of the plot, also. The two Misses Parker, Susan and Diana, are too old by contemporary standards to be in the marriage market, but through her interference the latter may eventually play a role in matchmaking. Their part in the novel is more that of comic relief, showing us their ludicrous fostering of symptoms of hypochondria that do not jibe with their hyperkinetic energy levels. Susan, the elder sister and probably the senior sibling of the Parker family, is reported as being very talkative, but not a single word of her dialog is reported, as though none of it is worth recording and passing along. In contrast, Diana's dialog—which more than compensates for the silence of most of the other female characters—takes up much of each scene in which she appears, even indirectly through a long letter that her brother Thomas reads to Charlotte. There are no precedents in earlier novels for these two remarkable sisters although the interminable babble of Miss Bates prepares us for chatter without content. (It must be said for Miss Bates, however, that if we read between the words, we may detect hints about some important elements of the plot.)

A more sinister figure, intent on fostering financial interests over sentiment and personal attachment, dubiously distinguished by "false values, insufficient education, and plain cupidity" (Halperin, 1983: 189), is now a dowager Lady instead of an autocratic General Tilney or vilifying Aunt Norris. Although Lady Denham, "the most complex figure in the story" (Southam, 1986: 371), owes some of her features to the villains of earlier novels, there is a liveliness and engaging candor suggesting a happier role for her. Less malicious than Mrs. Norris (who is not?) and not as menacing as General Tilney (who as a carryover from the Gothic horror tradition is essentially a caricature), perhaps she was intended to be the *dea ex machina* who would in the final scene bring together in blessed matrimony the various bachelors and bachelorettes. For most readers, however, she is a thoroughly unattractive character. David Selwyn's summary, reflecting almost universal revulsion to the great Lady of the Neighbourhood, that she was "born into a petty trade, inherits her first husband's estate and her second husband's title" (2007: 325), fails to account for her entering the first marriage as a very wealthy young Miss Brereton, possibly even more affluent than Mr. Hollis. And although she retains the distinction of "Lady Denham," the actual title of the Baronetcy is passed on to Sir Harry's nephew, now Sir Edward Denham. In addition, although it could well be that the Brereton money came from trade (perhaps not so petty considering the "munificent sum of £30,000" that she brought to the union), there is no information on this point anywhere in the text.

True, there are other elements in the story that could have become significant, like investment in questionable real estate, exploitation and speculation, greed and gluttony, the development of seaside communities, valetudinarianism. But just as *Sense and Sensibility* merely touches on the dangers to young men of attending schools where they can be preyed upon by unscrupulous young women, and *Pride and Prejudice* does not dwell on the evils of entailed estates, and *Mansfield Park* never really delves into the issue of ordination (despite what Jane Austen suggests in a famous passage in one of her letters) or the tragic history of slave labor, and *Emma* does not produce an essay on the sad life of a governess (Charlotte Brontë was to have the final word here), and the last completed manuscript falls short of describing the life of an officer's wife on a war ship, so this final effort merely glances at a number of topics of contemporary interest without ever departing from the central theme that informs all of Jane Austen's work.

The manuscript rolls on much like a series of tableaux, like a play in the making. Interspersing authorial narrative and Charlotte's own thoughts with dialog, Jane Austen spins out a tale about young love set in a romantic and at the same time challenged village that is undergoing difficult changes. With only a small portion of the novel before us, we have to guess at its direction. But on the basis of all her preceding work, it is safe to conclude that despite some glances at entrepreneurship, speculation, and the risks of investment, the core of the story—like all others from her pen—was the search and discovery of a life-long mate.

The case for the central theme of the novel cannot be more succinctly stated than Richard Jenkyn's observation that "all of her novels follow the simple pattern 'girl meets boy, girl marries boy'" (34). I entirely concur with his summary statement that "the sixty or so existing pages of *Sanditon* mostly study the growth of a new town and its inhabitants; but insofar as Jane Austen had a clear notion of where this book was to go, it too was evidently to be built around a young woman eventually marrying the man of her heart" (34).

However, there is a caveat that with so little of the text available we do not know anything about how the story was to work itself out. Whereas in the earlier novels we are occasionally kept on the edge of our seats wondering (and worrying) about the outcome, there is sound evidence in *Persuasion* that Jane Austen was ready to move forward in her craft.

It is clear that Elinor cannot have her Edward once news reaches her that "Mr. Ferrars is married," and following Willoughby's abandonment Marianne is left with no one to love since Colonel Brandon already has at least one foot in the grave. Although it seems inevitable that Bingley will return to Longbourn to declare his love to Jane, there is no one for Elizabeth, who has turned down Mr. Collins, has lost Wickham to her younger sister, and has consistently found Mr. Darcy the most obnoxious man on the face of the earth.

Mary Crawford may not win Edmund Bertram, but Fanny is obviously not the woman whom he wants to marry, and the field may be open for Henry Crawford to capture the heroine of the novel. Even less likely is it that Emma will find someone to marry since she refuses Mr. Elton and has no serious interest in Frank Churchill (who is, anyway, engaged elsewhere). Her unusual brother/sister relationship with Mr. Knightley cannot lead to marriage, so she will be at the end of the novel just as she is at the opening, the young and self-centered great lady of the neighborhood. Despite the obvious attraction between Catherine Morland and Henry Tilney, parental opposition is so strong that only a miracle can bring them together in holy matrimony.

In *Persuasion* alone do we know from the start that whatever vicissitudes may interfere with Anne's reconciliation with Frederick, they will come back together again by the end of the novel. Anne cannot marry William Elliot any more than Wentworth can marry Louisa Musgrove. What can be seen, then, is that in the last completed novel Jane Austen ventured not so much into new territory as a new spin on old material. Whether she was going to continue to develop this newer plot structure or was going to return to her older pattern in the new novel remains a mystery, but I am convinced that once Charlotte and Sydney meet on that dusty road almost unaware in their mutual attraction of the presence of Mrs. Parker, little Mary, and the unnamed servant, the succeeding course of the story is inevitable.

Jane Austen has often been criticized for neglecting large areas of the contemporary scene, and to the other extreme she has been elevated to the role of mistress of all that she surveys and a wise commentator on everything that has ever occurred or ever will take place in the world. The latter hyperbolic praise is hardly worth commenting on since it is not based on the reality of her life and art. The former criticism, however, is equally poorly founded since Jane Austen remained firm in her conviction that she should write only about what she knew firsthand, avoiding many topics because she had no interest in them, was ignorant about them, or was certain that her audience already knew about them and therefore had no need of her opinion. As Paul Johnson put it so well in his address to the Annual General Meeting of the Jane Austen Society in July 1996, "It was one of her most cherished artistic principles, which she observed however great the temptation to depart from it, only to deal with subjects she knew intimately and intuited strongly" (50–51).

With her roots in the eighteenth century and therefore cognizant of the need for financial security and social standing, Jane Austen is nevertheless enough a daughter of the nineteenth century to recognize the role of love as the most important ingredient for a successful marriage. We see few happy conjugal pairings in the novels, but those based upon affection are invariably gratifying. *Persuasion* is a happy exception since the Crofts enjoy an ideal union, and the future life together of Anne and Frederick is in part foreshadowed:

> Anne was tenderness itself, and she had the full worth of it in Captain Wentworth's affection. His profession was all that could ever make her friends wish that tenderness less, the dread of a future war all that could dim her sunshine. She gloried in being a sailor's wife, but she must pay the tax of quick alarm for belonging to that profession which is, if possible, more distinguished in its domestic virtues than in its national importance.

In marked contrast we have the discomfort of the Bennets and Sir Thomas and Lady Bertram, tolerating without much respect the folly of an unexamined union.

The details of how this novel was to continue and end will never be known, but there can be no doubt that it was to be in the same line as earlier attempts to show young people in the pursuit of love and happiness. By the final page, as is appropriate to this genre, each maid will catch her man, pairing off to initiate the next, unrecorded chapter in their history.

Scholars remain divided on how much, if any, Jane Austen's own state of health early in 1817 had an influence in forming the plot line and characters of the new effort. Her own letters from the time are the most reliable source of information, and they suggest that although it was impossible for her to remove her mind from current afflictions, she did not regard herself as in peril of imminent death. As always, she turned her discomfort into a source of humor.

Typically, Jane Austen wrote nothing in extant correspondence about the new work upon which she was engaged in 1817, the only hint anywhere in her letters being a possibly half-joking suggestion in a letter to Cassandra

Austen dated October 11/12, 1813, "I admire the Sagacity & Taste of Charlotte Williams. Those large dark eyes always judge well.—I will compliment her, by naming a Heroine after her" (*Letters*: 235; Modert: F-275). But this letter preceded the start of composition by several years, and there is no evidence that even Cassandra knew about the new novel.

Although it is traditional to regard the *Sanditon* manuscript as a product of Jane Austen's declining health, a "brave defiance against the depression of illness" (Grey: 282), if we are to believe her extant letters somewhat the contrary was true as she began work. She wrote on Thursday, January 23, 1817, to Caroline Austen, her 12-year-old niece (the youngest daughter of James Austen and goddaughter of Cassandra Austen), "*I* feel myself getting stronger than I was half a year ago, & can so perfectly well walk to Alton, *or* back again, without the slightest fatigue that I hope to be able to do both when Summer comes" (*Letters*: 326; Modert: F-423). This report might be taken for excessive optimism in writing to a child if not for a letter written to her old friend, Alethea Bigg, on the next day, Friday, January 24, 1817, repeating the good news: "We are all in good health [&] *I* have certainly gained strength through the Winter & am not far from being well" (*Letters*: 326; original lost). Three days later, Monday, January 27, 1817, in what she believed was improving health and in exuberant high spirits she began work on the manuscript, with its carefree, rollicking opening passage.

Despite a great deal of uneven handwriting and what must have been a difficult period when she used pencil instead of ink, for the most part she remained stable during the composition of the work, writing to her niece, Fanny Knight, on Thursday and Friday, February 20/21, 1817, "I am almost entirely cured of my rheumatism; just a little pain in my knee now & then, to make me remember what it was, & keep on flannel" (*Letters*: 329; Modert: 426).

But a slightly later letter to Fanny Knight, dated Thursday, March 13, 1817, is more ominous, suggesting a recent relapse: "I am got tolerably well again, quite equal to walking about & enjoying the air" (*Letters*: 333; Modert: F-434). Five days later, she completed her last sentence at the top of folio 60v of the new manuscript, inscribed the date "March 18" (Tuesday), and put down her pen. Writing to Fanny Knight a few days later, on Sunday, March 23, 1817 (the letter was concluded on Tuesday, March 25), she reveals the dreaded news: "I certainly have not been well for many weeks, & about a week ago I was very poorly." (*Letters*: 335; Modert: 440). "About a week ago," of course, she had been bringing the manuscript to a close. Despite what she thought was improving health—she continues to Fanny Knight, "I have had a good deal of fever at times & indifferent nights, but am considerably better now, & recovering my Looks a little, which have been bad enough, black & white & every wrong colour. I must not depend upon being ever very blooming again. Sickness is a dangerous Indulgence at my time of Life" (*Letters*: 335–336; Modert: 440)—she did not resume work on the manuscript, leaving it in a state that continues to tantalize, confuse, and challenge readers.

R.W. Chapman regards the manuscript as "a first draft, heavily corrected and revised" (*OIJA*–VI: 363), and for R. Brimley Johnson, "the style… is clearly a form of notes, not of composed narrative" (49). In contrast, B.C. Southam's carefully balanced estimate is that to some degree it is a fairly finished product: "No interpretation or description of this work can safely be developed unless we keep in mind that the manuscript is a first draft… [but] if… we judge that the corrected and revised first draft goes a long way towards fulfilling the author's intention, our opinion of the fragment, with regard to its literary importance and its place in Jane Austen's development, can be reached with some assurance" (1964: 107–109). In Mr. Southam's enthusiastic opinion (one with which I thoroughly agree), "*Sanditon* is the most vigorous of all Jane Austen's writing. There is not the least sign of fatigue in its style, invention, or design" (1964: 102).

The contrasting views of these great scholars can be reconciled through a hypothesis that the manuscript represents several stages of composition. Hence, whereas some pages or passages are almost certainly Jane Austen's earliest attempts and would require serious rethinking on her part, others are just as certainly finished products, at least at the point where she stopped revising them. It is therefore not so much *a* manuscript as a *series* of mini-manuscripts, each at a different stage of development.

For at least one important critic, however, both R.W. Chapman and R. Brimley Johnson are insufficiently harsh in their verdicts. "Dismiss[ing] it as the last gasp of a dying woman" (Halperin, 1983: 183), E.M. Forster, that self-avowed Janeite and most successful of her literary heirs, asserts in his review of the first edition of *Sanditon* in 1925:

> The fragment known to Miss Austen's family as *Sanditon* is of small literary merit, but no one is to blame for this: neither the

authoress, who left it a fragment, nor the owner of the MS, who has rightly decided on publication, nor the editor of the text, who has done his work with care and skill. Though of small merit, it is of great interest, for it was written after *Persuasion*, and consequently may throw light on the last phase of the great novelist. In 1817 she had reached maturity, but she was also ill, and these are the two factors we must bear in mind while we read. Are there signs of new development in *Sanditon*? Or is everything overshadowed by the advance of death?

The MS. (the editor tells us) is firmly written. Nevertheless, the fragment gives the effect of weakness, if only because it is reminiscent from first to last. It opens with a Mr. and Mrs. Parker falling out of a carriage (*cf. Love and Freindship*), and Mr. Parker, like Marianne Dashwood, sprains his ankle. A Mr. Heywood rescues him. The Parkers and Heywoods both have large families, and when the former return to their seaside home they take with them Miss Charlotte Heywood, "a very pleasing young woman of two-and-twenty," who is destined to be the heroine. Charlotte belongs to a type which has attracted Miss Austen all the way from *Sense and Sensibility* to *Persuasion*, and naturally dominates her pen when vitality is low; she is the well-scoured channel through which comment most readily flows. But whereas Eleanor Dashwood, Fanny Price, Anne Elliot, were real people whose good sense, modesty, and detachment were personal qualities, Charlotte turns these qualities into labels, and can be seen from some distance as she sits observing other labels upon the sea-front. It is a procession of adjectives. Here comes Clara Brereton, talented, good-looking, dependent, and not wholly trustworthy, whom we knew in a more living state as Jane Fairfax. Here is Clara's patroness, Lady Denham, who is jolly and downright like Mrs. Jennings, but domineers like Lady Catherine de Burgh. Here are the Miss Beauforts—shadows of the shadow of Isabella Thorpe, and the harp on which they perform echoes the dying echo of Mary Crawford's, even as the gruel of Mr. Woodhouse mingles with the cocoa of Arthur Parker a just perceptible aroma. And here come other labels, and in their midst sits the "very pleasing young woman" reading them out loud for our advantage and finding none of them quite to her taste. Clearly, so far as character-drawing is concerned, Jane Austen is here completely in the grip of her previous novels. She writes out of what she has written, and anyone who has himself tried to write when feeling out of sorts will realize her state. The pen always finds life difficult to record; left to itself, it records the pen. The effort of creating was too much, and the numerous alterations in the MS. are never in the direction of vitality. Even the wit is reminiscent. This is the best it can do:

"All that he understood of himself he readily told, for he was very open-hearted; and where he might be himself in the dark, his conversation was still giving information to such of the Heywoods as could observe."

It is the old flavour, but how faint! Sometimes it is even stale, and we realize with pain that we are listening to a slightly tiresome spinster, who has talked too much in the past to be silent unaided. "Sanditon" is a sad little experience from this point of view, and sentimentalists will doubtless say that it ought not to have been published lest it performs the mysterious operation known as "harming an author."

But meanwhile Charlotte sits on the sea-front. Why a sea-front?

Since the book promises little vigour of character and incident, one is tempted to assume that atmosphere and outline will be reminiscent also, and that the scene is laid in a watering-place because the writer had recently dealt with Lyme Regis and found marine humours easiest to handle. Nevertheless, there is a queer taste in these eleven chapters which is not easily defined: a double-flavoured taste—half topography, half romance. Sanditon is not like Lyme or Highbury or Northanger or the other places that provide scenes or titles to past novels. It exists in itself and for itself. Character-drawing, incident, and wit are on the decline, but topography comes to the front, and is screwed much deeper than usual into the story. Mr. Parker is an Enthusiast for Sanditon. He has invested money in the resort, so has Lady Denham; and not only their humours but their fortunes depend on its development and the filling of its lodging-houses. Isn't this new? Was there anything like it in the preceding novels which were purely social?

And—now for the romantic flavour—is there not a new cadence in this prose?

"Charlotte having received possession of her apartment, found amusement enough in standing at her ample Venetian window and looking over the miscellaneous foreground of unfinished Buildings, waving Linen, and tops of Houses, to the Sea, dancing and sparkling in Sunshine and Freshness."

"Found amusement enough" is typical Jane Austen, but the conclusion of the sentence belongs to someone else—to someone who has been laughed out of court but who now returns in more radiant garb. It is Mrs. Radcliffe. She is creeping back attired as a Nereid, and not without hope of brandishing some day the sword Excalibur.

"Poor Burns's known irregularities greatly interrupt my enjoyment of his Lines."

Very proper that they should, but why enjoy such lines at all? Why read and discuss Burns, Wordsworth, and Scott? The new literature rises over old landmarks like a tide, and not only does the sea dance in freshness, but another configuration has been given to the earth, making it at once more poetic and more definite. Sanditon gives out an atmosphere, and also exists as a geographic and economic force. It was clearly intended to influence the faded fabric of the story and govern its matrimonial weavings. Of course, Miss Austen would not have stressed this, and her book, even if conceived with vigour, would not have marked a turning-point in the English novel or overshadowed *Waverley*. The change is merely interesting because it took place in her mind—that self-contained mind which had hitherto regarded the face of the earth as a site for shrubberies and strawberry beds, and had denied it features of its own. Perhaps here, too, we can trace the influence of ill-health: the invalid looks out of her window, weary of her invaluable Cassandra, weary of civility and auntish fun, and finds an unexpected repose in the expanses of Nature:

"At last, from the low French windows of the Drawing-room, which commanded the road and all the Paths across the Down, Charlotte and Sir Edward, as they sat, could not but observe Lady Denham and Miss Brereton...."

"The road and all the Paths across the Down." The cadence is curious again: Henry Tilney would have pricked up his ears. After all, they have not been exorcized—those ebony cabinets and massive chests that so disquieted Catherine's sleep. The Lady of the Lake is creeping out of them, followed by her entire school. (148–152)

Even more devastating is Marilyn Butler's dismissal of what advocates of *Sanditon* find its most attractive quality, the refreshing new prose technique.

> The sensitive, new-style descriptions in *Sanditon* occur in isolated passages, and the ordinary narrative prose is often so crude that it startles: it is surprising that even a first draft by the author of *Emma* would be quite like this. (288)

However, for many other commentators, such as John Halperin, despite its unfinished state the novel is theoretically a magnificent achievement and a high-water mark in Jane Austen's career:

> [We] must... bitterly regret the catastrophic illness which put a stop to the writing of *Sanditon*. It promised to be one of her greatest achievements; her critics and students ignore it at their peril. (1983: 189)

Marvin Mudrick is of the same persuasion as John Halperin that in *Sanditon* we see, at least potentially, the best work produced by Jane Austen.

> Uncertainty of development may, indeed, mean complexity of development. (242)

> In her final work... her irony finds its renewed and, at least potentially, most uninhibited opportunity; it is, in fact, her irony that is dynamic, changing or expanding at last into an authentically unrestricted... point of view. (257)

Although the *Sanditon* manuscript bears certain similarities to the *Persuasion* manuscript, written less than a year earlier, there are many remarkable differences. In contrast to composing her work on the small, individual sheets of paper, as tradition tells us was her habitual practice, she penned the fragment preserved in Cambridge in three sewn booklets. Whereas the *Persuasion* manuscript (admittedly, only the partly rejected closing chapters, now in the British Library, exist) has the consistent character of a draft with numerous revisions, some of them extensive, the *Sanditon* manuscript is to a far greater extent lacking in uniformity. Some pages, like the first, are heavily revised, some pages are lightly revised, and a few pages are so clean that they could pass for final drafts.

Further, whereas the short extant *Persuasion* manuscript occupied only a few days, the longer *Sanditon* manuscript is dated over a much longer period, during a time that her health was failing rapidly. There is evidence throughout of changing states of health: the passage originally written in pencil and revised in ink, and some pages written in the bold, clear hand recognizable from the earlier letters contrasting with some sheets on which the writing is so poor that a reader can only wonder at her determination to continue while experiencing the worst imaginable physical discomfort.

A prevailing feeling in working with this manuscript is that some of the problems suggest not merely carelessness or illness, but the possibility of her copying—sometimes inaccurately—from another source, perhaps the small slips of paper that she had used a year earlier for the *Persuasion* manuscript, serving as scratch sheets before being transferred to the more permanent form of the stitched booklets. There are also a few suggestions of inaccurate transcription from dictated material.

How long, then, is a first draft a "first draft" when it contains changes that can be considered "corrected and revised" and going "a long way towards fulfilling the author's intention"? Even a "final draft" undergoes last-minute changes in galley proof. And in the case of a process writer like Jane Austen, there was perhaps no "final draft" until her family wrested the manuscript away from her to send it to the publisher. There is every likelihood that she continued to make changes on the copy that she would have kept for herself.

Sanditon opens up new vistas of narrative style with its detailed descriptions of the sea and surrounding area as well as delineations of characters, both eccentric and normal, beyond anything seen in her earlier work. Completed, it might have been her undoubted masterpiece, and perhaps her own consciousness of the power of the piece drove her to work despite failing health. The most frustrating thing about this manuscript, of course, is that during the time that she spent revising the existing 120 pages, she could probably have written an additional 120 pages, giving us perhaps two-fifths of a novel and a much clearer idea of what direction it was taking. However, this was clearly not her method of writing. Sometimes corrections are made immediately and sometimes shortly after composition. Obviously she did not think in terms of committing an entire book to paper before revising it.

Perhaps the most remarkable thing about the revisions in the *Sanditon* manuscript is that one entire page-length (middle of page 69 [f35r] to middle of page 70 [f35v]) was originally in pencil, presumably because Jane Austen, at that moment too ill to sit up at her desk and write with ink and quill, instead perhaps assumed a reclining position wherein she could work more easily in pencil. And soon thereafter, in extremely faltering handwriting, she not only wrote over this penciled material in ink, but she made several significant revisions. In one instance, she changed a verb, thereby improving the point of the text. In another place, she probably accidentally repeated a word and therefore crossed through the repeat. Two words added above the line were not in the penciled original. Even in what would appear to be the mechanical act of covering pencil with ink, our author has taken steps to improve her text.

II. The Manuscript

I f family legend is true that Jane Austen composed her novels on small slips of paper—and supporting evidence can be seen in the 16 leaves written in 1816 constituting the canceled chapters of *Persuasion* now in the British Library (Egerton 3038)—she departed dramatically from this practice during the last year of her life.

Now preserved in the Library of King's College, Cambridge, the autograph manuscript of what is known as *Sanditon* consists of 80 paper leaves distributed into three stitched gatherings of 16, 24, and 40 leaves. Brian Southam suggests in the Introduction (v) to his facsimile publication of the manuscript that Jane Austen herself may have stitched together these three booklets. Although the number of words is generally estimated to be about 24,000 ("Total text lines: 1350; Total word count: 23493" [*The Victorian Literary Studies Archive Hyper-Concordance*]), if all corrections are included the total is closer to 28,000 (Teran Lee Sacco reports that she transcribed "24,804 words" [175] but does not specify if she is including changes). If this total is divided by the 119 pages bearing text (the final folio, 60v, contains only a single line of seven words), each page has an average of 235 words. In the 51 days between Monday, January 27, 1817, and Tuesday, March 18, 1817 (1817 was not a leap year), Jane Austen wrote an average of 549 words a day or about two and one-third pages. This estimate does not include what may have been earlier drafts on lost pieces of paper.

The first gathering, of wove paper (writing paper with a very faint mesh pattern and a virtually uniform texture, produced by pressing the pulp against a very fine netting) watermarked "KENT 1812," measures about 7

1/2 inches high by about 4 1/2 inches wide. The foliation extends from 1r to 16v. At the top left of folio 1r is the date "Jan. 27, 1817," and centered at the top of the page is a large numeral "1," which may represent both "Chapter 1" and that the first two gatherings are seen as continuous (although the second gathering was probably not ready when she reached the last side of the first gathering). "Chapter 2" begins on folio 8v, and "Chapter 3" begins on folio 13r. That the second gathering was not ready as the author completed work on this portion of the novel is suggested by her writing the closing line of the third chapter at the bottom of folio 1r.

The second gathering, also of wove paper and watermarked "KENT 1812," likewise measures about 7 1/2 inches high by about 4 1/2 inches wide. The foliation extends from 17r to 40v. At the top of folio 17r appears "Chapter 4." "Chapter 5" begins on folio 21r, "Chapter 6" begins on folio 25r, "Chapter 7" begins on folio 29v, "Chapter 8" begins on folio 36v, and "Chapter 9" begins on folio 39v. That the third gathering was ready as the author completed work on this portion of the novel is suggested by the continuation of "Chapter 9" from folio 40v to folio 41r.

The third gathering, of laid paper (a paper which shows thick and thin lines at right angles to each other, produced by having thin wires placed very close together and fastened to thicker wires running at right angles at intervals of about 1 inch) watermarked "Joseph Coles 1815," measures about 6 1/4 inches high by almost 4 inches wide. The foliation of the used portion of this gathering extends from 41r to 60v (the last 20 leaves are blank). At the top of folio 41r is the date "March 1st." and a large numeral "2." The text continues from the preceding folio 40v. Since the first folio opens with a large numeral "1," the author may have thought of the first two gatherings as "Number 1," to be followed by (perhaps pairs of) gatherings numbered "2" and so on. "Chapter 9" is continued from the preceding gathering, with "Chapter 10" beginning on folio 45v, "Chapter 11" beginning on folio 52v, and "Chapter 12" beginning on folio 55v. Below the seven words on folio 60v, the author's final effort on this novel, Jane Austen wrote "March 18," four months before her death on July 18, 1817. Her dating this last gathering "March 1st." only 17 days before she stopped, with many blank pages awaiting composition, suggests that she felt well enough to assume that her illness was not fatal and that despite suffering she would complete this new work.

The projected length of the finished novel remains uncertain. If it was intended to replace "Susan"/"Catherine," then it may have been meant to be more or less the same length as the manuscript posthumously published as *Northanger Abbey* with *Persuasion* in December 1817. However, the fairly leisurely pace (we reach Chapter 12 without any certainty about the direction of the plot) suggests that it was meant to be more on the order of *Mansfield Park* and *Emma*. There is no evidence that she planned to publish "Susan"/"Catherine" with another manuscript, so there is no way to establish that this updated version was to be part of a two-novel set.

As an aside, there is no hint in extant correspondence that Jane Austen intended publishing the manuscript now known as *Persuasion* with another work. Quite the contrary is suggested by the only two references to the recently completed novel, both in letters to her niece, Fanny Knight:

> "I have a something ready for Publication, which may perhaps appear about a twelvemonth hence. It is short, about the length of Catherine." (Thursday, March 13, 1817; *Letters*: 333; Modert: F-433)

> "Do not be surprised at finding Uncle Henry acquainted with my having another ready for publication. I could not say No when he asked me, but he knows nothing more of it.—You will not like it, so you need not be impatient. You may *perhaps* like the Heroine, as she is almost too good for me." (Sunday, March 23, 1817; *Letters*: 335; Modert: F-439–F-440)

Comparison with the novels published during her lifetime may (or may not) shed some light on the question of the intended length of the unfinished manuscript. *Sense and Sensibility* may occasionally feel like the longest of the novels, but at about 119,000 words it is actually the shortest, handily topped—despite the second novel's being "lopt & cropt" as she reports to Cassandra on Friday, January 29, 1813 (*Letters*: 202; Modert: F-237)—by *Pride and Prejudice*, which feels too short since we want to know so much more about these people, at nearly 122,000 words. For sheer mass, *Mansfield Park* exceeds both of its predecessors, taking the reader through just short of 170,000 words. *Emma*, which does not contain a single word that feels as though it could be expunged, is slightly shorter than its immediate predecessor at almost 160,000 words.

By any standards, these four novels are very long and complex, leading to the conviction that Jane Austen's oft-quoted lines to her 18-year-old nephew James Edward Austen (known to the family as "Edward," he did not become

Austen-Leigh until 1836), "What should I do with your strong, manly, spirited Sketches, full of Variety & Glow?—How could I possibly join them on to the little bit (two Inches wide) of Ivory on which I work with so fine a Brush, as produces little effect after much labour?" (Monday, December 16/Tuesday, December 17, 1816; *Letters*: 323; Modert: 416), constitute mere pleasantries to compliment his youthful efforts rather than a serious description of her own published work.

The idea that Jane Austen's novels, despite their considerable length, can be likened to charming painted miniatures like that of the late Mr. Hollis inconspicuously displayed in his own sitting room in Sanditon House, has caught the fancy of commentators, with Lloyd W. Brown using *Bits of Ivory* as the title of his fine study published in 1973. However, Richard Jenkyns, by posting a disclaimer in the Preface to his insightful "Appreciation" of Jane Austen, *A Fine Brush on Ivory*, attempts to set the record straight about this famous passage: "My title derives, as many readers will recognise, from Jane Austen's notorious description of her work as 'the little bit (two Inches wide) of Ivory on which I work with so fine a Brush, as produces little effect after much labour'. The context of these words is flippant, however; they come from a letter to her nephew in which she plays with a fantasy about stealing some of his adolescent prose to use in a novel of her own. In Jane Austen's writings—in her titles, even—we should always be ready for irony" (ix). Thus we should not take these two titles—or Jane Austen's lighthearted "self-assessment" to her nephew—too literally. Or too seriously.

Described by the author as a "short" novel, *Persuasion*, totaling a mere 83,386 words, is presumably in the final form that Jane Austen intended. Her comments to Fanny Knight on March 13, 1817, suggest that she saw some advantages in writing shorter novels or at least recognized that it was not necessary to add and pad if a story could be told with brevity. And since the manuscript of "Susan"/"Catherine," to appear as *Northanger Abbey*, was even more concise at about 78,000 words, making it a suitable publishing mate for the book completed in 1816, we have a further suggestion that Jane Austen now thought in terms of writing shorter, more compact works. If (and this remains an enormous "IF") the final, unfinished manuscript was a replacement for the rejected "Susan"/"Catherine," then it may also have been planned to contain about 80,000 words.

If (again a huge "IF") this is a logical assumption, it is not supported by the views of some notable contemporary scholars that this new manuscript was meant to be a lengthy work. For example, Jon Spence writes that "if you compare the twelve chapters of *Sanditon* to the first twelve chapters of Austen's completed novels, you see how radically different *Sanditon* was to have been. The story has hardly begun. It was apparently to have been a very long novel" (232), and Deirdre Le Faye reminds her readers that Jane Austen "put the manuscript aside for the last time on 18 March, having drafted the first twelve chapters of what was evidently planned to be a long and most amusing story" (2002: 38).

In contrast, and in addition to stating that in "Susan"/"Catherine" we have the genesis of the final manuscript, Brian Southam indirectly suggests that if anything the work now known as *Sanditon* may have been intended to be shorter than its original because its plot and settings have been simplified:

> *Sanditon* repairs a slight clumsiness in the structure of *Northanger Abbey*, which, according to one theory, may have been first put together by joining two of the childhood pieces—a pastiche of the Fanny Burney situation and a Gothic satire—and running the two stories together, with a single heroine, using Bath as the stage for the parade of character types and the round of embarrassments and the Abbey as the setting for the Gothic reversal. In *Sanditon*, the two locations are combined. (1976: 8)

If this final manuscript is really "Susan"/"Catherine" in new garb, it is also presumably more or less the same length, particularly if there was any plan to publish it jointly with its immediate predecessor. Possibly *Persuasion* and *Northanger Abbey* were issued together because Jane Austen had shared such an idea with family members. With no way of knowing how the story was to proceed or how rapidly the events were to evolve, we can only hypothesize on the question of its length when completed. Thus, just as we wonder about the fate of Edwin Drood following his disappearance or ponder the awful decision about which is behind the sealed door, the lady or the tiger, we must continue to formulate educated… guesses.

That there are also several letters from this period suggests that she was spending a good deal of her enforced rest at her little writing desk. On Thursday, January 23, 1817, only four days before commencing work on the manuscript, she wrote a short, cheery letter to Caroline (Mary Craven) Austen (1805–1880, the youngest of James Austen's three children and younger sister of James Edward Austen-Leigh) (*Letters*: 325–326; Modert:

F-421–F-423). The lighthearted text—including a near-pun on "Better" and "Butter"—is filled with small details of family business. In reference to her own health, she reports, "I feel myself getting stronger than I was half a year ago, & can so perfectly walk to Alton, *or* back again, without the slightest fatigue that I hope to be able to do both when Summer comes." The handwriting is firm and clear, but if she has a new novel in mind she says nothing about it.

The next day, Friday, January 24, 1817, in her familiar firm and clear handwriting she wrote a long letter to her old friend, Alethea Bigg (d. 1855) (*Letters*: 326–328; original lost). Again there is no suggestion that she is about to begin work on a new piece of fiction. The chatty letter is mostly about things happening in the family, with especially good news about her health: "We are all in good health [&] I have certainly gained strength through the Winter & am not far from being well; & I think I understand my own case now so much better than I did, as to be able to care to keep off any serious return of illness. I am more & more convinced that *Bile* is at the bottom of all I have suffered, which makes it easy to know how to treat myself." There is light humor about her donkeys' having forgotten their education from not being used on a regular basis to draw their carriages. Preferring it to much of Robert Southey's earlier work, she has "been reading the 'Poet's Pilgrimage to Waterloo' [published in 1816], & generally with much approbation.... The opening—the *Proem* I beleive he calls it—is very beautiful. Poor Man! One cannot but grieve for the loss of the Son so fondly described. Has he at all recovered it?" Southey's 10-year-old son, Herbert, had died in April 1816 (*Letters*, Chapman: Note to Letter 139), almost a year after the great Battle of Waterloo (June 18, 1815). The child is referred to several times in the most tender and loving language:

Proem

VI.
Aloft on yonder bench, with arms dispread,
My boy stood, shouting there his father's name,
Waving his hat around his happy head;
And there, a younger group, his sisters came:
Smiling they stood with looks of pleased surprize,
While tears of joy were seen in elder eyes.

XV.
But there stood one whose heart could entertain
And comprehend the fullness of the joy;
The father, teacher, playmate, was again
Come to his only and his studious boy;
And he beheld again that mother's eye,
Which with such ceaseless care had watched his infancy.

XVIII.

…

The hope, the wonder, and the restless joy
Of those glad girls, and that vociferous boy!

In *The Poet's Pilgrimage to Waterloo*, the long poem that won Jane Austen's approval, Southey took stock of the recent turbulent and bitter course of history which Napoleon's defeat promised finally to check. Officially the work is a laureate's ode of national thanksgiving, but Southey was unprepared for the suffering that he witnessed on his visit to the hospital at the site of the battle—privately describing it as 'the real face of war', and the *Pilgrimage* unfolds his struggle with a deeply invasive experience of desolation before returning to a festive major key. In keeping with this positive mood, the poem moves from realism to allegory, from descriptions of Flanders and the scene of war to a visionary part II dominated by the rival figures of Wisdom and the Heavenly Muse. To Wisdom, a latter-day spokesman for the Enlightenment, falls the task of evoking the disillusion and ruin that have followed in the wake of the glorious days of Revolution. To Urania, who fills the poet with a spirit of renewal,… goes the brief of restoring faith in a benign providence and the power of mystery. But despite the high drama of the poet's conversion, the poem's most remembered lines come from its evil prophet who pictures a universe as callous and imperfect as man.…

History seems to have conspired against the overt optimism of the *Pilgrimage*, for the glowing scene of family reunion with which the poem opens was overshadowed, shortly after publication, by the death of Southey's only son. The news was widely known, and coloured the reception of the poem for many, including Jane Austen.…

Southey designed his poem to celebrate not merely British victory over the French but the triumph of religion over 'gross material philosophy'. Though the theodicial and other doctrinal aspects of Southey's poem are likely to strike readers today as the least satisfactory part of it, there can be little question that they appealed to Jane Austen. Nine months before Napoleon's defeat she ventured a view on the providential guidance of war very similar to that in the *Pilgrimage*. Writing to the wife-to-be of Francis, the elder of her two sailor brothers, she holds out for eventual victory over America on the grounds that Britain has the stronger 'claim to the protection of Heaven, as a Religious Nation, a Nation inspite of much Evil improving in Religion.' [note 19: To Martha Lloyd, 2 Sept. 1814, *Letters*, pp. 273-4.] (Knox-Shaw: 157–159)

Shortly after the publication of the poem, many people, including Jane Austen, learned of the death of Southey's son. There is special interest in Mr. Knox-Shaw's line, "The news was widely known, and coloured the reception of the poem for many, including Jane Austen." One has the impression that her condolences are directed entirely toward the grieving father, with no consideration of the desolation of the mother (Edith Fricker Southey, sister of Sara Fricker Coleridge, wife of Samuel Taylor Coleridge) nor of what the child may have experienced in pain and fear in the process of dying. Jane Austen was not the most tender-hearted person in regard to suffering if we are to believe passages in her extant letters, and her sympathy here seems to lie more in what she estimates to be a well-written Proem than in the tragedy itself. The combination of reference to Waterloo and this cool indifference to illness and death could have been the germ from which the idea of the final manuscript came to her.

Before coming to the real reason for the letter to Alethea Bigg, a request for the "receipt" (that is, "recipe") for orange wine, she particularly hopes that Miss Betsy Williams is well, and that her sister, Charlotte (born ca. 1783), is likewise in good health. In her letter to Cassandra Austen dated Monday/Tuesday October 11/12, 1813, she had confided, "I admire the Sagacity & Taste of Charlotte Williams. Those large dark eyes always judge well. — I will compliment her, by naming a Heroine after her" (*Letters*: 235, Modert: F-275).

On January 27, 1817, three days after writing her letter to Alethea Bigg, Jane Austen began work on the manuscript now known as *Sanditon*, including the character Charlotte Heywood as the most likely candidate for romantic heroine. In the course of discussing Elizabeth Bennet, David M. Shapard indirectly suggests that Charlotte Williams has a rival in Jane Austen's favorite novel ("It has long been known to us that Richardson was her favourite novelist, and *Grandison* her favourite novel" [Austen, *Sir Charles Grandison*, 1980: 3]) as the source of the name of the new Susan/Catherine: "[Her] strongest literary affinity is probably with a character who is mostly a humorous supporting figure: Charlotte Grandison, the sister of the hero in Richardson's *Sir Charles Grandison*, and in many ways the most interesting and vital figure in that novel" (xxviii).

The name Charlotte was one that Jane Austen had already used several times, most notably in *Pride and Prejudice*, where we meet Elizabeth Bennet's best friend and the eventual wife of Mr. Collins, Charlotte Lucas. In *Sense and Sensibility*, Jane Austen introduces the character of Charlotte Palmer, a good-tempered young woman. And in *Northanger Abbey* there is a very minor character named Charlotte Davis. The name was a popular one at the time, no doubt in honor of both Queen Charlotte (1744–1818), consort of George III, and the beloved daughter of the Prince Regent, Princess Charlotte Augusta of Wales (January 7, 1796–November 5, 1817), who married Prince Leopold of Saxe-Coburg in 1816 and died the following year in childbirth. At the time of the composition of *Sanditon*, the Princess had been married less than a year and appeared to be second in line to the throne.

Fanny Knight (1793–1882, elder daughter of Edward Austen-Knight) was the recipient of Jane Austen's next letter, dated Thursday, February 20, 1817 (*Letters*: 328–331; Modert: F-425–F-428), twenty-five days into the composition of *Sanditon* (with a possible 13,725 words, or half the manuscript, already composed). Writing at length, Jane Austen expresses her deep love of her niece in a playful tone remarkably reminiscent of some passages in *Sanditon*: "You are worth your weight in Gold, or even in the new Silver coinage.... You are the Paragon of all that is Silly & Sensible, common-place & eccentric, Sad & Lively, Provoking & Interesting.—Who can keep pace with the fluctuations of your Fancy, the Capprizios of your Taste, the Contradictions of your Feelings?—You are so odd!" With so much work already accomplished on her new manuscript, and the prospect before her of bringing to completion a major work of her mature period, Jane Austen had every reason to be drunk with joy in writing to Fanny. Her own health is of minor concern: "I am almost entirely cured of my rheumatism;

just a little pain in my knee now & then, to make me remember what it was, & and keep on flannel." Characteristically, despite all the chatter and loving confidences—including reference to praise of *Emma*, the perfect opportunity to mention the project underway—there is no suggestion that she is currently well into her newest and most innovative novel.

A very short letter to Caroline Austen followed on Wednesday, February 26, 1817 (*Letters*: 331; Modert: F-429–F-430), which despite references to her niece's writing interests—"I look forward to the 4 new Chapters with pleasure.—But how can you like Frederick better than Edgar?—You have some eccentric Tastes however I know, as to Heroes & Heroines."—fails to suggest in any way that she herself is engaged in writing a new novel.

By the time that Jane Austen wrote her next preserved letter, a long one to Fanny Knight, dated Thursday, March 13, 1817 (*Letters*: 331–334; Modert: F-431–F-435), she was only five days short of completing the manuscript to its present point. For the most part the handwriting is firm, showing none of the apparent distress seen in parts of the manuscript. Typically, she avoids any reference to her work in progress despite her restatement in "Single Women have a dreadful propensity for being poor" of Lady Denham's cold dismissal of Miss Esther Denham's plight ("Ah, young ladies that have no money are very much to be pitied!"). She does confide, however, that one novel ("Susan"/"Catherine") known to the family will not be published whereas another, not yet known (and apparently not yet named by her but to appear posthumously as *Persuasion*), will soon appear—"Miss Catherine is put upon the Shelve for the present, and I do not know that she will ever come out;—but I have a something ready for Publication, which may perhaps appear about a twelvemonth hence. It is short, about the length of Catherine.—This is for you alone." Whatever may be the downward slide of her own state of health, she is optimistic about her improvement: "I am got tolerably well again, quite equal to walking about & enjoying the Air; & by sitting down & resting a good while between my Walks, I get exercise enough." She must have been confident that her current effort, now well underway despite constant textual revisions, would be a well-wrought, updated version of the rejected "Susan">"Catherine" and a worthy companion or successor to the work later published as *Persuasion*.

The final letter preceding March 18 is the short one to Caroline Austen, dated Friday, March 14, 1817 (*Letters*: 334–335; Modert: F-437–F-438). The writing is large and clear but with some decline in neatness near the end. Despite her delight in reporting some financial gain from her first publication—"I have just recd nearly twenty pounds myself on the 2d Edit. of S & S- which gives me this fine flow of Literary Ardour"—there is again nothing to suggest that she is well along in her new novel, filled with fascinating creatures both normal and eccentric, not the least of them Sir Edward Denham, whose thrice-repeated "Ardour" fails to convince Charlotte Heywood of his exquisite sensibilities.

There is, then, no reference in any extant letters to her work on this final manuscript.

After Jane Austen died, the manuscript passed to her niece, Jane Anna Elizabeth Austen (1793–1872, eldest daughter of James Austen and only child of his first wife, Anne Mathew Austen), who upon marrying Benjamin Lefroy on November 8, 1814, became Anna Lefroy. "After Anna's death it remained in the Lefroy family until in 1930 it was presented by Anna's grand-daughter Mary Isabella Lefroy (1860–1939) to the Library of King's College, Cambridge, in memory of the donor's sister Florence Emma Austen-Leigh (1857–1926) and the latter's husband Augustus Austen-Leigh (1840–1905), sixth son of Jane Austen's nephew and first biographer James Edward Austen-Leigh and Provost of King's College, Cambridge, from 1889 until his death" (Gilson, 2003: viii).

John Halperin is but one of many critics who regard the manuscript as "only a first draft" (1983: 183). However, I remain convinced on the basis of examining every word of the manuscript (including corrections) that it is in part close to a finished product. The amount of labor, the detailed revisions that used up precious time that could have been employed in advancing the story, the obvious care in bringing every line up to a personal standard— all suggest that we have in part a fairly finished product lacking only a sympathetic editor's hand. As I attempt to show in *Jane Austen Caught in the Act of Greatness*, this final manuscript was, at the time that the author stopped working on it, well on its way to becoming her finest effort.

III. The History of the Text

T here is no reference to the incomplete manuscript in the biographical material that Jane Austen's brother, Henry Austen, wrote for the posthumous joint-publication of *Northanger Abbey* and *Persuasion* (1817/1818), nor does her nephew, James Edward Austen-Leigh, mention it in the first edition of his biography, *A Memoir of Jane Austen*, published in 1870 by Richard Bentley.

The first announcement to the world outside the family of the existence of the manuscript now known as *Sanditon* came in the second edition of James Edward Austen-Leigh's *Memoir of Jane Austen, to which is added Lady Susan, and fragments of two other unfinished tales by Miss Austen,* published in London in 1871 by Richard Bentley and Son. At 364 pages a much-expanded version of the 236-page-long first edition of 1870, this book presents a summary of the novelist's last effort along with excerpts, some rendered verbatim and some paraphrased.

I have followed James Edward Austen-Leigh's punctuation despite occasional ambiguity (clearly Jane Austen's nephew, like his aunt before him, did not write for dull elves). The manuscript readings are in square brackets.

CHAPTER XIII.

The last Work.

Jane Austen was taken from us: how much unexhausted talent perished with her, how largely she might yet have contributed to the entertainment of her readers, if her life had been prolonged, cannot be known; but it is certain that the mine at which she had so long laboured was not worked out, and that she was still diligently employed in collecting fresh materials from it. 'Persuasion' had been finished in August 1816; some time was probably given to correcting it for the press; but on the 27th of the following January, according to the date on her own manuscript, she began a new novel, and worked at it up to the 17th of March. The chief part of this manuscript is written in her usual firm and neat hand, but some of the latter pages seem to have been first traced in pencil, probably when she was too weak to sit long at her desk, and written over in ink afterwards. The quantity produced does not indicate any decline of power or industry, for in those seven weeks twelve chapters had been completed. It is more difficult to judge of the quality of a work so little advanced. It had received no name; there was scarcely any indication what the course of the story was to be, nor was any heroine yet perceptible, who, like Fanny Price, or Anne Elliot, might draw round her the sympathies of the reader. Such an unfinished fragment cannot be presented to the public; but I am persuaded that some of Jane Austen's admirers will be glad to learn something about the latest creations which were forming themselves in her mind; and therefore, as some of the principal characters were already sketched in with a vigorous hand, I will try to give an idea of them, illustrated by extracts from the work.

The scene is laid at Sanditon, a village on the Sussex coast, just struggling into notoriety as a bathing-place, under the patronage of the two principal proprietors of the parish, Mr. Parker and Lady Denham.

Mr. Parker was an amiable man, with more enthusiasm than judgment, whose somewhat shallow mind overflowed with the one idea of the prosperity of Sanditon, together with a jealous contempt of the rival village of Brinshore, where a similar attempt was going on. To the regret of his much-enduring wife, he had left his family mansion, with all its ancestral comforts of gardens, shrubberies, and shelter, situated in a valley some miles inland, and had built a new residence—a Trafalgar House—on the bare brow of the hill overlooking Sanditon and the sea, exposed to every wind that blows; but he will confess to no discomforts, nor suffer his family to feel any from the change. The following extract brings him before the reader, mounted on his hobby:—

'He wanted to secure the promise of a visit, and to get as many of the family as his own house would hold to follow him to Sanditon as soon as possible; and, healthy as all the Heywoods undeniably were, he foresaw that every one of them would be benefitted by the sea. [He wanted to secure the promise of a visit—to get as many of the Family as his own house wd. contain, to follow him to Sanditon as soon as possible—and healthy as they all undeniably were—foresaw that every one of them wd. be benefited by the sea.] He held it indeed as certain that no person, however upheld for the present by fortuitous aids of exercise and spirit in a semblance of health, could be really in a state of secure and permanent health without spending at six weeks by the sea every year. [He held it indeed as certain, that no person cd. be really well, no person, (however upheld for the present by fortuitous aids of exercise & spirits in a semblance of Health) could be really in a state of secure & permanent Health without spending at least 6 weeks by the Sea every year.] The sea air and sea-bathing together were nearly infallible; one or other of them being a match for every disorder of the stomach, the lungs, or the blood. [The Sea air & Sea Bathing together were nearly infallible, one or the other of them being a match for every Disorder, of the Stomach, the Lungs or the Blood;] They were anti-spasmodic, anti-pulmonary, anti-bilious, and anti-rheumatic. [They were anti-spasmodic, anti-pulmonary, anti-sceptic anti-bilious & anti-rheumatic.] Nobody could catch cold by the sea; nobody wanted appetite by the sea; nobody wanted spirits; nobody wanted strength. [Nobody could catch cold by the Sea, Nobody wanted appetite by the Sea, Nobody wanted Spirits, Nobody wanted Strength.] They were healing, softening, relaxing, fortifying, and bracing, seemingly just as was wanted; sometimes one, sometimes the other. [They were healing, softing, relaxing—fortifying & bracing—seemingly just as was wanted—sometimes one, sometimes the other.] If the sea breeze failed, the sea-bath was the certain corrective; and when bathing disagreed, the sea breeze was evidently designed by nature for the cure. [If the Sea breeze failed, the Sea-Bath was the certain corrective;—& where Bathing disagreed, the Sea Breeze alone was evidently designed by Nature for the cure.] His eloquence, however, could not prevail. Mr. and Mrs. Heywood never left home.... . [His eloquence however could not prevail. Mr— & Mrs. H— never left home. Marrying early & having a very numerous family... a Winter at Bath;] The maintenance, education, and fitting out of fourteen children demanded a very quiet, settled, careful course of life; and obliged them to be stationary and healthy at Willingden. [but the maintenance, Education & fitting out of 14 children demanded a very quiet, settled, careful course of Life—& obliged them to be stationary & healthy at Willingden.] What prudence had at first enjoined was now rendered pleasant by habit. [What Prudence had at first enjoined, was now rendered pleasant by Habit.] They never left home, and they had a gratification in saying so.' [They never left home, & they had a gratification in saying so.]

Lady Denham's was a very different character. She was a rich vulgar widow, with a sharp but narrow mind, who cared for the prosperity of Sanditon only so far as it might increase the value of her own property. She is thus described:—

'Lady Denham had been a rich Miss Brereton, born to wealth, but not to education. [Lady D. had been a rich Miss Brereton, born to Wealth but not to Education.] Her first husband had been a Mr. Hollis, a man of considerable property in the country, of which a large share of the parish of Sanditon, with manor and mansion-house formed a part. [Her first Husband had been a Mr. Hollis, a man of considerable Property in the Country, of which a large share of the Parish of Sanditon, with Manor & Mansion House made a part.] He had been an elderly man when she married him; her own age about thirty. [He had been an elderly Man when she married him;—her own age about 30.] Her motives for such a match could be little understood at the distance of forty years, but she had so well nursed and pleased Mr. Hollis that at his death he left her everything—all his estates, and all at her disposal. [Her motives for such a Match could be little understood at the distance of 40 years, but she had so well nursed & pleased Mr. Hollis, that at his Death he left her everything—all his Estates, & all at her Disposal.] After a widowhood of some years she had been induced to marry again. [After a widowhood of some years, she had been induced to marry again.] The late Sir Harry Denham, of Denham Park, in the neighbourhood of Sanditon, succeeded in removing her and her large income to his own domains; but he could not succeed in the views of permanently enriching his family which were attributed to him. [The late Sir Harry Denham, of Denham Park in the Neighbourhood of Sanditon had succeeded in removing her & her large Income to his own Domains, but he cd. not succeed in the veiws of permanently enriching his family, which were attributed to him.] She had been too wary to put anything out of her own power, and when, on Sir Harry's death, she returned again to her own house at Sanditon, she was said to have made this boast, "that though she had *got* nothing but her title from the family, yet she had *given* nothing for it." [She had been too wary to put anything out of her own Power—and when on Sir Harry's Decease she returned again to her own House at Sanditon, she was said to have made this boast to a friend "that though she had <u>got</u> nothing but her Title from the Family, yet she had <u>given</u> nothing for it."] For the title it was to be supposed that she married. [For the Title, it was to be supposed that she had married—& Mr. P. acknowledged… "There is at times… you will judge for yourself."]

'Lady Denham was indeed a great lady, beyond the common wants of society; for she had many thousands a year to bequeath, and three distinct sets of people to be courted by:—her own relations, who might very reasonably wish for her original thirty thousand pounds among them; the legal heirs of Mr. Hollis, who might hope to be more indebted to *her* sense of justice than he had allowed them to be to *his*; and those members of the Denham family for whom her second husband had hoped to make a good bargain. [Lady D. was indeed a great Lady beyond the common wants of Society—for she had many Thousands a year to bequeath, & three distinct sets of People to be courted by; her own relations, who might very reasonably wish for her Original Thirty Thousand Pounds among them, the legal Heirs of Mr. Hollis, who must hope to be more endebted to <u>her</u> sense of Justice than he had allowed them to be to <u>his</u>, and those Members of the Denham Family, whom her 2d. Husband had hoped to make a good Bargain for.] By all these, or by branches of them, she had, no doubt, been long and still continued to be well attacked; and of these three divisions Mr. Parker did not hesitate to say that Mr. Hollis's kindred were the least in favour, and Sir Harry Denham's the most. [By all of these, or by Branches of them, she had no doubt been long, & still continued to be, well attacked;—and of these three divisions, Mr. P. did not hesitate to say that Mr. Hollis' Kindred were the <u>least</u> in favour & Sir Harry Denham's the <u>most</u>.] The former, he believed, had done themselves irremediable harm by expressions of very unwise resentment at the time of Mr. Hollis's death: the latter, to the advantage of being the remnant of a connection which she certainly valued, joined those of having been known to her from their childhood, and of being always at hand to pursue their interests by seasonable attentions. [The former he beleived, had done themselves irremediable harm by expressions of very unwise & unjustifiable resentment at the time of Mr. Hollis's death;—the Latter, to the advantage of being the remnant of a Connection which she certainly valued, joined those of having been known to her from their Childhood & of being always at hand to preserve their interest by reasonable attention. Sir Edward, the present Baronet... to the greater part of all that she had to give—] But another claimant was now to be taken into account: a young female relation whom Lady Denham had been induced to receive into her family. [but there was now another person's claims to be taken into the account, those of the young female relation, whom Lady D. had been induced to receive into her Family.] After having always protested against any such addition, and often enjoyed the repeated defeat she had given to every attempt of her own relations to introduce 'this young lady, or that young lady,' as a companion at Sanditon House, she had brought back with her from London last Michaelmas a Miss Clara Brereton, who bid fair to vie in favour with Sir Edward Denham, and to secure for herself and her family that share of the accumulated property which they had certainly the best right to inherit.' [After having always protested against any such Addition, and long & often enjoyed the repeated defeats she had given to every attempt of her relations to introduce this young Lady, or that young Lady as a Companion at Sanditon House, she had brought back with her from London last Michaelmas a Miss Brereton, who bid fair by her Merits to vie in favour with Sir Edward, & to secure for herself & her family that share of the accumulated Property which they had certainly the best right to inherit.]

Lady Denham's character comes out in a conversation which takes place at Mr. Parker's tea-table.

'The conversation turned entirely upon Sanditon, its present number of visitants, and the chances of a good season. [The

Conversation turned entirely upon Sanditon, its present number of Visitants & the Chances of a good Season.] It was evident that Lady Denham had more anxiety, more fears of loss than her coadjutor. [It was evident that Lady D. had more anxiety, more fears of loss, than her Coadjutor.] She wanted to have the place fill faster, and seemed to have many harassing apprehensions of the lodgings being in some instances underlet. [She wanted to have the Place fill faster, & seemed to have many harassing apprehensions of the Lodgings being in some instances under-let.—Miss Diana Parker's two large Families... a French Boarding School, is it?] To a report that a large boarding-school was expected she replies, 'Ah, well, no harm in that. [No harm in that.] They will stay their six weeks, and out of such a number who knows but some may be consumptive, and want asses' milk; and I have two milch asses at this very time. [They'll stay their six weeks.—And out of such a number, who knows but some may be consumptive & want Asses milk—& I have two Milch asses at this present time.] But perhaps the little Misses may hurt the furniture. [But perhaps the little Misses may hurt the Furniture.] I hope they will have a good sharp governess to look after them.' [I hope they will have a good sharp Governess to look after them.—"] But she wholly disapproved of Mr. Parker's wish to secure the residence of a medical man amongst them. [Poor Mr. Parker... Going after a Doctor!] 'Why, what should we do with a doctor here? [Why, what shd. we do with a Doctor here?] It would only be encouraging our servants and the poor to fancy themselves ill, if there was a doctor at hand. [It wd. be only encouraging our Servants & the Poor to fancy themselves ill, if there was a Dr. at hand.] Oh, pray let us have none of that tribe at Sanditon: we go on very well as we are. [Oh! pray, let us have none of the Tribe at Sanditon. We go on very well as we are.] There is the sea, and the downs, and my milch asses: and I have told Mrs. Whitby that if anybody enquires for a chamber horse, they may be supplied at a fair rate (poor Mr. Hollis's chamber horse, as good as new); and what can people want more? [There is the Sea & the Downs & my Milch- asses—& I have told Mrs. Whitby that if any body enquires for a Chamber-House, they may be supplied at a fair rate—(poor Mr. Hollis's Chamber Horse, as good as new)—and what can People want for more?] I have lived seventy good years in the world, and never took physic, except twice: and never saw the face of a doctor in all my life on my own account; and I really believe if my poor dear Sir Harry had never seen one neither, he would have been alive now. [Here have I lived 70 good years in the world & never took Physic above twice—and never saw the face of a Doctor in all my Life, on my <u>own</u> account.—And I verily beleive if my poor dear Sir Harry had never seen one neither, he wd. have been alive now.] Ten fees, one after another, did the men take who sent him out of the world. [Ten fees, one after another, did the Man take who sent <u>him</u> out of the World.] I beseech you, Mr. Parker, no doctors here.' [I beseech you Mr. Parker, no Doctors here."]

This lady's character comes out more strongly in a conversation with Mr. Parker's guest, Miss Charlotte Heywood. Sir Edward Denham with his sister Esther and Clara Brereton have just left them.

'Charlotte accepted an invitation from Lady Denham to remain with her on the terrace, when the others adjourned to the library. [but when there was a proposition for going into the Library she felt that she had had quite enough of Sir Edw: for one morng, & very gladly accepted Lady D.'s invitation of remaining on the Terrace with her.—The others all left them,… that is,] Lady Denham, like a true great lady, talked, and talked only of her own concerns, and Charlotte listened. [Lady Denham, like a true great lady, talked & talked only of her own concerns, & Charlotte listened—amused in considering… Lady D's discourse.] Taking hold of Charlotte's arm with the ease of one who felt that any notice from her was a favour, and communicative from the same sense of importance, or from a natural love of talking, she immediately said in a tone of great satisfaction, and with a look of arch sagacity:— [Taking hold of Charlotte's arm with the ease of one who felt that any notice from her was an Honour, & communicative, from the influence of the same conscious Importance or a natural love of talking, she immediately said in a tone of great satisfaction—& with a look of arch sagacity—]

'Miss Esther wants me to invite her and her brother to spend a week with me at Sanditon House, as I did last summer, but I shan't. ["Miss Esther wants me to invite her & her Brother to spend a week with me at Sanditon House, as I did last summer.— But I shan't.] She has been trying to get round me every way with her praise of this and her praise of that; but I saw what she was about. [She has been trying to get round me every way, with her praise of this, & her praise of that; but I saw what she was about.] I saw through it all. [I saw through it all.—] I am not very easily taken in, my dear.' [I am not very easily taken-in my Dear."]

Charlotte could think of nothing more harmless to be said than the simple enquiry of, 'Sir Edward and Miss Denham?' [Charlotte cd. think of nothing more harmless to be said, than the simple enquiry of—"Sir Edward & Miss Denham?"]

'Yes, my dear; *my young folks*, as I call them, sometimes: for I take them very much by the hand, and had them with me last summer, about this time, for a week—from Monday to Monday—and very delighted and thankful they were. ["Yes, my Dear. <u>My young Folks</u>, as I call them sometimes, for I take them very much by the hand. I had them with me last Summer, about this time, for a week; from Monday to Monday; and very delighted & thankful they were.] For they are very good young people, my dear. [For they are very good young People my Dear.] I would not have you think that I only notice them for poor dear Sir Harry's sake. [I wd. not have you think that I <u>only</u> notice them, for poor dear Sir Harry's sake.] No, no; they are very deserving themselves, or, trust me, they would not be so much in my company. [No, no; they are very deserving themselves, or, trust me, they wd. not be so much in <u>my</u> Company.] I am not the woman to help anybody blindfold. [I am not the Woman to help any body blindfold.] I always take care to know what I am about, and who I have to deal with before I stir a finger. [I always take care to know what I am about, & who I have to deal with, before I stir a finger.] I do not think I was ever overreached in my life; and that is a good deal for a woman to say that has been twice married. [I do not think I was ever over-reached in my Life; & That is a good deal for a Woman to say that has been married twice.] Poor dear Sir Harry (between ourselves) thought at first to have got more, but (with a bit of a sigh) he is gone, and we must not find fault with the dead. [Poor dear Sir Harry (between ourselves) thought at first to have got more.—But (with a bit of a sigh) He is gone, & we must not find fault with the Dead.] Nobody could live happier together than us: and he was a very honourable man, quite the gentleman, of ancient family; and when he died I gave Sir Edward his gold watch.' [Nobody could live happier together than us—& he was a very honourable Man, quite the Gentleman of ancient Family.—And when he died, I gave Sir Edwd. his Gold Watch."]

This was said with a look at her companion which implied its right to produce a great impression; and seeing no rapturous astonishment in Charlotte's countenance, she added quickly, [She said this with a look at her Companion which implied its' right to produce a great Impression—& seeing no rapturous astonishment in Charlottes countenance, added quickly—]

'He did not bequeath it to his nephew, my dear; it was no bequest; it was not in the will. ["He did not bequeath it to his Nephew, my dear—It was no bequest. It was not in the Will.] He only told me, and *that* but *once*, that he should wish his nephew to have his watch; but it need not have been binding, if I had not chose it.' [He only told me, & that but once, that he shd. wish his Nephew to have his Watch; but it need not have been binding, if I had not chose it.—"]

'Very kind indeed, very handsome!' said Charlotte, absolutely forced to affect admiration. ["Very kind indeed! very Handsome!"—said Charlotte, absolutely forced to affect admiration.—]

'Yes, my dear; and it is not the only kind thing I have done by him. ["Yes, my dear—& it is not the only kind thing I have done by him.] I have been a very liberal friend to Sir Edward; and, poor young man, he needs it bad enough. [I have been a very liberal friend to Sir Edwd. And poor young Man, he needs it bad enough;] For, though I am only the dowager, my dear, and he is the heir, things do not stand between us in the way they usually do between those two parties. [For though I am only the Dowager my Dear, & he is the Heir, things do not stand between us in the way they commonly do between those two parties.—] Not a shilling do I receive from the Denham estate. [Not a shilling do I receive from the Denham Estate.] Sir Edward has no payments to make *me*. [Sir Edw: has no Payments to make me.] *He* don't stand uppermost, believe me; it is *I* that help *him*.' [He don't stand uppermost, beleive me.—It is I that help him."]

'Indeed! he is a very fine young man, and particularly elegant in his address.' ["Indeed!—He is a very fine young Man;— particularly Elegant in his Address."—]

This was said chiefly for the sake of saying something; but Charlotte directly saw that it was laying her open to suspicion, by Lady Denham's giving a shrewd glance at her, and replying, [This was said cheifly for the sake of saying something—but Charlotte directly saw that it was laying her open to suspicion by Lady D.'s giving a shrewd glance at her & replying—]

'Yes, yes; he's very well to look at; and it is to be hoped that somebody of large fortune will think so; for Sir Edward *must* marry for money. ["Yes, yes, he is very well to look at—& it is to be hoped some Lady of large fortune will think so—for Sir Edwd—must marry for Money.] He and I often talk that matter over. [He & I often talk that matter over.] A handsome young man like him will go smirking and smiling about, and paying girls compliments, but he knows he *must* marry for money. [A handsome young fellow like him, will go smirking & smiling about & paying girls compliments, but he knows he must marry for Money.] And Sir Edward is a very steady young man, in the main, and has got very good notions.' [And Sir Edw: is a very steady young Man in the main, & has got very good notions."]

'Sir Edward Denham,' said Charlotte, 'with such personal advantages, may be almost sure of getting a woman of fortune, if he chooses it.' ["Sir Edw: Denham, said Charlotte, with such personal Advantages may be almost sure of getting a Woman of fortune, if he chuses it."—]

This glorious sentiment seemed quite to remove suspicion. [This glorious sentiment seemed quite to to remove suspicion.]

'Aye, my dear, that is very sensibly said; and if we could but get a young heiress to Sanditon! ["Aye my Dear—That's very sensibly said cried Lady D— And if we cd. but get a young Heiress to S!] But heiresses are monstrous scarce! [But Heiresses are monstrous scarce!] I do not think we have had an heiress here, nor even a Co., since Sanditon has been a public place. [I do not think we have had an Heiress here, or even a Co— since Sanditon has been a public place.] Families come after families, but, as far as I can learn, it is not one in a hundred of them that have any real property, landed or funded. [Families come after Families, but, as far as I can learn, it is not one in an hundred of them that have any real Property, Landed or Funded.—] An income, perhaps, but no property. [An Income perhaps, but no Property.] Clergymen, may be, or lawyers from town, or half-pay officers, or widows with only a jointure; and what good can such people do to anybody? [Clergymen, may be, or Lawyers from Town, or Half pay officers, or Widows with only a Jointure. And what good can such people do anybody?] Except just as they take our empty houses, and (between ourselves) I think they are great fools for not staying at home. [—except just as they take our empty Houses—and (between ourselves) I think they are great fools for not staying at home.] Now, if we could get a young heiress to be sent here for her health, and, as soon as she got well, have her fall in love with Sir Edward! [Now, if we could get a young Heiress to be sent here for her health—(and if she was ordered to drink asses milk I could supply her)—and as soon as she got well, have her fall in love with Sir Edward!—"] ["That would be very fortunate indeed."] And Miss Esther must marry somebody of fortune, too. ["And Miss Esther must marry somebody of fortune too—] She must get a rich husband. [She must get a rich Husband.] Ah! young ladies that have no money are very much to be pitied.' [Ah! young Ladies that have no Money are very much to be pitied!—] After a short pause: 'If Miss Esther thinks to talk me into inviting them to come and stay at Sanditon House, she will find herself mistaken. [But—after a short pause—if Miss Esther thinks to talk me into inviting them to come & stay at Sanditon House, she will find herself mistaken.—] Matters are altered with me since last summer, you know: I have Miss Clara with me now, which makes a great difference. [Matters are altered with me since last Summer you know—. I have Miss Clara with me now, which makes a great difference." She spoke this... followed only by—"I have no fancy for... as an Hotel.] I should not choose to have my two housemaids' time taken up all the morning in dusting out bedrooms. [I should not chuse to have my 2 Housemaids Time taken up all the morng, in dusting out Bed rooms.—] They have Miss Clara's room to put to rights, as well as mine, every day. [They have Miss Clara's room to put to rights, as well as my own every day.—] If they had hard work, they would want higher wages.' [If they had hard Places, they would want Higher Wages.—" For objections of this Nature... Charity begins at home you know."—]

Charlotte's feelings were divided between amusement and indignation. [Charlotte's feelings were divided between amusement & indignation—but indignation had the larger & the increasing share.—] She kept her countenance, and kept a civil silence; but without attempting to listen any longer, and only conscious that Lady Denham was still talking in the same way, allowed her own thoughts to form themselves into such meditation as this:— [She kept her Countenance & she kept a civil Silence. She could not carry her forbearance farther; but without attempting to listen longer, & only conscious that Lady D. was still talking on in the same way, allowed her Thoughts to form themselves into such a meditation as this.—] 'She is thoroughly mean; I had no expectation of anything so bad. ["She is thoroughly mean.—I had not expected any thing so bad.] Mr. Parker spoke too mildly of her. [Mr. P. spoke too mildly of her.—His Judgement is evidently not to be trusted. His own Goodnature misleads him.] He is too kind-hearted to see clearly, and their very connection misleads him. [He is too kind hearted to see clearly.—I must judge for myself.—And their very <u>connection</u> prejudices him.] He has persuaded her to engage in the same speculation, and because they have so far the same object in view, he fancies that she feels like him in other things; but she is very, very mean. [He has persuaded her to engage in the same Speculation—& because their object in that Line is the same, he fancies she feels like him in others.—But she is very, very mean.—] I can see no good in her. [I can see no Good in her.—] Poor Miss Brereton! [Poor Miss Brereton!—] And it makes everybody mean about her. [And she makes every body mean about her.—] This poor Sir Edward and his sister! [This poor Sir Edward & his Sister—,] how far nature meant them to be respectable I cannot tell; but they are obliged to be mean in their servility to her; and I am mean, too, in giving her my attention with the appearance of coinciding with her. [how far Nature meant them to be respectable I can not tell,—but they are <u>obliged</u> to be Mean in their Servility to her.—And I am Mean too, in giving her my attention, with the appearance of coinciding with her.—] Thus it is when rich people are sordid.' [Thus it is, when Rich People are Sordid."]

Mr. Parker has two unmarried sisters of singular character. They live together; Diana, the younger, always takes the lead, and the elder follows in the same track. It is their pleasure to fancy themselves invalids to a degree and in a manner never experienced by others; but, from a state of exquisite pain and utter prostration, Diana Parker can always rise to be officious in the concerns of all her acquaintance, and to make incredible exertions where they are not wanted.

It would seem that they must be always either very busy for the good of others, or else extremely ill themselves. [It should seem that they must either be very busy for the Good or others, or else extremely ill themselves.] Some natural delicacy of constitution, in fact, with an unfortunate turn for medicine, especially quack medicine, had given them an early tendency at various times to various disorders. [Some natural delicacy of Constitution in fact, with an unfortunate turn for Medecine, especially quack Medecine, had given them an early tendency at various times, to various Disorders;—] The rest of their suffering was from their own fancy, the love of distinction, and the love of the wonderful. [the rest of their sufferings was from Fancy, the love of Distinction & the love of the Wonderful.—] They had charitable hearts and many amiable feelings; but a spirit of restless activity, and the glory of doing more than anybody else, had a share in every exertion of benevolence, and there was vanity in all they did, as well as in all they endured. [They had Charitable hearts & many amiable feelings—but a spirit of restless activity, & the glory of doing more than anybody else, had their share in every exertion of Benevolence—and there was Vanity in all they did, as well as in all they endured.—]

These peculiarities come out in the following letter of Diana Parker to her brother:—

'MY DEAR TOM,—We were much grieved at your accident, and if you had not described yourself as having fallen into such very good hands, I should have been with you at all hazards the day after receipt of your letter, though it found me suffering under a more severe attack than usual of my old grievance, spasmodic bile, and hardly able to crawl from my bed to the sofa. ["My dear Tom, We were all much greived at your accident, & if you had not described yourself as fallen into such very good hands, I shd. have been with you at all hazards the day after the recpt. of your Letter, though it found me suffering under a more severe attack than usual of my old greivance, Spasmodic Bile & hardly able to

60

crawl from my Bed to the Sofa.—] But how were you treated? [But
how were you treated?—] Send me more particulars in your next.
[Send me more Particulars in your next.—] If indeed a simple
sprain, as you denominate it, nothing would have been so judicious
as friction—friction by the hand alone, supposing it could be
applied *immediately*. [If indeed a simple Sprain, as you denominate
it, nothing wd. have been so judicious as Friction, Friction by the
hand alone, supposing it could be applied <u>instantly</u>.—] Two years
ago I happened to be calling on Mrs. Sheldon, when her coachman
sprained his foot, as he was cleaning the carriage, and could hardly
limp into the house; but by the immediate use of friction alone,
steadily persevered in (I rubbed his ancle with my own hands for
four hours without intermission), he was well in three days.…
[Two years ago I happened to be calling on Mrs— Sheldon when
her Coachman sprained his foot as he was cleaning the Carriage
& cd. hardly limp into the House—but by the immediate use of
Friction alone, steadily persevered in, (& I rubbed his Ancle with
my own hand for six Hours without Intermission)—he was well
in three days.— Many Thanks my dear Tom, for the kindness
with respect to us, which had so large a share in bringing on your
accident—But] Pray never run into peril again in looking for an
apothecary on our account; for had you the most experienced man
in his line settled at Sanditon, it would be no recommendation to
us. [pray never run into Peril again, in looking for an Apothecary
on our account, for had you the most experienced Man in his Line
settled at Sanditon, it wd. be no recommendation to us.] We have
entirely done with the whole medical tribe. [We have entirely
done with the whole Medical Tribe.] We have consulted physician
after physician in vain, till we are quite convinced that they can
do nothing for us, and that we must trust to our knowledge of
our own wretched constitutions for any relief; but if you think it
advisable for the interests of the *place* to get a medical man there,
I will undertake the commission with pleasure, and have no doubt
of succeeding. [We have consulted Physician after Phyn— in
vain, till we are quite convinced that they can do nothing for us
& that we must trust to our own knowledge of our own wretched
Constitutions for any releif.—But if you think it advisable for the
interest of the <u>Place</u>, to get a Medical Man there, I will undertake
the commission with pleasure, & have no doubt of succeeding.]
I could soon put the necessary irons in the fire. [I could soon put
the necessary Irons in the fire.] As for getting to Sanditon myself,

it is an impossibility. [As for getting to Sanditon myself, it is quite an Impossibility.] I grieve to say that I cannot attempt it, but my feelings tell me too plainly that in my present state the sea-air would probably be the death of me; and in truth I doubt whether Susan's nerves would be equal to the effort. [I greive to say that I dare not attempt it, but my feelings tell me too plainly that in my present state, the Sea air wd. probably be the death of me.—And neither of my dear Companions will leave me, or I wd— promote their going down to you for a fortnight. But in truth, I doubt whether Susan's nerves wd. be equal to the effort.] She has been suffering much from headache, and six leeches a day, for ten days together, relieved her so little that we thought it right to change our measures; and being convinced on examination that much of the evil lay in her gums, I persuaded her to attack the disorder there. [She has been suffering much from the Headache, and Six Leaches a day for 10 days together releived her so little that we thought it right to change our measures—and being convinced on examination that much of the Evil lay in her Gum, I persuaded her to attack the disorder there.] She has accordingly had three teeth drawn, and is decidedly better; but her nerves are a good deal deranged, she can only speak in a whisper, and fainted away this morning on poor Arthur's trying to suppress a cough.' [She has accordingly had 3 Teeth drawn, & is decidedly better, but her Nerves are a good deal deranged. She can only speak in a whisper—and fainted away this morning on poor Arthur's trying to suppress a cough.... Yours most affecly— &c"]

Within a week of the date of this letter, in spite of the impossibility of moving, and of the fatal effects to be apprehended from the sea-air, Diana Parker was at Sanditon with her sister. She had flattered herself that by her own indefatigable exertions, and by setting at work the agency of many friends, she had induced two large families to take houses at Sanditon. It was to expedite these politic views that she came; and though she met with some disappointment of her expectation, yet she did not suffer in health.

Such were some of the *dramatis personæ*, ready dressed and prepared for their parts. They are at least original and unlike any that the author had produced before. The success of the piece must have depended on the skill with which these parts might be played; but few will be inclined to distrust the skill of one who had so often succeeded. If the author had lived to complete her work, it is probable that these personages might have grown into as mature an individuality of character, and have taken as permanent a place amongst our familiar acquaintance, as Mr. Bennet, or John Thorp, Mary Musgrove, or Aunt Norris herself. (1872/1906: 181–194; Chapman, 1926: 192–206; Weldon, 1989: 170–182)

James Edward Austen-Leigh implies that the final page of the manuscript is dated March 17, and it is possible that despite writing "March 18" Jane Austen had actually ceased working the day before. His tentative statement that "some of the latter pages seem to have been first traced in pencil," perhaps based on Anna Lefroy's account, misrepresents the true picture that only a short passage in Chapter 7, running from about the middle of folio 35r (page 69) to about two-thirds down folio 35v (page 70), a total of about 30 lines, is an ink-over-pencil palimpsest. In his closing line, Austen-Leigh misspells "Thorpe." Unlike some later commentators, James Edward Austen-Leigh understands that Miss Diana Parker is the younger sister and that Miss Susan Parker is the older sister.

The next published reference to the manuscript appeared in *Jane Austen: Her Life and Letters, a Family Record*, by William Austen-Leigh and Richard Arthur Austen-Leigh, published in London by Smith, Elder & Co. in 1913. Heavily indebted to the work of James Edward Austen-Leigh, they present only a basic summary of the final novel.

Three days later [than January 24, 1817], Jane felt well enough to set to work on a fresh novel: thoroughly fresh, for it bore no resemblance to any of her previous stories. A short *résumé* of this beginning is given in the *Memoir*, and from it the reader will see that the scene is laid at a new watering-place, [Note: The watering-place is called "Sanditon," and this name has been given to the twelve chapters by the family.] which is being exploited by two of the leading characters. In the twelve chapters that she wrote, the *dramatis personae* are sketched in with vigour and decision; but there is little of the subtle refinement which we are accustomed to associate with her work, and certainly nothing of the tender sentiment of *Persuasion*. It is unfair, however, to judge from the first draft of a few introductory chapters, written as they no doubt were to relieve the tedium of long hours of confinement, and written perhaps also to comfort her friends by letting them

> see that she was still able to work. It is probable, too, that a long
> step in the downward progress of her condition was taken in the
> course of the seven weeks during which she was writing for the
> last time. It began "in her usual firm and neat hand, but some of
> the latter pages were first traced in pencil—probably, when she
> was too ill to sit long at a desk—and afterwards written over in
> ink." [Note: *Memoir*, p. 181.] The last date on the MS. is March
> 17. (381–382)

Misunderstanding their predecessor's remark that she "worked at it up to
the 17th of March," they inaccurately report the date on the last page (an
easy mistake if they have not studied the original manuscript). They also
misquote James Edward's suggestion that "some of the latter pages seem
to have been first traced in pencil," unhesitatingly stating that "some of
the latter pages were first traced in pencil." Both passages, of course, are
incorrect in suggesting that more than one page in the latter part of the work
was originally written in pencil. More careful study would have shown them
that the lines originally in pencil cover only the bottom half of f35r and the
top two-thirds of f35v, just over halfway into the manuscript. The note that
the title *Sanditon* "has been given to the twelve chapters by the family" is a
strong if indirect indication that Jane Austen did not have this title in mind
as she worked on the manuscript.

Unfavorably comparing the tone of this light satire with that of the sober
Persuasion is an unwitting compliment to Jane Austen's artistry in adapting
her style to fit the story and its diverse characters. Their observation that the
reader should not expect too much from the completed lines, "written as they
no doubt were to relieve the tedium of long hours," fails to take into account
that she was by this time a professional novelist, not an amateur seeking
ways to divert her attention from physical discomfort. The suggestion that
the new novel was "written perhaps also to comfort her friends by letting
them see that she was still able to work" would be more persuasive if there
were evidence that she told anyone about the project in hand.

The first printed version of the entire text of the manuscript, edited
anonymously by R.W. Chapman, appeared in 1925. Published in Oxford
at the Clarendon Press,

FRAGMENT
of a
NOVEL
written by
JANE AUSTEN
January–March 1817
————————

now first printed from
the manuscript

was issued in two different editions, both with black label "Sanditon" on the spine—an indirect way of assigning a title but very effective since it has never been seriously challenged.

The larger volume (limited to 250 copies), bound in gray/green Ingres paper boards, is printed on hand-made paper. The frontispiece is a collotype facsimile of the first page of the manuscript that is even better than the one which appeared some years later in the complete facsimile. This is as close as anyone can come to owning a page of this manuscript, and I gladly paid £48 for the copy that I found in Bath in 1996. David Gilson describes the volume in detail in his *Bibliography* (376).

The contents of the slightly smaller standard edition, bound in blue-gray boards, on regular paper and lacking the frontispiece, are identical to those of its sibling. Whereas in my copy of the less expensive version, identified as a "Second Impression," the last word of the text on page 169 is incorrectly printed as "saw," David Gilson's copy has the correct "was."

The two editions open with an unpaginated Preface by the anonymous editor admitting the uncertainty of the title of the work—"The fragment of a novel, written by Jane Austen in the first three months of the year in which she died, has no name; but it has long been known to members of her family as *Sanditon*"—and the manuscript's provenance. The transcription offers what the editor believes is the final state of the text with no indication of the original distribution of pages as found in the manuscript. He closes with Notes on the "erasures" (crossed-out words) and emendations in the manuscript.

The editor observes that "the manuscript contains a very large number of erasures and interlineations. It is so neat, and so uniformly spaced, that it is almost everywhere possible to distinguish what was first written from what was added, or substituted between the lines," an optimistic assessment in view of the many difficulties in transcribing it accurately. The text contains two notable misreadings: "no shiney rocks" for "no slimey rocks" on page 15, and "Sagacity" for "Ingenuity" on page 109 (see my articles in *Persuasions*, 1997 and 1995). Unknown to me until recently, F.P. Lock reported the latter correction in his 1977 review of the facsimile: "I read 'Ingenuity' instead of 'Sagacity' (p. 75)" (279).

In 1934, the text of the unfinished manuscript finally appeared as part of a complete modern edition in *Sanditon, The Watsons, Lady Susan And Other Miscellanea* ("The Plan of a Novel" and the "Cancelled Chapter of 'Persuasion'"), in the final volume of the seven-volume set, *The Works of Jane Austen*, edited by R. Brimley Johnson and published in London by J.M. Dent & Sons Ltd.

The eight delightful illustrations (four-color half-tone on a grained paper) by Maximilien Vox (né Samuel-William-Théodore Monod, 1894-1974) include three scenes from *Sanditon*. Facing page 10, we find "He was obliged... to sit down on the bank... unable to stand," showing a prematurely balding Mr. Parker grimacing in pain while holding his left ankle, a smiling Mr. Heywood standing over him. The unfortunate traveler's hat and a carryall lie nearby, along with what appear to be broken pieces of the carriage. Facing page 49, "A young Whitby running off with five volumes under his arm" depicts the librarian's single-pigtailed son carrying a stack of large tomes. Behind him is the far more important figure of Sir Edward Denham himself, every bit the wasp-waisted dandy presumed from the text but never described in detail. In his right hand he balances a fine cane while holding in his left hand a monocle, never mentioned in the manuscript but an expected adjunct to his sartorial splendor. And facing page 64 we find "The whole-length portrait of a stately gentleman," Sir Harry Denham (in half-length) surveying Mr. Hollis's sitting room from over the mantelpiece, viewed by a seated young woman dressed very fashionably and holding a square-framed lorgnette, sometimes carried as a piece of jewelry rather than to enhance vision. We have already seen that Charlotte has excellent eyesight, and it is difficult to visualize her so elegantly dressed and with this particular affectation.

R. Brimley Johnson does not make clear in his Introduction that he has consulted the manuscript, but his correct printing of "no slimy rocks" (15) suggests that R.W. Chapman, whose "generous courtesy" he cites, has shared with him some corrections to the earlier text. Unfortunately, the "Sagacity" wrongly attributed to Sir Edward Denham haunts page 52 and will continue to appear in later editions of the novel.

Hence although the text of *Sanditon* included in *Minor Works*, Volume VI of *The Works of Jane Austen* (*The Oxford Illustrated Jane Austen*), edited by R.W. Chapman in 1954 with revisions by Brian C. Southam starting in 1969, correctly reads "no slimey rocks" (309), on page 404 we find the erroneous "Sagacity."

In 1974, when Margaret Drabble edited *Lady Susan, The Watsons, Sanditon*, the correct state of the text had not yet been established. Although she published "no slimey rocks" (160), which was by then recognized as the true reading, she preserved the faulty "sagacity" (191), at this point an accepted although obviously incorrect reading. This state of the text was standard by 1975, when "Another Lady" (Marie Dobbs/Anne Telscombe) completed *Sanditon*. As expected, we find "no slimey rocks" on page 6 and "sagacity" on page 46.

Scholars who did not have ready access to the collection of King's College, Cambridge, were finally granted a view of the entire manuscript in 1975. To mark Jane Austen's two hundredth birthday, the Clarendon Press in Oxford in association with the Scolar Press in London issued *Sanditon, An Unfinished Novel by Jane Austen*, a facsimile of very fine quality. With an introduction by Brian C. Southam, this publication provided the necessary breakthrough for serious study of the manuscript.

Despite the availability of the facsimile (xxxiii-xxxiv) and his presentation of the text so that it closely resembles the original, in his edition of *Sanditon* that appeared in 1990 John Davie passed along "the Sagacity" (358) that had already become part of the textual history, thereby effectively legitimizing this false reading. That Sanditon did not, like its detested rivals, have "slimey rocks" (326) is correctly reported. The same combination of correct and incorrect readings—"no slimy rocks" (15) and "sagacity" (49)—is found in Julia Barrett's *Charlotte*, published in 2000.

Not until a full twenty years after the appearance of the facsimile, when in 1995 Teran Lee Sacco published *A Transcription and Analysis of Jane Austen's Last Work*, Sanditon, was the potential for a correct text available. With the facsimile as its source, her diplomatic transcription attempts to show in printed form the exact appearance of the manuscript. The accompanying notes shed a great deal of light on various aspects of the work, including spelling variants and a general analysis of the manuscript (164–176). "No slimey rocks" is correctly transcribed (14) as is, perhaps for the first time in print as part of the text, "Ingenuity" (111).

Already in preparation in 1995 but not issued until December 2003, *Jane Austen Caught in the Act of Greatness: A Diplomatic Transcription and Analysis of the Two Manuscript Chapters of* Persuasion *and the Manuscript of* Sanditon is a diplomatic transcription of the *Sanditon* pages based on direct examination of the manuscript in the Library of King's College, Cambridge, during the summers of 1993, 1994, and 1995, referring to R.W. Chapman's work for guidance in some challenging passages. In the summer of 1996, Teran Lee Sacco's transcription helped to clear up some final questions on difficult readings. Through margin notes, I show where my reading differs from those of R.W. Chapman and Teran Lee Sacco. In addition, every line in which Jane Austen made any kind of change is analyzed so that we can follow the progress of her work from initial concept to a finished product (that is, the state which satisfied her sufficiently at the time that she made no additional changes). Both "no slimey rocks" (147) and "Ingenuity" (205) are correctly transcribed. Perhaps for the first time, the palimpsest running from folio 35r to folio 35v is transcribed and analyzed.

The most recent diplomatic transcription of the manuscript, in *The Cambridge Edition of the Works of Jane Austen: Later Manuscripts*, correctly reports "no slimey rocks" (398) and "Ingenuity" (490). This transcription, based on the conviction that the manuscript is in "a first-draft state," does not "indicate whether revisions were made at the time of first writing or later (on which one can speculate only when examining the manuscript in its material state)" (xvi). However, acknowledgment of the assistance of Patricia McGuire, Archivist of the King's College, Cambridge, collection, suggests that the text is based on examination of the original manuscript. Although R.W. Chapman's work receives due acknowledgment, neither Teran Lee Sacco's groundbreaking diplomatic transcription nor my diplomatic transcription with detailed textual notes is recognized.

Until editors consult Teran Lee Sacco's work or mine or *CUPLM* (or *read* the original manuscript or its facsimile), a misrepresentation of the young Baronet—claiming a "Sagacity" that is neither possessed by the "heroes" of the novels that he admires nor a trait which Sir Edward Denham could imaginably achieve—will continue to contaminate modern texts of the novel.

When R.W. Chapman's transcription appeared in 1925, scholars were finally able to read the work beyond the running summary in the *Life Records*. Unfortunately, the first person to write a review of the newly published text was the great English novelist, E.M. Forster, who, despite being an avowed Jane Austen enthusiast, found the work in no way a credit to her memory. His evaluation, just short of scathing contempt, does not encourage future study of this hitherto unknown novel.

He opens with a skillfully calculated condemnation balanced by a refusal to pin the blame for its inferiority on anyone in particular.

> The fragment known to Miss Austen's family as *Sanditon* is of small literary merit, but no one is to blame for this: neither the authoress, who left it a fragment, nor the owner of the MS, who has rightly decided on publication, nor the editor of the text, who has done his work with care and skill. (148)

As work attempted after *Persuasion*, however, it offers some insight into that novel.

> Though of small merit, it is of great interest, for it was written after *Persuasion*, and consequently may throw light on the last phase of the great novelist. (149)

Among its major flaws, Mr. Forster informs his reader, is its lack of originality (the one quality that virtually every subsequent commentator has praised) and character (again a feature now considered a major factor in its success).

> It is reminiscent from first to last. It opens with a Mr. and Mrs. Parker falling out of a carriage (*cf. Love and Freindship*), and Mr. Parker, like Marianne Dashwood, sprains his ankle. A Mr. Heywood rescues him. The Parkers and Heywoods both have large families, and when the former return to their seaside home they take with them Miss Charlotte Heywood, "a very pleasing young woman of two-and-twenty," who is destined to be the heroine. Charlotte belongs to a type which has attracted Miss Austen all the way from *Sense and Sensibility* to *Persuasion*, and naturally dominates her pen

when vitality is low; she is the well-scoured channel through which comment most readily flows. But whereas Eleanor Dashwood, Fanny Price, Anne Elliot, were real people whose good sense, modesty, and detachment were personal qualities, Charlotte turns these qualities into labels, and can be seen from some distance as she sits observing other labels upon the sea-front. (149)

The indebtedness to earlier material even extends to the unlikely parallel of poor Arthur and the valetudinarian Mr. Woodhouse.

The gruel of Mr. Woodhouse mingles with the cocoa of Arthur Parker a just perceptible aroma. (149)

At the end of her life and with all creativity spent, Mr. Forster avers, Jane Austen merely rewrites (and not very well) what she has already written.

Clearly, so far as character-drawing is concerned, Jane Austen is here completely in the grip of her previous novels. She writes out of what she has written, and anyone who has himself tried to write when feeling out of sorts will realize her state. The pen always finds life difficult to record; left to itself, it records the pen. (149-150)

Although it is possible to accept Mr. Forster's view with modifications, he completely misses the mark since he failed to examine the emendations with care:

The effort of creating was too much, and the numerous alterations in the MS. are never in the direction of vitality. (150)

As I believe that I have demonstrated in *Jane Austen Caught in the Act of Greatness* and as has been observed by many commentators, the changes in the manuscript invariably add to the characterization and zest of the material. By starting out with a determination to come up with a negative view, E.M. Forster misrepresents the work, depriving us of what could have been a truly valuable evaluation. Because "[some of his] remarks are deceptively credible" (Southam, 1976: 1), his condemnation could well have returned the manuscript to the obscurity in which it had dwelt until its first publication.

Fortunately, the reading public has taken a completely different view as have almost all commentators, recognizing it as Jane Austen's potential masterpiece. Both R.W. Chapman and Brian B. Southam have found in the manuscript a balance between the author's first attempts and something that might have been ready for publication.

Writing in 1948, R.W. Chapman acknowledges E.M. Forster's negative review: "In his review of *Sanditon* (*Nation*, 21 March 1925) he found in the fragment not only evidence of fatigue but also a change of tone which might have led her to a new criticism of life" (171). The great editor of Jane Austen's works finds more to approve in the manuscript than the great novelist following in her footsteps. "We possess an early version, much corrected as it was written, of a book which from the width of its canvass and its leisurely procedure I guess to have been planned on the scale of *Emma*.... The fragment has a certain roughness and harshness of satire.... This might be due to failing powers; I doubt it. It is due in part to lack of revision; she would have smoothed these coarse strokes, so strikingly different from the mellow pencillings of *Persuasion*. But a degree of savagery would, I think, have persisted" (207–208).

In Brian C. Southam's carefully balanced view (which is much closer to mine), despite its roughness the manuscript is in part close to a final product.

> While some critics believe that the text is reasonably close to the form in which it would one day have been sent to the printer (needing only paragraphing, the expansion of abbreviations and other trivial tidying-up), others view it as a rough draft, not a document upon which to base confident critical judgement.[1] (1976: 1)

An important adjunct to this passage is the footnote attached:

> I belong to the former group and my argument for regarding the manuscript as a developed work is set out in Chapter 7 of *Jane Austen's Literary Manuscripts* (London, 1964). (1976: 25)

A more extreme view, one diametrically opposite to that of E.M. Forster, is John Bailey's enthusiastic support of the manuscript just as it stands in the 1925 edition: "Perhaps the readings cannot strictly be called 'various': what we get in the text is her final corrections.... An examination of the manuscript has shown that the author of the *Memoir* was wrong in supposing that the substitution of a pencil for a pen in part of it was due to weakness preventing her from sitting at her desk. The place in which the pencil appears is about the middle of what was written; and the last part of the manuscript is as accurate and legible as the beginning" (132–133). This praise, however, is conditional: "Of course it is a fragment and both story and character might have come later" (134).

To this day, critics remain divided in their estimates of the quality of the composition and how close the extant manuscript is to a finished product. At the very least meriting painstaking scrutiny, the work now known as *Sanditon* is a mirror of her last creative efforts, buoyantly optimistic, with every expectation of completing and publishing one more in a short chain of superb novels.

IV. The Title

The proper title for the work remains uncertain. The manuscript, of course, bears no title. Jane Austen refrained from mentioning the work in progress in any of her extant letters from this period, and Cassandra Austen did not record it as among her deceased sister's oeuvre (Pinion: 325; *Minor Works*, facsimile facing 242). Neither reference to the work nor its title appears in the first edition (1870) of James Edward Austen-Leigh's *Memoir*, but in the revised edition (1871) he refers to it merely as "The Last Work." Publishing early in the twentieth century, William Austen-Leigh and Richard Arthur Austen-Leigh for the first time in print assigned the title as we know it by observing in a footnote that "the watering-place is called 'Sanditon,' and this name has been given to the twelve chapters by the family" (*Life*: 381, footnote 2). In no way does this report suggest that the author had this title in mind.

How carefully the family members read the manuscript to determine its content other than the location of most of the action is unclear. John Halperin narrows the "family" to a single member: "Jane Austen's brother Henry, who was her literary executor, gave the fragment the posthumous title by which it has come down to posterity: *Sanditon*" (1983: 183). There is evidence that as early as 1862 some members of the family who were familiar with the manuscript were calling it "Sanditon":

> I am much obliged for your letter, & especially for your devoting so much of it to 'Sanditon'

(Letter from Anna Austen Lefroy to her brother James Edward Austen-Leigh, August 8, 1862 [see Appendix D, Continuations])

When the complete text was published for the first time in 1925, R.W. Chapman called it *Fragment of a Novel Written by Jane Austen, January–March 1817*. In his Preface, the editor acknowledges that the author never gave a title to her unfinished manuscript but that the family has for a long time referred to it by a now-familiar title. "The fragment of a novel, written by Jane Austen in the first three months of the year in which she died, has no name; but it has long been known to members of her family as *Sanditon*" ([1]; the Preface is not paginated). Although he gives no information about how long ago the name was assigned or whether or not he agrees that it is what the author intended, he (or his publisher) affixed small labels to the spine reading "Sanditon." My copy of the "cheap" edition of 1925 is thus identified, as is my copy of the "expensive" edition of 1925. The former, David Gilson reports (1985: 376), has a "spare label tipped in at the end" (missing from my copy but clearly indicated by a discolored rectangle of the right size), and the latter has a "spare label as before" (present in my copy). I find it difficult to regard this label, in the absence of R.W. Chapman's using the title on his title page or in his Preface, as evidence that the work was decisively entitled as we now know it in 1925. The title did become official, however, when in 1934, R. Brimley Johnson published *The Works of Jane Austen. Sanditon and Other Miscellanea.*

I would like to think that Jane Austen would have had no difficulty with *Sanditon*, and some commentators observe that this was the third of her novels to be named after a location, citing *Mansfield Park* and *Northanger Abbey* as its precedents. Although the former novel was named thus by its author, there is no evidence suggesting that the adventures of Catherine Morland were to be titled after General Tilney's home, where she spends only a short time. The title was chosen by Jane Austen's literary executors for its "romantic" sound (in the sense of the preceding Gothic novels) to accompany *Persuasion* (likewise a title not specified by its author although it would be difficult to find one more appropriate) when they appeared together in December 1817.

Advocates of this accepted title prove its suitability and correctness through a sort of circular reasoning that goes roughly like this: Jane Austen left her manuscript untitled. However, most of the story as we have it takes place in Sanditon, a former fishing village, now a young resort by the sea. Therefore the town of Sanditon and its development must be at least one of the major themes of the intended novel, perhaps even more important than the usual marriage theme seen in all of Jane Austen's preceding works. The town itself, as a matter of fact, is not merely the setting but one of the major actors if not *the* major actor in the novel. Therefore it follows inevitably that the title is *Sanditon*.

Ironically, support for this title rests in part because of the assumption that "Sanditon" means "Sandy Town." However, "-ton" really means "enclosure," "farm village," "estate," "manor" (from Old English "tun"). Jane Austen probably would not know about name derivations and might well have thought, regardless of the title, that "Sanditon" means "Sandy Town." Naming it thus might emphasize the beach in contrast to the high-saline water of rival Brinshore (perhaps thought of as "brine-shore").

That as far as the family members were concerned the title is "Sanditon" would appear to be settled but for one small problem: In the February 19, 1925, issue of *TLS* (120), Janet R. Sanders, granddaughter of Francis Austen, claimed that according to family tradition Jane Austen had intended naming her final novel, *The Brothers*.

"SANDITON."

Sir,—Some years ago my father, the late Rev. Edward Austen, then rector of Barfrestone, Kent, son of Admiral Sir Francis Austen, told me he had heard his Aunt Jane had intended to name her last novel (unfinished) "The Brothers." This may interest some of your readers.

I am, Sir, yours faithfully,
J.R. SANDERS.

It is unclear if Janet R. Sanders' letter was in any way connected with R.W. Chapman's publication of the manuscript in 1925, serving either as a piece of additional information or a corrective note. In any event, I believe that we can safely dismiss this contention. The very long time between the author's death (followed by Anna Lefroy's acquisition of the manuscript) and the emergence of "The Brothers" as the intended title casts serious doubt on the validity of the *TLS* article. The absence of any reference to "The Brothers" in James Edward Austen-Leigh's *Memoir* weakens but fails to destroy the argument, but the specific statement in the 1913 *Life* that according to family tradition the manuscript was to be called *Sanditon* pretty much nullifies the claim for "The Brothers."

Furthermore, it seems unlikely that Francis Austen's granddaughter would know more about this manuscript, which did not pass down through her immediate branch of the family, than would members of the branch dedicated to publishing records of family history. Sir Francis-William Austen (1774–1865), Admiral of the Fleet, moved to the Great House in 1814, then to Alton. Hence he was close to his sister during her work on *Mansfield Park*: "Now that Frank was living at the [Chawton] Great House, Jane had been able to discuss the book with him personally" (Le Faye, 1989: 197). One of the few members of the family to attend his sister's funeral—"Only three of the brothers—Edward, Henry and Frank—were present" (Le Faye, 1989: 231)—he was clearly close to her and may have had some unique knowledge about her work. If so he never shared it with anyone in the other branches (no doubt there was some rivalry about the now-famous writer in the family). There are no extant letters from 1817 from Jane Austen to Francis Austen. One wonders if the idea of "The Brothers" came about because of the presence of three of the Austen brothers at their sister's funeral.

Peggy Huey (253) refers to Brian C. Southam's Introduction to the facsimile of the manuscript to offer support for "The Brothers":

> This final, partially completed Jane Austen work is referred to variously as "The Last Work" (in the King's College listings), *Sanditon* (after the town where most of the action occurs) or "Two [sic] Brothers" (the planned title for the work according to Austen family tradition) (Southam, Introduction vii).

I believe, though, that in the cited passage Mr. Southam advocates this possible title far more tentatively than Peggy Huey suggests:

> It was there [*Memoir*, 2nd edition, 1871] formally referred to as 'The Last Work', a convenient label since the manuscript itself is untitled and the name *Sanditon* is really an unofficial title invented by the family. According to another family tradition, Jane Austen herself intended to call it 'The Brothers'. There is a copy of the manuscript made by Cassandra Austen; but, like the original, this is untitled. (Southam, Introduction vii)

William Austen-Leigh (son of James Edward Austen-Leigh) and his nephew, Richard Arthur Austen-Leigh, in contrast to Janet Sanders, were in the direct line of Jane Austen biographers. Significantly, no editor since the appearance of the J.R. Sanders article has renamed the work, to this day consistently called *Sanditon*.

In the Preface (dated 1953) to the 1954 OUP edition of *Minor Works*, R.W. Chapman reports that "Mr. Austen-Leigh… printed in the second (1871) edition… an account, with quotations, of 'the last work', which came to be known in the family as 'Sanditon.'" He does not mention the *TLS* assertion. Nor does B.C. Southam refer to the *TLS* letter in his Note to the Revised Impression (dated 1967) of *Minor Works*.

Despite general support for *Sanditon* as the publishing title, at least one critic remains convinced that Mrs. Sanders had it right. Thus, John Halperin unhesitatingly asserts that "On 27 January 1817, six months before her death, Jane Austen began a novel [which] she called… 'The Brothers.'… Less than two months later, on 18 March, she abruptly stopped writing 'The Brothers,'… 'The Brothers,' then, is her last piece of sustained fiction-writing" (1983: 183). Helen Baker has made a brave attempt to establish this as the true title in her continuation, *The Brothers by Jane Austen and Another Lady*.

To summarize the problems with "The Brothers": The title was apparently unknown to James Edward Austen-Leigh as well as to William Austen-Leigh and Richard Arthur Austen-Leigh. It was subsequently apparently unknown to R.W. Chapman and was not used in his Oxford University edition. It was not used for the first separate edition (R. Brimley Johnson, *Sanditon and Other Miscellanea*, 1934). It has apparently never been used by anyone, save Helen Baker for her continuation. Nothing in earlier work by Jane Austen suggests that she would have named a novel after her male characters (although the possible *The Elliots* would include Sir Walter), and there is nothing in the extant manuscript—in which the focus is so clearly on Charlotte Heywood— to hint that the three Parker brothers would have made up the central point of the book. Thomas has done his job of transporting Charlotte to Sanditon and gossiping about some of the other residents; Arthur has nowhere to go since any changes would negate the original portrait; Sidney alone can be developed, and presumably he will appear frequently as the hero of the tale destined to marry our heroine, Charlotte. Therefore, I think it unlikely that she ever considered *The Brothers* as the title for this novel.

One more complication in the matter of "The Brothers" is the assertion by Kathryn Sutherland that "the manuscript left unfinished at her death, had, according to Cassandra, the working title of 'The Brothers'" (2007: 18). Unfortunately, she offers no support for Cassandra Austen's alleged affirmation, which would be a strong argument for the title.

Jane Austen liked to use titles identifying her eponymous heroines—*Emma*, *Lady Susan*, and various early works, such as "The Beautiful Cassandra," "Amelia Webster," and "Catharine, or the Bower." The first version of what was later published as *Northanger Abbey* was "Susan," and as "Miss Catherine" she was put "upon the Shelve" on March 13, 1817 (*Letters*: 333). That this was to be the name of the novel if ever published is even more emphatically stated elsewhere in the same letter when she confides to her niece, Fanny Knight, that she has "a something ready for Publication, which may perhaps appear about a twelvemonth hence [sadly, as *Persuasion*, the novel appeared much earlier but only after her death]. It is short, about the length of Catherine." Strong support for this theory is found in Ellen Moody's online review of "Oxford's *Northanger Abbey, Lady Susan, The Watsons* and *Sanditon*," in which she asserts, I am convinced correctly, that "*Northanger Abbey*... [was]... first drafted 1793–94, [was] written 1798–99, [and underwent] revisions (1803 as *Susan* and 1816 as *Catherine*)." Anthony A. Mandal states unhesitatingly that "Austen's own work ["Susan"] was renamed *Catherine* after its repurchase [in 1816]" (524).

I believe that as the new novel was the successor to "Susan," later revised and known as "Catherine," the logical, inevitable, and most appropriate title of this work—as Julia Barrett declares in her continuation of the fragment— was to be (and should be) *Charlotte*.

It is a truth universally acknowledged, that a single young woman not in possession of a good fortune, must be in want of a husband, preferably possessed of a good fortune (and a title, however humble, does not work to his disadvantage).

V. Text and Commentary

Having already accounted for and commented upon each progressive stage of textual revision in *Jane Austen Caught in the Act of Greatness*, here I shall cite only the most interesting early readings along with the final one in the manuscript. Study of the sequence of composition shown in my earlier book reveals Jane Austen's close attention to the process of assembling her characters and creating for them the best narrative and dialog, along with her acute sense of style and rhetoric. She was clearly a process writer who would be revising her text up to the moment of sending it to the printer. Although this last version may not be what Jane Austen would have submitted to a publisher, as there is no other text to fall back on, of necessity it must be the one regarded as her final decision.

[Chapter 1]

Jan: 27.—1817.   (1)

[The number "1" appears to represent both "Chapter 1" and that the first two gatherings are regarded as a single piece, to be followed by "2" on the first page of the third gathering.]

A Gentleman & Lady travelling from Tunbridge towards that part of the Sussex Coast which lies between Hastings & E. Bourne, were on quitting the high road, & toiling up a very long steep hill through a rough Lane overturned in toiling up its' long ascent.

>

A Gentleman & Lady travelling from Tunbridge towards that part of the Sussex Coast which lies between Hastings & E. Bourne, being induced by Business to quit the high road, & toil up a very long steep hill through a rough Lane overturned in toiling up its' long ascent.

>

A Gentleman & Lady travelling from Tunbridge towards that part of the Sussex Coast which lies between Hastings & E. Bourne, being induced by Business to quit the high road, & attempt a very rough Lane, overturned in toiling up its' long ascent.

>

A Gentleman & Lady travelling from Tunbridge towards that part of the Sussex Coast which lies between Hastings & E. Bourne, being induced by Business to quit the high road, & attempt a very rough Lane, were overturned in toiling up its' long ascent half rock, half sand.

[That Jane Austen started out with something in the way of a plan for her new work is indicated in her numbering each new section beginning with the second chapter. Perhaps eventually someone will discover a solitary sheet of paper in her handwriting revealing the basic outline of the novel.

With so few samples of Jane Austen's novels in manuscript we cannot be certain of her practice, but on the basis of this fragment and the chapters of *Persuasion* in the British Library, it appears that she carefully dated her work. The question is why she would maintain such a record unless to keep track of her progress on a new novel. Her habitual neatness did not abandon her even in these last months of her life.

The opening line of this new novel clearly cost Jane Austen a great deal of trouble. She had never before started a tale in such a manner, and although some—who possibly have not consulted the original manuscript to see that she worked her way through four versions before continuing—have suggested that it is just a preliminary draft awaiting smoothing-out into more conventional sentences, it is certainly exactly what she sought as a rough-and-tumble effect. "The difficulty of the syntax [on the first page] is not the fault of haste or confusion, but a carefully worked-for effect" (Lock: 279).

Despite the clearly rural setting, the story is to be about the class of people, distinctly above a particular social level, who always inhabit Jane Austen's literary world. In no way does she attempt to present a full picture of life in her time, limiting herself from beginning to end to the class to which she belonged, with darting glances at those immediately contiguous, rarely lower but occasionally higher.

Although technically a "gentleman" is a man of gentle birth, not a member of the nobility but entitled to bear heraldic arms, the word can also designate a man of distinction without precise definition of rank—as one dictionary puts it so well, "an armigerous commoner." By "Gentleman" Jane Austen always means far more than merely a man of gentle and cultivated manners. He must be born at a sufficiently high social and economic level—it comes down to wealth and leisure—that he does not have to work for a living, in particular never descending to engaging in trade. "A gentleman was defined by the law as someone with no regular trade or occupation" (Pool: 44). Since the eldest son, like Mr. Thomas Parker, generally inherited the family estate intact through the law of entail, he would seek a profession only if the land failed to yield enough income to support him and his family. The younger brothers were expected to enter a profession, generally the military, the clergy, or the law. What we now consider noble professions like medicine were not suitable for the sons of gentlemen. A gentleman farmer could, like Mr. Heywood, work alongside his employees, but at the end of the day he retreated to a fine home to spend the evening at leisure with his lady and offspring. A gentleman scholar could also, like Mr. Bennet, spend his entire day closeted in his sacrosanct library, undisturbed by the vulgarities of the real world.

Central to Jane Austen's view of the decorous society that she created in her novels was the concept of a gentlemanly hero. Nowhere is her male protagonist's self-confidence in his possessing all the attributes of a gentleman more shaken than when a mortified Elizabeth Bennet hurls an indignant retaliatory reply to Mr. Darcy's insulting proposal:

"You are mistaken, Mr. Darcy, if you suppose that the mode of your declaration affected me in any other way, than as it spared the concern which I might have felt in refusing you, had you behaved in a more gentlemanlike manner."

And what for contemporaries of Jane Austen were the most important criteria for a gentleman? "A very decent shot, and there is not a bolder rider in England," declares Sir John Middleton, ironically describing that least gentlemanly of gentlemen, John Willoughby. Most of a gentleman's activities took place with other gentlemen, to the exclusion of ladies, "after breakfast [going] out, to the woods (to shoot), or the fields (to hunt), or the streams (to fish)" (Jones). In general, contemporary sportsmen distinguished between "Hunting," which was "the mounted pursuit of foxes and stags," and "Shooting," "the pursuit of wildfowl, hares and rabbits on foot" (Cain).

The term "lady" was more specific in Jane Austen's day than in ours, referring not merely to a woman or even to a woman deserving of respect but to a woman of a certain social standing. That her husband is a "gentleman" in itself makes her a "lady." The presumption is that she is the female head of a household with servants. Jane Austen rarely writes of a woman below this social level, and when she appears (like Nurse Rooke) it is as part of her service to a lady.

Throughout the manuscript, Jane Austen blends real places with fictional to create an effect of verisimilitude. In this opening line we find locations readily known to all her contemporary readers.

In principle, Jane Austen could be referring here to either Tunbridge (modern Tonbridge) or Tunbridge Wells (modern Royal Tunbridge Wells). Both Tonbridge—a busy shopping and market town boasting the remnants of a Norman castle—and Tunbridge Wells—fashionable since the eighteenth century for the Pantiles, a tree-shaded, colonnaded promenade where you can savor its famous natural chalybeate spring water (containing iron salts), perhaps surpassing in aroma and taste for its assault on the palate even what is dispensed in the Bath Pump Room—are in the county of Kent, between London and Sussex.

Someone traveling south from London toward the Sussex Coast would pass in succession through the first and then the second of the similarly named towns. A map of early nineteenth-century Sussex (Le Faye, 2002: 301) shows Tunbridge, later respelled Tonbridge, lying just north of and connected by road to what was then called Tunbridge Wells, now called Royal Tunbridge Wells.

Tonbridge (historic spelling *Tunbridge*) is a market town in the English county of Kent, with a population of 30,340 in 2007. It is located on the River Medway, approximately four miles north of Tunbridge Wells, 12 miles south west of Maidstone, and 25 miles south east of London. It belongs to the administrative borough of Tonbridge and Malling (population 107,560 in 2001).

> Until 1870, the "Tonbridge" name was actually known as *Tunbridge*: old maps prior to this date show it as such, as does the 1871 Ordnance Survey map and contemporary issues of the Bradshaw railway guide. In 1870, this was changed to *Tonbridge* by the GPO as it caused confusion with Tunbridge Wells, a much more recent town. The latter has always spelt its name that way. ("Tonbridge." *Wikipedia*)

Because George Austen was "born in Tonbridge in 1731 [and] educated at Tonbridge School,… return[ing from Oxford] to Tonbridge School for a few years as Second Master or 'Usher,'" Jane Austen would have known of the town's existence. "Despite the many family links with Tonbridge, there is no firm evidence that Jane Austen herself ever came here, though it is quite possible—even likely—that she would have done so" ("Tonbridge History.").

> Royal Tunbridge Wells is a town in west Kent in England, on the northern edge of the Weald. In general usage the appellation "Royal" is dropped from its title. Its boundaries lie across the border of Kent with East Sussex. It has a population of approximately 56,500. The town is the administrative centre of Tunbridge Wells Borough.

The town came into being as a spa in Georgian times and had its heyday as such in the seventeenth and eighteenth centuries, when the popularity of sea-bathing took away much of its clientele. Today the town is a relatively affluent place, within commuting distance of London.

The similar names—Tonbridge and Tunbridge Wells—have been a source of confusion ever since, especially to rail travellers.

The 1680s was a building boom in the town: carefully-planned shops were built beside the 175-yard (156m) long Pantiles (then known as the Walks); and the road Mount Sion, on which lodging house keepers were to build, was laid out in small plots. Careful attention was paid to the height and sewerage along the Pantiles: all so that the fashionable visitors should not be discouraged. ("Royal Tunbridge Wells." *Wikipedia*)

It may be possible to determine from her biography and other writings which town Jane Austen is referring to when she says "Tunbridge."

As Deirdre Le Faye (2002: 63) recounts, Jane Austen may have visited Tunbridge Wells as a girl:

When she and her parents visited Kent in 1788 they may perhaps have spent a day or two at Tunbridge Wells on the way. These wells, famous for their iron-impregnated water, had first become known in the seventeenth century, but the spa-town did not grow up around them until much later. The springs here were not thermal, and not nearly so copious as those at Bath; hence the water was used for medicinal drinking rather than bathing. Nevertheless, Tunbridge Wells had all the necessary spa attributes of assembly rooms [venues for balls], theatre, libraries, luxury shops, paved promenades and a bandstand in the centre of the little town, as well as elegant lodging-houses and pretty walks and rides, and the advantage of being only thirty-six miles south of London. It had been very fashionable in the middle of the eighteenth century, but was now starting to decline as the fashion leaders moved elsewhere.

In the very early *Lesley Castle*, Jane Austen writes, "We might meet at Bath, at Tunbridge, or anywhere else indeed, could we but be at the same place together." The reference to Bath suggests that she means Tunbridge Wells, the other important watering place of the time.

Writing from Southampton to Cassandra on Friday, February 20, and Sunday, February 22, 1807, Jane Austen reports, "It is beleived at Tunbridge that he [a relative] has left everything [to certain family members]" (*Letters*: 122).

In *Mansfield Park*, Mary Crawford's line, "I do not call Tunbridge or Cheltenham the country," probably refers to Tunbridge Wells since she would be more likely to be familiar with a fashionable watering place than a simple market town.

In *Emma*, we learn that "within abundance of silver paper was a pretty little Tunbridge-ware box, which Harriet opened." This particular kind of decorative art was apparently made in both Tunbridge (modern Tonbridge) and Tunbridge Wells:

> Later [in the 18C], the town [Tunbridge, modern Tonbridge] and its surroundings became famous for the production of finely inlaid wooden cabinets, boxes and other objects called Tunbridgeware, which were sold to tourists who were taking the waters at the nearby springs at Tunbridge Wells. ("Tonbridge." *Wikipedia*)

> The town [Tunbridge Wells] also had its own souvenir industry, "Tunbridge ware"—trinkets decorated with patterns or pictures made in coloured woods such as cherry, plum or yew. (Le Faye, 2002: 63)

> Tradesmen in the town [Tunbridge Wells] dealt in the luxury goods demanded by their patrons. These would have included Tunbridge ware, wood-inlaid objects. ("Royal Tunbridge Wells." *Wikipedia*)

The Thorpe family has visited "Tunbridge," and Isabella's comparing its balls with those of Bath points to Tunbridge Wells:

> Miss Thorpe, however, being four years older than Miss Morland, and at least four years better informed, had a very decided advantage in discussing such points; she could compare the balls of Bath with those of Tunbridge; its fashions with the fashions of London. (Facsimile: 31)

> Mrs. Thorpe, the not very rich widow from Putney—then a village on the outskirts of London—brings her daughters here [to Tunbridge Wells], and Isabella can awe the naïve Catherine by her ability to compare the balls of Bath with those of Tunbridge. (Le Faye, 2002: 63)

Jane Austen apparently refers to the spa town by its complete name only in *Persuasion*: "This was the letter, directed to 'Charles Smith, Esq. Tunbridge Wells,' and dated from London, as far back as July, 1803." Here the complete name would be necessary to avoid confusion and make sure that the letter is not sent to nearby Tunbridge (Tonbridge).

The weight of evidence clearly favors "Tunbridge Wells" as the town cited in the text as "Tunbridge." That in the early nineteenth century the two towns were not merely spelled the same but shared a common name explains the wisdom of attempting to distinguish them by changing the "u" to an "o" later in the century.

David Selwyn "can easily trace the Parkers' journey homewards from Tunbridge (where they have presumably either been taking the waters or, more likely, looking for ideas for their own resort)" (57), the implication being that in "travelling from Tunbridge towards... the Sussex Coast" they have visited Tunbridge Wells rather than Tunbridge (modern Tonbridge), not merely passing through or by the town but spending some time there. For other commentators, "Tunbridge," another name for "Tunbridge Wells, Kent," is merely "a stage in the Parkers' journey from London to Sanditon" (Bok: 484).

Because Mr. Thomas Parker would no more need the services of Tunbridge Wells than those of any of the detested rival health resorts along the Sussex Coast, Jane Austen probably mentions the town only as one of those through which they must pass, perhaps one of those where they change post-horses. Further, the text suggests that they are in such a hurry upon leaving London—taking a detour only to find the advertised surgeon, whom Mr. Parker would want to hire while still available—that they are unlikely to be planning any prolonged stops along the way. For her part, Mrs. Parker would be eager to return home as quickly as possible to be with her four young children. And since the carriage and horses have been hired, the shorter the time that they keep them, the lower the cost.

As for Jane Austen's abbreviated manner of referring to "Tunbridge Wells" merely as "Tunbridge," I cite the long-standing habit practiced by those of us from the Big Apple of meaning by "New York" not "New York State," with its implications of various places somewhere to the north along the Canadian border, but "New York City," meaning the five boroughs—and sometimes only the island of Manhattan, outside of which few civilized persons need to venture.

Without any explanation, *CUPLM* assumes that Jane Austen's "Tunbridge" is "Tonbridge": "The town of Tonbridge is about thirty miles south of London, on one of the main coach roads to the south coast. The road divides at the spa town of Tunbridge Wells, with one branch of the road going south-east to Hastings, and the other south-west to Eastbourne, both towns about sixty miles south of Tonbridge on the south coast" (629). Likewise reaching a decision on this perplexing issue without explanation, Margaret Drabble asserts that "Jane Austen spells Tonbridge as 'Tunbridge'" (218).

Sussex, a narrow county stretching along the English Channel for about 90 miles, is famous for the grass-covered chalk hills of the South Downs and its fortifying air. Many important seaside resorts, most notably Brighton, are found on its coast.

The town of Hastings is of course renowned as the site of the Norman Conquest in 1066, the last time that a foreign army, led by Duke William of Normandy, assuming the throne as King William I (more famously, "the Conqueror"), invaded the island. The actual battle, it must be noted, took place several miles inland in the smaller town of Battle.

Eastbourne, a former fishing village now famous for its gardens and architectural variety, is immortalized in one of Jane Austen's masterly early poems:

Mr. Gell and Miss Gill

On Reading in the Newspaper, the Marriage of "Mr. Gell of Eastbourne to Miss Gill."

Of Eastbourne Mr. Gell
From being perfectly well

Became dreadfully ill
For the love of Miss Gill.

So he said with some sighs
"I'm the slave of your *eyes*.
Oh! restore if you please
By accepting my *ease*."
(*Minor Works*, 444)

With a good magnifying glass you can find your way around the sites mentioned in the manuscript by consulting the early nineteenth-century map of Sussex provided by Deirdre Le Faye (2002: 301), showing only Bexhill lying between Hastings and Eastbourne. A map of Sussex in 1814, taken from John Cary's *Cary's Traveller's Companion*, can be found at:

http://freepages.genealogy.rootsweb.ancestry.com/~genmaps/genfiles/ COU_files/ENG/SSX/cary_ssx_1814.html.

Jane Austen fairly consistently writes "its'" for modern "its" despite its not making any sense. R.W. Chapman transcribes her error as "its" without comment.

Although commentary that this rough opening scene is an adumbration of the eventual financial ruin of Mr. Parker and the fall of Sanditon itself, I think it far more likely that it was Jane Austen's best attempt to revise the very uninteresting episode of her heroine's trip to Bath in "Susan"/"Catherine." Whereas it was easy enough to transport Susan/Catherine from her home in Fullerton to Bath as a companion to Mr. and Mrs. Allen, it was more difficult to work out how Charlotte Heywood would leave her comfortable home in Willingden to visit Sanditon. Thus instead of being chaperoned by a couple known to her parents, our new heroine will accompany strangers. And these strangers have come to Willingden in search of something that will enhance the "curb appeal" of Sanditon. The rough road and even more the angry coachman are the cause of the accident, which occurs not near Sanditon (seen by some commentators as at serious risk of disruption) but near Willingden, depicted as a stable home for virtuous English folk.]

The accident happened just beyond the only Gentleman's House near the Lane — the House, which their Driver on being required to turn that way, had conceived to be necessarily their object, & had with most unwilling Looks been constrained to pass two minutes before grumbling so much indeed, & looking so black, & pitying & cutting his Horses so much, that he might have been open to the suspicion of overturning them on purpose (especially as the Carriage was not the Gentleman's own) if the road had not indisputably & evidently become much worse than before, as soon as the premises of the said House were left behind — as Bad as it had been before the Change and seeming to say, that beyond it no wheels but cart wheels had ever thought of proceeding.

>

The accident happened just beyond the only Gentleman's House near the Lane — a House, which their Driver on being first required to take that Direction, had conceived to be necessarily their object, & had with most unwilling Looks been constrained to pass by —. He had grumbled & shaken his shoulders so much indeed, and pitied & cut his Horses so sharply, that he might have been open to the suspicion of overturning them on purpose (especially as the Carriage was not his Masters the Gentleman's own) if the road had not indisputably become considerably worse than before, as soon as the premises of the said House were left behind — saying with a most intelligent and seeming portentous countenance that beyond it no wheels but cart wheels could safely proceed.

>

The accident happened just beyond the only Gentleman's House near the Lane — a House, which their Driver on being first required to take that Direction, had conceived to be necessarily their object, & had with most unwilling Looks been constrained to pass by —. He had grumbled & shaken his shoulders so much indeed, and pitied & cut his Horses so sharply, that he might have been open to the suspicion of overturning them on purpose (especially as the Carriage was not his Masters the Gentleman's own) if the road had not indisputably become considerably worse than before, as soon as the premises of the said House were left behind — expressing with a most intelligent and portentous countenance that beyond it no wheels but cart wheels could safely proceed.

[Again Jane Austen goes through multiple revisions before continuing, refuting allegations that this is just a very rough draft barely representing a finished sentence.

We soon learn, of course, that the house is not occupied by a gentleman as Mr. Parker has assumed. Many critics have suggested that the text offers ambiguities at every turn to illustrate the contrast between illusion and reality. Hence, Mr. Parker will go to the wrong place in search of someone who is not there, Charlotte will form a favorable first impression of a titled stranger that she has to retract almost immediately, Clara Brereton will appear to be a helpless young woman caught in straitened financial circumstances and yet apparently in complete control during her secret meeting with Sir Edward, the catastrophically sick Miss Parkers turn out to be the most energetic people in the entire novel, the reportedly fragile Arthur Parker is discovered to be a large-sized gourmand with a fear of fresh air, and the saucy and irresponsible Sidney Parker proves to be an amiable gentleman beloved of his young niece. We are warned through this bizarre and unsettling opening scene that very few things—if any—will be quite as they seem.

The text never specifies if there are two or four horses drawing the carriage. Although the gentleman and his lady are traveling in a rented carriage, the driver may be their own servant, who has accompanied them from their home in Sanditon. The precise reference of "them" in "overturning them" is vague, but it probably refers to the general concept of the carriage rather than the horses or the gentleman and his lady. The horses are rented along with the carriage, accounting for the driver's unkindness.

The driver, riding postilion, probably on the near horse of one of the pairs, can be indifferent to toppling the carriage since he risks little personal injury. As usual in Jane Austen, he says nothing because he is of the servant class. Also as usual, despite his importance in developing the story, he remains nameless.

Jane Austen's use of "pity" here appears to mean not "feeling compassion for" but "deserving of compassion." The *OED* comes closest to this usage with "To move to pity, excite the compassion of; to grieve. Now *regional*." "Cut: struck with his whip" (*CUPLM*: 629). The phrasing "pitied & cut his Horses so sharply" may describe the anonymous driver's feelings about "his horses" (although not owned by him, nevertheless under his charge). Because of the impossible terrain which he has been ordered to attempt, he must drive his horses beyond their capability, whipping them but feeling compassion for them. Only a human agent can feel pity, and in this context that agent must be the driver.

We soon learn from Mr. Heywood that Mr. and Mrs. Parker have been traveling in a "post-chaise," a phrase that for Jane Austen's reader would suffice to describe their means of conveyance from their stay in London back to their home in Sanditon. "Post-chaises were owned by innkeepers, who hired them out together with horses and postboys (postillions) to ride them" (Le Faye, 2002: 58). For a contemporary reader it would be clear that while in London Mr. Parker hired from his innkeeper a chaise equipped with horses (which would be changed periodically as they advanced on their journey) and a driver, sometimes called a postboy or a postilion, who was usually mounted "on the near horse of a pair or of one of the pairs attached to the post-chaise" ("Chaise." *Wikipedia*).

It appears that on occasion the postilion rode not on one of the rear pair of horses but on the leading left-hand horse of a team of horses. The illustration on page 29 of Marylian Watney's *Royal Cavalcade* describes a safety device designed to separate the front and rear pairs of horses in case the driver falls off one of the leading horses, as is seen in the print.

As I show in *Jane Austen Caught in the Act of Greatness* (247–249), although she changed this line perhaps six times before proceeding, leading to the reasonable assumption that as it presently reads it more or less reflects her final intention, the passage as it stands leaves her exact meaning in limbo.

Despite her revisions, the text is unclear about who owns the carriage and who has employed the driver. The original material in parentheses, "(especially as the Carriage was not the Gentleman's own)," is self-explanatory, merely reiterating that the so-far unnamed gentleman traveling with his lady does not own the carriage since a post-chaise would obviously not belong to the person hiring it. But the use of "Gentleman" here so soon after the phrase "The only Gentleman's House" may have struck the author as potentially confusing. Hence she may have decided to clarify the second occurrence of the word by altering the parenthetical material to read "(especially as the Carriage was not his Masters the Gentleman's own)." The passage still means, as we expect, that the carriage does not belong to the traveling Gentleman, soon to be identified as Mr. Thomas Parker of Sanditon. But unexpectedly we are to understand that the rider regards the traveler as "his Master," meaning that he is in Mr. Parker's employ, making the situation very different from the usual practice of hiring horses and a postilion along with the post-chaise. In modern punctuation, we might write the passage as "especially as the Carriage was not his Master's, the Gentleman's, own," making the meaning clear through an appositional construction. If this is the correct reading, Mr. Thomas Parker may have brought his servant with him from Sanditon to London, to drive him back and forth in a rented carriage. Since he appears to take little interest in the safety of his two passengers, he who was at one time a trusted household servant will probably be seeking new employment upon their return to Sanditon. His manner suggests that he is not entirely sober, but the text is silent on this point. We never learn the name of this driver nor if he is still in charge of the horses when the Parkers and their charming young guest arrive in Sanditon.

Despite all the changes in this passage, Jane Austen never removed either "his Masters" or "the Gentleman's," leading to the assumption that she intended keeping the entire construction. The OUP reading, "the carriage was not his Masters own" (*OIJA*–VI: 364), leaves unanswered the question of who is the rider's "Master" and poorly matches the manuscript.

CUPLM offers a reading that may not match the manuscript: "JA wrote 'not his Masters' above the line though she did not delete the words they were intended to replace, 'the Gentleman's own.' Either formulation suggests that the travellers had hired horses, and a driver, to pull their own carriage, a common practice" (630). There is an assumption here that Jane Austen left the first page in an incomplete stage. However, she worked and reworked this page many times, so it is unlikely that she failed to cross out words that she had rejected. The original line reads "(especially as the Carriage was not the Gentleman's own.)" At this point it is clear that the occupant, soon found to be Mr. Parker, does not own the carriage. In the changed reading, "the" before "Gentleman" has been crossed out, and above "the Carriage" the author has inserted "not his Masters." The final reading is therefore likely to be "(especially as the Carriage was not his Masters the Gentleman's own)." Regardless of the final reading, the text strongly suggests that the carriage does not belong to Mr. Parker, who seems unconcerned over the condition of the vehicle, an understandable indifference if he does not own it. Deirdre Le Faye states unambiguously that "the Parkers have been driving in their hired post-chaise" (2002: 298). The observation by Mr. Heywood, who owns his own carriage although he rarely uses it, that "if Gentlemen were to be often attempting this Lane in Post-chaises, it might not be a bad speculation for a Surgeon to get a House at the top of the Hill" strongly points to the carriage's not belonging to Mr. Parker.

There is yet another possibility: The "Master" is the innkeeper who pays the postboy, and Jane Austen means that the carriage belongs neither to the innkeeper back in London, "his Master," nor to Mr. Parker, "the Gentleman."

In any event, we must be eternally grateful to this anonymous character, without whose ill temper and poor handling of his horses the accident would never have taken place and we would have followed Mr. and Mrs. Parker back home without the pleasure of Charlotte Heywood's company.

Many commentators see in this opening passage a foreshadowing of a dark future for Sanditon. I believe that a whole new interpretation of the novel is due. Instead of being a serious treatise on economic greed and hypochondria, it is far more likely in the tradition of the preceding novels, a lighthearted, romantic romp, surely ending with the marriage of the leading protagonists—Charlotte Heywood and Sidney Parker—and the success of Sanditon as a seaside attraction for people of wealth and taste. It is inconceivable after the glorification of love in *Persuasion* (by whatever title she intended) and her decision to shelve "Susan"/ "Catherine" that she would turn her attention to a tale of woe and misery. *Sanditon* (again, by whatever title it was meant to carry) was planned to be the best combination of the zany life created in her early writings and the perfection of narrative technique learned over her years of professional writing. Everything that follows is interpreted, therefore, in the light of the novel's being a series of humorous episodes, ending in success and universal joy.]

The severity of the fall was broken by their slow pace & the narrowness of the Lane, & the Travellors found themselves at first only shaken & bruised.

>

The severity of the fall was broken by their slow pace & the narrowness of the Lane, & the Gentleman having scrambled out & helped out his companion, they niether of them at first felt more than shaken & bruised.

[The emendation is essential because it accounts for the gentleman's leaving the carriage, thereby spraining his ankle. This change suggests that Jane Austen is making up the story line as she works through the text. Some commentators have suggested that Mr. and Mrs. Parker fall out of the carriage, but it is a closed carriage, holding them in as it topples.]

But the Gentleman had in the course of the extrication sprained his foot — & becoming sensible of it in a few moments, was obliged to cut short, both his remonstrance to the Driver & his self congratulations — & sit down on the bank, unable to stand.

>

But the Gentleman had in the course of the extrication sprained his foot —
& soon becoming sensible of it, was obliged in a few moments to cut short,
both his remonstrance to the Driver & his congratulations to his wife &
himself — & sit down on the bank, unable to stand.

[By "extrication" Jane Austen could mean either the Gentleman's scrambling
out of the overturned carriage or his helping his companion to free herself.
There is some initial confusion about precisely what the Gentleman has
sprained, identified here as his foot but shortly to be transferred to his ankle
(and eventually to his leg).

The Gentleman had good cause to offer congratulations to his wife and
himself since accidents involving horses—as the author knew to her personal
grief—were often fatal. "Jane Austen's great friend Madam Lefroy of Ashe
was killed in 1804 when she threw herself off a runaway horse" (Le Faye,
2002: 60). Another tragic event took place just two years later, when, as
Deirdre Le Faye records, "in October 1806 there was a fatal accident at
Leatherhead in Surrey, and the Austens would have read the inquest report
in the *Hampshire Chronicle*. The Princess of Wales and two of her ladies-
in-waiting, Lady Sheffield and Miss Harriet Cholmondeley [pronounced
"Chumly"], had been visiting Surrey and were returning to London in an
open barouche-landau, the impatient Princess urging the post-boys who
drove the four horses to travel at top speed. The horses took a corner too
fast and too wide, the off-wheels ran up the roadside bank and the carriage
overturned. The three ladies were flung out; Miss Cholmondeley was picked
up bleeding copiously from mouth and ears and died a few minutes later"
(2002: 61).

As *CUPLM* notes, "carriage accidents were common in fact and in fiction"
(629), and Jane Austen used the incident in her early comic "Love and
Freindship." This disrupted journey is in marked contrast to the safe one
experienced by Catherine Morland and the Allens, who were able to travel
to Bath avoiding a "lucky overturn to introduce them to the hero." Although
Emily St. Aubert and her father likewise experienced no accident, they
did encounter the story's hero—later identified as the suitably named
Valancourt— during their journey.

> They travelled on, sunk in that thoughtful melancholy, with which
> twilight and solitude impress the mind. Michael had now ended
> his ditty, and nothing was heard but the drowsy murmur of the

breeze among the woods, and its light flutter, as it blew freshly into the carriage. They were at length roused by the sound of fire-arms. St. Aubert called to the muleteer to stop, and they listened. The noise was not repeated; but presently they heard a rustling among the brakes. St. Aubert drew forth a pistol, and ordered Michael to proceed as fast as possible; who had not long obeyed, before a horn sounded, that made the mountains ring. He looked again from the window, and then saw a young man spring from the bushes into the road, followed by a couple of dogs. The stranger was in a hunter's dress. His gun was slung across his shoulders, the hunter's horn hung from his belt, and in his hand was a small pike, which, as he held it, added to the manly grace of his figure, and assisted the agility of his steps.

Brian Southam has suggested a source for the coach trip and the accident in Thomas Love Peacock's *Headlong Hall*. "The beginning of *Sanditon* is a playful version of Thomas Love Peacock's *Headlong Hall*, published in 1816, which opens with the four 'illuminati' in a coach heatedly discussing 'improvements.' Soon there is the comedy of a twisted ankle and an intrusive coachman" (1986: 371) (also 1976: 17-18). (See Appendix A.)]

"There is something wrong here, said he — putting his hand to his ancle — But never mind, my Dear — (looking up at her with a smile) — It c^d— not have happened, you know, in a better place. — Good out of Evil —. The very thing perhaps to be wished for. We shall soon get releif. —

[Mr. Thomas Parker, who can smile even when he is sitting in the dust alongside his overturned carriage in a strange neighborhood, is one of the cheeriest characters in Jane Austen's novels. Throughout the manuscript he succeeds in finding the good side of every person of his acquaintance however undeserving, with the sole exception of his younger brother, Sidney, one of the few people of his acquaintance likely to be found eventually worthy of praise.

The injury has now moved from the Gentleman's foot to his ankle. His wife, who is apparently standing at this point since he is looking up at her, has survived the accident intact.

The filler "you know" will characterize Thomas Parker's dialog throughout the fragment, sometimes appearing in a first version and occasionally being added in a revision.

Although there is nothing in the text about religion (other than the expected presence of a church in Sanditon and the name of at least one man of the cloth in the subscription book), Jane Austen's readers would not be surprised to find in a book written by a clergyman's daughter some reflections of scriptural passages, such as St. Augustine's pronouncement, "God judged it better to bring good out of evil, than to suffer no evil to exist." Or Thomas Parker may be paraphrasing Genesis 50:20, "You plotted evil against me, but God turned it into good." But he more likely expresses this sentiment as a platitude than as a paraphrase of one of the Fathers of the Church or a passage in the Old Testament. We learn soon that he has read some Cowper, but no more is disclosed about his literary interests]

<u>There</u>, I fancy lies my cure" — pointing to the neat-looking end of a Cottage, which was seen peeping out from among wood, and romantically situated on a high Eminence at some little Distance —

>

<u>There</u>, I fancy lies my cure" — pointing to the neat-looking end of a Cottage, which was seen romantically situated among wood on a high Eminence at some little Distance —

[This passage makes gentle fun of the current Romantic passion for cottages surrounded by natural beauty. The reader soon learns that there is nothing even remotely interesting in this cottage, which now houses no more than a shepherd and three old women.]

"Does not <u>that</u> promise to be the very place? —"

His wife fervently hoped it was — but stood, terrified & anxious, neither able to do or suggest anything — & receiving her first real comfort from the sight of several persons now coming to their assistance.

[The author remains unsympathetic to Mrs. Parker, who later in the fragment will be seen as unable to fulfill a simple although presumptuous request made by her husband and sister-in-law. Like everyone standing around and peering down at the fallen Louisa Musgrove, except the ever-resourceful Anne Elliot, she is frozen with fear.]

The accident had been discerned from a Hay field adjoining the House they had passed — & the persons who approached, were a well-looking Hale, Gentlemanlike Man, of middle age, the Proprietor of the Place, who happened to be among his Haymakers at the time, & three or four of the ablest of them summoned to attend their Master — to say nothing of all the rest of the field, Men, Women & Children — not very far off. —

[The author makes clear from the start that her characters are of the gentry, with a gentleman experiencing an accident and another gentleman coming to his rescue. That we may be surrounded by country bumpkins does not mean that we have to recognize their existence as individuals. Although Emma is commended for her visits to the poor of her village, she does not invite them to her home or think about them the moment she steps out of their humble abodes. Working comfortably alongside his employees, Mr. Heywood is presumably one of the "many landowners [who] were actively concerned in ensuring reasonable standards of living for the families of workers on their estates" (Pinion: 37).

With generally much shorter lives than we now enjoy, Jane Austen's contemporaries by "middle age" may have meant something rather younger than the OED definition of "between about forty-five and sixty." Mr. Heywood will shortly proclaim his age as "57," just short of what Jane Austen might uncharitably call "old" if Colonel Brandon is considered senescent at a mere 35.

As expected, only Mr. Heywood will speak. All the men, women, and children, being of a lower class and unnamed in the text, must remain silent. The workers carry scythes (long handles) and sickles (short handles) to cut the hay, but as usual the author pays no attention to secondary characters.

> Hay making is the longest established method of conserving grass for feeding cattle and sheep through the winter and has been an important function of the farming calendar in the UK for the last six thousand years. Successful haymaking relies on the crop of grass being thoroughly dried before it is baled or stored.

> The first step in hay making is the mowing of the grass crop. This usually starts in late June just before flowering; however, many crops are cut during flowering itself when lots of pollen is being produced (hence hay fever). Cutting must be done when the weather is fine and several continuous dry days are expected. Hay that has been rained on is of poorer quality and may be unpalatable.

> After the crop has been cut it is allowed to dry in the sun. ("Hay Making")

This passage in the manuscript may set the precise time of year in which the story takes place: "Haymaking normally takes place in July, so this places the opening of the novel in high summer" (*CUPLM*: 630). This dating is supported by Mr. Parker's dismay that Sanditon boasts few visitors although the summer is already well underway. Deirdre Le Faye, however, suggests an earlier opening date: "The story begins in June 1816, at hay-making time" (2002: 298). Contemporary evidence points to late June as haymaking time: "We are in the midst of our hay here" (Mrs. Piozzi to Dr. Whalley, Monday, June 29, 1812) (Whalley: 355).]

M^r. Heywood, such was the name of the said Proprietor, advanced with a very civil salutation — much concern for the accident — some surprise at any body's attempting that road in a Carriage — & ready offers of service.
>
M^r. Heywood, such was the name of the said Proprietor, advanced with a very civil salutation — much concern for the accident — some surprise at any body's attempting that road in a Carriage — & ready offers of assistance.

[There can be no surprise that a "Hale"-looking man working in a "Hay field" among his "Haymakers" is named... "Heywood." Like "Morland," the name to some degree describes the man's land-holding status. Jane Austen occasionally uses names to convey something about her characters. "Dashwood" may suggest lost hope. "Price" certainly suggests Fanny's great if little-appreciated value. "Knightley" (and "George," no less) cries out for a heroic character, and his estate known as "Donwell" matches him perfectly. One would expect the "Morlands" to be wealthier than they are, and the name may have misled the General into thinking Catherine a great heiress. Later in this manuscript we shall hear about the timid "Miss Lambe," who has come to Sanditon to be shorn of her wealth.]

Some critics have pointed to the broken construction here as evidence of an early draft, but I believe that the disjointed narrative is meant to summarize a complex of reactions in a brief space, and this it does very successfully. Jane Austen worked over every line on the opening page, so it is unlikely that it does not reflect her considered judgment as exactly what she intended writing.]

His courtesies were received with Goodbreeding & gratitude & while one or two of the Men lent their help to the Driver in getting the Carriage upright again, the Travellor said — "You are extremely obliging Sir, & I take you at your word.—

[For the last time we hear directly of the driver, who remains nameless, although he is presumably back on the job as they return to Sanditon. That the carriage is not very heavy is indicated in its being righted by only two or three men. Jane Austen customarily pays little attention to people below the status of gentleman and lady, and so the precise number of helpers is not specified. If several ladies or gentlemen had been involved, their number would probably have been faithfully reported.

The text does not state that any of Mr. Heywood's sons are working with him in the field or assisted in lifting the carriage. If any of them are still at home, they are too young to be part of this episode.]

The injury to my Leg is I dare say very trifling, but it is always best in these cases to have a Surgeon's opinion without loss of time; & as the road does not seem at present in the best possible state for my getting up to his house myself, I will thank you to send off one of these good People for the Surgeon."
>
The injury to my Leg is I dare say very trifling, but it is always best in these cases to have a Surgeon's opinion without loss of time; & as the road does not seem at present in a favourable state for my getting up to his house myself, I will thank you to send off one of these good People for the Surgeon."

[Like Dr. Watson's notorious wandering wound, mysteriously migrating from his left shoulder to other parts of his body, Mr. Parker's injury has traveled from his foot to his ankle and thence to his leg. Perhaps it was considered more genteel to refer to larger limbs than to small ones.

Jane Austen does not always seem to distinguish carefully among the several medical professions practiced at the time. "Surgeons were qualified medical men, trained and licensed to perform surgical operations" (*CUPLM*: 630), but there is no suggestion that Mr. Parker is looking for someone who will perform surgery in Sanditon. Rather, he seems to be looking for someone who will recommend immersion as a cure for any disease that afflicts (in reality or in imagination) the visitor to Sanditon.]

"The Surgeon Sir! — replied M^r. Heywood — I am afraid you will find no Surgeon at hand here, but I dare say we shall do very well without him."

[Mr. Heywood and Lady Denham probably never meet, but they are in total agreement on the questionable value of men of the medical profession. On the basis of her visit to Dr. Spence with her three young nieces, Jane Austen certainly had the same low opinion of dentists.]

"Nay Sir, if <u>he</u> is not in the way, his Partner will do just as well — or better —. I w^d. rather see his Partner indeed — I would have his Partner by preference.

>

"Nay Sir, if <u>he</u> is not in the way, his Partner will do just as well — or rather better —. I w^d. rather see his Partner indeed — I would prefer the attendance of his Partner. —

["Just as only a licensed surgeon could legally perform surgical operations, so only a licensed apothecary could dispense drugs, and it was therefore common for an apothecary to practise in partnership" (*CUPLM*: 630). It is difficult to understand Thomas Parker's preference.]

One of these good people will be there in three minutes I am sure.

>

One of these good people can be with him in three minutes I am sure.

[Mr. Parker is if nothing else determined to bring his adventure to a successful conclusion despite being told in clear terms that there is no surgeon nearby. His poor judgment here—an uncharitable person might call him obtuse— is an ominous sign about his business acumen as an entrepreneur at home in Sanditon as well as a foreshadowing of the questionable accuracy of his narrative to Charlotte on their way to Sanditon.]

I need not ask whether I see the House; (looking towards the Cottage). for Excepting your own, we have passed none in this place, which can be the Abode of a Gentleman."

Mr. H. looked very much astonished & replied — "What Sir! are you expecting to find a Surgeon in that Cottage? —We have neither Surgeon nor Partner in the Parish I assure you." —

[Although strictly speaking "Parish" is an ecclesiastical term referring to an area under the control of a bishop, here Mr. Heywood is more likely using the word in the general secular sense of a part of the county. Although the daughter and sister of clergymen, Jane Austen appears reluctant to introduce religion into her novels unless, as in *Mansfield Park*, it constitutes part of the plot.]

"Excuse me Sir — replied the other. I am sorry to have the appearance of contradicting you — but though from the extent of the Parish or some other cause you may not be aware of the fact; —— Stay — Can I be mistaken in the place? Am I not in Willingden? — Is not this Willingden?"

[The dialog here is very "stagey," especially the "Stay" and the rhetorical questions. Jane Austen regularly writes as "is not" the construction that we would write as the contraction, "isn't." In general, she reserves spoken contractions for characters with poor language skills. Her contemporaries would presumably recognize the distinction between people of quality and the others without the author's being more specific.]

"Yes Sir, this is certainly Willingden."

"Then Sir, I can bring proof of your having a Surgeon in the Parish — whether you may know it or not. Here Sir — (taking out his Pocket book —) if you will do me the favour of casting your eye over these advertisements, which I cut out myself from the Morning Post & the Kentish Gazette, only yesterday morn^g. in London — I think you will be convinced that I am not speaking at random.

[A "Pocket book," just as its name suggests, was a small book carried in a pocket to record notes and hold papers (Shapard: 529). "Both men and women kept 'pocket-books'—very small printed diaries with room for just a few words on the page, what we would now call engagement diaries" (Le Faye, 2002: 110).

The *Morning Post* was merged with the *Daily Telegraph* in 1937, just a month short of its one hundred and sixty-fifth birthday. "In the course of its long life, it had acquired an individuality not surpassed by that of any other newspaper" (Hindle: 1), with contributors including some of the most famous names in English literature, such as Dr. Johnson, Coleridge, and Wordsworth (Hindle: 4). That Mr. Parker read this popular newspaper, which "claimed sales of 5,000 copies per day in 1778" (Olsen: 505) is entirely in character and demonstrates Jane Austen's sensitivity to accurate reporting since "in its opinions... the *Morning Post*... belonged to one class exclusively;... it was very much the organ of the leisured classes" (Hindle: 5), "the most important newspaper for the monied and fashionable" (*CUPLM:*

631). Jane Austen herself may not have thought much of it, despite its being "the most important... [of] several daily papers published in London" (Borer: 205), because of its excessive support of the Prince Regent, not one of her favorite royals. "The *Morning Post* showed a remarkable affection for George IV both when Regent and when King" (Hindle: 107), "in verse and in prose, in season and out, during his Regency and during his reign,... praising George IV as probably no English king, and certainly no more worthless king, had ever been praised before" (Hindle: 110). As a member of the landed gentry and an advocate for seaside health resorts, Mr. Parker supports conservative politics and the Prince Regent's interest in the Sussex Coast.

Along with the increase in readership in London, by the beginning of the nineteenth century, "the number of provincial papers also rose dramatically. There had been only ten newspapers outside London in 1710, but this had grown to somewhere between sixty-five and seventy in the 1790s" (Olsen: 505). Originally published as *The Kentish Post*, founded in 1717, the county's first newspaper was renamed *The Kentish Gazette* in 1768, coming "out twice weekly, with a catchment area of Kent and nearby counties including Sussex" (*CUPLM*: 631).

Although the precise location of Willingden is unclear, it is probably in Kent as the advertisement is carried in a newspaper that "aims to bring results through a top quality and comprehensive service to the people and businesses of the county. **Just as it has for almost 300 years**" ("KM History"). Jane Austen was clearly aware of the specialties of the newspapers of her time, because in citing *The Kentish Gazette* she must have known that "in the 1810s it regularly carried advertisements by medical men" (*CUPLM*: 631). It is always difficult to determine if Jane Austen is creating a location or borrowing one that already exists but with a small twist: "There is no village of this name [Willingden] in the immediate vicinity described here, but there is a village more commonly spelled Willingdon just inland from Eastbourne" (*CUPLM*: 631).

His cutting out the articles instead of copying the information demonstrates reckless extravagance on Thomas Parker's part since at the time newspapers were "very expensive because of high stamp taxes placed on them" (Shapard: 609). "In the era of the Napoleonic Wars, newspapers won more and more readers.... [but] the average Englishman... could not buy them outright; increasing taxation had sent their price to 6*d.* by 1800, and after 1815 they rose to 7*d*.—a price prohibitive even to most middle-class families with an income of less than, say, £300 a year. Most copies of a daily paper in the first third of the century passed through a dozen or even scores of hands" (Altick, 1957: 322). With modern inventions, however, the newspaper in time came within the buying power of the average Englishman. "Advances in printing technology during the Industrial Revolution were responsible for turning the newspaper into a widely circulated means of communication. In 1814, *The Times* of London acquired a printing press capable of making 1,100 impressions per minute. Soon, it was adapted to print on both sides of a page at once. This innovation made newspapers cheaper and thus available to a larger part of the population" ("Newspaper." *Wikipedia*).

It is impossible to tell from the text at what point Mr. Parker decided to seek a surgeon for Sanditon. Possibly the notion did not strike him until he was in London and serendipitously found both a London and a Kentish paper with the identical ad for a surgeon who was seeking a new post. Or perhaps finding the advertisements reinforced an idea already percolating in his brain. If so, he made up his mind without discussing the issue with Lady Denham, who he knew would oppose the plan. This scenario would bolster the impression that that theirs is an uneasy business relationship, with Mr. Parker primarily interested in developing the community and Lady Denham primarily interested in making a large profit as quickly as possible.]

You will find it an advertisement Sir, of the dissolution of a Partnership in the Medical Line — in your own Parish — extensive Business — undeniable Character — respectable references — wishing to form a separate Establishment — You will find it at full length Sir" — offering him the two little oblong extracts. —

[Again we have a fragmented passage that could indicate an early draft, but I very much doubt that Jane Austen intended expanding this material into a more conventional paragraph. It perfectly conveys the stream of conversation, especially a mix of what Mr. Parker is reading and what he is saying to convince Mr. Heywood that there must be a surgeon living here in Willingden. Roger Sales makes an interesting point that "the search for a medical man seems to overturn his argument that Sanditon's air and sea will cure all known diseases" (202), but Thomas Parker may be seeking a surgeon not so much for his ability to cure illnesses as for the cachet—hence more and wealthier visitors—of having one in the town. "By the end of the eighteenth century no seaside resort was considered really established until it had its own resident physician" (Howell: 18).]

"Sir — said M^r. Heywood with a good humoured smile— if you were to shew me all the Newspapers that are printed in one week throughout the Kingdom, you w^d. not persuade me of there being a Surgeon in Willingden, — for having lived here ever since I was born, Man & Boy 57 years, I think I must have <u>known</u> of such a person, at least I may venture to say that he has not <u>much Business;</u> —

[Mr. Heywood's disclosure of his age is rare in Jane Austen's novels, where the older characters are rarely so specifically described. Later, in conversation with Charlotte, Lady Denham will share this same kind of information: "Here have I lived 70 good years in the world." For critics who believe that Sir Edward Denham's use of "Samphire" is a reference, conscious or otherwise, to the chameleonic Edgar's lines in *King Lear* ("Half-way down, Hangs one that gathers samphire; dreadful trade!"), that "Man & Boy" is taken from *Hamlet* should be an attractive suggestion. It seems unlikely that Jane Austen ever saw the Melancholy Dane on stage since in April 1811 she wrote from Sloane Street, while visiting Henry, to Cassandra, who was staying with Edward at Godmersham Park, "of a very unlucky change of the Play for this very night—Hamlet instead of King John—& we are to go on Monday to Macbeth, instead, but it is a disappointment to us both" (*Letters*: 181).]

To be sure, if Gentlemen were to be often attempting this Lane in Post-chaises, it might not be a bad speculation for a Surgeon to get a House at the top of the Hill.

["A chaise, unlike other carriages, was normally used for long-distance travel" (Shapard: 519). "The post-chaise was a fast carriage for traveling post in the 18th and early 19th centuries. It usually had a closed body on four wheels, sat two to four persons, and was drawn by two or four horses. The driver, especially when there was no coachman, rode postillion on the near horse of a pair or of one of the pairs attached to the post-chaise" ("Chaise." *Wikipedia*). "Post-chaises were owned by innkeepers, who hired them out together with horses and postboys (postillions) to ride them" (Le Faye, 2002: 58). "Postillion riders normally rode the left hand horse of a pair because of the ease of mounting a horse from the left. With a double team, a postillion would ride on the left rear horse in order to control all four horses" ("Postillion." *Wikipedia*). Quoting a journalist of 1791 writing about post-chaises, Deirdre Le Faye tells us that "'they are good carriages with four wheels, shut close... hold three persons in the back with ease; are narrow, extremely light, well hung, and appear the more easy, because the roads are not paved with stone... the postillions are not only civil but even respectful'" (2002: 58). Mr. Parker's rebellious postilion—perhaps his own servant—was clearly an exception. "Traveling post... was very expensive, as the rate was a minimum of one shilling per horse per mile, plus a tip to the postboy and tips to all inn servants along the way" (Le Faye, 2002: 58).

Mr. Heywood's identifying the overturned carriage as a "Post-chaise" tells us that Mr. Parker is not its owner. More expensive than a stagecoach, "a post chaise... cost 1s. 6d. per mile, plus a 3d.-per-mile tip to the postboys who rode and directed the horses, plus sixpence to each inn's ostler for tending to the horses" (Olsen: 109). A post chaise, or post coach, was usually a four-wheeled carriage for conveying passengers who travel post, stopping at a series of stations for refreshment and new horses and drivers. It was a "four-wheeled, closed carriage, containing one seat for two or three passengers, that was popular in 18th-century England. The body was of the coupé type, appearing as if the front had been cut away. Because the driver rode one of the horses, it was possible to have windows in front as well as at the sides. At the post chaise's front end, in place of the coach box, was a luggage platform. The carriage was built for long-distance travel, and so horses were changed at intervals at posts (stations)" ("Post Chaise." *Britannica Online Encyclopedia*).

It is possible, though, that the Parkers are traveling in "a hack or hackney coach[, which] was simply a rented vehicle, which might or might not come with its own coachman; the Parkers, in *Sanditon*, rent a coach but bring their coachman from home" (Olsen: 111). If this is true, then Mr. and Mrs. Parker presumably brought with them to London the unnamed coachman without whose short temper there would be no novel. The text does not specify if he is riding one of the horses or is on the coach, but the former is more likely as he seems to be unaffected by the overturn. The text never tells us how they return the coach, which perhaps they can hold until they next visit London. How the Parkers, and their coachman if he is one of their servants, reached London in the first place is also unclear. If what they have is a hackney coach, Mr. Heywood out of courtesy refers to it as a post chaise, thus elevating them socially; he himself owns a coach although an old one. Jane Austen surely knew all about these matters, but she is always reluctant to clutter her text with details that even dull elves like her readers were familiar with.]

But as to that Cottage, I can assure you Sir that it is in fact — (inspite of its spruce air at this distance—) as indifferent a double Tenement as any in the Parish, and that My Shepherd lives at one end, & three old women at the other."

[A double tenement is "a house divided and let to two separate tenants or tenant families" (*CUPLM*: 631). His generosity to strangers suggests that Mr. Heywood does not charge rent for these accommodations. That the house is "indifferent" may not reflect well on Mr. Heywood as a landlord. If by this adjective Jane Austen means "Not definitely possessing either of two opposite qualities; *esp.* (in current use), Neither good nor bad; of neutral quality" (*OED* with a citation as recent as 1821), then the structure is merely a modest one not worthy of the attention that Mr. Parker has given it. But it is possible— albeit it unlikely—that Mr. Heywood uses this word in a much less attractive sense: "Not particularly good; poor, inferior; rather bad" (*OED* with a quotation from *Pride and Prejudice* and a citation as recent as 1878).]

He took the bits of paper as he spoke — & having looked them over, added — "I beleive I can explain it Sir. —
>
He took the peices of paper as he spoke — & having looked them over, added — "I beleive I can explain it Sir.—

Your mistake is in the place. — There are two Willingdens in this Country — & your advertisements refer to the other — which is Great Willingden, or Willingden Abbots, & lies 7 miles off, on the other side of Battel — quite down in the Weald. And <u>we</u> Sir — (speaking rather proudly) are not in the Weald." —

[Here, as usual in the literature of the time, "country" means "county." Upon exclaiming in astonishment, "Willoughby! what, is HE in the country?" Sir John Middleton is obviously not expressing surprise that Willoughby is in England. When the Bennet sisters walked to Meryton, "however bare of news the country in general might be, they always contrived to learn some from their aunt," who was better prepared to gossip about her neighbors than events elsewhere in the United Kingdom. In reassuring her titled brother-in-law that young Fanny Price "would be introduced into the society of this country under such very favourable circumstances," Mrs. Norris has no thoughts of national recognition for her insignificant niece. And Harriet Smith, in boasting to Emma that her Mr. Martin "had been bid more for his wool than any body in the country," would be surprised if Miss Woodhouse thought that the frame of reference went far beyond the young man's Abbey-Mill Farm in Donwell parish. Lady Russell, eager as she was for the Elliots to retrench and "extremely glad that Sir Walter and his family were to remove from the country," had no intentions of banishing her old friends to foreign climes. Finally, when young and fortuneless Frederick Wentworth "left the country in consequence" of Anne's breaking off their engagement, he probably removed himself no farther than to his brother's house in Shropshire (although his naval adventures would eventually take him to faraway scenes of battle).

By interspersing real places among her fictional sites, Jane Austen succeeds in creating the effect of verisimilitude. The moment her tale fails to feel like true history, it fails to entertain and hold our interest. In this instance she throws in cities, mostly in the south of England—London, Chichester, Brighton, "Battel," Hailsham, Tunbridge, Tunbridge Wells, Bath, Hastings—that her readers would recognize. It follows, then, that "Willingden" and "Great Willingden/Willingden Abbots" are real places. But Sussex can claim no historic "Willingden"—and definitely not two. Jane Austen's "Willingden," the home of the Heywoods, is somewhere between London and the coast, south of Tunbridge and north of Hailsham, "a market town thirteen miles south-west of Battle and ten miles north of Eastbourne" (*CUPLM*: 632), not so far off the main road that Thomas Parker cannot reach it without a major deviation from his intended route home. Willingden is close enough to Tunbridge Wells that the Heywoods could—if they would—spend some time there but sufficiently far from London that a visit to the capital requires serious planning.

What confuses the issue about the location of fictional "Willingden" is that there is a real Willingdon here in Sussex, but it is in the wrong place to be the home of the Heywoods. "There is a Willingdon and Willingdon Hill just to the north of the town of Eastbourne" (Le Faye, 2002: 299) as can be seen on the early nineteenth-century map supplied by Deirdre Le Faye (2002: 301), who suggests that Jane Austen did not entirely invent the name of the town: "Did Jane Austen see [Willingdon] on some map, as she thought about the location for her story, and did the name perhaps stick in her memory?" Deirdre Le Faye obliquely suggests Jane Austen's additional indebtedness to an external source in noting that "a contemporary guidebook mentions Willingdon as being 'a pleasant village, about two miles from East Bourne, in which is a handsome house belonging to Mr Thomas, who has a park, decoy-pond, gardens, pleasure grounds, &c.'" (2002: 299).

"Battel" is of course Battle, "short for 'Battle Abbey' after the church built by William I of England to commemorate the Battle of Hastings (1066)" (*CUPLM*: 632).

The Weald, rising to more than 800 feet, is an area of clays and sandstones lying between the North Downs in Kent and the South Downs in Sussex. "It was formerly woodland ('weald' is the Old English word for 'forest') but by Austen's day it was mostly used for pasture" (*CUPLM*: 632).]

"Not <u>down</u> in the Weald I am sure Sir, replied the Travellor, pleasantly. It took us half an hour to climb your Hill. — Well Sir — I dare say it is as you say, & I have made an abominably stupid Blunder. —

All done in a moment; — the advertisements did not catch my eye till the last half hour of our being in Town; — when everything was in the hurry & confusion which always attend a short stay there — nothing able to be completed in the way of Business you know till the Carriage is at the door — and accordingly satisfying myself with a breif enquiry, & finding we were actually to pass within a mile or two of a <u>Willingden</u>, I sought no farther.
>
All done in a moment; — the advertisements did not catch my eye till the last half hour of our being in Town; — when everything was in the hurry & confusion which always attend a short stay there — One is never able to be complete anything in the way of Business you know till the Carriage is at the door — and accordingly satisfying myself with a breif enquiry, & finding we were actually to pass within a mile or two of a <u>Willingden</u>, I sought no farther.

[By "Town," of course, Jane Austen always means London, the largest of all English cities. In turn, when in London someone says "the City," he means the mile-square financial and commercial district. Technically, a city contains a cathedral and hence has a bishop. Below a town in size are villages and finally hamlets. We never learn why the Parkers have taken the long ride up to London, only to enjoy a "short stay there," but it must have been to conduct business of some sort. Lady Denham also periodically visits London, as do other characters throughout the novels.

Mr. Parker is more impetuous than one might expect, but without such a spontaneous impulse the story would never have come into existence.]

My Dear — (to his wife) I am very sorry to have brought you into this awkward Predicament.

>

My Dear — (to his wife) I am very sorry to have brought you into this Scrape.

[As expected, Mr. Parker speaks to his wife with less strict formality than he would to a stranger. Jane Austen is always sensitive to the precise form of address between a husband and his wife. The parenthetical "(to his wife)" seems unnecessary since he would obviously not be addressing Mr. Heywood in such terms, but it supplies a virtual stage direction so that we can imagine his turning in her direction.]

But do not be alarmed about my Leg. It gives me no pain while I am quiet, — and as soon as these good people have succeeded in setting the Car^{ge}. to rights & turning the Horses round, the best thing we can do will be to measure back our steps into the Turnpike road & proceed to Hailsham, & so Home, without attempting anything farther. — Two hours take us home, from Hailsham —

[Fortunately, Mr. Heywood prevails upon Thomas to rest before continuing the journey home, especially as the carriage has sustained some damage. If not for the two-week visit, we would miss out on the entire adventure that Jane Austen has in store for us.

"The turnpike system led to a considerable improvement of the main roads in the eighteenth century, especially in the second half, when better and faster coaches became more numerous. With continued road improvements private carriages appeared" (Pinion: 28). The creation of "turnpike trusts... peaked during the third quarter of the eighteenth century. The trusts, formed by means of a private act of Parliament (private because the drafting and passage were privately funded), built and maintained the turnpikes. Most people, livestock, carts, wagons, and carriages were subject to a toll every time they passed a gate, though mail coaches and troops were exempt. As soon as it was clear that turnpikes could be profitable, they snaked across the map of England like the roots of some fast-growing plant... [and were] naturally placed along the busiest city-to-city routes" (Olsen: 684).

> Road maintenance was then the responsibility of the parishes
> through which the road passed; local rates were raised for the
> purpose.… In the past, parish councils had rightly complained
> that non-resident travellers added to the wear on the roads but
> contributed nothing towards their upkeep, and in the seventeenth
> century Turnpike Trusts were created as a means of combating
> this problem. A group of local gentlemen, the Trustees, would
> arrange for a stretch of the main road, where it passed through
> their parish, to be closed off at each end and at intermediate
> cross-roads by means of heavy gates (turnpikes), with a little toll-
> house beside each gate; anyone wishing to use that section of road
> had to pay a toll for the gate to be opened and the tolls collected
> were then used for the maintenance of the road. Country lanes,
> however, were still left unimproved. (Le Faye, 2002: 55)

The turnpikes themselves were "barriers where people using a road
would have to stop and pay tolls. To improve its long-distance roads the
English government had granted authority to local turnpike trusts, private
enterprises that built new roads and then garnered the income generated by
tolls on travelers" (Shapard: 501). "The name derives from a spiked barrier
placed as a form of defence" (*CUPLM*: 609).

Writing as though living in London in 1800, Mary Cathcart Borer gives a
vivid picture of the role played by this innovation and the rapid growth of
its implementation.

> The increase in the number of Turnpike Trusts has brought about
> an improvement—and has taken the burden of payment for road
> repairs off local people, who formerly complained vociferously
> against having to pay for the upkeep of roads used by strangers
> on their travels. Turnpike Trusts are small companies empowered
> by Parliament to erect gates and toll bars on the road, at which
> they exact a fee from riders and coach-travellers, using a stipulated
> percentage of the money received to pay for the upkeep of roads.
> It has been estimated that today there are no fewer than 8,000
> tollgates on the roads. (49)

Now that the locals need not complain about the use of their roads
gratis by strangers, it is the turn of travelers to complain—albeit not
vociferously—about paying. The subject of turnpikes would obviously not
figure prominently in Jane Austen's correspondence, but in 1801, writing

in a particularly lighthearted mood to Cassandra from Bath, she reports a successful arrival after a long journey, having "changed Horses at the end of every stage, & paid at almost every Turnpike" (*Letters*: 81).

Hailsham is directly north of historic Willingdon—see an early nineteenth-century map in Le Faye, 2002: 301. The text suggests that "Willingden" is north of Hailsham and therefore not identical with the real Willingdon, which is south of Hailsham. "Journeys were undertaken at an average speed of seven miles an hour, either on horseback or in a carriage drawn by one or more horses" (Le Faye, 2002: 54), so Sanditon is about 14 miles from Hailsham.

We learn for the first time that the gentleman and lady are traveling to their home, which, lying between Hastings and Eastbourne, would be not far from Bexhill-on-Sea, generally called simply Bexhill. This seaside resort, with a history going all the way back to 772, is in an area in which "smuggling was rife… in the early nineteenth century" ("Bexhill-on-Sea." *Wikipedia*), a crime used as part of the story line of at least one of the continuations of the unfinished manuscript. The town has the distinction of being "the site of the 'first mixed bathing' in the UK; men and women could finally swim at the same beach" ("Bexhill-on-Sea." *Wikipedia*).]

And when once at home, we have our remedy at hand you know.

[A perfect segue into the core of the novel, the purported salutary effects of a visit to Sanditon. And as expected, "you know" is here to mark the line as Mr. Parker's. We are not such dull Elves that by now we do not recognize his distinctive voice.]

A little of our own Bracing Sea Air will soon set me on my feet again. — Depend upon it my Dear, it is exactly a case for the Sea.

Saline immersion will be the very thing. —
>
Saline air & immersion will be the very thing. —

["Then as now, sea air and salt water were both regarded as having healing properties, a belief supported by a range of enthusiastic treatises beginning with Sir John Floyer's *The Ancient Psychrolousia Revived; or, An Essay to prove Cold Bathing both Safe and Useful* (1702) and continuing throughout the eighteenth century" (*CUPLM*: 632).]

My sensations tell me so already." —

In a most friendly manner M^r. Heywood here interposed, entreating them not to think of proceeding till the ancle had been examined, & some refreshment taken, & very cordially pressing them to make use of his House for both purposes. — "We are always well stocked, said he, with all the common remedies for Sprains & Bruises — & I will answer for the pleasure it will give my Wife & daughters to be of service to you & this Lady in every way in their power. —"

[Recommendations on home remedies for sprains and bruises, including various poultices, were published by William Buchan and Richard Reece among others (*CUPLM*: 632–633). In *Emma*, Jane Austen casts doubt on the efficacy of sea bathing without placing much faith in other so-called cures. Isabella Woodhouse Knightley and her father, the valetudinarian Mr. Woodhouse, are discussing their favorite topic of conversation, sickness.

> "Oh! my dear sir, her throat is so much better that I have hardly any uneasiness about it. Either bathing has been of the greatest service to her, or else it is to be attributed to an excellent embrocation [a liniment] of Mr. Wingfield's, which we have been applying at times ever since August."

> "It is not very likely, my dear, that bathing should have been of use to her."

Again Mr. Heywood does not mention any sons in the household although they would be unlikely as nurses for either Mr. or Mrs. Parker.]

A twinge or two, in trying to move his foot disposed the Travellor to think rather more as he had done at first of the benefit of immediate assistance — & consulting his wife in the few words of "Well my Dear, I beleive it will be better for us" — turned again to M^r. H — & said — "Before we accept your Hospitality Sir, — & in order to do away any unfavourable impression which the sort of wild goose-chase you find me in, may have given rise to — allow me to tell you who we are.

[Jane Austen's use of "to do away" as a transitive verb meaning "to put an end to, abolish, destroy, undo" is cited in the *OED* as late as 1855.]

My name is Parker. — Mr. Parker of Sanditon; —this Lady, my wife M^{rs}. Parker. We are on our road home from London; <u>My</u> name perhaps — tho'

I am by no means the first of my Family, holding Landed Property in the Parish of Sanditon, may be unknown at this distance from the Coast — but Sanditon itself — everybody has heard of Sanditon, — the favourite — for a young & rising Bathing-place, certainly the favourite spot of all that are to be found along the coast of Sussex; — the most favoured by Nature, & promising to be the most chosen by Man." —

[Brian Southam suggests a source for this novel about sea resort speculation: "Jane Austen conducts a… burlesque comedy based on *The Magic of Wealth*, a 'Vehicle of Opinions.' The propaganda novel by Thomas Skinner Surr, published in 1815, tells the story of Mr. Flim-Flam, a tradesman turned banker, who transforms the fishing village of Thiselton into the resort of Flimflamton" (1986: 371). (See Appendix B.)

Although Sanditon is of course a fictional location, various attempts have been made to find its origins in a real town, such as David Selwyn's admittedly speculative suggestion that Thomas Parker's stating that "from Hailsham… it is two hours' journey to Sanditon, which, allowing for the state of even the turnpike roads, suggests a location somewhere near Bexhill. At that time Bexhill was a village standing on a hill overlooking Pevensey Bay, about half a mile from the sea, with a population of about 1700; occupying, in the words of an advertisement in the *Star* newspaper, 'one of the most healthy and pleasant situations on the coast of Sussex', it was 'well adapted for sea bathing', a purpose for which it was 'occasionally resorted to'. [footnote 116: "Quoted in L.J. Bartley, *The Story of Bexhill* (Bexhill, 1971), p. 28."]… I am of course indulging in a speculation almost as great as Mr Parker's own. Sanditon is an imaginary place, and it was important for Jane Austen's purpose that it should be so" (1999: 56–58).]

"Yes — I have heard of Sanditon, replied M^r. H. — Every five years, one hears of some new place or other starting up by the Sea, & growing the fashion. —

How they can half of them be filled, is amazing to me!
>
How they can half of them be filled, is the wonder!

<u>Where</u> People can be found with Money & Time to go to them!
>
<u>Where</u> People can be found with Money or Time to go to them!

["A frenzy of building took place in all the seaside resorts in the last decades of the eighteenth century, and the early nineteenth century" (Sutherland 1997: 62). Therefore, if the story takes place in 1816 as Deirdre Le Faye maintains (2002: 298), Jane Austen is writing well into the history of seaside resorts rather than about a new fad.]

Bad things for a Country; — sure to raise the price of Provisions & make the Poor good for nothing as — I dare say you find, Sir."

[Expectedly as a conservative, landed proprietor, Mr. Heywood may have drawn his views on economy from the Scottish Adam Smith's *Inquiry into the Nature and Causes of the Wealth of Nations*, published in 1776 (*CUPLM*: 635), "advocating a free market economy as more productive and more beneficial to society" ("The Wealth of Nations"). It is difficult to decide if by "country" Mr. Parker means "county" (the usual meaning in the novel) or England as a whole.]

"Not at all Sir, not at all — cried M^r. Parker eagerly. Quite the contrary I assure you. — A common idea — but a mistaken one. It may apply to your large, overgrown Places, like Brighton, or Worthing, or East Bourne —

["JA visited a number of seaside resorts on the south coast, including Worthing in 1805, for recreational rather than for health reasons" (*CUPLM*: 634). In her extant correspondence, the only location named here to which Jane Austen seems to have referred in her letters is Worthing. On Sunday, August 24, 1805, writing to Cassandra from Godmersham Park, she reports, "Little Edw:^{d} is by no means better,... Unless he recovers his strength beyond what is now probable, his brothers will return to School without him, & he will be of the party to Worthing.—If Sea-Bathing should be recommended he will be left there with us" (*Letters*: 107). "By mid-September [1805] the house-party was reassembled at Godmersham and on 17 September they set off for Worthing.... Mrs. Austen and her daughters... stayed in Worthing until at least early November" (Le Faye, 1989/2003: 134). Hence Jane Austen may have known the Sussex Coast well enough to write about it with confidence some years later.]

but not to a small Village like Sanditon, precluded by its size from experiencing any of the evils of Civilization, while the growth of the place, the Buildings, the Nursery Grounds, the demand for every thing, & the sure resort of the very best Company, those regular, steady, private Families of thorough Gentility & Character, who are a blessing everywhere, excite the industry of the Poor and diffuse comfort & improvement among them of every sort. — No Sir, I assure you, Sanditon is not a place —"

[Nursery grounds are "the fields where vegetables and fruits were cultivated" (*CUPLM*: 635). Private families did not "maintain a public position, and therefore [were] not of the highest social status; but the word also carries an implication of domesticity and respectability, in contrast to fashion and display" (*CUPLM*: 638).]

"I do not mean to take exceptions to <u>any</u> place in particular Sir, answered M^r. H. — I only think our Coast is too full of them altogether — But had not we better try to get you" —

[Very much in the manner an actor delivering scripted dialog, Mr. Heywood breaks into Mr. Parker's disquisition on the glories of Sanditon.]

"Our Coast too full" — repeated M^r. P. — On that point perhaps we may not totally disagree; — at least there are <u>enough</u>. Our Coast is abundant enough; it demands no more. — Everybody's Taste & everybody's finances may be suited —

[Continuing the natural dialog, Mr. Parker in turn breaks into Mr. Heywood's admonition that the injured ankle should receive immediate attention.]

And those good people who are trying to add to the number, are in my opinion excessively absurd, & I have no doubt will find themselves in the end the Dupes of their own fallacious Calculations. —
>
And those good people who are trying to add to the number, are in my opinion excessively absurd, & must soon find themselves the Dupes of their own fallacious Calculations. —

Such a place as Sanditon Sir, I may say was wanted, was called for. — Nature had marked it out — had spoken in most intelligible Characters — The finest, purest Sea Breeze on the Coast — acknowledged to be so — Excellent Bathing — fine hard Sand — Deep Water 10 yards from the Shore — no Mud — no Weeds — no slimey rocks — Never was there a place more palpably designed by Nature for the resort of the Invalid — the very Spot which Thousands seemed in need of. —

[John Halperin observes that as a "spa[,] like Bath, Brighton, and Cheltenham, [Sanditon] caters primarily to invalids" (1983: 185), but none of the main characters have come here for reasons of health. As a matter of fact, neither of the Parker sisters appears to have any interest in trying out the salutary effects of immersing herself in or imbibing the seawater, and Arthur Parker would certainly catch yet another dread disease if he approached the beach. Charlotte has no interest in getting into one of those strange machines, and Sidney sounds like someone who might enjoy swimming in the ocean just for the joy of it. The Beaufort sisters are obviously here in search of husbands. The Denhams—Lady, Sir Edward, and Miss Esther—clearly avoid the crowds on the sand. We hear about elderly men taking walks for their health and ladies dressed in white, seated on campstools sketching in their notebooks, but we are not told that they are invalids. Only Miss Lambe, off stage, specifically enters the water, and we know that she is "chilly and tender," which may or may not mean that she is an invalid who has been able to travel a long distance from her native West Indies. What use the various other people named make of the beachside amenities is never disclosed. The story feels as though it is going in a direction entirely different from a denunciation of hypochondria once Charlotte meets Sidney Parker and detects the Baronet and Miss Brereton in their tryst. Romance (or something) is now in the air.]

The most desirable distance from London! One complete, measured mile nearer than East Bourne. Only conceive Sir, the advantage of saving a whole Mile, in a long Journey.

[Since a carriage traveled only about seven miles an hour, a shorter distance to London was a major factor in choosing a seaside vacation.]

But Brinshore Sir, which I dare say you have in your eye — the attempts of two or three speculating People about Brinshore, this last Year, to raise that paltry Hamlet, situated between a stagnant marsh, & the constant effluvia of a ridge of putrifying Sea weed, can end in nothing but their own Disappointment.
>
But Brinshore Sir, which I dare say you have in your eye — the attempts of two or three speculating People about Brinshore, this last Year, to raise that paltry Hamlet, lying, as it does between a stagnant marsh, a bleak Moor & the constant effluvia of a ridge of putrifying Sea weed, can end in nothing but their own Disappointment.

[Although Mr. Parker does not specify the health dangers of Brinshore, contemporary scientists would have regarded the site as described as risky: "Buchan wrote of 'effluvia from putrid stagnant water' and 'vegetable effluvia' as causes of malignant fevers" (*CUPLM*: 636).]

What in the name of Common Sense is to <u>recommend</u> Brinshore? — A most insalubrious Air — Roads proverbially detestable — Water Brackish beyond example, impossible to get a good dish of Tea within 3 miles of the place — & as for the Soil —

[Mr. Parker's litany of charges against the detested rival, Brinshore, has been well rehearsed. The air, the roads, the water, and the soil are equally foul. Even worse, neither in the town itself nor in the surrounding countryside can one find an acceptable cup of tea. And yet something must have been attracting visitors to Brinshore.

The phrase "a dish of tea" is found in the literature of the time and simply means a cup of tea. Mrs. Price, flustered upon receiving Fanny after a long absence, gabbles, "I could not tell whether you would be for some meat, or only a dish of tea, after your journey, or else I would have got something ready." "In 1657 the British East India Company held the first public sale of tea in England, while that same year Thomas Garraway began offering tea at his London coffee house. In 1662 tea received a big boost in England when the Portuguese Catherine of Braganza, married King Charles II and introduced tea drinking to the British court. Gradually, the British fell in love with tea.... In 1768 the East India Company imported 10 million pounds of tea to Britain" ("History of Tea").]

it is so cold & ungrateful that it can hardly be made to grow a Cabbage.
—

>
it is so cold & ungrateful that it can hardly be made to pro[duce?] a Cabbage.
—

>
it is so cold & ungrateful that it can hardly be made to yeild a Cabbage.
—

[Although he will later cast aspersions on this lowly vegetable, here it serves Mr. Parker well to illustrate the sterility of even Brinshore's soil.]

Depend upon it Sir, that this is a faithful Description of Brinshore — not in the smallest degree exaggerated — & if you have heard it differently spoken of —"

"Sir, I never heard it spoken of in my Life before, said M^r. Heywood. I did not know there was such a place in the World." —

"You did not! — There my Dear — (turning with exultation to his Wife) — you see how it is. So much for the Celebrity of Brinshore! — This Gentleman did not know there was such a place in the World. Why, in truth Sir, I fancy we may apply to Brinshore, that line of the Poet Cowper in his description of the religious Cottager, as opposed to Voltaire — "She, never heard of half a mile from home." —

[Mr. Parker's addressing his wife as "my Dear" is not only a display of fondness but part of the social code of the time, when first names are used only within a family or among good friends. We again have a stage direction in "(turning with exultation to his Wife)."

Mr. Parker here refers to a passage from William Cowper's "Truth" (*Poems*, 1782, lines 323–336) in which the brilliant but misguided French Voltaire is unfavorably compared with a humble English peasant woman:

> She, for her humble sphere by nature fit,
> Has little understanding, and no wit,
> Receives no praise; but though her lot be such,
> (Toilsome and indigent) she renders much;
> Just knows, and knows no more, her Bible true—
> A truth the brilliant Frenchman never knew;
> And in that charter reads, with sparkling eyes,
> Her title to a treasure in the skies.
> Oh, happy peasant! Oh, unhappy bard!
> His the mere tinsel, hers the rich reward;
> He prais'd, perhaps, for ages yet to come;
> She never heard of half a mile from home;
> He, lost in errors, his vain heart prefers;
> She, safe in the simplicity of hers.

The text does not make clear that Mr. Parker has actually read anything by Voltaire ("writer, wit and iconoclast" [*CUPLM*: 636]), nom de plume of

François-Marie Arouet (1694-1778), nor is the reference necessarily apropos of the present situation.

Although Jane Austen mentions him in none of her extant letters and his name does not appear anywhere in her novels, she obviously knew enough about him to identify him as "the brilliant Frenchman" in this pointedly condemnatory passage by Cowper. The conflict between the English poet and the Gallic author and philosopher reflects current attitudes of anti-intellectualism, especially following the excesses of the French Revolution.

> How does the cottager "know her bible true"?… she is presumably neither a theologian nor a Hebraic philologist. Her reading of the Bible must be informed either by humble "common sense" or by the supernatural workings of the Holy Spirit. The former may well be historically determined, while the latter is hard to authenticate, although with the appreciative revaluation of the intuitive faculties effected by contemporary Scottish philosophy it is possible to see how the two could be conflated. Cowper retains a common belief in *both* the supremacy of scripture, and of a traditional "plain reading" of the same difficult text. The correct attitude with which to encounter God's word is one of reverence and humility. Cowper continues his homily with a denunciation of the fragility of worldly acclaim; Voltaire… becomes the archetypal victim of intellectual pride. (Brunström: 83)

Generally considered an infidel because of the compounded anomalies of his dedicating the church at his estate at Ferney directly to God and having within it inscribed the dedication "Deo erexit Voltaire" ("Erected to God by VOLTAIRE"), with the author's name written in the largest characters, Voltaire is further singled out for condemnation by Cowper:

> Nor he who, for the bane of thousands born,
> Built God a church, and laughed His Word to scorn.

A more reasoned view of Voltaire is that he was a Deist rather than an atheist, opposed to practices of organized religion rather than to religion itself.

Perhaps even more heinous than his theological irregularities was Voltaire's criticism of Shakespeare, the Sacred Cow (or Sacred Bull, if you prefer) of the time and since. In criticizing the Bard of Avon for deviating from neoclassical standards and assorted barbarities, the Frenchman stepped over the line of polite debate to literary blasphemy, inciting votaries to bitter counter-attacks.

> Cowper's hostility toward Voltaire may have been exacerbated by Voltaire's attack on Shakespeare. He greatly admired Elizabeth Montagu's reply to Voltaire and had a patriotic, indeed Gallophobic, preference for Shakespearean "noble irregularity" in composition— in opposition to "coldly correct" classicism (in this, as in so many things, he is almost tediously representative of mainstream English eighteenth-century opinion). For Cowper, French classicism is the literary architecture of systematic egotism.... Voltaire's impious cleverness is earthbound and sophistical: his slavishly neoclassical Gallic intellect habitually confines and categorizes, delimits and demoralizes, conquering literature only because of his cramped conception of what literature is. (Brunström: 83–84)

Jane Austen was familiar with and admired the works of William Cowper (1731–1800; pronounced "Cooper" according to some sources but "Cowper" according to others)—he "was, perhaps, Jane Austen's favourite poetical moralist" ("Poetic Pain"). Thus specifying that Thomas Parker reads his poetry is a tribute to that gentleman's well-cultivated taste, suggesting interests on his part beyond multiplying the Parker brood and speculating on seaside property.

In late November of 1798, Jane Austen wrote to Cassandra that "some money... is to be laid out in the purchase of Cowper's works" (*Letters*: 22), apparently a successful plan since she wrote again only a few weeks later, "My father reads Cowper to us in the evening, to which I listen when I can" (*Letters*: 27). Almost ten years later, in 1807, she again adverted to him in a letter to her sister: "Our Garden is putting in order, by a Man who bears a remarkably good Character, has a very fine complexion & asks something less than the first. The Shrubs which border the gravel walk he says are only sweetbriar & roses, & the latter of an indifferent sort;—we mean to get a few of a better kind therefore, & at my own particular desire he procures us some Syringas. I could not do without a Syringa, for the sake of Cowper's Line" (*Letters*: 119), referring to

Laburnum rich

In streaming gold; syringa, iv'ry pure.
("The Winter Walk at Noon," *The Task*, vi, lines 149–150)

In September 1813, Cassandra received yet another letter in which the poet is lauded: "I am now alone in the Library, Mistress of all I survey—at least I may say so & repeat the whole poem if I like it, without offence to anybody.—" (*Letters*: 228), with reference to "Verses supposed to be written by Alexander Selkirk." Two months later, now with Cowper's "Epitaph on a Hare" in mind, Jane Austen shared with Cassandra her view that William, Henry Austen's manservant "has more of Cowper than of Johnson in him, fonder of Tame Hares & Blank verse than of the full tide of human Existence at Charing Cross" (*Letters*: 250).

Several other characters in the novels—Mr. Knightley is familiar with his works, as are Fanny Price and Marianne Dashwood—are also readers of this popular eighteenth-century poet.]

"With all my Heart Sir — Apply any Verses you like to it — But I want to see something applied to your Leg — & I am sure by your Lady's countenance that she is quite of my opinion & thinks it a pity to lose any more time — And here come my Girls to speak for themselves & their Mother. (two or three genteel looking young Women followed by as many Maid servants, were now seen issueing from the House) — I began to wonder the Bustle should not have reached them. — A thing of this kind soon makes a Stir in a lonely place like ours. — Now Sir, let us see how you can be best conveyed into the House." —

[Puns are a rarity in Jane Austen although one would expect that someone with her delight in language would exult in them. It is unacceptable to think that Mr. Heywood, the creator of such a good one at this point —"Apply any Verses you like to it — But I want to see something applied to your Leg"—will not re-appear later in the text.

The text does not specify the nature of the "Bustle" that has drawn the female members of the family to the scene of the accident. Perhaps there was a louder crash than is described, or they are naturally curious about what they have seen through their windows. For all of the Heywoods, this is a welcome change from routine despite the inconvenience forced on the Parkers. If there were young boys in the household, it seems likely that they would be eager to see the spectacle of an overturned carriage and the gentleman and gentle lady so indecorously removed from it. There cannot be so many visitors to the farm that these unexpected intruders would not generate interest even among the children of the family.

One wonders how painful the ankle sprain is that Mr. Parker can take so much time discoursing on Sanditon and its medical marvels. But perhaps even thinking about the seaside village—and more so speaking about it— alleviates the suffering. We do not yet know that among Mr. Heywood's "Girls" is his daughter Charlotte, through whose eyes much of the balance of the tale will be narrated.]

The young Ladies approached & said every thing that was proper to recommend their Father's offers; & in an unaffected manner calculated to make the Strangers easy — And as M^{rs}. P. — was exceedingly anxious for relief — and her Husband by this time, not much less disposed for it — a very few civil scruples were enough — especially as the Carriage being now set up, was discovered to have received such Injury on the fallen side as to be unfit for present use. — M^{r}. Parker was therefore carried into the House, & his Carriage wheeled off to a vacant Barn. —

[The author achieves perfect structure in this chapter, starting and closing with the carriage, damaged as the tale opens and hauled off at the end for repairs.

Although this opening episode would be difficult to stage, Jane Austen casts it in real time, as though a scene in a play. A few of the major actors are introduced, including indirectly Charlotte, our heroine, as one of the daughters of the Heywood household. Some of the succeeding chapters are also in real time and in a single setting, much like a play. The dialog is at times very close to a script, including several possible stage directions (most notably Lady Denham's sigh in Chapter 7).]

[Chapter 2]

Chapter 2. —

The acquaintance, thus oddly begun, was neither short nor unimportant.

The Parkers were the Guests of the Heywoods a fortnight; The sprain was too serious for M^r. Parker to be sooner able to move

>

For a whole fortnight the Travellors were fixed at Willingden; M^r. P.'s sprain proving too serious for him to move sooner. —

[During this two-week stay, the Heywoods must have asked some neighbors over to meet their guests, and the Parkers, to the extent that Mr. Thomas could leave his sick-bed, must have made the acquaintance of some of the local inhabitants. Later we read that "M^{rs}. Heywood's Adventurings were only now & then to visit her Neighbours," and so we know that she has a social life, albeit a limited one, outside her home. With marriageable daughters in the house, these visits are not merely matters of courtesy. "Charlotte's parents are pointedly praised for doing as much as they can in the small village in which the Heywoods live to enable their daughters to come in the way of husbands" (Halperin: 190).

The Heywoods must have neighbors with whom they deal for business or for basic socializing like exchanging recipes, bringing together children to play, and even more to the point arranging for some wooing of daughters and wooing by sons. Mr. Heywood would be eager to introduce his new friends to the neighboring families and even give Mr. Parker a chance to advertise Sanditon.

But if any of this activity took place during these two weeks, our author is silent, raising suspicion that the famous lines written from Chawton on Friday, September 9, 1814, to her niece, Anna Austen—"You are now collecting your People delightfully, getting them exactly into such a spot as is the delight of my life;—3 or 4 Families in a Country Village is the very thing to work on—& I hope you will write a great deal more, & make full use of them while they are so very favourably arranged" (Le Faye, 2002:

275)—are a reflection of what the young woman has written rather than what her aunt has been doing in practice.

As a matter of fact, it is difficult to regard most of the extant novels as fitting the model suggested in this famous quotation. *Sense and Sensibility* certainly does not match this formula, nor does *Pride and Prejudice*, with only the Lucases to exchange visits with the Bennets. *Mansfield Park* also falls short of meeting these criteria for a satisfactory novel. *Persuasion* comes close at times, but the novel is not about families in a country village, and *Northanger Abbey* bears no relation to this prescription for a successful story. Only *Emma*, published in December 1815, a year after the letter to Anna, qualifies with the Woodhouses, the Knightleys, the Westons, the Bateses, the Martins, the Coles, and the Eltons filling the small stage. Nevertheless, commentators continue to refer to this passage as Jane Austen's confidential revelation to her niece of what she herself has been writing.

It is possible, however, to regard *Sanditon* as more or less a story of "3 or 4 Families in a Country Village" if we disregard the fact that Sanditon is not a country village and that the families do not all live there. Only Thomas Parker and his immediate family (wife and children) are permanent residents in Sanditon, the Parker sisters and the younger brothers being distributed in various unspecified locales. The Heywoods are represented in Sanditon by Charlotte, but the rest of her family is happily enjoying life in Willingden. The Denhams, if we can consider Lady Denham, Sir Edward Denham, and Miss Esther Denham a family, live within and close to Sanditon. The few tradespersons mentioned, like the Whitbys and the Woodcocks, are not people of quality, and no one else in the extant manuscript reasonably qualifies as part of the formula for delight.

If the Parkers were in Willingden for a fortnight, they spent at least one Sunday with the Heywoods. Although the text never specifies that they attended church services, it does not report that they did not. Jane Austen took such attendance so much for granted that she saw no need to mention it.

Roger Sales believes that this two-week visit is a sign that Thomas shares the family propensity for enjoying illness: "Parker stays at Willingden much longer than is really necessary and so displays signs of the hypochondria that is, as will be seen, much more rampant in some of the other members of his family. He likes being nursed" (202). The text does, however, tell us that "M^r. P.'s sprain [was] too serious for him to move sooner." In addition, the Parkers as gregarious people would enjoy being with this wholesome family, and Mrs. Heywood, recognizing this golden opportunity to find husbands for her remaining daughters, would encourage a long stay. And then there is the matter of repairing the damaged carriage, which may need parts not readily available. There are no indications elsewhere in the text that Mr. Thomas Parker has any particular inclinations toward imaginary illnesses, being like his immediately younger brother, Sidney, too busy to indulge in nonsense.]

He had fallen into very good hands. The Heywoods were a thoroughly respectable family, & every possible attention was paid in the kindest & most unpretending manner, to both Husband & wife. <u>He</u> was waited on & nursed, & <u>she</u> cheered & comforted with unremitting kindness — and as every office of Hospitality & friendliness was received as it ought — as there was not more good will on one side than Gratitude on the other — nor any deficiency of generally pleasant manners on either, they grew to like each other in the course of that fortnight, exceedingly well. —

M^r. Parker's Character & History were soon made known.
>
M^r. Parker's Character & History were soon unfolded.

All that he understood of himself, he readily told, for he was very openhearted; — & where he might be himself in the dark, he was still giving information unconsciously, to such of the Heywoods as could observe.
>
All that he understood of himself, he readily told, for he was very openhearted; — & where he might be himself in the dark, his conversation was still giving information, to such of the Heywoods as could observe.

By such he was perceived to be an Enthusiast; — on the subject of Sanditon, a complete Enthusiast. — Sanditon, — the success of Sanditon as a small, fashionable Bathing Place was the object, for which he seemed to live.

[It does not speak well for Mr. Parker that he is established as "an Enthusiast," even worse "a complete Enthusiast," "carrying hints of the older meaning of visionary and self-deluded" (*CUPLM*: 637).]

A very few years ago, & it had been a simple Village of no consideration inhabited by one Family of consequence, his own, of secondary pretensions;

>

A very few years ago, & it had been a quiet Village of no pretensions; but some natural advantages in its position & some accidental circumstances having suggested to himself, & the other principal Proprietor of the Land, the probability of its' being a profitable Speculation, he had engaged in it, & planned & built, & praised & puffed, & raised it to a Something of note

>

A very few years ago, & it had been a quiet Village of no pretensions; but some natural advantages in its position & accidental circumstances having suggested to himself, & the other principal Proprietor of the Land, the probability of its' being a profitable Speculation, they had engaged in it, & planned & built, & praised & puffed, & raised it to a Something of young notoriety, —

>

A very few years ago, & it had been a quiet Village of no pretensions; but some natural advantages in its position & some accidental circumstances having suggested to himself, & the other principal Land Holder, the probability of its' becoming a profitable Speculation, they had engaged in it, & planned & built, & praised & puffed, & raised it to a Something of young Renown, — and M^r. Parker could now think of very little besides.

[Jane Austen rarely enjoyed herself so much as in the creation of this story. The proof? The exuberant humor of this long, complicated sentence, perfectly executed and amusingly worded: "they had engaged in it, & planned & built, & praised & puffed, & raised it to a Something of young Renown" is a remarkable piece of mockery. I suspect that she shared this manuscript with no one in the family because she was saving it as a great surprise upon its completion.

Jane Austen does not frequently use figurative language or onomatopoeia, so her use of "puffed" is doubly noteworthy. As recorded in her early *History of England* ("I have nothing to say in praise of [Sir Walter Raleigh], & must refer all those who may wish to be acquainted with the particulars of his Life, to Mr Sheridan's play of the Critic, where they will find many interesting Anecdotes"), she and her family were particularly fond of Richard Brinsley Sheridan's comedy, *The Critic; or, A Tragedy Rehearsed. A Dramatic Piece in*

Three Acts (1781). Here we find the character Mr. Puff, who shortly after entering the scene (Act I, Scene 2) expands on the appropriateness of his name: "I make no secret of the trade I follow: among friends and brother authors, Dangle knows I love to be frank on the subject, and to advertise myself viva voce.—I am, sir, a practitioner in panegyric, or, to speak more plainly, a professor of the art of puffing, at your service—or anybody else's." His particular talent is teaching people how to inflate their diction so that they can "'enlay their phraseology with variegated chips of exotic metaphor" and "crowd their advertisements with panegyrical superlatives." This use of as many difficult words as possible while saying as little as possible may have been the inspiration for Sir Edward Denham, who shares this dubious talent.]

The Facts, which in more direct communication, he laid before them were that he was about 5 & 30 — had been married, — very happily married 7 years — & had 4 sweet Children at home; — that he was of a respectable Family, & easy though not large fortune; — no Profession — succeeding as eldest son to the Property which 2 or 3 Generations had been holding & accumulating before him; — that he had 2 Brothers & Sisters — all single & all independant — the eldest of the two Brothers in fact, by collateral Inheritance, quite as well provided for as himself. —
>
The Facts, which in more direct communication, he laid before them were that he was about 5 & 30 — had been married, — very happily married 7 years — & had 4 sweet Children at home; — that he was of a respectable Family, & easy though not large fortune; — no Profession — succeeding as eldest son to the Property which 2 or 3 Generations had been holding & accumulating before him; — that he had 2 Brothers & 2 Sisters — all single & all independant — the eldest of the two former indeed, by collateral Inheritance, quite as well provided for as himself. —

[This passage is certainly reported speech, replacing rapid narrative for more leisurely dialog. The second chapter is transitional and was meant to be no more than a summary of what happened between the arrival of the Parkers at Willingden and their departure two weeks later with Charlotte.

That Mr. Thomas Parker has "no Profession" is no surprise upon learning that he is the eldest son and therefore has inherited the entire property. "Normally the eldest son of a gentleman's family would inherit the family estate and its income on the death of his father; until that date he would expect an allowance, and he would not usually take on a profession" (*CUPLM*: 637–638), which in those days was usually the law, the Church, or the military (with the navy apparently more prestigious than the army).

Mr. Thomas Parker's being specifically described as "eldest son," not as "eldest offspring," lends support to my contention below that Miss Susan Parker is the senior member of the family. As eldest (or even elder) son he would by contemporary law of primogeniture inherit the property, as noted. If he were the eldest sibling, there would be no need to mention his right to inheritance.

We never learn the precise source of Mr. Sidney Parker's "collateral Inheritance," but since "collateral heirs [include relatives] such as nieces and nephews" (Redmond) it came to him presumably through an uncle, perhaps their mother's childless brother. Certainly his generous "inheritance from a relative with no direct heir, who might choose to benefit a younger son rather than leave his estate to someone unknown or already well provided for" (*CUPLM*: 638) has given Sidney Parker the opportunity to pursue a life of leisure despite not inheriting the family estate. But it was not the normal fate of "Younger sons[, who] could inherit money, but not real property, so they generally went into the military or the church, and looked for heiresses to marry" (Redmond). Sidney's being on a par financially with his older brother cannot go unnoticed by Mrs. Heywood, who like Mrs. Bennet remains faithful to her mission of pairing off her unmarried daughters. Charlotte—and we—must ponder for some time over the exact source of Sidney's fortune as we puzzle over his true nature.

The text does not disclose the source or extent of income enjoyed by Susan, Diana, and poor Arthur, but they are sufficiently comfortable financially to take rooms at the hotel in Sanditon instead of staying with their brother and sister-in-law. We never learn, incidentally, how long they plan to remain in Sanditon, but Miss Diana Parker is determined to interfere with Mrs. Griffiths' most valuable student as long as that party is in town.

Although in this manuscript Jane Austen has written "independant," in the *OIJA* edition of *Emma* we find "dependence," "independence," and "independent." In the *OIJA* edition of *Persuasion* we find "independence" and "independent." Presumably R.W. Chapman either normalized spellings found in the first editions or they had already been normalized. But in the "canceled chapters" of the manuscript published as *Persuasion* we find

"Independant" and "independant," clearly indicating the author's preference. It seems unlikely that she was alone in using this spelling at a time when the language was much more flexible than it has become. That all of the *OED* quotations use the "e" spelling may merely reflect normalization rather than the history of the word. The author may have been influenced by analogy with "pendant," a word that appears later in this manuscript.

Here as elsewhere Jane Austen uses the superlative form—"eldest"— where we would use the comparative—"elder."

The change from "2 Brothers & Sisters" to "2 Brothers & 2 Sisters" removes ambiguity about the gender distribution of the members of the Parker family. Through a small touch like this, Jane Austen shows that she regards the sisters as equal to the brothers in having their number specified, perhaps further argument against her plan to name the novel, "The Brothers."]

His object in quitting the high road, to hunt for an advertising Surgeon, was also plainly stated; — it had not proceeded from any intention of spraining his ancle or doing himself any other Injury for the good of such Surgeon — nor (as M^r. H. had been apt to suppose) from any design of entering into Partnership with him —; it was merely in consequence of a wish to establish some medical Man at Sanditon, which the nature of the Advertisement induced him to expect to accomplish in Willingden. —

["as M^r. H. had been apt to suppose" sounds like free indirect discourse.]

He was convinced that the advantage of a medical Man at hand w^d. very materially promote the rise & prosperity of the Place — w^d— in fact tend to bring a great influx; — nothing else was wanting.
>
He was convinced that the advantage of a medical Man at hand w^d. very materially promote the rise & prosperity of the Place — w^d— in fact tend to bring a prodigious influx; — nothing else was wanting.

[This passage suggests that the medical skills of the sought-after surgeon were less important than having it known that Sanditon boasted such a practitioner. Nothing in the text suggests confidence in the current medical fraternity.]

He had <u>strong</u> reason to beleive that <u>one</u> family had been deterred last year from trying Sanditon on that account — & probably very many more — and his own Sisters who were sad Invalids, & whom he was very anxious to get to Sanditon this Summer, could hardly be expected to hazard themselves in a place where they could not have immediate medical advice. — Upon the whole, M^r. P. was evidently an amiable, family-man, fond of Wife, Child^n —, Brothers & Sisters — & generally kind-hearted; — Liberal, gentlemanlike, easy to please; — of a sanguine turn of mind, with more Imagination than Judgement.

[That Mr. Thomas Parker is stated to be "fond of [his] Brothers" supports the argument that in railing against Sidney he is doing nothing more than carrying on a conversation in the course of which he admits that his younger brother leads an active social life, something that he might enjoy if he were not in the possession of a wife and many children. Nothing is said at this point about poor Arthur as yet another sad Invalid, and perhaps the special attributes of the character were not yet in the author's mind. Any sympathy that we might have for the sisters, any suggestion that the author is not being very sardonic, is thrown out when we find that the youngest brother is just like them.

The author—or perhaps the Heywoods—has cast Mr. Parker in an unfavorable light, mixing good qualities with some that are hardly commendable. A man who is "Liberal, gentlemanlike, easy to please; — of a sanguine turn of mind, with more Imagination than Judgement" is not what Jane Austen regards as her ideal. "Liberal" contains many possible meanings, including "of superior social station" and "bountiful, generous, open-hearted." It is unlikely that the word is here used to mean "Unrestrained by prudence or decorum, licentious" although the harsh judgment may be Mr. Heywood's uncharitable assessment of his new acquaintance.]

And M^{rs}. P. was as evidently a gentle, amiable, sweet tempered Woman, the properest wife in the World for a Man of strong Understanding, but not of capacity to supply the cooler reflection which her own Husband sometimes needed, & so entirely waiting to be guided on every occasion, that whether he were risking his Fortune or spraining his Ancle, she remained equally useless. —

[Jane Austen is not very kind to Mrs. Parker in this part of the novel, but in later passages she is treated a little more sympathetically. Mr. Parker is clearly not the easiest man to live with. It is difficult to reconcile the earlier description of him as having "more Imagination than Judgement" and his being "a Man of strong Understanding." Jane Austen may be in the process of shaping this character and has not yet decided on exactly who he is. The author could be basing the comic contrast of the tragedy of losing his fortune and spraining his ankle on the famous lines from Alexander Pope's *The Rape of the Lock,*

> Some dire Disaster, or by Force, or Slight,
> But what, or where, the Fates have wrapt in Night.
> Whether the Nymph shall break Diana's law,
> Or some frail China jar receive a Flaw,
> Or stain her Honour, or her new Brocade,
> Forget her Pray'rs, or miss a Masquerade,
> Or lose her Heart, or Necklace, at a Ball;
> Or whether Heav'n has doom'd that Shock must fall. (Canto II)]

Sanditon was a second Wife & 4 Children to him — hardly less Dear — & certainly more engrossing. — He could talk of it for ever. —

[And to the amusement of the Heywoods, he does.]

It had indeed the highest claims; — Birthplace, Property, Home, — it was also his Mine, his Lottery, his Speculation & his Hobby Horse; his Hope & his Futurity. —

>

It had indeed the highest claims; — not only those of Birthplace, Property, and Home, — it was his Mine, his Lottery, his Speculation & his Hobby Horse; his Occupation his Hope & his Futurity. —

[It is difficult to determine if this passage is indirect discourse or the author's comment on Thomas Parker's enthusiastic nature. On the whole, the impression is not favorable, especially if he has been buying expensive lottery tickets. "A variety of lotteries operated successfully through the eighteenth century, including the State lottery, which ran from 1694 to 1826, offering cash prizes as large as £30,000 in reward for tickets costing at least £3 (many gamblers bought only a share in a ticket). Lotteries were, however, always controversial and there was a new flurry of debate about the lottery in 1816" (*CUPLM*: 638), with one side condemning it as immoral and the other side defending it as a source of income for the government. That it was discontinued in 1826 tells us which side finally won the argument.

131

Referring to Thomas Parker's passion for the development of Sanditon as his "Hobby Horse" is another rare example of Jane Austen's use of figurative language in this manuscript. The phrase sounds like mild mockery on the part of the author rather than something that Parker would claim as applying to himself. The image of "a toy consisting of a long stick with a horse's head at one end" (*CUPLM*: 639) is ironic following the disastrous opening passage of the manuscript. It could well be one of the favorite toys of the Parker children.

Beyond the *CUPLM* commentary that "the usual meaning of the word ["Futurity"] is simply 'the future' or 'what will happen in the future' but JA seems to intend a stronger sense of confidence in future events" (639), I believe that Jane Austen is saying here that Thomas Parker has staked his entire fortune on the success of this entrepreneurial speculation. In doing so, he risks losing not only his present quality of life but his eldest son's patrimony and his daughters' dowries. If the project does fail, as many critics have suggested is the likely denouement of the novel, I would like to think that (like Darcy in a completely different context) Sidney steps in to rescue his brother as well as his nephews and nieces (especially little Mary, with whom he has a special relationship) from financial ruin.]

He was extremely desirous of drawing his good friends at Willingden thither; and his endeavours in the cause, were as grateful & disinterested, as they were warm.

He wanted to secure the promise of a visit — to get as many of the Family as his house w^d. contain, to follow him to Sanditon as soon as possible — and healthy as they all undeniably were — foresaw that every one of them w^d. be benefited by the sea air.

>

He wanted to secure the promise of a visit — to get as many of the Family as his own house w^d. contain, to follow him to Sanditon as soon as possible — and healthy as they all undeniably were — foresaw that every one of them w^d. be benefited by the sea.

[Deletion of the final "air" places focus on the curative powers of water. She picks up "Sea air" two sentences later, so we see some careful editing taking place in the course of composing the passage.]

He held it indeed as certain, that no person c^d. be really well, no person, (however upheld for the present by fortuitous aids of exercise & spirits in a semblance of Health) could be really in a state of secure & permanent Health without spending at least 6 weeks by the Sea every year. —

The Sea air & Sea Bathing together were almost infallible, one or the other of them being a match for every Disorder, In cases of the Stomach, the Lungs or the Blood; they were equally sovereign; They were anti-spasmodic, anti-pulmonary, anti-sceptic & anti-rheumatic.
>
The Sea air & Sea Bathing together were nearly infallible, one or the other of them being a match for every Disorder, of the Stomach, the Lungs or the Blood; anti-spasmodic, anti-pulmonary, anti-sceptic & anti-rheumatic.
>
The Sea air & Sea Bathing together were nearly infallible, one or the other of them being a match for every Disorder, of the Stomach, the Lungs or the Blood; They were anti-spasmodic, anti-pulmonary, anti-sceptic anti-bilious & anti-rheumatic.

[Jane Austen's spelling vagaries leave the matter uncertain, but her "sceptic" may be one of several possible puns in the manuscript. "It is impossible to be certain whether JA's spelling involved a deliberate allusion to Mr Parker's lack of skepticism" (*CUPLM*: 639). As though gilding the lily, our author could not resist adding "anti-bilious" to the other symptoms relieved by exposure to the natural elements found in Sanditon. This kind of overkill suggests that the novel is in part a farce like her *Juvenilia*. Gone are the restraints of the preceding manuscript, published as *Persuasion*, since the characters and the story are now on a very different plane. Anyone suggesting a diminishment of Jane Austen's powers has been misled by her failing handwriting on some pages since the text shows authority and precision in thought. The author "is satirizing the medical jargon of the time, which specialized in 'anti-' words" (*CUPLM*: 639). She often shows an interest in contemporary events and language, challenging the claim by critics that she is isolated from the real world around her.

The addition of "anti-bilious" to the final version of this line may be a comic response to her own illness (letter of January 24, 1817, to Alethea Bigg [*Letters*: 326-328]): "I am more & more convinced that *Bile* is at the bottom of all I have suffered."

Bile (also known as gall) "is a bitter yellowish, blue and green fluid secreted by hepatocytes from the liver of most vertebrates. In many species, bile is stored in the gallbladder between meals and upon eating is discharged into the duodenum where the bile aids the process of digestion of lipids by emulsification.... Yellow bile (sometimes called ichor) and black bile were two of the four vital fluids or humors of ancient and medieval Greco-Roman alternative medicine (the other two were phlegm and blood). The Greek names for the terms gave rise to the words "choler" (bile) and "melancholia" (black bile). Excessive bile was supposed to produce an aggressive temperament, known as "choleric." This is the origin of the word "bilious." Depression and other mental illnesses (melancholia) were ascribed to a bodily surplus of black bile. This is the origin of the word "melancholy." ("Bile")]

Nobody could catch cold by the Sea, Nobody wanted appetite by the Sea, nor c^d. the most obstinate Cougher retain a cough there 4 & 20 hours. —
>
Nobody could catch cold by the Sea, Nobody wanted appetite by the Sea, Nobody wanted Spirits, Nobody wanted Strength.

[Unexpectedly, the revision shows a reduction in the farcical tone. Perhaps Cassandra, looking over her sister's shoulder, remarked on the unnecessary excess of levity.

Although Dr. Richard Russell's work was recognized as a major treatise on the salutary effects of seawater, it was by no means the only one. "Dr Robert Squirrel advised that bathing could be used to advantage... [for] 'Indigestion, Gout, Fever, Jaundice, Dropsy, Hæmorrhages, Violent Evacuations, or any other disorder.' *An Essay on Indigestion and its Consequences... also Remarks on Sea or Cold Bathing... explaining the reason Why inspiring* [breathing in] *the Sea Air contributes more to the Recovery of Health than that of Cities and Inland Places* (1795), pp. 64–5" (*CUPLM*: 639–640).]

They were healing, softing, relaxing — fortifying & bracing — seemingly just as was wanted — sometimes one, sometimes the other. —

[This is apparently the only appearance in Jane Austen's writings of "softing," which she definitely wanted since this page in the manuscript shows several changes but not to this word. The handwriting is clear and strong, and she could not have missed an error of this sort. In this manuscript, the author plays with words far more than in earlier novels, and in this instance the onomatopoeic effect of "softing" is more convincing than that of the more common and therefore expected "softening" (which she had used in *Emma* and "Susan"/"Catherine"). I do not believe that "possibly JA meant the more usual 'softening'... [although] [w]hen Cassandra copied the manuscript she wrote 'softening'" (*CUPLM*: 640). Perhaps not trusting Jane Austen to say what she means, Jocelyn Harris quotes the line as: "They were healing, softing [sic], relaxing" (156). The choice of word by the author and the change by her sister well illustrate the difference between a genius and an ordinary mortal. The *OED* recognizes "soft" as a verb but marks it as obsolete with several related meanings, including: "To render (a person, the heart, etc.) less harsh, severe, or obdurate; to mollify, appease, pacify.... To render physically soft. Also in fig. context.... To become or grow soft in various senses." Although the *OED* editors missed out on quoting Jane Austen for its use, they do account for the participle "softing": "**1611** COTGR., *Amollissement*, a softing, mollifying, making tender. *Ibid.*, *Amollissant*, softing, mollifying." For all practical purposes, Jane Austen, in choosing the right term to express her meaning here, resurrected a venerable word and restored it to our vocabulary. *The Victorian Literary Studies Archive Hyper-Concordance* reports that the word "softing" does not appear in *Sense and Sensibility*, *Pride and Prejudice*, *Mansfield Park*, *Emma*, *Northanger Abbey*, *Persuasion*, "The Three Sisters," "Lady Susan," "The Watsons," or "Love and Friendship [sic]." This online Concordance reports "No entry found for query: softing" in *Sanditon*, but "softening" is reported for this passage. The sole use of the word is reported correctly in *Concordance*, Vol. II, 1064.]

If the Sea breeze failed, the Sea-Bath was the certain corrective; — & where Bathing disagreed, the Sea Breeze alone was palpably designed by Nature for the cure. —

>

If the Sea breeze failed, the Sea-Bath was the certain corrective; — & where Bathing disagreed, the Sea Breeze alone was evidently designed by Nature for the cure. —

[Mr. Thomas Parker's enthusiastic praise of the therapeutic power of seawater and sea air was of course not original to this manuscript. At least as early as the mid-eighteenth century the culture of sea bathing and imbibing was under development, its official acceptance in the scientific community perhaps sanctioned through the publication in 1750 of Dr. Richard Russell's *De tabe glandulari, sive de usu aqua marine in morbis glandularum dissertatio,* an account of his twenty-five years of studying the effects of the use of seawater both internally and externally, particularly in patients afflicted with glandular disease.

His father was practicing as a surgeon and apothecary when Richard Russell (1687-1759) was born in Lewes, so it was not unexpected that upon completing studies at the Grammar School of Southover, Lewes, the young man decided upon a medical career. In 1724 he received the degree of Doctor of Medicine in Leyden, returning to Lewes to resume his practice. From his early years he had been interested in the medical efficacy of seawater, a concept already in general circulation but attracting increased attention in England at the time. Hence his publication in 1750 served more to support an already popular concept than to initiate it. Displeased with the unauthorized English translations that began to appear in 1752, Dr. Russell published his own translation as *A Dissertation concerning the Use of Sea Water in Diseases of the Glands* in 1753. In the same year, 1753, Dr. Russell moved to Brighthelmston(e) (modern Brighton), thereby turning a small fishing and farming village into a major seaside community by introducing "modern" medical theory. The famous Brighton Pavilion—in a style sometimes called "Hindoo-Gothic"—as we now know it was not completed until 1823, leading Jane Austen's famously humorous Sydney Smith to declare that "it looked for all the world as if the Dome of St. Paul's had come down to Brighton and pupped."

> Dr. Richard Russell may well be said to be the father of Brighton and indeed of the seaside and bathing resorts of Britain and perhaps even of the Continent in that his book led to a general interest and acceptance of sea bathing if not as a method of cure, then certainly of health. (Lauste: 330)

Ted Power has published details, including contemporary drawings, on the January 7, 2001, exhibition at the Royal Pavilion honoring the work of Dr. Russell.

> Dr. Richard Russell's dissertation convinced other doctors and their patients that both drinking and bathing in (Brighton) sea-water provided treatment for many conditions, especially diseases of the glands. Dr. Russell was particularly interested in the remedial effects of the iodine in sea-water. Rich Londoners often ate too much food and did not take enough exercise. The coastal resort of Brighton was one of the nearest beaches (just 6 hours from London

by stagecoach) where they could get the form of hydrotherapy that Dr. Russell recommended.

Access to the sea was provided by **bathing machines**, small boxes on wheels in which Dr. Russell's patients were seated while bathing attendants transported them from the beach to the water.

Once the doctor's patients were surrounded by sea-water, **dippers** (for ladies) and **bathers** (for gentlemen) were employed to make sure that the patients' heads were dipped into the water. This provided jobs for people who had previously worked in the fishing trade. By 1790, Brighton had about twenty dippers and bathers. The practice began to die out at the end of the 19th century. Old pictures of the bathing machines on Brighton beach can be bought at the Royal Pavilion Gift Shops and may be found in books on sale at Sussex Stationers in East Street.

Ted Powers continues with what appear to be contemporary advertisements and hyperbolic claims about Dr. Russell's services.

1753: Dr Russell moves to Brighton

Lewes Doctor sets up sea-cure clinic on future site of Royal Albion Hotel

A new clinic has been set up very close to Brighton's seafront at Russell House.

It will be staffed by Dr. Richard Russell MD, FRS, formerly of Lewes, East Sussex. Patients will be able to benefit from Dr. Russell's special prescriptions containing organic ingredients mainly from the English Channel plus a few home-produced woodlice. Sea-bathing facilities will be at hand. A range of new bathing machines will be provided on the beach, staffed by trained bathing attendants. Robust ladies called "dippers" and strong men called "bathers" will be standing among the waves waiting for your arrival from dawn onwards. A wetting will be guaranteed for even the most reluctant patient. Special November offer—three dippings for the price of two!

Dr. Russell guarantees that fresh air and exercise will not damage your health. Each dipping will strengthen your brain and revitalize your nerves.

If you suffer from glandular fever, consumption, cancer, ruptures or madness (especially the latter), Brighton sea-water is for you!

In keeping with his scientific training, however, Dr. Russell made much more modest claims for the cure.

The conditions he describes seem to be mainly diseases of the lymphatic glands, mostly tuberculous in nature; Russell's treatment was based upon taking sea water in prescribed amounts internally, by sea bathing under appropriate conditions and by the external application of sea water and sea weeds, all associated with a strict regime and various medicines. Russell made it clear that treatment with sea water should not be used for all diseases, nor indeed for all stages of the same disease, but the method should be used with caution and only under the direction of a physician well versed in its use. (Lauste: 329)

Although Mr. Parker never refers to Dr. Russell's work and probably never read the full text, he would probably have been familiar with commentary on it. But he was clearly unaware of the strict conditions under which the good doctor had recommended the use of seawater, which was by no means—as our friend Thomas, seduced by extravagant advertisements, misconstrues—a panacea for every ill that has ever afflicted humankind. Jane Austen's humor here is very broad, indeed. (See Appendix C.)

We see here the expected reduction in figurative language. Later, in the descriptions of the sea, Jane Austen will let loose her range in this kind of rhetoric, normally absent from her prose. There is a loss, though, in the change from "palpable" to the prosaic "evidently," suggesting a self-editing not always to the advantage of the manuscript.]

His eloquence however could not prevail. M^r— & M^rs. H— never left home. Marrying early & having a very numerous Family, their movements had been long limitted to one small circle; & they were older in Habits than in Age. —

[The normal marrying age in Jane Austen's novels is never clear. Here we are told that the Heywoods married early, whereas Thomas Parker, at age 35, has been married for only seven years. His marrying at 28 matches the ages that we see in most of Jane Austen's male characters except for those whose more advanced age is part of the plot, like Colonel Brandon, labeled ancient at 35 by 17-year-old Marianne Dashwood.

It is difficult to determine the reasoning, if any, behind the spelling, "limitted." Although we do not have any really useful rules for spelling our language, we generally do not double the final "-t" unless that syllable receives primary stress, like "committed" and "permitted." Sadly, spelling was not Jane Austen's strong suit.]

Excepting two Journeys to London in the year, to receive his Dividends, M^r. H. went no farther than his feet, or his well-tried old Horse could carry him, and M^{rs}. Heywood's Adventurings were only now & then to visit her Neighbours, in the old Coach which had been new when they married & fresh lined on their Eldest Son's coming of age 10 years ago. —

They had very pretty Property — enough, had their family been of reasonable Limits to have allowed them a very gentlemanlike share of Luxuries & Change — enough for them to have indulged in a new Carriage & better roads, a Summer occasionally at Tunbridge Wells, & symptoms of the Gout to make a Winter at Bath; — but the maintenance, Education & fitting out of 14 Children demanded a very quiet, settled, careful course of Life — & obliged them to be stationary & healthy at Willingden.
>
They had very pretty Property — enough, had their family been of reasonable Limits to have allowed them a very gentlemanlike share of Luxuries & Change — enough for them to have indulged in a new Carriage & better roads, an occasional month at Tunbridge Wells, & symptoms of the Gout and a Winter at Bath; — but the maintenance, Education & fitting out of 14 Children demanded a very quiet, settled, careful course of Life — & obliged them to be stationary & healthy at Willingden.

[The comic message is clearly that you have to be able to afford to indulge hypochondria, to "enjoy ill health." Despite their wealth, the Heywoods have learned to limit themselves to the necessities of life with perhaps the occasional reasonable luxury. In contrast, Sir Edward will be seen to engage in expenditures—either real or planned—that are beyond his present means. Lady Denham's searches for a wealthy wife for her nephew-through-marriage because she is aware of his lack of fiscal responsibility.

Like Jane Austen's own, there are large families in many of her novels, but *fourteen* children is somewhat overdoing it and surely meant to be humorous. The slight exaggeration in reporting that the Morlands are a "family of ten children" has been extended for comic effect to virtual ridicule. In novels of the nineteenth century, perhaps only Mr. and Mrs. Quiverful can match this record. There is no indication about how many sons the Heywoods have nor if any of them are still at home. Charlotte is asked to bring back gifts for her sisters, suggesting that there are no young boys at home.]

What Prudence had at first enjoined, was now rendered pleasant by Habit. They never left home, & they had a gratification in saying so. — But very far from wishing their Children to do the same, they were glad to promote their getting out into the World, as much as possible.

They staid at home, that their Children might get out; — and while making that home extremely comfortable, welcomed every change from it which could lead them into respectable Company.
>
They staid at home, that their Children might get out; — and while making that home extremely comfortable, welcomed every change from it which could give useful connections or respectable acquaintance to Sons or Daughters.

[This is an open acknowledgement that the Heywoods welcome the unexpected arrival of the Parkers as an opportunity to seek a husband for their eldest daughter. Mrs. Bennet is not the only mother eager to settle her daughters.]

When M^r. and M^rs. Parker therefore ceased from soliciting a family-visit, and bounded their veiws to carrying back one young Lady with them, no difficulties were started.
>
When M^r. and M^rs. Parker therefore ceased from soliciting a family-visit, and bounded their veiws to carrying back one Daughter with them, no difficulties were started.

It was general pleasure & consent. — Their invitation was to Miss Charlotte Heywood, a very pleasing young woman of two & twenty, the eldest of the

Daughters at home, & the one, who under her Mother's directions had been particularly useful & obliging to them; who had attended them most, & knew them best. —

[It is not surprising that in her new appearance, Susan/Catherine, no longer an unformed girl of 17, is now a mature young woman of 22 ready to deal with the world outside her home and definitely ready for marriage. Having recently entered full womanhood, she presents a midpoint of Jane Austen's other heroines: at the lower end of the scale we have Fanny Price, initially seen at 10 and later at 15/16, and Catherine Morland, almost pretty at 17, followed by the preternaturally mature Elinor Dashwood at 19 and the sparkling Elizabeth Bennet at 20. Also age 20 is Emma Woodhouse, wise beyond her years, at least in her own eyes. At the upper end of the scale, of course, is the fading beauty of 27-year-old Anne Elliot.

One of the most dramatic and, I believe, significant alterations that Jane Austen made in discarding "'Susan"/"Catherine" was changing her heroine from a clergyman's daughter to that of a gentleman-farmer. Aside from Susan/Catherine, none of the heroines is from a clerical family although two of them marry clergymen. In many ways Elinor's marriage to Edward comes about because of his plan to enter the church rather than something more ambitious and socially acceptable to his mother. And whether or not the plot of *Mansfield Park* was to be "ordination" as arguably suggested in one of Jane Austen's letters, the whole point of the tale is that Fanny is destined to be the wife of a humble man dedicated to caring for the souls of his parishioners. But her other heroines are more worldly, and so Elizabeth as the daughter of a gentleman-recluse successfully moves all the way up the social scale to become the mistress of Pemberley, Emma remains on the same exalted level as her birth in marrying the wealthiest man in the neighborhood of Highbury, and Anne finally marries her Captain, who despite not being on the same social level has considerably more money than her retrenching father. It is therefore very much in the new romantic spirit that our author takes Charlotte from her comfortable, middle-class farm to the big city (well, more like a village by the sea), where she will meet and marry an independently wealthy younger son.

Mrs. Heywood has wisely seized on this opportunity to send out her eldest daughter, next in line to secure a husband, to find an eligible bachelor. The text is silent on the matter, but no doubt Mr. and Mrs. Parker have mentioned several times that young blades come to the seaside resort, although it is doubtful that they have nominated either Arthur or Sidney Parker at this point.

Although technically our heroine is "Miss Heywood," the initial introduction demands that we learn her first name, by which we will know her henceforth.]

Charlotte was to go, — with excellent health, to bathe & be better if she could — to receive every possible pleasure which Sanditon could be made to supply by the gratitude of those she went with — & to buy new Parasols, new Gloves, & new Broches, for her sisters & herself at the Library, which M^r. P. was anxiously wishing to support. —

[The first short clause—"Charlotte was to go"—has the sound of reported speech, very much in the tone of Mrs. Bennet's decisions about which of her girls will be next in leaving home to seek a husband and is probably pronounced by Mrs. Heywood. Her parents cannot possibly think of the health benefits and shopping opportunities as the primary reasons for sending Charlotte on such a long trip. Like Mrs. Allen, they are "aware that if adventures will not befall a young lady in her own village, she must seek them abroad." Mr. Parker has obviously been touting the merits of Sanditon as a buyer's paradise as well as a growing health resort, but he would have been remiss in not mentioning the eligible bachelors flocking there in search of brides, a remark that would inevitably cause Mrs. Heywood's ears to perk up. It is not clear how many unmarried daughters remain, but it is her duty to find husbands for them in seniority order.

The admonition "to buy new Parasols, new Gloves, & new Broches, for her sisters & herself at the Library" surely comes from Mrs. Heywood, who wants to placate all her daughters who must remain at home while their older sister goes off to a vacation by the sea. David Selwyn avers, however, that the suggestion comes from their guest, with a different and more mercenary motive: "Charlotte Heywood feels herself under the double pressure of being 'among so many pretty Temptations' and of wishing to please Mr Parker, who, 'anxiously wishing to support' the library, has already urged her to buy 'new parasols, new Gloves, & new Broches, for her sisters & herself'" (2007: 224).

There is no indication that Charlotte is as ungifted musically as Catherine, who, because she "was very fond of tinkling the keys of the old forlorn spinnet... learnt a year, and could not bear it," and "whose taste for drawing was not superior." But if Miss Heywood possesses any skills in these two womanly accomplishments they are not revealed in the manuscript.

The text suggests that Mr. Parker has some financial commitment to the Sanditon library although nothing is specific in the later passages.]

All that M^r. Heywood himself could be persuaded to promise was, that he would recommend everyone to Sanditon, who asked his advice, & that nothing should ever induce him (as far the future could be answered for) to spend even one night at Brinshore. —
>
All that M^r. Heywood himself could be persuaded to promise was, that he would send everyone to Sanditon, who asked his advice, & that nothing should ever induce him (as far the future could be answered for) to spend even 5 shillings at Brinshore. —

[Unlike the opening chapter, which is in real time, the second chapter is a summary of the two weeks that the Parkers stay with the Heywoods. Some of the narrative sounds like reported speech.]

[Chapter 3]

Chapter 3.

Every Neighbourhood should have a great Lady. — The great Lady of Sanditon, was Lady Denham; & in their Journey from Willingden to the Coast, M^r. Parker gave Charlotte a more detailed account of her, than had been called for before. —

[This opening lays out unambiguously the major tenor of Mr. Parker's chatty conversation on the journey from Willingden to Sanditon. Lady Denham has to be his major concern since his entire financial security depends on her willingness to cooperate with his ambitious plans for the seaside resort.

As in so many other passages in this manuscript, Jane Austen successfully engages the reader through use of an ambiguous narrative voice, starting the chapter in a sententious tone reminiscent of the opening lines of *Pride and Prejudice*, which are Mrs. Bennet's mantra. That every neighborhood should have a great lady, if from the author, drips with a sardonic tone. If from Mr. Parker, the inner narrator, it smacks of sycophancy. And if from Lady Denham, who has been reminding Sanditonians for a long time now that she has a special place in the community, it is merely self-serving. Charlotte is more reserved about the necessity for such a person, who is unlikely to be part of the social scene in Willingden.

In this context, "Neighbourhood," meaning something very different from and more elevated than merely "the general area," consists of "not all the people of the town but only those with whom it was appropriate to socialize" (Olsen: 130).

> When Jane Austen speaks of a "neighborhood"… she does not mean it in the sense we use today, that is, in the sense of a geographical area.… She means a social neighborhood, a community of people of approximately the same economic and cultural class who pay calls on each other and are entertained at each other's houses. In country villages… the neighborhood could be quite small, and genteel villagers… often had to walk or ride for miles in order to

visit a decent number of people…. With few options for guests for tea, let alone for marriage partners, neighborhoods could be very small indeed. (Olsen: 504–505)

Jane Austen had used "neighborhood" in the same sense in *Emma*, when Frank Churchill in his first scene with the heroine of the novel, in a scattered manner well reflecting his uncertain mental state, asks her about details of her life that he cannot possibly be interested in.

Their subjects in general were such as belong to an opening acquaintance. On his side were the inquiries,—"Was she a horsewoman?—Pleasant rides?—Pleasant walks?—Had they a large neighbourhood?—Highbury, perhaps, afforded society enough?—There were several very pretty houses in and about it.— Balls—had they balls?—Was it a musical society?"

Aside from being an impressive use of indirect discourse, this passage employs the same broken dialog that we find in *Sanditon*, the difference being that here in *Emma* it is considered a sign of remarkable narrative technique but in the final manuscript evidence of a failing mind.

Like the Beaufort sisters, Lady Denham "w^d. have been nothing at Brighton," and in London, without any doubt, she would have no callers.

We learn later that Lady Denham's title is derived from her union with Sir Harry Denham, a Baronet, the lowest hereditary rank and with the status of a commoner. She is perhaps not a great lady, but she is definitely a grand lady, in a class by herself among Jane Austen's varied actors. She may be an original creation, or she may be based on some earlier literary character. *CUPLM* notes that "there is a Lady Denham in Hannah Moore's *Cœlebs in Search of a Wife* (1808), who bears some resemblance to JA's character" (641). It seems unlikely, though, that Jane Austen would not merely borrow a character from an earlier novel but that she would use the same name with unlimited possibilities available. See Appendix B for two remarkable passages about Mrs. Flimflam—"a woman past the middle age of life, corpulent in person, coarse in her manners, vulgar in her speech, proud, and hard-hearted, bold, but grossly ignorant"— that could have inspired this colorful portrait.]

She had been necessarily often mentioned at Willingden, — for being his Colleague in Speculation, Sanditon itself could not be talked of long, without the introduction of Lady Denham & that she was a very rich old Lady, who had buried two Husbands, who knew the value of Money, was very much looked up to & had a poor Cousin living with her, were already well known, but some further particulars of names & places, & some hints of Character (though given with the light touch of a very friendly hand) were

>

She had been necessarily often mentioned at Willingden, — for being his Colleague in Speculation, Sanditon itself could not be talked of long, without the introduction of Lady Denham & that she was a very rich old Lady, who had buried two Husbands, who knew the value of Money, was very much looked up to & had a poor Cousin living with her, were already well known, but some further particulars of names & places, & some hints of Character served to lighten the tediousness of a long Pull, or a heavy bit of road, and to give the visiting Young Lady a suitable Knowledge of the Person with whom she might now expect to be daily associating. —

>

She had been necessarily often mentioned at Willingden, — for being his Colleague in Speculation, Sanditon itself could not be talked of long, without the introduction of Lady Denham & that she was a very rich old Lady, who had buried two Husbands, who knew the value of Money, was very much looked up to & had a poor Cousin living with her, were facts already well known, but some further particulars of her history, & her Character served to lighten the tediousness of a long Hill, or a heavy bit of road, and to give the visiting Young Lady a suitable Knowledge of the Person with whom she might now expect to be daily associating. —

[There is some hint here of the obsequious Mr. Collins in his sycophantic encomia on the glories of Lady Catherine de Bourgh. The manuscript shows that Jane Austen was particularly intent on creating effective first-impression descriptions of her leading characters. Hence the many levels of composition of this single line show that she regarded Lady Denham as a significant factor in her projected tale. Gossip about his co-investor obviously helped pass time during the two weeks of recuperation.]

Lady D. had been a rich Miss Brereton, born to Wealth but not to Education.

[The logic here is challenging. It is easy to understand that Miss Brereton was fortunate enough to become a member of a wealthy family, but she could not be expected, like Athena, to come into the world with comprehensive knowledge. The implication is that despite the opportunities that her wealth and therefore leisure have afforded, she has remained as ignorant as the day that she was born. And everything that she says once upon the stage reinforces this initial thumbnail sketch. It may be significant that we meet her as she approaches the library in Sanditon, not within its walls, where she would encounter alien books.]

Her first Husband had been a M^r. Hollis, a man of considerable Property in the Country, of which a large share of the Parish of Sanditon, with Manor & Mansion House made a part.

[At this point the narrative shifts to Mr. Parker in a kind of reported speech. Mr. Hollis's "considerable property" may be more extensive than specified in the text. "In medieval times many rural settlements were structured as 'manors' containing the local church, houses and agricultural land, all within the ownership of the lord of the manor.... In the early nineteenth century... the term 'manor'... continued to suggest control over the village" (*CUPLM*: 641-642). It is unclear who assumed this role while Lady Denham, formerly Mrs. Hollis, resided with her new husband in Denham Park. But she is back in Sanditon, reaping the benefits of her own personal wealth, the wealth and authority of her first husband, and the title of her second spouse. For good reason she is a "great lady" in this small setting, a very large fish in a very small tank.]

He had been quite an elderly Man when she married him; — her own age about 30. —
>
He had been an elderly Man when she married him; — her own age about 30. —

[Mr. Hollis's age is never disclosed, but at that time "elderly" was somewhat younger than we now apply the term. Marianne Dashwood regards Colonel Brandon as elderly although from our point of view he is still a young man of 35. "His appearance however was not unpleasing, in spite of his being in the opinion of Marianne and Margaret an absolute old bachelor, for he was on the wrong side of five and thirty." Like Marianne, Miss Brereton may have been many years younger than her suitor and so she has spoken of him as "elderly." Mr. Parker (like Colonel Brandon, 35 years old) certainly has all this information directly from the great lady herself since he had probably not yet been born at the time of Mr. Hollis's death some undisclosed years earlier. Jane Austen's change from "quite an elderly man" suggests that she does not envision him as truly ancient. We never learn how long this marriage lasted so we do not know when the former Miss Brereton became a widow for the first time.]

Her motives for such a Match could be little understood at the distance of 40 years, but she had so well nursed & pleased M^r. Hollis, that at his Death he left her everything — all his Estates, & all at her Disposal.

[Some commentators have denounced the "rich Miss Brereton, born to Wealth," as a gold digger, marrying Mr. Hollis for his money. Hence, "Lady Denham did not get her original capital by commerce of this kind [operating a gift shop like Mrs. Whitby], or by speculation, but rather in woman's old way—by marrying" (Taylor: 430). B.C. Southam likewise condemns her with faint praise for marrying for money: "Her wits have already won her a fortune" (1964: 114). The text, however, is clear that she came to the marriage as a very wealthy young woman. That her motives for the match were not understood at the time suggests that her contemporaries did not view her as marrying Mr. Hollis for his wealth. Quite the opposite of the charges against her is probable, since a man of means like Mr. Hollis would seek an heiress to increase his own fortune. Most likely it was an ideal match between two affluent and selfish people, if not made in heaven, conceived elsewhere. Mr. Hollis obviously had no interest in enriching his younger male relatives, since "unusually, [his] property was not entailed on to male heirs and he had chosen to leave it to his widow without conditions" (*CUPLM*: 642).

And if marrying for money is reprehensible, what are we to make of Elizabeth Bennet, who finds the repugnant Mr. Darcy increasingly attractive upon touring his extensive estate and viewing the splendors of his sumptuous mansion? How fortunate is Emma, with a handsome dowry of her own, to decide to marry the wealthiest single man in the neighborhood. Anne Elliot was perhaps ready to marry a penniless Frederick Wentworth, but upon seeing the abject poverty of her old friend Mrs. Smith she cannot regret that in the interval of their broken engagement and their reconciliation he has amassed twenty thousand pounds, enough to keep her from the want haunting her father and older sister. Perhaps only Lydia Bennet is worthy of praise in eloping with the ne'er-do-well Wickham, knowing that she can never be accused of pursuing him for his fortune. Throughout her novels,

Jane Austen makes clear her formula for a good life: Money may not bring happiness, but you cannot be happy without money.]

After a widowhood of some years, she had been induced to marry again. The late Sir Harry Denham, of Denham Park in the Neighbourhood of Sanditon had succeeded in removing her & her large Income to his own Domains, but he c^d. not succeed in the veiws of permanently enriching his family, which were attributed to him. She had been too wary to put anything out of her own Power — and when on Sir Harry's Decease she returned again to her own House at Sanditon, she was said to have made this boast to a friend "that though she had <u>got</u> nothing but her Title from the Family, still she had <u>given</u> nothing for it. —"

[Perhaps the novel would have taken us to the interestingly named Denham Park, suggesting a large estate with extensive grounds. But without adequate funds, the present Sir Edward would be unable to give his inheritance its proper care.

This passage reinforces the author's point that Mrs. Hollis did not marry Sir Harry for money, but he clearly had her fortune in his sights. It is very difficult to determine how much Jane Austen knew about the details of legal matters that she introduces in her novels, such as the important issue of "entail" that underlies part of the plot of *Pride and Prejudice*. Equally important for the story line of the incomplete manuscript is Lady Denham's wealth, which she initially inherited, over which she may have temporarily lost control upon marrying Mr. Hollis, and which she apparently reclaimed with profit upon his death. The problem, of course, is that "the Married Women's Property Act of 1882 provid[ing] that married women could acquire, hold and dispose of property 'as though they were single'" (Redmond, 1989) obviously does not apply to this case, and so there are questions about the disposal of that munificent sum of £30,000 that she possessed as Miss Brereton, brought to her first marriage with Mr. Hollis, and still holds as the widow of Sir Harry.

Because only an attorney can attempt to unravel such a tangled skein, I quote at length from a series of emails from Luane Bethke Redmond in response to my inquiry about the retained and even expanded wealth of Miss Brereton/Lady Denham:

First, recall that the English common law rules discussed in my JASNA article ("Land, Law and Love." *Persuasions*, 11 [1989], 46-

52) were intended to operate if there was no will, or where there was a will but it was poorly drafted or unclear. By will, property owners could dispose of their lands with considerable freedom; it was in instances of intestacy that the common law stepped in. Likewise, property dispositions such as entailments were intended to operate where wills were poor or absent, the idea being to keep the land in the families, protecting careless landholders and their heirs from themselves. Of course, if there were an entailment, it would supersede a bequest by will where there was a conflict, but we have no textual evidence of such an encumbrance here. In the absence of a legal encumbrance, where specific, clear wills existed, the results could be very different.

There are several missing documents in this story. One is the prenuptial agreement (then called a marriage settlement) between Mr. Hollis and Miss Brereton. Those agreements were very specific and could say pretty much anything the parties desired. It is quite possible that by the terms of the settlement, Miss Brereton, upon her husband's decease, would retain everything she had brought to the marriage, with the result that when he bequeathed her everything, it included his estates as well as whatever estate and income she had when they were first married. Your statement that she "never lost control over her fortune" may not be entirely accurate. Her husband could have controlled her money during the marriage if he wished, though in this case it sounds as if she had him wrapped around her little finger and perhaps he did not care to.

Remember that widowhood was a state of comparative freedom for women of that period. With no husband or father to tell her what to do with her money, a widow's independence was unique and even enviable. It sounds to me as if Mr. Hollis married chiefly for companionship, while Sir Harry Denham married for the money she brought to his titled but possibly financially strapped estates. Then we hear that Sir Harry "could not succeed in the views of permanently enriching his family which were attributed to him. She had been too wary to put anything out of her own power." This suggests that Sir Harry's demise before his wife, and her caution (which probably meant she did not, in her own will or by any transfer during her lifetime, give over any of her property to him or anyone else), left her with the title but his estates much as they were before. There could also have been a marriage settlement agreement specifying that her property remained in her name.

The second document we do not know anything about is Sir Harry's will. He may have left everything to her as well. We are told that she moved back to her own house at Sanditon but we are not told why—whether she had to because somebody else got Sir Harry's real estate, or she just preferred Sanditon. She did say she had not got anything for the title, which suggests there was not much money in Sir Harry's estate. The fact that she was still courted by his relatives could mean she got his money and land and they were hoping to get some on her demise if they stayed in her good graces, but it could also mean they hope to be or remain close enough to her to get some of her own property by the same means. (Redmond, 2008)

The last line—"she was said to have made this boast to a friend 'that though she had got nothing but her Title from the Family, still she had given nothing for it'"—is certainly indirect discourse, now very much a part of Jane Austen's arsenal of rhetorical devices and here very subtly treated since it is part of Mr. Parker's reported speech. He is obviously one of the busiest gossips in the village.]

For the Title, it was to be supposed that she had married — & Mr. P. acknowledged there being just such a degree of value for it apparent now, as to give her conduct that natural explanation.

[Women in Jane Austen's novels marry for a variety of reasons, sometimes practical (like Charlotte Lucas) but more often romantic (like Elizabeth Bennet). Marrying for a title would have been another legitimate reason.]

"There is at times said he — a little self-importance — but it is not offensive; — & there are moments, there are points, when her Love of Money is carried greatly too far.

[Mr. Parker's reported speech is here interrupted for direct speech. Although Charlotte is through this line prepared for Lady Denham's two most objectionable features—self-importance and cupidity—the reality will prove to be much worse than expected.]

But she is a goodnatured Woman, a very goodnatured Woman, — a very obliging, friendly Neighbour to us — and her faults are to be cheifly imputed to the want of Education.

>

But she is a goodnatured Woman, a very goodnatured Woman, — a very obliging, friendly Neighbour; a chearful, independant, valuable character. — and her faults may be entirely imputed to her want of Education.

She has good natural Sense, but quite uncultivated. — She has a fine active mind, as well as a fine healthy frame for a Woman of 70, & enters into the improvement of Sanditon with a spirit truly admirable — though now & then, a Littleness <u>will</u> appear.

She cannot look forward quite as I would have her — & takes alarm at a trifling present expence, without considering what returns it <u>will</u> make her.

>

She cannot look forward quite as I would have her — & takes alarm at a trifling present expence, without considering what returns it <u>will</u> make her in a year or two.

[The addition of a time element is significant. Lady Denham expects to see an immediate gain in any investment, in contrast to Mr. Parker's long-term vision. But for that period she is an elderly person and has no reason to be sanguine about what will happen in the distant future.]

That is — we think <u>differently</u>, we now & then, see things <u>differently</u> Miss H. —

Those who tell their own Story must be listened to with Caution.

>

Those who tell their own Story you know must be listened to with Caution.

[We have yet another inserted "you know"—here rhetorically meaningful but also part of Mr. Parker's characteristic speech pattern—a construction that Mrs. Parker uses once, undoubtedly in imitation of her husband, who in his turn has probably picked it up from Lady Denham.]

When you see us in contact, you will judge for yourself. —"

Lady D. was indeed a great Lady beyond the common Social order for she had many Thousands a year to bequeath, & three distinct sets of People to be courted by; her own relations, who might very reasonably wish for her Original Thirty Thousand Pounds among them, the legal Heirs of M^r. Hollis, who must hope to be more endebted to <u>her</u> sense of Justice than they c^d. be to <u>his</u>, and those Members of the Denham Family, whom her 2^d. Husband had hoped to make a good Bargain for. —

>

Lady D. was indeed a great Lady beyond the common wants of Society — for she had many Thousands a year to bequeath, & three distinct sets of People to be courted by; her own relations, who might very reasonably wish for her Original Thirty Thousand Pounds among them, the legal Heirs of M^r. Hollis, who must hope to be more endebted to <u>her</u> sense of Justice than he had allowed them to be to <u>his</u>, and those Members of the Denham Family, whom her 2^d. Husband had hoped to make a good Bargain for. —

[Aspersions on the young Miss Brereton's character, such as that she "did not get her original capital by commerce... , or by speculation, but rather in woman's old way—by marrying" (Taylor: 430), fail to take into account the clear statement in the text that she entered the marriage-market with "her Original Thirty Thousand Pounds." She certainly increased her assets through marrying Mr. Hollis, but her personal fortune was considerable at the time. "Landed estates... provide the most prominent unit for measuring competences in Austen's novels.... An heiress's fortune, in contrast, is given as a lump sum figure, which then must be calculated for the annual income it yields, the presumption being that it is invested in the government funds at an annual interest rate of 5 per cent" (Copeland, 2007: 321).

Miss Brereton's £30,000 in Jane Austen's day would now be worth—depending on which method of calculation is used—between £1,350,000 and £1,700,000, a considerable amount at a time when although goods were expensive, human labor was very cheap. Mr. Darcy is much wealthier, of course, since his *annual* income is £10,000, the current equivalent of at least £450,000. Someone good in mathematics can perhaps work out what his total assets are to bring in the equivalent of at least three-quarters of a million dollars a year (with no income tax to pay). It is hardly surprising that three separate parties are vying to inherit even a portion of Lady Denham's capital. Other great heiresses, like Miss Gray or the "young ladies that [Mr. Elton's] sisters are intimate with, who have all twenty thousand pounds apiece," are comparative paupers, coming to the marriage bargaining table a full £10,000 short of Miss Brereton's inheritance.

W.H. Auden has famously versified Jane Austen's preoccupation with money.

> There is one other author in my pack:
> For some time I debated which to write to.
> Which would be least likely to send my letter back?
> But I decided I'd give a fright to
> Jane Austen if I wrote when I had no right to,
> And share in her contempt the dreadful fates
> Of Crawford, Musgrave, and Mr. Yates.
> She was not an unshockable blue-stocking;
> If shades remain the characters they were,
> No doubt she still considers you as shocking.
> But tell Jane Austen, that is, if you dare,
> How much her novels are beloved down here.
> She wrote them for posterity, she said;
> 'Twas rash, but by posterity she's read.
> You could not shock her more than she shocks me;
> Beside her Joyce seems innocent as grass.
> It makes me uncomfortable to see
> An English spinster of the middle class
> Describe the amorous effects of "brass,"
> Reveal so frankly and with such sobriety
> The economic basis of society.
> ("Letter to Lord Byron," from *Letters from Iceland*, by W.H. Auden
> [and Louis MacNeice], London: Faber & Faber, 1937.)

As tempting is it is to think of Jane Austen's novels as primarily about the successful pursuit of love, a realistic look at them reveals that they are at least as much about money and the power and independence that it bestows upon its fortunate possessor. A simple caveat runs through all the novels: Marry for love, but be sure that there is enough money for a (very) comfortable lifestyle.]

By all of these, or by Branches of them, she had no doubt been long, & still continued to be, well attacked; — and of these three divisions, M^r. P. did not hesitate to say that M^r. Hollis' Kindred were the <u>least</u> in favour & Sir

Harry Denham's the <u>most</u>. — The former he beleived, had done themselves irremediable harm by expressions of very unwise & unjustifiable resentment at the time of M^r. Hollis's death; — the Latter, to the advantage of being the remnant of a Connection which she certainly valued, joined those of having been known to her from their Childhood & of being always at hand to preserve their interest by reasonable attention.

[The former Miss Brereton's two marriages are reported in marked contrast—and perhaps unfavorable distinction—to the marital conservatism of an earlier character: "That Lady Russell, of steady age and character, and extremely well provided for, should have no thought of a second marriage, needs no apology to the public, which is rather apt to be unreasonably discontented when a woman does marry again, than when she does not."

Jane Austen remained uncertain about how to show possession, especially with proper nouns ending in "-s." Hence on the same page she writes "Hollis' Kindred" and "Hollis's death."]

Sir Edward, the present Baronet, nephew to Sir Harry, resided constantly at Denham Park; & M^r. P— had little doubt, that he & his Sister Miss D— who always lived with him, w^d. be very principally remembered in her Will.
>
Sir Edward, the present Baronet, nephew to Sir Harry, resided constantly at Denham Park; & M^r. P— had little doubt, that he & his Sister Miss D— who lived with him, w^d. be principally remembered in her Will.

[This initial introduction to Sir Edward Denham does very little to prepare us for the gentleman himself. Only his own dialog and manner would suffice to describe him, so our author wisely waits for that passage to delight and entertain Charlotte Heywood and us. A Baronetcy is the lowest ranking hereditary title although at the level of a commoner.

> There were two ranks among the upper gentry that merited special titles, and they were very similar in their usage. Both baronets and knights were referred to as Sir Robert Smith or Sir Robert, but never Sir Smith. One difference between them was that a baronet could add an abbreviation after his name in writing: Sir John Smith, Bart., or Sir John Smith, Bt. A more important difference between the two titles was that a baronetcy could be inherited, while a knighthood could not. The wives in both cases were referred to as

> Lady Smith [so Lady Denham], as the use of a first name would have made it seem as if the woman in question was a peer's daughter rather than a knight's wife. (Olsen: 679-680)

The full range of English titles:

The Peerage (hereditary titles)

Royals
   Monarch (King/Queen, members of the Royal Family)
The Upper Nobility
   Duke (Duchess)
   Marquess (or Marquis) (Marchioness)
   Earl (Countess)

The Lower Nobility
   Viscount (Viscountess)
   Baron (Baroness)
Commoners
   Baronet (title is inherited)
   Knight (title is not inherited)
   (Beverley)

Jane Austen introduces very few titled characters in her novels, most notably the Baronets Sir Thomas Bertram, Sir Walter Elliot, Sir Edward Denham, and, possibly, Sir John Middleton. In the first two cases, that their titles are hereditary is important to the plot. Sir William Lucas is a mere Knight.

The highest-ranking character who appears on stage is the Dowager Viscountess Dalrymple, Anne Elliot's distant cousin through marriage. As part of a surprise ending, Eleanor Tilney marries a Viscount, thereby becoming a Viscountess.

The precise location of Denham Park or its proximity to Sanditon is never disclosed, but it is obviously a short distance away and "further inland" (Le Faye, 2002: 305). The text never specifies that along with the Baronetcy Sir Edward inherited Denham Park, so it is possible that it still belongs to Lady Denham as Sir Harry's widow. If so, she may have left Denham Park for her earlier home at Sanditon House to be closer to the sea and for the opportunity to engage in speculation, as well as to avoid the dampness that Miss Esther enjoys complaining about. We do not learn if she allows her nephew and niece through marriage to reside in her former home gratis or if she exacts rent (I think that we can guess that the latter is the answer). If Sir Edward now owns Denham Park, perhaps acquired through his uncle's will, he certainly lacks the money to maintain it at the level that his sister believes is her due. It is not clear if Sir Harry left his nephew any capital assets—other than the gold watch that Lady Denham was so generous in passing along since she had no personal use for it.

If Sir Harry left all his assets, including the estate, to his wife, she still owns Denham Park and allows her nephew and niece by marriage to reside there. How much money she provides to maintain the residence and their lifestyle is not reported, but she does hint that she supports them in some way rather than receiving anything from them. Everything in passages on the relationship between Lady Denham and the Denham siblings suggests avarice and small-mindedness on the part of the great lady of the neighborhood, and Jane Austen allows the reader to increase or reduce the level of her mean-spiritedness.]

He sincerely hoped it. — Miss Denham had a very small provision — & her Brother was a poor Man for his rank in Society.

[We never learn the details of Miss Denham's "very small provision," but it would be short of her ambitions whatever its amount. Nor do we ever learn how much Sir Edward brings in a year to support his living style, which is much more restrained than he would like. He must be aware of—and consequently envious of—Sidney Parker's relaxed mode of life with no financial constraints.]

"He is a warm friend to Sanditon, — said M^r. Parker — & his hand w^d. be as liberal as his heart, had he the Power. — He would be a noble Coadjutor! — As it is, he does what he can — & is running up a tasteful little Cottage Ornèe, on a strip of Waste Ground Lady D. has granted him, which I have no doubt we shall have many a Candidate for, before the end even of <u>this</u> Season".

[A "coadjutor" is "One who works with and helps another; a helper, assistant, fellow-helper" (*OED*). I think that Mr. Parker has "co-investor" more in mind. Like the gold watch, the strip of waste land is freely granted because Lady Denham can see no personal profit in it. Desperate for income, Sir Edward is ready to become a landlord, charging rent for the use of his property. On the basis of the failure of Sanditon to catch on as a major attraction, he may be investing precious resources only to be disappointed.

It is in no way clear where the strip of waste ground is, but it is presumably in the Sanditon area rather than inland as part of the Denham Park property, so it may well be a part of the Sanditon House lands. If so, Lady Denham has shown some generosity in granting the land to Sir Edward although the text does not state that he now owns it irrevocably nor that she does not expect to make a profit out of the lease of the planned tasteful little cottage ornèe.

Jane Austen may or may not mean by "grant" the *OED* definition: "in *Law*, to transfer (property) from oneself to another person, especially by deed." As a past participle, "granted" is defined by the *OED* as "Bestowed, allotted." It is hard to see why Lady Denham would relinquish property, even that of no immediate value, when she can just as easily allow its use but retain possession. Therefore I believe that the meaning here is "allowed him the use of." Elsewhere Jane Austen uses "granted" in a clearly non-legal sense. For example, Emma "was quite convinced of Harriet Smith's being exactly the young friend she wanted—exactly the something which her home required. Such a friend as Mrs. Weston was out of the question. Two such could never be granted." The more common meaning is seen when "Sir Thomas thought it best for each daughter that the permission should be granted," that is, given but without legal implications. There is certainly no implication of a permanent gift in Sir Walter Elliot's declaration to Mr. Shepherd that he is "very little disposed to grant a tenant of Kellynch Hall any extraordinary favour." The word is used even more loosely in *Sense and Sensibility*: Willoughby asks for the honour of calling the next day to inquire after Miss Dashwood, and "The honour was readily granted."

This is Jane Austen's only use of "cottage ornèe" (properly "cottage ornée"), "a mock-rustic detached house designed for the use of the gentry, and to be picturesque" (*CUPLM*: 642).

> In many respects the cottage ornée was the upmarket version of the primitive rustic cottage. "Though humble in its appearance it affords the necessary conveniences for persons of refined manners and habits," explained Richard Pocock, introducing his book of cottage ornée designs in 1807.
>
> But there were some very important additional elements aside from scale and class of occupant. It had, first of all, a deliberately complicated shape, form, texture and plan. There was the

characteristic thatch, but it was likely to be in the form of a set of roofs joined and angled together into a complicated and irregular silhouette, often with eyebrow eaves, curly carved bargeboards, dormer windows and highly decorative chimneys poking through the summit. Instead of a few rooms neatly arranged underneath, there was a plan of often considerable complexity which was echoed on the outside by a rambling irregularity, freedom of form and selection of materials which, a few years before, in the eighteenth century, would have been unthinkable from the drawingboard of an architect who wanted to be taken seriously.

It is not as if the description "cottage ornée" itself was all that serious. It is, of course, a made-up term and was probably invented by Robert Lugar, the great exponent of cottage ornée design. At all events, he was the first to use it in print in 1805, and it soon became part of the language despite an attempt two years later by Richard Pocock to clean up the suspect term with the more correct "cabane ornée." As it happens, the French already used the term *chaumier* (and the Germans *Strohhütte*) for ornamental rustic buildings in their English Gardens. The British prefer their own variants on French language and grammar, and so "cottage ornée" stuck. It belongs to the same etymological family as the term "ferme orneé."... Like the early nineteenth-century cottages ornées, they combined practicality with decorativeness.

That is not to say that the cottage ornée was not intended to be taken with the utmost seriousness, but it was a different kind of seriousness from that of the past. The cottage ornée's design should, said Pocock, be "calculated for comfort and convenience without minute attention to the rules of art, every part having its use apparent and the appearance in no way sacrificed to regularity [strict symmetry]... every other part must appear conducive to this one end... the comfort and convenience of its inhabitants."

At the same time, starting off from a practical rather than theoretical design premise allowed the designers of cottages ornées a tremendous freedom in what they could do with the appearance of their cottages.

. . .

In the end the cottage ornée was satisfying as an experiment in incorporating nature into architecture, but it was not necessarily an experiment in integrating or incorporating architecture into nature—which is what the Picturesque at its best was about. However charming as designs they were, the naturalism was self-conscious. With their shaggy, irregular thatch, diamond-paned windows, porches and the occasional tree-trunk veranda columns, they were rather more symbolic of an association with nature—a somewhat crude attempt to imitate its forms rather than its qualities—than an attempt to consider seriously the problem of designing for the spirit of a place. (Lyall: 73–79)

Sir Edward will have to build quickly because we are now in late July and "the end of the current 'season'... would probably be in October" (*CUPLM*: 643).]

Till within the last twelvemonth, M^r. P. had considered Sir Edw: as standing without a rival, as having the fairest chance of succeeding to the greater part of all that she had to give — but there was now another person's claims to be taken into the account, those of the young female relation, whom Lady D. had been induced to receive into her Family.

After having always protested against any such Addition, deprecating the idea of a Companion, defying & enjoying the repeated defeats she had given to every attempt of her relations to introduce this young Lady, or that young Lady as a Companion at Sanditon Hall House, she had brought back with her from London last Michaelmas a Miss Brereton, who bid fair by her Merits to vie in favour with Sir Edward, & to secure for herself & her family that share of the accumulated Property which they had certainly the best right to inherit. —

>

After having always protested against any such Addition, and long & often enjoyed the repeated defeats she had given to every attempt of her relations to introduce this young Lady, or that young Lady as a Companion at Sanditon House, she had brought back with her from London last Michaelmas a Miss Brereton, who bid fair by her Merits to vie in favour with Sir Edward, & to secure for herself & her family that share of the accumulated Property which they had certainly the best right to inherit. —

[The word "Companion" here has a specific denotation. "It was common for wealthy families, and particularly wealthy women living alone, to take into their households a gentlewoman in poverty, perhaps a family member, to provide company and companionship in return for her keep... who inhabited an uncomfortable position between employer and servants" (*CUPLM*: 643). Although we never see Clara Brereton at Sanditon House, she is clearly distinct from the housemaids and is rightly taken seriously as a likely heir to Lady Denham's fortune.

"House" is a replacement for "Hall," which at the time "meant that the house had centered on a great hall for entertainment, dining, and ceremonial living on a grand scale.... The term thus connoted both a certain grandeur... and the sort of ancient architecture likely to be associated with an old, august family" (Pool: 195). This was apparently not the kind of home that Jane Austen wanted to give to Lady Denham. The somewhat humbler and perhaps more generic "House" "reflects a period when residential comfort was increasingly of concern, and the period of naming things 'castle,' 'abbey,' or 'manor' was long past" (Pool: 195). Aside from the image produced by the choice of word, the author may have "wished to keep the name consistent with her earlier reference to 'manor and mansion house'" (*CUPLM*: 643).

Michaelmas (MIHK uhl muhs), the feast day of St. Michael the Archangel, falls on September 29. It is one of the four quarter days (the other three are Christmas [December 25], Lady Day [March 25], and Midsummer Day [June 24]) of the year when rents and bills come due. The text does not tell us why Lady Denham has gone to London at this time, but if it was a business matter she would probably want to handle it personally rather than entrust it to an agent. Unlike Sir Walter Elliot, who somewhat extravagantly uses Mr. Shepherd to handle his business, she watches her farthings and pence. Because it is close to the equinox it marks the beginning of autumn. There may be some symbolism here: Acknowledging that her active days are coming to a close (at 70 she is considerably older than most of her contemporaries), Lady Denham must plan on the transfer of her wealth in the near future.

Jane Austen would have had good feelings about Michaelmas after the success of *Pride and Prejudice*, which opens close to that date and ends shortly after one year later. In addition to referring to this holiday twice in *Pride and Prejudice*, she refers to it four times in *Sense and Sensibility*, three times in *Persuasion*, twice in *Mansfield Park* and *Sanditon*, and once in *Emma*.]

M^r. Parker spoke warmly of Clara Brereton, & the interest of his story increased very much with the introduction of such a young Woman.
>
M^r. Parker spoke warmly of Clara Brereton, & the interest of his story increased very much with the introduction of such a Character.

[One can only wonder at Mrs. Parker's reaction to her husband's warm words about a beautiful young woman that the married ladies of Sanditon could well regard as a predatory interloper. The transition from "Woman" to "Character" reflects the influence of Charlotte's imagination in shaping Clara Brereton's role in the unfolding drama. This needy but initiatory young lady—the very prototype of the romantic heroine—is exactly what Charlotte hoped to find among her new story-book acquaintances, just as Catherine Morland sought real-life parallels to the macabre horrors that she had found in her reading.]

Charlotte listened with more than amusement now; — it was solicitude & Enjoyment, as she heard her described to be lovely, amiable, gentle, unassuming, conducting herself uniformly with great good sense, & evidently gaining by her innate worth, on the affections of her Patroness. — Beauty, Sweetness, Poverty & Dependance, do not want the imagination of a Man to operate upon. With due exceptions — Woman feels for Woman very promptly & compassionately. —

He gave the particulars which had led to Clara's admission at Sanditon, as no bad exemplification of that mixture of Character, that union of Littleness with Kindness with Good Sence with even Liberality which he saw in Lady D. — After having avoided London for many years, principally on account of these very Cousins, who were continually writing, inviting & tormenting her, & whom she was determined to keep at a distance, she had been obliged to go there last Michaelmas with the certainty of being detained at least a fortnight. —

She had gone to an Hotel — living by her own account as prudently as possible, to defy the proverbial expensiveness of such a home, & at the end of three Days called for her Bill, that she might judge of her state.
>

She had gone to an Hotel — living by her own account as prudently as possible, to defy the reputed expensiveness of such a home, & at the end of three Days calling for her Bill, that she might judge of her state.

[Lady Denham's electing to stay in a hotel is an unexpected extravagance on her part, perhaps something that she is ready to show in London but not in Sanditon. At this time "hotels" are "'taverns or inns, under a new name, so called from the hotels in Paris, where you may be better accommodated than at the inns in and about London, but at a much greater expence'" (*CUPLM*: 644). This must have been her first experience with an accommodation of this sort since she is staggered by the bill.

The change from "proverbial" to "reputed" is disappointing, but Jane Austen avoids non-literal language whenever possible.]

Its' amount was such as determined her on staying another hour
>
Its' amount was such as determined her on staying not another hour in the House, & she was preparing in great anger & perturbation which a beleif of very gross imposition here,
>
Its' amount was such as determined her on staying not another hour in the House, & she was preparing in great anger & perturbation which a beleif of very gross imposition there, & an ignorance of where to go for better usage, to leave the Hotel at all hazards, when the Cousins, the politic & lucky Cousins, who seemed always to have spy on her, introduced themselves at this important moment, & learning her situation, induced her to accept such a home as their humbler house in very inferior part of London, c^d. offer for the rest of her stay. —
>
Its' amount was such as determined her on staying not another hour in the House, & she was preparing in all the anger & perturbation which a beleif of very gross imposition there, & an ignorance of where to go for better usage, to leave the Hotel at all hazards, when the Cousins, the politic & lucky Cousins, who seemed always to have a spy on her, introduced themselves at this important moment, & learning her situation, persuaded her to accept such a home for the rest of her stay as their humbler house in a very inferior part of London, c^d. offer. —

[I have shown all states of this sentence because it so well supports my theory that at least parts of this manuscript were initially composed on one piece of paper, perhaps a loose sheet, and later transferred to the present booklet. The initial version makes no sense, but it is quickly corrected with the insertion of "not." An additional emendation—the insertion of an initial "t"— turning the original "<u>here</u>" into "<u>there</u>" is additional evidence of an incorrect transcription. The transition from the next-to-the-last to the last version shows other possible transcription errors in the odd phrasings "to have spy on her" and "in very inferior part," both emended by the insertion of "a." In her final review of the line, such a simple passage in principle but one that clearly cost no end of difficulty, she moved "for the rest of her stay" to avoid the excessive alliteration of "home/humbler house," a sequence that would sound particularly funny if the initial "h" was suppressed. The initial "its'" is Jane Austen's usual rendering of the possessive form "its."]

She went; was delighted with her welcome & the hospitality & attention she received from every body — found her good Cousins the B— beyond her expectation worthy people — & finally was impelled by a personal knowledge of their narrow Income & pecuniary difficulties, to invite one of the girls of the family to pass the Winter with her.

The invitation was to <u>one</u>, for six months — with the probability of another being then to take her place; — but in <u>selecting</u> the one, Lady D. had shewn the good part of her Character — for passing by the actual <u>daughters</u> of the House, she had chosen Clara, a Neice —, more helpless & more pitiable of course than any — a dependant on Poverty — an additional Burthen on an encumbered Circle — & one, who had been so low in every worldly veiw, as with all her natural endowments & powers, to have been preparing for situation little better than a Nursery Maid. —

>

The invitation was to <u>one</u>, for six months — with the probability of another being then to take her place; — but in <u>selecting</u> the one, Lady D. had shewn the good part of her Character — for passing by the actual <u>daughters</u> of the House, she had chosen Clara, a Neice —, more helpless & more pitiable of course than any — a dependant on Poverty — an additional Burthen on an encumbered Circle — & one, who had been so low in every worldly veiw, as with all her natural endowments & powers, to have been preparing for a situation little better than a Nursery Maid.

—

[The addition of "a" — "preparing for situation" > "preparing for a situation" — again strengthens my argument that at least parts of the present manuscript have been transcribed from an earlier draft.

A nursery maid was one of the lowest-ranking and poorest-paid domestics in elite households of the period, "receiving perhaps £6 or £8 a year" (*CUPLM*: 644). She worked directly under the nanny, with supportive duties like cleaning the nursery. In some instances she might become a surrogate mother, raising the children of a busy woman or a widower. The future as a governess feared by Jane Fairfax is glorious by comparison.

The parallel between Charlotte and Clara is now established, both having been brought to Sanditon as an act of kindness and both in search of what every single young woman not in possession of a good fortune must be in want of.]

Clara had returned with her — & by her good sense & unpretending manners had now, to all appearance secured a very strong hold in Lady D.'s regard.
>
Clara had returned with her — & by her good sense & sweetness had now, to all appearance secured a very strong hold in Lady D.'s regard.
>
Clara had returned with her — & by her good sense & merit had now, to all appearance secured a very strong hold in Lady D.'s regard.

[I have reproduced all three versions of this sentence because they show Thomas Parker's changing view of Clara Brereton. In the third version her "good sense & merit" is almost an objective description of her behavior, whereas her "good sense & unpretending manners" suggests that he has been watching her closely, an attention that could not please Mrs. Parker. Even worse is "good sense & sweetness," her good sense being clear to all but her sweetness not a trait that a married man with four young children should notice and subsequently be praising in front of his wife to a strange young woman. Clara Brereton clearly has a powerful effect on all the men who encounter her, an effect that she cultivates for maximum advantage over Sir Edward Denham. It is not clear if the author, who has the right to do so, is familiarly calling her character "Clara," or if Mr. Parker, forgetting protocol (and the proximity of Mrs. Parker) has slipped into a less formal manner in speaking of this beautiful young woman who has caught his attention.]

The six months had long been over — & not a syllable was breathed of any change, or exchange. —

[Figurative language—such as the metonymy "not a syllable"—is more frequent in this manuscript than in earlier novels. The author appears to feel a new freedom from the constraints of conventional diction and a readiness to experiment with language.]

She was a general favourite; — the influence of her good Judgement & mild, unassuming, gentle Temper was felt by everybody.

\>

She was a general favourite; — the influence of her steady conduct & mild, gentle Temper was felt by everybody.

[Mr. Parker again seems to step back in his profuse praise of this young woman.]

The prejudices which had met her at first in some quarters, were all dissipated. She was felt to be worthy of Trust — to be the very companion who w^d. guide & soften Lady D — who w^d. enlarge her mind & open her hand. —

[The end of the second line sounds very much in the manner of Mr. Parker's continued efforts to encourage his business partner to be more ready to spend money on their joint enterprise. There may be a significant difference between the verbalized "she was felt" and unspoken "she was."]

She was as thoroughly amiable as she was lovely — & since having had the advantage of their Sanditon Breezes, that Loveliness was complete.

[Mr. Parker would not utter this line about a young woman in the presence of his wife, so it represents our author's summation on the glowing attributes of Miss Clara Brereton. Because of earlier skepticism about the salutary effects of Sanditon and its air, water, and all other natural features, the line carries a good deal of mockery.

Unlike the real-time construction of the opening chapter and the two-week-long summary of the second, this third chapter covers the journey from Willingden to Sanditon. Through a mix of extensive narrative and sparse dialog, Jane Austen gives us the amazing character of Lady Denham, as close to the villain of the piece as any in the extant manuscript. In contrast, we have the beautiful Clara Brereton, who in Charlotte's inner monolog becomes the expected if not the real heroine of the piece.

If there were any evidence that Jane Austen knew the works of Geoffrey Chaucer, one might be tempted to suggest that she has here added a new story to *The Canterbury Tales*, one that supplies information about the much-married Good Wife of Bath.]

[Chapter 4]

Chapter 4.

"And whose very snug-looking Place is this?" — said Charlotte, as in a sheltered Dip within 2 miles of the Sea, they passed close by a moderate-sized house, well fenced & planted, & rich in the Garden, Orchard & Meadows which are the best embellishments of such a Dwelling. "It seems to have as many comforts about it as Willingden." —

[Jane Austen seems not to have been interested in variety in verbs. In a construction where anyone else in completing Charlotte's question would have used "asked," or "queried," or "inquired," or some other verb denoting that it is an interrogative sentence, she uses the colorless verb "said." If she has a script in mind, only the dialog matters.

When Jane Austen writes "garden," she means "fruit and vegetable gardens, rather than flowerbeds, which would form part of the pleasure gardens around a house" (*CUPLM*: 644).

Not surprisingly, Charlotte, with a very limited experience outside her home, compares each new discovery with what she has experienced in Willingden. It is likely that if she ever visits London she will again find that it compares favorably with her small village.]

"Ah! — said M^r. P. — This is my House — the house of my Forefathers — the house where I & all my Brothers & Sisters were born & bred — & where my own 3 eldest Children were born — where M^rs. P. & I lived till within the last 2 years — till our new House was finished. —
>
"Ah! — said M^r. P. — This is my old House — the house of my Forefathers — the house where I & all my Brothers & Sisters were born & bred — & where my own 3 eldest Children were born — where M^rs. P. & I lived till within the last 2 years — till our new House was finished. —

[In saying "This is my House" Mr. Parker is probably stating that he still owns the property and is merely leasing it to Mr. Hillier. H. Abigail Bok correctly, I believe, identifies Mr. and Mrs. Hillier as "the tenants of the

Parkers' old house outside Sanditon" (442) as does the compiler of the List of Characters in the novel in the Kingdom of Pemberley site in citing Hillier as "tenant in Thomas Parker's old house." It is as unlikely that Mr. Hillier could afford to buy this expensive piece of real estate as that Mr. Parker, particularly with brothers and sisters to placate, would permanently dispose of the parental home. In addition, since he inherited it as first-born son, he must in turn pass it on to his first-born son. Identifying it as "the Parkers' former family estate" (Huey: 173) suggests that it has passed out of Thomas Parker's possession, an implausible interpretation of the text.

It is hard to believe that the inserted "old" was not part of an original draft since the word makes the point of the line. Mr. Parker would have to know that saying "This is my house" would mean to Charlotte Heywood that they have reached the end of their journey.]

I am glad you are pleased with it. — It is an honest old Place — and Hillier keeps it in very good order.

I have given it up to the Man who occupies the cheif of my Land.
>
I have given it up you know to the Man who occupies the cheif of my Land.

[The inserted "you know" adds nothing to the meaning of the sentence but helps stamp it as coming out of Thomas Parker's mouth. The parenthetical expression is here literally meaningless since of course Charlotte knows no such thing.]

<u>He</u> gets a better House by it — & I, a rather better situation! — one other ascent brings us to the heart of Sanditon — we shall soon catch the roof of my new house; my real home, — a beautiful Spot. —
>
<u>He</u> gets a better House by it — & I, a rather better situation! — one other Hill brings us to Sanditon — modern Sanditon — a beautiful Spot. —

[The original reading is much fuller but perhaps focuses more on the house itself than on its site, which was what led Mr. Parker to change the location of his residence.]

Our Ancestors, you know always built in a hole. — Here were we, pent down in this little contracted Nook, without Air or Veiw, only one mile &

3 q^{rs}. from the noblest expanse of Ocean between the South foreland & the Land's end, & without the smallest advantage from it. You will not think I have made a bad exchange, when we reach Trafalgar House — which by the bye, I almost wish I had not named Trafalgar — for Waterloo is more the thing now.

[Thomas Parker's rhetoric is meant to convince himself that he has made a wise choice: "Ancestors" suggests old-fashioned and hence in need of updating; "a hole" is never an appealing place to locate a home; "pent down" or "penned or shut up, confined," is a serious condemnation of the location; and who would want to live in a "little contracted Nook," especially one "without Air or Veiw"? Charlotte—and we—might wonder how all the Parkers survived growing up in this horrendous residence and why Mr. Parker allows the Hilliers to live in such an inferior place. As usual, Thomas Parker is exaggerating, perhaps even performing here for the pretty Miss Heywood.

Thomas now turns his rhetoric 90 degrees in relating to Charlotte the superiority of his new home's location. Jane Austen is attributing to Mr. Parker the extravagant claim that his expanse of ocean is the noblest of "the full length of England's south coast from South Foreland near Dover in the east to Land's End at the tip of Cornwall to the west" (*CUPLM*: 644). His frequent use of hyperbole should be kept in mind when he condemns his younger brother, Sidney, for what at the time would have been the normal lifestyle of a young, wealthy, unattached gentleman.

On October 21, 1805, Admiral Horatio Nelson's fleet defeated a combined French and Spanish fleet off Trafalgar, a cape on Spain's southern coast, delivering a crushing blow to Napoleon and assurance to the English that the French could not invade their island.

Ten years later, Napoleon sailed from Elba to attempt a return to power. On June 18, 1815, he attacked the Duke of Wellington's army at Waterloo, a small town near Brussels, only to be defeated again, this time with no choice but to abdicate and return to exile. Reference to this battle is the only internal evidence of the date of the novel, which presumably is set in the summer of 1816. Deirdre Le Faye is confident that "The story begins in June 1816" (2002: 298).

These two references to recent military victories give the lie to the oft-repeated canard that Jane Austen's novels lack reference to the political life of her times. In *Persuasion* and again in this revision of "Susan"/"Catherine," she uses contemporary events for a historic perspective and to create verisimilitude. Alluding to a recent historic event, one that every reader would know well, establishes this novel as reflecting "period, places, manners, books, and opinions" belonging to the present day, in marked contrast to what the Advertisement (written by Jane Austen or someone else) to *Northanger Abbey* promised its readers.

Although Mrs. Parker looks back with nostalgia at her former home, her husband never admits to an error in judgment. His regret extends only to his haste in naming his home "Trafalgar House" when if he had waited only a short time he could have called it the newly sensational "Waterloo House." In observing that "with no financial embarrassment to impel him, [Mr. Thomas Parker] abandons the home of his forefathers and builds himself a new house whose name, Trafalgar House, he is already starting to regret" (2007: 233), Claire Lamont focuses on his significant weakness of impetuosity with the subsequent regret that often follows acts undertaken without full consideration of their consequences. It is only one small step from regret at the choice of name for the new house to regret that he moved in the first place.]

However, Waterloo is in reserve — & if we have encouragement enough this year for the little Crescent to be ventured on — (as I trust we shall), & a Crescent is a building that always takes —) then, we shall be able to call it Waterloo Crescent — & the very name will give us choice of Lodgers. —
>
However, Waterloo is in reserve — & if we have encouragement enough this year for a little Crescent to be ventured on — (as I trust we shall), then, we shall be able to call it Waterloo Crescent — & the name joined to the form of the Building, which always takes, will give us the command of Lodgers —.

[The original version sounds garbled, perhaps from inaccurate transcription.

"The great debt to the spas is still visible in many old-established English seaside resorts; their Regency crescents and terraces echo those built decades earlier in Bath or Buxton" (Howell: 18). The beautiful Royal Crescent in Bath, built between 1767 and 1775, can hardly be called "little," but Mr.

Parker is probably determined to out-build it in size and architectural splendor.]

In a good Season We sh^d. have more applications than we could attend to." —

"It was always a very comfortable House — said M^{rs}. Parker — looking through the back window with a great deal of something like the fondness of regret. —

>

"It was always a very comfortable House — said M^{rs}. Parker — looking at it through the back window with something like the fondness of regret. —

[This account of Mrs. Parker's facial expression may be filtered through Charlotte. In the revised version she sees only a mild regret on her hostess's part for the change of home-site.]

And such a nice Garden — such an excellent Garden."

"Yes, my Love, but <u>that</u> we may be said to carry with us. — <u>It</u> supplies us, as before, with all the fruit & vegetables we want; & we have in fact all the comfort of an excellent Kitchen Garden, without the constant Eyesore of its formalities; or the yearly nuisance of its decaying vegetation. — Who can endure a Cabbage Bed in October"?

[By "formalities" Jane Austen may mean "outward form or appearance" or "the formal rows and squares" of the vegetables and fruit trees (*CUPLM*: 646).

Despite Mr. Parker's low opinion of cabbage, it was a popular culinary staple, "often boiled as a whole head and served in one gigantic lump, sometimes with interior hollowed out and filled with forcemeat, or with forcemeat layered between the leaves" (Olsen: 282).]

"Oh! dear — yes. — We are quite as well off now for Gardenstuff as we used to be — for if it is forgot to be brought at any time, we can always buy what we want at Sanditon-House. —

>

"Oh! dear — yes. — and We are quite as well off for Gardenstuff as ever we were — for if it is forgot to be brought at any time, we can always buy what we want at Sanditon-House. —

>

"Oh! dear — yes. — We are quite as well off for Gardenstuff as ever we were — for if it is forgot to be brought at any time, we can always buy what we want at Sanditon-House. —

[This sequence is interesting in showing how ready Jane Austen was to remove an added word, in this instance the unnecessary "and." Her care here and elsewhere in the manuscript to balance each sentence and rewrite until completely satisfied with the results belies the claims by critics that they detect a falling-off of her powers in this last year of her life.]

The Gardiner there, is glad enough to supply us —. But it was a nice place for the Children to run about in. So shady in Summer! —"

"My dear, we shall have shade enough & more than enough about us in the course of a very few years; — My Plantations astonish everybody by their Growth.

>

"My dear, we shall have shade enough on the Hill & more than enough in the course of a very few years; —The Growth of my Plantations is a general astonishment.

[The revised version reflects the occasional pomposity that Mr. Parker assumes in speaking of his belongings, in this instance the fine trees on the property.]

In the mean while we have the Canvas Awning, which gives us the most complete comfort within doors — & you can get a Parasol at Whitby's for little Mary at any time, or a large Bonnet at Jebb's — and as for the Boys, I must say I w^d. rather <u>them</u> run about in the Sunshine than not. I am sure we agree my dear, in wishing our Boys to be as hardy as possible." —

[Canvas awnings, "evidently mounted against the windows of the house, [provided a] form of shelter [that] had recently been adapted from [their] use on board ship" (*CUPLM*: 646).

Among the many things for sale at Mrs. Whitby's library are parasols, "introduced into Britain from south and south-east Asia, and… fashionable in the early nineteenth century for women to carry to protect the skin from sunshine and maintain a desirable paleness of complexion" (*CUPLM*: 646). Probably on the basis of the information that one can buy parasols at "Whitby's," H. Abigail Bok suggests that is was "originally a general store in

Sanditon run by the Whitby family; Mrs. Whitby added a lending library to it" (489).

We learn here that the millinery shop belongs to "Jebb," possibly Mrs. or Miss Jebb since it was generally a female profession. Just as the library, owned and run by Mrs. Whitby, is referred to as "Whitby's," so the millinery shop goes as mere "Jebb's" even if it is operated by Mrs. Jebb. The placement of the apostrophe in the manuscript (folio 18r) is uncertain. Chapman and I read the entry as "Jebb's," in contrast to a plural possessive "Jebbs'" in Sacco (45) and *CUPLM* (430). The surname "Jebb" is not uncommon, whereas "Jebbs" seems to be unusual.

Mr. Parker's construction "I w^d. rather <u>them</u> run about" may be meant to show his poor sense of language or it may have been acceptable at the time. It may be an abbreviated form of "I would rather have them run about."]

"Yes indeed, I am sure we do — & I will get Mary a little Parasol, which will make her so proud!
>
"Yes indeed, I am sure we do — & I will get Mary a little Parasol, which will make her as proud as can be!

[Mrs. Parker occasionally follows her husband's practice of expanding dialog without saying anything new.]

It will be delightful to see her walking about with it, so gravely. — She will fancy herself quite a little Woman. —
>
How Grave she will walk about with it, and fancy herself quite a little Woman. —

[The poor grammar—"Grave" substituted for "gravely"—indicates Mrs. Parker's inadequate education. Jane Austen is very sensitive to the literacy level of her characters as expressed through their dialog.]

Oh! I have not the smallest doubt of our being a great deal better off where we are now. If we any of us want to bathe, we have not a q^r. of a mile to go. — But you know, (still looking back) one loves to look at an old friend, at a place where one has been happy. —

[After the solecism of the preceding sentence, Mrs. Parker successfully negotiates the possessive pronoun before a gerund in "our being." "Bathe," of course, means immersion in the nearby sea. It is hardly surprising that Mrs. Parker occasionally inserts the familiar "you know" that characterizes her husband's lines.]

The Hilliers did not seem to feel the Storms last Winter as we did. —
>
The Hilliers did not seem to feel the Storms last Winter at all. —

I remember seeing M^rs. Hillier after one of those dreadful Nights, when <u>we</u> had been literally rocked in our bed, and she did not seem at all aware of the Wind being anything more than common."

[Here Mrs. Parker misses the possessive preceding a gerund in "the Wind being," but the more correct construction would be very formal for this level of friendly conversation. We never learn about her education, but it is presumably no more extensive than that of other women of her class. This calm discussion of stormy weather hardly prepares us for Sir Edward's later rhapsodies on the excitements of meteorological events.]

"Yes, yes — that's likely enough.

[Jane Austen rarely uses contractions like "that's," probably meant here to indicate Mr. Parker's lack of a formal education.]

<u>We</u> have all the Grandeur of the Storm, with less real danger, because the Wind meeting nothing to oppose or confine it around our House, simply rages & passes on — while down in this Pit,
>
<u>We</u> have all the Grandeur of the Storm, with less real danger, because the Wind meeting nothing to oppose or confine it around our House, simply rages & passes on — while down in this Gutter — nothing is known of the state of the Air, below the Tops of the Trees — and the Inhabitants may be taken totally unawares, if one of those dreadful Currents should pour through the Valley, which do more mischeif than an open Country ever knows
>
<u>We</u> have all the Grandeur of the Storm, with less real danger, because the Wind meeting nothing to oppose or confine it around our House, simply rages & passes on — while down in this Gutter — nothing is known of the state of the Air, below the Tops of the Trees — and the Inhabitants may be taken totally unawares, if one of those dreadful Currents should pour

through the Valley, which do more mischeif than an open Country ever experiences in the heaviest Gale. —

>

<u>We</u> have all the Grandeur of the Storm, with less real danger, because the Wind meeting with nothing to oppose or confine it around our House, simply rages & passes on — while down in this Gutter — nothing is known of the state of the Air, below the Tops of the Trees — and the Inhabitants may be taken totally unawares, by any of those dreadful Currents which do more mischief when they <u>do</u> arise in a Valley, when they <u>do</u> arise than an open Country ever experiences in the heaviest Gale. —

>

<u>We</u> have all the Grandeur of the Storm, with less real danger, because the Wind meeting with nothing to oppose or confine it around our House, simply rages & passes on — while down in this Gutter — nothing is known of the state of the Air, below the Tops of the Trees — and the Inhabitants may be taken totally unawares, by one of those dreadful Currents which do more mischief in a Valley, when they <u>do</u> arise than an open Country ever experiences in the heaviest Gale. —

[I have shown all states of this sentence to illustrate again how much attention Jane Austen pays to the minutiae of phrasing and balance. There is no indication here of a failing mind. Mr. Parker is very much attuned to the new Romantic movement in his view that rather than carrying danger, storms have grandeur.]

But my dear Love — as to Gardenstuff; — you were saying that any accidental omission is supplied in a moment by Ly D.'s Gardiner — but it occurs to me that we ought to deal with all our

>

But my dear Love — as to Gardenstuff; — you were saying that any accidental omission is supplied in a moment by Ly D.'s Gardiner — but it occurs to me that we ought to get

>

But my dear Love — as to Gardenstuff; — you were saying that any accidental omission is supplied in a moment by Ly D.'s Gardiner — but it occurs to me that we ought to go elsewhere upon such occasions — & that old Salmon & his son have a higher claim.

>

But my dear Love — as to Gardenstuff; — you were saying that any accidental omission is supplied in a moment by Ly D.'s Gardiner — but it occurs to me that we ought to go elsewhere upon such occasions — & that old Stringer & his son have a higher claim.

[And the next sentence shows the same attention to detail, including a last-minute change of name from "Salmon" to "Stringer."]

I encouraged him to set up — & am afraid he does not do very well — that is, there has not been time enough yet. —

He <u>will</u> do very well — but at first it is Uphill work; and therefore we must give him what encouragement we can — & when any Vegetables or fruit happen to be wanted — & it will not be amiss to have them forgotten, to have something or other forgotten most days; — Just to have a nominal supply you know, that poor old Andrew may not lose his daily Job — but in fact to buy the cheif of our consumption of the Stringers. —"
>
He <u>will</u> do very well beyond a doubt — but at first it is Uphill work; and therefore we must give him what Help we can — & when any Vegetables or fruit happen to be wanted — & it will not be amiss to have them often wanted, to have something or other forgotten most days; — Just to have a nominal supply you know, that poor old Andrew may not lose his daily Job — but in fact to buy the cheif of our consumption of the Stringers. —"

"Very well my Love, that can easily done
>
"Very well my Love, that can be easily done — & Cook will be satisfied I hope — which will be a great comfort, for she is always complaining of old Andrew now, he never brings her what she wants. —
>
"Very well my Love, that can be easily done — & Cook will be satisfied — which will be a great comfort, for she is always complaining of old Andrew now, & says he never brings her what she wants. —

[The first version again suggests incorrect transcription from an earlier draft. And the revised version also sounds incomplete without the finally added "& says." Every household of quality had a cook, and in the better households she is often known simply as "Cook." Some cooks doubled as housekeepers, but there is no evidence of such an arrangement in the Parker home.]

There — now the old House is quite out of
>
There — now the old House is quite left behind. —

[The revised version loses some of the dramatic visual effect suggested by the original "quite out of (sight)," but it gives a better sense that the carriage is in motion. We are rapidly approaching the physical core of the novel.]

What is it, your Brother Sidney says about its' being a Hospital?"

[Sidney, ever healthy and vigorous, grew up in a household with two older sisters dedicated to self-medication for imagined illnesses and a sickly younger brother.]

"Oh! my dear Mary, merely a Joke of his. Sidney says any thing you know.
>
"Oh! my dear Mary, merely a Joke of his. He pretends to advise me to make a Hospital of it. He pretends to laugh at my Improvements. Sidney says any thing you know.

[The inserted sentences are of interest because Jane Austen takes special care in developing the character of Sidney Parker, her destined hero, who will not appear personally—and even then for only a brief moment—for several chapters. Mr. Parker feels very comfortable with Charlotte in addressing his wife as "Mary," the common practice being a more formal "Mrs. Parker."]

He has always said what he chose of his eldest B^r— & to his Eldest B^r &
>
He has always said what he chose of & to us, all.

[The revised version is only marginally less awkward than its original.]

A young Man of Abilities & Address, & general ease of manner Miss H. — who says anything
>
Most Families have such a member among them I beleive Miss Heywood. — There is a someone in most families who is privileged to say anything.
>
Most Families have such a member among them I beleive Miss Heywood. — There is a someone in most families privileged by superior abilities or spirits to say anything.

[All versions of lines introducing us to Sidney Parker merit close reading since Jane Austen is careful in preparing the reader for this new version of Henry Tilney. Like his literary predecessor, lightly censured by his sister Eleanor for his waggish tongue, the middle Parker brother has given himself the privilege of untrammeled speech. If we had had the privilege of reading the shelved manuscript of "Susan"/"Catherine," upon arriving at this passage in the unfinished manuscript we would have spotted immediately that Jane Austen has used the same material to a similar effect. In the earlier work, Elinor Tilney berates her brother (who may have indicated to his sister directly or inadvertently some interest in young Catherine) for his waggish tongue:

> "Henry," said Miss Tilney, "you are very impertinent. Miss Morland, he is treating you exactly as he does his sister. He is forever finding fault with me, for some incorrectness of language, and now he is taking the same liberty with you. The word 'nicest,' as you used it, did not suit him; and you had better change it as soon as you can, or we shall be overpowered with Johnson and Blair all the rest of the way." (253)

In this later reworking of the material, Thomas Parker similarly affectionately censures his brother to a young woman who he must know is single and in need of a husband. Jane Austen's indebtedness to her own work and her ability to improve upon what in the earlier novel is perfection are ample testimony to the healthy state of her mind in early 1817 despite her physical decline.]

Sidney is very clever
>
In ours, it is Sidney; who is a very clever Young Man, — very lively, very pleasant — living very much in the World & liked by everybody. I should
>
In ours, it is Sidney; who is a very clever Young Man, — and with great powers of pleasing. — He lives too much in the World to be settled; that is his only fault. — I wish we may
>
In ours, it is Sidney; who is a very clever Young Man, — and with great powers of pleasing. — He lives too much in the World to be settled; that is his only fault. — He is here & there & every where. I wish we may get him to Sanditon.

[With all his faults, Sidney Parker is an admirable young man much esteemed by his family, and his presence in Sanditon is seen by his older brother as a powerful asset in attracting the right crowd by bringing to the resort the ton with which he associates. That Sidney wants to be "here & there & every where" may be a family trait shared with his older brother.]

I should like to have you acquainted with him. —

[And so Mr. Parker hopes to play the role assumed by Mr. King in *Northanger Abbey* in introducing our young couple.]

And it would be a credit to the Place! —
>
And it would be a fine thing for the Place! —

Such a young Man as Sidney, with his neat equipage & fashionable air, — You & I Mary, know what effect it might have:" Many a respectable Family, many a careful Mother, many a pretty Daughter, might it secure us, to the prejudice of E. Bourne & Hastings." —

[We are here prepared for the "neat equipage" —in marked contrast to what Sir Edward can claim—of which Sidney is master when he arrives in the twelfth chapter.

The quoted material may have originally been meant to end with "it might have," and upon continuing the speech the author neglected to remove the terminal double quotation marks. The "careful Mother" and her "pretty Daughter" in close conjunction with Sidney Parker suggests that his brother regards him as somewhat of a ladies' man, a description that he may perhaps better apply to himself.

Or possibly the second half of this passage is spoken by Mrs. Parker, Jane Austen having failed to insert quotation marks:

Such a young Man as Sidney, with his neat equipage & fashionable air, — You & I Mary, know what effect it might have:" "Many a respectable Family, many a careful Mother, many a pretty Daughter, might it secure us, to the prejudice of E. Bourne & Hastings." —

Mr. Parker, however, is far more likely to have observed the pretty daughters of Sanditon, and he is even more foolish than generally regarded to talk about them in front of his wife.

Exactly who these pretty daughters are is left unclear. They may be residents of Sanditon, who appear to be mostly invisible in the text, or visitors, none of whom we meet except for a brief glance at the Misses Beaufort.]

They were now approaching the Church & village of original Sanditon, which stood at the foot of the Down they were afterwards to ascend — a Hill, whose side was covered with the Woods & enclosures of Sanditon House but whose Top was an open Down overlooking the Sea.
>
They were now approaching the Church & real village of Sanditon, which stood at the foot of the Hill they were afterwards to ascend — a Hill, whose side was covered with the Woods & enclosures of Sanditon House and whose Height ended in an open Down where the new Build$^{gs.}$ might soon be looked for.

[This reference to a church, however normal in such a village, is the only overt nod to religion in the manuscript. Of the men in Mrs. Whitby's subscription book, the Reverend Mr. Hanking is obviously a man of the cloth as is probably Mr. Brown. There is no indication if either is living in Sanditon and assigned to the village church or a summer visitor.

The topographical detail here is in marked contrast to Jane Austen's earlier generalities about the appearance of locations.

As noted in *Jane Austen Caught in the Act of Greatness* (337), whereas R.W. Chapman suggests "neat village" as the revision of "original village," I am confident that the true reading is "real village." Although difficult to decipher, the word is similar to a very legible "real" elsewhere in the manuscript. *CUPLM* agrees that the word is "real" (435).]

A branch only, of the Valley, wound towards the Sea, giving a passage to an inconsiderable Stream, & forming at its mouth, a 3^d Habitable Division, in a small cluster of Fisherman's Houses. —
>
A branch only, of the Valley, winding more obliquely towards the Sea, gave a passage to an inconsiderable Stream, & formed at its mouth, a 3^d Habitable Division, in a small cluster of Fisherman's Houses. —

[The original and its revision offer a fascinating glimpse into the delicacy of phrasing that Jane Austen could achieve through balancing conjugated verbs and participles. Is it only my imagination that "winding" is far more suggestive of the appearance and motion of the stream than the mundane "wound"? I think not. And the added "obliquely" does a great deal to create a mental picture, something that Jane Austen rarely strives for.]

The Village contained little more than Cottages, but the Spirit of the day had been caught, as M^r. P. observed with delight to Charlotte, & two or three of the best of them were smartened up with a white Curtain & "Lodgings to let" —, and farther on, in the little Green Court of an old Farm House, two Females in elegant white were actually to be seen with their books & camp stools — and in turning the corner of the Baker's shop, the sound of a Harp might be heard through the upper Casement. —

[And so our travelers—and we—have arrived in Sanditon, where art and music are enlisted by elegant young women as part of their arsenal in securing husbands. White was very much in style at the time, and most of the unmarried ladies in the novel can be assumed to be wearing that fashionable color, which also proclaimed their chastity. Although the setting is on the other side of the Atlantic and somewhat later in the century, Angela L. Miller well describes the typical scene: "The tiny figure of the painter who appears with easel, campstool, and umbrella in the right foreground of the painting is a portrait of Cole himself" (118). By "books" Jane Austen probably means drawing books or sketch pads, not novels, which the young ladies are unlikely to be reading out of doors, especially on uncomfortable folding stools, designed for artistic pursuits rather than leisure. The harp, favored by young ladies like Mary Crawford, was enjoying great popularity at the time as an instrument of choice to show off musical talents and physical attractions. The Misses Beaufort will find upon arriving in Sanditon that their rivals in artistic and musical skills are already here in full force. Wilks (75) offers a scene that would have been typical in Jane Austen's day of a young woman and her musical trawling for a husband.]

Such sights & sounds were highly exhilarating to M^r. P. —
>
Such sights & sounds were highly Blissful to M^r. P. —

Not that he had any personal concern in the success of the Village itself; for considering it as too remote from the Beach, he had done nothing there — but it was a most valuable proof of the increasing fashion of the place altogether.

[A great deal of this material is reported speech, Mr. Parker's dialog converted into narrative.]

If the <u>Village</u> could attract, the Hill must be nearly full.
>
If the <u>Village</u> could attract, the Hill might be nearly full.

At the same time last year, (late in July) there had not been a single Lodger in the Village! — nor did he remember any the whole Season, excepting one family of children who came from London for sea air after the hooping Cough, but whose Mother c^d not bear to have them nearer for fear of their tumbling in. —
>
At the same time last year, (late in July) there had not been a single Lodger in the Village! — nor did he remember any during the whole Summer, excepting one family of children who came from London for sea air after the hooping Cough, and whose Mother would not let them be nearer the shore for fear of their tumbling in. —

[This passage is just a short step away from indirect discourse. If it is now late in July, the story could open at the beginning of July, making it just possible that the novel is set in 1815 rather than 1816 despite the unlikelihood that a battle won as recently as June 18, 1815, would lend its name to real estate. The argument for 1815 is even weaker if Deirdre Le Faye is right in asserting that "the story begins in June 1816" (2002: 298), presumably late enough in the month that the hay is ready to be mowed.

Hooping cough (that is, whooping cough) is a contagious disease characterized by convulsive coughs. "It was believed that one of the most effective remedies was a change or air... and a trip to the seaside was desirable" (*CUPLM*: 648). The word was variably written with or without the initial "w."]

"Civilization, Civilization indeed! — cried M^r. P—, delighted —.

[One of Jane Austen's favorite verbs is "to cry," denoting merely an exclamation of some intensity.]

Look my dear Mary — Look at old Heeley's windows. —
>
Look my dear Mary — Look at William Heeley's windows. —

[The change may indicate Mr. Parker's familiarity with the shopkeeper or a sense of propriety that referring to someone as "old" is discourteous.]

Blue Shoes, & nankin Boots! —

[High fashion has arrived in Sanditon, blue shoes "from the 1790s [having] become fashionable for women, replacing the more serviceable black shoes which had previously been worn" (*CUPLM*: 648).

> Half boots were designed for morning wear and especially for walking outdoors. Their increasing adoption by women as walking shoes is reflected in their appearance in three of the later novels, *Emma, Persuasion,* and *Sanditon.* In the example from *Sanditon,* they are made of "nankin" or nankeen, which was a sturdy yellow-brown or buff cotton fabric named for Nanking, China. Lord Osborne [*The Watsons*], in his recommendation of nankin boots, suggests not unreasonably that they be "galoshed with black," that is, partially covered with black leather. (Olsen: 635)

Nankin boots were "more a fashion boot than a boot for muddy lanes" (Drabble: 217), so only wealthy ladies would wear them.]

Who w^d. have expected such a sight in old Sanditon! — Glorious indeed! —

>

Who w^d. have expected such a sight at a Shoemaker's in old Sanditon! — Glorious indeed! —

>

Who w^d. have expected such a sight at a Shoemaker's in old Sanditon! — This is new within the Month. There was no blue Shoe when we passed this way a month ago. — Glorious indeed! —

[All this attention to expanding the text—adding and padding in contrast to lopping and cropping—indicates Jane Austen's sharp-minded interest in supplying details as well as Mr. Parker's effusive garrulousness and redundancy when discoursing on his favorite topic.]

Well, I think I <u>have</u> done something in my Day. — Now, for our Hill, our health-breathing Hill. —" In ascending, they passed the Lodge-Gates of Sanditon House, & saw the top of the House itself among its Groves.

It was the last Building of old erection in that line of the Parish.
>
It was the last Building of former Days in that line of the Parish.

A little higher up, the Modern began; & in crossing the Down, a Prospect House, a Bellevue Cottage, & a Denham Place were to be looked at by Charlotte with the calmness of amused Curiosity, & by M^r. P. with the eager eye which hoped to see scarcely any empty houses. —

[The mix of English "Prospect" and the French "Bellevue"—to some extent meaning the same thing in this context—would probably not have taken place if the British were still engaged in a war with their enemy on the other side of the Channel. Denham Place is not to be confused with Denham Park, the residence of Sir Edward and Miss Esther, but a new construction named after the family, perhaps by Lady Denham.]

More Bills at the Window than he had reckoned on; — fewer and a smaller shew of company on the Hill — Fewer Carriages, fewer Walkers.
>
More Bills at the Window than he had calculated on; — and a smaller shew of company on the Hill — Fewer Carriages, fewer Walkers.

[That visitors are not flocking to Sanditon is reflected in the bills, or advertisements of available rooms, on many of the newly constructed houses.

The change avoids repetition of "fewer." If the sentence is not indirect discourse it at least conveys Mr. Parker's sensory reaction to the scene before him more than the author's narration.]

He had fancied it just the time of day for them to be all returning from their Airings to dinner — but there were the Sands — the Sands always attracted some —. Tide must be flowing — about half in. —
>
He had fancied it just the time of day for them to be all returning from their Airings to dinner — But the Sands & the Terrace always attracted some —. and the Tide must be flowing — about half-Tide now. —

[The revised version is less stream-of-consciousness than the original. Jane Austen is creating a new prose style for herself here, but she is essentially conservative and checks herself from excessive looseness of form.]

He longed to be on the Sands, the Cliffs, at his own House, & everywhere out of his House at once.

[Like his younger brother, Thomas Parker wants to be "here & there & every where." The two older brothers and Diana Parker share this need for nonstop activity. Susan Parker may have at one time also been all over the place. Poor Arthur, of course, has always been the slow-moving member of the family.]

His Spirits rose with the very sight of the Sea & c^d — almost feel his Ancle getting stronger already. —
>
His Spirits rose with the very sight of the Sea & he c^d — almost feel his Ancle getting stronger already. —

[The added "he" is more than just an emendation but a necessary pronoun to make grammatical sense. This may be another example of a line that was incorrectly transcribed.]

Trafalgar House, on the most elevated spot of any, was an elegant Building, separated from the Down only by a
>
Trafalgar House, on the most elevated spot of any, was an elegant Building, standing in a small Lawn with very young plantations over it, not an hundred yards from the brow of the Cliff, which was
>
Trafalgar House, on the most elevated spot of any, was an elegant Building, standing in a small Lawn with very young plantations over it, not an hundred yards from the brow of a steep, but not lofty Cliff — and the nearest to it, of every Building, excepting one row of smart-looking Houses, called the Terrace, with a broad walk in front, aspiring to be the Mall of the Place.
>
Trafalgar House, on the most elevated spot on the Down was a light elegant Building, standing in a small Lawn with a very young plantation round it, about an hundred yards from the brow of a steep, but not very lofty Cliff — and the nearest to it, of every Building, excepting one short row of smart-looking Houses, called the Terrace, with a broad walk in front, aspiring to be the Mall of the Place.

[As we would expect, Jane Austen works carefully on this initial description of Trafalgar House, the new Parker residence. "The terrace was another form of building which came into fashion towards the end of the eighteenth century, much favoured by the new spa and seaside resorts: a terrace denoted a line of houses, attached to each other, and raised up from the natural street level in order to provide a wide walkway outside, as a formal promenade" (*CUPLM*: 649). "Mall" is here used in the sense of "a sheltered walk serving as a promenade" (*OED*) rather than a shopping street, which is "Chiefly *N. Amer., Austral.*, and *N.Z.*" (*OED*).]

In this row were the best Milliner's shop

["During the 18th century, milliners took the hat-making art out of the home and established the millinery profession. Today, a 'milliner' defines a person associated with the profession of hat making. In the 18th century however, a milliner was more of a stylist. Traditionally a woman's occupation, the milliner not only created hats or bonnets to go with costumes but also chose the laces, trims and accessories to complete an ensemble. The term 'milliner' comes from the Italian city of Milan, where in the 1700's, the finest straws were braided and the best quality hat forms were made" ("The History of Women's Hats).

In the milliner's shop (amusingly illustrated in Wilks: 65), fashionable ladies could buy "lace, ribbons, accessories and knick-knacks as well as hats" (*CUPLM*: 649). Few items of clothing were closer to the hearts of early nineteenth-century ladies than their headgear.

> Outdoors, women wore hats or bonnets. The technical difference between them was that hats had a brim all the way around, while bonnets had no brim in back, or only the barest hint of a brim. Hats and bonnets came in many styles and were made of many materials. Hats and bonnets for walking outdoors, for example, could be soft and made of muslin, beaver, or velvet; or, quite commonly, stiffer and made of straw decorated with sewn-on or pinned-on ribbons. (Olsen: 349-350)

A very stylish lady might combine various elements, wearing "a straw bonnet trimmed with green ribbon over a lace mob cap" ("1795–1820 in Fashion").

Very much interested in remaining à la mode, Jane Austen frequently mentions bonnets in her letters. For example, in one of her earliest preserved letters, dated Tuesday/Wednesday, December 18/19, 1798, she expands at length to Cassandra on her plans for her newest bonnet:

> I took the liberty a few days ago of asking your Black velvet Bonnet to lend me its cawl [caul, net], which it very readily did, & by which I have been enabled to give a considerable improvement of dignity to my Cap, which was before too *nidgetty* to please me.—I shall wear it on Thursday, but I hope you will not be offended with me for following your advice as to its ornaments only in part—I still venture to retain the narrow silver round it, put twice round without any bow, & instead of the black military feather shall put in the Coquelicot one, as being smarter;—& besides Coquelicot is to be all the fashion this winter.—After the Ball, I shall probably make it entirely black. (*Letters*: 25–26)

Many years later, writing to Cassandra on Thursday, April 18, 1811, she is still preoccupied with details of her newest extravagant purchase:

> Miss Burton has made me a very pretty little Bonnet—& now nothing can satisfy me but I must have a straw hat, of the riding hat shape… & a young woman in this Neighbourhood is actually making me one. I am really very shocking; but it will not be dear at a Guinea. (*Letters*: 180)

We never learn how many millinery shops there are in Sanditon, but Mr. Parker earlier recommended to his wife that she buy "a large Bonnet at Jebb's"—presumably "the best Milliner's shop"—for little Mary.]

& the Library —

[The "lending library… , besides books, newspapers and magazines, had all the functions of a gift shop, corner store and stationers combined. It was the social centre of the town—here one registered one's arrival, looked for the names of old acquaintances, met friends, planned expeditions, shared gossip and news" (Sutherland, 1997: 66). In Wilks (76) we see a very large circulating library, well filled with patrons and their dogs.

> The circulating libraries made reading fashionable when books were very expensive. By 1800, most copies of a novel's edition were sold to the libraries, which were flourishing businesses to be found in every major English city and town, and which promoted the sale

of books during a period when their price rose relative to the cost of living. The libraries created a market for the publishers' product and encouraged readers to read more by charging them an annual subscription fee that would entitle them to check out a specified number of volumes at one time. (Erickson: 573)

The library has a double function in this novel, as metaphor and as the core of the social and intellectual scene in Sanditon. As metaphor, it is the place of dreams and the nurturing of economic and romantic fantasies. The books and the characters in them are as unreal as the aspirations of the dramatis personae. In its second function, the library is the central meeting place, the final point of convergence, of the major characters who are destined to assemble in the village of Sanditon.

Without being specific about its function, David Selwyn has likewise pointed out the special role played by this library, "the only shop that Jane Austen created to exist, as it were, in its own right, to play its part in expressing the meaning of the work" (2007: 223). Replacing other possible common-ground institutions, like the church or town hall, it offers a full range of opportunities for good or ill, books filled with life-enhancing or misleading information, and items of use or vanity. Thus like the fair field full of folk celebrated by William Langland's anonymous narrator, Mrs. Whitby's emporium is a place of assembly in which significant decisions are made, choices that will determine the outcome of the novel.

Sir Edward has here in the circulating library found the poems that cloud his mind as well as the novels whose libertine "heroes" have befuddled the little bit of intelligence that he possesses into the notion that he is destined to walk in their boots. Charlotte enters with the certainty of virtue in rejecting Fanny Burney's novel about youthful romantic entanglements, only to find a real-life "heroine" in her circle of new acquaintances, a young woman who shortly thereafter is detected in a tryst directly borrowed from a sensationalist work of fiction. We have yet to see how other characters have been affected by the works available on Mrs. Whitby's crowded shelves. Even Mr. Thomas Parker has been influenced by the wares of this collection in referencing Cowper during his conversation with Mr. Heywood. No one is safe from the influence of the library—Sanditon in metaphor—as source of new and frequently insidious ideas. Sanditon is in turn a microcosm of English Regency society—which is, needless to say, in Jane Austen's view a microcosm of the civilized world.

A feature of the watering-place is the library, from which Isabella Thorpe at Bath obtained the novels with astonishing titles which so alarmed and delighted Catherine Morland. Novels are the main supply of libraries, and supply primarily the wants of women. They are obtained by an annual subscription of up to one guinea for membership and a small payment of a penny for each volume borrowed. (Craik: 137)

Resorts vied with one another for visitors, so a range of amenities had to be provided. Daily life at a watering place generally followed a pattern. Bathing very early in the morning was followed by a walk or ride along the cliffs or downs, or a stroll in the public gardens. Much of the social life of the day was centred on the circulating libraries (in Brighton, Fishers and Donaldsons). These were not only lenders of books, but centres for men and women to gossip, read current periodicals and shop. Lydia, obviously not a great reader, writes to her mother that "they were just returned from the library, where such and such officers had attended them, and where she had seen such beautiful ornaments as made her quite wild." Since they were places where patrons loitered, they also became places for casual meeting and conversation, and even assignations. (Jones: 2003)

As a mundane business enterprise in the village of Sanditon, Mrs. Whitby's subscription library is part of an important growing trend at the time to make books available to the reading public at an affordable price. By the end of the eighteenth century, which saw the development of the novel into what became and has remained the dominant form of fiction in our language, literacy was a given. But merely being able to read does not guarantee access to this outpouring from the press since prices of books kept them beyond the reach of the average reader.

It was these impecunious booklovers who were in some degree responsible for the development of the circulating library, the principal means by which the eighteenth-century reader circumvented the high purchase price of books. (Altick, 1957: 59)

Some unknown person of deep intelligence and imagination came up with a new concept, that it might not be necessary to invest the large amounts of cash required to acquire books.

The first real circulating library in Britain seems to have been that of Allan Ramsay, the poet and ex-wigmaker of Edinburgh, who began to rent books from his shop in 1725. Within a very few years circulating libraries appeared at some of the spas, where books were ideal to relieve the boredom of taking the waters. (Altick, 1957: 59–60)

What was good for the people of Scotland was surely just as good for the people to the south in England, and so "the circulating library... arrive[d] in the capital [in] the early 1740's" (Altick, 1957: 60).

From these beginnings, the practice of lending books on a subscription basis developed into two quite separate kinds of libraries during the remainder of the [eighteenth] century.... These were either separate institutions or collections attached to the "literary and philosophical societies" that sprang up in the larger towns during the second half of the century, and they were important agencies for the extension of learning among the better-educated portion of the middle and upper classes.

But far more important to the growth of the mass reading audience were the commercial libraries that dispensed fiction and other "light literature." While it may have been only a coincidence that a few obscure book and pamphlet vendors were experimenting with the lending of their wares at the very time of the *Pamela* craze, the circulating library was destined shortly to complete the triangle whose other legs were the expanded middle-class audience and the new fascination of the novel. As the fiction-reading habit spread, circulating libraries sprang up in London, the watering places, the provincial towns, and even in small villages. (Altick, 1957: 60–61)

. . .

In 1801 there were said to be 1,000 circulating libraries in England. (Erickson: 574)

In a classic instance of the chicken and the egg, we see the simultaneous establishment of the novel as the staple of the general reading public and the business acumen of shopkeepers who saw that there was a good living to be had from stocking and lending—rather than selling—samples of this new form of domestic entertainment.

> It was the circulating libraries' chief stock in trade, the ordinary novel, that, more than any other form of literature, helped democratize reading in the eighteenth century. (Altick, 1957: 62–63)

Like a self-fulfilling prophecy, the novel in the form that we know it today thereby became the most popular form of modern literature.

> Then, when the writing and sale of fiction became the occupation of hacks and booksellers who cultivated a shrewd awareness of the special interests and limitations of their semi-educated audience, the novel became the favorite fare of the common reader, a distinction it has had ever since. (Altick. 1957: 63)

As expected, this appealing new way to acquire the newest fictional publications along with many other amenities quickly spread beyond London.

> Circulating libraries were a feature of most sizable towns. Often run by people who ran a side-business such a bookbinding or trinket-selling, they served not only as libraries but also as social centers. Advertisements for lodgings to rent or servants for hire were sometimes placed there, and the list of subscribers offered, at a glance, a sense of the sort of middle- and upper-class society present in town.... A share in a more genteel library might cost anywhere from one to five guineas, with an annual subscription costing perhaps six to ten shillings. The stock of books might be anywhere from a few hundred to a few thousand.... Circulating libraries could be found in increasing numbers in resort towns such as Bath, where a subscription cost 15s. a year or 5s. a quarter from 1789. (Olsen: 593–595)

The social implications of this spread of literacy and the sheer weight of this accumulation of publications had significance far beyond mere entertainment, coming as it did at a precise moment in political history.

> When novels became easily available through circulating libraries, their popularity (and, by association, that of the libraries themselves) touched off the first widespread discussion of the social effects of a democratized reading audience. (Altick, 1957: 63)

At the same time, of course, there was some alarm at the spread of literacy among common people, especially with dangerous notions so easily acquired. Attacks on fiction and the novel in particular failed to spread its widening appeal, but sides were now taken on whether or not Pandora's Box had been opened.

> In the latter half of the [eighteenth] century the appearance of hundreds of trashy novels every year and the establishment of ever more libraries to distribute their "poison" among the populace greatly strengthened opposition to the spread of education. From the prevalent climate of social opinion sprang the fatalistic conviction that the inferior orders, simply because they *were* inferior, intellectually as well as socially, would never be capable or desirous of reading anything but the hair-raising, scandalous, or lachrymose tales upon which they then battened. Every new reader would automatically and irreparably become a victim of circulating library fiction. So it was futile, indeed dangerous, to promote the extension of literacy. (Altick, 1957: 64)

Such a popular form of entertainment, now available to the masses at a price within their means, called out for attacks. The world as we knew it was threatened, and only the suppression of the nefarious source of these dangerous specimens of prose might save it from coming to an ignominious end.

> The hostility to novels which had been building up for several decades reached its peak in the early nineteenth century. The primary target was the circulating-library novel, compact of sensationalism, sentimentality, and (in the evangelical view) salaciousness. It was this very kind of book, however, which was best adapted to the taste of the reader whose limited education equipped him to relish little else. (Altick, 1957: 123)

Ironically, one of the major volleys directed against the new literature appeared in the same issue of *Flowers of Literature* that advertised *Susan*. In theory, she could have begun publishing as early as 1803, with the possibility of a longer and even more productive creative life. Jane Austen presumably saw this issue of *Flowers of Literature*, and such a passage may have directed her attention in a rewrite of her manuscript to the need to defend the contemporary novel.

Our domestic Novelists, absurdly imitating the German literati, have long dealt in the marvellous; and, though they seem for the present to have abandoned the idle and frightful dreams of a distorted imagination, they are nevertheless to be deprecated for teaching youth to mistake loose sentiments for liberal opinions, heedless profligacy for benevolent disposition, and impiety for strength of mind. Happy would it be, for the welfare of the present generation, if those ridiculous fabrications, of weak minds and often depraved hearts, which constitute the enchantment of circulating libraries, could be entirely annihilated! Our readers cannot expect that we should give them a catalogue of those pernicious publications, which increase the laxity of manners and debility of character, already so prevalent in all degrees of society: we will, on the contrary, content ourselves with specifying a few novelists, in whose works, instead of poisonous, they will find a grateful and nutritive combination. (Introduction: 29)

. . .

We will, before we conclude this article, and our rapid view of the state of domestic and foreign literature, earnestly entreat our young and fair readers, who are seeking for materials to amuse their imagination and gratify their curiosity, to turn from the perusal of those idle, dangerous, and unfaithful pictures of human life, (the trash of Circulating Libraries,) to those faithful descriptions contained in authentic travels, which display the wonders of nature in remote regions, trace the intellectual characters of men, savage or civilized, and mark, with the pencil of truth, the variations of customs, and the shades of national manners. By such a change in their taste, we will venture to assert, that, however great may be their eagerness after rational entertainment, they will never want the means to satisfy their inclination for reading. For, we may sincerely, and with justice, congratulate our countrymen, on the immense store of knowledge, and means of improvement, which the numberless and successful exertions of our judicious writers have laid open to our view. (Introduction: 31)

At some point in her work on the manuscript that eventually became *Northanger Abbey*, Jane Austen entered the debate on the status of the novel. Hers is a spirited defense, one that I believe in its present state came late in the history of this manuscript.

Yes, novels;—for I will not adopt that ungenerous and impolitic custom so common with novel writers, of degrading by their contemptuous censure the very performances, to the number of which they are themselves adding—joining with their greatest enemies in bestowing the harshest epithets on such works, and scarcely ever permitting them to be read by their own heroine, who, if she accidentally take up a novel, is sure to turn over its insipid pages with disgust. Alas! if the heroine of one novel be not patronized by the heroine of another, from whom can she expect protection and regard? I cannot approve of it. Let us leave it to the Reviewers to abuse such effusions of fancy at their leisure, and over every new novel to talk in threadbare strains of the trash with which the press now groans. Let us not desert one another; we are an injured body. Although our productions have afforded more extensive and unaffected pleasure than those of any other literary corporation in the world, no species of composition has been so much decried. From pride, ignorance, or fashion, our foes are almost as many as our readers. And while the abilities of the nine-hundredth abridger of the History of England, or of the man who collects and publishes in a volume some dozen lines of Milton, Pope, and Prior, with a paper from the Spectator, and a chapter from Sterne, are eulogized by a thousand pens,—there seems almost a general wish of decrying the capacity and undervaluing the labour of the novelist, and of slighting the performances which have only genius, wit, and taste to recommend them. "I am no novel-reader—I seldom look into novels—Do not imagine that *I* often read novels—It is really very well for a novel."—Such is the common cant.—"And what are you reading, Miss——?" "Oh! it is only a novel!" replies the young lady; while she lays down her book with affected indifference, or momentary shame.—"It is only Cecilia, or Camilla, or Belinda;" or, in short, only some work in which the greatest powers of the mind are displayed, in which the most thorough knowledge of human nature, the happiest delineation of its varieties, the liveliest effusions of wit and humour are conveyed to the world in the best-chosen language. Now, had the same young lady been engaged with a volume of the Spectator, instead of such a

> work, how proudly would she have produced the book, and told its name; though the chances must be against her being occupied by any part of that voluminous publication, of which either the matter or manner would not disgust a young person of taste: the substance of its papers so often consisting in the statement of improbable circumstances, unnatural characters, and topics of conversation, which no longer concern anyone living; and their language, too, frequently so coarse as to give no very favourable idea of the age that could endure it. (Facsimile: 61–65)

With or without Jane Austen's enthusiastic support, the novel flourished as the nineteenth century progressed, and as subscription libraries were built, an increasing number of people had access to the new literature. In the capital by 1800, especially, the new business venture thrived—"There are a number of circulating libraries in London these days" (Borer: 208). But rental costs were still high, and it would be many years before anything like a free public library would be available.

> Early in the [nineteenth] century there were at least twenty such libraries in the City. Their subscription fees, however, confined their clientele to the well-to-do. In 1814, the Minerva, for example, charged two guineas a year for an ordinary subscription and five guineas for one that entitled a patron to borrow twenty-four volumes at a time if he lived in London, thirty-six if he lived in the country. (Altick, 1957: 217)

And, as we see in the village of Sanditon, there are additional reasons to support an establishment such as Mrs. Whitby and her family operate since it also functions as a general store. "For readers there were 'circulating libraries,' which were often shops where 'pretty temptations' such as gloves, parasols, and brooches could be bought" (Pinion: 45). To these wares, Lee Erickson, quoting Thomas Wilson (1797), adds "Haberdashery, Hosiery, Hats, Tea, Tobacco and Snuffs; or Perfumery, and… Patent Medicines" (581).

Such a business was now indispensable for the success of a new watering place. "The new circulating libraries, by now grandly known as marine circulating libraries, were perhaps most important to the social life of a new resort. They did not just lend out books, but also sold novelties, organized raffling—which had long been a popular pastime at the spas—and soon built rooms for cards, billiards and concerts. When visitors first arrived, they paid a subscription which allowed them to use all the library's facilities, and writing their name in the library visitors' book was a way of introducing themselves to the town" (Howell: 27). Equally important, "Libraries were also social centers. Thus [people's] going to the library regularly does not necessarily indicate any interest in books on their part" (Shapard: 53). In addition, "The earliest seaside visitors… seem to have felt the urge to buy keepsakes that would remind them of the pleasures of their stay long after they had returned home" (Howell: 27). "In the early days of the nineteenth century there were three circulating libraries in Brighton" (*CUPLM*: 641). We never learn how many are operating in Brinshore, but it is possible that no one involved with that hated rival can even read or write.

Although on the surface the circulating library appeared to be a source of culture and education, it was obviously primarily meant to enrich the proprietor. "Dramatic techniques complemented libraries' lending policies. Since novelty was a library's bread and butter, especially in London and fashionable watering places like Bath, proprietors urged patrons to read quickly. Turner's insisted that, 'New novels must not be kept longer than a week, and new plays and pamphlets not longer than two days'" (Benedict: 78).

Despite the colorful depiction of Sir Edward as a major patron of Mrs. Whitby's shop, the primary target of the new institution was the impressionable female reader. "Within the catalogs of circulating libraries, however, comparison worked to reinforce the charms of each composition, rather than to elevate one at the expense of another. Novels trained readers in reading novels, through their intertexuality or their repetitions of tropes that with increasing efficiency induced the desired, sentimental responses. The characteristics of female heroines accumulated in the mind of the reader to form an idea heroine, a composite Emma—the character parodied in Austen's 'Plan of a Novel.' This comparative, heroine-centered evaluation reflects the ways novels were presented: as exegeses of female virtue" (Benedict: 81).

Unfortunately, there was also a darker side to the picture. "Libraries, as well as lenders of books, were shops…. Since they are places where patrons, in the nature of their business, have to loiter, they become places for casual meetings, for conversation, and society; it is an easy step to becoming places of assignation and dubious repute" (Craik: 138).

There are few specific references to circulating libraries in the other novels. The passing reference in *Pride and Prejudice* ("Mamma," cried Lydia, "my aunt says that Colonel Forster and Captain Carter do not go so often to Miss Watson's as they did when they first came; she sees them now very often standing in Clarke's library."), gives us no assurance that Lydia goes to the library to find a book although she spends a good deal of time there. In her long-expected and very short letters to her mother from Brighton, Lydia reports "little else than that they were just returned from the library, where such and such officers had attended them, and where she had seen such beautiful ornaments as made her quite wild." We also learn that someone in the Bennet household borrows books from such an institution: "Mr. Collins readily assented, and a book was produced; but, on beholding it (for everything announced it to be from a circulating library), he started back, and begging pardon, protested that he never read novels."

An entirely different use of circulating libraries is seen in the next published novel, where Fanny Price, an avid reader while growing up at Mansfield Park, finds a new world upon her visit to her family in Portsmouth. "After a few days, the remembrance of the said books grew so potent and stimulative, that Fanny found it impossible not to try for books again. There were none in her father's house; but wealth is luxurious and daring—and some of hers found its way to a circulating library. She became a subscriber—amazed at being any thing *in propria persona*, amazed at her own doings in every way; to be a renter, a chuser of books!" (398) Jane Austen thereby makes her point clear: there is no inherent evil in novels or the institution of the circulating library, their being available to be used for good or bad according to the intelligence of the subscribers. Nor surprisingly, the unstable Mary Elliot Musgrove is not among the more intelligent of them, "[getting] books from the library, and chang[ing] them so often, that the balance had certainly been much in favour of Lyme."

In contrast, in *Northanger Abbey* we find numerous indirect references to circulating libraries, which supply the books that keep Isabella and Catherine enthralled with their unspeakable horrors for hour upon hour. And as expected, it is Henry Tilney who raises the issue in one of his bantering harangues over a misunderstanding between Catherine and his sister Eleanor.

> The general pause which succeeded his short disquisition on the state of the nation, was put an end to by Catherine, who, in rather

a solemn tone of voice, uttered these words, "I have heard that something very shocking indeed, will soon come out in London."

Miss Tilney, to whom this was chiefly addressed, was startled, and hastily replied, "Indeed!—and of what nature?"

"That I do not know, nor who is the author. I have only heard that it is to be more horrible than any thing we have met with yet."

"Good heaven!—Where could you hear of such a thing?"

"A particular friend of mine had an account of it in a letter from London yesterday. It is to be uncommonly dreadful. I shall expect murder and every thing of the kind."

"You speak with astonishing composure! But I hope your friend's accounts have been exaggerated;—and if such a design is known beforehand, proper measures will undoubtedly be taken by government to prevent its coming to effect."

"Government," said Henry, endeavouring not to smile, "neither desires nor dares to interfere in such matters. There must be murder; and government cares not how much."

The ladies stared. He laughed, and added, "Come, shall I make you understand each other, or leave you to puzzle out an explanation as you can? No—I will be noble. I will prove myself a man, no less by the generosity of my soul than the clearness of my head. I have no patience with such of my sex as disdain to let themselves sometimes down to the comprehension of yours. Perhaps the abilities of women are neither sound nor acute—neither vigorous nor keen. Perhaps they may want observation, discernment, judgment, fire, genius, and wit."

"Miss Morland, do not mind what he says; —but have the goodness to satisfy me as to this dreadful riot."

"Riot!—what riot?"

"My dear Eleanor, the riot is only in your own brain. The confusion there is scandalous. Miss Morland has been talking of nothing more dreadful than a new publication which is shortly to come out, in three duodecimo volumes, two hundred and seventy-six pages in each, with a frontispiece to the first, of two tombstones and a lantern—do you understand?—And you, Miss Morland— my stupid sister has mistaken all your clearest expressions. You talked of expected horrors in London—and instead of instantly conceiving, as any rational creature would have done, that such words could relate only to a circulating library, she immediately pictured to herself a mob of three thousand men assembling in St. George's Fields; the Bank attacked, the Tower threatened, the streets of London flowing with blood, a detachment of the 12th Light Dragoons (the hopes of the nation,) called up from Northampton to quell the insurgents, and the gallant Capt. Frederick Tilney, in the moment of charging at the head of his troop, knocked off his horse by a brickbat from an upper window. Forgive her stupidity. The fears of the sister have added to the weakness of the woman; but she is by no means a simpleton in general."

Catherine looked grave. "And now, Henry," said Miss Tilney, "that you have made us understand each other, you may as well make Miss Morland understand yourself— unless you mean to have her think you intolerably rude to your sister, and a great brute in your opinion of women in general. Miss Morland is not used to your odd ways." (Facsimile: 264-269)

If the final, incomplete manuscript is really a rewrite of "Susan"/"Charlotte," there would be some reflection of this material, and so as expected the social life of Sanditon is centered on Mrs. Whitby's emporium. And we can hope to revisit some of Henry Tilney's amusing banter in as yet unwritten scenes between Charlotte and that saucy fellow, Sidney Parker.

Mrs. Whitby's establishment is a major asset to the developing community, and as "the circulating library was expected to be centrally located in a resort's organization of pleasure" (Erickson: 575) its location is not surprisingly in the best part of town.

Circulating libraries, then, were an important part of the social fabric in Austen's England and materially affected the conditions in which her own novels were produced. They helped to create an audience for the ephemeral novel when books were expensive and, in particular, made reading a social activity in which women could usually properly participate. (Erickson: 585)] a little detached from it, the Hotel & Billiard Room —

[Although we never visit the Billiard Room, we can be sure that Sidney Parker and his friends will spend a good deal of time here. That it was "a popular entertainment among gentlemen" (*CUPLM*: 649) assures us that it is many notches up on the social scale from the grimy, smoke-filled pool hall of the traditional modern film noir. Sir Edward Denham may play, but nothing in the text connects him with the Room, and he may not be able to afford the luxury even if he is a skilled player and would not lose bets on the outcome. "For men, one of the principal social games" (Olsen: 313), billiards may go back as far as the fourteenth century, originating in England, France, Italy, Spain, or China depending on the nationality of the advocate. By 1800 the game was probably fully developed in its present form. "Always a popular game, it had a revival at the turn of the century. An advertisement in the *Morning Post* of 28 September 1809 declares:

> Billiards are becoming very fashionable: it is an amusement of a gentlemanly cast—giving at once activity to the limbs, and grace to the person." (Craik: 27)

Although usually thought of as a male sport, billiards historically has also been a woman's game, with no less than Marie Antoinette known to be an enthusiastic player.

Jane Austen refers only twice in her extant correspondence to billiards, with no details about the game or its being one that ladies played. In a letter to Cassandra from Godmersham Park, dated Thursday, October 14/Friday, October 15, 1813, she observes a little tartly, "The Comfort of the Billiard Table here is very great.—It draws all the Gentlemen to it whenever they are within, especially after dinner, so that my B^r Fanny & I have the Library to ourselves in delightful quiet" (*Letters*: 239). Her comment in her letter dated Tuesday, October 26, 1813, also to Cassandra from Godmersham Park, again suggests that she has no enthusiasm for the game: "We have had another of Edward Bridges' Sunday visits.—I think the pleasantest part of his married Life, must be the Dinners & Breakfasts & Luncheons & Billiards that he gets in this way at Gm. [Godmersham Park]" (*Letters*: 246).

Within the novels, she never shows anyone actually at play although some of her characters are perhaps excessively preoccupied with the game. Mr. Palmer, who "was nice in his eating, uncertain in his hours; fond of his child, though affecting to slight it; and idled away the mornings at billiards, which ought to have been devoted to business," rudely and somewhat blasphemously for the period questions, "What the devil does Sir John [Middleton, his brother-in-law, who favors outdoor sports] mean by not having a billiard room in his house?"

As expected, the despicable John Thorpe is an enthusiast, boasting to Catherine that among his acquaintances is General Tilney, whom he has vanquished at the table:

> "Know him!—There are few people much about town that I do not know. I have met him for ever at the Bedford; and I knew his face again to-day the moment he came into the billiard-room. One of the best players we have, by the bye; and we had a little touch together, though I was almost afraid of him at first: the odds were five to four against me; and, if I had not made one of the cleanest strokes that perhaps ever was made in this world—I took his ball exactly—but I could not make you understand it without a table;—however, I *did* beat him." (Facsimile: 220–221)

In her other novels, the game is barely mentioned. Although somewhere within Lady Catherine de Bourgh's elegant Rosings is a billiard-table, we never see either Mr. Darcy or Colonel Fitzwilliam at play despite their having nothing else to do indoors now that all field sports are over. Mansfield Park also boasts a billiard-room, which Tom implies is actually used as such, but within the novel it serves as the setting for the disastrous attempt at mounting a play during Sir Thomas's absence. In neither *Emma* nor *Persuasion* do we find any reference to billiards, but neither Mr. Knightley nor Captain Frederick Wentworth is likely to engage in anything so frivolous.

With Mr. Palmer and John Thorpe the only active players in the novels, Jane Austen pretty clearly demonstrates her opinion of this game.]

Here began the Descent to the Beach, & to the Bathing Machines — & this was therefore the favourite spot for Beauty & Fashion. —

[There is something delightfully condemnatory in the phrase "Beauty & Fashion," as though the author is saying that they are only conventionally twinned. The phrase—perhaps another example of synecdoche, the use of a part to represent a more complex whole—conjures up an image of immaculately dressed ladies and gentlemen promenading in their best and most expensive attire while judging others for style and complexion. Sir Walter Elliot, strolling in this manner in Bath, was comforted with the observation that he alone looked presentable:

The worst of Bath was the number of its plain women. He did not mean to say that there were no pretty women, but the number of the plain was out of all proportion. He had frequently observed, as he walked, that one handsome face would be followed by thirty, or five-and-thirty frights; and once, as he had stood in a shop on Bond Street, he had counted eighty-seven women go by, one after another, without there being a tolerable face among them. It had been a frosty morning, to be sure, a sharp frost, which hardly one woman in a thousand could stand the test of. But still, there certainly were a dreadful multitude of ugly women in Bath; and as for the men! they were infinitely worse. Such scarecrows as the streets were full of! It was evident how little the women were used to the sight of anything tolerable, by the effect which a man of decent appearance produced.]

At Trafalgar House, rising at a little distance behind the Terrace, the Travellors were safely set down, & all was happiness & Joy between Papa & Mama & their Children; while Charlotte having received possession of her apartment, found amusement enough in standing at her window, & looking over the miscellaneous foreground of unfinished Buildings, waving Linen, & tops of Houses, to the Sea, dancing & sparkling under a Sunshiny Breeze.

>

At Trafalgar House, rising at a little distance behind the Terrace, the Travellors were safely set down, & all was happiness & Joy between Papa & Mama & their Children; while Charlotte having received possession of her apartment, found amusement enough in standing at her ample, Venetian window, & looking over the miscellaneous foreground of unfinished Buildings, waving Linen, & tops of Houses, to the Sea, dancing & sparkling in Sunshine & Freshness.

[Exploiting her new freedom of style, Jane Austen here expands a long, complicated sentence into one with even more detail. Several very different scenes—the arrival home, the onslaught by the children, and Charlotte's discovery of the sea—are skillfully melded here.

"Papa" and "Mama," being the excited cries of the children upon the return of their father and mother, is a kind of reported dialog constituting virtual stage directions. Throughout, Jane Austen comes close to acting as a playwright. Catherine Morland in the same affectionate terms refers to her parents: "If I could but have Papa and Mamma, and the rest of them here, I suppose I should be too happy!"

Charlotte's "apartment," surely much more commodious and private than what she enjoys back home in Willingden, where she would probably have to share a bedroom with several younger sisters, denotes a "room or set of rooms… frequently… a combination bedroom and dressing-room" (Shapard: 521).

The description of the window is perhaps unique since Jane Austen virtually never discloses details of architectural features. That she furnishes this information has to mean that it is somehow important to understanding the scene. In this instance, it tells us how expensive and fashionable the new Parker home is, including a window that would be highly taxed and therefore symbolic of its proprietor's wealth. The Venetian—also known as Palladian—window consists of a main window with an arched head, flanked on each side by a long and narrow window with a square head. It was popular in seventeenth- and eighteenth-century England, inspired by the work of the sixteenth-century Italian architect, Andrea Palladio.

The "Window Tax" was imposed by William III in 1696 to collect revenues on the basis of a taxpayer's prosperity while avoiding hated income tax. Anyone who could afford a large house obviously had many windows and hence would pay more tax. As a status symbol the wealthiest families commissioned houses with many windows just to show how exceptionally affluent they were. The window tax was finally repealed in 1851.

Growing up inland, Charlotte—like Jane Austen—would rarely have an opportunity to see long stretches of seacoast, and this is probably her first view of what the author obviously relishes describing in detail.

> The later, more fashionable homes were built on wide crescents and terraces, parallel to the beach, with large windows to afford the best view of the sea. In these early years, the resorts were frequented by the upper and middle classes—the same people who visited the inland spas. Houses and streets were given eye-catching names:

Trafalgar Court, Nelson Close, Waterloo House, Marine Parade.
(Sutherland 1997: 63)

Charlotte's delight in the natural beauty before her, because that is what
Jane Austen here describes along with the literal scene of what lies between
the house and the horizon, reflects the author's own happiness at visiting the
coast on occasion. Like Charlotte and her earlier avatar, Catherine Morland,
Jane Austen grew up inland, and it appears that only in her mature years
she had the opportunity to view the open sea that surrounds her native
country. She assigns her own appreciation of the sea to her heroine in
Mansfield Park:

> The day was uncommonly lovely. It was really March; but it was
> April in its mild air, brisk soft wind, and bright sun, occasionally
> clouded for a minute; and every thing looked so beautiful under
> the influence of such a sky, the effects of the shadows pursuing each
> other, on the ships at Spithead and the island beyond, with the
> ever varying hues of the sea now at high water, dancing in its glee
> and dashing against the ramparts with so fine a sound, produced
> altogether such a combination of charms for Fanny, as made her
> gradually almost careless of the circumstances under which she
> felt them.

This fourth chapter is again almost in real time, taking our travelers and
us from their first view of Sanditon to Trafalgar House. Consisting mostly
of dialog, with some carefully wrought narrative, it indirectly introduces
the next important character (and hero of the novel), the middle brother,
Sidney Parker.]

[Chapter 5]

Chapter 5.

When they met before dinner, M^r. P. was looking over Letters. — "Not a Line from Sidney! — said he. — He is an idle fellow. —

[As an inveterate letter writer—"at a conservative estimate, Jane Austen probably wrote about 3,000 letters during her lifetime, of which only 160 are known and published" (Le Faye, 2007: 33)—Jane Austen frequently shows her characters involved with written correspondence, either producing it or receiving it. Her original version of *Sense and Sensibility*—as was possibly that of *Pride and Prejudice*—was a novel-in-letters, and *Lady Susan* remained in that genre despite its being a very eighteenth-century form of narrative.]

I sent him an account of my accident from Willingden, & thought he would have vouchsafed me an Answer. — perhaps it implies that he is coming himself. — Not unlikely. —
>
I sent him an account of my accident from Willingden, & thought he would have vouchsafed me an Answer. — But perhaps it implies that he is coming himself. — I trust it may. —

[Jane Austen employs many examples of litotes in her manuscript, but perhaps feeling that its use was excessive, especially from the mouth of someone as forthright and unimaginative as Thomas Parker, she changed "not unlikely."]

But here is a Letter from one of my Sisters. They never fail me. — Women are the only Correspondents to be depended on. — Now Mary, (smiling at his Wife) — before I open it, what shall we guess as to the state of health of those it comes from — or rather what w^d. Sidney say if he were here? — Sidney is a saucy fellow, Miss H. —

[Thomas Parker here is presumably using "saucy" in the more usual sense of "impertinent" or "cheeky," almost an affectionate term (rather than "wanton" or "lascivious"). Jane Austen liked the adjective and applied it to several of her characters, usually in the same sense as that used by Thomas Parker.

"Should not you, Marianne? Forgive me, if I am very saucy." [Edward, always apologetic, asking that his informal manner be excused]

They owed the restoration of Lydia, her character, every thing, to him. Oh! how heartily did she grieve over every ungracious sensation she had ever encouraged, every saucy speech she had ever directed towards him. [Elizabeth lightly condemning herself about her manner toward Darcy]

"How often, when you were a girl, have you said to me, with one of your saucy looks—'Mr. Knightley, I am going to do so-and-so; papa says I may, or I have Miss Taylor's leave'—something which, you knew, I did not approve. In such cases my interference was giving you two bad feelings instead of one." [Knightley in a humorously reminiscent and affectionate tone to Emma]

"Do not you think, Miss Woodhouse, our saucy little friend here is charmingly recovered?" [Miss Bates with affection for Jane to Emma]

The implications of the word, however, are very different—perhaps not quite "wanton" but definitely neither humorous nor affectionate—in *Mansfield Park* when Edmund relates to Fanny his last interview with Mary Crawford. Jane Austen knew exactly how to paint a portrait in words of a young and beautiful seductress.

"'Mr. Bertram,' said she. I looked back. 'Mr. Bertram,' said she, with a smile; but it was a smile ill-suited to the conversation that had passed, a saucy playful smile, seeming to invite in order to subdue me; at least it appeared so to me."]

And you must know, he will have it there is a good deal of Imagination in my Sisters' complaints — but it really is not so — or very little — They have wretched health, as you have heard us say, & are at times Martyrs to very dreadful Disorders. —
>
And you must know, he will have it there is a good deal of Imagination in my two Sisters' complaints — but it really is not so — or very little — They have wretched health, as you have heard us frequently say, & are subject to a variety of very serious Disorders. —

[In line with her general avoidance of metaphoric language, especially from someone as unimaginative as Thomas Parker, Jane Austen drops the effective "Martyrs" of her first version (perhaps quoting one of Sidney's gibing pleasantries about their sisters), gaining literalness at the expense of entertainment.]

Indeed, I do not beleive they know what a day's health is; — & at the same time, they are such excellent useful Women & have so much energy of Character that, where any Good is to be done, they force themselves on exertions which to those who do not thoroughly know them, have an extraordinary appearance. — But there is really no affectation about them. They have only weaker constitutions & stronger minds than are often met with, either separate or together. —

[Miss Susan Parker displays no evidence in the manuscript of the "energy of Character" and the "exertions" in the behalf of other people for which her brother praises her. But her younger sister more than makes up for whatever the senior member of the family lacks in frenetic activity.]

And our Youngest B[r]. — who lives with them, & who is not above 22, I am sorry to say, is almost as great an Invalid as themselves. —
>
And our Youngest B[r]. — who lives with them, & who is not above 20, I am sorry to say, is almost as great an Invalid as themselves. —
>
And our Youngest B[r]. — who lives with them, & who is not much above 20, I am sorry to say, is almost as great an Invalid as themselves. —

[In the first detailed description of Mr. Arthur Parker, the author initially makes him the same age as Charlotte and in his majority. She then lowers his age to make him technically a minor and younger than Charlotte Heywood and then proceeds to raise it slightly. As she revises Thomas Parker's dialog, she generally removes meiotic phrases like "not above 22" and "not above 20." A few lines further on, poor Arthur is "1 & 20," legally in his majority.]

He is so delicate that he can engage in no Profession, which is most unfortunate. —
>
He is so delicate that he can engage in no Profession. —

[The implications of these two versions are very different, the first suggesting that Arthur may be in straitened circumstances and therefore at risk by having no profession, the latter excusing him from any such pursuit without condemning him to eventual penury. There is no suggestion anywhere in the manuscript that any member of the Parker clan is in other than a comfortable financial state.]

Sidney laughs at him — but it really is no Joke — tho' Sidney often makes me laugh at them all inspite of myself. — Now, if he were here, I know he w^d. be offering odds, that either Susan, Diana or Arthur w^d. appear by this letter to have been at the point of death within the last month." —

[This is a more realistic picture of Sidney than previously disclosed by Thomas, who finally admits that his younger brother has both a sense of humor and an understanding of the ridiculous. Although Thomas is probably using no more than a metaphor in suggesting that Sidney would place a bet on his siblings' survival chances, he could also be disclosing that his younger brother occasionally engages in gambling.

The order of names suggests that Susan is the elder of the two sisters. She is ostensibly the weaker of the two and more in need of constant medical attention, an impression belied by her demonstration of brute strength upon arriving at Sanditon. It is a cute touch on Jane Austen's part to give Miss Parker the original name of the heroine of the unpublished manuscript languishing on a shelf.]

Having run his eye over the Letter, he shook his head & began —: "No chance of seeing them at Sanditon I am sorry to say. — A very indifferent account of them indeed. Seriously, a <u>very</u> indifferent account. — Mary, you will be quite sorry to hear how ill they have been & are. — Miss H., if you will give me leave, I will read Diana's Letter aloud. — I like to have my friends acquainted with each other — & I am afraid this is the only sort of acquaintance I shall have the means of accomplishing between you. — And I can have no scruple on Diana's account — for her Letters shew her exactly as she is, the most active, friendly, warmhearted Being in existence, & therefore must give a good impression."

[That Thomas Parker can run his eye over the letter to pick up its salient points suggests that despite its considerable length Diana Parker did not cross-write (that is, turn the paper 90° and write at a right angle over the earlier text), a common practice. He is using "indifferent" in the sense possibly meant earlier by Mr. Heywood, "Not particularly good; poor, inferior; rather bad" (*OED*).]

He read. — "My dear Tom, We were all much greived at your accident, & if you had not described yourself as fallen into such very good hands, I sh^d. have been with you at all hazards the day after the rec^pt. of your Letter, though it found me hardly able to crawl from my Bed to the Sofa under a more severe attack than usual of my old greivance, Spasmodic Bile. —

>

He read. — "My dear Tom, We were all much greived at your accident, & if you had not described yourself as fallen into such very good hands, I sh^d. have been with you at all hazards the day after the rec^pt. of your Letter, though it found me suffering under a more severe attack than usual of my old greivance, Spasmodic Bile & hardly able to crawl from my Bed to the Sofa. —

[The inverted final clause—"though... Bile" > "though... Sofa"—gains in dramatic effect by being split into two parts through the connecting "&." Miss Diana Parker is the mistress of effective rhetorical devices. In this instance, by reporting her own suffering, which nothing can alleviate, she upstages her brother's injury, quickly attended to.]

But how were you treated? — Send me more Particulars in your next. — If indeed a simple Sprain, as you denominate it, nothing w^d. have been so judicious as Friction, Friction by the hand alone, supposing it could be applied <u>instantly</u>. —

["The medical advice of the time rarely recommended friction [vigorous chafing or rubbing] for sprains or strains" (*CUPLM*: 651), but Diana Parker rejects all conventional treatments. The use of "denominate" for the expected "name" suggests that Miss Diana Parker is either fairly well educated or pretentious in her choice of vocabulary.]

Two years ago I happened to be calling on M^rs— Sheldon when her Coachman sprained his foot as he was cleaning the Carriage & c^d. hardly limp into the House — but by the immediate application of Friction alone, well persevered in, (& I rubbed his Ancle with my own hand for 4 Hours without Intermission) — he was well in three days. —

>

Two years ago I happened to be calling on M^rs— Sheldon when her Coachman sprained his foot as he was cleaning the Carriage & c^d. hardly limp into the House — but by the immediate use of Friction alone, steadily persevered in, (& I rubbed his Ancle with my own hand for six Hours without Intermission) — he was well in three days. —

[As part of her instinct for drama, Miss Diana Parker raises the initial and unlikely "4 Hours" to an unimaginable "six Hours." Although she applies therapeutic stimulation to his injured joint as an act of kindness, imposing herself on her friend's Coachman would have caused intense embarrassment. And after three days the Coachman should have recovered from a minor sprain even without the application of long-sustained rubbing.]

Many Thanks my dear Tom, for the kindness with respect to us, which had so large a share in bringing on your accident — But pray never run into Peril again, in looking for an Apothecary on our account, for had you the most experienced Man in his Line settled at Sanditon, it w^d. be no recommendation to us. We have entirely done with the whole Medical Tribe. We have consulted Physician after Phy^n— in vain, till we are quite convinced that they can do nothing for us & that we must trust to our own knowledge of our own wretched Constitutions for any releif. —

[Diana Parker is confused about her brother's search for a medical man for Sanditon in her specifying an apothecary as his target. The text is clear that he was seeking to employ a surgeon, who might or might not have had an apothecary as partner. But since the partnership had been dissolved, presumably only the surgeon would be brought to Sanditon.]

I know where to apply
>
I could soon put the necessary Irons in the fire. —

[Whereas Jane Austen removes some metaphoric language from Thomas Parker's dialog, she adds it to that of his far more outspoken and imaginative younger sister.]

As for getting to Sanditon myself, it is quite an Impossibility. I greive to say that I dare not attempt it, but my feelings tell me too plainly that in my present state, the Sea air w^d. probably be the death of me. — And neither of my dear Companions will leave me, or I w^d— promote their going down to you for a fortnight. But in truth, I doubt whether Susan's nerves w^d. be equal to the effort.

[It seems bizarre that the sea air that her brother has been touting as a panacea for all known ailments would be detrimental to Diana Parker's health, especially since she presumably grew up in the old Parker residence here in Sanditon by the sea. The tone of "dear Companions" suggests that Arthur continues to live with his much older sisters.]

She has been suffering much from the Headache, and Six Leaches a day for the last week have releived her so little that we thought it right to change our measures — and being convinced on examination that much of the Evil lay in her Gum, I persuaded her to attack the disorder there.
>
She has been suffering much from the Headache, and Six Leaches a day for 10 days together releived her so little that we thought it right to change our measures — and being convinced on examination that much of the Evil lay in her Gum, I persuaded her to attack the disorder there.

[The *OED* recognizes the spelling "leach" as an acceptable variant of "leech" through the eighteenth century and even into the nineteenth century. With so little accurate information about disease and its cure, physicians and their patients had no choice but to resort to whatever traditions had been handed down to them. "Treatments for disease ranged from the noninvasive to the dramatic.... Others resorted to the time-honored practices of purging... , bleeding with leeches, and 'cupping'" (Olsen: 441). "Medicinal leeches were specifically bred for the purpose. The average leech spent fifteen minutes sucking about half a teaspoonful of blood" (*CUPLM*: 651).

Again seeking more drama through exaggeration, Miss Diana Parker increases her sister's suffering from "the last week" to "10 days together."]

She has accordingly had 3 Teeth drawn, & is decidedly better, but her Nerves are a good deal deranged.

[The drawing of teeth to cure all sorts of ailments was common at the time.

Dentistry was still emerging as a serious medical practice. No specialized training was required to set up shop, and the treatment afforded by most dentists tended to be limited to pulling offending teeth.... The tooth-drawer was the more common practitioner, and all he required was a pair of forceps or, if he were especially well equipped, a dental key, a tool that looked rather like a large house

key with a claw at one end. The tooth-drawer used this key to grab
the tooth, twist, and wrench it out with one enormous pull.... The
local tooth-drawer was as likely as not to be a farrier [who trims and
shoes horses' hooves] or blacksmith; he rarely knew anything more
advanced about dentistry than how to grab and pull. (Olsen 661)

Jane Austen never discloses personal encounters with dentists, but she does
report some unpleasant family experiences.

"Going to [the London dentist] Mr Spence's was a sad Business &
cost us [her young nieces Lizzy, Marianne, and Fanny Knight] many
tears, unluckily we were obliged to go a 2^d time before he could do
more than just look:—we went 1st at ½ past 12 and afterwards at
3. Papa with us each time—&, alas! we are to go again to-morrow.
Lizzy is not finished yet. There have been no Teeth taken out
however, nor will be I believe, but he finds *hers* in a very bad state,
& seems to think particularly ill of their Durableness.—They have
been all cleaned, *hers* filed, and are to be filed again. There is a
very sad hole between two of her front Teeth." (*Letters*: 220; to
Cassandra, dated Wednesday, September 15, 1813)

"The poor Girls & their Teeth!—I have not mentioned them yet, but
we were a whole hour at Spence's, & Lizzy's were filed & lamented
over again & poor Marianne had two taken out after all, the two
just beyond the Eye teeth, to make room for those in front.—When
her doom was fixed, Fanny Lizzy & I walked into the next room,
where we heard each of the two sharp hasty Screams.—Fanny's
teeth were cleaned too.... The little girls teeth I can suppose in a
critical state, but I think he must be a Lover of Teeth & Money &
Mischeif to parade about Fannys. I would not have had him look
at mine for a shilling a tooth & double it.—It was a disagreeable
hour." (*Letters*: 223-224; to Cassandra, dated Thursday, September
16, 1813)

Such skepticism about the medical tribe puts Jane Austen very much
in Diana Parker's camp. Later we shall read a similar verdict by Lady
Denham.]

She can only speak in a whisper — and fainted away twice this morning on poor Arthur's sneezing.

>

She can only speak in a whisper — and fainted away twice this morning on poor Arthur's trying to suppress coughing.

>

She can only speak in a whisper — and fainted away twice this morning on poor Arthur's trying to suppress a cough.

[We never learn Miss Susan Parker's age—nor apart from her being "Miss Parker" is the text specific about which of the sisters is indeed the elder—but she is certainly in fragile health according to this letter. How delicate she really is will be revealed upon their arrival at Sanditon.]

He, I am happy to say is tolerably well — tho' more languid than I like — & I fear for his Liver. — I have heard nothing of Sidney since your being together in Town,

[Although the author prepares us for the introduction to Arthur Parker, he will still be a total surprise. "It was believed that a sedentary or languid habit could be both cause and symptom of liver problems" (*CUPLM*: 652), but among his many and varied ailments Arthur Parker never identifies his liver as a source of his imaginary problems.

Apparently Mr. and Mrs. Thomas Parker met with his younger brother while in London. Sidney, as an unattached, wealthy young man has the luxury of freedom of motion and takes full advantage of it. Unlike his sister, Sidney is not a habitual letter-writer.]

but conclude his scheme to the I. of Wight has not taken place, or we should have seen him in his way. —

[The Isle of Wight, covering 147 square miles and separated from the mainland by a strait called The Solent, is close to Hampshire, which we later learn is the county in which the Parker sisters and Arthur Parker reside. The text suggests that Sidney lives somewhere to the north of Hampshire and hence would naturally pass by his siblings' home. It would be interesting to speculate on why these family members, who presumably grew up in the original Parker home in Sanditon, have moved to another county. Perhaps their mother, through whom the siblings other than Thomas may have inherited their wealth, was from Hampshire. In any case, its being Jane

Austen's own beloved native county would make it a natural second home. That Sidney Parker ends up in Sanditon, however briefly, suggests that he has abandoned his plan to visit the Isle of Wight, directly south of the county of Hampshire and not as easily reached from Sussex. A complete romantic would hypothesize that he has come to Sanditon in response to his brother's correspondence about the charming young guest staying in the new family home.

Where Sidney Parker is coming from at this point in the story is unclear. The *CUPLM* editor states that he "is presumably traveling from London, and his route would therefore be through Hampshire, where the Parker sisters… live" (652). This itinerary is logical regardless of where Sidney makes his home, which could be in London. Or he could be proceeding south without returning first to his own residence after visiting the capital city while his older brother and sister-in-law were there.]

Most sincerely do we wish you a good Season at Sanditon, & though we cannot contribute to your Beau Monde in person, we are doing our utmost to send you Company worth having; & think we may safely reckon on securing you two large Families, one, a rich West Indian from Surry, the other, a most respectable Girls Boarding School, or Academy, from Camberwell. —

[Diana Parker's inserting a French phrase like "Beau Monde" suggests some level of education or at least a pretense to one. It is difficult to determine if she is being somewhat ironic because to date there do not appear to be any people from the fashionable world among the visitors to Sanditon.

Although "West Indian" at one time meant "The original inhabitants of the West Indies," this definition was obsolete by Jane Austen's time, being supplanted by "An inhabitant or native of the West Indies, of European origin or descent" (OED). The identity of the people who lived on the islands before European incursions was thus effectively obliterated.

In the early nineteenth century, "Surry" (now spelled "Surrey") extended sufficiently to the north and east to include Southwark (maps, Le Faye, 2002: 68, 253). Modern Camberwell, no longer in Surrey, now forms part of the London Borough of Southwark. The school group would be coming to Sanditon for the social life rather than for reasons of health, since "up to the mid-nineteenth century, Camberwell was visited by Londoners for its rural tranquillity and the reputed healing properties of its mineral springs" ("Camberwell." *Wikipedia*). The coincidence of the two groups' being from the same part of England clearly never struck anyone in the Parker family.]

I will not tell you how many People I have employed in the business — Wheel within wheel. — But Success more than repays. Yours most affec^ly — &c"

[As unlikely as it may be that Diana Parker would be quoting religious sources, her "Wheel within wheel" sounds like what the Prophet Ezekiel saw in a vision. It is difficult to imagine her reading the Bible on a regular basis, so perhaps the most recent Sunday sermon contained this striking and memorable image:

"The appearance of the wheels and their work was like a beryl: and the four of them had one likeness; and their appearance and their work was as it were a wheel within a wheel" (1:16).

A more likely explanation is the one offered by *CUPLM* that "the reference is to the old saying, 'wheels within wheels', a complex network of influences and circumstances, not all of which are apparent" (653).]

"Well — said M^r. P. — having finished & refolded his Letter — I suppose if Sidney w^d—
>
"Well — said M^r. P. — as he concluded
>
"Well — said M^r. P. — as he finished it.
>
"Well — said M^r. P. — as he finished. Though I dare say Sidney w^d—
>
"Well — said M^r. P. — as he finished. Though I dare say Sidney might find something very amusing in this Letter I declare I̲ can see nothing in it — but what is very pitiable or very creditable. —
>
"Well — said M^r. P. — as he finished. Though I dare say Sidney might find something to laugh at in this Letter I declare I̲ by myself, can see nothing either in it — but what is very pitiable or very creditable. —
>
"Well — said M^r. P. — as he finished. Though I dare say Sidney might find something extremely entertaining in this Letter & make us laugh for half

an hour together I declare I̱ by myself, can see nothing in it — but what is either very pitiable or very creditable. —

[It is disappointing that "refolded his Letter," an excellent stage direction, was dropped after the first version of this line.

"Because paper was sold already folded in half, it became customary to write letters… as if the folded paper were a little, four-page book…. When the letter was finished, it was folded with the blank space on the fourth page on the outside. The address, 'or direction'… was written here" (Olsen: 728). Occasionally a letter was enclosed in an envelope, which "was merely another sheet of paper, wrapped and folded around the letter and sealed…. an envelope in this sense was generally reserved for messages carried by servants from one house to another" (Olsen: 729). The addressee paid the postage since there were no stamps to lick and stick (the first adhesive postage stamp, the Penny Black, issued on May 1, 1840, can be found now for prices ranging from a few dollars to several thousand dollars, depending on condition). Jo Modert well illustrates how letters were addressed in her facsimile edition of the letters. Sometimes the address was complex—"Nov. 1800, Miss Austen [meaning Cassandra Austen as the elder sister], Edward Austen's Esq,, Godmersham Park [the estate of Edward Austen, after 1812 known as Edward Austen-Knight], Faversham, Kent" (F–156) or "Miss Austen, 10. Henrietta Street [the home of Henry Austen], Covent Garden, London"—and sometimes simple—"Miss Austen, Chawton."

Jane Austen indirectly, through another Jane (Fairfax), heaps praise on the performance of the contemporary post office.

> "The post-office is a wonderful establishment!" said she.— "The regularity and despatch of it! If one thinks of all that it has to do, and all that it does so well, it is really astonishing!"

In keeping with his waggish tongue and saucy manner, if Sidney Parker took the time to correspond with his brother he would probably write far more to address the letter than necessary, perhaps "Mr. Thomas Parker, Trafalgar House, Sanditon, Sussex, England, Great Britain, United Kingdom of Great Britain, Europe, Earth, World." We would love to have a letter from Thomas to Sidney because that might reveal the latter's place of residence. His meeting with his older brother and sister-in-law in London could mean that he lives in London, evidence of considerable wealth.

Clearly what Mr. Sidney Parker would have said if he had been present is so important that our author takes the passage through multiple revisions. We are meant to anticipate his entrance on the scene since he will prove to be an updated Henry Tilney. Thomas Parker may make disparaging remarks about his brother, but he brings him up on every apposite occasion. It is a pity that the manuscript did not extend far enough for us to share in some of Sidney's side-splittingly humorous remarks. This trait certainly suggests some indebtedness to his namesake Sydney Smith (frequently considered the original of Henry Tilney), likewise famous for inducing long bouts of laughter.

Sydney Smith was famous for his witticisms, any of which could have come from Henry Tilney and might in time have been produced by Sidney Parker. Much of his best humor can be found in his letters. The first and last would be particularly appropriate coming from Sidney Parker, skeptical as he is about sea cures and hypochondria.

> I have great pleasure in informing you Mrs. S is better, the Sea air has revived her, and she has made a very considerable, and satisfactory progress in the course of the 3 or 4 days last past. We are very delightfully situated in this place—opposite to Edinburgh on the other side of the Firth, and under the high woods of Aberdour Lord Morton's property. The little Town hitherto only celebrated for the cure of herrings will I hope in future be equally so for the cure of Wives. (18)

> I take the liberty to send you two brace of grouse, curious, because killed by a Scotch metaphysician; in other and better language they are mere ideas, shot by other ideas, out of a pure intellectual notion called a gun. (42)

> What is real piety? What is true attachment for the Church? How are these fine feelings best evinced? The answer is plain: by sending strawberries to a clergyman. Many thanks. S.S. (148)

> Knowing (as you do my dear Lady Grey) Lady Holland so well, and having known her so long, you will I am sure be sorry to hear the misfortune that has befallen her. You know how long she has been alarmed by diseases of the heart; terrified to an agony by some recent death from that cause, she was determined that Brodie should examine the chest thoroughly with a stethoscope. He spent

a long time there, bestowed the greatest attention upon the case, and ended with saying that in the course of his practice he had never witnessed a more decided case of healthy circulation, and that she had not a single complaint belonging to her. I have seen her since, and never saw anyone so crestfallen and desponding. She did all she could to get me to help her to some fresh complaint, but I was stubborn. (154)]

With all their sufferings, you perceive how much they are occupied in promoting the Good of others! So anxious for Sanditon! Two large Families — One, for Prospect House probably, the other, for N°. 2. Denham Place — or the end house of the Terrace, — & extra Beds at the Hotel. — I told you my Sisters were excellent Women, Miss H —."

"And I am sure they must be very extraordinary ones. — said Charlotte.

I am quite astonished at the chearful style of the Letter, considering the state in which both Sisters appear to be.
>
I am astonished at the chearful style of the Letter, considering the state in which both Sisters appear to be.

[So that her forthright view can be demonstrated, Charlotte's dialog is slightly reduced with the removal of the unnecessary "quite."]

Three Teeth drawn at once! — It is really frightful!
>
Three Teeth drawn at once! — frightful!

[Again Charlotte's dialog is reduced to indicate her directness of thought and economy of speech, in marked contrast to the tone of Miss Diana Parker's letter.]

Your Sister Diana seems almost as ill as possible, but those 3 Teeth of your Sister Susan's, are most distressing to one's imagination than all the rest. —"
>
Your Sister Diana seems almost as ill as possible, but those 3 Teeth of your Sister Susan's, are most distressing than all the rest. —"
>

Your Sister Diana seems almost as ill as possible, but those 3 Teeth of your Sister Susan's, are more distressing than all the rest. —"

[Yet again Charlotte's dialog is simplified to reflect her realistic view of the use of language. It is hard to understand why Jane Austen had to go through two initial versions of this line to correct the comparative "more," but the distinction at the time between comparative and superlative adjectives was less prescriptive than now.]

"Oh! — they are so used to the operation — to every operation — & have such Fortitude! —"

"Your Sisters know what they are about, I dare say, but their Measures seem to touch on Extremes. — I feel that in any illness, I should be so anxious for Professional advice, so very little venturesome for myself, or any body I loved! — But then, <u>we</u> have been so healthy a family, that I can be no Judge of what the habit of self-doctoring may do. —"

"Why to say the truth, said M^rs. P. — I <u>do</u> think the Miss Parkers carry it too far sometimes — & so do you my Love, you know. —
>
"Why to own the truth, said M^rs. P. — I <u>do</u> think the Miss Parkers carry it too far sometimes — & so do you my Love, you know. —

[The change from the literal and formal "say" to the more conversational and colloquial—perhaps even bucolic—"own" reduces the level of Mrs. Parker's dialog to something appropriate to a character who is not a woman of the world. And, of course, our author (sensitive to the sound of her prose) avoids the proximity of "say" and "said."]

You often think they w^d. be better, if they w^d. leave themselves more alone — & especially p
>
You often think they w^d. be better, if they w^d. leave themselves more alone — & especially Arthur.

[Mrs. Parker was, of course, about to say "poor Arthur," the familial epithet most consistently used to describe his precarious physical state.]

I know you think it a great pity they sh^d. give <u>him</u> such a turn for being ill. —"

"Well, well — my dear Mary — I grant you, it <u>is</u> unfortunate for poor Arthur, that, at his time of Life he sh^d— be encouraged to give way to Indisposition.

It <u>is</u> bad; — it <u>is</u> bad that he should be fancying himself too sickly for any Profession — & sit down at 1 & 20, idle & indolent, on the interest of his own little Fortune, without any idea of attempting to improve it, or any prospect of engaging in any occupation that may be of use to himself or others. —

>

It <u>is</u> bad; — it <u>is</u> bad that he should be fancying himself too sickly for any Profession — & sit down at 1 & 20, on the interest of his own little Fortune, without any idea of attempting to improve it, or the slightest plan of engaging in any occupation that may be of use to himself or others. —

>

It <u>is</u> bad; — it <u>is</u> bad that he should be fancying himself too sickly for any Profession — & sit down at 1 & 20, on the interest of his own little Fortune, without any idea of attempting to improve it, or of engaging in any occupation that may be of use to himself or others. —

[Poor Arthur's age is perhaps finally established as 21, so he has just arrived at his majority—"One came of age, and legally became an adult, at twenty-one" (Shapard: 29); "Twenty-one was the coming of age for men" (Ray: 119); "Until 1823, a man or woman under the age of twenty-one could not marry without parental permission" (Pool: 180)—and is only slightly younger than Charlotte. Each of the Parkers appears to be well provided for financially. Thomas is contrasting Arthur's indifference to expanding his resources with his own real estate speculations and Arthur's aloofness to Diana Parker's determination to play a significant role in the life of everyone around her, particularly that of total strangers. Ironically, Arthur's *not* engaging in any "regular trade or occupation" is what legally defines him as a gentleman (Pool: 44).]

But let us talk of pleasanter things. — These two large Families are just what we wanted — But — here is something at hand, pleasanter still — Morgan, with his "Dinner on Table." —

[Aside from Morgan the butler no other household servant is named although we know that the Parkers keep a cook and certainly have at least one maid, along with the nursery maid who takes care of the children, and possibly the man who accompanies them and acts as postilion when they leave home. Jane Austen never examines the lives of people at this level of society, in part because she has no interest in them and in part because she knows that she has insufficient knowledge to include them in her tales.

Morgan—upper servants are always addressed by surname alone—has many grave responsibilities in the Parker household, among them

> [taking] care of the estate's wine, beer, glassware, and plate. When new wine was purchased in large casks, it was his job to bottle it and then to serve it with dinner. He took on the duties of the valet in households where there was none and, in any case, supervised the setting out of the breakfast things.... The butler would carry the "eatables" and possibly wait on the table during the meal.... At dinner he released the requisite articles of plate from their locked chest, carried in the first dish, and served wine throughout the meal.... He was also in charge of serving supper if it was wanted. (Olsen: 617)

As we shall soon see, he also has the major responsibility of greeting visitors at the front door, a daunting task that requires him to decide for whom his master and mistress are "at home." We would recognize Morgan immediately upon meeting him since "butlers used to always be attired in a special uniform, distinct from the livery of junior servants" ("Butler." *Wikipedia*). As expected, Jane Austen refrains from quoting any of Morgan's dialog directly: the line is constructed so that Thomas Parker says what he knows that his butler is about to pronounce. Although Jane Austen must have heard servants speaking, she appears to be reluctant to give them speaking parts in her script.

Although very few household servants appear on stage in the earlier novels, when there is a butler he is generally mentioned. Despite their comparative poverty, even the Bennets have a butler:

> They ran through the vestibule into the breakfast-room; from thence to the library; their father was in neither; and they were on the point of seeking him upstairs with their mother, when they were met by the butler, who said: "If you are looking for my master, ma'am, he is walking towards the little copse."

The Dashwoods do not include a butler among their meager, severely curtailed staff (one that any present-day family of wealth would be happy to claim), but Sir John and Mrs. Jennings would certainly have one apiece. General Tilney, the Woodhouses, and the Bertrams, of course, have butlers. Even in his enforced state of retrenchment, Sir Walter Elliot maintains a full staff befitting his blemished dignity, including "a butler and foot-boy."

Dinner was the main meal of the day, sometimes served as early as three o'clock (Borer: 60) but increasingly later and later into the evening depending on social status (or pretense thereto) and location (the country vs. London)— "The dinner-hour varied according to the family's place of residence and social status" (Le Faye, 2002: 119).

> After breakfast, the day continues without formal interruption until dinner, whose hour varies according to the inclination, age, and pretensions to fashion of the household, being generally (then as now) later in London than elsewhere. Four o'clock is an early hour, suiting the old-fashioned and fairly countrified habits of Emma's father, Mr Woodhouse; the pretentious but not up-to-date or fashionable General Tilney in *Northanger Abbey* dines exactly at five; the stylish Bingleys, bringing their London ways into Hertfordshire in *Pride and Prejudice*, dine as late as half-past six. (Craik, 1969: 14)

Most people of class "ate a multicourse dinner anywhere between 5 p.m. and 7 p.m." (Ray: 98). "In her own letters Jane Austen most often mentions eating dinner around five" (Shapard: 121).

A formal meal for which ladies and gentlemen "dressed," dinner was served in courses (Ray: 210). "Meat was the centerpiece of every dinner among prosperous people" (Olsen: 262). Among "the nobility and the gentry," dinner consists of "soup, poultry, butcher's meat, and sweets; the wine, port, and sherry" (Olsen: 266–267).

The Parkers may be besotted with their children, but they do not tolerate them at the dinner table. "Young children ate dinner in the nursery with their governess, but might to be brought to their parents before or after dinner" (Ray: 209).

This fifth chapter is again in real time, beginning shortly before dinner is announced and ending with Morgan's formal invitation to the family to enter the dining room. It consists almost entirely of dialog, and we now meet primarily through her letter Miss Diana Parker and her older sister, Miss Susan Parker. Mr. Arthur Parker is barely hinted at, but in an ensuing chapter we shall encounter first-hand all the obsessions that only a confirmed hypochondriac can fully enjoy. The long letter here is standard in late eighteenth-century fiction, especially those known as novels-in-letters or epistolary novels, and many letters continue to appear in Jane Austen's works despite her re-casting the novels in third-person omniscient-author style. Although *Lady Susan* stands as testimony to Jane Austen's skill in this old-fashioned genre, we remain eternally grateful that *Sense and Sensibility*—probably originally consisting primarily of correspondence—was published in its present form. I have seen no hypotheses that the unpublished "Susan" was an epistolary novel, and there is little in *Northanger Abbey* to suggest that in an earlier version the narration was significantly different. Catherine Morland enjoys reading, but although there is no evidence of her skills in writing, she might have written more or less faithfully to a favorite sister back in Fullerton, the duplicitous Isabella Thorpe, or Eleanor Tilney. The Parkers clearly enjoy each other's company and therefore engage in active correspondence.]

[Chapter 6]

The Party were very soon moving after Dinner.

[It is disappointing that Jane Austen chose to pick up again only after dinner has been completed. Her contemporary audience might have been bored with the details, but for us it would have been an interesting peek into family life at the time. The children, of course, do not dine with the adults. The time of this dinner varies according to the authority that one reads, but the consensus is that the morning lasted all the way up to about 3 or 5 p.m., when dinner was served. This particular dinner obviously ends early enough that they can proceed to the Library and later return home to have tea with Lady Denham and Miss Clara Brereton.]

M^r- P. could not be satisfied without an early visit to the Library, & the Library Subscription book, & Charlotte was glad to see as much, as quickly as possible, where all was new.
>
M^r- P. could not be satisfied without an early visit to the Library, & the Library Subscription book, & Charlotte was glad to see as much, & as quickly as possible, where all was new.

[Mr. Parker is of course far more interested in the names entered in the Library Subscription book than in the printed matter available in the Library. He is perhaps too busy with speculation to spend much time on literature although we learned in the opening chapter that he has read some poetry by William Cowper.

That everything is "new" to Charlotte reinforces her role as heroine, through whose inquiring eyes we see the story unfolding. Jane Austen's technique is by now so well developed that she can assume the roles of narrator and lead character simultaneously.

No less conservative in this manuscript than in her preceding novels, Jane Austen in citing something as "new" cannot be assumed to be admiring it. Charlotte may be momentarily dazzled by the panoply of goods before her, but her solid country values—those of the author—warn her that frequently underneath false tinsel lurks real tinsel.]

They were out in the very quietest part of a Watering-place Day, when the important of Dinner or of sitting after Dinner was going on in almost every inhabited Lodging; —

>

They were out in the very quietest part of a Watering-place Day, when the important Business of Dinner or of sitting after Dinner was going on in almost every inhabited Lodging; —

[A phrase like "the important of Dinner" again suggests that we are dealing with a transcription from an earlier sheet of paper.]

— here & there a solitary Elderly Man might be seen, who was forced to move early & walk for health — but in general, it was a thorough pause of Company, it was Emptiness & Tranquillity on the Terrace, the Cliffs, & the Sands. —

[As has frequently been observed, Jane Austen adopts for this manuscript an allusive tone rarely found in her earlier work. It is almost as though some of the elements later to be found in Impressionist, and even Pointillist, art are anticipated through verbal means.]

The Shops were deserted — the Straw Hats & pendant Lace seemed left to their fate both within & without, and M^rs. Whitby at the Library was sitting in the little inner parlour, reading one of her own Novels, for want of something better to do. —

>

The Shops were deserted — the Straw Hats & pendant Lace seemed left to their fate both within the House & without, and M^rs. Whitby at the Library was sitting in her inner room, reading one of her own Novels, for want of Employment. —

[Our characters have moved quickly from Trafalgar House past shops empty of customers to the Library, likewise lacking business. We find here more description of the setting than is usual in Jane Austen, and perhaps more than found in any of her earlier novels. For example, the town of Meryton, a frequent resort of the Bennet sisters, is summarily dismissed in a few words: "The village of Longbourn was only one mile from Meryton; a most convenient distance for the young ladies, who were usually tempted thither three or four times a week, to pay their duty to their aunt and to a milliner's shop just over the way." Other than cloth for new dresses or hats, it has nothing to interest the girls or the reader: "In pompous nothings on his side, and civil assents on that of his cousins, their time passed till they entered Meryton. The attention of the younger ones was then no longer to be gained by him. Their eyes were immediately wandering up in the street in quest of the officers, and nothing less than a very smart bonnet indeed, or a really new muslin in a shop window, could recall them." Although the shopping possibilities here in Sanditon are much greater, the material is at best vague and superficial. Not even the lending library, the focus of this particular scene, is described in any detail. Here, as in all previous work, Jane Austen's interest lies in the characters, not the rooms through which they pass or the streets that they traverse. The projected novel was to be about people *in* the village of Sanditon, not about the village itself. Hence although the locale is inseparable from the story, it is not in itself the subject of the work.

The metaphoric language occasionally encountered in this manuscript, like "the Straw Hats & pendant Lace," is new to Jane Austen, who up to now has generally avoided such non-literal images. In what may be an example of synecdoche, the author summarizes in two articles of clothing the entire fashion scene in Sanditon.

Straw bonnets ("Women's or girl's head-dress, with deep brim and ribbons to tie under the chin" ["Bonnets"]), which "in the 1810's... were de rigueur" ("The History of Women's Hats"), perhaps represent daytime wear while promenading along the beach. In Vic's "Seaside Fashion, Regency Style," we find a description of a contemporary beach scene.

> Famed illustrator James Gillray showed seaside fashion in all its glory. From the high tide hem of the lady in the center, to the completely covered up garb of the women sitting on the beach. This lovely illustration from 1810, "The Calm," shows the seashore on a calm day, with our fashionable miss as exposed as she can decently be—her arms and neck bare, her head covered by a small straw bonnet, and her tiny parasol barely protecting her delicate skin from Sol's harmful rays. (Vic, 2009)

At the other end of the fashion spectrum is the "pendant lace," more likely worn in the evenings for more formal occasions. Lacemaking began in Europe in the sixteenth century, with Italy and Belgium as the major suppliers of this luxury item, a decorative fabric consisting of an open, netlike pattern of threads. It was made by hand and therefore considered a rare luxury item until the invention in the early nineteenth century of a lacemaking machine.

> England originated lace machines, and France may claim to have perfected them. The stocking machine was no doubt the parent of lace-making machinery. The machines were started at Nottingham in England, early in the nineteenth century, and were called bobbin-net, or point-net, or warp-net, machines, and the lace first made was often finished and enriched by hand. Owing to the destruction of more than a thousand stocking frames and lace machines by rioters, it was made a capital offence in 1812 to destroy machines. ("Lace")

If it is true that over a thousand machines were destroyed before 1812 but the industry continued to thrive, there must have been many thousands of such machines to fill an ongoing demand. It is possible that Jane Austen is commenting on "pendant lace" not so much to praise its fashionableness as to point out its being common and readily available.

Despite her modest lifestyle, Jane Austen was always interested in the newest fashions. But information about dress is rare in the novels.

> Her letters, by contrast, are full of witty references to changes in fashions and personal tastes, her own and other people's. Although Austen often portrays fashion-consciousness as a sign of foolish or frivolous behavior in her novels… , she was as concerned with cutting a fine figure as everyone else.

> One reason for the many references to fashion in Austen's letters is that, in a sense, people were closer to fashion then than they are now. The making, purchasing, and care of clothing were different in Austen's day than they are in our own. Certain items, like bonnets or cloaks, could be bought ready-made, but in most cases, necessary materials were purchased at a linen draper's shop and the garments would be made at a tailor's or dressmaker's shop… , or by family or servants at home. (Nigro)

Although Mrs. Whitby is not a servant, she is nevertheless in trade. Hence she is given no explicit dialog although some of her chatter is implied.

CUPLM (453) transcribes "Whitby" as "Whilby" through a misunderstanding about how Jane Austen formed her letters. Although the medial "t" is not crossed, so that it has the general appearance of the letter "l," examination of the manuscript (folio 25v) shows that it is like a form of a terminal "t" that Jane Austen often used (such as in the following word, "at") and is still in use today, a vertical line followed by a small upward diagonal line with no crossbar. In this case Jane Austen has used what is ordinarily a form of a terminal "t" as a medial "t." Chapman (70), Johnson (36), and Sacco (74) concur in reading the name as "Whitby."]

The List of Subscribers was but commonplace.

[The subscription book serves as a roster of the leading characters, in part in seniority order to recognize that we have very clear social levels present. More stage action is implied, such as Mr. Parker's careful scrutiny of the Subscription Book with perhaps a scowl on his face. The text is visually ironic in capitalizing "List" and "Subscribers," only to identify it as "commonplace." Jane Austen has again successfully blended her authorial voice with that of one of her characters. Capitalizing nouns was a common practice in the eighteenth century, and in this way Jane Austen continues to show her indebtedness to her immediate predecessors.

The list suggests a certain level of cross-section of middle and lower upper-class society, the kind of people whom Mr. Parker and Lady Denham are trying to attract to Sanditon:

> The resorts were centres of wealth and conspicuous consumption among the upper-class residents and visitors. A middle class was present in the legal and medical professionals, teachers and private tutors, military officers, owners of shops and businesses. A large group was formed by those in personal service: domestic servants, laundry workers, cooks and landladies. At the base of the social structure were the local labourers, fishermen, boat builders, construction workers. (Sutherland, 1997: 68)

Marilyn Butler takes a less sympathetic view of what is happening in and to Sanditon:

> The people who flock to Sanditon are of the type of gentry Jane
> Austen always censures: urban, rootless, irresponsible, self-
> indulgent. (286)

Nothing in the text supports this strong condemnation since we have
learned nothing so far about most of the people whose names appear in
the subscription book, and nothing in the text points in the direction that
they will make a personal appearance. Mr. Parker is optimistic that in time
more people will come to the seaside resort, but for now very few people
have chosen to "flock" to Sanditon. The financial danger that he and Lady
Denham face is that people will *not* flock to Sanditon.

We find in this manuscript a wider range of social types, especially at
the lower end, than previously seen in Jane Austen's novels. "Characters
from classes never before allowed subjective presence in Austen's novels
make their appearance in *Sanditon*: a circulating library mistress idled by
a failing business, a mulatto heiress just arrived from the West Indies to
be exploited, a distressed family singled out for charity subscription, a
local gardener whose income must be supported against the prices of the
current market" (Copeland, 2007: 325). However, in the extant text not
one of these people cited speaks a single word. To them we can add many
other important characters, similarly silent: the coachman without whose
poor management of his horses the story would never have taken place; the
unnamed apothecary and the unnamed and elusive surgeon who decided
to dissolve their partnership, hence Mr. Parker's precarious voyage up the
road near the Heywood home; Mrs. Heywood, without whose initiative
Charlotte would probably not visit Sanditon, a journey that constitutes
the plot; Morgan, the butler, who must speak to announce that dinner is
ready and to greet Diana Parker when she comes to Trafalgar House; the
Beaumont sisters, Miss Beaumont and Miss Letitia, who mirror all of the
worst of contemporary young ladies in search of a husband; Mrs. Griffiths,
who brings Miss Lambe to Sanditon; Miss Susan Parker, who is extensively
described but despite great volubility never utters a word.

And then there are all the minor characters, some nameless, who are at the
edges of society but essential for the plot: Sir Edward's groom (perhaps his
only servant), patiently walking the horse (perhaps his only horse) back and
forth; the Brereton family, without whose intervention Lady Denham would
never have met Clara; Hillier, whose dependability enables Mr. Parker
to abandon his family home, and Mrs. Hillier; the milliner Jebb; Lady

Denham's servants and gardener, perhaps "poor old Andrew," "a purveyor of vegetables and fruits in Sanditon, possibly employed by Lady Denham" (Bok: 402); the Parkers' cook, who enjoys complaining about "old Andrew"; the various people who inscribed their names in the subscription book, any one of whom could loom larger in the continuing story; the shoemaker William Heeley; Miss Whitby and young Whitby; Mrs. Sheldon and her anonymous coachman; Lady Denham's two housemaids, probably not the same as the two servants who admit Charlotte, Mrs. Parker, and little Mary to Sanditon House; Mr. Woodcock; Old Sam; Miss Capper and Fanny Noyce and Mrs. Darling and Mrs. Charles Dupuis, to name them as a short but unbroken chain; poor Mullins; and finally the various people hired by Diana Parker—including "Cooks, Housemaids, Washer women [*OED*: "A woman whose occupation is the washing of dirty linen; one who takes in washing"] & Bathing Women [who like Martha Gunn immersed the terrified ladies]"—engaged in menial occupations rarely specified in contemporary novels but without whose labor daily life as enjoyed by the middle and upper classes would come to a jarring halt. This is a long cast of characters who in a Dickens novel would not only be mentioned but would be seen and heard.]

The Lady Denham, Miss Brereton, M^r. and M^{rs}. P. — Sir Edw: Denham & Miss Denham, whose names might be said to lead off the Season, were followed by nothing better than such as these. — Mrs Mathews — Miss Mathews, Miss E. Mathews, Miss H. Mathews. — D^r. and M^{rs}. Henderson — M^{r-} Richard Pratt. — M

>

The Lady Denham, Miss Brereton, M^r. and M^{rs}. P. — Sir Edw: Denham & Miss Denham, whose names might be said to lead off the Season, were followed by nothing better than — Mrs Mathews — Miss Mathews, Miss E. Mathews, Miss H. Mathews. — D^r. and M^{rs}. Brown — M^{r-} Richard Pratt. — Lieut: Smith R.N. Capt: Little, — Limehouse. — M^{rs}. Jane Fisher. Miss Fisher. Miss Scroggs. — Rev: M^r. Hanking. M^r. Beard — Solicitor, Grays Inn. — M^{rs}. Davis. & Miss Merryweather. —

[It is impossible to tell from this list which are residents of Sanditon, like Lady Denham and the Parkers, which are frequent visitors like Sir Edward and Miss Denham, and which are summer visitors although the text implies that some are in this category.

"Since every genteel visitor would be expected to subscribe to the library, the subscription book served as a kind of social registry" (*CUPLM*: 653). This list does not, of course, reflect all of the people who enter Mrs. Whitby's establishment. There are many Sanditon residents who cannot qualify as "genteel" but are necessary to accommodate visitors and keep the local businesses, including Mrs. Whitby's, flourishing throughout the year.

Jane Austen's writing "The Lady Denham" raises the interesting point of how aware she was of titular protocol. "The prefix 'The' would normally be correct only if Lady Denham had been the widow of a peer rather than of a baronet [a hereditary title but along with knighthood of the common class rather than nobility], so either JA was suggesting that Sanditon was attempting to exaggerate Lady Denham's importance or she made a slip" (*CUPLM*: 653). Since it is likely that Jane Austen knew precisely how titles were used and it was Lady Denham who inscribed her name in the book, the stronger likelihood is that the great lady of the neighborhood has added the article to give herself a status that is not hers but that guarantees the deference that she expects from her acquaintances.

The early position of Miss Brereton, immediately following Lady Denham and ahead of Sir Edward—and, even more to that lady's chagrin, ahead of Miss Denham—hints at her being the presumptive heiress. Far from the "helpless &… pitiable… dependant on Poverty—an additional Burthen on an encumbered Circle—& one, who had been so low in every worldly veiw, as with all her natural endowments & powers, to have been preparing for situation little better than a Nursery Maid," Clara Brereton has successfully transitioned into the beau monde and is now second only to Lady Denham in social standing. Of course, it is Sanditon, not London, where her credentials might be more carefully scrutinized. The authority of Lady Denham, extending from the financial to the social world of Sanditon, is powerfully illustrated in this successful advancement of her humble ward.

One or both of the two clergymen—the Reverend Mr. Hanking and Dr. Brown, assuming that the latter is a member of this profession—may be assigned to the village church and therefore resident in Sanditon. Will we ever learn why "Dr. and Mrs. Henderson" abandoned Sanditon, to be replaced by "Dr. and Mrs. Brown"?

Here as in earlier novels, Jane Austen limits her clerics to Priests (Rectors, Vicars, Curates), with no representation of members of the higher orders of the Church of England, Archbishops (Canterbury and York) or Bishops.

The name "Hanking" presents major problems to the reader of this manuscript. Chapman (70) and Johnson (36) agree on "Hanking," whereas Sacco (74) and *CUPLM* (453) cast a vote for "Hankins," a fairly common surname. Although the final letter of the word, on the right-hand edge of the sheet, is very difficult to decipher and does not look like any other terminal "g" on the page, after long sessions of staring at the manuscript I am inclined to concur with Chapman and Johnson that the correct reading is "Hanking," which also occurs as a surname.

That Captain Little is identified as from Limehouse suggests that he is among the visitors, as is likely Mr. Beard, a solicitor normally plying his trade in Gray's Inn, London. There is no way of telling if either of these gentlemen has any role in the unfolding story, but in light of the hint in "Susan"/"Catherine" that Northanger Abbey has entertained a gentleman who left behind a washing-bill for shirts, stockings, cravats, and waistcoats, a gentleman who turns out to be a titled lord, a member of the peerage, who marries Eleanor Tilney, we cannot lightly dismiss any male visitors to Sanditon.

As a "solicitor" Mr. Beard is "a lawyer in one of the Inns of Court in London, at the centre of the English legal system" (*CUPLM*: 654). "A solicitor is a lawyer operating directly with his/her client as opposed to a barrister that operates indirectly or is called upon by a solicitor to advocate in a case" ("The Jane Austen Regency Glossary").

Founded in the thirteenth century, the four Inns of Court—Gray's Inn, the Inner Temple, the Middle Temple, and Lincoln's Inn—provide living and work space for London-based lawyers and judges. There is, however, a problem in Jane Austen's assigning Mr. Beard, a solicitor, to Gray's Inn. "The four Inns of Court have the exclusive right to Call men and women to the Bar - ie to admit those who have fulfilled the necessary qualifications to the degree of Barrister-at-Law, which entitles them, after a period of pupillage (vocational training) either to practise as independent advocates in the Courts of England and Wales or to take employment in government or local government service, industry, commerce or finance. Thus, to qualify as a barrister, everyone must join an Inn and keep a qualifying session on at least twelve occasions" ("The Honourable Society of Gray's Inn").

Unless a significant change has taken place since, Mr. Beard as a solicitor could not have lived or worked in Gray's Inn or any of the other three Inns of Court. Just as one sometimes has the feeling that Jane Austen uses "doctor," "physician," and "surgeon" interchangeably although they were technically distinct, it is possible that she did not know the difference between a "solicitor" and a "barrister" (the former word appears only in this manuscript and the latter word never appears in her published novels). We are told that Mr. John Knightley is a "lawyer" practicing in London, but we never learn if he is a solicitor or a barrister. There is also "a pert young lawyer" named William Cox(e), scion of a family of lawyers in Highbury. Miss Maria Ward, better known to us as the languid Lady Bertram, has an uncle identified as a "lawyer." Catherine Morland tells Eleanor Tilney that the late Mr. Thorpe had been a "lawyer." Mr. Shepherd is "a civil, cautious lawyer." Mrs. Ferrars seeks advice from "her lawyer" about disinheriting Edward. It is puzzling that Jane Austen formerly referred to members of the profession as "lawyers" but in this manuscript specifies "solicitor" and then places him in one of the Inns of Court, reserved for barristers.

Equally unclear is who is with whom aside from the obvious family groups like Mrs. Mathews and her three unmarried daughters, who are probably here like the Beaufort girls in search of a husband. It is possible, for example, that "Lieut: Smith R.N. Capt: Little, — Limehouse." means that Lieutenant Smith and Captain Little have come to Sanditon together from Limehouse. If they are bachelors in want of wives, they could not have arrived at a more opportune moment as the Beaufort sisters are still available and unattached.

Limehouse, in the London Borough of Tower Hamlets on the northern bank of the River Thames, has been a major port since late medieval times. In the eighteenth and nineteenth centuries, it played an important role in the Port of London's international trade. Just for the record: "The sometimes pejorative term *Limey* for Englishman, erroneously thought to derive from the sailors of Limehouse, derives from the unrelated term *lime-juicer,* from the use of lime juice by sailors to prevent scurvy" ("Limehouse." *Online Encylopædia Britannica*).

Through its punctuation—"Captain Little—Limehouse; Mrs. Jane Fisher, Miss Fisher, Miss Scroggs; Reverend Mr. Hanking;"—the continuation published by Another Lady in 1975 suggests a party of three women (30). If Miss Scroggs has come to Sanditon with Mrs. Jane Fisher and Miss Fisher, she is perhaps the latter's governess or companion. This is an intriguing possibility except that the punctuation in the manuscript in no way indicates this relationship. Adhering more closely to the original punctuation, the 1934 text, edited by R. Brimley Johnson, suggests that the three ladies are not here together: "Capt. Little, Limehouse; Mrs. Jane Fisher, Miss Fisher; Miss Scroggs; Rev. Mr. Hanking" (36). The OUP text maintains the ambiguity of the original by following the punctuation of the manuscript: "Capt: Little,—Limehouse.—Mrs Jane Fisher. Miss Fisher. Miss Scroggs.—Rev: Mr Hanking" (*Minor Works*: 389).

It is a pity that we do not learn more about Miss Scroggs, who promises to be Miss Bates with a nautical air. Jane Austen enjoyed the sounds of unusual names.

CUPLM well points out that "significantly none of the visitors matches the residents in rank" (653), gratifying Lady Denham that she remains the great lady of the neighborhood but at the same time disappointing the partners as well as all the entrepreneurs of the village that Sanditon has not caught on as a major vacation spot for the rich and powerful.]

M^r. P. could not but feel that the List was not only without Distinction, but less numerous than he had hoped. It was but July however, & August & September were the Months; —

[Although the precise beginning of the novel is uncertain, we now know that we are in the month of July. The second sentence is probably indirect discourse. Because "the summer holiday season extended from May to October but was at its height in September" (*CUPLM*: 654), Thomas Parker has reason to be as optimistic about the near future as he is about his "futurity."

The great victory achieved by the Duke of Wellington (born Arthur Wellesley, 1769–1852) at Waterloo took place on June 18, 1815, so "the story begins in June 1816, at hay-making time, and the fragment ends only a few weeks later, in July or August of the same year" (Le Faye, 2002: 298).]

And besides, the promised large Families from Surry & Camberwell, was an ever-present source of Joy. —

>

And besides, the promised large Families from Surry & Camberwell, were an ever-ready consolation. —

[These preceding lines are close to imagined dialog. Whereas much of the manuscript is told through Charlotte's point of view, here we certainly look through Mr. Parker's optimistic eyes. The erroneous "was" in the first version is difficult to explain other than poor copying, unless the author momentarily had "Camberwell was" in her ear.]

M^rs. Whitby came forward immediately from her Literary recess, delighted to see M^r. Parker again, whose manners recommended him to every body, & they were fully occupied in their various Civilities & Communications, while Charlotte having added her name to the List with all becoming alacrity as the first offering to the success of the Season, was proceeding to some immediate purchases for the good of Every body, as soon as Miss Whitby could be hurried down from her Toilette, with all her glossy Curls & ornamented Combs to wait on her. —

>

M^rs. Whitby came forward without delay from her Literary recess, delighted to see M^r. Parker again, whose manners recommended him to every body, & they were fully occupied in their various Civilities & Communications, while Charlotte having added her name to the List as the first offering to the success of the Season, was busy in some immediate purchases for the further good of Every body, as soon as Miss Whitby could be hurried down from her Toilette, with all her glossy Curls & smart Trinkets to wait on her.

[Our author continues to labor with care over one-sentence summaries of complex scenes. Although *CUPLM* (654) suggests a possible source for "literary recess" in Clara Reeve's *The Recess; or, a Tale of Other Times* published as far back as 1785, I believe that it is far more likely a mocking quotation from Mrs. Whitby herself, her vocabulary affected by the romantic novels that she has been reading, who would refer in such an elevated manner to what is no more than a chair in a small room. The passage also indicates, of course, that she has so little business that she has time to read her own wares. Just as her mother's dialog is implied, Miss Whitby's is left unspoken, no loss to Charlotte or the reader because of the unlikelihood that she has much to say of import.]

In adding her name to the list with the "becoming alacrity" of the initial version of the line, Charlotte is following standard protocol of the time "since it was the custom to subscribe to the libraries immediately upon arrival in the watering places and resorts, [so that] their subscription books became a useful guide to who was in town" (Erickson: 576).

David Selwyn may be suggesting that Jane Austen made an error in shifting from "M^{rs}. Whitby" to "Miss Whitby" because he accounts for only one lady on the premises, "a proprietress who has to be 'hurried down from her Toilette, with all her glossy Curls & smart Trinkets' to attend to her customers" (2007: 223–224). I believe, however, that the author has clearly distinguished between Mrs. Whitby, engaged in reading her latest romantic acquisition, and her daughter, occupied with attempts to improve upon nature before presenting herself to her mother's patrons. Her abundance of "glossy Curls" must have been fashionable at the time and hence mocked by the author. That "ornamental Combs" was changed to "smart Trinkets" suggests that the young woman has decorated herself in all the most fashionable but inexpensive accoutrements. The *OED* offers several meanings for "trinket," the most likely one in this context being "a small ornament or fancy article, usually an article of jewellery for personal adornment." To her "ornamental Combs" Miss Whitby has added various bits and pieces consisting of necklaces, rings, bracelets, and brooches, no doubt another current dress fashion adopted by ladies with less discriminating taste than Jane Austen.

In Chapter 8 we learn that there is at least one "young Whitby." There is no Mr. Whitby in the manuscript, but since Mrs. Whitby is not referred to as a widow, he may be somewhere around the premises.

The medial "t" in "Whitby" is identical to the one transcribed earlier by *CUPLM* as "l" except this time there is a heavy crossbar.]

The Library of course, afforded every thing; all the useless things in the World that c^d. not be done without, & among so many pretty Temptations, & with so much good will for M^r. P. to encourage Expenditure, Charlotte began to feel that she must check herself — or rather she reflected that at two & Twenty there c^d. be no excuse for her doing otherwise — & that it w^d. not do for her to be spending all her Money the very first Evening.

[Mr. Heywood has followed the example set by Mr. Morland, who "instead of giving [his daughter, Catherine] an unlimited order on his banker, or even putting an hundred pounds bank-bill into her hands, gave her only ten guineas, and promised her more when she wanted it" (*Northanger Abbey*, 1817: 15). Charlotte's commendable determination to spend her small amount of money wisely is an interesting reflection of Mrs. Morland's advice to Catherine on her departure for Bath: "I beg, Catherine, you will always wrap yourself up very warm about the throat, when you come from the Rooms at night; and I wish you would try to keep some account of the money you spend;—I will give you this little book on purpose" (*Northanger Abbey*, 1817:14).

David Selwyn suggests that in addition to selling "all the useless things in the World that c^d. not be done without," the library "is also a toyshop" (2007: 223). There are no references to toys in the text, and since Charlotte has not been asked to bring back gifts for the younger children at home, she is not seeking any.

David Selwyn sees this passage as significant in the development of Jane Austen's portrait of Charlotte Heywood: "At a period in which the production, sale and acquisition of goods had reached unprecedented heights, it was a striking and timely innovation on Jane Austen's part to invoke the lure of rampant consumerism to test her heroine's character" (2007: 224).]

A vol: of <u>Camilla</u> happened to lie on the Counter.
>
She took up a Book; it happened to be a vol: of <u>Camilla</u>.

[In light of the indebtedness of this manuscript to the shelved "Miss Catherine," it can be no surprise that as part of her vigorous defense of the novel in the published text of *Northanger Abbey* we find references to Burney's "Camilla" (along with "Cecilia" and "Belinda") in the conversation between two imaginary people:

> "And what are you reading, Miss——?" "Oh! it is only a novel!" replies the young lady; while she lays down her book with affected indifference, or momentary shame.— "It is only Cecilia, or Camilla, or Belinda;" or, in short, only some work in which the greatest powers of the mind are displayed, in which the most thorough knowledge of human nature, the happiest delineation of its varieties, the liveliest effusions of wit and humour are conveyed to the world in the best chosen language. (Facsimile: 63–64)

Perhaps demonstrating her naïveté nowhere more than in her attempt to discuss literature seriously with the painfully obtuse John Thorpe, Catherine Morland is led to the work by Fanny Burney through the boorish young man's confusing one writer with another:

> "I think you must like Udolpho, if you were to read it; it is so very interesting."
>
> "Not I, faith! No, if I read any, it shall be Mrs. Radcliff's; her novels are amusing enough; they are worth reading; some fun and nature in *them*."
>
> "Udolpho was written by Mrs. Radcliff," said Catherine, with some hesitation, from the fear of mortifying him.
>
> "No sure; was it? Aye, I remember, so it was; I was thinking of that other stupid book, written by that woman they make such a fuss about, she who married the French emigrant."
>
> "I suppose you mean Camilla?"
>
> "Yes, that's the book; such unnatural stuff!… as soon as I heard she had married an emigrant, I was sure I should never be able to get through it."
>
> "I have never read it."
>
> (Facsimile: 93–95)]

Catherine Morland is definitely not speaking for Jane Austen since the Burney book was so well known in the Austen household after it came out in 1796 that reference to it needed no elaboration.

> In a letter written home to Cassandra from Rowling (Edward's house in Kent) in 1796, soon after the publication of Frances Burney's Camilla, Austen alludes to that novel in explaining her inability to return when she chooses, since Henry, whom she requires to escort her, is about to leave instead for Yarmouth:
>
> To-morrow I shall be just like Camilla in Mr Dubster's summerhouse; for my Lionel will have taken away the ladder by which I came here, or at least by which I intended to get away, and here I must stay till his return. My situation, however, is somewhat

239

preferable to hers, for I am very happy here, though I should be glad to get home by the end of the month. (1 September 1796)

Cassandra would immediately have recognized this parallel between Jane's situation and that of Camilla, stranded by her brother Lionel's thoughtless joke, since the sisters shared the experience of reading Burney's novel. Austen closed her next letter to Cassandra with another allusive joke: "Give my Love to Mary Harrison, & tell her I wish whenever she is attached to a young Man, some respectable Dr Marchmont may keep them apart for five Volumes" (5 September 1796). Works like Camilla thus served Austen's family and friends as common sources for allusions, metaphors, and jokes such as the juvenilia. ("Jane Austen's Letters: Facts and Fictions")

Like its antecedent, "Susan"/"Catherine," this new manuscript is even for Jane Austen very "literary" in containing far more references to published authors than her earlier novels.

The story deals with the matrimonial concerns of a group of young people, Camilla Tyrold and her sisters, the daughters of a country parson, and her cousin Indiana Lynmere; and centres round the love-affair of Camilla herself and her eligible suitor, Edgar Mandlebert. Its happy consummation is delayed over five volumes by intrigues, contretemps, and misunderstandings. The book, especially in its earlier chapters, contains some of the comic situations and absurd characters in which Miss Burney excelled. Among the latter are Sir Hugh Tyrold, Camilla's good-natured but unpractical uncle; the grotesque tutor, Dr. Orkborne, so wrapt up in his own studies that he can give no attention to the duties for which he is engaged; and the fop Sir Sedley Clarendel. But the drollery soon gives place to overstrained romance. (Harvey: 133)

The first edition of *Camilla*, published in five volumes in 1796, was dedicated to Queen Charlotte, wife of George III:

**TO THE
QUEEN**

MADAM,

THAT Goodness inspires a confidence, which, by divesting respect of terror, excites attachment to Greatness, the presentation of this little Work, to Your Majesty must truly, however humbly, evince; and though a public manifestation of duty and regard from an obscure Individual may betray a proud ambition, it is, I trust, but a venial–I am sure it is a natural one.

In those to whom Your Majesty is known but by exaltation of Rank, it may raise, perhaps, some surprise, that scenes, characters, and incidents, which have reference only to common life, should be brought into so august a presence; but the inhabitant of a retired cottage, who there receives the benign permission which at Your Majesty's feet casts this humble offering, bears in mind recollections which must live there while 'memory holds its seat,' of a benevolence withheld from no condition, and delighting in all ways to speed the progress of Morality, through whatever channel it could flow, to whatever port it might steer. I blush at the inference I seem here to leave open of annexing undue importance to a production of apparently so light a kind yet if my hope, my view–however fallacious they may eventually prove, extended not beyond whiling away an idle hour, should I dare seek such patronage?

With the deepest gratitude, and most heart-felt respect, I am,

MADAM,

Your Majesty's

Most obedient, most obliged,
And most dutiful servant,
F. d'Arblay.

Bookham,
June 28, 1796

The advertisement acknowledges the warm reception accorded her two earlier novels.

ADVERTISEMENT

THE Author of this little Work cannot, in the anxious moment of committing it to its fate, refuse herself the indulgence of expressing some portion of the gratitude with which she is filled, by the highly favourable reception given to her *TWO* former attempts

> in this species of composition; nor forbear pouring forth her
> thanks to the many Friends whose kind zeal has forwarded the
> present undertaking: from amongst whom she knows not how to
> resist selecting and gratifying herself by naming the Hon. Mrs.
> BOSCAWEN, Mrs. CREWE, and Mrs. LOCKE.

Knowing of his daughter's admiration of the earlier works by Fanny
Burney D'Arblay (1752-1840), *Evelina* (1778) and *Cecilia* (1782), in 1796
the Reverend George Austen bought her a subscription to the first edition
of *Camilla*, and her name is on the list of subscribers (Olsen: 589).]

She had not <u>Camilla</u>'s Youth, & had no intention of having her Distress,
— so, she turned from the Drawers of rings & Broches repressed farther
solicitation & paid for what she bought. —

[The text implies that Charlotte has read *Camilla*, with the logical extension
that she has read other books of the same type. Although nothing is said
during the episode at Willingden about its having a circulating library, there
must be one close enough for the young women of the Heywood household
to indulge in their reading fantasies. Although circulating libraries were
common in the cities, they also appeared in rural communities as the idea of
reading for pleasure spread across the country. Like the Bennet girls visiting
Meryton to pick up small purchases and big gossip, the Heywood daughters
would make regular excursions to the local shops, among which would be a
general goods store along with circulating library like the one operated by
Mrs. Whitby. Lee Erickson, however, is doubtful that Willingden would
provide a source for Charlotte's books: "In rural areas circulating libraries
did not exist, since a bookseller needed an urban population of about 2,000
to make a living" (578).

Charlotte's admission that "she had not <u>Camilla</u>'s Youth" is not merely
a realistic assessment of herself but a reference to the book's subtitle, "A
Picture of Youth" (at the beginning of the novel, the heroine is introduced
at only 9 years of age, but she is 17 for the major part of the novel). "Her
distresses include financial embarrassments through overspending a small
allowance in the purchase of 'little keep-sakes' at the beginning of a visit
to the fashionable spa of Tunbridge Wells" (*CUPLM*: 654). Charlotte's
moderated frugality is also a confirmation that despite her enjoyment of
romantic novels, like a good daughter of a gentleman-farmer, she has her feet
firmly planted on terra firma. Since Catherine Morland admitted to John

Thorpe that she had not read Burney's novel, it is possible that Charlotte Heywood has also decided to forgo its attractions. We never learn what she bought, by the way, but no doubt she has found some small souvenirs, the "new Parasols, new Gloves, & new Broches, for her sisters & herself," as requested by Mrs. Heywood. There does not appear to be anything in the library for the boys at home if there are any young Heywoods in Willingden. If it is also a toyshop, Charlotte has been given no commission to bring back any.

For "Broches repressed" Jane Austen probably meant "Broches, repressed," but there is no comma in the manuscript.]

For her particular gratification, they were then to take a Turn on the Cliff — but as they quitted the Library they were met by two Ladies whose arrival made an alteration necessary, Lady Denham & Miss Brereton. —

[Jane Austen enjoys changing the direction of a plot, here postponing the planned walk on the cliff because of the unexpected arrival of Lady Denham and Clara Brereton. She had created the same effect in *Pride and Prejudice* when Elizabeth and the Gardiners are forced to substitute for the distant Lakes the closer attractions of Derbyshire. And guess who owns a magnificent estate in that county?

The cast of characters is now almost complete, with only Sir Edward Denham and Miss Esther Denham yet to appear on stage. Jane Austen skillfully introduces her characters slowly so that we can learn who they are, primarily through their conversation but sometimes exclusively through narration. Thus we have Lady Denham and Clara Brereton in this scene, to be followed shortly by the entrance of Sir Edward and Esther Denham. Lady Denham and Sir Edward make their impression on us through their dialog, but neither Clara nor Esther utters a word in the extant text.

It may be significant that Lady Denham does not enter the library, where she would have no interest other than entering her name in the subscription book.]

They had been to Trafalgar House, & been directed thence to the Library, & though Lady D. was a great deal too active to regard the walk of a mile as anything requiring rest, & talked of going home again directly, the Parkers knew that to be pressed into their House, & obliged to take her Tea with them, would suit her best, — & therefore the stroll on the Cliff gave way to an immediate return home. —

[The opening is probably indirect discourse with Lady Denham's recounting the steps in her reaching her friends, who have been away.]

"No, no, said her Ladyship — I will not have you hurry your Tea on my account. — I know you like your Tea late. — My early hours are not to put my Neighbours to inconvenience. No, no, Miss Clara & I will get back to our own Tea. — We came out with no other Thought. —

[First impressions are everything in Jane Austen, and our first impression of Lady Denham is of a woman accustomed to getting her own way with a minimum of fuss. Her open admission that she knows that the Parkers have a late tea is evidence of her readiness to impose herself upon anyone in her path. Her insincerity is strongly suggested in her asserting that she has taken this long walk from Trafalgar House, where she must have expected to be invited in for an early tea, to the Library in order to return home—sans tea—to Sanditon House. Tea was expensive, and Lady Denham knows how to cut down on her expenses by visiting neighbors at particular hours of the day. By "Neighbours" she presumably means those few people in Sanditon who are sufficiently genteel to merit her attention, not merely someone who lives nearby.]

We wanted just to see our good Neighbours, & be sure of their being really come —, but we get back to our own Tea." —
>
We wanted just to see you & make sure of you being really come —, but we get back to our own Tea." —
>
We wanted just to see you & make sure of your being really come —, but we get back to our own Tea." —

[Surprisingly, the author revises her material to return to the original, and grammatically correct construction ("be sure of their being really come" > "make sure of you being really come" > "make sure of your being really come") despite the better illustration in the second version of Lady Denham's lack of formal education and indifference to the niceties of the language.]

She went on however towards Trafalgar House & took possession of the Drawing room very quietly — without seeming to hear a word of M^{rs}. P.'s orders to the Servant as they entered, to bring Tea directly.

[This is obviously a scene that has taken place on a regular basis since the Parkers moved into Lady Denham's sphere of influence.]

Charlotte was fully consoled for the loss of her walk, by finding herself in company with those, whom the conversation of the morn^g. had given her a great curiosity to see. —

>

Charlotte was fully consoled for the loss of her walk, by finding herself in company with those, whom the conversation of the morn^g. had given her a great curiosity to see. She observed them well. —

[The added second sentence makes clear that the following passage is through Charlotte's all-observing and judgmental eyes.]

Lady D. was of middle height, stout, upright & alert in her motions, with a shrewd eye, & self-satisfied air — but not an unagreable Countenance — & tho' her manner was rather downright & abrupt, as of a person who valued herself on being free-spoken, there was a good humour & cordiality about her — a civility & readiness to be acquainted with Charlotte herself, & a heartiness of welcome towards her old friends, which was inspiring the Good will she seemed to feel; —

[*CUPLM* suggests "strong, robust" (655) as Jane Austen's meaning for "stout." However, her earlier description of Mrs. Jennings, a far more affable antecedent of the great lady of Sanditon, as "a good-humoured, merry, fat, elderly woman, who talked a great deal, seemed very happy, and rather vulgar," may indicate that Jane Austen is using the word "stout" in *Sanditon* in its current sense of "corpulent." Jane Austen appears to have used the word "fat" only one other time in her novels, and it clearly means "corpulent" in this passage from *Emma*.

Jane Fairfax['s]… height was pretty, just such as almost every body would think tall, and nobody could think very tall; her figure particularly graceful; her size a most becoming medium, between fat and thin.

Her parsimoniousness suggests that Lady Denham buys as little food as possible, and we never see her eating (only cadging tea off her neighbors), so we do not know if she is more like Arthur Parker or Diana Parker in her dietary habits and appearance.

The word "stout" has additional meanings as recorded in the *OED* that could be implied. "Proud, haughty, arrogant," now obsolete but used well into the nineteenth century and apropos to Lady Denham as her character is developed. The *OED* cites Jane Austen's use of the word in *Sense and Sensibility* to illustrate the meaning "strong in body; of powerful build": "**1796** JANE AUSTEN *Sense & Sens.* xxxviii, They must get a stout girl of all works." This early dating, long before the publication date of 1811, must be based on the unprovable assumption that the text as we know it is close what it had been in "Elinor and Marianne." "In robust health," used well into the nineteenth century, is a good fit with the general impression of Lady Denham. An unlikely meaning here, used through the nineteenth century, was "valiant, brave."

Jane Austen had used the word "stout" several times in earlier novels, generally in the likely sense of robust or healthy, such as

> Lydia was a stout, well-grown girl of fifteen, with a fine complexion and good-humoured countenance. (*Pride and Prejudice*)

or

> The younger boy [2-year-old Walter Musgrove], a remarkable stout, forward child, of two years old, having got the door opened for him by some one without, made his determined appearance among them. (*Persuasion*)

or

> "He is a fine old fellow, upon my soul! Stout, active—looks as young as his son." (*Northanger Abbey*, John Thorpe on General Tilney)

The word could possibly mean corpulent, however, in

> "A neighbour of ours, Dr. Skinner, was here for his health last winter, and came away quite stout." (*Northanger Abbey*, Mrs. Allen to Henry Tilney)

or

[John Thorpe] was a stout young man of middling height, who, with a plain face and ungraceful form, seemed fearful of being too handsome unless he wore the dress of a groom.

Since the "great boy" could well have a fat mother, something more than merely robust is suggested in

Harriet was soon assailed by half a dozen children, headed by a stout woman and a great boy. (*Emma*)

Charlotte betrays her own readiness to be flattered, as she will soon be by Sir Edward's insincere notice, by Lady Denham's apparently friendly manner. But Lady Denham has yet to learn that Charlotte is not an heiress and is therefore not suitable for her nephew-through-marriage. This Catherine/General Tilney relationship has been borrowed from the rejected manuscript. That Lady Denham can at best claim "not an unagreable Countenance" is a deliberately evasive description of her appearance. Because of her habitual penny pinching she is probably not overweight, so "stout" is probably here used to mean "strong."]

And as for Miss Brereton, her appearance so completely justified M^r. P.'s praise that Charlotte thought she had never beheld a more lovely, or more Interesting young Woman. —

["Interesting" was "a popular adjective in the fiction of the period, with a stronger meaning than now, often used to indicate that something about the person being described has an air of mystery, or possibly a significant or unusual history which will inevitably be told during the course of the novel" (*CUPLM*: 655). Although Jane Austen probably never uses "interesting" in its extended sense of "to be pregnant"— *OED*: "3. (to be) in an interesting condition, situation, state: (to be) pregnant"—she must have been aware of its use in contemporary writing. Is she perhaps planting a subtle hint about what is to come in the ensuing story?]

Elegantly tall, regularly handsome, with great delicacy of complexion & soft Blue eyes, a sweet modesty yet natural gracefulness of Address, Charlotte could see her only as
>
Elegantly tall, regularly handsome, with great delicacy of complexion & soft Blue eyes, a sweet modesty & yet natural gracefulness of Address,

Charlotte could see in her only the most perfect representation of all the most beautiful & bewitching Heroines

>

Elegantly tall, regularly handsome, with great delicacy of complexion & soft Blue eyes, a sweet modesty & yet natural gracefulness of Address, Charlotte could see in her only the most perfect representation of whatever Heroine might be most beautiful & bewitching, in all the numerous vol:ˢ they had left behind them in Mʳˢ. Whitby's

>

Elegantly tall, regularly handsome, with great delicacy of complexion & soft Blue eyes, a sweet modesty & yet natural gracefulness of Address, Charlotte could see in her only the most perfect representation of whatever Heroine might be most beautiful & bewitching, in all the numerous vol:ˢ they had left behind them on Mʳˢ. Whitby's shelves. —

>

Elegantly tall, regularly handsome, with great delicacy of complexion & soft Blue eyes, a sweetly modest & yet naturally graceful Address, Charlotte could see in her only the most perfect representation of whatever Heroine might be most beautiful & bewitching, in all the numerous vol:ˢ they had left behind them on Mʳˢ. Whitby's shelves. —

[The description of Clara Brereton matches that assumed to belong to every fictional heroine of the time. The passage may be unique in Jane Austen's novels in delineating in detail someone's appearance, with most of her heroines merely sketched, such as Elizabeth with her "fine eyes" or Emma, "handsome, clever, and rich."

Again our author stresses the importance of first impressions, this time of the young woman who in any conventional novel would be the heroine, like Marianne Dashwood, Jane Bennet, Jane Fairfax, and perhaps Mary Crawford. Charlotte may not be a Camilla, but she looks at the world around her as though inhabiting a romantic novel. Jane Austen rarely describes a character in such physical detail, but since Clara is a traditional heroine she must be shown to fit the traditional mold.

Jane Austen's concept of sentence structure is very different from ours: by current standards, "Elegantly tall... graceful Address" would modify "Charlotte." But only very dull Elves would misunderstand the passage and fail to connect the phrase with the beautiful Clara.

CUPLM transcribes the medial "t" of "Whitby" as "l" to give us "Whilby" (458). Again the uncrossed letter is a final "t" (minus the crossbar) used medially. It is very similar to the "t" in "partly" that ends the page (folio 27r). Chapman (75), Johnson (38), and Sacco (78) concur in reading the name as "Whitby."]

Perhaps it might be partly oweing to her having just issued from a Circulating Library — but she c^d. not separate the idea of a complete Heroine from Clara Brereton. Her situation with Lady Denham so very much in favour of it! — She seemed placed with her on purpose to be ill-used. — Such Poverty & Dependance joined to such Beauty and Merit, seemed to leave no choice in the business. —

[There is no "perhaps" about the influence of the Library on her first reaction to Miss Clara Brereton, but Charlotte, fresh from the country, is almost as much in search of a real-life manifestation of a romantic heroine as she is of a husband. "Many novels of the period showed genteel but impoverished heroines being ill treated by wealthy older women who were ostensibly offering them protection... for example, Emily St. Aubert and Madame Cheron in Ann Radcliffe's *The Mysteries of Udolfo* (1794)" (*CUPLM*: 655). The Cambridge University Press editor's introducing Mrs. Radcliffe's novel as though it constituted part of Charlotte's reading brings us right back to Catherine Morland, as the text specifies that it is one of her favorite books. Even the boorish John Thorpe is aware of it although we never learn if he has actually read any of it.

Henry Tilney, of course, has read it, and he confesses great pleasure in it (although I suspect some irony in his hyperbolic praise): "The person, be it gentleman or lady, who has not pleasure in a good novel, must be intolerably stupid. I have read all Mrs. Radcliffe's works, and most of them with great pleasure. The Mysteries of Udolpho, when I had once begun it, I could not lay down again; I remember finishing it in two days—my hair standing on end the whole time."]

These feelings were not the result of any spirit of Romance in Charlotte herself. No, she was a very sober-minded young Lady, sufficiently well-read in Novels to supply her Imagination with amusement, but not at all unreasonably influenced by them;

[The author does perhaps protest too much, since Charlotte shows every sign of transferring what she had read to real life.]

249

& while she pleased herself the first 5 minutes with fancying the Persecutions which <u>ought</u> to be the Lot of the interesting Clara, especially in the form of the most barbarous conduct on Lady Denham's side, she found no reluctance to admit from subsequent observation, that they appeared to be on very comfortable Terms. — She c^d. see nothing worse in Lady Denham, than the sort of oldfashioned formality of always calling her <u>Miss Clara</u> — nor anything objectionable in the degree of observance & attention which Clara paid. —

[Clara is again "interesting," an adjective assigned to no one else in the text. Lady Denham's addressing her young guest as "Miss Clara" is open to several interpretations. She may not want to enter the level of comfortable familiarity that would be reached if she called her "Clara." More likely, Lady Denham does not want to refer to her as "Miss Brereton" since that was her own name at one time.

Jane Austen liked the word "barbarous," using it in several of her novels, each time in a slightly different sense. The word carries various connotations, ranging from fairly mild—"uncultured, uncivilized, unpolished; rude, rough, wild, savage"—to the most extreme sadism—"savage in infliction of cruelty, cruelly harsh" (*OED*).

In *Northanger Abbey*, she uses the word in its most extreme sense, which may match what she has in mind in the final manuscript in her description of Charlotte's imagined relationship between Lady Denham and Clara Brereton.

> To what might not those doors lead? In support of the plausibility of this conjecture, it further occurred to her, that the forbidden gallery, in which lay the apartments of the unfortunate Mrs. Tilney, must be, as certainly as her memory could guide her, exactly over this suspected range of cells, and the stair-case by the side of those apartments of which she had caught a transient glimpse, communicating by some secret means with those cells, might well have favoured the barbarous proceedings of her husband. Down that staircase she had perhaps been conveyed in a state of well-prepared insensibility! (*OIJA–V*: 188)

Because Catherine's fertile imagination has led her to the conviction that General Tilney has either imprisoned his wife in some darkened cell or even murdered her, she could well mean "cruelly harsh" at the very least. In using the word in almost as extreme a sense as Catherine, Charlotte reveals her origins in the young lass from Fullerton. She also announces to us that she has been reading some of the same sensationalist novels that infected the mind of her younger avatar.

In *Sense and Sensibility*, in contrast, the word is used in a much less extreme sense. She assigns the word three times, and as expected it is always to Marianne, who for the most part speaks in the most hyperbolic tone. In each instance, though, her use of the word suggests unkindness rather than extreme cruelty.

> "This woman of whom he writes—whoever she be—or any one, in short, but your own dear self, mama, and Edward, may have been so barbarous to bely me."

> "Willoughby, where was your heart when you wrote those words? Oh, barbarously insolent!—Elinor, can he be justified?"

> "Oh! Elinor," she cried, "you have made me hate myself for ever.— How barbarous have I been to you!"

It would be surprising to find the cool and self-controlled Charlotte Heywood emoting at the level of a much younger and self-indulgent Marianne Dashwood.

Mere "unkindness" is all that can be meant in *Pride and Prejudice* when Mrs. Bennet frets over Mr. Collins's successful proposal to Charlotte Lucas.

> Two inferences, however, were plainly deduced from the whole: one, that Elizabeth was the real cause of the mischief; and the other that she herself had been barbarously misused by them all; and on these two points she principally dwelt during the rest of the day.

No higher level of cruelty is suggested in the unusual instance of Fanny Price's momentary loss of self-control in her concern over her cousin's feelings.

> Fanny, not able to refrain entirely from observing them, had seen enough to be tolerably satisfied. It was barbarous to be happy when Edmund was suffering.

Finally, Jane Austen uses the word in an unexpectedly comic manner in *Pride and Prejudice*.

Bingley, from this time, was of course a daily visitor at Longbourn; coming frequently before breakfast, and always remaining till after supper; unless when some barbarous neighbour, who could not be enough detested, had given him an invitation to dinner which he thought himself obliged to accept.]

On one side it seemed protecting kindness, on the other grateful & affectionate respect. —

[The controlling word is "seemed," as this favorable assessment is Charlotte's first impression based on only a very short acquaintance with the two women. As the story progresses, Charlotte will frequently learn that her initial impressions, especially pre-judgments, are faulty. She has to re-evaluate Lady Denham following Thomas Parker's fairly flattering summary, finding her to be much worse than expected. Her first impression of Sir Edward is that she likes him and that he is attracted to her. Both ideas are quickly quashed when he shows that he is merely using her to make Clara Brereton jealous and is essentially a bubble head. She initially sees Clara Brereton as the besieged heroine of a sentimental novel, only to see that she is apparently well treated by Lady Denham and clearly in charge of the situation near the end of the fragment when Charlotte espies her with Sir Edward in what could be a lovers' tryst. Sidney Parker, reported by his older brother to be a somewhat useless and saucy fellow, turns out to be an affectionate uncle, a highly regarded brother-in-law, and a complete gentleman. We have yet to see how many other surprises are in store for our heroine.]

The Conversation turned entirely upon Sanditon, its present number of Visitants & the Chances of a good Season. It was evident that Lady D. had more anxiety, more fears of loss, than her Coadjutor. She wanted to have the Place fill faster, & seemed to have many harassing apprehensions of the Lodgings being in some instances under-let. — Miss Diana Parker's two large Families were not forgotten.

[The text does not specify how Lady Denham learned of Diana Parker's success in bringing two families to Sanditon. Nor will it state her reaction upon learning that the two families are one family. We never see Diana Parker with Lady Denham, and a confrontation between these two powerful personalities would make for interesting dialog.]

"Very very good, very good, said her Ladyship. —
>

"Very good, very good, said her Ladyship. —

[The repeated "Very very" again strongly suggests inaccurate transcription.]

A West Indy Family & a school. That sounds well. That will bring Money." —

"No people spend more freely, I beleive, than W. Indians." observed M^r. Parker. —

[Thomas Parker's observation is based on stereotypes of residents in that distant part of the world. There may also be a twinge of envy about the great wealth of these alien people. There is certainly no expression of dismay that their comfort was bought through human enslavement and forced labor. "Huge fortunes were to made in the eighteenth and early nineteenth centuries by people who owned plantations, and traded goods such as sugar, produced by means of cheap slave labour; those who came back to Britain, or sent relatives to Britain, for education, leisure or retirement, were therefore likely to be very wealthy. People who lived in the West Indies were regarded as prone to temperamental and emotional extremes, from indolence on the one hand to passion on the other, because of the hot climate" (*CUPLM*: 655). As is clearly seen in *Mansfield Park*, such holdings are the main source of Sir Thomas Bertram's fortune. Jane Austen must have known about contemporary efforts to stop traffic in slave labor, such as the ban on importing African slaves in British colonies in 1807, finally abolished in the British Empire in 1833.]

"Aye — so I have heard — and because they have full Purses, think themselves equal, may be, to your old Country Families.
>
"Aye — so I have heard — and because they have full Purses, fancy themselves equal, may be, to your old Country Families.

[There is a far more scornful tone in "fancy" than in "think." The text fails to prove that Lady Denham is herself from an "old Country Family," but now that she is a titled widow she can pass judgment on other people.]

But then, they who scatter their Money so freely, never think of whether they may not be doing mischeif by raising the price of Things — And I have heard that's very much the case with your West-injines — and if they come among us to raise the price of our necessaries of Life, we shall not much thank them M^r. Parker." —

[Again we have a rare contraction in "that's," perhaps once more indicating poor education. Lady Denham is one of the few characters in Jane Austen to use this now-standard construction.

The form "West-injines" does not itself receive *OED* recognition, but as noted in *CUPLM* (656) it appears in the *OED*'s citation of the meaning of "West Indians" contemporaneous with the fragment: "**1817** JANE AUSTEN *Sanditon* (1925) 78 And I have heard that's very much the case with your West-injines."]

"My dear Madam, They can only raise the price of consumeable Articles, by such an extraordinary Demand for them & such a diffusion of Money among us, as must do us more Good than harm. — Our Butchers & Bakers & Traders in general cannot get rich without bringing Prosperity to <u>us</u>. — If <u>they</u> do not gain, our rents must be insecure — & in proportion to their profit must be ours eventually in the increased value of our Houses."

[Thomas Parker is by far the more sanguine and imaginative of the two business partners. The text never tells us how much money each has invested in the development of Sanditon as a seaside resort, and it is possible that Lady Denham, with an enormous fortune, has contributed more than her co-adjutor, who has a comfortable but not exceptional bank account. When men in Jane Austen's novels are really wealthy, like Rushworth and Darcy, we are told their impressive annual income. In the case of the Parkers, we are told only that they have a good life and are in no way needy. But that is a long way from the affluence enjoyed by the former Miss Brereton, now Lady Denham, with her original fortune plus whatever she inherited from Mr. Hollis and Sir Harry. Hence she is far more apprehensive about each detail of Sanditon's future than Thomas Parker, who must have kept some resources in reserve for all the little Parkers, those already at home and those who will on an annual basis certainly join the family, now very small by contemporary standards.]

"Oh! — well. — But I should not like to have Butcher's meat raised, though — & I shall keep it down as long as I can. — Aye — that young Lady smiles I see; — I dare say she thinks me a odd sort of a Creature, — but <u>she</u> will come to care about such matters herself in time.

[This passage supplies stage action of Charlotte's smiling, suggesting that she lacks sufficient control over her facial expression to conceal her real reactions to the people around her. As a young woman raised to distinguish between fact and fantasy, she has never had to develop the skills to hide her thoughts.]

Yes, Yes, my Dear, depend upon it, you will be thinking of the price of Butcher's meat in time — tho' you may not happen to have quite such a Servants Hall full to feed, as I have. —
>
Yes, Yes, my Dear, depend upon it, you will be thinking of the price of Butcher's meat in time — tho' you may not happen to have quite such a Servants Hall to feed, as I have. —

[Despite disclaimers of being "a Woman of Parade," Lady Denham hints occasionally about all the staff employed at Sanditon House, with the original "full" suggesting more servants than we see later and possibly even "an army of servants" (Knox-Shaw: 244–245).

I am not a Woman of Parade, as all the World knows, & if it was not for what I owe to poor M^r. Hollis's memory, I should never keep up Sanditon House as I do; — it is not for my own pleasure. — Well M^r. Parker — and the other is a Boarding school, a French Boarding School, is it? — No harm in that. — They'll stay their six weeks. — And out of such a number, who knows but some may be consumptive & want Asses milk —& I have two Milch asses at this present time. — But perhaps the little Misses may hurt the Furniture. — I hope they will have a good sharp Governess to look after them. —"

[A "French Boarding School" was "run by a Frenchwoman, or a woman purporting to be French" (*CUPLM*: 656). It was fashionable at the time for English women to assume Gallic names to add a cachet of authenticity to their institution. "In 1785, [Cassandra and Jane Austen and their cousin Jane Cooper] briefly attended Mrs. La Tournelle's [aka Sarah Hackitt] Ladies' Boarding School in Reading, Berkshire, also known as Abbey House school, but the fees ["about £35 a year for each pupil" (Le Faye, 2002: 20)] proved too expensive for the rector to continue" ("Jane Austen." *BBC America Shop*).

"Asses' milk was considered to resemble human milk closely, and therefore to be superior to other milk. It was seen as particularly suitable for asthmatics and consumptives" (*CUPLM*: 656).

In his book originally published in 1750, Dr. Richard Russell included milk, presumably that of an ass, in his cures for various illnesses.

> And tho' I am far from affirming this Method of Salt Water will do every Thing, there being some obstinate Tumours, and cutaneous [skin] Eruptions, which will elude it's Force; yet after Trials of this, and other Medicines, which has stimulated too much, I have committed the Patients some Months to drink of Water, and a Milk Diet; and then, the Acrimony being abated, I have cured them by those very Remedies, which did not answer before. (83)

> XV.

> In Cases attended with great Acrimony, I have sometimes thought Sea Water irritated too much; but a Milk Diet, and Absorbents will alter that State; and I have seen Sea Water cure those Cases afterwards. (197)

In writing to one of his medical correspondents, Dr. Frewin, Dr. Russell is more specific about the source of the salutary milk.

> I have remarked in my Essay, that where *Sea Water* and *cold Bathing* failed, I thought it a sufficient Reason to try a quite contrary Method; and found, that after a Course of *tepid Bathing* and Asses Milk, I could cure many Diseases, which Sea Water, and cold Bathing, would not reach before. (252) (Appendix C. Dr. Richard Russell)

In 1785 (second edition; first edition 1769), when Lady Denham would have been about 40 years old and aware of contemporary medical practice, Dr. William Buchan (1729–1805) recommended in his *Domestic Medicine; or, the Family Physician*, that asses' milk be consumed in large doses.

> ASSES milk is commonly reckoned preferable to any other; but it cannot always be obtained; besides, it is generally taken in a very small quantity; whereas, to produce any effects, it ought to make a considerable part of the patient's diet. It is hardly to be expected, that a gill or two of asses milk, drank in the space of twenty-four

hours, should be able to produce any considerable change in the humours of an adult; and when people do not perceive its effects soon, they lose hope, and so leave it off. Hence it happens that this medicine, however valuable, very seldom performs a cure. The reason is obvious; it is commonly used too late, is taken in too small quantities, and is not duly persisted in.

I HAVE known very extraordinary effects from asses milk in obstinate coughs, which threatened a consumption of the lungs; and do verily believe, if used at this period, that it would seldom fail; but if it be delayed till an ulcer is formed, which is generally the case, how can it be expected to succeed?

ASSES milk ought to be drank, if possible, in its natural warmth, and, by a grown person, in the quantity of half an English pint at a time. Instead of taking this quantity night and morning only, the patient ought to take it four times, or at least thrice a day, and to eat a little light bread along with it, so as to make it a kind of meal.

IF the milk should happen to purge, it may be mixed with old conserve of roses. When that cannot be obtained, the powder of crabs claws may be used in its stead. Asses milk is usually ordered to be drank warm in bed; but as it generally throws the patient into a sweat when taken in this way, it would perhaps be better to give it after he rises.

By no means did interest in asses' milk commence in the eighteenth century. Asses (also known as donkeys) were first domesticated as early as 5500 B.C. in the Nile valley as work animals to pull ploughs. In the closing years B.C.E., asses' milk acquired a reputation for improving the complexion because Cleopatra bathed in it. Closely resembling human milk, it may be better for medicinal purposes than cow's milk. In Jane Austen's day, "Wealthy individuals, especially those with tuberculosis, [drank] asses' milk, which had fewer nutrients than cows' or goats' milk but also had less protein and fat and was thus more easily digested" (Olsen: 77).

Lady Denham's concern for the condition of furniture is seen in the closing lines of the fragment when we visit her drawing room.

CUPLM suggests a meaning for "governess" in this passage—a "teacher, particularly the chief teacher who might own the school (that is, the woman who governs the establishment)" (657)—that is different from what we find elsewhere in Jane Austen's novels. In an exception to her usual use of the word, Jane Austen had in mind someone higher on the social scale when she created Mrs. Weston (née Miss Taylor).

> Sixteen years had Miss Taylor been in Mr. Woodhouse's family, less as a governess than a friend, very fond of both daughters, but particularly of Emma. Between *them* it was more the intimacy of sisters.

In contrast, in the worst possible meaning of the word, becoming a governess—"A female teacher; an instructress; now chiefly, one so employed in a private household" (*OED*)—is the dreaded fate awaiting Jane Fairfax if her secret engagement comes to nothing. As she attempts to explain to a deaf Mrs. Elton,

> "I did not mean, I was not thinking of the slave-trade," replied Jane; "governess-trade, I assure you, was all that I had in view; widely different certainly as to the guilt of those who carry it on; but as to the greater misery of the victims, I do not know where it lies."

Despite her general lack of sympathy for Miss Bates' impoverished niece, from Emma's point of view it is clearly a demeaning position, the worst possible employment for a woman, and entirely unsuitable for Jane Fairfax.

> "Jane actually on the point of going as governess!"

In *Mansfield Park*, the governess presumably lived in the house to instruct Miss Bertram and Julia.

> Had she [Lady Bertram] possessed greater leisure for the service of her girls, she would probably have supposed it unnecessary, for they were under the care of a governess, with proper masters, and could want nothing more.

The governess employed for Anne Elliot and her two sisters must also have lived in the family home, Kellynch Hall.

> She had called on her former governess, and had heard from her of there being an old school-fellow in Bath, who had the two strong claims on her attention of past kindness and present suffering.

The most amusing passage on a governess, and again a conventional denotation, comes during Elizabeth Bennet's visit to Lady Catherine.

"Has your governess left you?"

"We never had any governess."

"No governess! How was that possible? Five daughters brought up at home without a governess! I never heard of such a thing…. Then, who taught you? who attended to you? Without a governess, you must have been neglected."]

Poor M^r. Parker got no more credit from Lady D. than he had from his Sisters, for the Object which had taken him to Willingden.

[It appears that most members of the Parker family are "poor" in some way.]

"Lord! my dear Sir, she cried, how could you think of such a thing? I am very sorry you met with your accident, but upon my word you deserved it. — Going after a Doctor! — Why, what sh^d. we do with a Doctor here? It w^d. be only encouraging our Servants & the Poor to fancy themselves ill, if there was a D^r. at hand. — Oh! pray, let us have none of the Tribe at Sanditon. We go on very well as we are.

[Lady Denham's use of "Doctor"—Mr. Parker very distinctly attempted to retain the services of a surgeon—may be meant to indicate her lack of discernment: whereas nowadays the word represents anyone with a license to practice medicine, at the time there were fairly strict distinctions to be made. At the top were the physicians (such as those consulted by the Parker sisters), who had studied "physics" or what passed for medical studies at the time. Below them were the surgeons (among them the man sought by Thomas Parker), whose specialties included blood-letting and removal of limbs. And below them were the apothecaries, who prepared such medications as were available.

In 1800, "doctor" generally meant a "physician," with functions distinct from those of a surgeon.

When a physician recommends blood-letting he will be present, but the operation is done by a surgeon—those who cannot afford a surgeon will go to an apothecary. The incision is usually made in the neck or arm. First a handkerchief is thrown over the patient's head, so that he will not see the blood. The doctor then places a ball of wool in the patient's hand, and as he presses it, the vein of the arm swells. The surgeon touches a blue vein with his lancet, and as the blood spurts out the doctor catches it in a basin. He orders the blood-letting to stop when he considers the right amount has been taken, which in the case of a fever is eight ounces. (Borer: 170)

To practice either as a physician or surgeon in 1800 required advanced training.

No one can legally practise in London today as a physician or surgeon without a licence or diploma from the Royal College of Physicians or the Royal College of Surgeons. (Borer: 165)

It is worth remembering that in Jane Austen's time the title "Doctor" was used differently from its current meaning.

Doctor [was] a title used in Jane Austen's novels, usually only to designate a doctor of divinity. It was also applied to physicians, but generally not to surgeons, who were known as 'Mr.' (Pool: 299)

There is the Sea & the Downs & my Milch-asses — & I have told M^{rs}. Whitby that if any body enquires for a Chamber-House, they may be supplied at a fair rate — (poor M^{r}. Hollis's Chamber House, as good as new) — and what can People want for more? —
>
There is the Sea & the Downs & my Milch-asses — & I have told M^{rs}. Whitby that if any body enquires for a Chamber-House, they may be supplied at a fair rate — (poor M^{r}. Hollis's Chamber Horse, as good as new) — and what can People want for more? —

[The handwriting on "House" is uneven but clear enough. The error may be another indication that at least some of the pages of this manuscript are transcriptions.

The chamber horse, an item no longer found in most households, "was the Regency equivalent of an exercise bicycle or similar fitness machine, being a wooden chair with a box seat containing concertina-like springs, upon which the user would bounce up and down as if trotting on a horse, in order to stimulate the system" (Le Faye, 2002: 307; illustration: *"A Sheraton*

design for a chamber-horse, 1793, with a cutaway sketch showing the four tiers of spiral springs inside the seat."). A superbly restored chamber-horse from about 1790 can be seen at:
www.eronjohnsonantiques.com/dynapage/IP17766.htm

"Literally a hobby-horse for adults to use in exercise when troubled by melancholia, the chamber horse was used by such notables as Samuel Richardson, whose physician Dr. Cheyne 'promised "all the good and beneficial Effects of a hard Trotting Horse except the fresh Air"'" (Blackwell, note 51).

> George Cheyne [was] a popular 18th century diet doctor—this despite his weighing 440 pounds at the height of his popularity. Cheyne was also responsible for a long-forgotten exercise fad:

> Cheyne championed the "chamber horse," a chair sporting an elevated seat on what resembled an accordion bellows. Inside was a large spring, and by gripping the chair's arms you could bounce up and down in a simulation of horse-riding.... Even the dour Methodist theologian John Wesley spent time each day bouncing up and down on one. Cheyne recommended to Samuel Richardson that he compose his novel *Pamela* by dictating it while bouncing on a chamber horse.... Nearly a century later the physician Benjamin Rush was still prescribing chamber-horses, and Jane Austen's characters also resorted to them. Throughout the 18th and 19th centuries estate sales regularly turned up abandoned chamber-horses—though any resemblance to our own garages of dusty treadmills and exercise bicycles is, of course, surely coincidental. (Collins, Paul)

CUPLM (464) transcribes the medial "t" of "Whitby" as "l" to give us "Whilby." Jane Austen has again used a form of the terminal "t" in a medial position. Examination of the manuscript page (folio 29r) shows a considerable variety in how she wrote the letter "t": in line 1, "it" has a final "t" without a crossbar; in line 10, "credit" has a final "t" that does not need a crossbar but has one; in line 12, "to" is written with a kind of short-hand "t" without a crossbar linked to the "o"; in line 15, "accident" closes with a final "t" that does not need a crossbar but has one; line 16 contains "it" with what may be a terminal "t" that does not need a crossbar but has one; again in line 16 we find "after" with a barely crossed conventional medial "t"; and still on line 16, "Doctor" has a medial "t" that is not only crossed but looks far more like a large looped "l"; in line 20 we find "let" with a terminal "t" that does not need a crossbar but has one; and in "the Sea & the Downs" on line 23 she uses an initial "t" unlike what we find in the middle or at the end of words on this page. Chapman (81), Johnson (41), and Sacco (82) concur in reading the name as "Whitby."]

Here have I lived 70 good years in the world & never took Physic above twice — and never saw the face of a Doctor in all my Life, on my <u>own</u> account. —

[Lady Denham is now old enough that she can announce with pride that she has survived seven decades, no thanks to the medical profession. She is probably the oldest person whose age is specified in Jane Austen's novels, but she is also one of the most vigorous. Although it is inconceivable that she is in any way based on Jane Austen's mother, Cassandra Leigh Austen (1739-1827), who celebrated her eighty-seventh birthday in the year that the manuscript was written, that a woman could reach this age and still be strong and active must have been seen inside the Austen household. In contrast, aging men, like Mr. Henry Woodhouse, who is probably no more than 50 years old and may be somewhat younger, become housebound valetudinarians. Jane Austen's sympathy for Lady Denham is tempered by the great lady's arrogance and stinginess, but the underlying admiration remains.]

And I verily beleive if my poor dear Sir Harry had never seen one neither, he w^d. have been alive now. — Ten fees, one after another, did the Man take who sent <u>him</u> out of the World. — I beseech you M^r. Parker, no Doctors here." —

The Tea things were brought in. —

[Some of the beautiful tables and serving pieces can be seen at "On the Tea Table" (www.georgianindex.net/Tea/ttable.html).

In Jane Austen's time, "tea was frequently offered after dinner, when the ladies and gentlemen had gathered together in the drawing room" (Pool: 209), "where tea with cold snacks or cakes was served about seven or eight" (Le Faye, 2002: 119).

The last official function of the day is tea, with which goes some light refreshment, some hours after dinner if that has been an early one, and at the end of the stay of any guests there may have been. The intervening interval is filled with some sort of recreation.... Tea, as now, is an occasion rather than a beverage, a light supper which, like the mid-day cold meat, is not eaten at a table, or formally laid out. (Craik, 1969: 19)

The Thomas Parkers and their guests assemble in this scene for a light repast, and in a later chapter Charlotte will visit the Parker sisters and poor Arthur for "tea," where hot cocoa as well as tea is available, along with toast (well buttered is best, according to young Mr. Parker). The practice— "'Taking tea' is a vulgar expression. Drinking tea is considered the proper phrase" (Vic)—is seen frequently in the novels, in which it is generally accepted that friends and family will assemble in the late afternoon or early evening to enjoy each other's company over a cuppa.]

"Oh! my dear M^{rs}. Parker — you should not indeed — why would you do so? — I was just upon the point of wishing you good Evening.

[It is hard to believe that Lady Denham thinks that her neighbors accept her apologies for forcing an early tea upon them. It is clear from the beginning that any "conversation" with the haughty and opinionated Lady Denham is a one-way discourse.]

But since you are so very neighbourly, I beleive Miss Clara must stay." —
>
But since you are so very neighbourly, I beleive Miss Clara & I must stay." —
—

[The omitted "& I" suggests again that at least in part this manuscript is a transcription from an earlier source.

The sixth chapter is again almost in real time, beginning at the end of dinner and closing as tea is about to commence. We meet Lady Denham at last, and much of her dialog confirms what we suspected from Mr. Parker's long revelation in the third chapter. We also meet Miss Clara Brereton, but neither in this chapter nor in any of the rest of the extant manuscript does she utter a word.]

[Chapter 7]

The popularity of the Parkers brought them some visitors the very next morning; — amongst them, Sir Edw.ᵈ Denham & his Sister, who having been at Sanditon H— drove on to pay their Compliments; & the duty of Letter-writing being accomplished, Charlotte was settled with Mʳˢ P.— in the Drawing room in time to see them all. —

[Tea has been consumed, Lady Denham and Miss Brereton have returned to Sanditon House, the Parker household has enjoyed a good night's sleep, and now visitors—unidentified except for the brother and sister from Denham Park—arrive the next morning to welcome Mr. and Mrs. Thomas Parker back from their short journey to London. Because "morning" at the time extended to a much later time than now, it may not be an early hour. Most important among the guests, of course, is Sir Edward Denham, about whom Mr. Parker had much to say in the third chapter. But nothing there prepares us for the Baronet in person. Sir Edward is so important to the progress of the plot that none of the other visitors are even identified by name. His sister, Miss Esther Denham, is a pale companion, and none of her dialog is ever reported although we learn that she conducts an energetic conversation with Lady Denham for an invitation that will never come. The siblings' stopover at Sanditon House was probably in pursuit of the same favor from their aunt-through-marriage.

Despite Henry Tilney's condemnation of women as inherently unable to write intelligibly, writing letters was a fine art practiced by young ladies. If Jane Austen herself had not from an early age corresponded with Cassandra during the few occasions that they were apart, we would be the poorer in knowing even less about her personal life than we do. Charlotte has written at least one letter, presumably to her parents or favorite younger sister. Since postage—paid by the recipient—was expensive, she would more likely write to her mother, who would share the contents with the older members of the family, than to individual sisters. Obviously they would all be eager to hear of her adventures, and therefore the content would probably be very close to what we have just read about her conversations with the Parkers during their journey and her arrival at Sanditon. The females in the family would be particularly interested in learning of the latest fashions, since Sanditon like all watering places aspired to be a center of fashion even if far removed from London. The letter itself was usually a single sheet of paper, folded several times and sealed with wax. The address would be written on the outside. Again because of the cost of postage, the writing was often very small and cramped, and if Charlotte followed the author's practice she may have cross-written, so that after the page was filled, it was turned ninety degrees and new lines were written at right angles to the originals. Jo Modert's facscimile edition of Jane Austen's letters illustrates the challenging appearance of these letters.

The letter as a literary device was central to the development of the novel in the late eighteenth century, when many novels-in-letters, epistolary novels, were published. Jane Austen's own *Lady Susan* is such a production. *Sense and Sensibility*, then called *Elinor and Marianne*, "according to Austen family tradition… was originally composed as a novel-in-letters" (Le Faye, 2002: 154). I do not recall seeing any suggestions that the origin of *Northanger Abbey*, the elusive "Susan"/"Catherine," was an epistolary novel although it would seem to be a good candidate for such a theory. Catherine is away from home for most of the story, just as Charlotte is in the present manuscript, and it is expected that she would keep her family back in Willingden informed of her progress among her new friends, in particular her introduction into good society and encounters with wealthy young (preferably titled) bachelors.]

The Denhams were the only ones to excite particular attention. Charlotte was glad to complete her knowledge of the family by an introduction to them, & found them, the better half at least — (for while single, the <u>Gentleman</u> may sometimes be thought the better half, of the pair) —

[It is tempting to guess at the identity of the other guests, perhaps drawn from the residents and guests in the subscription book. *CUPLM* notes that the colloquial "better half" is "almost exclusively used for a wife" (657), and most often by her husband. The phrase, though, means a husband, wife, or partner. In this context, it has no literal meaning since a brother and sister do not make up a social pair. By "while single" Jane Austen could mean "although single," but a more interesting reading is "as long as he is a bachelor." Why is it no surprise that a young woman in search of a husband is more attracted to a young gentleman—with a hereditary title to boot—than to his sullen sister?

The *OED* entry—"**c. better half…** esp. (after Sidney [**1580** SIDNEY *Arcadia* III. 280]) used for 'my husband' or 'wife'; now, jocularly appropriated to the latter"—suggests that until recently the term could be applied equally to a man or a woman. The term appears nowhere else in Jane Austen's novels, and its colloquial nature characterizes her adventurous new prose style.]

not unworthy notice. —

[More of Jane Austen's habitual litotes. In any lesser writer it would be intolerable, but even here it can become mannered.]

Miss D. was a fine young woman, but cold & reserved, giving the idea of one who felt her consequence with Pride & her Poverty with Discontent, & who was immediately gnawed by the want of an handsomer Equipage than the simple Gig in which they travelled, & which their Groom was leading about still in her sight.

[That the Denhams overshadow all other visitors is clearly a matter of Charlotte's viewing Sir Edward as a potential suitor. Like all the other young women in the novel, she is here in Sanditon to hunt down and snare a suitable husband. Jane Austen successfully sums up Miss Denham as proud but discontent, with her comparatively modest means of travel a pain gnawing at her innards. "A gig—two wheels and one horse—was the cheaper small carriage used by most people" (Le Faye, 2002: 60) and keenly embarrassing to the distaff member of the Denham household. If the definition of "gig" as offered by "The Regency Period Glossary" is applicable here—"A two-person horse-drawn carriage that was light-weight, inexpensive and driven by one of the two passengers"—then it follows that the groom did not drive the carriage to Sanditon but must have sat facing the rear behind Miss Denham and her brother, who drove the carriage (as does Sidney Parker later in the manuscript). Miss Denham's chagrin may be based on her carriage's having a single horse since that immediately identifies it as a gig rather than the more fashionable curricle, "which was drawn by a pair of horses" (Pinion: 28), as seen in Marghanita Laski's illustration of the Prince Regent by Thomas Rowlandson (100–101). The gig is an open carriage and of doubtful comfort in this rainy part of the world. Because "the gig was driven by its owner" (Ray: 216), there was no need of a coachman, but Sir Edward has brought along one of his household servants, perhaps one of his "stable boys [hired] to help groom the horses and tend to their feed and bedding" (Olsen: 123). The appearance of this servant, a mere groom instead of a liveried coachman and perhaps a lad fresh from the country or a grizzled old holdover from the employ of Sir Harry, can only add to Miss Denham's mortification. Since the seat would be just wide enough for Sir Edward as driver and his sister as passenger, the groom probably rode behind facing the rear. In the 2007 version of *Persuasion*, Captain Wentworth (Rupert Penry-Jones) unceremoniously hoists the footsore Anne (Sally Hawkins) onto the back end of the Crofts' gig.]

Sir Edwd. was much her superior in air & manner; — certainly handsome, but yet more to be remarked for his very good address & wish of paying attention & giving pleasure. —

[The narrative is very much through Charlotte's eyes, thus greater attention to the brother than to the sister, with whom she would immediately feel some rivalry. He is introduced to us as though vastly superior to that saucy fellow, Sidney Parker, and so the initial impression—first impressions again—is that he must be the hero of this novel.]

He came into the room remarkably well, talked much — & very much to Charlotte, by whom he chanced to be placed — & she soon perceived that he had a very fine Countenance, a most pleasing gentleness of voice, & a great deal of Conversation.
>
He came into the room remarkably well, talked much — & very much to Charlotte, by whom he chanced to be placed — & she soon perceived that he had a fine Countenance, a most pleasing gentleness of voice, & a great deal of Conversation.

[Every important quality of a gentleman is seen in this brief passage of first impressions: how he enters the room, how he carries himself, his attention to young ladies, his general appearance, his voice, and his ability to talk with ease. For the moment, he is someone for whom Charlotte might very well set her cap, and she is already planning a full report about this potential catch in the next letter home.]

Charlotte liked him. —
>
She liked him.

[The change from "Charlotte" to "She" places the material more into her perspective. We have here one of the most important first impressions of the novel. Forthright herself, Charlotte assumes that each new acquaintance is likewise as advertised, only to reveal his or her real character through dialog.]

Sober-minded as she was, she thought him very agreable, & did not quarrel with the notion of his finding her equally so, which might be implied from his evidently disregarding his Sisters' motion to go, & persisting in his station & his discourse. —

>

Sober-minded as she was, she thought him agreable, & did not quarrel with the suspicion of his finding her equally so, which arose from his evidently disregarding his Sisters' motion to go, & persisting in his station & his discourse. —

>

Sober-minded as she was, she thought him agreable, & did not quarrel with the suspicion of his finding her equally so, which <u>would</u> arise from his evidently disregarding his Sisters' motion to go, & persisting in his station & his discourse. —

[Jane Austen worked carefully on this passage, since as always first impressions are important even if they must be amended later. Sir Edward's blandishments are working on Charlotte as they would on any impressionable young woman, but he will soon overplay his hand. Jane Austen's confusion about how to show possessives is well demonstrated in the meaningless "Sisters' motion"—a form that Mr. Parker could use with two sisters but not Sir Edward with only one.]

I make no apologies for my Heroine's vanity. —

[For a moment our author speaks directly to us, forcing us to excuse Charlotte's vanity as natural in the circumstances. In light of Jane Austen's specifically identifying Charlotte Heywood as her "Heroine," it is difficult to understand the occasional suggestion that Charlotte is not the heroine of the novel.]

If there are young Ladies in the World at her time of Life, more Dull of Mind & more ind

>

If there are young Ladies in the World at her time of Life, more Dull of Mind & more careless of pleasing, I know them not, & never wish to know them. —

>

If there are young Ladies in the World at her time of Life, more simple & more careless of pleasing, I know them not, & never wish to know them.

—

>

If there are young Ladies in the World at her time of Life, more dull of Fancy & more careless of pleasing, I know them not, & never wish to know them.

[This simple passage exonerating Charlotte from accusations of excessive vanity has gone through four stages of revision. Jane Austen needs to be very clear in her development of Charlotte, who is not merely the heroine of the novel but the spokesperson for the author.]

At last, from the low French windows of the Drawing room which commanded the road & all the Paths across the Down, Charlotte & Sir Edw: as they sat, could not but observe Lady D. & Miss B. walking by — & there was instantly a slight change in Sir Edw:'s countenance — with an anxious glance after them as they proceeded — followed by an early proposal to his Sister — not merely for moving, but for walking on together to the Terrace — which altogether gave an hasty turn to Charlotte's fancy, cured her of her halfhour's fever, & placed her in a more capable state of judging, when Sir Edw: was gone, of how agreable he had actually been. —

[We have a second description of the elegant windows in Mr. Parker's new residence, in this instance French windows or doors, a pair of long windows like doors, hinged at the sides and opening in the middle.

This long single sentence covers a series of short episodes, and like Henry James at his best our author suggests the inner thoughts—the exquisite sensibilities—of first Sir Edward and in consequence those of Charlotte Heywood. As outsiders, we now know exactly what game Sir Edward is playing as he flirts with Charlotte but is interested in Clara. Charlotte's rapid—almost instantaneous—recovery is good evidence of her practical nature and sound upbringing, exhibiting a sensible, clear-headed view of the world that supplies a welcome change from what we suffer through while following Marianne Dashwood in her self-inflicted torments.]

"Perhaps there was a good deal in his Air & Address; And his Title did not hurt him."

>

"Perhaps there was a good deal in his Air & Address; And his Title did him no harm."

[Charlotte is far luckier in the possibilities of an advantageous match than in her earlier state as Sudan/Catherine, for whom "there was not one lord in the neighbourhood; no—not even a baronet." For all young women on the prowl for a husband, his money came first, but a title was a desirable extra attraction.]

She was very soon in his company again. The first object of the Parkers, when their House was cleared of morn^g. visitors was to get out themselves; — the Terrace was the attraction to all; — Every body who walked, must begin with the Terrace,

["In every town trying to turn itself into a sea-bathing place one particular walk... was adopted for fashionable promenading. Here in the evening everyone strolled about bowing to their new acquaintances. It was the place where one went 'to be stared at and stare'" (Howell: 26–27).]

& there, seated on one of the two Green Benches by the Gravel walk, they found the united Denham Party; — but though united in the Gross, very distinctly divided again — the two superior Ladies being at one end of the bench, & Sir Edw: & Miss B. at the other. —

[Like a stage play, the text gives specific locations of the actors and actresses. Colors are rarely stated in Jane Austen's text, so her noting that the benches—two of them!—are green indicates a new interest in specificity, again as though instructing a stage designer on how to set up the props. And instructing the characters to be seated in pairs intensifies the visual sense. "In the gross," *CUPLM* notes, means "generally, in a general way" (657). The complete *OED* entry is a little more complete: "**in gross, in the gross.** [F. *en gros.*] **a.** In a general way, generally, without going into particulars; in the main, on the whole." Although Jane Austen often uses "gross" in various senses including "unattractive," "flagrant," "vulgar," or "repulsive," this appears to be her only use of this phrase with this meaning.]

Charlotte's first glances told her that Sir Edw.'s air was that of a Lover. — There could be no doubt of his Devotion to Clara. —

[This first impression comports well with Charlotte's interpretation of the tryst near the end of the fragment, but it does not gibe with his plans to seduce Clara Brereton. Obviously the character of Sir Edward is either more complex than revealed on the very shallow surface or the author is in the process of shaping his precise nature. Because Charlotte's first-hand experience of lovers and their airs is limited or naught, she has derived her perception from amorous passages in novels.]

How Clara received it, was less obvious — but she was inclined to think not very favourably; for tho' sitting thus apart with him (which probably she might not have been able to prevent) her air was calm & grave. —

[This scene is almost repeated near the end of the fragment when Sir Edward and Clara are alone and believe themselves safe from observation. Clara is one of the most self-possessed young women anywhere in Jane Austen's novels. And so far we have not heard a word from her lips.]

That the young Lady at the other end of the Bench was doing Penance, was indubitable. The difference in Miss Denham's countenance, the change from Miss Denham sitting in cold Grandeur in M^{rs}. Parker's Draw^g-room to be kept from silence by the efforts of others, to Miss D. at Lady D.'s Elbow, listening & talking with smiling attention or solicitous eagerness, was very striking — and very amusing — or very melancholy, just as Satire or Morality might prevail. — Miss Denham's Character was pretty well decided with Charlotte. Sir Edward's required longer Observation.

[Like a good playwright, Jane Austen gives us specific stage directions, placing her characters strategically on the terrace. The entire remarkable passage allows us to see the scene through Charlotte's eyes, and thus we know that Miss Esther Denham, niece and then sister to a Baronet, is a shameless and unsuccessful sycophant, that Sir Edward Denham is a conscienceless flirt, and that Miss Clara Brereton is either a besieged young woman in need of rescue or a very clever manipulator. The social proprieties—she never thinks of Miss Denham as merely Esther, and of course her titled

271

brother is always *Sir* Edward—are part of Charlotte's makeup even in her private thoughts.]

He surprised her by quitting Clara immediately on their all joining & agreeing to walk, & by addressing his attentions entirely to herself. — Stationing himself Close by her, he seemed to mean to detach her as much as possible from the rest of the Party & to give her the whole of his Conversation.

[Sir Edward outdoes even himself in this open demonstration of flirtation with a young woman about whom he obviously cares nothing. Reference to Miss Brereton by her first name reflects Sir Edward's interest in her, whether real or pretended. We know as well as Charlotte that this entire scene is being played for what Sir Edward hopes is Clara Brereton's pain and despair upon seeing her suitor flirting with a rival. There is an element of Frank Churchill in Sir Edward, appearing to be courting one young lady while far more interested in another. But Clara Brereton is no Jane Fairfax, and we almost surely do not have a secret engagement, although the tryst scene makes that a possibility.]

He began, in a tone of great Taste & Feeling, to talk of the Sea & the Sea shore — & ran with Energy through all the usual Phrases employed in praise of their Sublimity,

[Ecstasy over the sublimity of nature was de rigueur for anyone posing as a lover of the new Romantic Movement. Far more from reading than from personal experience, Sir Edward attempts to present himself to Charlotte as very much in the current mode. "Novelists and poets, particularly those within the Gothic tradition, wrote at length of mountains, lakes and seas as productive of... sublime terror, until the heightened rhetoric of the sublime became a cliché, ripe for comic or satiric treatment" (*CUPLM*: 657). Jane Austen may or may not have delighted in the beauties of nature, but even in praise of the sublime—" Of things in nature and art: Affecting the mind with a sense of overwhelming grandeur or irresistible power; calculated to inspire awe, deep reverence, or lofty emotion, by reason of its beauty, vastness, or grandeur" (*OED*)—she favored moderation and self-control, neither of which Sir Edward has even considered mastering.

Only once earlier in her published novels had Jane Austen used the word "sublimity," and there it conveys a calm and rational view of nature.

Looking out of the window and sharing her thoughts with Edmund, Fanny exclaims,

> "Here's harmony!… Here's repose! Here's what may leave all painting and all music behind, and what poetry only can attempt to describe! Here's what may tranquillize every care, and lift the heart to rapture! When I look out on such a night as this, I feel as if there could be neither wickedness nor sorrow in the world; and there certainly would be less of both if the sublimity of Nature were more attended to, and people were carried more out of themselves by contemplating such a scene." (*OIJA*–III: 113)

The word "sublime" occurs in Jane Austen's earlier novels only in *Emma*, in both instances in a mock-serious sense reflecting the heroine's reaction to the amorous Mr. Elton.

> After this speech he was gone as soon as possible. Emma could not think it too soon; for with all his good and agreeable qualities, there was a sort of parade in his speeches which was very apt to incline her to laugh. She ran away to indulge the inclination, leaving the tender and the sublime of pleasure to Harriet's share. (*OIJA*–IV: 82)

> It was all the service she could now render her poor friend; for as to any of that heroism of sentiment which might have prompted her to entreat him to transfer his affection from herself to Harriet, as infinitely the most worthy of the two—or even the more simple sublimity of resolving to refuse him at once and for ever, without vouchsafing any motive, because he could not marry them both, Emma had it not. (*OIJA*–IV: 431)]

& descriptive of the <u>undescribable</u> Emotions

[The impossibility of describing the indescribable apparently does not occur to Sir Edward, now deep in the throes of sensibility, but Charlotte—as well as the reader—sees the problem at once. The spelling "undescribable" was not unusual at the time: "**1728** ELIZA HEYWOOD tr. *Mme. de Gomez's Belle A.* (1732) II. 201, I have heard it reported, resumed the Marquis with an undescribable Agitation, that he was in love with a Spanish Lady. **1768** STERNE *Sent. Journ.* 217, I felt such undescribable emotions within me. **1818** BYRON *Ch. Har.* IV. liii, Let these describe the undescribable" (*OED*). Lord Byron, of course, did not pick up the phrasing from Jane

Austen's manuscript, so it must have been part of the Romantic rhetoric of the day. The current spelling, "indescribable" did not appear until after 1794, when Jane Austen was already 19 years old and would already be long accustomed to the older form.]

they excite in the Mind of Sensibility. —

[In an earlier chapter we have already seen hyperbolic praise of the sea, but coming from Mr. Parker it rings true with conviction. Here it is merely an expression of false emotion calculated to produce an effect of being a Man of Sensibility. Many of the phrases here, like "undescribable Emotions" and "Mind of Sensibility" must be direct quotations from the young Baronet's impassioned address. What appears to be a considerable change in Sir Edward's manner, earlier speaking in such a way that Charlotte thought him accomplished and worthy of being liked, but now acting like a fool, is possibly no more than his unpracticed attempt to engage Charlotte in conversation that will attract Clara's attention and hopefully raise her level of jealousy.

The phrase "Mind of Sensibility" is a nod in the direction of the Cult of Sensibility as practiced by a Man of Feeling, discussed below.]

The terrific Grandeur of the Ocean in a Storm, its glassy surface in a calm, its' Gulls & its Samphire, & the deep fathoms of its' Abysses, its' quick vicissitudes, its' direful Deceptions, its' Mariners tempting it in Sunshine & overwhelmed by the sudden Tempest, All were eagerly & fluently touched; —

["Terrific" is to be taken in its most literal meaning, "Causing terror, terrifying; fitted to terrify; dreadful, terrible, frightful" (*OED*). Sir Edward is given not merely to long and difficult words but to hyperbole.

"Samphire is a succulent plant in the carrot family, similar to Queen Anne's Lace, but with yellow flowers. It grew abundantly on England's southern and eastern coasts, where it was gathered and the stalks and leaves pickled. Because the plant naturally grows very close to the ocean, where it is moistened by the salt spray, it is symbolic of coastal regions. Thus, Austen mentions it, along with gulls, fathoms, and mariners, to evoke the seaside context of Sanditon" (Olsen: 609). "Samphire is a name given to a number of very different, edible plants, that happen to grow in coastal areas. Rock samphire, *Crithmum maritimum*, is a coastal species with white flowers that grows in the United Kingdom" ("Samphire," *Wikipedia*).

That all these complex things were "fluently touched" suggests a good deal of rehearsal on Sir Edward's part. The entire scene is calculated to flatter Charlotte while catching the attention of Clara. He has not yet had enough experience with women to know not to play such a dangerous game.]

rather commonplace perhaps —

["Sir Edward's speech here is indeed reminiscent of a number of literary apostrophes to the sea… frequently quoted or anthologized" (*CUPLM*: 658). Sir Edward can be forgiven for not creating something new, but his confusion about who wrote what proves him to be a hopeless dilettante.]

but doing very well from the Lips of a handsome Sir Edward, — and she c^d. not but think him a Man of Feeling —

[In 1771, Henry Mackenzie (1745-1831) published his picaresque novel, *The Man of Feeling*, which "inaugurated a vogue for a new kind of hero, 'the man of feeling,' a sensitive male" ("The Man of Feeling." *Wikipedia*). This mawkish narrative, "in which the hero dies of joy, in which a dog drops dead from grief, and in which true sensibility is revealed by the shedding of tears" (Probyn), was so admired by Walter Scott that in 1814 he dedicated the *Waverley* novels to his elder fellow-Scotsman. The story of the lachrymose hero Harley and his love for Miss Walton would exert a pernicious influence on many of the writers of the time, who learned from him that when in doubt about the story line or dialog, merely have the character cry and cry again.

The introductory passage of the Project Gutenberg EBook warns the reader that *The Man of Feeling* "begins with imitation of Sterne, and proceeds in due course through so many tears that it is hardly to be called a dry book." The Author's Introduction brings us into the tale in the lugubrious spirit that will infuse the entire narrative:

> My dog had made a point on a piece of fallow-ground, and led the curate and me two or three hundred yards over that and some stubble adjoining, in a breathless state of expectation, on a burning first of September. It was a false point, and our labour was vain: yet, to do Rover justice (for he's an excellent dog, though I have

lost his pedigree), the fault was none of his, the birds were gone: the curate showed me the spot where they had lain basking, at the root of an old hedge. I stopped and cried Hem! The curate is fatter than I; he wiped the sweat from his brow. There is no state where one is apter to pause and look round one, than after such a disappointment. It is even so in life. When we have been hurrying on, impelled by some warm wish or other, looking neither to the right hand nor to the left—we find of a sudden that all our gay hopes are flown; and the only slender consolation that some friend can give us, is to point where they were once to be found. And lo! if we are not of that combustible race, who will rather beat their heads in spite, than wipe their brows with the curate, we look round and say, with the nauseated listlessness of the king of Israel, "All is vanity and vexation of spirit." I looked round with some such grave apophthegm in my mind when I discovered, for the first time, a venerable pile, to which the enclosure belonged. An air of melancholy hung about it. There was a languid stillness in the day, and a single crow, that perched on an old tree by the side of the gate, seemed to delight in the echo of its own croaking. I leaned on my gun and looked; but I had not breath enough to ask the curate a question. I observed carving on the bark of some of the trees: 'twas indeed the only mark of human art about the place, except that some branches appeared to have been lopped, to give a view of the cascade, which was formed by a little rill at some distance. Just at that instant I saw pass between the trees a young lady with a book in her hand. I stood upon a stone to observe her; but the curate sat him down on the grass, and leaning his back where I stood, told me, "That was the daughter of a neighbouring gentleman of the name of WALTON, whom he had seen walking there more than once. "Some time ago," he said, "one HARLEY lived there, a whimsical sort of man I am told, but I was not then in the cure; though, if I had a turn for those things, I might know a good deal of his history, for the greatest part of it is still in my possession." "His history!" said I. "Nay, you may call it what you please," said the curate; "for indeed it is no more a history than it is a sermon. The way I came by it was this: some time ago, a grave, oddish kind of a man boarded at a farmer's in this parish: the country people called him The Ghost; and he was known by the slouch in his gait, and the length of his stride. I was but little acquainted with him, for he never frequented any of the clubs hereabouts. Yet for all he used to walk a-nights, he was as gentle as a lamb at times; for I have seen him playing at teetotum with the children, on the great stone at the door of our churchyard. Soon after I was made curate, he left the parish, and went nobody knows whither; and in his room was found a bundle of papers, which was brought to me by his landlord. I began to read them, but I soon grew weary of the task; for, besides that the hand is intolerably bad, I could never find the author in one strain for two chapters together; and I don't believe there's a single syllogism from beginning to end." "I should be glad to see this medley," said I. "You shall see it now," answered the curate, "for I always take it along with me a-shooting." "How came it so torn?" "'Tis excellent wadding," said the curate.—This was a plea of expediency I was not in a condition to answer; for I had actually in my pocket great part of an edition of one of the German Illustrissimi, for the very same purpose. We exchanged books; and by that means (for the curate was a strenuous logician) we probably saved both. When I returned to town, I had leisure to peruse the acquisition I had made: I found it a bundle of little episodes, put together without art, and of no importance on the whole, with something of nature, and little else in them. I was a good deal affected with some very trifling passages in it; and had the name of Marmontel, or a Richardson, been on the title-page—'tis odds that I should have wept: But One is ashamed to be pleased with the works of one knows not whom.

As expected, in the succeeding fragmentary narrative the single word with the greatest number of occurrences is "tears."

Jane Austen did not have to write more than this three-word phrase— "Man of Feeling"—for a contemporary reader to know exactly what she was referring to. At least as early as *Sense and Sensibility*, with Marianne's preference for the false sentiment represented by John Willoughby over the solid feelings evinced by Colonel Brandon, she was using this trait as a target of mockery. Perhaps the most brilliant ridicule of this literary byway is demonstrated in Henry Tilney's dialog, which she would have had in mind when she turned from the "shelved" manuscript of "Susan"/"Catherine" to take up this new project. Never one to throw away usable muslin, she would now divide her original male protagonist into two new men, one the true hero and the other a villain manqué.

Although "Susan"/"Catherine" was clearly designed to ridicule the extremes of the Gothic tradition, there was enough nonsense prevalent in contemporary literature to allow Jane Austen to target additional shopworn devices worthy of contempt. And what could be more brilliant mockery of the Man of Sensibility theme than Henry's inquiry about Catherine's introduction to Bath society (a passage that I believe in its extraordinary level of composition reflects major revisions from the original)?

> They made their appearance in the Lower Rooms; and here fortune was more favourable to our heroine. The master of the ceremonies introduced to her a very gentlemanlike young man as a partner;— his name was Tilney. He seemed to be about four or five and twenty, was rather tall, had a pleasing countenance, a very intelligent and lively eye, and, if not quite handsome, was very near it. His address was good, and Catherine felt herself in high luck. There was little leisure for speaking while they danced; but when they were seated at tea, she found him as agreeable as she had already given him credit for being. He talked with fluency and spirit—and there was an archness and pleasantry in his manner which interested, though it was hardly understood by her. After chatting some time on such matters as naturally arose from the objects around them, he suddenly addressed her with—"I have hitherto been very remiss, madam, in the proper attentions of a partner here; I have not yet asked you how long you have been in Bath; whether you were ever here before; whether you have been at the Upper Rooms, the theatre, and the concert; and how you like the place altogether. I have been very negligent—but are you now at leisure to satisfy me in these particulars? If you are I will begin directly."
>
> "You need not give yourself that trouble, sir."
>
> "No trouble, I assure you, madam." Then forming his features into a set smile, and affectedly softening his voice, he added, with a simpering air, "Have you been long in Bath, madam?"
>
> "About a week, sir," replied Catherine, trying not to laugh.
>
> "Really!" with affected astonishment.
>
> "Why should you be surprized, sir?"

"Why, indeed!" said he, in his natural tone—"but some emotion must appear to be raised by your reply, and surprize is more easily assumed, and not less reasonable than any other.—Now let us go on. Were you never here before, madam?"

"Never, sir."

"Indeed! Have you yet honoured the Upper Rooms?"

"Yes, sir, I was there last Monday."

"Have you been to the theatre?"

"Yes, sir, I was at the play on Tuesday."

"To the concert?"

"Yes, sir, on Wednesday."

"And are you altogether pleased with Bath?"

"Yes—I like it very well."

"Now I must give one smirk, and then we may be rational again."

Catherine turned away her head, not knowing whether she might venture to laugh.

"I see what you think of me," said he gravely—"I shall make but a poor figure in your journal tomorrow."

"My journal!"

"Yes, I know exactly what you will say: Friday, went to the Lower Rooms; wore my sprigged muslin robe with blue trimmings— plain black shoes—appeared to much advantage; but was strangely harassed by a queer, half-witted man, who would make me dance with him, and distressed me by his nonsense."

"Indeed I shall say no such thing."

"Shall I tell you what you ought to say?"

"If you please."

"I danced with a very agreeable young man, introduced by Mr. King; had a great deal of conversation with him—seems a most extraordinary genius—hope I may know more of him. *That,* madam, is what I *wish* you to say."

"But, perhaps, I keep no journal."

"Perhaps you are not sitting in this room, and I am not sitting by you. These are points in which a doubt is equally possible. Not keep a journal! How are your absent cousins to understand the tenour of your life in Bath without one? How are the civilities and compliments of every day to be related as they ought to be, unless noted down every evening in a journal? How are your various dresses to be remembered, and the particular state of your complexion, and curl of your hair to be described in all their diversities, without having constant recourse to a journal?—My dear madam, I am not so ignorant of young ladies' ways as you wish to believe me; it is this delightful habit of journalizing which largely contributes to form the easy style of writing for which ladies are so generally celebrated. Every body allows that the talent of writing agreeable letters is peculiarly female. Nature may have done something, but I am sure it must be essentially assisted by the practice of keeping a journal."

"I have sometimes thought," said Catherine, doubtingly, "whether ladies do write so much better letters than gentlemen! That is—I should not think the superiority was always on our side."

"As far as I have had opportunity of judging, it appears to me that the usual style of letter-writing among women is faultless, except in three particulars."

"And what are they?"

"A general deficiency of subject, a total inattention to stops, and a very frequent ignorance of grammar."

"Upon my word! I need not have been afraid of disclaiming the compliment. You do not think too highly of us in that way."

"I should no more lay it down as a general rule that women write better letters than men, than that they sing better duets, or draw

280

better landscapes. In every power, of which taste is the foundation, excellence is pretty fairly divided between the sexes."

They were interrupted by Mrs. Allen:— "My dear Catherine," said she, "do take this pin out of my sleeve; I am afraid it has torn a hole already; I shall be quite sorry if it has, for this is a favourite gown, though it cost but nine shillings a yard."

"That is exactly what I should have guessed it, madam," said Mr. Tilney, looking at the muslin.

"Do you understand muslins, sir?"

"Particularly well; I always buy my own cravats, and am allowed to be an excellent judge; and my sister has often trusted me in the choice of a gown. I bought one for her the other day, and it was pronounced to be a prodigious bargain by every lady who saw it. I gave but five shillings a yard for it, and a true Indian muslin."

Mrs. Allen was quite struck by his genius. "Men commonly take so little notice of those things," said she: "I can never get Mr. Allen to know one of my gowns from another. You must be a great comfort to your sister, sir."

"I hope I am, madam."

"And pray, sir, what do you think of Miss Morland's gown?"

"It is very pretty, madam," said he, gravely examining it; "but I do not think it will wash well; I am afraid it will fray."

"How can you," said Catherine, laughing, "be so——" She had almost said, strange.

"I am quite of your opinion, sir," replied Mrs. Allen; "and so I told Miss Morland when she bought it."

"But then you know, madam, muslin always turns to some account or other; Miss Morland will get enough out of it for a handkerchief, or a cap, or a cloak.—Muslin can never be said to be wasted. I have heard my sister say so forty times, when she has been extravagant in buying more than she wanted, or careless in cutting it to pieces."

"Bath is a charming place, sir; there are so many good shops here.— We are sadly off in the country; not but what we have very good shops in Salisbury, but it is so far to go;— eight miles is a long way; Mr. Allen says it is nine, measured nine; but I am sure it cannot be more than eight; and it is such a fag—I come back tired to death. Now here one can step out of doors and get a thing in five minutes."

Mr. Tilney was polite enough to seem interested in what she said; and she kept him on the subject of muslins till the dancing recommenced. Catherine feared, as she listened to their discourse, that he indulged himself a little too much with the foibles of others.—"What are you thinking of so earnestly?" said he, as they walked back to the ballroom;—"not of your partner, I hope, for, by that shake of the head, your meditations are not satisfactory."

Catherine coloured, and said, "I was not thinking of any thing."

"That is artful and deep, to be sure; but I had rather be told at once that you will not tell me."

"Well then, I will not."

"Thank you; for now we shall soon be acquainted, as I am authorized to tease you on this subject whenever we meet, and nothing in the world advances intimacy so much."

They danced again; and, when the assembly closed, parted, on the lady's side at least, with a strong inclination for continuing the acquaintance. Whether she thought of him so much, while she drank her warm wine and water, and prepared herself for bed, as to dream of him when there, cannot be ascertained; but I hope it was no more than in a slight slumber, or a morning doze at most; for if it be true, as a celebrated writer has maintained, that no young lady can be justified in falling in love before the gentleman's love is declared, it must be very improper that a young lady should dream of a gentleman before the gentleman is first known to have dreamt of her. How proper Mr. Tilney might be as a dreamer or a lover, had not yet perhaps entered Mr. Allen's head, but that he was not objectionable as a common acquaintance for his young charge he was on inquiry satisfied; for he had early in the evening taken pains to know who her partner was, and had been assured of Mr. Tilney's being a clergyman, and of a very respectable family in Gloucestershire. (Facsimile: 29–43)

We would have to wait for the best of Oscar Wilde to find comic material of this luster and jewel-like precision.

Mackenzie wrote two more novels foreshadowing Sir Edward Denham, *The Man of the World* (1773), in which we find a villainous hero, and *Julia de Roubigné* (1777), an imitation of Richardson's *Clarissa*. Although Jane Austen never refers to Mackenzie or his work in her extant letters, her own writing and this phrase leave us in no doubt that she was familiar with his œuvre.]

till he began to stagger her by the number of his Quotations, & the bewilderment of some of his sentences. —

"Do you remember, said he, Scotts' beautiful Lines on the Sea? — Oh! what a description they convey! — They are never out of my Thoughts when I walk here. — That Man who can read them unmoved must have the nerves of an Assassin! —

[Villains, like Signor Montoni in *The Mysteries of Udolfo*, abound in Gothic literature, and they play an important part in Catherine Morland's reading. However, the lack of foreboding in the appearance of Northanger Abbey somewhat allays her fears, and "she had nothing to dread from midnight assassins or drunken gallants."]

Heaven defend me from meeting such a Man un-armed." —

[The meaning can go in two entirely different directions. Sir Edward could be praying that he will be fully armed and therefore able to defend himself if he encounters such a menacing person. Or that only Heaven could intercede to keep him from harming an unarmed enemy. Neither meaning, though, is to be taken literally since Sir Edward is not only unarmed but is unlikely to know how to use a weapon. "Gentlemen had stopped wearing swords well before the end of the eighteenth century, and would not usually carry knives or pistols so this is a figurative statement" (*CUPLM*: 639), and one that like all of Sir Edward's pronouncements must be considered show rather than substance. Charlotte is as little impressed by his pretence of bravado as is the reader.]

"What description do you mean? — said Charlotte. I remember none at this moment, of the Sea, in either of Scotts' Poems." —

[As she does so frequently, Jane Austen uses "to say" where logic dictates "to ask."

This passage is troublesome because although Sir Edward has uttered the name "Scott," he has mentioned no poem, and certainly not two of them, by this author, nor has he quoted yet from any of his published poems.

CUPLM suggests that "it is just possible that JA was using the word 'either' in the sense of 'any' but it is more likely that she was thinking of the two poems for which Walter Scott, the most popular poet of the period, was best known: *Marmion* (1808) and *The Lady of the Lake* (1810)" (659).

Although *OED* cites primarily the usual meaning, "one or the other of two," it does record the occasional meaning "any one (of more than two)," in use during Jane Austen's lifetime.

Examination of *Emma* (I use this novel because I believe that it demonstrates her art at its highest level) shows that Jane Austen almost always uses "either" in the usual sense of "one or the other of two."

> Mr. Woodhouse thought it no hardship for either James or the horses.

> She had never boasted either beauty or cleverness.

> "What say you to Mr. Weston and Mr. Elton? Compare Mr. Martin with either of *them*."

> She was not much deceived as to her own skill either as an artist or a musician.

Occasionally Jane Austen uses "either" in a slightly different sense.

> "What are Harriet Smith's claims, either of birth, nature or education, to any connexion higher than Robert Martin?"

> The morning of the interesting day arrived, and Mrs. Weston's faithful pupil did not forget either at ten, or eleven, or twelve o'clock, that she was to think of her at four.

In using the negative form, "neither," Jane Austen is less strict.

"I cannot wish to prevent it, provided the weather be what it ought, neither damp, nor cold, nor windy."

She had given them neither men, nor names, nor places, that could raise a blush.

In one instance there is the likelihood that Jane Austen is using "either" in a sense other than "one or the other of two."

> Mr. Woodhouse had so completely made up his mind to the visit, that in spite of the increasing coldness, he seemed to have no idea of shrinking from it, and set forward at last most punctually with his eldest daughter in his own carriage, with less apparent consciousness of the weather than either of the others.

Finally, there is one instance in which the use of "either" definitely refers to more than "one or the other of two."

> She would not acknowledge that it was with any view of making a match for her, hereafter, with either of Isabella's sons.

Isabella Woodhouse Knightley and John Knightley have three sons, Henry (named after his grandfather), John (named after his father), and George (named after his uncle). They also have two daughters, Bella (a shortened version of her mother's name) and Emma (no need to explain whom she was named after).

There are at least five possible explanations to make sense out of what Charlotte says:

1. By "either" she means "any," that is, "I have read all of Scott's poetry and remember no description of the sea in any of them."

2. At the time of the story, probably summer 1816, although Scott had already published several poems, two of them—*Marmion* and *The Lady of the Lake*—were so well known that for all practical purposes anyone discussing his poetry would be referring to these two titles. Walter Scott's enormous popularity and his influence over the contemporary literary scene must be taken into account as part of the history of modern publishing.

> The effect of Scott's popularity upon English book-trade economics, and therefore upon the rate at which the reading public was to grow, can hardly be overestimated. The commercial success of his

poems, and even more of his novels, seemed at the time to prove that exorbitant prices were no bar to large sales.... Scott's first novel, *Waverley* (1814), cost 21*s.*, at a time when the customary price of a three-volume novel was 15*s.* or 18*s.*, and went through eight editions (11,500 copies) in seven years. (Altick, 1999: 262–263)

Scott's successive volumes of poetry were clear record-breakers: *The Lay of the Last Minstrel* (1805) sold 15,000 copies in five years, *Marmion* (1808) 13,000 in the first six months and six editions by the end of the year, and *The Lady of the Lake* (1810) 30,000 or more in the first year. (Altick, 1999: 292)

3. In *Persuasion*, Captain Benwick "tr[ied] to ascertain whether Marmion or The Lady of the Lake were to be preferred," and the author may have subconsciously linked them in anticipation of Sir Edward's quotations.

4. Charlotte has a prescience not seen elsewhere that tells her that Sir Edward is about to offer quotations from these two particular poems.

5. This is additional evidence to support my unprovable theory that the present manuscript is in part a copy from an earlier, lost first draft, and so in the process of assembling this complex passage Jane Austen has reversed some of her material. Hence Charlotte appears to know which of Scott's poems Sir Edward is referring to ahead of his specific quotations.

With the exception of William Wordsworth, Sir Edward has a strong predilection for writers of Scottish heritage, perhaps foremost among them Sir Walter Scott, Bart.—so appropriately named—born in Edinburgh in 1771 and one of the most beloved novelists and poets of his time. His death in 1832 is generally seen as marking the end of the Romantic Movement in English literature.

Although he has presumably lived all his life on the Sussex Coast, Sir Edward may be aware that his family name "Denham" can be traced to Scotland. The Denham crest bears the motto, "Cura dat victoriam" ("Caution gives victory"), an admonition that the impetuous young Baronet would be wise to heed.

The name is an ancient one that can be traced back to the eleventh century, with members of the family being "first found in Suffolk where they had been granted lands by William the Conqueror for their assistance at the Battle of Hastings in 1066." The name is spelled variously Denham, Denholm, Denholme, and Dennam ("Denham Family Crest and Name History").

There is no one by the name of Denham anywhere in Jane Austen's extant letters, nor does the name occur elsewhere in her prose writings. However, she may have created it as a reflection of her signing as "Mrs. Ashton Dennis" when she wrote to Messrs. Crosbie & Co. in 1809 asking about the long-unpublished manuscript of "Susan" (*Letters*: 174–175; see note, page 400, on this signature as an afterthought).

Aside from references to him in Jane Austen's novels and letters, Walter Scott is very important in being the first major critic who wrote in praise of her work. In 1816 he wrote an unsigned review of *Emma* that appeared in the *Quarterly Review* (October 1815, issued March 1816, xiv, 188-201). "The publisher of *Emma*, John Murray, invited Scott to review the novel [so although it was published without a signature, anyone bothering to inquire of John Murray could learn the identity of the writer].... This is the first major critical notice of Jane Austen" (*Jane Austen, The Critical Heritage*, Vol. 1: 58–69). His praise of the novel as being one of "a class of fictions which has arisen almost in our own times, and which draws the characters and incidents introduced more immediately from the current of ordinary life than was permitted by the former rules of the novel" (59), and "copying from nature as she really exists in the common walks of life, and presenting to the reader, instead of the splendid scenes of an imaginary world, a correct and striking representation of that which is daily taking place around him" (63), was only the first of many critical assessments during the nineteenth century and beyond that propelled her into the first tier of writers of prose fiction in the English language. Who—least of all then-Mr. Walter Scott or Miss Jane Austen—could have imagined at the time of the publication of his lengthy review that before many years would pass she would reach the pinnacle of success and he would be relegated to little more than a footnote?

After Jane Austen's death, Walter Scott—Sir Walter as of 1820, when he was created Baronet—continued to record in letters and his journal his admiration for this woman whom he had never met. Of the five items reprinted in Vol. 1 of *Jane Austen, The Critical Heritage* (106), perhaps the most insightful is that entered in his journal on March 14, 1826:

Also read again and for the third time at least Miss Austen's very finely written novel of *Pride and Prejudice*. That young lady had a talent for describing the involvement and feelings and characters of ordinary life which is to me the most wonderful I ever met with. The Big Bow-wow strain I can do myself like any now going, but the exquisite touch which renders ordinary commonplace things and characters interesting from the truth of the description and the sentiment is denied to me. What a pity such a gifted creature died so early!

"In neither *Marmion* nor *The Lady of the Lake* are there prominent lines on the sea, though in *Marmion*, during an account of a voyage, there is the near-couplet 'The whitening breakers sound so near/Where, boiling through the rocks they roar" (*CUPLM*: 660). I think that we can take it as a given that Sir Edward did not recall these specific lines although Charlotte's memory is not perfect, either.]

"Do not you indeed? —

[Although to our ears this construction sounds bizarre, for Jane Austen's contemporaries the common contraction based on this sequence of words, "Don't," might sound equally strange.]

— Nor can I exactly recall the beginning at this moment — But — you cannot have forgotten his description of Woman. —

"Oh! Woman in our Hours of Ease —"

Delicious! Delicious! — Had he written nothing more, he w^d. have been Immortal.

[The quotation, "com[ing] from a moment of high drama late in Scott's long narrative poem when the knight Marmion has been fatally wounded and the maiden, whose name in fact is Clara, comes to his aid" (*CUPLM*: 660), is from Walter Scott's *Marmion*:

O, Woman! in our hours of ease,
Uncertain, coy, and hard to please,
And variable as the shade
By the light quivering aspen made;
When pain and anguish wring the brow,
A ministering angel thou!

(VI, XXX, 902–907)

Walter Scott recognized Jane Austen as a contemporary novelist, and in her turn, of course, she was very much aware of his publications that appeared during her lifetime. Her letters indicate special familiarity with *Marmion: A Tale of Flodden Field*, an epic poem published in 1808, most famous now for its frequently misattributed couplet

> O, what a tangled web we weave,
> When first we practise to deceive!
> (Canto Sixth, The Battle, XVII, 532-533)

Although Jane Austen never quotes these lines, she would have found them apropos as she developed the character of Henry Crawford.

References to *Marmion* do, however, show up in three of her letters, where she expresses little enthusiasm for the events of 1513.

> Ought I to be much pleased with Marmion?—as yet I am not.— James reads it aloud in the Even^g—beginning at about 10, & broken by supper. (to Cassandra, June 20, 1808; *Letters*: 131)

> Charles's rug will be finished today, & sent tomorrow to Frank, to be consigned by him to Mr Turner's care—& I am going to send Marmion out with it;—very generous in me, I think. (to Cassandra, January 10, 1809; *Letters*: 164) (Deirdre Le Faye's note, p. 397: "The first edition of *Marmion*, in quarto, cost 31s. 6d., but several octavo editions appeared in 1808, so we need not suppose that J. A. laid out more than 12s." (*Letters*, ed. Chapman, note to letter 63)

Her most famous indebtedness to Scott, though, appears in her letter to Cassandra dated January 29, 1813 (*Letters*: 202). Explaining to her sister that although here and there in *Pride and Prejudice* for greater clarity as to who is speaking she might have interpolated a "he said" or "she said,"

> "I do not write for such dull Elves"

paraphrasing a line from *Marmion*,

> I do not rhyme to that dull elf,
> Who cannot image to himself,
> That all through Flodden's dismal night,
> Wilson was foremost in the fight.

(Canto Sixth, The Battle, XXXVIII, 1147–1150)]

And then again, that unequalled, unrivalled address to Parental affection —

"Some feelings are to Mortals given
With less of Earth in them than Heaven" &c

[The couplet is from Scott's "Lady of the Lake." Sir Edward starts out with confidence but falls back on the ubiquitous "&c" as his memory fails him. This is what he has forgotten:

Some feelings are to mortals given
With less of earth in them than heaven;
And if there be a human tear
From passion's dross refined and clear,
A tear so limpid and so meek
It would not stain an angel's cheek,
'Tis that which pious fathers shed
Upon a duteous daughter's head!
And as the Douglas to his breast
His darling Ellen closely pressed,
Such holy drops her tresses steeped,
Though 't was an hero's eye that weeped.
Nor while on Ellen's faltering tongue
Her filial welcomes crowded hung,
 Marked she that fear—affection's proof—
Still held a graceful youth aloof;
No! not till Douglas named his name,
Although the youth was Malcolm Graeme.
(Canto II, St. 22)]

But while we are on the subject of Poetry, what think you Miss H. of Burns Lines to his Mary?" —

[Robert Burns (1759–1796), more familiarly known as Bobbie Burns (as well as Rabbie Burns, Scotland's favourite son, the Ploughman Poet, the Bard of Ayrshire, and in Scotland as simply The Bard), born in Alloway, South Ayrshire Scotland, is generally considered the national poet of Scotland. As a pioneer of the Romantic Movement and a source of inspiration to supporters of liberalism and socialism, he would not be likely to be one of Jane Austen's favorite poets. These political concepts might not be especially appealing to Sir Edward, either, but the possible Denham origins in Scotland along with Burns's reputation for "casual love affairs [that] did not endear him to the elders of the local kirk and created for him a reputation for dissoluteness amongst his neighbours" ("Robert Burns." *Wikipedia*) would automatically make him a model for the young Baronet to admire and even attempt to emulate.

Burns wrote several poems "to his Mary," none quoted by Sir Edward. But Donald A. Low (*Robert Burns: The Critical Heritage*: 294, note 3) votes for "Highland Mary" (to the tune "Katherine Ogie"), which certainly contains its share of pathos and could well be the one to which the young Baronet refers. "Highland Mary" was "Mary Campbell… with whom he planned, for a brief intense period before her sudden death in late 1786, to share his life" (*CUPLM*: 661).

> Ye banks, and braes, and streams around
> The castle o' Montgomery!
> Green be your woods, and fair your flowers,
> Your waters never drumlie:
> There Simmer first unfauld her robes,
> And there the langest tarry;
> For there I took the last Farewell
> O' my sweet Highland Mary.
>
> How sweetly bloom'd the gay, green birk,
> How rich the hawthorn's blossom,
> As underneath their fragrant shade,
> I clasp'd her to my bosom!
> The golden Hours on angel wings,
> Flew o'er me and my Dearie;
> For dear to me, as light and life,
> Was my sweet Highland Mary.
>
> Wi' mony a vow, and lock'd embrace,
> Our parting was fu' tender;
> And, pledging aft to meet again,
> We tore oursels asunder;
> But oh! fell Death's untimely frost,
> That nipt my Flower sae early!
> Now green's the sod, and cauld's the clay
> That wraps my Highland Mary!

O pale, pale now, those rosy lips,
I aft hae kiss'd sae fondly!
And clos'd for aye, the sparkling glance
That dwalt on me sae kindly!
And mouldering now in silent dust,
That heart that lo'ed me dearly!
But still within my bosom's core
Shall live my Highland Mary.

The element of "Pathos" is also particularly strong in "To Mary in Heaven."

Thou ling'ring star, with lessening ray,
That lov'st to greet the early morn,
Again thou usher'st in the day
My Mary from my soul was torn.
O Mary! dear departed shade!
Where is thy place of blissful rest?
See'st thou thy lover lowly laid?
Hear'st thou the groans that rend his breast?

That sacred hour can I forget,
Can I forget the hallow'd grove,
Where, by the winding Ayr, we met,
To live one day of parting love!
Eternity will not efface
Those records dear of transports past,
Thy image at our last embrace,
Ah! little thought we 'twas our last!

Ayr, gurgling, kiss'd his pebbled shore,
O'erhung with wild-woods, thickening green;
The fragrant birch and hawthorn hoar,
'Twin'd amorous round the raptur'd scene:
The flowers sprang wanton to be prest,
The birds sang love on every spray;
Till too, too soon, the glowing west,
Proclaim'd the speed of winged day.

Still o'er these scenes my mem'ry wakes,
And fondly broods with miser-care;
Time but th' impression stronger makes,
As streams their channels deeper wear,
My Mary! dear departed shade!
Where is thy blissful place of rest?
See'st thou thy lover lowly laid?
Hear'st thou the groans that rend his breast?

For lyric charm and gentle sorrow it would be hard to surpass his "Sweet Afton."

Flow gently, sweet Afton! amang thy green braes,
Flow gently, I'll sing thee a song in thy praise;
My Mary's asleep by thy murmuring stream,
Flow gently, sweet Afton, disturb not her dream.

Thou stockdove whose echo resounds thro' the glen,
Ye wild whistling blackbirds in yon thorny den,
Thou green-crested lapwing thy screaming forbear,
I charge you, disturb not my slumbering Fair.

How lofty, sweet Afton, thy neighbouring hills,
Far mark'd with the courses of clear, winding rills;
There daily I wander as noon rises high,
My flocks and my Mary's sweet cot in my eye.

How pleasant thy banks and green valleys below,
Where, wild in the woodlands, the primroses blow;
There oft, as mild Ev'ning weeps over the lea,
The sweet-scented birk shades my Mary and me.

Thy crystal stream, Afton, how lovely it glides,
And winds by the cot where my Mary resides;
How wanton thy waters her snowy feet lave,
As, gathering sweet flowerets, she stems thy clear wave.

Flow gently, sweet Afton, amang thy green braes,
Flow gently, sweet river, the theme of my lays;
My Mary's asleep by thy murmuring stream,
Flow gently, sweet Afton, disturb not her dream.

Less tragic but still intensely heart-felt is "My Bonie Mary"

> Go, fetch to me a pint o' wine,
> And fill it in a silver tassie;
> That I may drink before I go,
> A service to my bonie lassie.
> The boat rocks at the pier o' Leith;
> Fu' loud the wind blaws frae the Ferry;
> The ship rides by the Berwick-law,
> And I maun leave my bonie Mary.
>
> The trumpets sound, the banners fly,
> The glittering spears are ranked ready:
> The shouts o' war are heard afar,
> The battle closes deep and bloody;
> It's not the roar o' sea or shore,
> Wad mak me langer wish to tarry!
> Nor shouts o' war that's heard afar—
> It's leaving thee, my bonie Mary!

Sir Edward could have in mind any of these poems, or several others by Burns addressed "to his Mary." It is just as likely, though, that the young Baronet has heard that Burns wrote poems to various young ladies, including Mary, and he hopes to impress Charlotte with his sensitivity to the great poet's skill in evoking pathos.]

Oh! Pathos that maddens one!
>
Oh! "there is Pathos to madden one! —

If ever there was a Man who <u>felt</u>, it was Burns.

— Montgomery has all the Fire of Poetry,

[James Montgomery (1771–1854) was born at Irvine, in Ayrshire, located in south-west Scotland on the shores of the Firth of Clyde. Since Sir Edward makes no attempt to quote from one of his poems, it is possible that the Baronet knows yet another name of a Scottish writer without having read him. Montgomery demonstrates considerable skill at creating a very complex stanza as seen in this poem to his parents, who had died in the West Indies:

The loud Atlantic ocean,
On Scotland's rugged breast,
Rocks, with harmonious motion,
His weary waves to rest,
And gleaming round her emerald isles
In all the pomp of sunset smiles.
On that romantic shore
My parents hailed their first-born boy;
A mother's pang my mother bore,
My father felt a father's joy;
My father, mother—parents now no more!
Beneath the Lion Star they sleep,
Beyond the western deep,
And when the sun's noon-glory crests the waves,
He shines without a shadow on their graves.]

Wordsworth has the true soul of it —

[We have here Jane Austen's only reference to William Wordsworth (1770–1850) in a novel (he is never mentioned in an extant letter), and "since it is an enthusiastic allusion by Sir Edward Denham, it is of doubtful significance" (Williams: 194). That the foolish young Baronet is drawn to his lines is not a favorable sign of the poet's standing in the Austen household. Not even Marianne Dashwood at her most maudlin or Captain Benwick in his most sentimental mood ever refers to the co-author of *The Lyrical Ballads*—which John Halperin believes that Jane Austen "surely… had been reading" (1983: 186)—and many other works now considered cornerstones of early Romantic poetry. He is the only English writer praised by Sir Edward, and it is possible that the Baronet knows him only by name, having noticed his works among those in Mrs. Whitby's library. If Sir Edward read *The Lyrical Ballads* he would know about Wordsworth's collaborator, Samuel Taylor Coleridge, but we are not told if he was familiar with the work of this major poet.]

Campbell in his pleasures of Hope has touched the extreme of our Sensations —

"Like Angel's visits, few & far between."

[Sir Edward is nearly correct in his quotation from *The Pleasures of Hope* (1799), by Thomas Campbell (1777–1844), born in Glasgow:

> Cease, every joy, to glimmer on my mind,
> But leave, oh! leave the light of Hope behind!
> What though my wingèd hours of bliss have been,
> Like angel-visits, few and far between?
> Her musing mood shall every pang appease,
> And charm—when pleasure lose the power to please!
> (*The Complete Poetical Works*: 33)

Sir Edward's memory for selected snatches of poetry is commendable although it is possible that he has been reading not the poems but a selection from anthologies of "memorable quotations" intended to impress the fair sex. As seen in a later passage, his more serious reading is probably devoted to eighteenth-century novels about libidinous heroes.]

Can you conceive any thing more subduing, more melting, more fraught with the deep Sublime than that Line? — But Burns — I confess my sense of his Pre-eminence Miss H. —

If Scott has a fault, it is the want of Passion. — Tender, Elegant, Descriptive — but Tame. —The Man who cannot do justice to the attributes of Woman is my contempt. — Sometimes indeed a flash of feeling seems to irradiate him — as in the Lines we were speaking of — "Oh! Woman in our hours of Ease" — .

[Sir Walter Scott, *Marmion*; see above. Since Sir Edward twice quotes this line but never goes past it, it is possible that it is all that he has read of the poem, picked up from a miscellany of lines selected to move the soul to transports of transcendently ethereal joy.]

But Burns is always on fire. — His Soul was the Altar in which lovely Woman sat enshrined, his Spirit truly breathed the immortal Incence which is her Due. —"

"I have read several of Burn's Poems with great delight, said Charlotte as soon as she had time to speak, but I am not poetic enough to separate a Man's Poetry entirely from his Character; — & poor Burns's known Irregularities, greatly interrupt my enjoyment of his Lines. — I have difficulty in depending on the Truth of his Feelings as a Lover. I have not faith in the sincerity of the affections of a Man of his Description. He felt & he wrote & he forgot."

[Jane Austen, here speaking through Charlotte Heywood, thought somewhat less of Burns than did Sir Edward, regarding him as a talented poet but too unconventional in his personal life to be recommended reading for a young person of good society. (Insistence on equating a poet's genius and morals requires dismissing out of hand the works of that most prolific of all writers, "anon.") She mentions him in no extant letter, and no one in any of the novels reads his work. Thus Jane Austen indirectly but distinctly condemns Sir Edward by telling us that instead of reading poets beloved by her for their moral vision, like Cowper and Crabbe, he indulges in the works of Scottish poets, including at least one of irregular moral standards.

Jane Austen's understanding of the poet's name is questionable when she writes first "Burn's Poems" and then "Burns's known Irregularities." Spelling and punctuation were far more "flexible" at that time than nowadays, but such variety is unsettling.

Surprisingly (perhaps amazingly), Sir Edward makes no reference to the works of George Gordon, Lord Byron (1788–1824), who had already published *Childe Harold's Pilgrimage* (1812), *The Bride of Abydos* (1813), and *The Corsair* (1816). If Charlotte is indeed "not poetic enough to separate a Man's Poetry entirely from his Character," she could not have found anything to praise in his work as after rumors of an incestuous relationship with his half-sister, Augusta Leigh, he left England in 1816, never to return. That Jane Austen herself knew Lord Byron's work is seen in *Persuasion*.

> Anne found Captain Benwick getting near her, as soon as they were all fairly in the street. Their conversation, the preceding evening, did not disincline him to seek her again; and they walked together some time, talking as before of Mr. Scott and Lord Byron, and still as unable as before, and as unable as any other two readers, to think exactly alike of the merits of either. (*OIJA–V*: 107)

. . .

> Anne found Captain Benwick again drawing near her. Lord Byron's "dark blue seas" could not fail of being brought forward by their present view, and she gladly gave him all her attention as long as attention was possible. (*OIJA–V*: 109)

. . .

> He [Captain Benwick] would gain cheerfulness, and she [Louisa
> Musgrove] would learn to be an enthusiast for Scott and Lord
> Byron. (*OIJA–V*: 167)

Anne Elliot, as a spokesperson for Jane Austen, is skeptical about the effect
on a depressed spirit, like that of Captain Benwick, of "all the impassioned
descriptions of hopeless agony" found in Lord Byron.

> For, though shy, he did not seem reserved; it had rather the
> appearance of feelings glad to burst their usual restraints; and
> having talked of poetry, the richness of the present age, and gone
> through a brief comparison of opinion as to the first-rate poets,
> trying to ascertain whether *Marmion* or *The Lady of the Lake*
> were to be preferred, and how ranked the *Giaour* and *The Bride
> of Abydos*; and moreover, how the *Giaour* was to be pronounced,
> he shewed himself so intimately acquainted with all the tenderest
> songs of the one poet [Scott], and all the impassioned descriptions
> of hopeless agony of the other [Byron]; he repeated, with such
> tremulous feeling, the various lines which imaged a broken heart,
> or a mind destroyed by wretchedness, and looked so entirely as if
> he meant to be understood, that she ventured to hope he did not
> always read only poetry; and to say, that she thought it was the
> misfortune of poetry, to be seldom safely enjoyed by those who
> enjoyed it completely; and that the strong feelings, which alone
> could estimate it truly, were the very feelings which ought to taste
> it but sparingly. (*OIJA–V*: 100–101)

Sir Edward's failure to refer to Lord Byron's poetry deprives us not only
of Charlotte's opinion but indirectly that of Jane Austen in her last year.
However, since she had already stated her view through Anne Elliot in the
preceding year, it is unlikely that her original opinion had been altered.]

"Oh! No no — exclaimed Sir Edw: in an extasy. He was all ardour &
Truth! — His Genius & his Susceptibilities might lead him into some
Aberrations — But who is perfect? — It were Hyper-criticism, it were
Pseudo-philosophy to expect from the soul of high toned Genius, the
grovellings of a common mind. —

[As *CUPLM* observes, the *OED* cites Jane Austen for "the first recorded
appearance" (663) of "pseudo-philosophy": "**1817** J. AUSTEN *Sanditon*
(1925) vii. 92 It were Hyper-criticism, it were Pseudo-philosophy to expect

from the soul of high toned Genius, the grovellings of a common mind." This may be a rare instance of Jane Austen's creating a new word. It should be kept in mind that the *OED* editors have here cited the first known *instance* of the word, not its first known *publication*, which may not have been until 1897. They do, however, supply the earliest publication date of the word as used by Jane Austen, in the R.W. Chapman edition of 1925. The passage did not appear in James Edward Austen-Leigh's *Memoir*, where Sir Edward has no on-stage dialog.

"The usual meaning of ["Genius"] at the turn of the eighteenth–nineteenth centuries would be 'natural ability' or 'quality of mind', but the more modern meaning of a particular kind of intellectual power proceeding from divine or otherwise miraculous inspiration may also be intended here" (*CUPLM*: 663). In her completed novels, the word is generally used in its earlier sense.

[Wentworth's] genius and ardour had seemed to foresee and to command his prosperous path.

"To be sure, my dear, that is very stupid indeed, and shows a great want of genius and emulation." (Mrs. Norris on Fanny)

She [Mrs. Allen] had neither beauty, genius, accomplishment, nor manner.

Occasionally, however, the meaning may include the newer sense of divine inspiration.

"Only think what grand things were produced there by our all going with him one hot day in August to drive about the grounds, and see his genius take fire." (Mary Crawford speaking hyperbolically about her brother Henry)

"I danced with a very agreeable young man, introduced by Mr. King; had a great deal of conversation with him—seems a most extraordinary genius—hope I may know more of him. That, madam, is what I wish you to say." (Henry Tilney to Catherine)

Having reached the ornamental part of the premises, consisting of a walk round two sides of a meadow, on which Henry's genius had begun to act about half a year ago, she [Catherine] was sufficiently recovered to think it prettier than any pleasure-ground she had ever been in before, though there was not a shrub in it higher than the green bench in the corner.

At times she uses the word in an ironic sense that could be either the original or newer meaning.

He [Sir Thomas] was aware that he must not expect a genius in Mr. Rushworth.

I [Knightley] do not pretend to Emma's genius for foretelling and guessing.

Perhaps Sir Edward can come down to earth long enough to explain his mixed metaphor in which the "mind" can "grovel."]

The Corascations of Talent, elicited by impassioned feeling in the breast of Man, are perhaps incompatible with some of the prosaic Decencies of Life; —
>
The Coruscations of Talent, elicited by impassioned feeling in the breast of Man, are perhaps incompatible with some of the prosaic Decencies of Life; —

[In "Corascations" > "Coruscations" we have one of the few instances in which Jane Austen corrects her spelling. It appears to be her first and last use of the word, and perhaps its newness to her vocabulary led to the misspelling.

Alternatively, the original spelling may be meant to represent Sir Edward's pretentious, incorrect pronunciation of the word, but the author decided that this was too subtle and revised to what she knew to be the correct spelling. It is likely that Sir Edward uses many words that he does not understand and frequently mispronounces them.

The *OED* cites primarily literal uses of the word, "A vibratory or quivering flash of light, or a display of such flashes." But it was also occasionally used figuratively as we see in this manuscript. The *OED* does not cite any work that Jane Austen can be assumed to have read, and so where she found this unusual word must remain a mystery. The only early nineteenth-century appearance in print that *OED* quotes is from 1810, an unlikely source in the writings of Gouverneur Morris (1752–1816), an American statesman who was born in New York but represented Pennsylvania at the Convention in Philadelphia in 1787 and who is credited with writing much of our Constitution.

Certainly the most important appearance of this word in modern literature, at least as far as we devoted Sherlockians are concerned, is in *The Valley of Fear* (published 1914–1915), where the great detective pays Dr. Watson as high a compliment as he can muster: "Surely you do yourself an injustice. One more coruscation, my dear Watson. Yet another brain-wave." This passage is not cited in *OED*, which records the last figurative use in 1880.]

nor can you, loveliest Miss Heywood — (speaking with an air of deep sentiment) — nor can any Woman be a fair Judge of what a Man may be propelled to say, write or do, by the sovereign impulses of illimitable Ardour."

This was very fine; — but if Charlotte understood it at all, not very moral. — & being moreover by no means pleased with his extraordinary stile of compliment, she gravely answered "I really know nothing of the matter. — This is a charming day. The Wind I fancy must be Southerly."

[Charlotte's sophistication in bringing this nonsensical discussion to a close is commendable. But the indomptible Sir Edward continues unfazed in the same vein.]

"Happy, happy Wind, to engage Miss Heywood's Thoughts! —" She began to think him downright silly. —

[The long preceding scene, from "He began, in a tone of great Taste & Feeling" to "She began to think him downright silly," is so remarkably free of revisions (see facsimile, folios 31v–33r, or Axelrad, 2003: 193–195) that it seems impossible that it was initially written as we now have it. I offer such a passage as evidence to support my contention that at least part of what is extant was copied from an earlier, lost draft.

As is the nature of language, "silly" has been transformed over time from a word of praise—"deserving of pity, compassion, or sympathy" or "plain, simple, rustic, homely"—to one with a pejorative meaning—"weak or deficient in intellect; feeble-minded, imbecile" or "lacking in judgement or common sense; foolish, senseless, empty-headed" (*OED*). Jane Austen uses the word in the more recent sense, but exactly how imbecilic or merely foolish someone is the author leaves to our judgment.

Chiding his daughter in the fondest terms, Mr. Woodhouse uses the word as no more than a mild rebuke.

> "Emma never thinks of herself, if she can do good to others," rejoined Mr. Woodhouse, understanding but in part. "But, my dear, pray do not make any more matches; they are silly things, and break up one's family circle grievously."

George Knightley's use of the word in speaking to Emma is somewhat more acerbic.

> "Men of sense, whatever you may chuse to say, do not want silly wives."

Emma, as only Emma can do, attempts to turn the word upside down and inside out.

> "I do not know whether it ought to be so, but certainly silly things do cease to be silly if they are done by sensible people in an impudent way."

For Mr. Bennet, indirectly alluding to their silly mother while affectionately chiding his daughters, the state of silliness is a normal and universal female condition.

> "They have none of them much to recommend them," replied he; "they are all silly and ignorant like other girls; but Lizzy has something more of quickness than her sisters."

Perfectly describing the vain and foolish Sir Walter Elliot, the adjective is by no means limited to women.

> Three girls, the two eldest sixteen and fourteen, was an awful legacy for a mother to bequeath, an awful charge rather, to confide to the authority and guidance of a conceited, silly father.

George Knightley uses the same adjective in dismissing Frank Churchill as almost not worth his consideration.

> "Hum! just the trifling, silly fellow I took him for."

But for Jane Austen's major stroke of genius in delineating the portrait of a silly man, we must consider Mr. Collins. The word is appropriately used as the culmination of a series of damning adjectives to summarize all that we know about this sycophantic cleric.

"Mr. Collins is a conceited, pompous, narrow-minded, silly man."]

His chusing to walk with her, she had learnt to understand. It was done to pique Miss Brereton. She had read it, in an anxious glance or two on his side — but why he sh^d— talk so much Nonsense, unless he could do no better, was un-intelligible. — He seemed very sentimental, very full of some Feelings or other, & very much addicted to all the newest-fashioned hard words — had not a very clear Brain she presumed, & talked a good deal by rote. —

The Future might explain him further — but when there was a proposition for going into the Library she felt that she had had quite enough of Sir Edw: for one morn^g, & very gladly accepted Lady D.'s invitation of remaining on the Terrace with her. — The others all left them, Sir Edw: with looks of very gallant despair in tearing himself away, & they united their agreableness — that is, Lady Denham like a true great Lady, talked & talked only of her own concerns, & Charlotte listened — amused in considering the contrast between her two companions. —

[Again like a skillful playwright, Jane Austen has changed the scene, with everyone leaving but Lady Denham and Charlotte. It is time for these two strong characters to have a direct, face-to-face encounter as Lady Denham has seen Sir Edward's performance and knows that she must warn off this unsuitable match for her impoverished nephew-by-marriage. Like him, Lady Denham hogs any conversation, but her point is reached much more directly.]

Certainly, there was no strain of doubtful Sentiment, nor any phrase of difficult interpretation in Lady D's discourse. Taking hold of Charlotte's arm with the ease of one who felt that any notice from her was an Honour, & communicative, from the influence of the same conscious Importance or a natural love of talking, she immediately said in a tone of great satisfaction — & with a look of arch sagacity — "Miss Esther wants me to invite her & her Brother to spend a week with me at Sanditon House, as I did last Summer — But I shan't. —

[Lady Denham's directness of vision and discourse are her chief characteristics. The rudeness of her disclosing to a stranger the subject of the importunities of her niece-by-marriage clarifies all that we were unsure about.]

She has been trying to get round me every way, with her praise of this, & her praise of that; but I saw what she was about. — I saw through it all. — I am not very easily taken-in my Dear."

[Although Lady Denham is perceptive about her niece, she remains in the dark about the machinations of her ward, Miss Clara Brereton.]

Charlotte c^d. think of nothing more harmless to be said, than the simple enquiry of — "Sir Edward & Miss Denham?" —

"Yes, my Dear. <u>My young Folks</u>, as I call them sometimes, for I take them very much by the hand. I had them with me last Summer, about this time, for a week; from Monday to Monday; and very delighted & thankful they were. — For they are very good young People my Dear. I w^d. not have you think that I <u>only</u> notice them, for poor dear Sir Harry's sake. No, no; they are very deserving themselves, or trust me, they w^d. not be so much in <u>my</u> Company. — I am not the Woman to help any body blindfold. — I always take care to know what I am about & who I have to deal with, before I stir a finger. — I do not think I was ever over-reached in my Life; & That is a good deal for a Woman to say that has been married twice. Poor dear Sir Harry (between ourselves) thought at first to have got more. —

But (with a bit of a sigh) He is gone, & we must not rip up the faults of the Dead.
>
But (with a bit of a sigh) He is gone, & we must not find fault with the Dead.

[Our author could not resist the stage direction sigh. Surprisingly, though, she modifies Lady Denham's vulgar "rip up" to the more conventional "find fault with."]

We lived perfectly happy together — & he was a very honourable Man, quite the Gentleman of ancient Family.
>

Nobody could live happier together than us — & he was a very honourable Man, quite the Gentleman of ancient Family.

[Here, however, Jane Austen changes her text to show Lady Denham's poor grasp of basic English grammar.]

And when he died, I gave Sir Edwd. his Gold Watch. —"

She said this with a look at her Companion which implied its' right to produce a great Impression — & seeing no rapturous astonishment in her countenance, added quickly — "He did not bequeath it to his Nephew, my dear — It was no legal bequest.
>
She said this with a look at her Companion which implied its' right to produce a great Impression — & seeing no rapturous astonishment in Charlottes countenance, added quickly — "He did not bequeath it to his Nephew, my dear — It was no bequest.

It was not in the Will. He only told me, & that but once, that he sh^d. wish his Nephew to have his Watch; but it need not have been binding, if I had not chose it. —"

[We find more evidence of Lady Denham's lack of education in the false participle "chose."]

"Very kind indeed! very Handsome!" — said Charlotte, absolutely forced to affect admiration. —

[For a straightforward young woman, especially one speaking here for the author, such required hypocrisy is painful and yet necessary. The passage illustrates how insidious Lady Denham is in forcing Charlotte to pretend admiration when her feelings are those of revulsion.]

"Yes, my dear — & it is not the only kind thing I have done by him. — I have been a very liberal friend to Sir Edwd.

And poor young Man, he needs it enough; —
>
And poor young Man, he needs it bad enough; —

[Another emendation to illustrate not merely Lady Denham's vulgarity but her poor education.]

305

For though I am <u>only</u> the <u>Dowager</u> my Dear, & he is the <u>Heir</u>, things do not stand between us in the way they commonly do between those two parties. — Not a shilling do I receive from the Denham Estate. Sir Edw: has no Payments to make <u>me</u>. He don't stand uppermost, beleive me. — It is <u>I</u> that help <u>him</u>."

[Lady Denham's referring to herself as "Dowager" is unnecessary: "When a titled lady is widowed she becomes a dowager, but the practice has generally been not to use that title until the heir takes a wife and there could be confusion as to who is the real Lady [Denham]" (Beverley). This is the only place in the manuscript where this term is used, perhaps because everyone else understands better than she how to use it properly. As Mr. Thomas Parker tells Charlotte, she has not had the advantages of an education. Both Sir Edward, as the hereditary holder of the title of Baronet, and his sister, as the niece and now sister of a Baronet, would certainly be aware of their social superiority to this woman despite her title and wealth.

Needless to say, these confidences to a total stranger are exceptionally vulgar, and Charlotte is both taken aback and amused by the situation. We already know that Lady Denham is poorly educated, and her faulty agreement—"He don't"—puts her in sharp contrast to most of the other characters in the story. Her correct "It is I" is surprising.]

"Indeed! — He is very fine young Man; — particularly Elegant Address." —

>

"Indeed! — He is a very fine young Man; — particularly Elegant in his Address." —

[A possible example of incorrect transcription although Charlotte could be speaking in a truncated manner since—contrary to habit—she is somewhat at a loss for words.]

This was said cheifly for the sake of saying something — but Charlotte imagined it was laying her open to suspicion by Lady D.'s giving a shrewd glance at her & replying — "Yes, yes, he is very well to look at — & it is to be hoped some Lady of large fortune will think so — for Sir Edwd— <u>must</u> marry for Money. —

>

This was said cheifly for the sake of saying something — but Charlotte directly saw that it was laying her open to suspicion by Lady D.'s giving a shrewd glance at her & replying — "Yes, yes, he is very well to look at — & it is to be hoped some Lady of large fortune will think so — for Sir Edwd— must marry for Money. —

[The change of "imagined" to "directly saw" is significant in establishing Lady Denham's suspicion of any unsuitable young lady who throws herself in Sir Edward's path. Oddly, the suspicion does not extend to the most obvious danger, Miss Clara Brereton.]

He & I often talk that matter over. — A handsome young fellow like him, will go smirking & smiling about & paying girls compliments, but he knows he must marry for Money. — And Sir Edw: is a very steady young Man in the main, & has got very good notions."

"Sir Edw: Denham, said Charlotte, with such personal Advantages may be almost sure of getting a Woman of fortune, if he chuses it." —

[Confident that he is as smooth as silk, Sir Edward has no idea that every woman with whom he comes in contact sees through his blandishments. He has been "smirking & smiling" too often and at too many young ladies for his aunt-by-marriage not to be aware of his random flatteries, and with her wider experience she knows better than he how they can lead to an unexpected misalliance. The plight of Mr. Edward Ferrars, inadvertently drawn into a secret engagement with the likes of Lucy Steele, must be avoided at all costs.]

This glorious sentiment seemed to to remove suspicion.
>
This glorious sentiment seemed quite to to remove suspicion.

[Both the original line and its revision are so clearly defective that even theorizing transcription from an earlier manuscript fails to explain the problem.]

"Aye my Dear — That's very sensibly said

cried Lady D — And if we c^d. but get a young Heiress to S! But Heiresses are monstrous scarce! I do not think we have had an Heiress here, or even a Co— since Sanditon has been a public place.

[The passage originally in pencil and over-written in ink begins at "cried." If John Halperin is right that "the writer, puffing and breathless, could not get it all down fast enough" (1983: 183), it is hard to see why she spent precious time writing in ink over what would have been sufficiently legible in pencil. For details on the pencil/ink differences, see Axelrad, 2003: 399–403.

By "Co—" Lady Denham means a "joint-heiress" (*CUPLM*: 663). Abbreviating in this manner may be meant to demonstrate her vulgarity. In contrast, Thomas Parker refers to the young Baronet more respectfully as a potential "noble Coadjutor!"]

Families come after Families, but as far as I can learn, it is not one in an hundred of them that have any Property. —

>

Families come after Families, but as far as I can learn, it is not one in an hundred of them that have any real Property, Landed or Funded. —

[The revised ending demonstrates Lady Denham's knowledge of the complexity of "Property." "Among the aristocracy and gentry, financial status depended on land, and the income coming from it, or money invested in government stocks, or funds, rather than money earned" (*CUPLM*: 663). A gentleman does not labor for wages.]

An Income perhaps, but no Property. Clergymen may be, or Lawyers from Town, or Half pay officers, or Widows with only a Jointure. And what good can such people do anybody? — except just as they take our empty Houses — and (between ourselves) I think they are great fools for not staying at home.

[Lady Denham's contempt is probably directed against the people in the current Subscription Book, where we find two likely clergymen (Dr. Brown and the Reverend Mr. Hanking), one lawyer from London (Mr. Beard), two officers (Lieutenant Smith and Captain Little), and several ladies who could be impoverished widows (perhaps Mrs. Mathews, Mrs. Fisher, or Mrs. Davis).

Lady Denham's confusing "solicitors" and "barristers" as "Lawyers from Town" may reflect Jane Austen's own uncertainty about the distinction. "Half pay officers," whether in the army or the navy, "were not on active service, either because they were between assignments or because they were unable to undertake active tasks" (*CUPLM*: 663–664). Among these half pay officers who can do nothing for Lady Denham would be men formerly engaged in the recent wars fought to protect her and her worldly possessions.

As the sister of two naval officers, Jane Austen allows Lady Denham to condemn herself through her own words as selfish and mercenary.

A jointure is "that part of an estate specifically willed from a husband to a wife, to provide for her after his death; it would usually be a small proportion, since the main part of the estate would go to the heir, most often the eldest son" (*CUPLM*: 664). Lady Denham can afford to scorn these poor widows because with no sons from either marriage, both husbands left her their entire property.]

Now, if we could but get a young Heiress to be sent here for her health — (and if she was ordered to take asses milk I could supply her) — and as soon as she got well, have her fall in love with Sir Edward! —"
>
Now, if we could get a young Heiress to be sent here for her health — (and if she was ordered to drink asses milk I could supply her) — and as soon as she got well, have her fall in love with Sir Edward! —"

[Lady Denham does not know yet, of course, that Miss Lambe is on her way to Sanditon, possibly fulfilling every one of the dowager's wishes.]

"That would be very fortunate indeed."

"And Miss Esther must marry somebody of fortune too — She must get a rich Husband. Ah! young Ladies that have no Money are very much to be pitied! — But — after a short pause — if Miss Esther thinks to talk me into inviting them to come & stay at Sanditon House, she will find herself mistaken. — Matters are altered with me since last Summer you know —. I have Miss Clara with me now, which makes a great difference."

[Lady Denham, after confiding in a stranger about personal family matters, returns to the original thread of her conversation, Miss Esther Denham's attempts to wangle an invitation for herself and her brother to Sanditon House.]

She spoke this so seriously that Charlotte

[The passage originally in pencil and over-written in ink ends at "Charlotte."]

instantly saw in it the evidence of real penetration & prepared for some fuller remarks — but it was followed only by — "I have no fancy for having my House as full as an Hotel. I should not chuse to have my 2 Housemaids Time taken up all the morn^g, in dusting out Bed rooms. — They have Miss Clara's room to put to rights as well as my own every day. — If they had hard Places, they would want Higher Wages. —"

[We never learn the full extent of Lady Denham's domestic support, but that she has abundant servants is clear from various remarks.]

For objections of this Nature, Charlotte was not prepared, & she found it so impossible even to affect simpathy, that she c^d. say nothing. —

Lady D. soon added, with great glee — "And besides all this my Dear, am I to be filling my House to the prejudice of Sanditon? — If People want to be by the Sea, why dont they take Lodgings? — Here are a great many empty Houses — 3 on this very Terrace; no fewer than three Lodging Papers staring us in the face at this very moment, Numbers 3, 4 & 8. 8, the Corner House may be too large for them, but either of the two others are nice little snug Houses, very fit for a young Gentleman & his sister — And so, my dear, the next time Miss Esther begins talking about the Dampness of Denham Park, & the Good Bathing always does her, I shall advise them to come & take one of these Lodgings for a fortnight. — Don't you think that will be very fair? — Charity begins at home you know." —

[The reputed dampness of Denham Park may be one of various reasons that Lady Denham vacated the home of her second husband and moved back to Mr. Hollis's Sanditon House, which she also apparently owned.]

Charlotte's feelings were divided between amusement & indignation — but indignation had the larger & the increasing share. — She kept her Countenance & she kept a civil Silence. She could not carry her forbearance farther; but without attempting to listen longer, & only conscious that Lady D. was still talking on in the same way, allowed her Thoughts to form themselves into such a Meditation as this. —

"She is much worse than I expected. — meaner — a great deal meaner —
>
"She is much worse than I expected. — She is very mean. —
>
"She is thoroughly mean. — I had not expected any thing so bad.

[Jane Austen labored over this simple passage so that Charlotte could state her impressions precisely.]

Mr. P. spoke too mildly of her. —

His own kind Disposition makes him judge too well of others. His Judgement is evidently not to be trusted in his opinion of others & —
>
His own kind Disposition makes him judge too well of others. His Judgement is evidently not to be trusted. His own Goodnature misleads him in judging of others.
>
His Judgement is evidently not always to be trusted. His own Goodnature misleads him.
>
His Judgement is evidently not to be trusted. His own Goodnature misleads him.

[This passage is an unusual example of Jane Austen's lopping and cropping in this manuscript, where she more often adds and pads as she revises.]

He is too kind hearted to see clearly. — I must judge for myself. — And their very <u>connection</u> prejudices him. — He has persuaded her to engage in the same Speculation — & because their object in that Line is the same, he fancies she feels like him in others. — But she is very, very mean. — I can see no Good in her. — Poor Miss Brereton! — And she makes every body mean about her. —

This poor Sir Edward & his Sister —, how far Nature meant them to be respectable I can tell, — but they are <u>obliged</u> to be Mean in their Servility to her. —
>
This poor Sir Edward & his Sister —, how far Nature meant them to be respectable I can not tell, — but they are <u>obliged</u> to be Mean in their Servility to her. —

[The omitted "not" is strong evidence that this manuscript is a transcription from an earlier copy.]

And I am Mean too, in giving her my attention, with the appearance of coinciding with her. — Thus it is, when Rich People are Sordid." —

[We meet Sir Edward Denham and learn of Lady's Denham's plans for him and Miss Denham, scornful of the low people about her and reserving her unreported dialog for sycophantic addresses to her aunt-by-marriage.

This chapter contains the famous palimpsest passage, running from the middle of folio 35r to about two-thirds down folio 35v. Over the pencil Jane Austen rewrote the passage in ink with a few changes (see *Jane Austen Caught in the Act of Greatness*: 399–403).]

[Chapter 8]

Chapter 8. —

The two Ladies continued walking together till rejoined by the others, who as they issued from the Library were followed by a young Whitby running off with 5 vols. under his arm to Sir Edward's Gig —

[Whereas the older woman is a "Lady" by virtue of her marriage, Charlotte is a "lady" because her father is a gentleman-farmer.

CUPLM makes an intriguing suggestion that the five volumes under young Whitby's arm are "possibly Burney's *Camilla*, which Charlotte had already seen on Mrs Whitby's counter and which consisted of five volumes altogether" (664), an argument with merit because most novels at the time were published in only three volumes, with a few in four and even fewer in five. If this hypothesis is sound, perhaps Sir Edward has somehow learned of Charlotte's interest in the book—Mrs. Whitby may have told the Baronet that the young visitor had picked up one volume of the set—and plans to impress her by spouting some choice passages during their next meeting. The text, however, in no way suggests that Sir Edward is interested in Burney's work or that the five volumes constitute a single novel. In illustrating this scene, Maximilien Vox does not show matching spines (*The Works of Jane Austen. Sanditon and Other Miscellanea*. Ed. R. Brimley Johnson. Facing page 49).

"The libraries' short lending period of two to six days for new books" proves what we can already guess, that Sir Edward reads very rapidly if extravagantly since generally for the considerable sum of "two guineas a year [he would] be entitled to have two volumes out and by paying more could have more volumes" (Erickson: 578).

Here we meet "young Whitby," of undisclosed age but charmingly pigtailed as drawn by Maximilien Vox. Because he is identified in the text as "a young Whitby" (rather than just "young Whitby"), it is possible that he has several brothers. Like his mother and sister, he has no dialog since he is in trade.

CUPLM (486) transcribes the medial "t" of "Whitby" as "l" to give us "Whilby." Jane Austen has again used a terminal "t" without a crossbar in a medial position (folio 36v). Chapman (105), Johnson (facing 49 and 51), and Sacco (107) concur in reading the name as "Whitby."]

and Sir Edw: approaching Charlotte, said "You may perceive what has been our Occupation. My Sister wanted my Counsel in the selection of some books.

[Sir Edward's selecting "some books" strongly argues against the preceding suggestion that he has borrowed Burney's five-volume *Camilla*. And if the text is to be read literally, the books are for Miss Esther Denham, who would certainly not be interested in anything admired by Charlotte Heywood. Miss Denham does not, however, seem like an avid reader, and it is likely that the five volumes are really for Sir Edward himself and he is twisting the truth to impress Charlotte with his sensitivity to the Fair Sex. Is it really likely that Miss Denham turns to her brother for any "Counsel"?]

We have many leisure hours, & read a great deal. —

[Again Sir Edward suggests that his sister is an avid reader, but the little bit that we see of her suggests otherwise. That they both have many leisure hours is certainly true since neither can work and neither has found a way to be useful. Jane Austen comments as much about social classes in this fragment as economy.]

I am no indiscriminate Novel-Reader. The mere Trash of the common Circulating Library, I hold in the highest contempt.

[The "Trash" of the circulating library had already been specifically condemned by an earlier foolish character.

> Mr. Collins readily assented, and a book was produced; but, on beholding it (for everything announced it to be from a circulating library), he started back, and begging pardon, protested that he never read novels.

"The Austens, however, found reading such novels an amusing pastime" (*CUPLM*: 664), and Jane Austen clearly regards them as entertainment not to be taken seriously.]

You will never hear me advocating those puerile Emanations which detail nothing but discordant Principles incapable of Amalgamation, or those vapid tissues of ordinary Occurrences from which no useful Deductions can be drawn. — In vain may we put them into a literary Alembic; — we distil nothing which can add to Science. — You understand me I am sure?"

[*CUPLM*, in suggesting that "Sir Edward's declaration ["ordinary occurrences... drawn"]... forms a neat companion-piece to the famous description of the novel in *NA*, a work 'in which the greatest powers of the mind are displayed; in which the most thorough knowledge of human nature, the happiest delineation of its varieties, the liveliest effusions of wit and humour are conveyed to the world in the best chosen language'" (664–665), perhaps inadvertently lends support to my argument that the fragment owes a great deal to "Susan"/"Catherine." It is unlikely that in abandoning the earlier manuscript Jane Austen would give up altogether this passage on which she must have labored hard and long.

"An alembic is a glass vessel with a top, traditionally used for the distilling of chemicals, but acquiring a figurative meaning towards the end of the eighteenth century" (*CUPLM*: 665). Jane Austen deliberately assigns figurative language to Sir Edward, whose imagination is stronger than his wit or intelligence.

"Despite the scientific words elsewhere in the sentence, 'science' has its traditional meaning of general knowledge" (*CUPLM*: 665). The earliest recorded use of "science" in its modern sense—"synonymous with 'Natural and Physical Science', and thus restricted to those branches of study that relate to the phenomena of the material universe and their laws"—is dated 1867 (*OED*).]

"I am not quite certain that I do. — But If you will describe the sort of Novels which you <u>do</u> approve, I dare say it will give me a clearer idea."

"Most willingly, Fair Questioner. —

[The *CUPLM* note is a little puzzling: "In Burney's *Camilla*, the former governess Miss Margland, trying to cajole the pretty, vain and vacuous Indiana Lynmere, 'began a negociation with the fair questioner....' *Camilla* is very far from the kind of novel Sir Edward says he admires" (666). Why, then, would he borrow Mrs. Whitby's copy of the five-volume *Camilla*? "Fair Questioner" is far enough over-the-top to be original with Sir Edward.]

315

The Novels which I approve are such as display Human Nature with Grandeur — such as shew her in the Sublimities of intense Feeling — such as exhibit the progress of strong Passion from the first Germ of Susceptibility to the utmost Energies of Reason half-dethroned, — where we see the strong spark of Woman's Captivations elicit such Fire in the Soul of Man as leads him — (though at the risk of some Aberrations from the strict line of Primitive Obligations) — to hazard all, dare all, encounter all, to obtain her. —

>

The Novels which I approve are such as display Human Nature with Grandeur — such as shew her in the Sublimities of intense Feeling — such as exhibit the progress of strong Passion from the first Germ of incipient Susceptibility to the utmost Energies of Reason half-dethroned, — where we see the strong spark of Woman's Captivations elicit such Fire in the Soul of Man as leads him — (though at the risk of some Aberrations from the strict line of Primitive Obligations) — to hazard all, dare all, atcheive all, to obtain her. —

[Sir Edward's approval of novels that "display Human Nature with Grandeur — such as shew her in the Sublimities of intense Feeling — such as exhibit the progress of strong Passion from the first Germ of incipient Susceptibility to the utmost Energies of Reason half-dethroned" allies him with Jane Austen, who says much the same thing, but in much better chosen language, in the assessment of the modern novel that she added to "Susan"/"Catherine." "'Primitive' here carries the meaning of 'original, basic'; and the obligations would include upholding moral principles with friends, family and society" (*CUPLM*: 666).

There are only two changes—"Germ of Susceptibility" > "Germ of incipient Susceptibility" and "encounter all" > "atcheive all"—in the revised version, but they successfully intensify the nonsense of Sir Edward's extravagant address. The spelling "atcheive" may be meant to record Sir Edward's mispronunciation, mixing "attain" and "achieve" to create an unintentional portmanteau word. The *OED* cites several occurrences of "atchieve" from the eighteenth century.]

Such are the Works which I peruse with ardour, & I hope I may say, with amelioration. They hold forth the most splendid Portraitures of high Conceptions, Unbounded Veiws, illimitable Ardour, unconquerable Decision — and even where the Event is mainly anti-prosperous to the

prime Character, the potent, pervading Hero of the Story, it leaves us full of Generous Emotions for him; — our Hearts are paralized —.
>
Such are the Works which I peruse with delight, & I hope I may say, with amelioration. They hold forth the most splendid Portraitures of high Conceptions, Unbounded Veiws, illimitable Ardour, indomptible Decision — and even where the Event is mainly anti-prosperous to the high-toned Machinations of the prime Character, the potent, pervading Hero of the Story, it leaves us full of Generous Emotions for him; — our Hearts are paralized —.

[Although the author again makes only a few revisions—"I peruse with ardour" > "I peruse with delight," "unconquerable Decision" > "indomptible Decision," and "anti-prosperous to the prime Character" > "anti-prosperous to the high-toned Machinations of the prime Character"—the new version is far more ridiculous than its nonsensical original. Sir Edwards's "indomptible" (correctly spelled "indomptable") is a rare variant of "indomitable," not a neologism. Our Baronet is no more capable of creating a new word than he is of fashioning an original idea.]

T'were Pseudo-Philosophy to assert that we do not feel more enwraped by the brilliancy of his Career, than by the tranquil & morbid Virtues of his Rival. Our approbation of the Latter is Eleemosynary. — These are the Novels which enlarge the primitive Capabilities of the Heart, & which it cannot impugn the Sense or be any Dereliction of the character, of the most sagacious Man, to be conversant with." —
>
T'were Pseudo-Philosophy to assert that we do not feel more enwraped by the brilliancy of his Career, than by the tranquil & morbid Virtues of any opposing Character. Our approbation of the Latter is but Eleemosynary. — These are the Novels which enlarge the primitive Capabilities of the Heart, & which it cannot impugn the Sense or be any Dereliction of the character, of the most anti-puerile Man, to be conversant with." —

[Not even a Romantic poet—which Sir Edward certainly is not—would have said "T'were" with a straight face in the course of a conversation. Exactly what the contraction represents is a mystery since there is no implied letter between "T" ("It") and "were." The proper contraction would be "'Twere" like the famous "'Twas" that opens the poem, "The Night Before Christmas." Since Sir Edward is saying it but Jane Austen has written it, although it demonstrates his affected diction it also shows again her problems with punctuation.

Sir Edward has become fond of "Pseudo-Philosophy," a phrase perhaps invented by Jane Austen. The *OED* does not cite this line. The spelling with a single "p" may reflect Sir Edward's mispronouncing "enwraped," his mind filled with images of seducing Clara Brereton, by force if necessary (or perhaps even by preference). Again the changes are minimal—"of his Rival" > "of any opposing Character," "is Eleemosynary" > "is but Eleemosynary," and "the most sagacious Man" > "the most anti-puerile Man"—but they bring Sir Edward's harangue to a crashing finale of nonsense. This prolonged passage on Sir Edward's poor reading habits may have been influenced by the defense of novels inserted at some time into the manuscript of "Susan"/"Catherine" and published in *Northanger Abbey*.

The word "Eleemosynary" ("charitable") appears nowhere else in Jane Austen's novels. She allows Sir Edward to enunciate this unusual word because "it also appeared (often for comic effect) in fiction" (*CUPLM*: 666).]

"If I understand you aright — said Charlotte — our taste in Novels is not at all the same."

[As expected, Charlotte summarizes the distinctions between her taste and that of Sir Edward in a simple and outright statement. Chacun à son goût. And some of us have no goût at all.]

And here they were obliged to part — Miss D. being too much tired of them all, to stay any longer. —

[Miss Esther Denham, besides mute as far as the reader is concerned, must be the dourest character in any of Jane Austen's novels.]

The truth was that Sir Edw: whom circumstances had confined very much to one spot had read more sentimental Novels than agreed with him. His fancy had been early caught by all the impassioned, & most exceptionable parts of Richardsons;

[The three epistolary novels by Samuel Richardson (1689–1761), *Pamela; or, Virtue Rewarded* (1740), *Clarissa; or, The History of a Young Lady* (1748), and Jane Austen's favorite, *Sir Charles Grandison* (1754), "attracted controversy because of the propensity of the first two novels in particular to wallow in their vivid explorations of virtue under siege and in peril" (*CUPLM*: 667).]

& such Authors as have since appeared to tread in Richardson's steps, so far as Man's determined pursuit of Woman in defiance of every opposition of feeling & convenience is concerned,

["Richardson's Lovelace was copied by a large number of novelists, including Richardson himself with the figure of Sir Hargrave Pollexfen in *Sir Charles Grandison*.... In most later novels Richardson's subtleties were replaced by a crude representation of a predatory male, who might appear appropriately within the pages of a melodramatic plot but who was completely out of place in a realistic representation of contemporary life" (*CUPLM*: 667). Unintentionally, Mrs. Whitby has brought Sir Edward to this dream-like state where he lives in a fictional world in which he is Lovelace reborn. The situation is comic despite the serious crimes of the real Lovelace.]

had since occupied the greater part of his literary hours, & formed his Character. — With a perversity of Judgement, which must be attributed to his not having by Nature a very strong head, the Graces, the Spirit, the Ingenuity, & the Perseverance, of the Villain of the Story outweighed all his absurdities & all his Atrocities with Sir Edward.

[Having left the nonsense of Gothic novels behind when she abandoned "Susan"/ "Catherine," Jane Austen now inveighs against sentimental novels, from which hyper-imaginative young readers like Sir Edward may be infected with a form of conversational insanity.

The correct reading, "Ingenuity," may be found in the most recent editions of the manuscript, all earlier editions incorrectly printing "Sagacity." See my article, "Sir Edward's 'Ingenuity': A Corrected Reading in the *Sanditon* Manuscript." *Persuasions*, 17 (1995), 47–48.]

With him, such Conduct was Genius, Fire & Feeling. — It interested & inflamed him; & he was always more anxious for its Success & mourned over its Discomfitures with more Tenderness than c^d. ever have been contemplated by the Authors. —

[Indirectly bowing to the old alchemical theory of the four basic elements, to air and water, already abundantly present in the novel, here Jane Austen adds fire. When poor Arthur Parker finally comes onstage, the author will complete the metaphor in observing that "a good deal of Earthy Dross hung about him." The former fishing village of Sanditon, transmuted into a risky business venture, has become a crucible in which speculators can accumulate gold—or go broke.]

Though he owed many of his ideas to this sort of reading, it were unjust to say that he read nothing else, or that his Language was not formed on a more general Knowledge of modern Literature. —

>

Though he owed many of his ideas to this sort of reading, it were unjust to say that he read nothing else, or that his Language were not formed on a more general Knowledge of modern Literature.

[Jane Austen's use of the subjunctive "were" must be based on her regarding the verb form as equivalent to "would be." However, the "were" replacing the original "was" reads poorly and was probably changed by some kind of attraction and desire for parallel construction despite sense.

By modern literature, Jane Austen means "literature from the eighteenth century, in contrast to the 'ancient' classical literature that still formed a large part of the reading particularly of men of the aristocracy and gentry" (*CUPLM*: 668). To his credit, Sir Edward has opened his mind (?) to contemporary literature.]

He read all the Essays, Letters, Tours & Criticisms of the day — & with the same ill-luck which made him derive only false Principles from Lessons of Morality, & incentives to Vice from the History of it's Overthrow, he gathered only hard words & involved sentences from the style of our most approved Writers. —

>

He read all the Essays, Letters, Tours & Criticisms of the day — & with the same ill-luck which made him derive only false Principles from Lessons of Morality, & incentives to Vice from the History of it's Overthrow, he gathered only hard words & involved sentences from the style of the most approved Writers. —

>

He read all the Essays, Letters, Tours & Criticisms of the day — & with the same ill-luck which made him derive only false Principles from Lessons of Morality, & incentives to Vice from the History of it's Overthrow, he gathered only hard words & involved sentences from the style of our most approved Writers. —

[The revision "our" > "the" and back again to "our" is an important touch showing Jane Austen's particular pride in English belles lettres. She may also be saying discreetly that Sir Edward Denham, with little formal education, can read only English. From the "Tours," which were "accounts of travels undertaken by young aristocrats on 'the grand tour', usually through the major capitals of western Europe, and also of increasingly popular general recreational tours within the UK and Europe" (*CUPLM*: 668), he would have learned about a world unavailable to him because of pecuniary restrictions. Among these readings he may have encountered something about the distant land of Timbuktu.]

Sir Edw:'s great object in life was to be seductive. — With such personal advantages as he knew himself to possess, & such Talents as he did also give himself credit for, he regarded it as his Duty. —

[As a latter-day Henry Crawford, Sir Edward is sadly deficient with neither the wealth nor the personal resources of his earlier incarnation.]

He felt that He was formed to be a dangerous Man — quite in the line of the Lovelaces. — To be generally gallant & assiduous about the fair, to make fine speeches to every pretty Girl, was but the inferior part of the Character he had to play. —
>
He felt that He was formed to be a dangerous Man — quite in the line of the Lovelaces. — The very name of Sir Edward he thought, carried some degree of fascination with it. — To be generally gallant & assiduous about the fair, to make fine speeches to every pretty Girl, was but the inferior part of the Character he had to play. —

[Jane Austen had used the word "dangerous" frequently in her preceding novels in a completely different sense of "fraught with danger or risk" (*OED*):

"Well, my dear," said Mr. Bennet, when Elizabeth had read the note aloud, "if your daughter should have a dangerous fit of illness—if she should die, it would be a comfort to know that it was all in pursuit of Mr. Bingley, and under your orders."

For Sir Edward, "formed to be a dangerous Man," the word takes on a slightly different meaning—"causing or occasioning danger" (*OED*)—not usually applied to a person in this manner. Again Jane Austen is more experimental in her language than in earlier writings, and she is particularly adventurous with Sir Edward since she must convey his somewhat twisted value system through what he says.

In 1748, Samuel Richardson published his very long epistolary novel, *Clarissa*, in which the unprincipled anti-hero Robert Lovelace pursues and finally ravishes the eponymous heroine, thus establishing a popular theme of the novels of the day. Jane Austen had mocked this tradition in "Susan"/"Catherine" (material that presumably has been preserved in the text of *Northanger Abbey*). While preparing Catherine for her great adventure in Bath, Mrs. Morland is sorely troubled about what warnings to impart to her naïve young daughter.

> When the hour of departure drew near, the maternal anxiety of Mrs. Morland will be naturally supposed to be most severe. A thousand alarming presentiments of evil to her beloved Catherine from this terrific separation must oppress her heart with sadness, and drown her in tears for the last day or two of their being together; and advice of the most important and applicable nature must of course flow from her wise lips in their parting conference in her closet. Cautions against the violence of such noblemen and baronets as delight in forcing young ladies away to some remote farm-house, must, at such a moment, relieve the fulness of her heart. Who would not think so? But Mrs. Morland knew so little of lords and baronets, that she entertained no notion of their general mischievousness, and was wholly unsuspicious of danger to her daughter from their machinations. Her cautions were confined to the following points. "I beg, Catherine, you will always wrap yourself up very warm about the throat, when you come from the rooms at night; and I wish you would try to keep some account of the money you spend;—I will give you this little book on purpose." (Facsimile: 13–14)

It is hardly surprising that we find such a link between two manuscripts that are so closely related.

Sir Edward's intense reading of this kind of eighteenth-century sensationalist fiction along with adventures of the newer Byronic-style hero has seriously addled what passes for his brain. Although his is not a high title, it is nevertheless a distinction that Sir Edward is keenly aware of, hence his delight in being called "Sir."

Like others in the tale, Sir Edward is a "Character" playing an assigned role. A good playwright, however, frequently has her puppets perform quite differently from what we expect. Just as despite the earlier passages Clara Brereton is revealed in the twelfth chapter to be other than a demure victim of circumstances, so Sir Edward may have more in him than appears on the very superficial surface. Beneath the veneer of false tinsel may lie many layers of genuine tinsel.]

Miss Heywood, or any other young Woman with some pretensions to Beauty, he was entitled (according to his own mistaken veiws of Society) to approach with high Compliment & Rhapsody on the slightest acquaintance; but it was Clara on whom he had serious designs; it was Clara whom he meant to seduce. —

>

Miss Heywood, or any other young Woman with any pretensions to Beauty, he was entitled (according to his own veiws of Society) to approach with high Compliment & Rhapsody on the slightest acquaintance; but it was Clara alone on whom he had serious designs; it was Clara whom he meant to seduce. —

[The revised version removes and adds but leaves the basic comedic picture intact. Young Baronets as habitual seducers was a theme dear to Jane Austen's authorial heart.]

Her seduction was quite determined on. Her Situation in every way called for it. She was his rival in Lady D.'s favour, she was young, lovely & dependant. — He had very early seen the necessity of the case, & had now been long trying with cautious assiduity to make an impression on her heart, and to undermine her Principles. — Clara saw through him, & had not the least intention of being seduced — but she bore with him patiently enough to confirm the sort of attachment which her personal Charms had raised. — A greater degree of discouragement indeed would not have affected Sir Edw: —. He was armed against the highest pitch of Disdain or

Aversion. — If she could not be won by affection, he must carry her off. He knew his Business. — Already had he had many Musings on the Subject.

[Sir Edward's "cautious assiduity" is our author's tongue-in-cheek way of mocking the young Baronet's misapplied ingenuity. The assurance that Miss Clara Brereton both sees through Sir Edward and has no intention of being seduced helps explain her composure in the later scene in the garden of Sanditon House. The text does not say, however, that she has no intention of seducing him.]

If he <u>were</u> constrained so to act, he must naturally wish to strike out something new, to exceed those who had gone before him — and he w^d have felt some curiosity to know whether the Neighbourhood of Tombuctoo might not afford some desola

>

If he <u>were</u> constrained so to act, he must naturally wish to strike out something new, to exceed those who had gone before him — and he w^d have felt some curiosity to know whether the Neighbourhood of Tombuctoo might not afford some solitary House adapted for Clara's reception; — but the Expence alas! of Measures in that masterly style was ill-suited to his Purse, & Prudence obliged him to prefer the quietest st

>

If he <u>were</u> constrained so to act, he must naturally wish to strike out something new, to exceed those who had gone before him — and he w^d have felt some curiosity to know whether the Neighbourhood of Tombuctoo might not afford some solitary House adapted for Clara's reception; — but the Expence alas! of Measures in that masterly style was ill-suited to his Purse, & Prudence obliged him to prefer the quietest sort of ruin & disgrace for the object of his Affections, to the more renowned. —

>

If he <u>were</u> constrained so to act, he must naturally wish to strike out something new, to exceed those who had gone before him — and he felt a strong curiosity to ascertain whether the Neighbourhood of Tombuctoo might not afford some solitary House adapted for Clara's reception; — but the Expence alas! of Measures in that masterly style was ill-suited to his Purse, & Prudence obliged him to prefer the quietest sort of ruin & disgrace for the object of his Affections, to the more renowned. —

[The working-out of Sir Edward's plans for the ruin of Clara Brereton cost Jane Austen a good deal of effort. The bottom line, however, is quickly reached: he cannot afford a high-class seduction and so will have to settle for something rather ordinary.

> He is still thinking of legendary Timbuctoo, fabled for its remoteness, its exotic pleasures and riches. But this romantic image had been shattered in the reports of Mungo Park and Robert Adams, which gave a disenchanted European view of Timbuctoo's alien and unpalatable native culture. These travellers' tales had only recently appeared—Mungo Mark had been reprinted in 1815, Adams was published in 1816, and both books were extensively reviewed and quote from in the monthlies and quarterlies. Incompetent as a latter-day Lovelace, Sir Edward is also laughably out of date in his Regency Afro-Gothicism. (Southam, 1976: 8)

It seems likely that the "cottage ornèe" is eventually built to serve as the site of Sir Edward's conquest of Clara Brereton. We can only imagine the hilarious turn of events as things do not work out as planned.]

[Chapter 8 is exceptionally compressed, with a good deal of script-like dialog and a good portion of authorial commentary. It is a rare example of Jane Austen's writing more than is necessary. We have already experienced a healthy dose of Sir Edward's nonsense, reassuring us that although he is essentially in the tradition of John Willoughby, George Wickham, and Henry Crawford, his is a much brighter and lighter character, with superficial charm covering a considerable amount of self-doubt. The only new information in this chapter is a revelation of Sir Edward's dark side, but we can be certain that he will never succeed in his goal of seducing Clara Brereton. This information could easily have been introduced in an earlier chapter, where we saw Sir Edward casting longing looks upon his intended victim. I suggest that Jane Austen wrote this chapter almost as an afterthought and that she might well have altered it substantially upon reviewing the completed manuscript. With such a leisurely approach to the novel, she may not have had a short work in mind.]

[Chapter 9]

Chapter 9.

One day, soon after Charlotte's arrival at Sanditon, she had the pleasure of seeing just as she ascended from the Sands to the Terrace,

[Charlotte's enjoyment of walking is very much in the tradition of Jane Austen's country-bred heroines like Elizabeth Bennet. Emma Woodhouse also does a considerable amount of walking, an exercise that is healthful and ladylike.]

a Gentleman's Carriage with Post Horses standing at the door of the Hotel, as very lately arrived, & by the quantity of Luggage taking off, bringing it might be hoped, some respectable family determined on a long residence. —

[Although the time scheme for the manuscript is undetermined because of Jane Austen's use of phrases like "soon after," which could be anything from a few days to a few weeks. Ellen Moody has attempted a chronology, which I have slightly modified.

1746: Lady Denham born; she is 70 in 1816.

1759: The year when Mr Heywood began to live in Willingden; perhaps the year of his birth?

1776: Lady Denham (née Miss Brereton) 30, marries Mr. Hollis.

1814: Until 2 years ago the Parkers lived in old house; since then they have been in Trafalgar House; since he now wishes he'd named it Waterloo, the year must be before 1815, but not too far before.

2 years ago Miss Diana Parker called on Mrs Sheldon when her coachmen sprained his foot; Miss Parker rubbed his ankle for 6 hours without intermission, and he was well in 3 days.

1815: A year ago, July, not a lodger in the village. Less than a year earlier, Michaelmas, Lady Denham obliged to go to London; sees bill after 3 days, outraged, and Hollis cousins present themselves as having a place for her to stay the necessary fortnight; she invites one of girls to come live with her for 6 months, and shows good side of her character by inviting Clara Brereton, a niece not a daughter so a dependent upon poverty.

1816?: Opens "late in July" or height of new season. A twelvemonth ago Miss Clara Brereton had come to live at Denham Park, last Michaelmas. An accident; two weeks pass; when we go to Sanditon we are told within a twelvemonth ago Miss Brereton had come to live with Lady Denham at Michaelmas. For "a whole fortnight" Mr. and Mrs. Parker fixed at Willingden. They travel home, taking 22-year-old Charlotte Heywood with them, and before dinner, Mr. Parker looks over his letters. Letter from Miss Diana Parker to Mr. Tom Parker; tells of how 2 years ago she rubbed a coachman's ankle for 6 hours and he was cured of a fall after 3 days; of how Susan Parker for 10 days endured 6 leeches a day; now has had 3 teeth drawn, fainted away twice this morning; fears sea air would be the death of her. After dinner Parkers and Charlotte go to library, subscribe, walk; they meet Lady Denham and Clara Brereton, walk home because Lady Denham doesn't mind smooching [*sic*, for "mooching"?] tea from them. The very next morning: Sir Edward Denham and his sister visit the Parkers and Charlotte; Sir Edward spies Lady Denham out walking with Miss Brereton, follows them; Parkers go to Terrace and meet foursome, both Charlotte's conversations with Sir Edward on literature, and that with Lady Denham on why she won't invite Miss Denham to Sanditon House occur on that day before dinner. One day before: Diana Parker set out, three days before she arrived, she has letter from Mrs. Charles Dupuis, assuring her Camberwell group is coming. Two days before Charlotte sees them, Parkers set out; they set out at six in the morning. Next day, they set out from Chichester at six in the morning. Next or "One day, soon after Charlotte's arrival," and, "after having been contending for the last two hours with a very fine wind blowing directly on shore," she hurries back; Diana, Susan, and Arthur Parker have arrived, travelling two nights from their home; Diana comes to tell of arrival, Arthur gone from hotel to secure lodgings in Terrace; it is now only half past four, she can take a house for Mrs. Griffiths before six when she and Susan and Arthur are to dine; this is less than a week after Diana wrote her letter to Mr. Parker telling him the sea air would be the death of her; Mr. and Mrs. Parker dine at the hotel that night. On the next morning Diana's plan is to take lodgings for herself, Susan, and Arthur directly after breakfast; Diana has not sat down once in seven hours when Charlotte and Mr. and Mrs. Parker go to drink tea in the evening at new lodgings in one of the Terrace houses; letter from Mrs. Dupuis saying Camberwell lady on the way, a Mrs. Griffiths, in charge of a Miss Lambe too. Ten days after Charlotte's arrival, Mrs. Parker and Charlotte set out at an early hour in order to visit Sanditon House, Mr. Parker and Diana want them to nag Lady Denham into giving money, Diana off to shore to help Miss Lambe bathe, but will be back by one o'clock to put leeches on Susan; they meet Sidney Parker, just arrived from Eastbourne, will stay at hotel, to be joined by a friend or two; carry on to Sanditon, see Clara and Sir Edward talking on a bank beyond the paling.]

Delighted to have such good news for M^r. & M^{rs}. P., who had both gone home some time before, she proceeded for Trafalgar House with as much alacrity as could remain, after having been contending for the last 2 hours with a very fine wind blowing directly on shore; but she had not reached the little Lawn, when she saw a Lady walking nimbly behind her at no great distance; and convinced that it could be no acquaintance of her own, she resolved to hurry on & get into the House if possible before her.

[Thus we have our first picture of the languishing Miss Diana Parker, too ill to travel or enjoy any of the pleasures of life, here seen rapidly catching up with the much younger and healthier Charlotte.]

But the Stranger's pace was too brisk for this to be accomplished; — Charlotte was on the steps & had rung, but the door was not opened, as the other crossed the Lawn; — and when the Servant appeared, they were just equally ready for entering the House. —
>
But the Stranger's pace did not allow this to be accomplished; — Charlotte was on the steps & had rung, but the door was not opened, when the other crossed the Lawn; — and when the Servant appeared, they were just equally ready for entering the House. —

[I prefer the "too brisk" of the earlier version to the vague revision. The changes in the manuscript, although usually very much to its advantage, are occasionally not well thought out.]

The ease of the Lady, her "How do you do Morgan? —" and Morgan's Looks on seeing her, were a moment's astonishment — but another moment brought M^r. P. into the Hall to welcome the Sister he had seen from the Draw^g. room, & she was soon introduced to Miss Diana Parker.

[This is Morgan's second appearance, and again although he must say something in the way of greeting Miss Diana Parker, Jane Austen deliberately suppresses his dialog.]

There was great astonis
>
There was much g
>
There was a great deal of surprise & great pleasure in seeing her. —
>
There was a great deal of surprise but still more pleasure in seeing her. —

[This sentence proves, if such proof were necessary, that Jane Austen was concerned over the details of each sentence as well as the general movement of her story. The last version is worth the trouble invested to reach it.]

How did she come? & with whom? —
>
Nothing c^d. be kinder than her reception from both Husband and Wife.
did she come? & with whom? —
>
Nothing c^d. be kinder than her reception from both Husband and Wife.
How did she come? & with whom? —

[The three stages here show some uncertainty on the author's part. Dropping the initial "How" to read "did she come?" makes no sense, but the word is restored in the third and last state. The closing words are clearly reported speech, a kind of indirect discourse. There may be a quotation mark before "How did she come?" but I cannot see it in the original manuscript.]

And they were so glad to find her equal to the Journey!—

And she was to belong to <u>them</u>, was a thing of course."

>

And that she was to belong to <u>them</u>, was a thing of course."

[The omitted "that" again suggests faulty transcription from an earlier source. The quotation, consisting of indirect discourse, closes although it never really opens in the manuscript.]

Miss Diana P. was about 4 & 30, of middle height & slender; — but rather delicate than absolutely sickly; in her

>

Miss Diana P. was about 4 & 30, of middle height & slender; — but rather delicate than absolutely sickly; with an agreable face, & a very animated eye; — and her manners resembled her Brother's in their ease & frankness, though there was more decision & less mildness in her Tone.

>

Miss Diana P. was about 4 & 30, of middling height & slender; — delicate looking rather than sickly; with an agreable face, & a very animated eye; — her manners resembling her Brother's in their ease & frankness, though with more decision & less mildness in her Tone.

[As always, the author works hard to establish a clear initial impression of a major character.]

She began an account of herself as soon as they were in the Drawing room — Thanking them for their Invitation, but "<u>that</u> was quite out of the question, for they were all three come, & meant to get into Lodgings & make some stay." —

>

She began an account of herself without delay. — Thanking them for their Invitation, but "<u>that</u> was quite out of the question, for they were all three come, & meant to get into Lodgings & make some stay." —

[The revised version omits what amounts to a stage direction, "as soon as they were in the Drawing room." The quoted material is more indirect discourse, by now a familiar technique. It is hard to determine the size of Thomas Parker's house since despite its cost it may be not large enough to accommodate his two sisters and his younger brother. Unlike Sir Edward and Miss Esther, the Parker siblings do not expect to be put up for free while visiting Sanditon.]

"All three come! — What! — Susan & Arthur! — Susan able to come too! —

This was a great increase of the Happiness! — "
>
This was better & better."

"Yes — we are actually all come. Quite unavoidable. — A case of Necessity. — You shall hear all about it. —
>
"Yes — we are actually all come. Quite unavoidable. — Nothing else to be done. — You shall hear all about it. —

[I rather prefer the earlier and more abrupt "A case of Necessity" to its slightly longer revised form, which is also abrupt as an incomplete sentence. Jane Austen is attempting through these revisions to establish a distinctive idiolect for Diana Parker.]

But my dear Mary, send for the Children; — I long to see them." —

"And how has Susan born the Journey? — & how is Arthur? — & why do not we see him here with you?"—

[The past participle "borne" was long established by the beginning of the nineteenth century. Here as elsewhere, Jane Austen's spelling is—to be generous—idiosyncratic. The dialog has shifted from indirect discourse to actual conversation. The construction "why do not we," common in Jane Austen, is the logical source of "why don't we."]

"Susan has born it wonderfully.

She had not a wink of sleep either the night before we set out, or last night which we spent at Chichester, and as this is not so common with her as with <u>me</u>, I have had a thousand fears for her — but she has kept up charmingly —.
>
She had not a wink of sleep either the night before we set out, or last night at Chichester, and as this is so not so common with her as with <u>me</u>, I have had a thousand fears for her — but she has kept up wonderfully —.

[As expected, Jane Austen knows this part of England well, and so Chichester, famous for its unusually interesting cathedral dating back to

1108 and beautiful market cross, is correctly cited as the first important city upon entering Sussex along the main highway that the Parkers would use traveling east from their home province of Hampshire to reach the beach resorts. Deirdre Le Faye has supplied an early nineteenth-century map of Sussex (2002: 301), with "E. Bourne" (Eastbourne) just northeast of the southernmost point, "Beachey Head," a site mentioned by William Price. "The fictional Sanditon is said to be one mile nearer to London than is Eastbourne" (Le Faye, 2002: 300).

"Charmingly" was a strange first choice, well changed to "wonderfully."]

and no Hysterics of consequence till we came to poor old Sanditon — and they were quite subsided by the time we reached your Hotel — so that we got her out of the Carriage extremely well, with only young Woodcock's help — & when I left her she was directing where all the Luggage, sh^d. be carried, & helping old Hannah uncord the Trunks. —
>
She had no Hysterics of consequence till we came within sight of poor old Sanditon — and the attack was not very violent — quite over by the time we reached your Hotel — so that we got her out of the Carriage extremely well, with only M^r. Woodcock's assistance — & when I left her she was directing the Disposal of the Luggage, & helping old Sam uncord the Trunks. —
>
had no Hysterics of consequence till we came within sight of poor old Sanditon — and the attack was not very violent — nearly over by the time we reached your Hotel — so that we got her out of the Carriage extremely well, with only M^r. Woodcock's assistance — & when I left her she was directing the Disposal of the Luggage, & helping old Sam uncord the Trunks. —

[As our initial view of Miss Susan Parker, whom we shall barely glimpse in the pages to follow, this passage required considerable revision to convey the necessary first impressions. This fragile and fainting lady's ability to supervise and even engage in the removal and disposal of heavy trunks parallels her sister's ability to walk even faster than the much younger Charlotte despite serious medical problems. That she supervises the details of her family's arrival at Sanditon suggests to me that she is the elder sister, probably the senior member of the Parker family. Critics have for good reason made much of the three hypochondriacs, Susan, Diana, and Arthur Parker, in this manuscript—for example, John Halperin writes that "the fragment bulges with invalids and hypochondriacs of various species (one of them cannot eat toast without huge amounts of butter—otherwise it acts on his stomach like a nutmeg-grater), each of whom is able to demonstrate astonishing strength and blinding energy on selected (and usually private and selfish) occasions" (1983: 185)—but once their scenes are over they seem secondary to the main plot, the pairing-off of the various young lovers.

"Hysterical fits or convulsions [were] associated rather with delicate fictional heroines than with real-life women taking a coach journey" (*CUPLM*: 669). Marianne nearly dies as a result of her hysteria because she had not read Jane Austen's warning in her early "Love and Freindship," Part 3.

> "Beware of fainting-fits. Though at the time they may be refreshing and agreeable, yet beleive me they will in the end, if too often repeated and at improper seasons, prove destructive to your Constitution."

There are several "old" people in this manuscript, the "three old women" sharing the cottage with Mr. Heywood's shepherd, the "very rich old Lady" who dominates Sanditon society, "old Salmon & his son" (replaced by "old Stringer & his son"), "poor old Andrew," and "Old Heeley's windows" (changed to "William Heeley's windows").

Neither "Old Hannah" (presumably a Parker servant or possibly in Mr. Woodcock's employ) nor "Old Sam" (perhaps Hannah's replacement or an additional Parker servant or possibly in Mr. Woodcock's employ) has made it to H. Abigail Bok's "Dictionary." I suspect that the reason for the change is the author's desire to intensify the disjuncture between Miss Parker's professed invalidism and the reality of her vital strength and health. If she were assisting another woman, "Old Hannah," she might be seen as merely wanting to relieve the burden of an elderly retainer despite her own fragility. But no woman in the condition that Diana Parker has painted about her sister would assist a man, even "Old Sam," unless she saw herself as at least his equal in physical vigor.]

She desired her best love, with a thousand regrets at her being so poor a Creature that she c^d not come with me.

>

She desired her best love, with a thousand regrets at being so poor a Creature that she c^d not come with me.

[The third gathering, folio 41r, page 81—headed "March 1.ˢᵗ" and a large "2"—begins at "with a thousand regrets."]

And as for poor Arthur, he wᵈ. not have been afraid for himself, but there is so much Wind that I did not think he cᵈ. safely venture, — for I am <u>sure</u> there is Lumbago hanging over him — and therefore helped him on with his great Coat & sent him off to take us Lodgings. —

>

And as for poor Arthur, he wᵈ. not have been unwilling himself, but there is so much Wind that I did not think he cᵈ. safely venture, — for I am <u>sure</u> there is Lumbago hanging about him — and so I helped him on with his great Coat & sent him off to the Terrace, to take us Lodgings. —

[Mr. Thomas Parker is not the only family member who always calls the youngest son "poor Arthur," clearly a family epithet for this character. We have only a hint here of his appearance, which will loom large—in every sense—in a later scene.

> The standard outer garment for men was the greatcoat. This, unlike the frock coat, did not shrink appreciably in size. It remained a large, comparatively shapeless garment and was worn at any time when an additional layer was deemed necessary for warmth or protection from rain. (Olsen: 162)

> A greatcoat, also known as a watchcoat, is a large overcoat typically made of wool designed for warmth and protection against the elements. Its collar and cuffs could be turned out to protect the face and hands from cold and rain, and the short cape around the shoulders provides extra warmth and repels rainwater (if made of a waterproof material). It was popular in the 15th Century as a military uniform and casual wear for the wealthy.... During the 17th and 18th century and the Industrial Revolution, greatcoats became available for all social classes. The coat generally hangs down below the knees and the cape is kept short, normally just above or below the elbows. It also sported deep pockets for keeping letters and food dry. ("Greatcoat." *Wikipedia*)

Diana Parker's continuing concern over her youngest brother, who has now reached his majority, extends to helping him don a heavy coat even in what must be warm weather. A more expected wearer of such a coat is the confirmed valetudinarian, Mr. Woodhouse, about whom Mr. Knightley is properly solicitous: "I will fetch your greatcoat and open the garden door for you." Mr. Allen takes his greatcoat along with him to Bath, where it will be useful when it rains. "I hope Mr. Allen will put on his greatcoat when he goes," chides Mr. Allen, "but I dare say he will not, for he had rather do anything in the world than walk out in a greatcoat; I wonder he should dislike it, it must be so comfortable." General Tilney has also brought with him to Bath "his greatcoat, [which] instead of being brought for him to put on directly, was spread out in the curricle in which he was to accompany his son." The fashionable dress of that witty young curate, Henry Tilney, when he drove Catherine to Northanger Abbey caused her to delight in how "the innumerable capes of his greatcoat looked so becomingly important!" William Walter Elliot apparently also owns such a garment, but although he carries it about he does not wear it, as Mary Elliot Musgrove regrets that "the great-coat was hanging over the panel, and hid the arms" on her cousin's carriage that would have established his identity.]

Miss Heywood must have seen our Carriage standing at the Hotel. —

[The formality of recent acquaintances is highlighted here. Although Miss Diana Parker is somewhat older than Charlotte, she cannot address her yet by her given name even if by now Mr. and Mrs. Parker have reached that stage of intimacy.]

I knew Miss Heywood the moment I saw her before me in the field
>
I knew Miss Heywood the moment I saw her before me on the Down. —

[It is difficult to determine what "field" Jane Austen had in mind since the area consists of gently rolling hills or downs. There is an implied exchange of letters in which Thomas wrote to Diana about his houseguest.]

My dear Tom I am so glad to see you walk so well. Let me feel your Ancle. — That's right; all right & clean.

[These lines are virtually stage directions: we see Thomas Parker walking and presumably sitting down so that Diana can feel his ankle.]

The play of your Sinews a <u>very</u> little stiffened: — barely perceptible. —
>
The play of your Sinews a <u>very</u> little affected:— barely perceptible. —

[Our author has decided to avoid any specifics about sinews, which may or may not stiffen after a major sprain. Without any medical training, and a long-standing conviction that a novelist must eschew nonsense, she prefers to write about things within her own range of knowledge.]

Well — now for the explanation of my being here. — I told you in my Letter, of the two considerable Families, I was hoping to secure for you — the West Indians, & the Seminary. —"

["In the eighteenth century, ['Seminary' was] a general synonym for school, but in the early nineteenth century particularly applied to a private school for young ladies" (*CUPLM*: 669). In *Emma* we read Jane Austen's skepticism about "a seminary, or an establishment, or any thing which professed, in long sentences of refined nonsense, to combine liberal acquirements with elegant morality, upon new principles and new systems—and where young ladies for enormous pay might be screwed out of health and into vanity."]

Here M^r. P. drew his Chair still nearer to his Sister, & took her hand again most affectionately as he answered "Yes, Yes; — How active & how kind you have been!" —

"The Westindians, she continued, whom I look upon as the <u>most</u> desirable of the two — as the Best of the Good — prove to be a M^{rs}. Griffiths & her family. I know them only through others.

[A usual, Jane Austen uses the superlative "most" where current usage requires the comparative "more." By "family," Jane Austen may mean "the body of persons who live in one house or under one head, including parents, children, servants, etc." (*OED*), but she supplies no information about the arrivals other than Mrs. Griffiths, Miss Lambe, and the Misses Beaufort.]

My friend Fanny Noyce
>
I dare say you have heard me mention Miss Capper, the particular friend of <u>my</u> very particular friend Fanny Noyce; — now, Miss Capper is extremely intimate with a M^{rs}. Darling, who is on terms of constant correspondence with M^{rs}. Griffiths herself. —
>
You must have heard me mention Miss Capper, the particular friend of <u>my</u> very particular friend Fanny Noyce; — now, Miss Capper is extremely

intimate with a M^rs. Darling, who is on terms of constant correspondence with M^rs. Griffiths herself. —

[Diana Parker's habitual garrulousness compelled our author to expand the line after writing only four words. Like Miss Bates, the younger sister is unable to limit herself to a brief account of how she came to learn about the visitors from Fanny Noyce, so she must introduce the notion of her friend indirectly through someone whom she has apparently never even met, Miss Capper, who in turn knows Mrs. Darling, yet another lady unknown personally to the speaker.]

Only a <u>short</u> chain, you see, between us, & not a Link wanting.

M^rs. G. meant to go to the Sea, for her Young People's benefit — had fixed on the coast of Sussex, but was undecided as to the Spot, wanted something Private, & wrote to ask the opinion of her friend M^rs. Darling. —
>
M^rs. G. meant to go to the Sea, for her Young People's benefit — had fixed on the coast of Sussex, but was undecided as to the where, wanted something Private, & wrote to ask the opinion of her friend M^rs. Darling. —

Miss Capper happened to be staying with M^rs. D. when M^rs. G.'s Letter arrived, & was consulted on the question; <u>she</u> wrote the same day to Fanny Noyce and mentioned it to her — & Fanny all alive for <u>us</u>, instantly took up her pen & forwarded the circumstance to me — except as to <u>Names</u> — which have but lately transpired. —

The was but <u>one</u> thing for <u>me</u> to do. —
>
There was but <u>one</u> thing for <u>me</u> to do. —

[The initial "The" again suggests a transcription error.]

I answered Fanny's Letter by the same Post & pressed for the recommendation of Sanditon. Fanny had feared your having no house large enough to receive such a Family. But I seem to be spinning out my story to an endless length. — You see how it was all managed.

[Unlike Miss Bates, Diana Parker is aware of how much she embellishes even the simplest sequence of events. Her "character" may be primarily that of a hypochondriac, but she is equally a gadabout and bore.]

I had the pleasure of hearing soon afterwards by the same simple link of connection that Sanditon <u>had been</u> recommended by M^{rs}. Darling, & that the Westindians were very much disposed to go thither. — This was the state of the case when I wrote to you; — but two days ago; — yes, the day before yesterday — I heard again from Fanny Noyce, saying that <u>she</u> had heard from Miss Capper, who by a Letter from M^{rs}. Darling understood that M^{rs}. G. — has expressed herself in a letter to M^{rs}. D. more doubtingly on the subject of Sanditon. — Am I clear? I would be anything rather than not clear." —

"Oh! perfectly, perfectly. Well?" —

[Thomas Parker is justifiably impatient with his sister, who spins short tales into novels. And no, she is not very clear.]

"The reason of this hesitation, was her having no connections in the place, & no means of ascertaining that she should have good accomodations on arriving there; — and she was particularly careful & scrupulous on all those matters more on account of a certain Miss Lambe a young Lady (probably a Neice) under her care, than on her own account or her Daughters. — Miss Lambe has an immense fortune — richer than all the rest — & very delicate health. —

[And so another young woman, perhaps also in search of a husband but with the enormous advantage of great wealth—her poor health makes her all the more appealing to a fortune-hunter like Sir Edward Denham—has come to Sanditon.]

One sees clearly enough by this, the <u>sort</u> of Woman M^{rs}. G. must be — as helpless & indolent, as Wealth & a Hot Climate are apt to make the English.
>
One sees clearly enough by all this, the <u>sort</u> of Woman M^{rs}. G. must be — as helpless & indolent, as Wealth & a Hot Climate are apt to make us.

[Jane Austen's emendation from "English" to the vague "us"—which may refer to women rather than to the general population—enables Diana Parker to avoid a blanket condemnation of all English people.]

But we are not all born to equal energy. — What was to be done? — I had a few moments indecision; — Whether to offer to write to <u>you</u>, — or to M^{rs}. Whitby to secure them a House? — but neither pleased me. —

[In addition to her other business, then, Mrs. Whitby is a real estate agent.]

I hate to employ others, when I ought to act myself — and my conscience told me that this was an occasion which called for my Exertions.
>
I hate to employ others, when I am equal to act myself — and my conscience told me that this was an occasion which called for me.

Here was a family of helpless Invalides whom I might essentially serve. — I sounded Susan — the same Thought had occurred to her. —

[The comic irony of the Parker sisters' wanting to assist "a family of helpless Invalides" cannot escape the reader's attention.]

Arthur made no difficulties — our plan was arranged immediately, we were off yesterday morn^g. at 6 —, at the same hour today — & here we are. —"
>
Arthur made no difficulties — our plan was arranged immediately, we were off yesterday morn^g. at 6 —, left Chichester at the same hour today — & here we are. —"

[The omitted "left Chichester" is a strong suggestion of an error in transcription since the first version makes little sense.]

"Excellent! — Excellent! — cried M^r. Parker. — Diana, you are unequal'd in serving your friends & doing Good to all the World. — I know nobody like you. — Mary, my Love, is not she a wonderful Creature? — Well — and now, what House do you design to engage for them? — What is the size of their family? —"

"I do not at all know — replied his Sister — have not the least idea; — never heard any particulars; — but I am very sure that the largest house at Sanditon cannot be <u>too</u> large. They are more likely to want a second. — I shall take only one however, & that, but for a week certain. — Miss Heywood, I astonish you. — You hardly know what to make of me. — I see by your Looks, that you are not used to such quick measures." —

[Like Lady Denham in a preceding scene, Diana Parker reads in Charlotte's face a strong reaction to the dialog. As a candid young woman, Charlotte has had no experience in masking her thoughts.]

The part of the story which was really astonishing Charlotte most, she could not noticed, she had just given it to herself the words of "Unaccountable Officiousness! — Activity run mad!" —

>

The part of the story which was really astonishing Charlotte most, she could not have noticed, she had just given it to herself the words of "Unaccountable Officiousness! — Activity run mad!" —

>

The part of the story which was really most astonishing to Charlotte, she could not have noticed, she had just given it to herself the words of "Unaccountable Officiousness! — Activity run mad!" —

>

the words of "Unaccountable Officiousness! — Activity run mad!" — but she could only give one explanation of the Amazement which she c^d. easily beleive to be painted in her face. —

>

The words "Unaccountable Officiousness! — Activity run mad!" — had just passed through Charlotte's brain — and collecting her Thoughts, she replied — "I dare say I <u>look</u> surprised, for I feel so,

>

The words "Unaccountable Officiousness! — Activity run mad!" — had just passed through Charlotte's mind — and collecting her Thoughts, she replied — "I dare say I <u>look</u> surprised, for I feel so,

>

The words "Unaccountable Officiousness! — Activity run mad!" — had just passed through Charlotte's mind —

[This brief passage obviously cost Jane Austen a great deal of trouble. After several attempts, she arrived at the only good solution, a very brief summary of Charlotte's response to Diana Parker's meandering tale. The first version, with its impossible "she could not noticed," again suggests careless copying from an earlier draft.]

but a civil answer was easy.

"I dare say I look surprised, said she — because these are very great exertions, & I know that both you & your Sister are sad sufferers as to Health

>

"I dare say I look surprised, said she — because these are very great exertions, & I know that both you & your Sister are Invalides. —"

>

"I dare say I do look surprised, said she — because these are very great exertions, & I know what Invalides both you & your Sister are."

"Invalides indeed. — & I trust there are not three People in England who have so sad a right to that name! —

>

"Invalides indeed. — & I trust there are not three People in England who have so sad a right to that appellation. —

[As an illustration of the blind leading the blind, this family of invalids has offered to assist a family of invalids soon to arrive in Sanditon. Diana Parker makes sure that poor Arthur is included in this sad family trio. Replacing "appellation" for "name" suggests some level of education on Diana Parker's part or just a hint of an interest in difficult words that has infected Sir Edward.]

But my dear Miss Heywood, we are sent into this World to be as extensively useful as possible, & where some degree of Strength of Mind is given, it is not a feeble body which will excuse us — or incline us to excuse ourselves. —

The World is pretty much divided between the Weak of Mind & the Strong — between those who can act & those who can act & it is the bounden Duty of the Capable to let none of their faculties be wasted. —

>

The World is pretty much divided between the Weak of Mind & the Strong — between those who can act & those who can not & it is the bounden Duty of the Capable to let none of their faculties be wasted. —

>

The World is pretty much divided between the Weak of Mind & the Strong — between those who can act & those who can not & it is the bounden Duty of the Capable to let no opportunity of doing Good be wasted. —

>

The World is pretty much divided between the Weak of Mind & the Strong — between those who can act & those who can not & it is the bounden Duty of the Capable to let no opportunity of being useful escape them. —

[The nonsensical repetition of the first version—"those who can act & those who can act"—is again evidence of faulty transcription from an earlier draft. Our author probably misread "not" as "act."]

My Sister's Complaints & mine are happily not often of a Nature, to threaten Existence <u>immediately</u> — & as long as we <u>can</u> exert ourselves to be of use of others, I am convinced that the Body is the better, for the refreshment the Mind receives in doing its' Duty. — While I have been travelling, with this object in veiw, I have been perfectly well." — The entrance of the Children ended this little panegyric on her own Disposition — & after having noticed & caressed them all, — she prepared to go. —

"Cannot you dine with us? — Is not it possible to prevail on you to dine with us?" was then the cry; and <u>that</u> being absolutely negatived, it was "And when shall we see you again? and how can we be of use to you?" — and M^r. P. warmly offered his assistance in taking the house for M^rs. G.— "I will come to you the moment I have dined, said he, & we will go about together." —

But this was immediately declined. — "No, my dear Tom, upon no account in the World, shall you stir a step on any business of mine. — Your Ancle wants rest. I see by the position of your foot, that you have used it too much already. — No, I shall go about my House-taking directly. Our Dinner is not ordered till six — & by that time I hope to have completed it. It is now only 1/2 past 4. — As to seeing <u>me</u> again today — I cannot answer for it; the others will be at the Hotel all the Even^g, & delighted to see you at any time, but as soon as I get back I shall hear what Arthur has done about our own Lodgings, & probably the moment Dinner is over, shall be out again on business relative to them, for we hope to get into some Lodgings or other & be settled after breakfast tomorrow. — I have not much confidence in poor Arthur's skill for Lodging-taking, but he seemed to like the commission."

[Again "poor Arthur," suggesting that within the family he is known only by this epithet. Six o'clock is a late dinnertime, suggesting that the Parker sisters are very much aware of social trends and seek to emulate the practices of London.]

"I think you are doing too much, said M^r. P. You will knock yourself up. You sh^d. not move again after Dinner."

[In British English, "knock up" means "to wear out" or "to exhaust." The phrase has not done well in crossing the Atlantic.]

"Oh! as to your Sisters Dinner cried his wife, that's never any thing more than a <u>name</u> with you all, that it can do you no good. —

>

"No, indeed you should not, cried his wife, for Dinner is such a mere <u>name</u> with you all, that it can do you no good. —

[The revised version makes logical sense, something lacking in the original.]

I know what your appetites are. —"

"My appetite is very much mended I assure you lately. I have been taking some Bitters of my own decocting, which have done wonders.

[By "bitters," Diana Parker means "either quinine… or bitter native herbs such as camomile and tansey—made into a medicine by boiling them down in water to a concentrate.… Bitters were used against a wide range of ailments, including fevers and upset stomachs" (*CUPLM*: 669–670).]

Susan never eats — & just at present <u>I</u> shall want nothing; I never eat for about a week after a Journey — but as for Arthur, he is much more likely to eat too much than too little on

>

Susan never eats — & just at present <u>I</u> shall want nothing; I never eat for about a week after a Journey — but as for Arthur, he eats enormously. We

>

Susan never eats — & just at present <u>I</u> shall want nothing; I never eat for about a week after a Journey — but as for Arthur, he is only too much disposed for Food. We are often obliged to check him." —

>

Susan never eats I grant you — & just at present <u>I</u> shall want nothing; I never eat for about a week after a Journey — but as for Arthur, he is only too much disposed for Food. We are often obliged to check him." —

[Although the chronology is not always clear, a passage in the next chapter—"She was not made acquainted with the others till the following day, when, being removed into Lodgings & all the party continuing quite well, their Brother & Sister & herself were entreated to drink tea with them."—suggests that Diana Parker had regained her appetite by the next afternoon. The report on poor Arthur's uncontrolled appetite just becomes more and more bleak.]

"But you have not told me any thing of the <u>other</u> Family coming to Sanditon, said M^r. P. as he walked with her to the door of the House — the Camberwell Seminary; have we a good chance of <u>them</u>? —"

"Oh! Certain — quite certain. — I had forgotten them for the moment, but I had a letter 3 days ago from my friend M^{rs}. Charles Dupuis which assured me of Camberwell. Camberwell will be here to a certainty, & very soon. — <u>That</u> good Woman (I do not know her name) not being so wealthy & independant as M^{rs}. G.— can travel & chuse for herself. — I will tell you how I got at <u>her</u>.

M^{rs}. Charles Dupuis lives almost next door to a Lady, who has a relation lately settled at Clapham, & attends some of the girls of the Seminary, to give them lessons in Botany & Belles Lettres
>
M^{rs}. Charles Dupuis lives almost next door to a Lady, who has a relation lately settled at Clapham, who actually attends the Seminary and gives lessons on Eloquence and Belles Lettres to some of the Girls. —

[Our author has decided that Eloquence is more appropriate subject matter for a girls' seminary than Botany, a branch of science that could lead to others of questionable decorum like anatomy. "The emphasis... on learning... for the girls [was on] such accomplishments as drawing, languages, and music" (Pinion: 40), hence the prevalence of harps and sketchpads. "'Accomplishments,' which took the form of some degree of skill in music, the visual arts, and the modern languages, were usually considered part of a girl's education and had their social importance" (McMaster, 1986:140).

"People of good education learned French, spoke French, read French, and aped French fashions in clothing and manners yet condemned the French and all they stood for. As members of the country gentry, the Austen children would certainly have been expected to be acquainted with French....

Jane... probably read it quite well. Austen's works are peppered with French phrases and references, [which] are never italicized to call attention to their foreign derivation" (Olsen: 292-293).

Various females in the novels have musical and artistic inclinations, but although they are presumed to have some learning in foreign languages, only occasionally do we witness their proficiency. Miss Bingley "play[ed] some Italian songs," but despite her lecture upon the awesome accomplishments of a young lady we never learn if she knows the language. As expected, before coming to live with her wealthy relatives little Fanny Price "had never learned French" (or very much else to win praise from her judgmental female cousins and fire-breathing Aunt Norris), but in time the governess "Miss Lee taught her French." Harriet Smith must have been subjected to some instruction in foreign languages, with the result that she now "hate[s] Italian singing" as expertly performed by Jane Fairfax. Not surprisingly, although Catherine Morland was "taught... French by her mother, her proficiency... was not remarkable." In contrast, Anne Elliot, despite modestly deprecating her skills—"I am a very poor Italian scholar"—"in the interval succeeding an Italian song,... explained the words of the song to Mr. Elliot."

Jane Austen may be using "belles lettres" in its broadest possible application, "elegant or polite literature or literary studies. A vaguely-used term, formerly taken sometimes in the wide sense of 'the humanities,' *literæ humaniores*; sometimes in the exact sense in which we now use 'literature'" (*OED*). Following up on her earlier "beau monde," Miss Diana Parker demonstrates a rudimentary knowledge of French, or at least of some common phrases.]

I got that Man a Hare from one of Sidney's friends —

["Rabbits and hares usually bred on estate land and though they were not officially classed as game they were regarded as belonging to the owner of the land; they were unlikely therefore to be readily available in butchers' shops" (*CUPLM*: 670). The line indirectly adds to our small store of information about Sidney Parker that among his friends is at least one wealthy, landed gentleman.]

and he recommended Sanditon; — Without <u>my</u> appearing however — M^{rs}. Charles Dupuis managed it all. —"

[The ninth chapter consists almost entirely of Miss Diana Parker's self-congratulatory account of how she found two large and separate parties for Sanditon.]

[Chapter 10]

Chapter 10.

It was not a week, since Miss Diana Parker had been told by her feelings, that the Sea Air w^d. probably in her present state, be the death of her, and now she was at Sanditon, intending to make some Stay, & without appearing to have the slightest recollection of having written or felt any such thing. — It was impossible for Charlotte not to suspect a good deal of fancy in such an extraordinary state of health. — Disorders & Recoveries so very much out of the common way, seemed more like the amusement of eager Minds in want of employment than of actual afflictions & releif. The Parkers, were no doubt a family of Imagination & quick feelings — and while the eldest Brother found vent for his superfluity of sensation as a Projector, the Sisters were perhaps driven to dissipate theirs in the invention of odd complaints. —

["Miss Diana Parker" is the younger sister since "Miss Parker" would be sufficient if she were the elder of the two. Although James Edward Austen-Leigh, who would have been raised with the social protocol familiar to his aunt, states unambiguously in 1871 that "Mr. Parker has two unmarried sisters of singular character. They live together; Diana, the younger, always takes the lead, and the elder follows in the same track," some later commentators have questioned his reading of the text.

"Cassandra was Miss Austen, and Jane was Miss Jane Austen. This is still correct" (Austen-Leigh, Joan).

Without actually saying it but certainly implying it, Linda Waldemar identifies Miss (Susan) Parker as the elder sister (and hence the eldest of the five siblings).

> There are a number of Parkers besides the above mentioned Mr. Tom Parker, 35, and his wife Mary and their four children. Mr. Parker's sisters and brothers visit; Miss Parker and Miss Diana Parker, 34, and Mr. Arthur Parker, 21, are notorious hypochondriacs.

Jenny Allan, reviewing the same book, also suggests but falls short of declaring the correct sibling order.

> Soon we meet the Parker's siblings Susan, Diana and Arthur who are all terrible hypochondriacs and whose antics provide much of the comic relief of the book.

Because G.L. Apperson may merely be placing their names in alphabetical order—"Parker, Diana and Susan, sisters of Thomas" (109)—it is impossible to determine which of the two sisters he believes is the elder. Ellen Moody leaves the issue undecided in noting under "1814" that "2 years ago Miss Diana Parker called on Mrs Sheldon when her coachmen [sic] sprained his foot; Miss Parker rubbed his ancle for 6 hours without intermission, and he was well in 3 days" ("Sands"). Among others, John Lauber has reversed the true order: "Diana Parker, the older sister, seems the most energetic woman in Austen's fiction" (114), as has H. Abigail Bok: "PARKER, SUSAN, Diana Parker's younger sister" (464).

Although Isaac Schapera offers abundant information about the naming practice at the time, he says nothing about its reason. Most likely designating the eldest unmarried daughter as Miss X, like Miss Bennet (for Jane Bennet), would advertise that she is the next in line to be wooed and married. If Jane Bennet married Bingley early in the novel, Elizabeth would automatically become Miss Bennet and so on down the line until it is Lydia's turn. But Lydia upsets the normal pattern by rushing off to be seduced and enter a shotgun marriage.

Although I doubt very much that this new novel was meant to be called *The Brothers*, I can well imagine that at one point Jane Austen thought of calling it *The Parkers* since this family is central to the plot up to this point. Although we have not yet met Arthur, Sidney, or Susan Parker in person, we have learned enough about them to be as eager as Charlotte to make their acquaintance.

A "projector" is "one who forms a project or enterprise; but the word could also pejoratively imply a misguided or foolish venturer" (*CUPLM*: 670).]

The <u>whole</u> of their mental vivacity was evidently not so employed; Part was laid out in a Zeal for being useful. — It should seem that they must either be very busy for the Good or others, or else extremely ill themselves. Some natural delicacy of Constitution in fact, with an unfortunate turn for

Medecine, especially quack Medecine, had given them an early tendency at various times, to various Disorders; — the rest of their sufferings was from Fancy, the love of Distinction & the love of the Wonderful. —

[The manuscript reads "Good or others," silently corrected by R.W. Chapman and Teran Lee Sacco as "Good of others."]

The mystery is how Thomas and Sidney have avoided what appears to be a pernicious family trait of hypochondria. No doubt the former is too busy creating and raising his family, and the latter is too occupied with worldly things like enjoying life and having fun.]

They had benevolent hearts & many amiable feelings — but the disease of activity, & the glory of doing more than anybody else, had their share in every exertion of Health, as well as in every inaction of Sickness — and there was Vanity in all they did, as well as in all they endured. —
>
They had Charitable hearts & many amiable feelings — but a spirit of restless activity, & the glory of doing more than anybody else, had their share in every exertion of Benevolence — and there was Vanity in all they did, as well as in all they endured. —

[It is important to note that in mocking the hypochondria of these fairly young and obviously vigorous people Jane Austen is not reflecting on her own mother's habit of complaining about her ill health. The revision is a marked improvement in substituting "Benevolence" for "Health." In order to effect this change she wisely amended "benevolent" to its synonymous "Charitable."]

M^r. & M^rs. P. spent a great part of the Even^g. at the Hotel; but Charlotte had only two or three veiws of Miss Diana posting over the Down after a House for this Lady whom she had never seen, & who had never employed her. She was not made acquainted with the others till the following day, when, being removed into Lodgings & all the party continuing quite well, their Brother & Sister & herself were entreated to drink tea with them. —

["Miss Diana" rather than "Miss Parker" again tells us that she is the younger of the two sisters. "Sister" here is of course really "Sister-in-law."

The *OED* defines "to post" as "to ride, run, or travel with speed or haste; to hurry, make haste," using a quotation from Jane Austen to illustrate the use of "posted" in the early nineteenth century: "**1801** J. AUSTEN *Let.* 21 May (1995) 87 In climbing a hill I could with difficulty keep pace with her. On plain ground I was quite her equal and so we posted away under a fine hot sun." Thus by "posting" Jane Austen means "hurrying (alluding to the swift movement of the post chaise)" (*CUPLM*: 670), which sped along at about a dizzying seven miles an hour.

Jane Austen creates ambiguity in observing that Diana Parker was "after a House for this Lady whom she had never seen, & who had never employed her," allowing us to decide if this an authorial comment, one by Charlotte, or an inextricable combination of the two points of view.

The use of "herself" here is very colloquial, suggesting the informality of the scene. The Parkers, we learn throughout the manuscript, are on very easy terms with one another.]

They were in one of the Terrace Houses — & she found them arranged for the Even^g. in a small neat Drawing room, with a beautiful veiw of the Sea if they had chosen it, — but though it had been a very fair English Summer-day, — not only was there no open window, but the Sopha & the Table, & the Establishment in general was all at the other end of the room by a brisk fire.

["Arranged for the Evening" suggests a stage setting, which is very much what this entire scene is. Charlotte has already met two of the most interesting characters in Sanditon, Lady Denham and Sir Edward Denham, and now for the first time she has the opportunity to meet the three visiting Parkers together. Charlotte notes to her dismay that the same splendid ocean view that she has from her bedroom window is here obstructed.

The *CUPLM* reading of "Establishment" as "arrangement, of the people and furniture" (670) is neither clearly cited in *OED*, with "organization" or "a settled arrangement" the closest matches, nor found in any of Jane Austen's completed novels.]

Miss P- whom, remembering the three Teeth drawn in one day, Charlotte approached with a peculiar degree of respectful Compassion, was not very unlike her Sister in person or manner — tho' more thin & worn by Illness & Medecine, more relaxed in air, & more subdued in voice.

[Although Susan Parker is sometimes believed to be the younger of the two sisters—for example, "Diana Parker's younger sister" (Bok: 464)—her being distinguished as "Miss P-" tells us that she is the elder sister since only the oldest unmarried daughter would properly be called "Miss Parker." (See Isaac Schapera's work on the complex kinship terminology of the early nineteenth century.) It is not always clear, however, that Jane Austen observes this protocol although of course she was aware of it, most notably in how a mother and her daughters visiting Sanditon have entered their names in the subscription book in Mrs. Whitby's Library: "Mrs. Mathews, Miss Mathews, Miss E. Mathews, Miss H. Mathews."

Jane Austen makes brilliant use of this distinction between an older and a younger sibling, creating a frisson because of our strong sympathy with Elinor Dashwood and at the same time showing ignorance of social protocol among the lower classes, when to the Dashwood women seated at table "their man-servant" (unusually, given a first name, Thomas) offers as a "voluntary communication—'I suppose you know, ma'am, that Mr. Ferrars is married.'… Mrs. Dashwood [asked,] 'Who told you that Mr. Ferrars was married, Thomas?' 'I see Mr. Ferrars myself, ma'am, this morning in Exeter, and his lady too, Miss Steele as was.'" Obviously the Dashwoods (and we), knowledgeable about the distinction, assume that "Mr. Ferrars" is the elder brother, Elinor's beloved Edward, rather than his foppish younger brother, properly Mr. Robert Ferrars. Jane Austen does, however, leave the matter slightly ambiguous when in reply to Mrs. Dashwood's questioning him, "Was Mr. Ferrars in the carriage with her?" Thomas replies, "Yes, ma'am, I just see him leaning back in it, but he did not look up;—he never was a gentleman much for talking." The possibility remains, then, that Thomas has mistaken one brother for the other. This is one of the rare instances in Jane Austen that a servant has a name and speaks some lines, but the exception is necessary to create the misunderstanding that leads to Elinor's temporary misery. No member of the Dashwood circle would be guilty of this solecism.

The important distinction is made unambiguously, however, in *Mansfield Park* during a conversation between Henry and Mary Crawford.

> "I like your Miss Bertrams exceedingly, sister," said he, as he returned from attending them to their carriage after the said dinner visit; "they are very elegant, agreeable girls."

"So they are indeed, and I am delighted to hear you say it. But you like Julia best."

"Oh yes! I like Julia best."

"But do you really? for Miss Bertram is in general thought the handsomest."

"So I should suppose. She has the advantage in every feature, and I prefer her countenance; but I like Julia best; Miss Bertram is certainly the handsomest, and I have found her the most agreeable, but I shall always like Julia best, because you order me."

As a writer of discrimination and good taste, Jane Austen carefully observes the distinction between "Mr. John Knightley" in the closing lines of Chapter XI and "Mr. Knightley," with whom she opens Chapter XII.

I believe that Susan is the elder sister and senior sibling, making her older than the 35-year-old Thomas, perhaps 36. Therefore I propose that the true order is the matriarchal head of the family, Miss (Susan) Parker, perhaps 36; the first-born son and therefore heir to the estate, Mr. (Thomas) Parker, 35; Miss Diana Parker, 34; Mr. Sidney Parker, 28; and finally poor Arthur at a recently attained 21.

One of the few published supports that I have found for my interpretation is at: http://www.pemberley.com/bin/regency/janames/janames.cgi?category=Sanditon, where Miss Susan Parker is identified as "Elder of two unmarried Parker sisters" and Miss Diana Parker is described as "Younger of two unmarried Parker sisters 'about 4 and 30.'"

However, the information at this site is not entirely reliable. This Republic of Pemberley page, which lists the characters named in the manuscript, identifies Miss Lambe as "'probably a niece' of Mrs Griffith [sic]," a misinterpretation by Diana Parker about the true relationship between the heiress and Mrs. Griffiths. Mr. Heywood is described as "of Willingden, Sussex, aged fifty-seven. Has wife and 'two or three' daughters, including Charlotte and at least one son," a total progeny well short of the fourteen reported in the text. Because there is a church in Sanditon, there may be a resident clergyman, but both Dr. Brown and Rev. Hanking are identified as "visitors to Sanditon." The entry for "Stringer" tells us that "there are two Stringers, referred to as 'old Stringer' and 'young Stringer'. One is shopkeeper at Sanditon," a fuzzy way to report that Mr. Parker ("of Traflagar [sic] House") has encouraged "old Stringer [originally "Salmon"] & his son" to set up a business supplying "Gardenstuff" ("Vegetables or fruit") to local residents. One would never know from the description of "Sir, Bart. Edward Denham" as "born to be a villain" that he is a comic character with little likelihood of fulfilling his erotic fantasies. An important part of the plot is distorted in reporting that Arthur Parker is "'not much above 20,'" concealing the fact that he has attained the age of 21 and is no longer a minor. No description is supplied for "Fanny Noyce," "Miss Capper," "Mrs. Charles Dupuis," "Mrs. Darling," "Mrs. Griffiths," or "Mrs. Sheldon." Mr. Hillier is noted but not his wife. In some ways the most important character in the novel, the unnamed coachman who overturns the carriage in the opening passage, is not mentioned. The mystery characters in this listing are "Mr. Heywood" (in addition to Mr. Heywood, Charlotte's father), "Son of Rev. Heywood, aged 31," and "Mrs. Heywood" (apparently distinct from "wife" of Mr. Heywood of Willingden, Sussex), "Wife to Rev. Heywood." It is possible, as Sherwood Smith has suggested, that these extra names are in continuations.

As might be expected if Susan is indeed the senior sister, her health may be even more precarious than that of Diana, and despite her vigorous exertions in the preceding scene—supervising the unloading of the carriage and the disposition of luggage, even physically engaging in handling the heavy trunks—she is here seen as the more moribund of the two, thinner and more exhausted by illness as well as quieter on the whole than Diana (although by no means taciturn) and hence likely to be of a greater age.

The litotic construction "was not very unlike" may have entertained Jane Austen's readers but is both affected and unnecessarily confusing.]

She talked however, the whole Evening as incessantly as Diana — & except that she sat with salts in her hand, took Drops two or three times from one, out of many Phials already domesticated on the Mantlepeice, — & made a great many odd faces & contortions, Charlotte could perceive no signs of illness which she, in the boldness of her own good health, w^d. not have undertaken to cure, by putting out the fire, opening the Window, & disposing of the Drops & salts by means of one or the other.
>
She talked however, the whole Evening as incessantly as Diana — & excepting that she sat with salts in her hand, took Drops two or three times

from one, out of the several Phials already at home on the Mantlepeice, — & made a great many odd faces & contortions, Charlotte could perceive no symptoms of illness which she, in the boldness of her own good health, w^d. not have undertaken to cure, by putting out the fire, opening the Window, & disposing of the Drops & the salts by means of one or the other.

[Susan Parker is not identified by her first name as is Diana, with whom Charlotte has already established some kind of friendly relationship. I think that we can safely assume that "Susan Parker" is *the* "Miss Parker."

"Smelling salts, consisting usually of ammonium carbonate, [are] used to combat faintness" (*CUPLM*: 670). Many "medicinal preparation[s were] taken in the form of drops of liquid…. usually… either laudanum, an opiate, or elixir of vitriol" (*CUPLM*: 670). Laudanum, "made of 10% opium and 90% alcohol,… flavored with cinnamon or saffron" ("Laudanum"), used so famously by Samuel Taylor Coleridge (1772–1834), was a very popular and highly addictive opiate in the nineteenth century. Elixir of vitriol is an aromatic sulfuric acid (a mixture of sulfuric acid, alcohol, and aromatics, usually ginger and cinnamon) prescribed as a tonic and for stomach disorders. Since alcohol is a major component of both laudanum and elixir of vitriol, it may be safe to assume that Miss (Susan) Parker's problem lies in hitting the bottle too frequently. Arthur is not the only Parker sibling who indulges in excess ingestion of fluids.

Although the *OED* reports that "There are no results" for "mantlepiece," under the more usual spelling—"mantelpiece"—it cites three instances of the rarer spelling: "**1742** W. ELLIS *Timber-tree Improved* II. iii. 53 This is the Reason, why a Chimney, or Mantle-piece, of Beech remains sound Time out of Mind. **1795** *French & Amer. Gaz.* 6 July 4/4 (*advt.*) For Sale. China figures for mantle pieces. **1827** G. BEAUCLERK *Journey to Marocco* viii. 92 A French mantle-piece clock." Thus Jane Austen is not alone in confusing "mantle" (a cloak) and "mantel" (a shelf), The "ei"/"ie" substitution was common at the time.

The word is correctly spelled in *Sense and Sensibility* ("Willoughby… was leaning against the mantel-piece with his back towards them"; "Over the mantelpiece still hung a landscape in coloured silks of her performance"; "[Willoughby] lean[ed] against the mantel-piece as if forgetting he was to go"), *Pride and Prejudice* ("The girls… examine[d] their own indifferent imitations of china on the mantelpiece"; "Mr. Darcy… was leaning against the mantelpiece"; "She… saw the likeness of Mr. Wickham… over the mantelpiece"), *Mansfield Park* (There was "a collection of family profiles… over the mantelpiece"), *Emma* (The "portrait was to… hold a very honourable station over the mantelpiece"), and *Persuasion* (There was an "elegant little clock on the mantel-piece"), but even if Jane Austen's editors had not already done so, R.W. Chapman would have normalized spellings, so we do not know if the odd spelling in the final manuscript is an anomaly.

Jane Austen is not as particular as an English teacher might be in a construction like, "excepting that she sat… Charlotte could perceive."]

She had had great curiosity to see M^r. Arthur Parker; & having fancied a very puny, delicate-looking young Man, the smallest very materially of not a robust Family, was astonished to find him quite as tall as his Brother & a great deal Stouter — Broad made & Lusty — and excepting
>
She had had great curiosity to see M^r. Arthur Parker; & having fancied a very puny, delicate-looking young Man, the smallest very materially of not a robust Family, was astonished to find him quite as tall as his Brother & a great deal Stouter — Broad made & Lusty — and with no other look of an Invalide, than a sodden complexion. —
>
She had had considerable curiosity to see M^r. Arthur Parker; & having fancied him a very puny, delicate-looking young Man, the smallest very materially of not a robust Family, was astonished to find him quite as tall as his Brother & a great deal Stouter — Broad made & Lusty — and with no other look of an Invalide, than a sodden complexion. —

[As usual, our author devotes care to her first impressions of a major character. In this instance, the reality is so far from what was expected that the level of comedy has reached a very high level.

Jane Austen again refers to a character as "stout," and again her meaning is ambiguous. "The modern meaning of 'stout'—plump, corpulent—was just coming into use in the early nineteenth century, and it is not clear whether JA intends this, or the earlier meaning of well- or strongly made" (*CUPLM*: 671). Although I think that the jury is out about what "stout" means in reference to Lady Denham, in this instance the humorous point is made only if it turns out that Arthur is fat and not merely well put together. The adjective is used to compare Arthur with Thomas, who is not undernourished and who handily freed himself and his wife from the overturned carriage. The author is saying that to Charlotte's surprise Arthur is as tall as Thomas and carries far more weight. Like "Big and Tall" and "Oversized," the added "Broad made & Lusty," i.e., "large or substantial" (*CUPLM*: 671), is merely a euphemism. The word "sodden" has undergone a considerable change since its early meaning of "boiled," by the nineteenth century meaning "having the appearance of, or resembling, that which has been soaked or steeped in water ["or alcohol" (*CUPLM*: 671)]; rendered dull, stupid, or expressionless, esp. owing to drunkenness or indulgence in intoxicants; pale and flaccid" (*OED*). His unhealthy lifestyle and excessive use of alcohol, a weakness shared with Miss Susan Parker, have turned the youngest of the siblings into a very "poor" Arthur indeed.]

Diana was evidently the cheif of the family; principal Mover & Actor; — she had been on her Feet the whole Morning, on M^rs. G.'s business, or their own, & was still the most alert of the three. —

[Diana's being the "cheif of the family; principal Mover & Actor"—phrasing that may have misled some readers to take Diana as the elder sister—merely means that she is the surrogate dominant member because of the frail health of the true head of the family, Miss (Susan) Parker. If Diana Parker were the elder sister, she would not be "evidently" the head of the family. By "family," Jane Austen presumably means here the Parker household consisting of Miss Parker, Miss Diana Parker, and Mr. Arthur Parker. Mr. Thomas Parker (the head of the Parker family as the eldest male) has a separate family in this sense, and Mr. Sidney Parker has yet to settle down and create a family. That Diana Parker is an "Actor" perhaps inadvertently reveals that we are watching a play in which characters read prepared scripts.

Diana Parker has been severely criticized, within the novel and by readers, for expending huge amounts of energy minding other people's business and investing her time in projects that are bound to fail, along with unceasing gabble. D.A. Miller offers a particularly detailed analysis of her "language of *chatter*":

> Here is Diana Parker's "explanation" of her arrival in Sanditon: "Well—now for the explanation of me being here… & here we are." I would regret the expense of a quotation so full and so inevitably out of proportion to my commentary on it, if it didn't point to a defining characteristic of chatter: namely, its excess—

its constant overproduction in relation to that which it can be said to communicate. "I seem to be spinning out my story to an endless length." The technique of Diana Parker's spinning out is hypotaxis. The humor of "only a *short* chain, you see, between us, & not a Link wanting" comes from our opposite sense that her language has more links than it really wants, just as it tells of more complications than really prove the case. We soon discover that "the Family from Surry & the Family from Camberwell were one & the same." What is threatened in Diana's discourse is perfectly clear ("Am I clear?—I would be anything rather than not clear"): clarity and—what clarity is a necessary condition of in Jane Austen— truth. This excessive and excessively differentiated language would seem basically a response to a lack of provision for discourse. It is a kind of linguistic hypochondria. Much as Diana fills her abundant leisure with the motions of bustle (mainly, only an active form of inefficaciousness), her language supplies its meager and trivial matter by overarticulating it, as though there were all too much to tell. (33–36)

But in fairness the text also shows another side of her: keeping the three-member household going, organizing the visit to Sanditon, and finding within a very short time all the domestic help that she believes will be needed by two vacationing families.]

Susan had only superintended their final removal from the Hotel, bringing two heavy Boxes herself, & Arthur had found the air so cold that he had merely walked from one House to the other as nimbly as he could, — & boasted much of sitting by the fire till he had cooked up a very good one. —

[Reference to Susan and Arthur by their first names is unlikely to be through Charlotte since she barely knows the sister and brother. The author herself is often the narrator, although her slipping into the identity of Charlotte occurs frequently and sometimes subtly.]

Diana, whose exercise had been too domestic to admit of calculation, but who, by her own account had not once sat down during the space of seven hours, confessed herself a little tired. She had been too successful however for much fatigue; for not only had she by walking & talking down a thousand difficulties at last secured a proper House at 8^g p^r. week for M^{rs}. G. —;

she had also opened so many Treaties with Cooks, Housemaids, Washer women & Bathing Women, that M^rs. G. would have little more to do on her arrival, than to wave her hand & collect them around her for choice. —

[Some of this passage sounds like reported speech, Diana's account of her frantic activities earlier in the day. The "thousand difficulties" is exactly the kind of exaggeration that we would expect from her. A guinea, called thus because the precious metal came from Guinea (Ghana) in Africa, was a British gold coin introduced in 1663 and as of 1717 worth 21 shillings or £1.05. Although traditionally used for stating prices of expensive purchases and still "much used in auctions (the bidder pays in guineas, the vendor gets paid the same number of pounds—the auctioneer gets the rest) and as the prizes… for horse races" ("Money & Coins"), the guinea has not been minted since 1813 and is now a value rather than a coin or note. Eight guineas a week was a considerable amount of money at the time, "the equivalent of something approaching £500 a week at early twenty-first-century prices" (*CUPLM*: 671).

The hiring of "Bathing Women" or "Dippers," who helped ladies in the bathing machines and then dunked them in the sea, is in anticipation that many of Mrs. Griffiths' charges and those of the lady bringing the second party will be enjoying the local specialty of sea immersion. Although Miss Diana Parker, having lived in Sanditon for part of her life, is familiar with the local bathing practices, there is no indication in the text that she or any other members of the family have ever actually participated in any of the much-touted seaside activities. Poor Arthur would in particular be a sight to behold on the beach, whether modestly garbed or in the men's section au naturel.]

Her concluding effort in the cause, had been a few polite lines of Information to M^rs. G. herself — time not allowing for the circuitous train of intelligence which had been hitherto kept up, — and she was now regaling in the delight of opening the first Trenches of an acquaintance with such a powerful discharge of unexpected Obligation.

["Regale" is now exclusively a transitive verb and has been throughout its history. However, it also appears as a reflexive verb with an understood but unspecified pronoun. Jane Austen, always "flexible" in her spellings and general handling of our language, had already used the verb in a "transferred" sense: "*transf.* **1814** JANE AUSTEN *Mansf. Park* ii, Mrs. Norris… thus regaled in the credit of being foremost to welcome her" (*OED*); the sense is of course "Mrs. Norris regaled herself." In a letter written to Cassandra on October 12, 1813, Jane Austen had used the word in the same manner: "Have you any Tomatas?—Fanny & I regale on them every day" (*Letters*: 235), with the clear sense of "Fanny and I regale ourselves." And so Miss Diana Parker "was now regaling herself" with the thoughts of all that she had accomplished for people who had not asked for her assistance.

Although Jane Austen as narrator says it, as part of indirect discourse it is likely that the word "Trenches" is in the report delivered by Diana Parker about her success in assisting Mrs. Griffiths without that lady's knowledge. Hence we have "a very unusual figurative use of the military term for the digging of hollows or ditches in the ground, reinforced by 'discharged' later in the sentence" (*CUPLM*: 671). More than most characters in Jane Austen's novels, Diana Parker has an idiolect replete with figurative language.]

M^r^. & M^rs^. P. — & Charlotte had seen two Post chaises crossing the Down to the Hotel as they were setting off, — a joyful sight — & full of speculation. — The Miss Ps — & Arthur had also seen something; — they could distinguish from their window that there <u>was</u> an arrival at the Hotel, but not its amount. Their Visitors answered for two Hack–Chaises. — Could it be the Camberwell Seminary? — No — No. — Had there been a 3^d^. carriage, perhaps it might; but it was very generally agreed that two Hack chaises could never contain a Seminary. — M^r^. P. was confident of another new Family. —

[A post chaise—the same as a "hack" or "hackney [a trotting horse used chiefly for driving] chaise"—is a hired carriage with horses that are changed along the way. Part of this passage is reported dialog, particularly the "No — No." And we can well imagine Thomas Parker's encouraging dialog as he expresses confidence that more visitors are on their way.]

When they were all finally seated, after some removals to look at the Sea & the Hotel, Charlotte's place was by Arthur, who was sitting next to the Fire with a degree of Enjoyment which gave a good deal of merit to his civility in wishing her to take his Chair. —

There was nothing dubious in her manner of declining it, & he sat down again with much satisfaction. She drew back her Chair to have all the advantage of his Person as a screen, & was very thankful for every inch of Back & Shoulders beyond her pre-conceived idea.

[The "firescreen, a common piece of furniture in the days of open fires, [was] used to protect people from the direct heat of the fire" (*CUPLM*: 671). A young lady who wanted to be fashionably pale would be sure to avoid the heat of the flames, but as a farm-bred girl Charlotte is accustomed to the warm rays of the sun. The text continues to suggest that Arthur Parker is very large indeed, perhaps even fat.]

He had in every respect a heavy Look. — Yet was not indisposed to talk; — and while the other 4 were very much engaged together, evidently felt it no penance to have a good-looking Girl next to him, requiring in common Politeness some attention — as his B^r— observed with much pleasure

>

He had in every respect a heavy Look. — Yet was not indisposed to talk; — and while the other 4 were very much engaged together, evidently felt it no penance to have a good-looking Girl next to him, requiring in common Politeness some attention — as his B^r— observed with gr pleasure

>

He had in every respect a heavy Look. — Yet was not indisposed to talk; — and while the other 4 were very much engaged together, evidently felt it no penance to have a good-looking Girl next to him, requiring in common Politeness some attention — as his B^r—, who felt the great want of some motive for action, of something

>

He had in every respect a heavy Look. — Yet was not indisposed to talk; — and while the other 4 were very much engaged together, evidently felt it no penance to have a good-looking Girl next to him, requiring in common Politeness some attention — as his B^r—, who felt the great want of some motive for action, of some source of animation for Arthur, observed with no inconsiderable pleasure. —

>

Arthur was heavy in Eye as well as figure, but by no means indisposed to talk; — and while the other 4 were cheifly engaged together, he evidently felt it no penance to have with a young agreable — Girl next to him, requiring in common Politeness some attention — as his B^r—, who felt the decided want of some motive for action, some Powerful object of animation for him, observed with considerable pleasure. —

>

Arthur was heavy in Eye as well as figure, but by no means indisposed to talk; — and while the other 4 were cheifly engaged together, he evidently felt it no penance to have a fine young Woman next to him, requiring in common Politeness some attention — as his B^r—, who felt the decided want of some motive for action, some Powerful object of animation for him, observed with considerable pleasure. —

[Our author again devotes considerable time to reworking her passage of first impressions of a new major character. As usual, Jane Austen resists describing her heroine, wavering from "a good-looking Girl" to "a young agreable Girl" to more vaguely "a fine young Woman." This passage may be in part Arthur Parker's reaction to his visitor, who offers him none of the special attractions of the Beaufort sisters, but it is also part of the author's strategy not to make her heroine the great beauty of the novel. Here, Charlotte must take second place to Clara Brereton, as Fanny Price does to Mary Crawford, as Elizabeth Bennet does to Jane Bennet, and as Emma Woodhouse does to Jane Fairfax. In these novels, the special strength of the heroine lies not in mere physical beauty but in personality, intelligence, and sheer intensity of spirit. The great beauties of the books tend to be shallow or merely objects to be admired. And if Charlotte is no more than pleasing to the eye, she is in line with her original in being "almost pretty today."]

Such was the influence of Youth & Bloom that he began even to make a sort of apology for having a Fire.

[We have already heard a good deal about Clara Brereton's personal charms, but it is important to note that Charlotte also has much in the way of youthful beauty to draw attention from all the unattached men assembled at Sanditon. A young woman's bloom or glowing complexion was indispensable to her attractiveness, as seen in *Persuasion*.

A few years before, Anne Elliot had been a very pretty girl, but her bloom had vanished early.]

"We sh^d. not have one at home, said he, but the Sea air is always damp. I am not afraid of any thing so much as Damp. —"

[Poor Arthur's condemnation of sea air as damp and therefore dangerous is in sharp contrast to his eldest brother's unlimited praise of its restorative powers.]

"I am so fortunate, said C. as never to know whether the air is damp or dry. It has always some property that is wholesome & invigorating to me. —"

[It is hard to determine how serious Charlotte is in conducting a conversation on the least rewarding topic imaginable, the salutary properties of air. By now she must have discerned that Sir Edward Denham is not the only foolish man among the population of Sanditon.]

"I like the Air too, as well as any body can; replied Arthur, I am very fond of standing at an open Window when there is no Wind — — but unluckily a Damp air does not like <u>me</u>. — It gives me the Rheumatism. — You are not rheumatic I suppose? —"

[On March 26, 1817, eight days after coming to the end of this manuscript, Jane Austen wrote to her niece, Caroline Austen, "A great deal of wind does not suit me.... I am a poor Honey at present" (*Letters*: 338). The novel is a case-study in wooing expertise, with Sir Edward going off into hyperbolic praise of fair ladies, poor Arthur discoursing on his stomach lining, and Sidney hopefully demonstrating the proper technique.]

"Not at all."

"That's a great blessing. — But perhaps you are nervous."

[Poor Arthur uses a contraction—"That's"—whereas the more cultivated Charlotte avoids them.]

"No — I beleive not. I have no idea that I am. —"

"I am very nervous. —

In my own opinion Nerves are the worst part of my Complaints —
>
To say the truth — Nerves are the worst part of my Complaints in <u>my</u> own opinion. —
>
To say the truth — Nerves are the worst part of my Complaints in <u>my</u> opinion. —

[Mrs. Bennet, then, is not the only character in a Jane Austen novel with this (imaginary?) ailment.

"Mr. Bennet, how CAN you abuse your own children in such a way? You take delight in vexing me. You have no compassion for my poor nerves."

"You mistake me, my dear. I have a high respect for your nerves. They are my old friends. I have heard you mention them with consideration these last twenty years at least."]

My Sisters think me Bilious, but I doubt it. —"

[Bile, a fluid secreted by the liver, helps the body digest and absorb fatty foods as well as ridding the body of certain waste products. Bile or liver problems may cause nausea and vomiting. If there is anything autobiographical in this fragment, this line is the most likely since Jane Austen believed in her final months that she was suffering from bilious attacks. On January 24, 1817, three days before beginning the final manuscript, she wrote to Alethea Bigg, "I am more & more convinced that *Bile* is at the bottom of all I have suffered, which makes it easy to know how to treat myself" (*Letters*: 326–327). Her home remedies were clearly inefficacious, and some days after abandoning the manuscript, she wrote to Charles Austen on April 6, 1817, "I have been suffering from a Bilious attack, attended with a good deal of fever" (*Letters*: 338).

Accepted for some years without much controversy, Sir Zachary Cope's diagnosis in 1964 of the exact cause of Jane Austen's death as tubercular Addison's disease has recently been challenged by K.G. White.]

"You are quite in the right, to doubt it as long as you possibly can, I am sure. —"

[The conversation here has some of the elements of Alice in Wonderland.]

"If I were Bilious, he continued, you know Wine w^d. disagree with me, but it always does me good. — The more Wine I drink (in Moderation) the better I am. — I am always best of an Even^g. —

[Jane Austen admitted in a letter to her sister dated November 20, 1800, that on occasion she was prone to excessive drinking.

"I believe I drank too much wine last night at Hurstbourne; I know not how else to account for the shaking of my hand today" (*Letters*: 60).

Thirteen years later (November 6, 1813), she wrote again to Cassandra,

"Bye the bye, as I must leave off being young, I find many Douceurs in being a sort of Chaperon for I am put on the Sofa near the Fire & can drink as much wine as I like" (*Letters*: 251).

It would be foolish to hazard a guess at what was in the many letters that Cassandra Austen destroyed after her sister's death.]

If you had seen me today before Dinner, you w^d. have thought me a very poor Creature. —"
>
If you had seen me today before Dinner, you w^d. have found me a very poor Creature. —"
>
If you had seen me today before Dinner, you w^d. have thought me a very poor Creature. —"

[This line shows Jane Austen's occasional practice of returning to an original reading.]

Charlotte could beleive it — . She kept her countenance however, & said — "As far as I can understand what nervous complaints are, I have a great idea of the efficacy of air & exercise for them; — daily, regular Exercise; — and I should recommend rather more of it to <u>you</u> than I suspect you are in the habit of taking. —"

[Charlotte is learning how to "keep her countenance" after revealing her true thoughts to Lady Denham and Diana Parker. The maturation process of not always sharing your thoughts is part of what this novel will demonstrate. Openness in a young lady does not require her to express her opinion on everything.]

"Oh! I am very fond of exercise myself — he replied — & mean to walk a great deal while I am here, if the Weather is temperate. I shall be out every morning before breakfast — & take several turns upon the Terrace, & you will often see me at Trafalgar House." —

[Although the usual "breakfast is a light meal of tea and bread and butter" (Borer: 60), we can safely assume that poor Arthur consumes some more, all well covered in butter.]

"But you do not call a walk to Traf: H. much exercise ? —"

"Not, in mere distance, but there is such a steep Hill to get up to it! —
>
"Not, as to mere distance, but the Hill is so steep! —

Walking up that Hill, in the middle of the day, would throw me into such a Perspiration! — You would see me all in a Bath, by the time I got there! — I am very subject to Perspiration, and there cannot be a surer sign of Nervousness. —"

[It is possible that in attributing this fear to Arthur Parker the author was unaware that "in fact, in most instances, perspiration was seen as health-giving rather than as a sign of illness" (*CUPLM*: 672). It is more likely—and far more comical—that Arthur is such a confirmed hypochondriac that he misreads evidence of good health as evidence of illness.]

They were now advancing so deep in Physics, that Charlotte veiwed the entrance of the Servant with the Tea things, as a very fortunate Interruption. — It produced a great & immediate change. The young Man's attentions were instantly lost.

[Jane Austen uses "Physics" in the obsolete sense of "the science of medicine."]

The text never specifies if the three Parkers have come with a servant (perhaps Old Hannah or Old Sam), who is here bringing tea, or if this servant is an amenity provided by their landlord. Jane Austen expects us dull elves to use our own imaginations.

Like Sir Edward in an earlier scene, Arthur Parker turns suddenly from lighthearted banter with Charlotte to something more to his liking, in this instance, edibles. Our heroine has good reason to be wary of the young men here, and so her meeting with Sidney Parker will be in startling contrast to her earlier experiences in Sanditon. Charlotte's ego is hardly being fed by first having Sir Edward flirt with her only to make another woman jealous and now being disregarded for a set of cups.]

He took his own Cocoa Pot from the Tray, — which seemed provided with almost as many Tea-pots &c as there were persons in company, Miss P. drinking one sort of Herb-Tea & Miss Diana another, & turning completely to the Fire, sat coddling & cooking it to his own satisfaction & toasting some Slices of Bread, ready-prepared in the Toast rack — and till it was all done, she heard nothing of his voice but in a faint murmur, & a few broken sentences of approbation of his own Doings & prosperity. —

>

He took his own Cocoa from the Tray, — which seemed provided with almost as many Tea-pots &c as there were persons in company, Miss P. drinking one sort of Herb-Tea & Miss Diana another, & turning completely to the Fire, sat coddling & cooking it to his own satisfaction & toasting some Slices of Bread, brought up ready-prepared in the Toast rack — and till it was all done, she heard nothing of his voice but the murmuring of a few broken sentences of self-approbation & success. —

[Jane Austen writes of Arthur Parker's indulgence in hot chocolate to show his extravagance as much as his love of sweets. "Chocolate ha[d] long since been a fashionable drink... for the few who could afford it" (Borer: 63). As early as 1657, Londoners could buy solid chocolate from which they made the beverage, soon available in chocolate houses throughout Europe. However, in Great Britain it remained a luxury, too expensive except for the wealthy—"Mixed with cocoa, milk became 'chocolate,' a luxurious drink enjoyed at the homes of the wealthy, and on special occasions" (Olsen: 77)—until the duty was lowered in the mid-nineteenth century.

> Jane Austen prepared hot cocoa for her family for breakfast. In *Northanger Abbey*, General Tilney enjoys it in the morning, as well, oblivious to his guests. Arthur Parker, an imaginary invalid in *Sanditon*, is nearly found out through his love of it. Chocolate has been for ages, one of the most beloved of all dessert and baking products. It did not, however, attain its recognizeable form until the mid 1800's. How then was it used before the invention of cocoa powder?

> Cocoa first arrived in Europe in 1528. The original hot cocoa recipe was a mixture of ground cocoa beans, water, wine and peppers. When the Spanish first brought chocolate back to Europe from the new world, it was served as a beverage, though the ingredients underwent a historic change: the chili pepper was replaced by sugar. After being introduced in England in 1652, milk was added to create an after dinner treat. The new, sweetened, chocolate beverage was a luxury few could afford, but by the 17th century the drink was common among European nobility. In England, which was somewhat more egalitarian than the rest of Europe, chocolate

was more widely available. Those who could afford it could enjoy chocolate drinks in the new coffee and chocolate houses of London. A few of the more famous were the Cocoa Tree Chocolate House (which served guests from 1799 to the early 19th c.) and Whites, which began its career as a Chocolate House before becoming a private club. Coffee and Chocolate Houses, like today's Starbucks and other such establishments, were popular places to drink with friends and talk politics or gossip. Each faction had their favorite spot and many were known by name as meeting houses for various political parties. While all of these establishments sold most beverages (coffee, chocolate, cider, coffee and tea, etc.) Coffee house customers who were less than affluent had to think of their purses: chocolate was dearer than coffee, but tea was the most expensive of them all. Coffee provided the most stimulation for the least outlay, which is probably why these were "coffee-houses" rather than "chocolate-houses."

In the 18th c. Cocoa powder for making hot chocolate was created in factories. There, workers would roast the beans in a cauldron, winnow to release inner nib, break nib in a mortar and a final grinding on the surface of a heated table. Once this had been done, the powder was able to be used. Creating it at home took time, skill and a special pot. The chocolate pot, looking like a small samovar stood on legs so that a heat source could be placed beneath it. Ingredients (milk, cocoa powder or chocolate, flavorings, and whatnot) were melted together, stirred from the top, by a whisk, poured out and, if served in a shop, whipped to a froth and drunk from tall chocolate cups which were meant to slow the cooling. ("A Passion for Hot Chocolate")]

When his Toils were over however, he moved back his Chair into as gallant a Line as ever, & proved that he had not been working only for himself, by his earnest invitation to her to take both Cocoa & Toast. — She was already helped to Tea — which surprised him — so totally self-engrossed had he been. —

"I thought I should have been in time, said he, but cocoa takes a great deal of Boiling." —

"I am much obliged to you, replied Charlotte — but I <u>prefer</u> Tea."

[As difficult as it may be to imagine, tea is not part of England's ancient heritage, having been introduced in comparatively modern times.

> The importing of tea into Britain began in the 1660s with the marriage of King Charles II with the Portuguese princess Catherine of Braganza where she brought to the court the habit of drinking tea.... In the same year Samuel Pepys records drinking "a china drink of which I had never drunk before." It is probable that early imports came via Amsterdam or through sailors on eastern boats.... It was initially promoted as a medicinal beverage or tonic. By the end of the seventeenth century tea was taken as a drink, albeit mainly by the aristocracy. In 1690 nobody would have predicted that by 1750 tea would be the national drink. ("Tea." *Wikipedia*)

> By the 1800s, [tea] rivaled beer in popularity even among the lower classes... and the fact that the water was boiled made it safe to drink.... Originally, tea was imported from China by the East India Company under a virtual monopoly, and for a long time it was so expensive that it was sometimes kept in locked boxes called tea caddies. (Pool: 208–209)

> Tea was such a precious commodity after its introduction in England during the mid 17th century, that servants were never entrusted with handling the loose leaves. The tea was... stored in the customer's caddy, or cannister, which came with a lock and key to prevent pilfering.

. . .

> By the 1800's tea was widely drunk by the middle classes.... However, tea remained expensive. The British East India Company, which held the monopoly on importing tea until 1834, held prices artificially high for centuries. In addition, the government kept raising taxes on tea in order to finance England's expensive wars. Smuggling tea became a lucrative business, and shopkeepers and individuals were not averse to purchasing tea leaves on the black market. Be that as it may, by Jane Austen's day, the drinking of tea had become a regular occurrence, both at home and in public. (Vic, 2007)

Tea became the favorite English beverage after 1750. In 1785, tea imports reached 11 million pounds. By 1797, tea consumption reached an annual rate of 2 pounds per capita and would increase five fold over the next ten years. ("On the Tea Table")

The escalation of tea importation and sales over the period 1690 to 1750 is mirrored closely by the increase in importation and sales of cane sugar: the British were not drinking just tea but *sweet* tea. Thus, two of Britain's trading triangles were to meet within the cup: the sugar sourced from Britain's trading triangle encompassing Britain, Africa and the West Indies and the tea from the triangle encompassing Britain, India and China ("Tea." *Wikipedia*)

We have here an unexpected and indirect link between Charlotte Heywood and Miss Lambe, which Jane Austen may (or perhaps may not) have meant us to perceive. Charlotte has been raised in some affluence if tea, then very expensive, is her beverage of choice.

Superficially, Jane Austen appears to give us a series of contrasting heroines of a considerably wide range in social standing, in a sense beginning with Susan/Catherine (daughter of a hardly impoverished but far from wealthy country cleric) and ending with Charlotte (daughter of a hardly impoverished but far from wealthy gentleman farmer). Between them we find the Dashwood sisters, brought up in comfort (extreme luxury, as a matter of fact, if we are to believe the appearance of Norland Park in some of the film versions); the Bennet girls, with all the advantages of being daughters of a landowning country gentleman but without any assurance of permanence because of the absence of a brother to inherit Longbourn; Fanny Price, of a poor background but well connected with the fairly wealthy family of a Baronet; Emma, wealthy in her own right; and finally Anne Elliott, the daughter of a Baronet and secure in her social standing, ready as a younger woman to marry a man with no immediate prospects but hardly displeased that by postponing her nuptials she can have a husband of considerable wealth.

Despite what appears to be wide diversity, however, there is a common element among all these heroines that is by far more important than their differences, their lack of aspiration to changing their social status, especially if that would require marrying without love. We are deliberately shown characters like Isabella Thorpe, Lucy Steele, Charlotte Lucas, and Maria

Bertram who for worldly considerations are ready to abandon all hope of happiness. For Jane Austen and her heroines, a loveless marriage would be a desecration of that time-honored institution. And for the author and her creations, love would obviously be found only in one's own or a higher social class, not among the workmen of the fields or (!) the tradesmen of the town. Jane Austen, essentially conservative, preserves the social order of the day by sorting like with like, as Harriet Smith marries her Mr. Robert Martin and Emma Woodhouse marries her Mr. George Knightley.

And Jane Austen writes from personal experience about the delicate matter of what a woman seeks most in marriage.

> In the winter of 1802,… while she and Cassandra were on a visit to their brother James back in the family rectory at Steventon, Jane received a proposal from Harris Bigg-Wither, the plain and awkward younger brother of some girlhood friends of hers, and heir to a pleasant country estate near Basingstoke. Perhaps from feelings of friendship or gratitude, she accepted his proposal in the evening; but by the next morning had evidently decided that worldly benefits would not outweigh the disadvantages of a loveless marriage, and so retracted her consent. (Le Faye, 2002: 29)

Could she do no less for Lizzy, Fanny, and Anne?]

"Then I will help myself, said he. — A large Dish of rather weak Cocoa every evening agrees with me better than any thing." —

[Possibly poor Arthur prefers to drink his cocoa out of the dish rather than directly from a cup. Some people reduce the scalding heat of the boiling water by pouring small amounts into the dish to avoid scorching the mouth. But he may be using "Dish" in a more general sense as suggested in the *OED*: "**3.** As a term of quantity more or less indefinite. **a.** As much or as many as will fill or make a dish when cooked. **b.** A dishful, a bowlful or cupful." Mr. Thomas Parker has already observed that it is "impossible to get a good dish of Tea within 3 miles of" Brinshore, so the phrase was standard at the time, and "dish" very likely means "cup."]

It struck her however, as he poured out this rather weak Cocoa, that it came forth in a very fine, dark coloured stream — and at the same moment, his Sisters both crying out — "Oh! Arthur, you get your Cocoa stronger & stronger every Even^g" —, with Arthur's somewhat conscious reply of "Tis rather stronger than it should be tonight" — convinced her that Arthur was by no means so fond of being starved as they could desire, or as he felt proper himself. — He was certainly very happy to turn the conversation on dry Toast, & hear no more of his sisters. —

[If Jane Austen means by "his Sisters both crying out" that Susan Parker as well as Diana Parker thus remonstrated with him, we have for one brief moment something directly from the lips of the elder sister.]

"I hope you will eat some of this Toast, said he, I reckon myself a very good Toaster; I never burn my Toasts — I never put them too near the Fire at first — & yet, you see, there is not a Corner but what is well browned. — I hope you like dry Toast." —

[Arthur's "but what" may be common at the time, but better-educated characters do not speak at this level.]

"With a reasonable quantity of Butter spread over it, very much — said Charlotte — but not otherwise. —"

"No more do I — said he very much obliged
>
"No more do I — said he very much pleased —
>
"No more do I — said he exceedingly pleased —

We think quite alike there. — So far from dry Toast being wholesome, I think it a very bad thing for the Stomach. Without a little butter to soften it, it hurts the Coats of the Stomach. I am sure it does. — I will have the pleasure of spreading some for you directly — & afterwards I will spread some for myself. — Very bad indeed for the Coats of the Stomach — but there is no convincing some people. — It irritates & acts like a nutmeg grater. —"

[There was some controversy at the time about the dangers of Arthur Parker's diet. Although

> breakfast in a substantial home might include... toast and butter... ,
> the anonymous author of *The Mirror of the Graces* (1811) took issue
> with... this... menu, which she claimed made women ugly:

Their breakfasts not only set forth tea and coffee, but chocolate and *hot* bread and butter. Both of these latter articles, when taken constantly, are hostile to health and female delicacy. The heated grease, which is their principal ingredient, deranges the stomach; and, by creating or increasing bilious disorders, gradually overspreads the before fair skin with a wan or yellow hue. (Olsen: 265)

The coats that Arthur Parker is eager to protect "are the protective layers of membrane lining the stomach" (*CUPLM*: 672).

Kirstin Olsen (253) has given us a contemporary print illustrating the fine art of toasting muffins.

Toasting Muffins, Vide Royal Breakfast, James Gillray, 1791. In this caricature of George III, the monarch toasts muffins by a small inset fireplace.

The Royals were regarded as particularly poor exemplars of diet, as seen in the frontispiece—"George IV *Gill Ray*"—to *The Regency Companion* (Laudermilk and Hamlin). The Prince Regent/George IV could well have served as a model for Arthur Parker if Jane Austen saw drawings of this nature. James Gillray (1757–1815) was a "savage caricaturist who alternately amused and outraged Georgian England" (Laudermilk: 286). The paragon of profligacy, the Prince was heartily disliked by Jane Austen (and many of her contemporaries), a revulsion not made the less powerful through her being almost forced to dedicate *Emma* to him.

As she does so frequently in the manuscript, Jane Austen implies a stage direction in underlining "<u>some</u>," which would be accompanied by a hostile glare or a movement of a shoulder and the head in the direction of his two sisters. The volume of his voice probably goes up as he speaks this word so that his two sisters are certain to know his reaction to their chiding.]

It was rather amusing to see
>
He could not get the command of the Butter however, without a struggle;
>
He could not get the command of the Butter Glass however, without a struggle;
>

He could not get the command of the Butter however, without a struggle;

[This line required some work, and again the author has restored a rejected reading.

The butter glass of the time was not like the narrow rectangle that we occasionally use to hold a stick or quarter-pound of butter. It may have been round and beautifully crafted, as seen at cgi.ebay.com/ Fenton-Ruby-Marble-8680RX-Regency-Covered-Butter-Dish_ W0QQitemZ380193409903QQcmdZViewItemQQptZLH_DefaultD omain_0?hash=item58854b0b6f#ht_1601wt_941.

Another possible type is a "sterling butter dish with glass liner," seen at

www.silverpattern.com/BIRKS%20STERLING%20AND%20 REGENCY%20PLATE.htm.

Although the *OED* cites "butter dish" ("**1572** *Wills & Inv. N.C.* (1835) 349, xxxix *butter Dishes. **1861** MRS. BEETON *Househ. Managem.* 814 An ornamental butter-dish"), it does not recognize "butter glass." It does, however, note "butter-boat" ("**1787** *Gentl. Mag.* Sept. 821/2 His mustard-glass and butter-boat were overturned. **1807** BYRON *To Miss Pigot* 5 July, Upset a butter-boat in the lap of a lady") and "Butter coolers" ("**1790** *Pennsylvania Packet* 7 Dec. 3/3 Butter coolers")].

His Sisters accusing him of eating a great deal too much, & declaring he was not to be trusted; — and he maintaining that he only eat enough to secure the Coats of his Stomach; — & besides, he only wanted it now for Miss Heywood.

[Although Arthur may be pronouncing "eat" (past tense) to rhyme with "late," he is more likely pronouncing it to rhyme with "let," a substandard pronunciation apparently still used. Since we cannot hear his spelling, there would be no point in Jane Austen's writing "eat" if Arthur pronounces it as "ate," so she almost certainly means a rhyme with "let." Like Lady Denham, his lack of education is demonstrated through his dialog. This line could be reported dialog shared by the two sisters and their brother or by Arthur alone, confiding to Charlotte how much they abuse him verbally.

In *Emma*, Jane Austen twice uses "ate" as past tense, the first time as part of the author's narrative and probably reflecting her own usage. "They had to listen to the description of exactly how little bread and butter she [Miss

Bates] ate for breakfast." However, if the line is indirect discourse, the verb choice matches that of a later speech by Miss Bates, who is poor but not ignorant: "As long as so many sacks were sold, it did not signify who ate the remainder." Elsewhere in the novel, we find one instance of "eat" as past participle, with the possibility of indirect discourse reflecting Mr. Woodhouse's speech: "The compliments of his neighbours were over; he was no longer teased by being wished joy of so sorrowful an event; and the wedding-cake, which had been a great distress to him, was all eat up." The normal past participle appears elsewhere: "but still the cake was eaten"; "if it is… eaten very moderately of… I do not consider it unwholesome"; "only too rich to be eaten much of."]

Such a plea must prevail, he got the butter & spread away for her with an accuracy of Judgement which at least delighted himself; but when that was done, & he took his own Toast in hand, Charlotte c^d. hardly contain himself as she saw him watching his sisters, while he scrupulously scraped off as much butter as he put on, & then seize an odd moment for adding a great dab just before it went into his Mouth. —

>

Such a plea must prevail, he got the butter & spread away for her with an accuracy of Judgement which at least delighted himself; but when her Toast was done, & he took his own in hand, Charlotte c^d. hardly contain herself as she saw him watching his sisters, while he scrupulously scraped off almost as much butter as he put on, & then seize an odd moment for adding a great dab just before it went into his Mouth. —

[It is amusing to conjecture if this passage finds its source in Jane Austen's report to Cassandra—in the same letter, dated October 11/12, 1813, in which she praises "the sagacity and taste of Charlotte Williams… [w]hose large dark eyes always judge well"—that "Mr. Rob. Mascall breakfasted here; he eats a great deal of butter" (*Letters*: 235). The original "Charlotte c^d. hardly contain himself" again suggests inaccurate copying from a lost original.]

Certainly, M^r. Arthur P.'s enjoyments in Invalidism were very different from his sisters — by no means so spiritualized. —

A good deal of Earth hung about him.

>

A good deal of Earthy Dross hung about him.

[The change here intensifies the image, another rare instance of Jane Austen's use of figurative language in this manuscript. The unusual adjective "earthy," which appears nowhere else in the novels, had several meanings that work in this phrase, such as "*fig.* grossly material, coarse, dull, unrefined" (*OED*). There is a certain amount of redundancy in matching "Earthy" with "Dross," which already contains the ideas of "Dreggy, impure, or foreign matter, mixed with any substance, and detracting from its purity," as well as "scum, recrement, or extraneous matter" and "refuse; rubbish; worthless, impure matter" (*OED*). The *CUPLM* editor well summarizes the phrase as "'common clay'" (673), but why would Charlotte have expected a more spiritual person in the Parker family?]

He seemed to have chosen that line of Life, cheifly for the indulgence of an indolent Temper — & to be determined on having no Disorders but such as called for warm rooms & good Nourishment. —
>
He seemed to have adopted that line of Life, cheifly for the indulgence of an indolent Temper — & to be determined on having no Disorders but such as called for warm rooms & good Nourishment. —
>
Charlotte could not but suspect him of having adopted that line of Life, cheifly for the indulgence of an indolent Temper — & to be determined on having no Disorders but such as called for warm rooms & good Nourishment. —
>
Charlotte could not but suspect him of adopting that line of Life, principally for the indulgence of an indolent Temper — & to be determined on having no Disorders but such as called for warm rooms & good Nourishment.
—

[We may see Mr. Woodhouse in his youth.]

In one particular however, she soon found that he had caught something from <u>them</u>. — "What! said he — Do you venture upon two dishes of strong Green Tea in one Even^g? — What Nerves you must have! — How I envy you. — Now, if <u>I</u> were to swallow only one such dish — what do you think its' effect would be upon me? —"

[Green tea, "made from fresh leaves dried immediately after picking... introduced to Britain in the mid seventeenth century... [claimed] health benefits [that] were disputed" (*CUPLM*: 673).]

"Keep you awake perhaps all night" — replied Charlotte, meaning to overthrow his attempts at Surprise, by the Grandeur of her own Conceptions. —

"Oh! if that were all! — he exclaimed. —

No — it w^d. entirely take away the use of my right side, before I had swallowed it 5 minutes.

—

>

[On the basis of a misreading of the manuscript (page 102, folio 51v),

> No — it
> acts on me like Poison and
> w^d. entirely take away the use of my
> right side,

Chapman (145), Johnson (67), Another Lady (62), *OIJA*–VI (418), Sacco (143), and Axelrad (2003: 229), recognizing that the five words of the second line have been interpolated, render the amended line,

"No—it acts on me like Poison and w^d. entirely take away the use of my right side."

CUPLM (530) transcribes the manuscript correctly ("act" rather than "acts),

> No — it
> act on me like Poison and
> w^d. entirely take away the use of my
> right side,

to read (*CUPLM*: 199),]

"No—it would act on me like poison and entirely take away the use of my right side."

[Jane Austen does not always write in a caret, and if one is implied between "w^d." and "entirely" to insert "act on me like Poison and," the line now reads as the author intended.]

It is a sort of thing hardly to be beleived but it has happened to me three times. —

\>

It is a sort of thing hardly to be beleived but it has happened to me several times. —

\>

It is a sort of thing hardly to be beleived but it has happened to me so often that I cannot doubt it. —

\>

It sounds almost incredible — but it has happened to me so often that I cannot doubt it. —

[Thus his malady escalates in severity each time he rehearses it.]

The use of my right Side is entirely taken away for several hours!"

"It sounds rather odd to be sure — answered Charlotte coolly — but I dare say it would be proved to be the simplest thing in the World, by those who have studied right sides & Green Tea scientifically & thoroughly understand all the possibilities of their action on each other." —

["A number of treatises were published in the eighteenth century considering the beneficial or otherwise qualities of tea" (*CUPLM*: 673). That Jane Austen has moved far from the original premises of "Susan"/"Catherine" is seen in Charlotte's sardonic summary, very much along the lines of Henry Tilney's usual bantering style but alien to the mind of his 17-year-old companion who has just come to sophisticated Bath from the country.

The nonsense of "those who have studied right sides & Green Tea scientifically" anticipates *Alice in Wonderland*.]

Soon after Tea, a Letter was brought to Miss D. P— from the Hotel. —

[The direction of the plot takes a sudden turn here, changing from Arthur Parker's ludicrous medical problems to the puzzle of the two expected arriving parties.]

"From M^{rs}. Charles Dupuis — said she. — some private hand." —

[A "private hand" was "a personal letter, delivered by private carrier" (*CUPLM*: 673). The phrase is not in the *OED*, but one of the definitions of "private"—"Of a conversation, communication, etc.: intended only for or confined to the person or persons directly concerned; confidential"—is found not many years after the composition of this manuscript in the work of one of Jane Austen's greatest adherents: "**1857** TROLLOPE *Barchester Towers* xlvii, He received a letter, in an official cover, marked 'private'." The phrase is in use, apparently as a kind of abbreviated description: On Google, one finds "Private Hand Delivery Network," a "Global Private Delivery service." Within the site, however, the phrase "private hand" is never used.

Exactly how this letter from Mrs. Charles Dupuis made its way to Diana Parker is unclear. The sisters and youngest brother left their home too precipitately for Diana to write to her friend that they were on their way to Sanditon.

"Yes — we are actually all come. Quite unavoidable. — Nothing else to be done. — You shall hear all about it.… What was to be done? — I had a few moments indecision.… our plan was arranged immediately, we were off yesterday morn^g. at 6 —, left Chichester at the same hour today — & here we are. —"

[The Parkers are people of swift and decisive action as seen in Thomas Parker's spontaneous search for a medical man to return with him to Sanditon and Diana Parker's hastily arranged trip to the seaside as well as Sidney Parker's unexpected change of plans, visiting Sanditon instead of going on to the Isle of Wight.

The letter could have been sent on from the Parker residence in Hampshire if the forwarding address was known. Alternatively, between Diana Parker's arrival in Sanditon and this scene she may have written letters to her various acquaintances, although it is difficult to see how she would have had time for correspondence while running around minding other people's business.]

And having read a few lines, exclaimed aloud "Well, this is very extraordinary! very extraordinary indeed! — That both should have the same name. — Two M^rs. Griffiths! — This is a Letter of recommendation & introduction to me, of the Lady from Camberwell — & <u>her</u> name happens to be Griffiths too. —"

[The joke here, of course, must be that we understand long before Diana Parker that there cannot possibly be *two* Mrs. Griffiths arriving in Sanditon at the same time.]

A few lines more however, and the colour rushed into her Cheeks, & with much Perturbation she added — "The oddest thing that ever was! — a Miss Lambe too! — a young Westindian of large Fortune. — But it <u>cannot</u> be the same. — Impossible that it should be the same." —

[And now we are to believe that *two* Miss Lambes are coming to Sanditon. Miss Diana Parker cannot be praised for her intelligence.]

She read the Letter aloud for comfort. — It was merely to "introduce the Bearer, M^{rs}. G.— from Camberwell, & the three young Ladies under her care, to Miss D. P.'s notice. — M^{rs}. G. — being a stranger at Sanditon, was anxious for a respectable Introduction — & M^{rs}. C. Dupuis therefore, at the instance of the intermediate friend, provided her with this Letter, knowing that she c^{d}. not do her dear Diana a greater kindness than by giving her the means of being useful. Mrs G.'s cheif solicitude w^{d}. be for the accomodation & comfort of one of the young Ladies under her care, a Miss Lambe, a young W. Indian of large Fortune, in delicate health." —

[Here Jane Austen successfully incorporates indirect discourse into a letter.]

"It was very strange! — very remarkable! — very extraordinary" but they were all agreed in determing it to be <u>impossible</u> that there should not be two Families; such a totally distinct set of people as were concerned in the reports of each made that matter quite certain. There <u>must</u> be two Families. — Impossible to be otherwise. "Impossible" & "Impossible," was repeated over & over again with great fervour. — An accidental resemblance of Names & circumstances, however striking at first, involved nothing really incredible — and so it was settled. —

[Jane Austen here combines reported speech with narrative. The spelling "determing" suggests carelessness.]

Miss Diana herself derived an immediate advantage to counterbalance her Perplexity. She must put her shawl over her shoulders, & be running about again. Tired as she was, she must instantly repair to the Hotel, to investigate the truth & offer her Services. —

[Reference to Susan Parker as "Miss P." indicates that she is the elder of the two sisters. That Diana Parker is generally called "Miss Diana Parker" creates a distinction that Jane Austen's readers would pick up on immediately. Diana is described as "the cheif of the family; principal Mover & Actor" on the basis of her activity, not seniority. The occasional reference to "Susan" and "Arthur" is more likely from Diana Parker than from Charlotte, who has just met them.

Despite being told that Susan Parker talked incessantly, we never get a snippet of her conversation. Like Miss Denham, Miss Brereton, and Miss Lambe, she has no reported dialog.]

[Chapter 11]

It would not do. —

[Jane Austen has supplied an amazing opening line for her new chapter, perfectly summarizing Diana Parker's dismay and disbelief that she could have misunderstood how many groups are coming to Sanditon. But her "indomptible" self-confidence is merely shaken, not seriously threatened, and as is her practice she throws herself into minimizing the disaster.]

Not all that the whole Parker race could say among themselves, c^d. produce a happier catastrophee than that the Family from Surry & the Family from Camberwell were one & the same. — The rich Westindians, & the young Ladies Seminary had all entered Sanditon in those two Hack chaises.

[We shall soon learn that aside from Miss Lambe, only the Misses Beaufort—not her niece and daughters as Diana Parker assumed—have come with Mrs. Griffiths, well short of the anticipated large numbers.]

We have an unusual oxymoron in "happier catastrophee" if the second word is taken in its usual sense of "a sudden disaster" (*OED*), but the word can also mean merely a dénouement or "the change or revolution which produces the conclusion or final event of a dramatic piece" (*OED*). In other words, "outcome." Since the scene is so close to that of a play, the idea of the climax of a "dramatic piece" is appropriate.

Jane Austen had difficulty writing the word "catastrophe," probably spelling it originally as "catastraphe." She changed the incorrect "a" to "o" and then did something to the final "e" that could be an added second "e." There is possibly an acute accent over the first "e," but I read it as double "e" without an accent: "catastrophee."

In 1925, R.W. Chapman transcribed it as "catastrophe" (149), a spelling followed by R. Brimley Johnson in 1934 (69). It appears for the first time, apparently, as "catastrophée" in 1954/1988 (*OIJA*–VI: 420), and the *CUPLM* editors believe that "JA wrote 'catastrophée'" (674).

Teran Lee Sacco transcribes the word as "catastrophe{e}" (145). "Curly brackets indicate where Austen changes her mind about a word she wrote originally and writes directly on the first word or letters to make the change. The original reading is in the brackets and the later, superimposed revision appears either before or after the brackets" (xiii). If I correctly understand, she is saying that Jane Austen originally wrote "catastrophee" and changed it to "catastrophe."

The word appears twice in earlier novels, both times as "catastrophe."

> [As] Mrs. Norris depended on being the first person made acquainted with any fatal catastrophe, she had already arranged the manner of breaking it to all the others. (*Mansfield Park*)

> As to the sad catastrophe itself, it could be canvassed only in one style by a couple of steady, sensible women. (*Persuasion*).

What would we not give to find Jane Austen's original manuscripts so that we could see how she spelled this word before editors intervened?]

The M^rs. G. who in her friend M^rs. Darling's hands, had wavered as to coming & been unequal to the Journey, was the very same M^rs. G. whose plans were at the same period (under an other representation) perfectly decided, & who was without fears or difficulties. — All that had the appearance of Incongruiety in the reports of the two, might very fairly be placed to the account of the Vanity, the Ignorance, or the blunders of the many engaged in the cause by the vigilance & caution of Miss Diana P—.

[There is only one instance of "Incongruity" in an earlier novel.

> But he [Mr. Elton] had fancied her [Emma] in love with him;... and after raving a little about the seeming incongruity of gentle manners and a conceited head, Emma was obliged... to... admit that her own behaviour to him had been... complaisant.

For "Incongruiety"—my reading and that of the editors of *CUPLM* (534)— both R.W. Chapman and Teran Lee Sacco read "Incongruity." There is no way to know how Jane Austen spelled the word in the manuscript of *Emma*. If her spelling "Incongruiety" is based on how she pronounced the word, she may have rhymed it with "society."]

<u>Her</u> intimate friends must be officious like herself, & the subject had supplied Letters & Extracts & Messages enough to throw everything into confusion.

>

<u>Her</u> intimate friends must be officious like herself, & the subject had supplied Letters & Extracts & Messages enough to make everything appear what it was not.

[The assumption that Diana Parker's friends matched her in officiousness is Charlotte's reported thought. Our narrator continually interweaves her own commentary with that of the heroine.]

Miss D. probably felt a little awkward on being first obliged to admit her mistake. A long Journey from Hampshire taken for nothing — a Brother disappointed — a House on her hands for a week, must have been some of her immediate reflections — & much worse than all the rest, must have been a sort of sensation of being less clear-sighted & infallible than she had supposed.

>

A long Journey from Hampshire taken for nothing — a Brother disappointed — an expensive House on her hands for a week, must have been some of her immediate reflections — & much worse than all the rest, must have been the sort of sensation of being less clear-sighted & infallible than she had beleived herself. —

[We learn here for the first time that the Parker sisters and youngest brother reside in Hampshire, Jane Austen's own native county. The "Brother disappointed" is presumably Mr. Thomas Parker since Arthur Parker appears to have no special expectations in regard to Sanditon other than yet another place to eat and consume hot beverages. This long, complicated sentence is a good example of free indirect discourse blended with narrative.]

There is an interesting similarity between this passage and one in the shelved manuscript eventually published as *Northanger Abbey*.

> A sacrifice was always noble; and if she had given way to their entreaties, she should have been spared the distressing idea of a friend displeased, a brother angry, and a scheme of great happiness to both destroyed, perhaps through her means. To ease her mind, and ascertain by the opinion of an unprejudiced person what her own conduct had really been, she took occasion to mention before

> Mr. Allen the half-settled scheme of her brother and the Thorpes
> for the following day.]

No part of it however seemed to trouble her long. There were so many to share in the shame & the blame, that probably when she had divided out their proper portions to M^rs. Darling, Miss Capper, Fanny Noyce, M^rs. C. Dupuis & M^rs. C. D.'s Neighbour, there might be a mere trifle of reproach remaining for herself. —

At any rate, she was seen all the following morn^g. walking about after Lodgings with M^rs. G. — as alert as ever. —

[This skip in time is unusual in the manuscript, where most chapters are in real time. The plot is picking up its pace, and we can expect events to proceed rapidly now that all the major characters have been met or at least mentioned.]

M^rs. G. was a very well-behaved, genteel kind of Woman, who supported herself by giving a home to great girls & young Ladies, who wanted either Masters for finishing their Education, or a home for beginning their Displays. —
>
M^rs. G. was a very well-behaved, genteel kind of Woman, who supported herself by receiving such great girls & young Ladies, as wanted either Masters for finishing their Education, or a home for beginning their Displays.

["Great girls" is not a comment on their corpulence but on the maturity level of these students, who are not yet classified as "young Ladies." "Great Girls—I have always taken this to mean gawky overgrown teenage girls, at the stage between childhood and young womanhood. Since for JA young womanhood started it would seem at about 17, when they were considered marriageable, then I would guess she considered Great Girls to be, say, 13–16, depending upon the individual's development. See Catherine Morland: 'At fifteen, appearances were mending;…' and so on to end of sentence.— and later on, specifying she is growing up into a heroine between ages 15 and 17" (Le Faye, 2010). The *OED* has somehow missed this phrase, which Jane Austen had used earlier in *Emma*, where "Mr. Elton [was] the adoration of all the teachers and great girls in the school."

The masculine version of the phrase occurs in *Emma*—"Harriet was soon assailed by half a dozen children, headed by a stout woman and a great boy"—with the more likely meaning of "corpulent" or at least "large."

This odd phrasing "as wanted"—deliberately created through a simple revision—is almost certainly Mrs. Griffiths' reported speech, so without even meeting her we know that despite being well-behaved and "genteel," she is not well educated. Young ladies were sent to such schools to "begin their displays," that is, to learn "music, dancing and drawing which would assist in their gaining husbands" (*CUPLM*: 674). The Misses Beaufort attempt the sketchpad and the harp, but we know nothing about their accomplishments on the dance floor, where a young Jane Austen spent many happy evenings.]

She had several more under her care than the three who were now come to Sanditon, but the others all happened to be absent. —

[Jane Austen piques our curiosity about the other young ladies under Mrs. Griffiths' care, who perhaps eventually arrive at Sanditon en masse to supply a bride for every eligible bachelor.]

Of these three, & indeed of all, Miss Lambe was beyond comparison the most important & precious, as she paid in proportion to her fortune. — She was about 17, half Mulatto, chilly & tender, had a maid of her own, was to have the best room in the Lodgings, & was always of the first consequence in every plan of M^{rs}. G. —

["Half Mulatto" may be Jane Austen's way of saying "Mulatto," that is, with one white and one black parent. Or she may be technically specific in reporting that one of Miss Lambe's parents is a mulatto and her other parent is white, so that she is a "Quadroon" or "Quarteroon." "The unusual identifier 'half mulatto' might indicate Austen's ignorance of the racial nomenclature of her time" (Salih: 352). The brief account of her is probably a rough sketch of Mrs. Griffiths' conversation with Diana Parker, whose report to her family may be summarized here in the text, perhaps reflecting a desire on the part of one of the women to minimize Miss Lambe's racial difference by calling her only a half mulatto. Or the unusual phrase may be just part of a redundant speech pattern.

In the period under discussion, the descriptors applying to people of mixed origin were... multifarious[,]... "West Indian" [being] used almost uniquely to describe inhabitants of the Caribbean who were of European origin or descent." (Salih: 333)

The imprecision of contemporary terminology allows Austen to play a joke on the unsuspecting reader. Up until this point in the narrative, only the term "West Indian" (along with its various corruptions by the ignorant Lady Denham) has been used to describe Miss Lambe and her non-existent family. Since, in this context, "West Indian" is a non-racial designator, the discussions preceding Miss Lambe's arrival would not have prepared the reader for the introduction of a "half mulatto," chilly, tender, or otherwise. Editing *Sanditon* more than a hundred and fifty years later in 1975, Margaret Drabble certainly seems to have been caught unawares. "I cannot help but comment on the extraordinary effect of the phrase 'half mulatto, chilly and tender,'" she remarks in an effusive endnote: "It is as though one had entered into another world. Who would ever have thought that Miss Lambe would prove to be half mulatto? And yet Jane Austen states the fact with the utmost calm. As for 'chilly and tender,' the words refer presumably to her state of health and response to the English climate, but if they were intended to describe her emotional nature, what an interesting character she might have proved." Drabble's reaction is instructive, for it highlights a critical tendency (dominant at least until the late 1970s, possibly into the early 1980s) to divorce broader social and political concerns from the apparently self-enclosed communities that Austen so succinctly describes. (Salih: 335–336)

"Half mulatto" (adopted so unquestioningly by twentieth-century writers, critics, and editors) is highly specific, perhaps without precedent. The phrase may indicate an awareness on Austen's part of contemporary codifications of "race," but the designator is not used in any of the fictional or non-fictional sources I have consulted.... Not one of these commentators uses the term "half mulatto" to describe the child of a mulatto woman and a white man. Unsurprisingly, no definition appears in *OED* for "half mulatto," whereas "quadroon" is defined as "one who is the offspring of a white person and a mulatto; one who has a quarter of Negro blood" (Salih: 337).

Mulatto and quadroon girls receiving their education in England could pass for white.... As for what the future might have held for Miss Lambe: some coloured girls did remain in England to marry white men, so Lady Denham's idea of making a match between Miss Lambe and Sir Edward Denham is not altogether out of the question.... Apparently, all that is required for social acceptance is a fortune large enough to pay for one's chronic medical condition. (Salih: 350-351)

Almost as intriguing is Miss Lambe's maid, a personal amenity far beyond the means of the two Misses Beaufort. The text never informs us if she was hired locally in Camberwell or if, as is more likely, she was already in the Lambe household employ before her young mistress was shipped off to England from an undisclosed homeland—Antigua according to Anne Telscombe's continuation or Barbados if Julia Barrett got it right in her continuation. In neither instance is it likely that she would have played a significant role in the comedy-drama of Sanditon, in part because Jane Austen was not interested in the lives of people on this low social order. However, her mentioning the maid could be a hint that yet another surprise—and the manuscript is filled with them—is in store for us. "The Unexpected" could well have served as a title to describe what she succeeded in producing during those few fleeting weeks between January and March of 1817.

Although the text of *Mansfield Park* is never explicit, there must have been mulattos and "half mulattos" among the slaves owned by Sir Thomas Bertram in Antigua. Following his address, "Jane Austen, Coleridge and Geopolitics," at the 1996 Annual General Meeting of the Jane Austen Society held in Chawton, Paul Johnson opened the floor to discussion, and at that time either someone in the audience or Mr. Johnson himself threw out the idea that Henry and Mary Crawford may be mulatto or to some degree of mixed racial origin, citing as textual support:

Miss Crawford's beauty did her no disservice with the Miss Bertrams. They were too handsome themselves to dislike any woman for being so too, and were almost as much charmed as their brothers with her lively dark eye, clear brown complexion, and general prettiness. Her brother was not handsome: no, when they first saw him he was absolutely plain, black and plain; but still he was the gentleman, with a pleasing address.

However, Jane Austen elsewhere uses similar words in situations where racial distinctions are not involved. In a letter to Cassandra dated Tuesday, June 11, 1799, she asserts "that Mr Elliott is handsomer than Mr. Lance— that fair Men are preferable to Black" (*Letters*: 44–45). And in *Northanger Abbey* we have an exchange between Isabella and Catherine on preferences in their male suitors:

> "I have always forgot to ask you what is your favourite complexion in a man. Do you like them best dark or fair?"

> "I hardly know. I never much thought about it. Something between both, I think. Brown—not fair, and—and not very dark."

> "Very well, Catherine. That is exactly he. I have not forgot your description of Mr. Tilney—'a brown skin, with dark eyes, and rather dark hair.'"

Precisely what Mr. Darcy likes about Elizabeth Bennet is unclear since she works very hard to irk him in every way, but entirely without volition and very much against his instincts he finds himself drawn to "the beautiful expression of her dark eyes." A person's temperament can be the source of a color used for description, as in *Persuasion* we learn that Captain Harville is a "tall, dark man" without possible reference to his race.

I recall no comment from anyone at the AGM on this suggestion about the Crawfords, and I am not aware of anything that has been published on the matter.

Miss Lambe's being "about 17" is Mrs. Griffiths' estimate since the narrator would know her precise age. The phrase "chilly and tender" may be taken from the clown Lavache (*All's Well that Ends Well*, IV, v): "but the many will be too chill and tender" (Keith: 99). Miss Lambe is the most exotic creature found anywhere in Jane Austen's extant work.]

The other Girls, two Miss Beauforts were just such young Ladies as may be met with, in at least one family out of three, throughout the Kingdom;

[The *OED* recognizes, with a preference, two different ways to refer to unmarried sisters: "When the title is applied to several persons of the same name at once, usage sanctions two forms, viz. *the Misses Smith* and *the Miss Smiths*, the former being regarded as the more formal."]

they had tolerable complexions, shewey figures, an upright decided carriage & an assured Look; — they were very accomplished & very Ignorant, their time being divided between such pursuits as might attract admiration, & those Labours & Expedients of dexterous Ingenuity, by which they could dress in a stile much beyond what they <u>ought</u> to have afforded; they were some of the first in every change of fashion — & the object of all, was to captivate some Man of much better fortune than their own. —

[The angry, certainly at least dismissive, tone here is not entirely in keeping with the rest of the manuscript. But the passage makes clear that the theme of the novel, like all those preceding it, is to find and seize a mate, preferably one of greater fortune and social standing. Love must be tempered with practicality.]

M^rs. G. had preferred a small, retired place, like Sanditon, on Miss Lambe's account — and the Miss Bs — , though naturally preferring any thing to Smallness & Retirement, yet having in the course of the Spring been involved in the inevitable expence of six new Dresses each for a three days visit, were constrained to be satisfied with Sanditon also, till their circumstances were retreived.

[The "three days visit" preceded this journey to Sanditon since there is no indication that Mrs. Griffiths plans to remain here for such a short time. We never learn if the two young ladies have brought all their new dresses with them.]

There, with the hire of a Harp for one, & the purchase of some Drawing paper for the other & all the finery they could already command, they meant to be very economical, very elegant & very retired; with the hope on Miss Beaufort's side, of praise & celebrity with all who walked within the sound of her Instrument, & on Miss Letitia's, of curiosity & rapture in all who came near her while she sketched — and to Both, the consolation of meaning to be the most stylish Girls in the Place. —
>
There, with the hire of a Harp for one, & the purchase of some Drawing paper for the other & all the finery they could already command, they meant to be very economical, very elegant & very secluded; with the hope on Miss Beaufort's side, of praise & celebrity from all who walked within the sound of her Instrument, & on Miss Letitia's, of curiosity & rapture in

all who came near her while she sketched — and to Both, the consolation of meaning to be the most stylish Girls in the Place. —

[Both the harp and the drawing paper could have been obtained from Mrs. Whitby's circulating library, which also served as a general goods store (*CUPLM*: 674).

Music and art, of course, are the traditional and requisite accomplishments of any well-bred young lady, although neither Charlotte Heywood nor her earlier avatar, Catherine Morland, can claim any skill in these endeavors:

> Her mother wished her to learn music; and Catherine was sure she should like it, for she was very fond of tinkling the keys of the old forlorn spinner; so, at eight years old she began. She learnt a year, and could not bear it; and Mrs. Morland, who did not insist on her daughters being accomplished in spite of incapacity or distaste, allowed her to leave off. The day which dismissed the music-master was one of the happiest of Catherine's life. Her taste for drawing was not superior; though whenever she could obtain the outside of a letter from her mother or seize upon any other odd piece of paper, she did what she could in that way, by drawing houses and trees, hens and chickens, all very much like one another.

The formal distinction is again made between the elder sister—Miss Beaufort—and her inferior younger sibling—Miss Letitia. Unfortunately, as we learned in an earlier passage when Charlotte and the Parkers arrive at Sanditon, sounds of harps are already emanating from upstairs rooms and ladies are already out on their stools sketching landscapes endlessly in the hope of drawing admiring looks from honorable bachelors in search of brides or young blades in pursuit of conquests. But so far the pickings are slim this summer with only Sir Edward Denham and Arthur Parker on the scene. The arrival of Sidney Parker, perhaps accompanied by some other young bachelors, will change the dynamics.

Some level of musical accomplishment was considered essential for young ladies, through their prowess winning admirers who could fantasize about long evenings of civilized entertainment. Occasionally an unconventional instrument, such as the cello or guitar, formed part of a young woman's arsenal in her search for a husband, but the most popular instruments were the keyboard and the harp (Olsen: 454, 455). Whereas the piano could be tackled without charges of his being effete—after all, Europe was resounding with encomia of dazzling performances by Mozart, Beethoven, Hummel, and Czerny—by a young gentleman so that he could accompany a young lady in duets or, more to his liking, entertain his friends with the latest rollicking, rowdy lyrics, the harp was the exclusive domain of the Fair Sex (Shapard: 87).

Although many of Jane Austen's secondary heroines, like Marianne Dashwood and Jane Fairfax, are talented pianists, a few—perhaps none more than Mary Crawford—have developed their skills on the harp. Mary chooses well in speaking of it in her campaign to draw Edmund Bertram's favorable attention:

> Edmund spoke of the harp as his favourite instrument, and hoped to be soon allowed to hear her.

> . . .

> The harp arrived, and rather added to her beauty, wit, and good-humour; for she played with the greatest obligingness, with an expression and taste which were peculiarly becoming, and there was something clever to be said at the close of every air. Edmund was at the Parsonage every day, to be indulged with his favourite instrument: one morning secured an invitation for the next; for the lady could not be unwilling to have a listener, and every thing was soon in a fair train.

> A young woman, pretty, lively, with a harp as elegant as herself, and both placed near a window, cut down to the ground, and opening on a little lawn, surrounded by shrubs in the rich foliage of summer, was enough to catch any man's heart.

It was considered a particularly graceful and feminine instrument, permitting young ladies to show off their unique charms. The shape of the instrument, with its balanced curves, complemented the figure even more than walking about the room, a fashionable woman's stratagem.

> (Mr. Darcy:) "You either choose this method of passing the evening because you are in each other's confidence, and have secret affairs to discuss, or because you are conscious that your figures appear to the greatest advantage in walking; if the first, I would be completely

in your way, and if the second, I can admire you much better as I sit by the fire."

The upright sitting position and occasional bending and swaying lent a sexual tension to what otherwise would be an impeccably chaste performance. And what better opportunity was there to show off perfectly shaped hands, used for nothing more demanding than needlework? The harp is an ancient instrument, but the substantial improvements made by Sébastien Érard (1752-1831), such as extending the range by allowing the flat, natural, and sharp notes to be played on each string, increased its appeal (Olsen: 458).

Drawing, the other requisite skill for a young lady in pursuit of a husband, is only occasionally seen as an accomplishment of one of the major Jane Austen heroines. Elinor Dashwood enjoys sketching, as does Emma Woodhouse, but it never plays the dominant role assigned to music. Jane Austen herself, a good pianist, apparently had no talents in this art form, one in which her elder sister Cassandra excelled.

As we should expect, the heroine of *Mansfield Park* is far above these mundane pursuits:

"But I must tell you another thing of Fanny, so odd and so stupid. Do you know, she says she does not want to learn either music or drawing."

We have yet to learn if Charlotte Heywood has any artistic leanings, but it is safe to assume that Clara Brereton can both play an instrument and draw, since these skills would help her pursue her original future as a nursery maid or perhaps even as a governess. Miss Esther Denham, I suspect, would like Miss Anne De Bourgh play excellently if not for the misfortune of "a sickly constitution, which has prevented her from making that progress in many accomplishments which she could not have otherwise failed of."

If any of the young gentlemen draw, they obviously keep this talent very much to themselves, since hunting and fishing were the manly exercises of the day.]

The particular introduction of M^rs. G. to Miss Diana Parker, secured them immediately an acquaintance with the Trafalgar House-family, & with the Denhams; — and the Miss Beauforts were soon satisfied with the Circle in which they moved to use a proper phrase, for every body must now "move in a Circle", — the prevalence of which rototary Motion, is perhaps to be attributed the Giddiness & false steps of many. —

\>

The particular introduction of M^rs. G. to Miss Diana Parker, secured them immediately an acquaintance with the Trafalgar House-family, & with the Denhams; — and the Miss Beauforts were soon satisfied with "the Circle in which they moved in Sanditon" to use a proper phrase, for every body must now "move in a Circle", — to the prevalence of which rototary Motion, is perhaps to be attributed the Giddiness & false steps of many. —

[The quoted material—"the Circle in which they moved in Sanditon… [like] every body… mov[ing] in a Circle"—is clearly indirect discourse, either part of the Beaufort girls' conversation or taken from a letter home to their hopeful parents, who have invested in their education and travels with hopes of advantageous marriages.

"Rototary" for "rotatory" probably reflects the author's incorrect pronunciation of the word and her failure to recognize its relation to "rotate."

R.W. Chapman (154) and *OI* VI (422) read the word as "rototory," and Teran Lee Sacco (150) reads it as "rotatary." R. Brimley Johnson (71) corrects it to "rotatory" as does Another Lady (67). *CUPLM* reads the word as "rototory" in the diplomatic transcription (539) but prints it as "rotatory" in the text (203). *CUPLM* notes that "Cassandra's copy has 'rotatory'" (674).

The word—spelled correctly or otherwise—appears nowhere else in Jane Austen's novels. It is tempting but misguided to suggest that her spelling is based on "rotor," a shortened version of "rotator" that did not appear in the language until 1873 (*OED*).]

Lady Denham had other motives for calling on M^rs. G. besides attention to the Parkers. — In Miss Lambe, here was the very young Lady, sickly & rich, whom she had been asking for; & she made the acquaintance for Sir Edward's sake, & the sake of her Milch asses.

[Linking Sir Edward and Lady Denham's asses cannot be accidental. Sadly, Jane Austen chose not to name him Nick.]

How it might answer with regard to the Baronet, remained to be proved, but as to the Animals, she soon found that all her calculations of Profit w^d.

be vain. M^{rs}. G. would not allow Miss L. to have the smallest symptom of a Decline, or any complaint which Asses milk c^d. possibly releive.

[A "Decline" was "not merely a general failure of health, but a more specific disease, such as tuberculosis, in which the bodily strength gradually fails" (*CUPLM*: 674)]

"Miss L. was under the constant care of an experienced Physician; — and his Prescriptions must be their rule" — and except in favour of some Tonic Pills, which a Cousin of her own had a Property in, M^{rs}. G. did never deviate from the strict Medecinal page. —

[Having a "Property" in something meant an investment for profit (*CUPLM*: 674). Jane Austen is silent on Lady Denham's reaction to this rebuff (written as indirect discourse), but her language upon returning to her own residence may have been such that it could not in all decorum be repeated. Mrs. Griffiths has already set herself up to take advantage of Miss Lambe's medical problems and has no intention of sharing the profits with an outsider. "Medecinal," like "rototary" and some other odd spellings, may reflect Jane Austen's pronunciation of the word, in this instance perhaps influenced by the French, "le médecin." Alternatively, because the passage is in part indirect discourse, it could record Mrs. Griffiths' affected speech.]

The corner house of the Terrace was the one in which Miss D. P. had the pleasure of settling her new friends, & considering that it commanded in front the favourite Lounge of all the Visitors at Sanditon, & on one side, whatever might be going on at the Hotel, there c^d. not have been a more favourable spot for the seclusions of the Miss Beauforts.

[A "Lounge," at that time "a place for strolling or lounging about" (*CUPLM*: 675), has come in more modern English to mean a room in which one lounges or the American equivalent of "living room" or "family room." The Misses Beaufort have elected a very public site for their seclusions.]

And indeed, long before they had suited themselves with an Instrument, or Drawing paper, they had, by the frequency of their appearance at the low Windows upstairs, in order to close the blinds, or open the Blinds, or arrange a flower pot on the Balcony, or look at nothing through a Telescope, attracted many eye upwards, & made many a Gazer gaze again. —
>

And indeed, long before they had suited themselves with an Instrument, or Drawing paper, they had, by the frequency of their appearance at the low Windows upstairs, in order to close the blinds, or open the Blinds, to arrange a flower pot on the Balcony, or look at nothing through a Telescope, attracted many an eye upwards, & made many a Gazer gaze again. —

>

And accordingly, long before they had suited themselves with an Instrument, or with Drawing paper, they had, by the frequency of their appearance at the low Windows upstairs, in order to close the blinds, or open the Blinds, to arrange a flower pot on the Balcony, or look at nothing through a Telescope, attracted many an eye upwards, & made many a Gazer gaze again. —

["In Georgian houses the living-rooms were often on the first floor, with large or full-length windows through which the occupants could see and—as here—be seen, and a balcony outside" (*CUPLM*: 675). "The astronomical discoveries of William Henschel... and his sister Caroline, did much to make astronomy popular in the early years of the nineteenth century as a pastime for both men and women" (*CUPLM*: 675). This appears to be the sole appearance of the word "telescope" in Jane Austen's novels. "Many eye" of the earliest version of this line is probably really "Many eyes" with the final "s" overwritten by the following word.]

A little Novelty has a great effect in so small a place; the Miss Beauforts, who w^d. have been nothing at Brighton, could not move here without being noticed; — and even M^r. Arthur Parker, though little disposed by habit for supernumerary exertion, always went out at this end of the Terrace, in his walk to Trafalgar H. by this corner House, for the sake of a glimpse of the Miss Bs —, though it was 1/2 a q^r. of a mile-about, & added two steps to the ascent of the Hill.

>

A little Novelty has a great effect in so small a place; the Miss Beauforts, who w^d. have been nothing at Brighton, could not move here without notice; — and even M^r. Arthur Parker, though little disposed for supernumerary exertion, always quitted the Terrace, in his way to his Brothers by this corner House, for the sake of a glimpse of the Miss Bs —, though it was 1/2 a q^r. of a mile round about, & added two steps to the ascent of the Hill.

[*CUPLM* transcribes the word as "noticed" (542) but prints it as "notice" in the text (204). Jane Austen's deletion of the final "d" after changing the phrase is usually bold, a heavy vertical line (page 110, folio 55v).]

Nothing can speak more cogently to the charm of these two young ladies than Arthur Parker's going so far out of his way to observe them at their window, either opening or closing, arranging, looking (at nothing), or otherwise drawing the gaze of amorous Gazers, among them the youngest Parker.

Jane Austen in being so harsh with the Beaufort sisters may be inveighing more against the society that has forced them into this situation than the young ladies themselves. With very little education and probably a modest dowry apiece, they are doomed to find a wealthy husband or fade into rejected spinsterhood.

This chapter is much more complex in time sequence than the others. It begins the preceding day with the shocking discovery that the two expected parties are one, proceeds to Diana Parker's meeting with Mrs. Griffiths, follows with Lady Denham's unsuccessful attempt to make a profit out of Miss Lambe's fragile state, and concludes with an undisclosed length of time during which Arthur Parker learns about the Beaufort girls and takes several atypical walks to steal a brief look at them. Romance is in the air!]

[Chapter 12]

Chap: 12.

Charlotte had been 10 days at Sanditon without seeing Sanditon House, every attempt at calling on Lady D. having been defeated by meeting with her beforehand. But now it was to be more resolutely undertaken, at a more early hour, that nothing might be neglected of attention to Lady D. or amusement to Charlotte. —

[We finally learn something specific about time lapse in "10 days," only part of which has been specifically accounted for. Jane Austen makes a point of Lady Denham's preferring to visit to being visited, no doubt to avoid having to offer tea to her guests. As during the Parkers' two-week sojourn with the Heywoods there is no reference to church attendance, so again there is nothing about it during this 10-day period. But the social leaders of the community, like Lady Denham and Mr. Thomas Parker, must have made it their responsibility to appear in church every Sunday, and Charlotte would have accompanied them. Lady Denham would claim the most important pew, and her friends might join her in that exalted site.

"More early" appears in no earlier novel, where the standard and expected "earlier" is consistently used.

> You had better come earlier another time.
> Mrs. Jennings left them earlier than usual.
> (*Sense and Sensibility*)

> I shall entreat his pardon for not having done it earlier.
> . . . which perhaps I ought to have mentioned earlier.
> (*Pride and Prejudice*)

> . . . the evil would have been earlier remedied.
> . . . his eldest son had duties to call him earlier home.
> (*Mansfield Park*)

... with the eagerness to arrive which had made him alter his plan,
and travel earlier, later, and quicker.
They would have solicited the honour earlier.
(*Emma*)

... would have bestowed earlier prosperity than could be reasonably
calculated on.
... to find that no earlier day could be fixed.
(*Persuasion*)

... had Thorpe, who joined her just afterwards, been half a minute
earlier.
... it would be only her retiring to dress half an hour earlier than
usual.
(*Northanger Abbey*)]

"And if you should find a favourable opening my Love, said M^r. P. (who did
not mean to go with them) — I think you had mention the poor Mullins's
situation, & sound her Ladyship as to a Subscription for them.
>
"And if you should find a favourable opening my Love, said M^r. P. (who did
not mean to go with them) — I think you had better mention the poor
Mullins's situation, & sound her Ladyship as to a Subscription for them.

[We come into the middle of a conversation, just as though the curtain has
parted and we are entering a domestic scene on stage.

In "had mention" we have another obvious error in transcription. "A
subscription was an arrangement whereby people signed up to make a
specific contribution to a worthy cause" (*CUPLM*: 675).]

I am not fond of charitable subscriptions in a place of this kind — It is a sort
of tax upon all that come — Yet as their distress is very great & I almost
promised the poor Woman yesterday to get something done for her, I
beleive we must set a subscription on foot & therefore the sooner the better,
— & Lady Denham's name at the head of the List will be a very necessary
beginning. — You will not dislike speaking to her about it, Mary? —"

[That Lady Denham's name would be the first on such a list, as in the
Subscription Book in Mrs. Whitby's library, is a convincing argument to

induce her to participate in this effort. Jane Austen continues to favor litotic phrases like "not dislike."]

"I will do whatever you wish me, replied his Wife — but you would do it so much better yourself. I shall not know what to say." —

"My dear Mary, cried he, it is impossible you can be really at a loss.

Nothing can be simple.
>
Nothing can be more simple.

[The original reading is so unidiomatic that it must be a transcription error.]

You have only to state the present afflicted situation of the family, their earnest application to me, & my being willing to promote a little subscription for their releif, provided it meet with her approbation." —

"The easiest thing in the World — cried Miss Diana Parker who happened to be calling on them at the moment —. All said & done, in less time that you have been talking of it now. — And while you are on the subject of subscriptions Mary, I will thank you to mention a very melancholy case to Lady D, which has been represented to me in the most affecting terms. — There is a poor Woman in Worcesteshire, whom some friends of mine are exceedingly interested about, & I have undertaken to collect whatever I can for her. If you w^d. mention the circumstance to Lady Denham! — Lady Denham <u>can</u> give, if she is properly attacked — & I look upon her to be the sort of Person who, when once she is prevailed on to undraw her Purse, would as readily give 10 ^{Gs} as 5. — And therefore, if you find her in a Giving mood, you might as well speak in favour of another Charity which I & a few more, have very much at heart — the establishment of a Charitable Repository at Burton on Trent. — And then, — there is the family of the poor Man who was hung last assizes at York, tho' we really <u>have</u> raised the sum we wanted for putting them all out, yet if you <u>can</u> get a Guinea from her on their behalf, it may as well be done. —"

[The geographical range of Diana Parker's philanthropy is impressive if she has managed to keep track of events as far away as Burton upon Trent, Worcestershire, and York, all well to the north of Diana Parker's home in Hampshire and even more distant from the Sussex coast. To expect Lady

Denham to "undraw," that is, "unfasten by pulling" (*CUPLM*: 675), her purse—especially to aid faraway strangers—tells us that Diana Parker does not well know the great lady of Sanditon.

A "charitable repository... the precursor of the modern-day charity shop, [w]as a place where donated goods were sold for the benefit of the poor" (*CUPLM*: 676). Burton upon Trent, a major brewery town in eastern Staffordshire, produces foodstuffs, hosiery, knitting machines, and steel goods. In Jane Austen's time it boasted "about 4000 inhabitants" (*CUPLM*: 675).

We never learn for what crime "the poor Man was hung," but this extreme punishment was meted out for a wide range of misdeeds, including smuggling (Borer: 64), a popular activity at the time because of very high import duties, along with "sheep stealing,... stealing something worth more than five shillings from a shop,... doing damage to Westminster Bridge, and about two hundred other offenses" (Pool: 134).

Diana Parker's "hung" for "hanged" was probably a common error then as it is now— the form "hanged" to mean "put to death by hanging by the neck" was in use from as early as 1470, and "in this sense, *hanged* is now the specific form of the pa. tense and pa. pple.; though *hung* is used by some, esp. in the south of England" (*OED*)—and it may not be part of the author's attempt to suggest a poor education. The form "hung" appears frequently in the novels but always as the past tense of "to hang" in a sense other than to be executed. Nowhere else in the novels is anyone unfortunate—or foolish—enough to be either hung or hanged. This may be the only reference anywhere in the novels to capital punishment, a dark moment in what is otherwise meant to be a lighthearted romp. Jane Austen has indeed entered a new century if she has any concern with the impossibly draconian penal laws of the time.

Assizes are "the sessions held periodically in each county of England, for the purpose of administering civil and criminal justice, by judges acting under certain special commissions (chiefly and usually, but not exclusively, being ordinary judges of the superior courts)" (*OED*).

The great walled city of York, located 175 miles north of London in Yorkshire, has long been a major manufacturing center. There is no evidence that Jane Austen ever traveled to this part of England. Her geographical references in this passage range farther from home than in earlier novels, with only "York" being used previously to convey the idea of a great distance:

"Aye, there she comes," continued Mrs. Bennet, "looking as unconcerned as may be, and caring no more for us than if we were at York, provided she can have her own way."

"Putting them all out" means "setting them up in apprenticeships or other ways of earning their own livings, which would require an initial premium to be paid on their behalf" (*CUPLM*: 676).]

"My dear Diana! exclaimed M^rs. P. — I could no more mention these things to Lady D. — than I c^d. fly." —

[Clearly for Mary Parker the most impossible thing imaginable would be her flying. In 1903, less than 100 years later, on December 17 (the day after Jane Austen's birthday!), the Wright brothers made the impossible happen.]

"Where's the difficulty? — I wish I could go with you myself — but in 5 minutes I must be at M^rs. G.— to encourage Miss Lambe in taking her first Dip.

[The morning hours, before any food had been consumed, were generally considered the best time to enjoy the new health cure.]

She is so frightened, poor Thing, that I promised to come & keep up her Spirits, & go in the Machine with her if she wished it — and as soon as that is all over, I must hurry home, for Susan is to have Leaches today which will be a three hours business, — therefore I really have not a moment to spare — besides that (besides
>
She is so frightened, poor Thing, that I promised to come & keep up her Spirits, & go in the Machine with her if she wished it — and as soon as that is all over, I must hurry home, for Susan is to have Leaches today which will be a three hours business, — therefore I really have not a moment to spare — besides that (between ourselves) I ought to be in bed myself at this present time, for I am hardly able to stand — and when the Leaches have done, I dare say we shall both go to our rooms for the rest of the day." —
>
She is so frightened, poor Thing, that I promised to come & keep up her Spirits, & go in the Machine with her if she wished it — and as soon as that is over, I must hurry home, for Susan is to have Leaches at one oclock which will be a three hours business, — therefore I really have not a moment to

401

spare — besides that (between ourselves) I ought to be in bed myself at this present time, for I am hardly able to stand — and when the Leaches have done, I dare say we shall both go to our rooms for the rest of the day." —

[The first version with the repeated "besides" is probably another instance of erroneous transcription.

There can be no surprise in Diana Parker's applying to Miss Lambe the same epithet that has become inextricably linked to her youngest brother's name. For her everyone is "poor" and hence in need of her unsolicited assistance.

The bathing machine was from an early date an essential part of the new practice of entering the sea for health and exercise.

> Bathing was a serious business, to be undertaken under medical supervision, with formality and attention to decorum. One hired a bathing-machine, in which one could disrobe privately, which was pulled into the water by a horse, and from which one could descend into the water under cover of a hood—all in strict seclusion. (Craik: 13)

The process was much more complicated than the current practice of merely running down to the shoreline and plunging into the oncoming waves with a shout of abandon. Without the assistance of the bathing machine, women in particular were unable to enjoy any of the salutary effects of the new panacea.

> If one wanted to swim in the sea one climbed into one of these things, which were basically large covered wagons attached to a horse who towed one out into several feet of water. There one was assisted down the steps and into the sea by a frequently unsober female attendant. This was after undressing inside the machines, which were small, uncomfortable, badly ventilated, and poorly lit, the only light coming from tiny openings placed high up to deter voyeurs. (Pool: 266)

> The bather climbed fully clothed into a wooden hut on wheels and undressed while a horse pulled the machine into the sea and turned it round so that the door was facing away from the beach. The water

was now lapping round the steps and one could descend straight into it. (Howell: 21)

A contemporary account, however, reports that the procedure was slightly different:

> You have never seen one of these machines—Image to yourself a small, snug, wooden chamber, fixed upon a wheel-carriage, having a door at each end, and on each side a little window above, a bench below—The bather, ascending into this apartment by wooden steps, shuts himself in, and begins to undress, while the attendant yokes a horse to the end next the sea, and draws the carriage forwards, till the surface of the water is on a level with the floor of the dressing-room, then he moves and fixes the horse to the other end—The person within, being stripped, opens the door to the sea-ward, where he finds the guide ready, and plunges head-long into the water—After having bathed, he re-ascends into the apartment, by the steps which had been shifted for that purpose, and puts on his clothes at his leisure, while the carriage is drawn back again upon the dry land; so that he has nothing further to do, but to open the door, and come down as he went up—

(Smollett: Volume II, 178–179)

Moving the horse from one end to the other while in the water would not be easy, but it sounds safer than attempting to turn the machine around while partly submerged. If this is how it worked, the machine would have a door at both ends and movable steps. It is unclear how many people are employed in this complicated process.

There are many contemporary illustrations of the bathing huts, the dippers, and their clients, with a particularly good one in Ivor Brown's *Jane Austen and Her World* (18–19). We see not only a trembling young woman being pulled into the sea by two rather fearsome dippers, but nearby another young woman appears to be swimming on her own, evidence that sea swimming along with sea bathing was practiced. The drawing may also establish that after pulling the hut into the water, the horse was unhitched and taken to the shore-side to return to the beach. In this illustration the man handling the horse is riding, not walking alongside the horse. The bathing machine seen in Ivor Brown's illustration has four enormous wheels. This description of the process casts doubt on another reported scenario: "The bathing machine was backed from the beach into the ocean.... After a dip, clients once more entered the machine to change clothes as the box was drawn back on to the beach by a reliable man who carefully guided the horse" (Laudermilk: 200).

Most of the first-time participants would have been terrified of this new experience since the sudden immersion was accompanied by the constant motion of the surrounding water. Few of the women would have been able to swim, so the best that they could do was cling for dear life to a rope. "In the water one either swam or hung onto the rope attached to the machine while the waves washed over one" (Pool: 266). Any possibility of male chivalry, along with the temptations to view young ladies in wet attire, was eliminated since "men and women swam many yards apart—partly because men swam nude until the 1870s" (Pool: 266).

Especially designed for female visitors, "the bathing machines proved indispensable and were to be found at every seaside resort. Some of the bathing women, or 'dippers,' became well known legends in their own time" (Sutherland 1997: 64). Dippers and bathing-women "helped the bathers undress in the machines and then, carrying out the instructions of Dr. Russell, they would grab them by the shoulders, and in spite of shrieks and pleadings, completely submerge them two or three times in the sea" (Howell: 24). If this was indeed the practice at Sanditon, it is easy to understand why Miss Lambe was so transfixed with fear from the experience.

Some of the women employed to service the machines became famous. Martha Gunn (born 1776), most notably, "was a landmark of Brighton and, as it says on her gravestone, 'particularly distinguished as a bather in this town for nearly seventy years'" (Howell: 24). A friend of the Prince of Wales, Martha Gunn can be seen in a portrait painted in 1796 by John Russell formerly hanging in the tea-room of the Royal Pavilion (present location uncertain), and it is believed that she lived in a house still standing in central Brighton at 36 East Street, not far from the seafront.

She died on May 2, 1815 (her grave is in the southeast corner of St. Nicholas's Churchyard in Brighton), and perhaps that sad event triggered Jane Austen's interest in the subject. More information— including four illustrations (Martha Gunn holding the "Prince of Wales" as a baby, although they did not meet until he was a young adult; her gravestone; bathing machines)—on the remarkable Martha Gunn can be found at:

http://www.womenofbrighton.co.uk/marthagunn.htm.

It is difficult to establish a secure date for when these devices were first used. Sarah Howell (11) reports that in *Letters of a Gentleman from Scarborough*, 1734, John Setterington "shows the first recorded bathing-machine. It is the little pavilion with four wheels and a pointed roof parked at the water's edge. A naked gentleman is descending from it into the waves while a door is held open for him by a liveried servant." Because Margate was so popular for sea bathing, its being "the first place to use bathing-machines, in 1750" (Le Faye 2002: 66), might have legitimized the "bathing-machine [as] an absolutely essential part of taking a dip" (Howell: 21). Indirectly, the popularity of these devices helped to maintain the essential division existing among social classes, as the high price of renting the bathing machines "must have had the effect of ensuring that bathing was a pastime only for prosperous visitors, and of keeping undesirable locals off the beaches" (Howell: 23).

Some commentators, however, assign a slightly later date for its invention.

> The year in which Dr. Russell moved to Brighton [1753] saw the advent of a device whose effect upon the life and aspect of our beaches was to be incalculable, and which was to remain almost unmodified for nearly a century and a half. At Margate, on the eastern extremity of the Kentish coast, whither the bathing fashion had already spread, the mind of a Quaker, Benjamin Beale by name, conceived a Bathing Machine, a hut on wheels, with a door at each end, which was drawn into the sea by a horse until the floor of the hut was level with the water. Undressing in the machine on the outward journey, the bather emerged from the seaward door when the horse stopped, to find himself enveloped in a kind of canvas umbrella, let down to the water's surface, not unlike the superstructure of an old-fashioned wagon. In the modest shade of this awning his dip could be conducted in private. He dressed again on the return journey. Beale's invention was widely copied, but he gained no financial success from it. He died in poverty and his widow ended her days in an almshouse. (Marsden: 12)

It is important to keep in mind that sea bathing was practiced only for medical reasons.

> There was no aspect of *pleasure* connected to sea bathing, in its early days. Bathing, and drinking sea water, were considered medicinal,

405

and the time and extent of the practice were strictly prescribed. Early morning, sometimes as early as 5 a.m., was considered the best time. (Sutherland 1997: 65)

Sarah Howell, however, believes that the "recommended hours [were] between six and nine in the morning" (23), perhaps giving us some time frame for this particular passage in the novel.

The Austen household was familiar with the use of leeches: "My Mother [is] no more in need of Leeches," the author wrote to Cassandra on September 16, 1813 (*Letters*: 222).]

"I am sorry to hear it, indeed; but if this is the case I hope Arthur will come to us." —

[This line is spoken by either Mr. or Mrs. Parker, but more likely the latter since his brother seems not to be sympathetic to poor Arthur.]

"If Arthur takes my advice, he will go to bed too, for if he stays up by himself, he will certainly eat & drink more than he ought; — but you see Mary, how impossible it is for me to go with you to Lady Denham's." —

"Upon second thoughts Mary, said her husband, I will not trouble you to speak about the Mullins's. — I will take an opportunity of seeing Lady D. myself. — I know how little it suits you to be pressing matters upon a Mind at all unwilling." —

His application thus withdrawn, his sister could say no more in support of hers, which was his object, as he felt all their impropriety & all the certainty of their ill effect upon his own better claim. —

M^rs. P. was delighted at this release, & set off very happy with her friend & her little girl, on this walk to Sanditon House. —

It was a close, misty morn^g, & when they reached the brow of the Hill, they could for some time make out what sort of Carriage it was, which they saw coming up it.
>
It was a close, misty morn^g, & when they reached the brow of the Hill, they could not for some time make out what sort of Carriage it was, which they saw coming up.

[The original "they could for some time make out" makes no sense and is almost certainly another transcription error.]

It appeared at different moments to be every thing from the Gig to the Pheaton, — from one horse to 4; & just as they were concluding in favour of a Tandem, little Mary's young eyes distinguished the Coachman & she eagerly called out, "T'is Uncle Sidney Mama, it is indeed." And so it proved. — Mʳ. Sidney Parker driving his Servant in a very neat Carriage was soon opposite to them, & they all stopped for a few minutes.

[The manuscript definitely reads "T'is" although the contraction does not mean anything. As in Sir Edward's earlier "T'were," Jane Austen is unclear about how apostrophes work.

We have here an amazing introduction for Sidney Parker, one very appealing to the impressionable Charlotte Heywood although far less wildly romantic than Rochester's first appearance on an enchanted horse accompanied by an unworldly dog—

> The din was on the causeway: a horse was coming; the windings of the lane yet hid it, but it approached... as I watched for it to appear through the dusk... now coming upon me. It was very near, but not yet in sight;... down by the hazel stems glided a great dog with strange pretercanine eyes.... The horse followed,—a tall steed, and on its back a rider.

—but an improvement over Catherine's prosaic introduction through Mr. King in the Lower Assembly Rooms to the arch Henry.

> They made their appearance in the Lower Rooms; and here fortune was more favourable to our heroine. The master of the ceremonies introduced to her a very gentlemanlike young man as a partner; his name was Tilney. He seemed to be about four or five and twenty, was rather tall, had a pleasing countenance, a very intelligent and lively eye, and, if not quite handsome, was very near it. His address was good, and Catherine felt herself in high luck. There was little leisure for speaking while they danced; but when they were seated at tea, she found him as agreeable as she had already given him credit for being. He talked with fluency and spirit—and there was an archness and pleasantry in his manner which interested, though it was hardly understood by her. After chatting some time

on such matters as naturally arose from the objects around them, he suddenly addressed her with—"I have hitherto been very remiss, madam, in the proper attentions of a partner here; I have not yet asked you how long you have been in Bath; whether you were ever here before; whether you have been at the Upper Rooms, the theatre, and the concert; and how you like the place altogether. I have been very negligent—but are you now at leisure to satisfy me in these particulars? If you are I will begin directly."

Charlotte has finally met the middle brother, and since he will definitely "do," she will be writing a long letter to her mother tonight. With the entrance on stage of Sidney Parker, we see that this novel is not, after all, to be a serious (or even comic) treatise on economy. Marvin Mudrick sees the final novel as primarily a comedy, a view with which I thoroughly agree. "Nothing but a wholly comic subject, without catastrophe or overt moral challenge (and only *Emma* and—tentatively—*Sanditon* meet these conditions), could free her altogether" (222). Like all of Jane Austen's previous works, it is a novel of romance, with a clearly defined heroine of charm and perception, a hero with many but forgivable faults, and a resolution in their marriage. Sidney is Henry Tilney redivivus, with the added advantages of more money and a sophistication born of travel and experience rather than isolation in a country parish. With *Persuasion* Jane Austen learned that a hero does not have to be either a fabulously wealthy landowner or a clergyman, and in Sidney we have the best of all possible combinations, an elegant young gentleman of independent means.

That the young eyes of little Mary not merely first recognize her uncle but that she announces the discovery with great elation produces an important psychological moment as Sidney Parker is revealed to be not merely an amiable young man but one who is beloved of his brother's children, qualifying him to be Charlotte's husband and the loving father of her children, and thus the undoubted hero of the novel. Edward Copeland praises the middle brother in the highest possible terms as "the likely hero of the piece—handsome, rich, twenty-seven or –eight, a good brother and a man who loves children" (1997: 126). As young adults, Charlotte and Mrs. Parker may already be suffering some sight loss, but young Mary still has perfect vision and can spot her favorite uncle from a great distance.

The passage has some striking similarities to what may have been its origin in "Susan"/"Catherine": "The chaise of a traveller being a rare sight in Fullerton, the whole family were immediately at the window; and to have it stop at the sweep-gate was a pleasure to brighten every eye and occupy every fancy—a pleasure quite unlooked for by all but the two youngest children, a boy and girl of six and four years old, who expected a brother or sister in every carriage. Happy the glance that first distinguished Catherine! Happy the voice that proclaimed the discovery! But whether such happiness were the lawful property of George or Harriet could never be exactly understood."

We see very few interactions in Jane Austen between young men and youngsters. In her Academy Award-winning screenplay for *Sense and Sensibility*, Emma Thompson retained scenes showing the amicable relationship between the precocious Margaret and the austere Edward. In creating a mock swordfight between the two, witnessed by Elinor (and us), she wisely supplied her hero with true character along with a sense of play despite his general lack of personality.

An amusing interchange between the hero and a young girl is found in the closing pages of *Northanger Abbey*. Henry Tilney, having come to Fullerton to declare himself to his Catherine, is uncomfortably seated with Mrs. Morland, at least one of the minor children, and the object of his desire. Eager to speak to Catherine in privacy, he comes up with the bright idea of inquiring about Mr. and Mrs. Allen, "ask[ing] her if she would have the goodness to show him the way. 'You may see the house from this window, sir,' was information on Sarah's side, which produced only a bow of acknowledgment from the gentleman, and a silencing nod from her mother." The brief passage makes clear that Henry has established easy terms with Sarah so that she can address him courteously but without awe. Like Sidney Parker, Mr. Knightley is comfortable with his nieces and nephews, who enjoy his company. As Emma observes upon seeing her friend admiring the new baby, "What a comfort it is, that we think alike about our nephews and nieces."

The confusion about the kind of carriage and the number of horses is a reflection of the varying reactions of the three witnesses, Charlotte, Mrs. Thomas Parker, and little Mary Parker. The mist that obscures the true nature of the arriving carriage is the same that will create the magical scene that follows, the rendezvous of Clara Brereton and Sir Edward. The horses' hooves raise a good deal of dust as they race toward the onlookers, also causing some uncertainty about their number.

We have already seen a gig, Sir Edward's humble equipage, the shame and embarrassment of his unhappy sister. It is very unlikely that Sidney would drive such a carriage since he can afford something much more expensive and fashionable.

He is more likely to be driving a "Pheaton" (properly "Phaeton"), a small open carriage that was generally owner-driven. "Of the four-wheeled carriages, the phaeton was the lightest and usually drawn by two horses" (Pinion: 28). By the end of the eighteenth century, the two-seater phaeton, or "Highflyer," with a small body perched above four large wheels and drawn by two or more horses, was popular with sporting young men wishing to display their skill at handling this riskily designed vehicle (Le Faye, 2002: 59).

Or Sidney Parker may be driving a two-wheeled curricle, popular with young men for its two matched horses (not specified here but almost certainly so) and speed. In *The Elegant Carriage* (22), Marylian Watney shows us a curricle in operation, the fashionable dressed owner flourishing his whip above two magnificent prancing horses. His servant, possibly a boy, is riding behind and just below him, facing forward. With no other guide in Jane Austen's text, I propose Plate III, "The Turn-out of the Season," as illustrating Sidney Parker as he arrives in Sanditon. His entrance onto the scene would have been even more dramatic, however, if he had followed the example of the Prince Regent, who, if we are to believe a contemporary drawing, rode his curricle drawn by two magnificent white horses—and accompanied by a no less magnificent lady—*standing up* (Wilks: 45)!

If Sidney Parker is driving one of these fashionable but potentially dangerous carriages, Jane Austen's contemporaries—and we—learn a great deal about him without further description. Boldly mastering equipage that Sir Edward would love to possess, he is temperamentally far from either the staid Thomas Parker or the timorous Arthur Parker.

> Some carriages were meant to be driven by a coachman, but not all. Well-to-do young men enjoyed showing off their prowess with the whip and reins, and therefore some carriages, such as gigs, curricles, and phaetons, were intended to be driven by the owner. The light weight of these carriages made them fast; the high springs, particularly toward the end of the eighteenth century, made them top heavy and likely to tip over if driven poorly. In other words, they were deliciously dangerous. (Olsen: 130)

It is also possible that he is driving a "tandem," one of the most popular but most dangerous carriages favored by adventurous young blades.

> From the end of the eighteenth century a number of daring young men, usually bucks of the Regency period, drove high-seated gigs or cocking carts with a pair or horses or ponies in tandem. This was highly dangerous, especially where there were many turnings and crossings, and almost suicidal in heavy traffic. (D.J. Smith: 19)

"A team of two horses harnessed one behind the other (as opposed to side by side) were said to be driven in "tandem'" (Pool: 379). "In the gig family... was the tandem, a variant of the dogcart... [a] two-wheeled carriage that seated four—two facing forward, two facing backward.... Beneath their joint seat was a box... for transporting hunting dogs.... The name 'tandem' simply meant that the carriage was pulled by two horses, one in front of the other, rather than side by side" (Olsen: 334).

Calling Sidney Parker, the proprietor of the carriage, the "Coachman" is an amusing touch. It was standard for the owner of this kind of carriage to drive it himself, so Sidney is accompanied by a servant to whom he is rendering a service. The text does not specify if the servant is enjoying the experience riding alongside his master (an unlikely arrangement) or is seated behind him, either facing forward or facing the rear and enjoying the dust raised by the horses' hooves and the wheels.

Although we never learn what kind of carriage Sidney Parker is driving, we can be certain that it is expensive, fashionable, and perfectly apposite to his bachelor lifestyle. Whatever it may be, it is exactly what Sir Edward Denham longs for but cannot afford.

As usual, Jane Austen does not describe how a character is dressed, but as a fashionable young man Sidney Parker probably wears clothes based on the standard riding costume: a top hat, a tail-coast with collar turned down, tight trousers, and riding boots (Wood: 41).

> Like women, men revolted at the end of the eighteenth century against the artificiality of the mannered clothing associated with the royal court. Instead, the new style of dress was to be natural, unartificial—it was modeled after the riding costume. This consisted of a linen shirt, a stiff neckband (a stock) or a cloth square that had been folded into a triangle and was tied around the neck (a

cravat). The pants were tights, with tall boots worn over them, and for the upper body there was a vest (a waistcoat),… and a "dress" riding coat, cut high up and double-breasted with large lapels in the front over the waist and long-tailed in back. This was the costume that would have been favored by Jane Austen's heroes. (Pool: 216)

Because the novel takes place in 1816, some of the features of the standard gentleman's outfit of 1800—"a plain tail coat, waistcoat and breeches of fine woollen cloth, and [a] tall silk hat" (Borer: 106)—may already be slightly passé. Men's clothing from 1811 can be seen in Wilks (61).

Sidney Parker's personal appearance is also, as expected, not described. At the time, "men were usually clean-shaven" (Pool: 217), and there is no reason to believe that he is other than conventional in this regard. If Sidney were sporting any facial hair, Thomas Parker would probably have mentioned it as part of his rant about his middle brother.]

The manners of the Parkers were always pleasant among themselves — & it was a very friendly meeting between Sidney & his sister in law, who was most kindly taking it for granted that he was on his way to Trafalgar House.

[Because Sidney Parker has two sisters, Mrs. Parker is specifically identified by the author as his "sister in law." In an earlier passage, when no ambiguity can take place, the Parker sisters regard Thomas and Mary Parker as "their Brother & Sister."]

This he declined however. "He was just come from Eastbourne, proposing to spend two or three days, as it might happen, at Sanditon — but the Hotel must be his Quarters — He was expecting to be joined there by a friend or two." —

[Sidney Parker's dialog, which helps introduce him formally, is cast as indirect discourse. The economy of expression—we do not have the opportunity to hear his clever and perhaps pungent bons mots—suggests speed and his decisive manner, and the quotation marks make clear that he is speaking even if in indirect discourse. For some commentators, however, this passage does not contain real dialog, and "the manuscript… ends before Sidney Parker ever speaks in person" (Knox-Shaw: 243). In a manner appropriate to an unattached, wealthy young man of the world, Sidney keeps his options open and does not commit himself to anyone's schedule.]

The rest was common enquiries & remarks, with kind notice of little Mary, & a very well-bred Bow & proper address to Miss Heywood on her being named to him — and they parted, to meet again within a few hours. —

[Sidney's brief but conventional courteous exchange with Charlotte is in marked contrast to the nonsensical behavior of Sir Edward Denham, with his false flattery, and the self-centered chatter of Arthur Parker. Perhaps nowhere in earlier novels has Jane Austen so successfully drawn contrasts among her leading male characters and so early in the proceedings. Charlotte would observe Sidney's benevolent avuncular notice of little Mary with approval as a promising mate and father of her children. It is impossible to visualize poor Arthur's interaction with his brother's offspring.]

Sidney Parker was about 7 or 8 & 20, very good-looking, with a
>
Sidney Parker was about 7 or 8 & 20, very good-looking, & very much the Man of fashion in his air
>
Sidney Parker was about 7 or 8 & 20, very good-looking, with a decided air of Ease & Fashion, and a lively countenance. —

[As the initial description of Sidney Parker, this single line required a good deal of attention on Jane Austen's part. His age is Charlotte's estimate since the author would know it to the precise year, and the rest of the line is very much through our heroine's interested eyes. She can write home tonight that her long journey to Sanditon has not been in vain. Perhaps the saddest loss in not having more of the manuscript is the series of conversations between our heroine and hero as they verbally fence before acknowledging their mutual attachment.]

This adventure afforded agreable discussion for some time. M^rs. P. entered into all her Husband's joy on the occasion, & exulted in the credit which Sidney's arrival w^d. give to the place.

[Charlotte unabashedly asks Mrs. Parker about her brother-in-law, and that lady, lacking any curiosity as to the purpose of the interest, is all too happy to discuss her fashionable relative.]

The approach to Sanditon H. was at first only a broad, handsome, planted road between fields, but ending in about a q^r. of a mile in the Grounds, which though extensive were

>

The approach to Sanditon H. was at first only a broad, handsome, planted road between fields, but ending in about a q^r. of a mile in the Grounds, which though not extensive had all the Beauty & Respectability which an abundance of very fine Timber could give. —

>

The approach to Sanditon H. was at first only by a broad, handsome, planted road between fields, of about a q^r. of a mile's length, & conducting into the Grounds, which though not extensive had all the Beauty & Respectability which an abundance of very fine Timber could give. —

>

The approach to Sanditon H. was at first only by a broad, handsome, planted road between fields, & conducting at the end of a q^r. of a mile through second Gates into the Grounds, which though not extensive had all the Beauty & Respectability which an abundance of very fine Timber could give. —

>

The road to Sanditon H. was a broad, handsome, planted approach between fields, & conducting at the end of a q^r. of a mile through second Gates into the Grounds, which though not extensive had all the Beauty & Respectability which an abundance of very fine Timber could give. —

[With five versions, this is one of the most-revised lines in the entire manuscript. Each succeeding line describing the estate will require rewrites. Jane Austen very rarely describes a scene in detail, but for some reason this one intrigued her and so she spent a great deal of precious, limited time on it.

By "planted approach," the author means that "the road leading to the house has been formally planted with trees on either side for an aesthetic effect that was becoming slightly outmoded by the 1810s" (*CUPLM*: 677). "Large quantities of mature trees were a valuable asset to a country estate, but took many decades to grow, and their presence indicated good and thoughtful management by the owner over several generations" (*CUPLM*: 677). This may be a very indirect compliment to Lady Denham, but it is clear that she has taken good care of the estate that she inherited from Mr. Hollis. "Strictly speaking, 'timber' denoted mature elm, oak, and ash, but its more general meaning included any mature tree that was capable of being used for structural purposes" (*CUPLM*: 677).]

They were so narrow at the Entrance, that <u>one</u> outside fence was at first almost pressing on the road — till an angle in one, & a curve in the other gave them a better distance.

>

These Entrance Gates were so much in a corner of the Grounds or Paddock, so near one of its Boundaries, that an outside fence was at first almost pressing on the road — till an angle <u>here</u>, & a curve <u>there</u>, threw them to a better distance.

The Fence was a proper Park paling in excellent condition; with vigorous Elms, or old Thorns & Hollies following its course almost every where.

—

>

The Fence was a proper Park paling in excellent condition; with rows of fine Elms, or old Thorns following its course almost every where. —

>

The Fence was a proper Park paling in excellent condition; with clusters of fine Elms, or rows of old Thorns following its line almost every where. —

["A paling was a solidly constructed fence with stakes driven into the ground, fixed to horizontal rails supported by posts, marking the boundaries of the park and keeping grazing animals secure within it; its presence is another sign of good management of the estate. Elm was one of the trees traditionally grown for its timber, and thorn was a prickly shrub traditionally grown in the English countryside" (*CUPLM*: 677). Jane Austen makes very clear that despite all her faults, Lady Denham has given Sanditon House all the care that it deserves despite what must be heavy expenditures.]

<u>Almost</u> must be stipulated — for there were intervals

>

<u>Almost</u> must be stipulated — for there were vacant spaces — & through one of them, Charlotte as soon as they entered the Enclosure, caught a glimpse of something White & Womanish over the pales, in the field on the other side; — it was something which immediately brought Miss B. into her head — & stepping to the pales, she saw indeed — & very distinctly, though at some distance before her Miss B— seated, not far before her, on

>

<u>Almost</u> must be stipulated — for there were vacant spaces — & through one of them, Charlotte as soon as they entered the Enclosure, caught a glimpse of something White & Womanish over the pales, in the field on

the other side; — it was something which immediately brought Miss B. into her head — & stepping to the pales, she saw indeed — & very distinctly, though at some distance before her Miss B— seated, not far before her, at the foot of the sloping bank which

>

Almost must be stipulated — for there were vacant spaces — & through one of them, Charlotte as soon as they entered the Enclosure, caught a glimpse of something White & Womanish over the pales, in the field on the other side; — it was something which immediately brought Miss B. into her head — & stepping to the pales, she saw indeed — & very distinctly, though at some distance before her Miss B— seated, not far before her, at the foot of the bank which sloped down from the outside of the Paling & at which

>

Almost must be stipulated — for there were vacant spaces — & through one of them, Charlotte as soon as they entered the Enclosure, caught a glimpse of something White & Womanish over the pales, in the field on the other side; — it was something which immediately brought Miss B. into her head — & stepping to the pales, she saw indeed — & very distinctly, though at some distance before her Miss B— seated, not far before her, at the foot of the bank which sloped down from the outside of the Paling & which a narrow track seemed to skirt along; — Miss Brereton seated, apparently very composedly — & Sir E. D. by her side. —

>

Almost must be stipulated — for there were vacant spaces — & through one of these, Charlotte as soon as they entered the Enclosure, caught a glimpse over the pales of something White & Womanish in the field on the other side; — it was something which immediately brought Miss B. into her head — & stepping to the pales, she saw indeed — & very decidedly in spite of the Mist; Miss B— seated, not far before her, at the foot of the bank which sloped down from the outside of the Paling & which a narrow Path seemed to skirt along; — Miss Brereton seated, apparently very composedly — & Sir E. D. by her side. —

[Our author labored through six versions to reach what she may have considered a final reading for this sentence, long and complex, unique in her writings in its insinuation and gentle atmosphere.

Perhaps no commentator has surpassed R.W. Chapman in his assessment of this amazing passage:

Others besides myself, I find, have been called to attention by a scene in the last chapter, where the observant, critical Charlotte identifies a "stolen interview" of "secret lovers." What she sees, as she walks, is "a glimpse of something white and womanish"; and she sees it on "a close, misty morning" and through a gap in the park paling. All the items of *chiaroscuro*—the mist, the treacherous fence, the ill-defined flutter of ribbons—add up to an effect which is as clearly deliberate as it is certainly novel. (1948: 209)

Not a word is spoken, but we can perhaps supply the dialog—as usual, Jane Austen avoids writing the script for a courting scene, if that is indeed what Charlotte and we are witnessing. Still blinded by her initial impression of the young woman as a romantic heroine drawn from contemporary novels and familiar with Sir Edward as a passionate admirer of women—with an all-too-obvious preference for the poor cousin from London—Charlotte leaps to the most obvious interpretation of the scene. At the time, merely exchanging letters would have been considered a breach of etiquette on a young lady's part in advance of a publicly recognized engagement, and such a one-on-one meeting of these two single people—neither related nor affianced—would be considered at least indecorous.

Clare Brereton has assumed a new persona here, no longer the lowly handmaiden accepting the crumbs of charity from a demanding and patronizing Lady Denham but a soft-spoken and yet obviously dominant mistress of the relationship. Between her earlier appearance in the manuscript as an ideal heroine according to contemporary romances and this idyllic scene, Clara has mutated into a bold and confident young woman, perhaps even an adventuress. She would have accepted this tryst (she may even have initiated it) knowing how contrary it is to the wishes of her benefactress and therefore must remain a secret if she is to continue to live comfortably ensconced here in Sanditon House. Whether or not this is the first or one of a series of such meetings may be disclosed later, but for now it may be safe to assume that Clara and Sir Edward have for some time had some kind of understanding, and mindful of the mystery pervading an earlier novel, we might think that like Jane Fairfax and Frank Churchill they are secretly engaged. Or perhaps they have not yet reached that stage in their covert relationship, and Clara is waiting for Sir Edward to propose a private marriage so that between them they can gather up Lady Denham's fortune.

Her plan would be to remain in thrall to Lady Denham in order to inherit at least a good portion of the original Brereton fortune, and his stratagem would be to remain on the best terms with his aunt-by-marriage in the hope that she will give him some of the money not set aside for Clara as well as any other incidental gifts of waste ground. Like Clara, Sir Edward must know how dangerous this clandestine meeting is, since he risks losing substantial financial advantages in contravening Lady Denham's wishes that he marry money.

While still in the process of creating the unique character of Sir Edward the author limns a very different picture of him here from what we saw in his earlier conversations with Charlotte. The brainless chatterer is now a silent, ardent lover, a persona learned through reading romantic novels, which dominate this work as Gothic novels had shaped the plot of "Susan"/"Catherine."

But Charlotte leaps to this most obvious interpretation of the scene, drawing us into what may be a misconstruction, because she is not privy as are we to Sir Edward's libidinous motives in pursuing the young woman from London—to seduce and then abandon her. We know that *Clara* knows that Sir Edward has licentious plans afoot, with a particularly shameful fate in store for her, and the scene suggests that whatever he thinks his plans are, she is at least one giant step ahead of him.

The passage is twice-distanced from the reader—the narration is Jane Austen's, but the take is Charlotte's. And although we can generally trust Charlotte as an honest and well-meaning secondary narrator, she admits that she can misjudge people. Hence her initial reaction to Sir Edward is that she likes him, primarily because he has flattered her with unctuous attention. But upon seeing that he is merely using her to incite Clara's jealousy, she recognizes that she not only no longer likes him but that she is as guilty as other people in reaching false conclusions when her vanity has been indulged. This portrait of the Baronet as an attentive listener is in sharp contrast to his earlier pose as a boorish monopolizer of conversation centered entirely around his own quirky reading choices and even more bizarre interpretation of them, leading us to wonder which is the true Sir Edward. Perhaps he is not after all a naïve and somewhat comic young man limited by experience and financial means but a skillful actor, uncomfortably close to Henry Crawford and a seducer to be reckoned with.

Because the story so far has been a series of unexpected twists and turns, it is possible that Charlotte—who sees everything in terms of what she has read in romantic novels—has misunderstood this scene, leading the reader into erroneous interpretations. For example, the purpose of the meeting may be no more sentimental than Sir Edward's asking for advice on how to wrangle an invitation for himself and his sister to Sanditon House. So far he and Miss Clara have never spent a night together under the same roof, and such a visit might combine rescuing Miss Denham from the damp of Denham Park and giving him easier access to the object of his lubricious desires.

From the beginning of the manuscript, we have been led in directions that turn out to be false, and the transfer of view from the author to Charlotte has only added to the effect of confusion. Jane Austen has once again succeeded brilliantly in creating characters and situations that defy easy analysis, and so despite Charlotte's confidence that she understands what she glimpses through a gap in the park paling, the precise nature of the dialog between Sir Edward and Clara remains as much a mystery to our heroine-observer as to us.

In this manuscript, as in the published novels, Jane Austen gives virtually no information about costuming, assuming that her contemporaries knew how ladies and gentlemen dressed and unaware that we would be reading her novels with undiminished pleasure into an indeterminate future. Hence there was no need for her to specific about many details of everyday life. Illustrations from the time give some idea of the clothing of the time, though, and the few hints that she drops are compatible with what is known from objective sources.

> Women's clothing… was filmy, gauzy, and virtually transparent at the beginning of the century… thin muslin with only light stays, if that, and a chemise underneath. The dresses were frocks—that is, they buttoned down the back. They were cinched high just under the breasts to suggest a high waist. They had no pockets, and personal items had to be carried in a small bag or "reticule." The more daring damped down their chemises underneath for a more revealing effect…. At the same time everyone looked innocent and girlish, in part because most frocks were white…. Headgear was always worn—caps could be worn indoors; bonnets invariably when outside. (Pool: 213–214)

Some fashionable dresses for women in Jane Austen's day can be found in Wilks (60–61).]

They were sitting so near each other & appeared so closely engaged in gentle conversation, that Ch— instantly felt that she had nothing to do but to step back again, & say not a word. —

>

They were sitting so near each other & appeared so closely engaged in gentle conversation, that Ch— instantly felt she had nothing to do but to step back again, & say not a word. —

Privacy was certainly their object. —

[For "privacy" one might better read "secrecy," since this assignation is surely unknown to Lady Denham, whose response would be swift and devastating to both parties. Clara would be cast off and returned to London in shame, and Sir Edward would be rebuked and lose whatever financial assistance his aunt-through-marriage has been providing. And Miss Esther, of course, would be furious with her brother for closing to them forever the doors of Sanditon House, with its absence of the dampness that makes her home in Denham Park so unpleasant.]

It could not but strike rather unfavourably with regard to Clara; — but hers was a situation which ought not to be judged with severity. —

>

It could not but strike her rather unfavourably with regard to Clara; — but hers was a situation which must not be judged with severity. —

[We are well before the Victorian Period with its excessively prudish attitudes about the relationships between young men and young women. Although her family felt concern over her safety and reputation for being seen too frequently with Willoughby, Marianne Dashwood never risked social ostracism. And long before such behavior would be intolerable, she was engaged in what appears to be a one-way correspondence with her admirer, leading Elinor to the logical assumption that her younger sister was secretly engaged. In this instance, Charlotte is torn between her loyalty to another young woman, presumably in love but with many reasons to conceal her passion, and her training in what was appropriate behavior on the part of a young lady, especially when a rather giddy and unpredictable gentleman was involved. On the whole, Charlotte's good nature allows her to sympathize with Clara despite misgivings about the wisdom of the clandestine tryst. If the line is Jane Austen's narrative, the reference to "Clara" suggests that for the author she is less than the "Miss Brereton" of earlier chapters. Likewise, if this line reflects Charlotte's thoughts, the familiar "Clara" suggests that the young woman has sunk considerably in Charlotte's opinion and no longer merits a formal title.]

She was glad to perceive that nothing of it had been seen by M^{rs}. Parker; she was considerably the tallest of the two, or Miss B.'s white ribbons might not have fallen within the ken of <u>her</u> more observant eyes. —

\>

She was glad to perceive that nothing had been discerned by M^{rs}. Parker; If Charlotte had not been considerably the tallest of the two, Miss B.'s white ribbons might not have fallen within the ken of <u>her</u> more observant eyes. —

[Although we never learn the precise heights of her characters, we have here a rare instance of learning at least that Charlotte is somewhat taller than Mrs. Parker. And if Charlotte is on the tall side for a woman of the time, then in turn Clara, admired by Charlotte as being "Elegantly tall," may be what would nowadays be considered a runway model.]

Among other points of moralising reflection which the sight of this Tete a Tete produced, Charlotte c^{d}. not but think of the extreme difficulty which secret Lovers must have in finding a proper spot for their stolen Interveiws. —

[In the spirit of her initial impression of Clara Brereton as a romantic heroine, Charlotte's immediate interpretation of the scene is that the pair are secret lovers, entirely at odds with our inside knowledge of Sir Edward's plans to seduce and thereby ruin Lady Denham's young companion. Perhaps the plot, not entirely worked out, is evolving before our eyes. Or perhaps—and just as likely—the author is giving us yet another illustration of Charlotte's leaping to conclusions based on her narrow range of experience and dependence on the stuff of romantic novels. As a new Susan/Catherine, our updated heroine may still be under the domination of the fantasy of the printed word.]

Here perhaps they had thought themselves so secure from observation! — the whole field open before them — a steep bank & Pales never crossed by the foot by Man behind them — and a great thickness of air, in aid — . Yet here, she had seen them.

>
Here perhaps they had thought themselves so perfectly secure from observation! — the whole field open before them — a steep bank & Pales never crossed by the foot by Man at their back — and a great thickness of air, in aid — . Yet here, she had seen them.

[The text reads "by the foot by Man" in both the first and revised versions, suggesting either lack of attention because of failing health or very careless copying from an earlier draft.]

They were really ill-used by her. —
>
They were really ill-used. —

[Charlotte, often accused of being coldly judgmental, is scarcely so in this episode. Always the romantic, she assumes that the relationship between Sir Edward and Clara is far more intimate than they have shown publicly, and she empathizes with their difficulty in securing a few minutes together. If we were reading *Emma*, we would assume that we have caught Frank Churchill and Jane Fairfax unawares, but the characters and the situations are very different. Such a private meeting would be considered indecorous later in the century, but with the less strict rules of the eighteenth century informing the morality of the book, the rendezvous is perhaps indiscreet but not scandalous. More to the point, it is secretive because neither Sir Edward nor Clara dares reveal to Lady Denham—who has plans for them that do not include their marrying—that they meet privately. The text is just ambiguous enough, though, that the possibility remains that Charlotte misunderstands the nature of this tête-à-tête.]

The House was large & handsome; two Servants appeared, to admit them, & every thing had a suitable air of Property & Order. —

[The transition from Charlotte's ruminations about the scene that she has just witnessed to Sanditon House itself is very abrupt, suggesting only a rough version of the chapter at this point.

We never have a clear picture of how many people are in Lady Denham's employ. These "two Servants" are possibly the "2 Housemaids" who are kept busy dusting out the bedrooms, but it seems unlikely that they would greet visitors at the front door. One can assume a butler and of course a cook. As expected, Jane Austen gives dialog to neither of the two servants. Her servants are as silent as they are almost invisible—and like others of their lowly class unnamed in the text—since they play no active role in her tale of romance. The unusual feature of prolonged speech from Mrs. Reynolds is necessitated by the author's having to show us—and Elizabeth—that the master of Pemberley is not the haughty snob hitherto assumed. But as Mr. Darcy's housekeeper, Mrs. Reynolds is at the top of the servant scale and will play an important role in the heroine's life when she become mistress of the great estate as well as of its amiable master.]

Lady D. valued herself upon her liberal Establishment, & had great enjoyment in the Importance of her style of living. —

>

Lady D. valued herself upon her liberal Establishment, & had great enjoyment in the order and the Importance of her style of living. —

They were shewn into the usual sitting room, well-proportioned & well-furnished; — tho' it was Furniture rather originally good & extremely well kept, than new or shewey — and as Lady D. was not there, Charlotte had leisure to look about, & to be told by M^rs. P. that the whole-length Portrait of a portly Gentleman, which placed over the Mantlepeice, caught the eye immediately, was the picture of Sir H. Denham — and that one among many Miniatures in another part of the room, little conspicuous, was M^r— Hollis.

>

They were shewn into the usual sitting room, well-proportioned & well-furnished; — tho' it was Furniture rather originally good & extremely well kept, than new or shewey — and as Lady D. was not there, Charlotte had leisure to look about, & to be told by M^rs. P. that the whole-length Portrait of a stately Gentleman, which placed over the Mantlepeice, caught the eye immediately, was the picture of Sir H. Denham — and that one among many Miniatures in another part of the room, little conspicuous, represented M^r— Hollis.

["The usual sitting room" would be used for "ordinary or everyday [visitors]. There would be another sitting-room for use on formal occasions" (*CUPLM*: 677). That Lady Denham takes care of her old furniture instead of replacing it with newer, more fashionable pieces is a backhanded compliment implying stinginess and lack of imagination. It is likely that she is still using the furniture that Mr. Hollis owned when he was living alone many years earlier in Sanditon House.

A whole-length portrait of Sir Harry Denham must have been brought over from Denham House, where it would more appropriately hang. Presumably upon quitting Denham House, Lady Denham left everything behind that was not personal property. Perhaps Sir Edward allowed her to move the portrait as a good-will gesture. Jane Austen might be familiar with full-length portraits from the famous one of her brother, Edward Austen-Knight, painted in 1789, when he was about 22 (Cecil: facing 176), now on display in the Chawton Cottage.

Jane Austen probably borrowed her famous line, "the little bit (two Inches wide) of Ivory on which I work with so fine a Brush," from the art of miniatures. Although silhouette cutouts were popular in middle-class families, miniatures were expensive and found in the homes of only the wealthy.]

Poor M^r. Hollis! —

It was impossible not to feel him hardly used; to be obliged to stand back in his room & see the best place by the fire constantly occupied by Sir H. D.
>
It was impossible not to feel him hardly used; to be obliged to stand back in his own House & see the best place by the fire constantly occupied by Sir H. D.

[As we can see, Jane Austen is revising right up to the very last line of the manuscript. One can only conjecture how much more of the story line would be extant if she had decided to hold off on self-editing and record her tale as it came to her. Although the ending is generally assumed to be incomplete, John Halperin has written that "twelve chapters were completed" (1983: 183). It is possible, of course, that the twelfth chapter was meant to end at this point since several important scenes have been included in it. This final chapter is very close to real time, but it covers a wider range of locations than most of the preceding chapters.]

March 18.

[Just as she had dated the beginning of the manuscript, so now Jane Austen affixes a date to her last line. Some commentators have suggested that this means that she knew that she would not be returning to work on the new novel, but it could just as well have been a way of recording when she paused in her work, a labor of love that would be resumed as soon as she felt ready to continue. There is no evidence that she believed in March of 1817 that she was fatally ill and would die in only four months' time.]

Appendix A.

In this short novel, published in December 1815 but advertised as appearing in 1816, we read about Sir Harry Headlong's invitation to three philosophers (Mr. Eston, Mr. Foster, and Mr. Jenkison) along with a divine (Mr. Gaster) and various other friends to his estate, Headlong Hill. There they discuss a wide range of issues, eat, drink, and find love. The prose is often lively and filled with commentary on contemporary matters. It is a "discussion" novel that Brian Southam believes may have given Jane Austen some ideas for her final manuscript.

However, despite the similarities, there are some significant differences. There is no coaching accident, the core of Jane Austen's opening. Instead, the Reverend Doctor Gaster's sprained ankle is a result of his hasty departure from the carriage, not the carriage's overturning:

> Here the coach stopped, and the coachman, opening the door, vociferated—"Breakfast, gentlemen"; a sound which so gladdened the ears of the divine, that the alacrity with which he sprang from the vehicle superinduced a distortion of his ankle, and he was obliged to limp into the inn between Mr. Escot and Mr. Jenkison.

The tale opens in December rather than in June. The four gentlemen in the coach—Mr. Foster, the perfectibilian; Mr. Escot, the deteriorationist; Mr. Jenkison, the statu-quo-ite; and the Reverend Doctor Gaster—are strangers rather than family members. The opening chapter recounts the spirited conversation among these characters, not their search for a doctor and the consequent accident. A group of strangers in a coach is not an unusual setting since that is how people traveled together, and unless they were sullen or aloof, they would have lightened the weary journey by engaging in a lively discussion of topics of contemporary interest, including the popular one of "improvements."

Although Thomas Love Peacock was well known in his own time, publishing a considerable amount of poetry between 1804 and 1817, *Headlong Hall* (published 1815 but dated 1816) and *Melincourt* (1817) were the only novels that appeared during Jane Austen's lifetime. Jane Austen never refers to him in her extant letters if R.W. Chapman is correct (*Letters*, 1952/1979: "Index V. Authors, Books, Plays"), nor does Deirdre Le Faye include his name in her "General Index" (*Letters*: 623–643). Oliver MacDonagh indirectly links Jane Austen and Thomas Love Peacock's *Nightmare Alley* (1818) and *Crotchet Castle* (1831), neither of which she could have read (18, 163).

The complete text of *Headlong Hall* can be found at the Thomas Love Peacock Society website: www.thomaslovepeacock.net.

Appendix B.

Thomas Skinner Surr (1770–1847), *The Magic of Wealth*

This long, three-volume novel published in 1815 relates how a mysterious figure of enormous wealth (known by many names but for much of the story called Lyttleton) rescues worthy people from distress and opposes evil people. His major adversary is the banker Flimflam, who builds the watering-place known as Flimflamton. The book covers a good deal of material beyond speculation in a seaside resort, but that element could have given Jane Austen the idea for her final manuscript, as Brian Southam suggests. Very much of mixed genre, like Jane Austen's work it mingles the characteristics of a novel and a play. The prose is turgid, but some of the characters (particularly the apothecary Christopher Crisp) lay the groundwork for what we shall later enjoy in Dickens.

Because the book is scarce and not available in its entirety online, I shall share some of the passages to which Jane Austen could have been indebted.

THE
MAGIC OF WEALTH.
A NOVEL.
IN THREE VOLUMES
······················
By T. S. SURR,
AUTHOR OF A WINTER IN LONDON, &c.
··············
VOL. I.
London:

PRINTED FOR T. CADELL & W. DAVIES, STRAND;
By G. SIDNEY, Northumberland Street.
1815.
ADVERTISEMENT.

In submitting to the Public a fifth production, under the popular form of a Novel, the author hopes that, as far as this species of work can properly be rendered a vehicle of opinions, he has not neglected the opportunity, which is furnished him, of making it an auxiliary of TRUTH.

He is not unconscious that, in the structure of his fable, and the conduct of his plot, he has occasionally infringed on the laws of refined criticism, for the purpose of producing EFFECT. A Novel, however, like a Play, is expected to afford its *surprises*; and to combine these in NEW FORMS, it will be admitted, was no easy task, when it was considered by what able hands the various scenes of human life, and the copious stores of literature, have been so often gleaned.

Islington,

March, 1815.

(Yates reading from a letter by his nephew, Matthew Mason:)
"Don't you know that within ten miles of Moreton, and not one from Beaumont Hall, there is a new and rising watering place, created, as it were, by magic, out of a few fishing huts, by the power and wealth of a rich banker of your county?—And don't you know that at this season of the year all the fashionable world are flying from this metropolis [London], as if the plague had broken out; and further, don't you know that several of the richest unmarried heiresses in the empire, have fixed upon this new watering place as their retreat for the summer; and that, therefore, for that, and other reasons, as well as its novelty, Flimflamton will be the most thronged with Fashionables, of all the marine refuges of fashion?... Margate is too hacknied to furnish a single new paragraph; Brighton is,—not as it has been—many other places once in vogue are gone by; but Flimflamton will be perfectly new, for this season at least."
(I, 263–265)

(Some of the features of "New Town":)

The Crescent, the new Squares, the Parade, and the Stein. (I, 272)

(Mr. Flimflam, the corrupt and evil banker:)

"Not a brick of Flimflamton shall be sold; on the contrary, I'll spend my last guinea in giving it the most brilliant eclat: I know I can make it in a month the magnet of fashion; and I will—for I'll lend money to princes and nobles, without any other security than their presence at Flimflamton. The bells and rattles shall be stationed there, and the ship of fools will soon sail to the port." (I, 276)

(Possible source for Sir Edward Denham's cottage, the idea of a new town, and dislike of innovation:)

Instead of these old-fashioned appendages to a country gentleman's domains, there had arisen, on one hand, as in scorn of the Old Manor house, a gew-gaw villa of a country banker; and, on the other, a new town, built on the sea-coast, and denominated after its founder Flimflamton. (II, 14)

(Mr. Lyttleton on studying fashionable "characters":)

"It is my intention to repair the Hall immediately; I shall, therefore, spend sometime at Flimflamton, which, I am told, is now the focus of what is called the Fashionable World. As studying characters is one of my favourite amusements, I am glad of this; for it is much pleasanter to me to view this *fantocini* of fashionables on the small stage of a watering-place; than to endure the fatigue of playing follow my leader over the larger theatre of London." (II, 37–38)

(Mr. Oldways' reply to Mr. Lyttleton in free indirect discourse:)

The reply of Mr. Oldways was characteristic; "he thanked Mr. Lyttleton sincerely, but he mixed very little with the mob of people." (II, 38)

(Chapter II, Scene 1, visitors arrive at Flimflamton:)

"Behold Flimflamton!" said the Countess St. Orville to Mr. White, as the carriage turned the corner of a green lane, and that paragon of all modern marine resorts came in view.

Mr. White. Have we then passed the village of Thistleton, where, as I told your Ladyship, I spent several of my youthful summers?

Countess. This spot was once called Thistleton.

Mr. White. Amazing! Where then is the steeple and tower of Thistleton church? What has become of the old Fort? Where are the fishermen's dwellings that dotted the coast? To the left too—all gone—all changed. Gracious Heavens! Surely hereabouts stood Sir Thomas Alder's noble mansion!—This road must have skirted the park wall. In the space, which my eye now scans, I am sure there, then, stood a score or two of cottages, besides several farm-houses—all vanished.—And instead of these objects, what metamorphoses are here! Stones for grass—chimneys for trees—a crowded town, instead of a retired village. (II, 40-41)

(Emma Clarendon, an impoverished beauty, as possible source for Clara Brereton? Many names in the book end in "–on":)

The carriage wheels now clattered through the streets of Flimflamton, and the Countess most affably pointed out to Mr. White and Emma Clarendon, the different buildings, as they passed them.—"The Hotel,"—"The Library,"—"The Baths,"—"The Concert Rooms,"—"Assembly Rooms,"—"The Theatre,"—"The Chapel,—and the Bank." (II, 41)

(Resistance to change and skepticism about speculation:)

Mr. White. Do I hear rightly? The establishment of a Bank wanted in the hamlet of Thistleton? Wanted here—may I ask by whom? For what? (II, 42)... I own, my Lady, that the old-fashioned notion, which "the Bank" conveys to my mind, rendered its association with a petty hamlet of cottagers and fishermen, ludicrous in the extreme. (II, 44)

Mr. Flirt. Villages are metamorphosed into watering-places;—and watering-places become the courts of Princes. (II, 49)

Mr. White. For since the spirit of speculation has taken a flight beyond the utmost bounds of real capital, the speculators, as well buyers as sellers, must, of necessity, be satisfied with a guarantee of credit in its place. (II, 50–51)

(Condemnation of the fashionable practice of leaving town, i.e., London, for the summer; *domophobia*; love of the sea likened to a madness; Mrs. Wilkins > Mrs. Whitby?:)

Chapter III.

It was now *"the season for watering-places,"* or in other words, it was the period of the year, when that tormenting disease, peculiar to the climate of England, *"the Domophobia,"* rages with all its violence. Foreigners have expressed more surprize at the effects of this distemper, upon our females especially, than at any other singularity which marks the national character.

When they behold the happiness of an English fireside, where reigns that tranquil felicity which we express by the word, COMFORT; a state of feeling not to be described in any other language than our own; when they perceive the attractions of "Home," a magnet which operates upon all ranks and classes of English society, each home drawing towards itself some share of the hearts of all, so that the whole population of the empire might be numbered by its domestic circles; they are eager to exclaim—"What magic must there be in an English home!"

Anon—the first symptoms of *domophobia* appear; varying, in their demonstration, according to the modes of life and habits of the persons affected; for no rank is free from the contagion. In the higher circles it begins to be visible generally about June; but is sometimes later in its appearance, the movements of the court, or the sittings of the parliament, having a certain influence on the progress of the disease. The observing foreigner is now amazed at the changes he every where perceives. In all parties, the chief conversation consists of—"When do you leave town? Where do you summer this season? Are you stationary? Do you go to the Lakes—Do you visit Brighton—Have you secured a house at Flimflamton?" (II, 53–55)

. . .

But it is remarkable, that water has quite opposite effects in the two species of madness—in domophobia it allays, in hydrophobia it excites the irritability of the patient. It is still, however, very doubtful, notwithstanding this fact, whether domophobia be the origin of water places, or whether these said watering places at first created, or now encourage, the continuance of the malady. However this point may be determined, there is no doubt, but that as watering places have increased, the disease domophobia has been more and more prevalent among all ranks of people.

Of all these modern *Fashion-traps*, Flimflamton was at the present epoch the most successful in its baits; and, consequently, contained a larger portion of the "Fashionable World," than any similar "decoy"; and, consequent on that, a larger portion of the inferior classes, who ever follow where Fashion leads.

No wonder, therefore, that arrogance and extortion became the marking features of the Flimflamtonians, whether house and lodging owners, shopkeepers or victuallers, among whom the widow Wilkins, landlady of the "Hotel," was a most distinguished personage. (II, 56–57)

(Lending libraries as the center of social life:)

Scene 1.

A few days after this contract had been made, and about that hour of the day when the real gentry at a watering-place are taking their wine and fruit after dinner, and the mock gentry are rummaging their bundles for clean gowns and caps, cravats and pantaloons, to dress for the libraries, a chaise and pair drove up to the "Hotel." (II, 59)

. . .

Miss Perryman. We shall meet often at the libraries. (II, 68)

(The curative powers of sea air are lauded:)

Crisp. Sea air makes you sharp. (II, 60)

. . .

Lyttleton [speaking to Lancaster]. I trust the air of Flimflamton will complete the restoration of your health. (II, 72)

(Reflections on meanness imposed upon poverty, like Charlotte Heywood's reaction to Lady Denham:)

Lancaster [in thought]. This is the bitter curse of a dependent state!—No action can be spontaneous—the tongue must wear a chain—the eyes must be centineled, each motion must be made with trembling care; and man, "*In form and attitude how like an Angel, in comprehension how like a God!*" must meanly crouch and fawn, and fetch and carry, and play all sorts of antics, like dancing dogs, or muzzled bears, that are starved and tortured into performances revolting to their natures, for the profit or the pleasure of their keepers! (II, 77)

(Reference to "romance":)

Lyttleton. I am myself well acquainted with many most striking instances of British benevolence and philanthropy, which, if published, would make as marvellous a chapter of romance, as the incidents, strange as they are, which have brought us four together in this pleasant little parlour. (II, 84)

(Disdain for lower-class vacationers:)

Lyttleton. Yon crowd of triflers are parading up and down the Steine there, echoing short nonsense sentences from group to group. (II, 89)

(Skepticism about the new wave of Philanthropy as seen in Miss Diana Parker:)

Mason. The consequence has been, a most grotesque and absurd conjunction of mirth and pity—of gaiety and compassion. Pleasure may be the real motive; but Philanthropy must be the pass-word, even to our amusements. (II, 199)

(Some worthless land given liberally, like Lady Denham to Sir Edward Denham:)

A plot of worthless ground, about a mile out of Flimflamton, was liberally given by the Banker. (II, 203)

(Sick people like the Parker sisters; bathing machines and dippers; asses, here probably for a ride; Clara Brereton's likely fate as a Nursery-maid:)

Mason. "Pleasure floating on every breeze, brought joy into every face;—e'en inanimate bathing-machines were moved merrily backwards and forwards; while dippers and guides, full of glee and good humour, wished the Duke at Flimflamton for ever. Donkies, ponies, and chaises, were in such requisition that nursery-maids and foot boys, were seen giggling and grinning, scampering and scrambling, and playfully wrestling, to obtain for their young lords and ladies the triumph of possessing on this gala day, the ass most in favour and fashion.

"Invalids shared the general inspiration, and smiled; even loungers forgot for an hour the horrors of *ennui*; and the countenance of every inhabitant and visitor of this delightful aquatic retreat evinced that, at least, the moments then fleeting were those of unalloyed joy." (II, 212–213)

(Seashore setting:)
The only sound that fell upon the listening ear of Lancaster was the monotonous dashing of the waves upon the pebbly shore they trod. (II, 223)

(Libraries less as a source of reading matter than as a place for the ton to be seen by the lower classes; the fashionable game of gazing and being gazed upon:)

Chapter VI.
Scene 1.
When one of Flimflam's friends suggested to him, with a sort of *eclectic spirit*, that Libraries were now become so common, it would be better to hit upon some novel substitute—he consulted his Oracle of High Fashion and Taste [the Marchioness], who exclaimed:
"The fool, the fool, what is a Watering-place without a Library? it would be like a church without a pulpit, or more *apropos*,—a bell without a clapper!… But let me repeat the *hint* to you, that to make the Library at a watering-place, at all adopted to the purposes of a staring-room for fashionables, it must have CAPACIOUSNESS— take that *hint*—let there be ample stage-room, and you will have a succession of actors from the great world, who will feel as much gratification in *walking in, walking round*, and *walking out*, as the humble sons and daughters of John Bull themselves experience in gazing at us, and guessing at our titles!" (II, 237–239)

(Splendid new library:)
The Pavilion Library, built on the plan of the Pantheon; decorated with the most tasteful ornaments; furnished magnificently; and stocked with every work of Literature, that could be bought. (II, 240)

(A fashionable young man visits the library to look in the Subscription Book:)
A young blood, from Throgmorton Street, who has got leave of old Daddy to spend a month and a few Bank notes where he pleases, puts up his horses, and with his head full of *high life*, trundles

himself into the library—and smacking his whip on his *bran* [sic] new Wellington overalls, turns over the *"Subscription Book,"* with the air of an accomplished lounger, and enquires; "Well, Mister, who has the Devil sent among you? Any body here? Any Fashion? Any High-flyers? Let's look at your book.—No, all cits—all cockneys—your place will never do at this rate." (II, 243–244)

(A passage that could well be the origin of Lady Denham:)

> An extraordinary bustle and pressure announced the arrival of the great patroness of Flimflamton. An equipage of prodigious splendour had conveyed her to the door—and the crowd on each side giving way, formed an alley, through which Mrs. Flimflam swam into the Library, in motion and appearance, like the fresh painted figure at the head of a ship, at a launch.—She was a woman past the middle age of life, corpulent in person, coarse in her manners, vulgar in her speech, proud, and hard-hearted, bold, but grossly ignorant. Her dress was a ludicrous specimen of extravagant profusion and bad taste, in form, fabric, and colours: and her head, neck, arms, and wrists, were loaded, but not ornamented, with diamonds. (II, 256)

(Mrs. Flimflam is a wealthy but uneducated snob like Lady Denham; she employs poor grammar, such as her incorrect use of "don't," and she has a generally vulgar manner:)

> The Marchioness solicited of her friend the Countess an introduction to Lyttleton, with whom she entered into conversation, as well as with White and Lancaster, to the great chagrin of Mrs. Flimflam, who had no other method at hand of venting her spleen, than by an indirect attack on the poverty of the Oldways. Addressing herself to Stanly, in a key of voice which the object of her attack could not avoid hearing, she said, "Poor Miss Oldways! I suppose she's come to hear *Thingummeeani*. At the Opera she may be heard for five shillings in the gallery—though my Box costs me seven hundred pounds for the season;—but to people that are buried by circumstances in the country, such a treat as this must be delicious. She's most charming in a private room—I had her at our party last night—we had a select hundred exactly. I'm sorry Mr. Oldways is so odd—for I'm sure I should have no objection to the young people being invited to our parties, without being asked again.—Indeed, we ask many respectable families to visit us, although we know it

don't suit them to give entertainments on the scale that we do. In this world of *ups* and *downs*, as the saying is, some grow richer and some poorer; but for my part, I'm sure I shall never shut my doors against a genteel family, merely because their fortune is the worse for wear." (II, 258–259)

(Mr. Lyttleton's closing condemnation of speculators and praise of conservative men:)

"In the mean time the *Bankruptcy* of *Mr. Flimflam*, which will be announced this evening, will occasion such an accumulation of distress in this immediate district, that I earnestly request the active co-operation of all present, in applying the MAGIC OF REAL WEALTH, in order to counteract the evils, which have originated in, or resulted from, the tricks and delusions of selfish impostors.

"Happy will it be for old England, for the British empire, for the Civilized World, when the manœuvres of such mischievous speculators as Flimflam shall be no longer successful; and when the character and conduct of such men as Mr. OLDWAYS shall be rightly understood, duly honoured, and generally imitated!" (III, 222)

Jane Austen never refers to Thomas Skinner Surr in her extant letters if R.W. Chapman is correct (*Letters*, 1952/1979: "Index V. Authors, Books, Plays"), nor does Deirdre Le Faye include his name in her "General Index" (*Letters*: 623–643).

Appendix C

Dr. Richard Russell.

The British Library owns two copies of Dr. Richard Russell's 1753 translation of his own book, originally published in Latin in 1750 as *De tabe glandulari, sive de usu aquæ marinæ in morbis glandularum dissertatio.* The copy in better overall condition, shelf mark 1171 h 11, was rebound in 1935 and measures about 6 inches by 9 inches. Cut down at some time to about 5 inches by 7 inches but otherwise identical, 7460 A.A.A. 32. is in poor condition, the front cover being detached. The special interest in this second copy lies in the inscription on the Imprimatur page, facing the title page:

S Durrant Surgeon Retherbridge [?]
MM Durrant 1791

This inscription may mean that M.M. Durrant gave the book to S. Durrant, a Surgeon living in Retherbridge (a town or village—or hamlet—that I cannot identify; the correct reading may be "Betherbridge," also a surname and equally unidentifiable as a geographical site) in 1791, the year in which Jane Austen celebrated her sixteenth birthday. There is no evidence that Jane Austen ever saw this book or even knew of its existence, but that it was being read as late as the final years of the eighteenth century suggests that it still had currency as a work of some scientific validity.

Facing the title page is the imprimatur:

Imprimatur,

J. Browne,
Vice-Can. *Oxon.*

Apr. 4. 1753.

The title page, as was typical at the time, offers a long title and other information:

CONCERNING THE USE
OF SEA WATER
IN DISEASES OF THE GLANDS, &c.
TO WHICH IS ADDED
AN EPISTOLARY DISSERTATION
TO R. FREWIN, M.D.
By Richard Russell, M.D. & F.R.S.
(passage in Greek)
Eurip. Iphigen. In Taur.

————————————————————————————————

(illustration)
OXFORD,
Printed at the Theatre: and Sold by James Fletcher
in the *Turl,* and J. and J. Rivington in St. *Paul's*
Church-Yard, London. MDCCLIII.

The dedication that follows is characteristic of the servile tone used by writers over many centuries in addressing themselves to people whom they deemed (and who deemed themselves) their social superiors.

TO HIS GRACE
THE DUKE OF NEWCASTLE

&c. &c. &c.

THIS WORK
IS HUMBLY INSCRIBED
BY HIS GRACE'S
MOST OBEDIENT SERVANT

RICHARD RUSSELL.

Although some commentators have suggested that Dr. Russell places more emphasis on sea bathing than on imbibing seawater, examination of the book shows that that is not really the case.

In the Preface, the author states his specific purpose for writing this long book.

PREFACE

I offer to the Reader's Perusal in the following Sheets some Cases, which were cured by Sea Water; wherein I have endeavoured to explain and illustrate, as far as I am able, by what Ways it produces its good Effects; in subduing Diseases of the Glands. (v)

Dr. Russell is clearly fascinated by the sea and the life-giving energy that it must contain.

That great Body of Water, therefore, which we call the Sea, and which is rolled with such Violence by Tempests round the World, passing over all the submarine Plants, Fish, Salts, Minerals, and in short, whatsoever else is found betwixt Shore and Shore, must probably wash off some parts of the whole, and be impregnated, or saturated with the Transpiration, if I may so term it, of all the Bodies it passes over: the finest Parts of which are perpetually flying off in Streams, and attempting to escape to the outward Air, till they are entangled by the Sea, and make Part of its Composition. Whilst the Salts also are every Moment imparting some of their Substances to enrich it, and keep it from Putrefaction. (vii)

On unnumbered page 1, Dr. Russell commences his report of his long studies of the salutary effects of seawater.

A DISSERTATION
UPON
GLANDULAR CONSUMPTIONS,
OR
The Use of SEA WATER
IN
Diseases of the Glands.

From the outset, Dr. Russell stresses his specific interest in the use of seawater to cure diseases of the internal glands and nothing else.

Under these Circumstances, I hope it will not be thought an unprofitable Thing to the Publick, if by introducing the Use of Sea Water, in Diseases of the internal Glands, a Way may be found out to prevent these most dangerous Distempers in the Beginning, and preserve the Lungs, a Bowel of that great Consequence, from being spoil'd and destroy'd by Apostemations [the formation of an "apostem" or abscess; the gathering of matter in a purulent tumour; festering]. (3)

Some pages later, in the course of noting that ancient physicians recommended seawater as a cure, Dr. Russell introduces the idea of bathing in the sea as a treatment supplementing ingestion of seawater. He is vague here about "other Helps," some of which may be the real cause of any improvement in the patient's condition.

From the Observations before made of the antient Medicine in these Cases, we may however draw two general Rules.... The other is, that by the Use of Sea Water, and other Helps, the Glands may be scour'd and cleans'd of their Obstructions; after which, the whole Habit of Body ought to be strengthen'd, and render'd firm by cold Bathing in the Sea, that it may be enabled to resist any new Fluxions [abnormal discharges of blood or other matter from or within the body]. (14–15)

However, the internal use of seawater is at this point in his treatise the primary curative treatment.

How far Sea Water might have assisted, if I had known the Use of it, as much then as I do now, I will not presume to say. For certainly I do not know a greater discutient [a medicine having the quality of "discussing" or dissipating morbid matter] than Sea Water, used internally; nor any better suited to answer the above-mentioned Intentions: which in that Case indeed, should have been drank by itself dayly, to prevent Constipation, before the Obstruction had been total; when it would have had this additional Advantage also, of being a Help to Digestion, and Chylification [the production of chyle, the fluid in the intestines just before absorption]. (41)

As a good scientist, Dr. Russell advocates the drinking of seawater not as the sole but as the follow-up treatment for glandular disorders, to be used only after traditional remedies, including bleeding, have been applied.

> Viewing Things in this Light, I was convinced that the Use of Sea
> Water might be of great Service, in preventing bilious Colics at Sea,
> from attacking the Mariner at all; and securing the Patient from
> Relapses, after the Inflammation had been carried off by Bleeding,
> the Use of the *Semicupium* [a hip-bath], and saline Purges. (42)

Continuing as a man of modern-day science, Dr. Russell observes that
although Greek and Roman physicians recommended drinking seawater,
they never understood its effects.

> Although the Antients gave Sea Water internally, in many Diseases,
> yet they were afraid of it, and never knew it's true Uses. (54) ["it's"
> is standard at the time for "its," not a printing error]

Despite his denial throughout that seawater is a universal panacea, as he
proceeds in extolling its virtues he moves from its effect on internal glands to
its effect on external glands, ending in some unexpected religious imagery.

> Having there considered first, the Use of Sea Water in the Internal
> Glands, let us see what Effect it has upon the external ones. And as
> these are more immediately under the Eye of the Physician, so in
> their Diseases, he will more immediately see, both the Change of
> the Disease, and the Effect of the Medication.... by [these] Means
> the Gracefulness of the Neck is restored, which was designed by our
> Maker as the Column, or ornamental Pillar, on which he intended
> to place the last, and most finished Part of his Creation. (61–62)

Dr. Russell remains uncertain about how long a patient must partake
of seawater for major improvement. From this passage it seems that sea
bathing—a follow-up of a treatment of imbibing seawater—is not viewed
as in itself a cure. He has a good idea, however, that seawater is a very
unpleasant palliative taken internally and that most patients will not be
able to endure the prolonged ingestion that he believes is necessary to effect
a full cure.

> For if the Patient has not Resolution enough to continue a great
> while the Use of Sea Water, and finish his Cure by cold bathing in
> the Sea, in all likelihood, upon the first Plenitudes arising in the
> Habit, the Disease will again shew itself. (67)

Again, as a modern practitioner of medicine and unwilling to step over the line of hyperbole in praise of this cure, Dr. Russell observes its limitations. The milk here recommended is presumably that of asses.

> And tho' I am far from affirming this Method of Salt Water will do every Thing, there being some obstinate Tumours, and cutaneous [skin] Eruptions, which will elude it's Force; yet after Trials of this, and other Medicines, which has stimulated too much, I have committed the Patients some Months to drink of Water, and a Milk Diet; and then, the Acrimony being abated, I have cured them by those very Remedies, which did not answer before. (83)

It is difficult to discern if Dr. Russell is aware that as long as he uses seawater as only part of a cure, along with other, more traditional methods, it is impossible to judge how effective it is.

> And tho' Sea Water will do a great deal by itself, in internal Tumours, yet, in Order to have it's right Effect upon Diseases of the Liver, and Kidneys, saponaceous [soapy] Medicines should be joined to it. (99–100)

Dr. Russell concludes this portion of his work by repeating his primary goal, to share with other physicians his experiences in what seawater can and cannot do to cure glandular problems.

> Thus have I at length performed my Promise; I have faithfully pointed out, as far as I was able, what Sea Water will, and what it will not do. (105)

In the following section, Dr. Russell offers thumbnail sketches about various patients. Of particular interest is his referring to the seaside resort that would in time be known as Brighton.

> But as a little Cough still remained, I sent him to Brighthelmstone, a Town on the Sea Coast, that he might have near him the Medicine destined to relieve his Obstructions. (111)

For another patient, prolonged drinking of seawater and applying it to her skin brought about a cure.

HIST. VI.
Of various Defœdations [pollutions] of the Skin.

I was called to a Woman with scorbutic Eruptions [scurvy] behind both Ears, and on her Face, which wet many Cloths every Day; and had a yellow mealy Crust over some Parts of them. She had used many Remedies, but nevertheless continued dayly to grow worse. She came at last to the Sea, where she took Antiscorbutics, and drank Sea Water every Morning, cleansing the Skin with the *Quercus Marina*, fresh out of the Sea. By this Method, she was cured in five Weeks or two Months. (124–125)

That some patients cannot tolerate a long period of ingesting seawater is a problem that Dr. Russell addresses in another history. Again the focus is on drinking rather than on bathing, although the latter practice is also advocated.

HIST. XII.

Of diseased uterine Glands.

I saw, not long ago, an obstinate *Fluoralbus* [a mucous discharge] cured, by bathing in the Sea, drinking Sea Water occasionally, and taking the following Remedies.... I must observe that the Purging by Sea Water is to be repeated, as often as the Patient can well bear it, especially if he be too costive [constipated]. (134–135)

Unfortunately, despite his enthusiasm, Dr. Russell cannot explain how or why this highly touted cure (if such it is) works.

HIST. XIV.

From all these Cases, we may see clearly that the Way, by which Sea Water produces it's good Effects, and relieves so powerfully many Diseases, is, by opening some new Secretion, and thereby easing and unloading the diseased Parts. (138–139)

Although the treatment seems unreliable, the town that would become Brighton is already identified as a health resort. As can be seen, Dr. Russell writes far more about drinking seawater than immersion in this main section of the book. I can find nothing in his treatise about the salubrious effect of sea air, so Mr. Thomas Parker must have another source for his extravagant claims.

HIST. XXVI.

A Girl of eleven Years old, had her upper Lip and Nostrils much swelled; but upon taking Sea Water, the Swelling sunk. However,

the Spring following, she consulted *Sr.* Edward Hulse, as the Disease
returned; and he advised her to resume the Method by Sea Water,
which she had before used successfully. He then prescribed the
following Medicines, which the Patient used to take with Whey,
whilst she was in *London*, and with Sea Water, after she came to
Brighthelmstone. (157)

Despite what must have been unpleasant side effects, some patients were
kept on a very long course of treatment that involved drinking seawater.
One can only surmise that the disease in this case ran its course and that
the patient would have had the same results without a pint of seawater every
morning for nine months.

HIST. XXXVI.
A dry *Lepra* came upon the Head, and almost all the Joints, and
leprous Spots were scattered over the Surface of the whole Body.
The Case was extreamly obstinate, and could not be cured without
great Patience and Perseverance. The Patient continued to drink
a Pint of Sea Water every Morning, for nine Months together
without the least Intermission; and, as the Reward of his Steadiness
and Resolution, in bearing the tedious Process of this Cure, was
restored to perfect Health. (187)

In contrast (and this observation should have suggested to Dr. Russell
that the drinking of seawater does not bring about a cure), some patients
endured this treatment for a very short time before they were whole again.
The very inconsistency of the "cure" argues against its efficacy.

HIST. XXXVII.
This Patient took a Pint of Sea Water every Morning, for a Week
only, and, as the Swelling entirely went away upon it, he recovered
without any farther Assistance. (188)

Satisfied that he has presented adequate anecdotal support for his theory,
Dr. Russell continues with a series of Aphorisms, beginning on page 92. In
one of them, his phrasing suggests that seawater although not a panacea is
useful in conjunction with other medical treatment.

VII.

If a diseased Gland of the Lungs, or any other Part, maturates [forms pus], Sea Water will do no Good, till that Matter is discharged. (194)

In a later Aphorism, Dr. Russell admits that ingestion of seawater may be excessively irritating, so that introduction of milk to the patient's diet may ease the problem. Lady Denham has good medical authority in promoting the use of asses' milk for sickly girls from overseas.

XV.

In Cases attended with great Acrimony, I have sometimes thought Sea Water irritated too much; but a Milk Diet, and Absorbents will alter that State; and I have seen Sea Water cure those Cases afterwards. (197)

Almost a panacea but recognized as ineffective against cancer, seawater is best mixed with a wide range of other remedies. Thus it is impossible to establish how efficacious seawater really is.

XXI.

Many Ulcers in the Mouth and Tongue, that approach nearly to Cancers, will be palliated, and some cured, by Sea Water and other Remedies. (198)

Occasionally, Dr. Russell cites specific illnesses for which seawater has effected a cure.

XXIV.

Sea Water prevents a Constipation of the Belly, and by that Means facilitates the coming away of Gall Stones and Gravel. (199)

Soap?!

XXV.

Sea Water, by dissolving and dissipating the tumefied Glands of the Liver, is the safest Purge, joined with Soap, in a curable *Icterus* [jaundice]. (199)

Despite his enthusiasm for the new cure, Dr. Russell advocates allowing nature to heal whenever possible, a useful caveat against introducing seawater into a patient's diet too soon.

XLII.
All Tumours that are the Crises of Fevers are to be left to Nature; that we may first see what she can do, towards suppurating [festering] or dispersing them, before we begin the Use of Sea Water. (205)

In his final Aphorism, Dr. Russell warns sternly about the dangers of seeking medical help from people who have not attained his level of expertise.

XLIX.
Sea Water has great, and various Excellencies, but it may be misapplied by unskilfull Persons. (208)

Thus ends the book proper, but Dr. Russell, very much interested in the medicinal properties of anything living in the sea, has more to say on his favorite topic:

Appendix of the Quercus Marina; discussion of the attributes and uses of the submarine plant that appears to have various medicinal applications.

Quercus Marina, also known as sea oak, kelp, black tang, rockweed, kelp-ware, bladderwrack, bladder, cutweed, Blasen-tang (blasentang), seetang, Meereiche (meeriche), brown algae, common seawrack, Dyers fucus, edible seaweed, fucoidan, fucoxantin, Fucus, green algae, Hai-ts'ao, knotted wrack, popping wrack, red algae, red fucus, rockrack, schweintang, sea kelp, seaware, seaweed, swine tang, tang, Varech vesiculeux, vraic, and wrack,

is a common seaweed in the form of long ribbons, about 1m long and 5cm across, leathery, shiny, olive-green to yellow-brown. Down the centre of each ribbon is a midrib, on either side of which are the air-filled bladders which keep the alga floating up from its rocky anchorages. It is found on the north Atlantic and Baltic coasts, the Irish and North Seas and is often washed up on beaches after storms.... It is best to collect bladderwrack from the sea in its healthy, live state than to gather it from beaches. It should be dried as soon as possible.... Fucus, rich in iodine, stimulates the thyroid gland, thereby increasing basal metabolism. It is a useful remedy in the treatment of hypothyroidism, goitre myxoedema and lymphadenoid goitre. By regulating thyroid function, there is an improvement in all the associated symptoms. Fucus also appears to assist in the problem of lipid balance associated with obesity, and where obesity is associated with thyroid dysfunction, this herb may help to reduce excess weight. It has a reputation in the relief of rheumatism and rheumatoid arthritis and may be used both internally and as an external application for inflamed joints. The main phytotherapeutic use of Fucus is during debility and convalescence, and also to remineralise the body.... This seaweed was the original source of iodine, discovered in 1812, and it was used extensively to treat goitre, a swelling of the thyroid related to lack of iodine. In the 1860s it was claimed that bladderwrack, as a thyroid stimulant, could counter obesity by increasing metabolic rate, and, since then, it has featured in numerous slimming remedies. Farmers in the south of England use bladderwrack as a potash fertilizer. (www.purplesage.org.uk/profiles/bladderwrack.htm)

Dr. Russel relates, that he found this plant an useful assistant to sea water in the cure of disorders of the glands: that he gave it in powder to the quantity of a dram, and that in large doses it nauseated the stomach: that by burning in the open air it was reduced into a black saline powder, which seemed, as an internal medicine, greatly to excel the officinal burnt sponge; which was used with benefit, as a dentifrice, for correcting laxities of the gums; and which shewed a notable degree of detergent virtue by its effect in cleaning the teeth: that the juice of the vesicles, after standing to putrefy, yielded, on evaporation, an acrid pungent salt, amounting to about a scruple from two spoonfuls: that the putrefied juice, applied to the skin, sinks in immediately, excites a slight sense of pungency, and deterges like a solution of soap: that one of the best applications for discussing hardness, particularly in the decline of glandular swellings, is a mixture of two pounds of the juicy vesicles, gathered in July, with a quart of sea water, kept in a glass vessel for ten or fifteen days, till the liquor comes near to the consistence of very thin honey: the parts affected are to be rubbed with the strained liquor twice or thrice a day, and afterwards washed clean with sea water. (William Lewis, "An Experimental History Of The Materia Medica." "Æthiops vegetabilis Dr. Russel," *Med. Eff. Edinb.* ii. 257.) (http://chestofbooks.com/health/materia-medica-drugs/ Experimental-History-Materia-Medica/Quercus-Marina.html))

In 1810, the plant was listed among many others that displayed medicinal qualities: "The Dublin Pharmacopœia, in regard to selection of articles, was characterized by the insertion of various articles, not in either the London or Edinburgh Pharmacopœias; and the omission of other articles contained in both. The following are the simples inserted:... Quercus marina (221)." (*Edinburgh Medical and Surgical Journal: Exhibiting A Concise View of the Latest and Most Important Discoveries in Medicine, Surgery, and Pharmacy.* 1810. Vol. Sixth. Second Edition.) (books.google.com/books?id=lnYBAA AAYAAJ&pg=PA221&lpg=PA221&dq=Quercus+marina&source=bl& ots=mAGfchkpsS&sig=fKtKwZXlwki9OcqBLJYDQSdduko&hl=en& ei=GNu0Ss-RA4at4gaKoaR8&sa=X&oi=book_result&ct=result&resn um=7#v=onepage&q=Quercus%20marina&f=false)

Although there is no reference in Jane Austen's text to Quercus Marina or any other specific sea-inhabiting plant, Mr. Thomas Parker does point out, in extolling the virtues of Sanditon over the inadequacies of other watering resorts, that on his beach a visitor will find

— no Weeds — no slimey rocks —

It seems, then, that if Mr. Parker was familiar with Dr. Russell's work, he specifically rejected this important part of the book. We can be certain that Quercus Marina, under any of its various nomenclatures, will never desecrate the waters of Sanditon.

Dr. Russell has one more section to support his passion for seawater. In a series of letters to and from medical colleagues, he shares his views and to some extent shifts his attention away from imbibing to swimming, or at least immersion.

Three Letters [and RR's replies] from Dr. Frewin, Dr. Wilmot, Dr. Lewis, to Richard Russell, M.D.

[Dr. Frewin to Dr. Russell]
I advised the Patient to take [various medications] twice a day, and to go to *Southamton* [sic], as soon as he could, both for the Benefit of drinking the Sea Water, and bathing there. When he came to *Southamton* he went into the Sea the 17th of *Nov.* in the Morning, and every Day afterwards.

Nov. 23. Having bathed four Times, he was much better, altho' the Symptoms encreased a little this Night, being near the full of the Moon.

Nov. 24. This Night, and every Day afterwards, he drank half a Pint of Sea Water, either when he went to Bed, or early in the Morning, and bathed every Day without Intermission.

Nov. 27. Things wore a better Face; the Gesticulations of his Hands and Fingers were less frequent, and he spoke better; but upon being tired of his Medicines, I advised him to drop them, and to trust to Sea Water and bathing only. (235–236)

. . .

Dec. 12. He grew dayly to have better Spirits; more Strength in his Limbs; and Facility in Speech; and upon the 9th of this Month, when there was a new Moon, there appeared no Spasms or Tremors.

Jan. 11. Upon being informed by a Letter that the Patient was entirely recovered, I advised him to return gradually to his former Manner of living, that is, to bathe first three Times a Week, then twice, and afterwards but once; to drink Sea Water not so often, and in less Quantities than before; not oftener than every other Night and Morning. (237)

. . .

[Dr. Russell to Dr. Frewin]

I shall therefore insert in this Epistle, what occurs to me on this Head, rather in the Manner they fall into my Mind, than in any exact Method, or with a View of giving any correct Things upon *cold Bathing*.

And in the first Place therefore, it will be needful to observe, that neither *warm* nor *cold Bathing* should be entered upon immediately after Eating or Drinking plentifully. The Ancients were so cautious of this, in *warm Bathing*, that they directed their Patients to abstain from Eating and Drinking, some Time after they came out of the Bath.... But in *cold Bathing* this Advantage is obtained by drinking a Glass of Sea Water, as soon as the Patient comes out of the Sea....

Great Quiet of Body and Mind should precede *cold Bathing*: the Parts should be as much at Rest as possible. (243–245)

. . .

As Sea Bathing is not so cold as some others are, I generally direct the Use of it early in the Morning; and in many Cases a Glass of Sea Water, as soon as the Patient comes out of the Bath; which passes off quick, and leaves the Person cheerful, and with a good Appetite. And instead of pouring Sea Water on the afflicted Parts, I generally advise a light Friction, with the *Quercus Marina*. (248–249) [Perhaps Diana Parker used Quercus Marina when she rubbed Mrs. Sheldon's Coachman's "Ancle."]

. . .

I have remarked in my Essay, that where *Sea Water* and *cold Bathing* failed, I thought it a sufficient Reason to try a quite contrary Method; and found, that after a Course of *tepid Bathing* and Asses Milk, I could cure many Diseases, which Sea Water, and cold Bathing, would not reach before. (252)

[Dr. Lewis to Dr. Russell]

There remained yet one, and only Remedy untried, which was *Sea Water*; the great Benefit of which our Surgeons are well acquainted with, in the Cure of scorbutic, and especially of scrophulous [scrofulous] Ulcers. The Patient therefore was removed to *Newport* in the *Isle of Wight*; not far from the Place where she lived. She drank Sea Water in the usual Manner, without any other Remedies except Asses Milk. (285) [Lady Denham may have a panacea, after all.]

Dr. Russell's long work ends with a document addressed to Dr. Richard Frewin about cures for scrofula.

OF
SOME ANTISTRUMOUS REMEDIES
USED BY THE ANTIENTS;
ALSO OF
TEPID BATHING, AND SEA BATHING:
AN EPISTOLARY DISSERTATION

TO
RICHARD FREWIN, M.D. (323)

. . .

Of Tepid Bathing. (362)

A Gentleman, aged 36, was sent me as a Patient from an eminent Physician in *London*.... When he got down to the Sea, he entered upon Sea Bathing immediately, and drank the Sea Water; but upon going into the Sea, the Eruptions were not only much teized [irritated], but became more general, and the Itching intolerable; his Clothes sticking to the Parts almost every where.

Under these Circumstances I was sent for to him, when he produced his Physician's Letter to me; in which he had wisely directed previous Evacuations [discharges]: but that Advice was either not known, or not followed by the Patient. Upon observing the Edges of the Eruptions to lye high on the Skin, and that they were very red, and the Fluxion [flowing] great, with large Incrustations on many Parts; I advised the laying aside Sea Bathing, and even the Water for some Time. (368–369)

. . .

I advised Bleeding [for a serious case of itching] once or twice, and that she should take the *vegetable Æthiops* [a charcoal prepared by the incineration in a covered crucible of the *fucus vesiculosus*, or common sea wrack], and *Lac. Sulphur*, with a medicated Whey, Night and Morning; and enter into the tepid Bath, as before described; with a third part of Whey or Buttermilk added to the Bath. By these Means the Irritation was taken off; and to recruit [reinvigorate] the Patient, I ordered warm Chicken or Mutton Broth to be drank Night and Morning, during the Time, she was in the Bath; which nourished her: and, as she was more at Ease, she slept better, and grew plump.... I then ventured upon Sea Water again, which soon took off the Fluxion; and the Cure was finished by Sea Bathing. (372–373)

[Having described an ideal locale eerily similar to that of Jane Austen's fictional Sanditon, Dr. Russell closes with the same caveat as used to conclude the aphorisms.]

> I distinguish Sea Bathing into *general*, and *topical*; by the former I mean, when the whole Body is immersed.... We will begin with the Consideration of the first: and that naturally suggests the Situation of the Place; which, I think, should be clean and neat, at some Distance from the opening of a River; that the Water may be as highly loaded with Sea Salt, and the other Riches of the Ocean, as possible, and not weakened by the mixing of fresh Water with it's Waves. In the next Place, one would choose the Shore to be sandy, and flat; for the Conveniency of going into the Sea in a Bathing Chariot. And lastly, that the Sea Shore should be bounded by lively Cliffs, and Downs; to add to the Chearfulness of the Place, and give the Person that has bathed an Opportunity of mounting on Horseback dry and clean; to pursue such Exercises, as may be advised by his Physician, after he comes out of the Bath.
>
> The Situation of the Place being premised; as to what regards the Patient, and his entering upon Sea Bathing, if he be an Invalid, he should not attempt it without advising with some skilful Person; as this Remedy, like others, may be misapplied. (379–380)
>
> > I am, Sir, &c.
> >
> > R. RUSSELL. [398]

Appendix D

Continuations

If it indeed be true that continuation is the sincerest form of flattery, then *Sanditon* has been subjected to more than its share of compliments.

Austen, Jane, and Another Lady (Marie Dobbs/Anne Telscombe). *Sanditon.* London: Peter Davies, 1975; Boston: Houghton Mifflin, 1975. The dust jacket on the hardcover edition shows a fort-like structure with various fashionably garbed ladies and gentlemen, two dogs at play, and a seaside vista with cliffs, homes, and some bathing machines at the edge of the water, whereas the paperback version offers four ladies, two of them standing and very elegantly dressed, along with two gentlemen in the high fashion of the day, serving as foreground to the view of the sea with bathing machines along the water's edge.

Baker, Helen. *The Brothers by Jane Austen and Another Lady.* UK: Lulu. com, 2009.

Barrett, Julia. *Jane Austen's* Charlotte: *Her Fragment of a Last Novel, Completed.* New York: M. Evans, 2000.

Cobbett, Alice. *Somehow Lengthened: A Development of* Sanditon. London: Ernest Benn Limited, 1932.

Eden, D.J. *Sanditon.* London: Minerva Press, 2002.

Hill, Reginald. *The Price of Butcher's Meat.* (UK title: *A Cure for All Diseases.*) New York: Harper Collins, 2008. A new take on life in Sandytown, featuring Andy Dalziel, Peter Pascoe, psychologist Charlotte Heywood, and Lady Daphne Denham.

Lefroy, Anna Austen. *Jane Austen's* Sanditon: *A Continuation by her Niece.* Transcribed, edited, and with an introduction by Mary Gaither Marshall. Chicago: The Chiron Press, 1983. An unfinished continuation.

There is some controversy over whether or not Jane Austen shared her intended plot with anyone. Whereas most critics believe that no one, including Anna Austen Lefroy, had any private information, David Hopkinson believes otherwise: "In this respect it [Anna Austen Lefroy's continuation] is a disappointment, the more so because James Edward Austen-Leigh had made an allusion in his *Memoir* of Jane Austen to what Cassandra might have told her nieces about the development of this story" (73). As Deirdre Le Faye has pointed out, Mary Gaither Marshall makes the same suggestion in her introduction to Anna Austen Lefroy's continuation:

> In her introduction to Anna's continuation Mary Marshall repeats several times the suggestion that Jane Austen probably discussed the plot of Sanditon with Anna and perhaps even asked her to complete the work along lines she had indicated.

> However, Anna's own comment on the original Sanditon text— "The story was too little advanced to enable one to form any idea of the plot"—together with her brother's [James Edward Austen-Leigh] similar statements—"It is more difficult to judge of the quality of a work so little advanced. It had received no name; there was scarcely any indication what the course of the story was to be, nor was any heroine yet perceptible"—show that this theory cannot be sustained. This ignorance of the plot of Sanditon is confirmed by a letter from Anna to James-Edward in the summer of 1862, by which time she had already written and abandoned her own attempt to complete the story:

> "Monk Sherborne
> Augt. 8th [postmarked "1862"]
> My dear Edward

I am much obliged for your letter, & especially for your devoting so much of it to 'Sanditon'. I agree with you that the M.S. as it stands is very inferior to the published works—and perhaps by no corrections could be worked up to an equality with any other 12 opening Chapters: for that I think the fairest sort of comparison. If publishing the M.S. can only gratify curiosity at the expense of the Authoresse's [sic] fame of course under ordinary circumstances it ought not to be attempted—but then comes the question of how entirely to prevent it."

. . .

It is apparent, therefore, that although Jane had to some extent discussed the characters of Sanditon with Anna in the early months of 1817, she had told neither her nor Cassandra how she intended to develop the plot. (1987: 57–59)

If we had evidence that Jane Austen discussed the plot of this novel with Anna, her continuation, however truncated, would be of inestimable value as at least giving us some notion of where the text was going. Writing in what sounds like an authoritative voice, Mary Gaither Marshall, in her introduction to Anna Austen Lefroy's continuation, maintains several times that the niece had directly from her aunt information about the manuscript shared with no one else.

Mary Gaither Marshall verbalizes her theory on different levels of conviction, concluding with an assurance that is not supported by existing evidence.

She might well have discussed her ideas for the continuation of the work with Lefroy. (xvi)

It is not inconceivable... that she wanted Lefroy to have *Sanditon* because the two women had discussed the future course of the work. (xxiv)

Perhaps Lefroy had promised Austen to continue *Sanditon*; perhaps, after Austen's death, Lefroy, in memoriam, recorded what her aunt had discussed concerning the novel. (xxv)

Perhaps she did not complete the novel because she had merely written down what her aunt had told her.... She might have added some of her own ideas to those which she and Austen had discussed. (xxvi)

Of course, if Austen had actually told her specifically how *Sanditon* was to continue, Lefroy was under the additional constraint of complying with her aunt's wishes. (xxxv)

Lefroy's work is of literary and historical significance as an indication of Jane Austen's own plans for the completion of her last work. (xliii)

In any event, Anna Lefroy adds so little of substance to the unfinished manuscript that what she knew or did not know hardly matters.

Measham, Donald. *Jane Austen Out of the Blue*. Morrisville, North Carolina: Lulu.com, 2006.

Shapiro, Juliette. *A Completion of* Sanditon, *Jane Austen's Unfinished Novel*. College Station, Texas: Virtualbookworm.com Publishing, Inc., 2003.

· · · · · · · · · · · · · · · ·

About continuations and completions:

Bander, Elaine. "The Significance of Jane Austen's Reference to 'Camilla' in 'Sanditon': A Note." *Notes and Queries* n.s. 25 (1978): 214–216.

Hopkinson, David. "Completions." *The Jane Austen Companion*, Ed. J. David Grey (Macmillan, 1986), 72–76.

James-Cavan, Kathleen Viola. *Readers as Writers: A Study of Austen's* The Watsons *and* Sanditon *and Their Completions by Subsequent Writers* (Queen's University dissertation, 1993).

Lambdin, Robert T. *A Companion to Jane Austen Studies*. Westport, Conn.: Greenwood Press, 2000, p. 257. Link+ Electronic Source.

Sachs, Marilyn. "The Sequels to Jane Austen's Novels." *The Jane Austen Companion*, Ed. J. David Grey (Macmillan, 1986), 374–376. (no mention of *Sanditon* continuations)

Appendix E

Errata in *Jane Austen Caught in the Act of Greatness*

Page 3

The cover illustration, by Hugh Thomson, reproduces the frontispiece to the edition of *Pride and Prejudice* published in London by George Allen in 1903 (from a copy of this edition in the collection of Mr. Christopher Viveash).
>
The cover illustration, by Hugh Thomson, reproduces the frontispiece to the edition of *Pride and Prejudice* published in London by George Allen in 1894 (Gilson E78) (from a copy of this edition in the collection of Mr. Christopher Viveash).

Page 141

Mr. H. Iooked very much astonished
>
Mr. H. looked very much astonished

Page 193

Heaven defend me from meeting such a
Man un-armed."
>
Heaven defend me from meeting such
a Man un-armed."

Page 197

& praise of that; but I saw what she was
about.
>
& praise of that; but I saw what she
was about.

Page 198

its' right to produce a great Impression —
seeing no rapturous astonishment
>
its' right to produce a great Impression — &
seeing no rapturous astonishment

Page 229

     No — it
acts on me like Poison and
w^d. entirely take away the use of my
right side,
>
     No — it
act on me like Poison and
w^d. entirely take away the use of my
right side,

Page 232

All that had the appearance of Incongruiety
>
All that had the appearance of Incongruiety

Page 236

The corner house ot the Terrace
>
The corner house of the Terrace

Page 243

never crossed by the foot of man

>

never crossed by the foot by man

Page 399

from "cried" to "Charlotte" in sentence 70.2

>

from "cried" to "Charlotte" in sentence 70.3

Bibliography

Allan, Jenny. Review of *Sanditon*, by Jane Austen and Another Lady. December 9, 2003. www.austenfans.com/Jane-Austen-Sequels/Sanditon.html

Altick, Richard D. *The English Common Reader: A Social History of the Mass Reading Public, 1800–1900*. Second Edition. Columbus, Ohio: Ohio State University Press, 1957, 1998.

_____. "Publishing." *A Companion to Victorian Literature & Culture*. Ed. Herbert F. Tucker. Chapter 20. Malden, Massachusetts: Blackwell, 1999.

Apperson, G[eorge].L[atimer]. *Jane Austen Dictionary*. New York: Haskell House, 1932, 1968.

Austen, Henry. "Biographical Notice of the Author." London, December 13/20, 1817. *Northanger Abbey and Persuasion*. London: John Murray, 1818. Pages iii–xix. London: Routledge/Thoemmes Press, 1994. A facsimile reprint.

Austen, Jane. "Advertisement, By the Authoress, to *Northanger Abbey*." *Northanger Abbey and Persuasion*. London: John Murray, 1818. Pages xxiii–xxiv. London: Routledge/Thoemmes Press, 1994. A facsimile reprint.

_____. *Fragment of a Novel (Sanditon)*. Ed. R.W. Chapman. Oxford: Clarendon Press, 1925. Dr. Chapman's transcription of the manuscript. The "cheap" edition contains no facsimiles; my copy of the second impression reads "saw" for "was" on the last line of p. 169. The "expensive" edition, limited to 250 copies on hand-made paper, contains a good facsimile of the first page of the manuscript; my copy, purchased in 1996 in Bath, bears no indication of its ownership history.

_____. *Jane Austen's "Sir Charles Grandison."* Ed. Brian C. Southam. Oxford: Clarendon Press, 1980.

_____. *Lady Susan, The Watsons, Sanditon*. Ed. Margaret Drabble. London: Penguin Books, 1974.

_____. *Letters*. Ed. Edward, Lord Brabourne. In two volumes. London: Richard Bentley & Son, 1884. My copy is signed "Mary Lascelles October 1934."

_____. *Letters*. Ed. R.W. Chapman. Second Edition. Oxford: Oxford University Press, 1952. Reprinted with corrections 1979. Supplanted by Deirdre Le Faye's edition but indispensable for the Indexes.

_____. *Letters*. Ed. Deirdre Le Faye. Third Edition. Oxford: Oxford University Press, 1997. An expanded version in paperback of the 1995 edition. All quotations from Jane Austen's correspondence are taken from this edition (*Letters*).

_____. *Northanger Abbey and Persuasion*, Volume I. 1817. London: Routledge/Thoemmes Press, 1994. A facsimile reprint. "Fascimile" quotations are taken from this text.

_____. *Northanger Abbey, Lady Susan, The Watsons, and Sanditon*. Ed. John Davie. Oxford: Oxford University Press, 1990.

_____. *Sanditon, An Unfinished Novel by Jane Austen*. Introduction by Brian C. Southam. Oxford: Oxford University Press, and London: The Scolar Press, 1975. A very good facsimile of the manuscript in King's College Library, Cambridge, but less faithful to the original than the frontispiece of Dr. Chapman's "expensive" 1925 edition, which in turn is but a pale version of the manuscript itself.

_____. *The Works of Jane Austen. The Oxford Illustrated Jane Austen*. Ed. R[obert].W[illiam]. Chapman. Volume I, *Sense and Sensibility*. Oxford: Oxford University Press, Third Edition, 1923, 1988. (*OIJA*–I)

_____. *The Works of Jane Austen. The Oxford Illustrated Jane Austen*. Ed. R.W, Chapman. Volume II, *Pride and Prejudice*. Oxford: Oxford University Press, Third Edition, 1923, 1988. (*OIJA*–II)

_____. *The Works of Jane Austen. The Oxford Illustrated Jane Austen*. Ed. R.W. Chapman. Volume III, *Mansfield Park*. Oxford: Oxford University Press, Third Edition, 1923, 1988. (*OIJA*–III)

_____. *The Works of Jane Austen. The Oxford Illustrated Jane Austen*. Ed. R.W. Chapman. Volume IV, *Emma*. Oxford: Oxford University Press, Third Edition, 1923, 1988. (*OIJA*–IV)

_____. *The Works of Jane Austen. The Oxford Illustrated Jane Austen*. Ed. R.W. Chapman. Volume V, *Northanger Abbey* and *Persuasion*. Oxford: Oxford University Press, Third Edition, 1923, 1988. (*OIJA*–V)

_____. *The Works of Jane Austen. The Oxford Illustrated Jane Austen*. Ed. R.W. Chapman. Revised by Brian C. Southam. Volume VI, *Minor Works*. Oxford: Oxford University Press, 1954, 1988. (*OIJA*–VI)

_____. *The Works of Jane Austen. Sanditon and Other Miscellanea*. Volume 7 but not indicated as such. Ed. R. Brimley Johnson. London: J. M. Dent & Sons, 1934. Illustrated by Maximilien Vox (Samuel-William-Théodore Monod, 1894–1974).

Austen, Jane, and Another Lady (Marie Dobbs/Anne Telscombe). *Sanditon*. London: Peter Davies, 1975. A continuation.

Austen-Leigh, James Edward. *A Memoir of Jane Austen by her Nephew J.E. Austen-Leigh, Vicar of Bray, Berks*. London: Richard Bentley, 1870.

_____. *A Memoir of Jane Austen by her Nephew J. E. Austen-Leigh*. Second Edition, 1871. Ed. R.W. Chapman. Oxford: Clarendon Press, 1926.

_____. *A Memoir of Jane Austen by her Nephew J.E. Austen-Leigh*. Third Edition. London: Richard Bentley and Son, 1872.

_____. *A Memoir of Jane Austen by her Nephew J.E. Austen-Leigh*. London: Macmillan and Co., 1906.

_____. *A Memoir of Jane Austen by her Nephew J.E Austen-Leigh*. Introduction by Fay Weldon. London: The Folio Society, 1989. "This text is taken from the second edition, as edited by R.W. Chapman for the Clarendon Press in 1926."

Austen-Leigh, Joan. "Forms of Address and Titles in Jane Austen." *Persuasions*, 12 (1990), 35–37.

Austen-Leigh, William, and Richard Arthur Austen-Leigh. *Jane Austen: Her Life and Letters, a Family Record*. London: Smith, Elder & Co., 1913.

Axelrad, Arthur M. "Jane Austen's 'Susan' Restored." *Persuasions*, 15 (1993), 44–45. www.jasna.org/persuasions/printed/number15/axelrad.htm

_____. "'Of which I avow myself the Authoress… J. Austen': The Jane Austen–Richard Crosby Correspondence." *Persuasions*, 16 (1994), 36–38. A corrected reading of this palimpsest. Includes a facsimile of Mr. Richard Crosby's letter.

_____. "Sir Edward's 'Ingenuity': A Corrected Reading in the *Sanditon* Manuscript." *Persuasions*, 17 (1995), 47–48.

_____. "No 'Shiney' Rocks at Sanditon; or, R.W. Chapman's Generosity Saves the Day." *Persuasions*, 19 (1997), 23–25.

_____. *Jane Austen Caught in the Act of Greatness: A Diplomatic Transcription and Analysis of the Two Manuscript Chapters of* Persuasion *and the Manuscript of* Sanditon. Introduction by David Gilson. Bloomington, Indiana: 1stBooks Library, 2003.

Bailey, John. *Introductions to Jane Austen*. London: Oxford University Press, 1931.

Baker, Helen. *The Brothers by Jane Austen and Another Lady*. UK: Lulu. com, 2009. A continuation.

Bander, Elaine. "*Sanditon, Northanger Abbey*, and *Camilla*: Back to the Future?" *Persuasions*, 19 (1997), 195–204.

Barrett, Julia. *Jane Austen's* Charlotte: *Her Fragment of a Last Novel, Completed*. New York: M. Evans, 2000. A continuation.

Barrett, Pam, Ed. *Insight Guide: England*. London: Insight Guides, 2000.

Batey, Mavis. *Jane Austen and the English Landscape*. London: Barn Elms, 1996.

Bell, David. "'Here & There & Every Where': Is Sidney Parker the Intended Hero of *Sanditon?*" *Persuasions*, 19 (1997), 160–166.

Benedict, Barbara M. "Sensibility by the Numbers: Austen's Work as Regency Popular Fiction." *Janeites: Austen's Disciples and Devotees*. Ed. Deidre Lynch. Princeton, New Jersey: Princeton University Press, 2000. Pages 63–86.

Benson, Mary Margaret. "Parasols & Gloves & Brooches & Circulating Libraries." *Persuasions*, 19 (1997), 205–210.

Benson, Robert. "Jane Goes to Sanditon: An Eighteenth Century Lady in a Nineteenth Century Landscape." *Persuasions*, 19 (1997), 211–218.

Beverley, Jo. "English Titles in the 18th and 19th Centuries." www.jobev.com/title.html

"Bile." *Wikipedia*.

Blackwell, Bonnie. "*Tristram Shandy* and the Theater of the Mechanical Mother." *English Literary History*, 68, 1 (2001), 81–133.

Bok, H. Abigail. "A Dictionary of Jane Austen's Life and Works." *The Jane Austen Companion*. Ed. J. David Grey. New York: Macmillan, 1986. Pages 399–493.

"Bonnets." www.hatsuk.com/hatsuk/hatsukhtml/bible/glossary.htm

Borer, Mary Cathcart. *An Illustrated Guide to London 1800*. New York: St. Martin's Press, 1988.

Bray, Joe. *The Female Reader in the English Novel: From Burney to Austen*. New York: Routledge, 2009.

Brodey, Inger Sigrun. "Resorting and Consorting with Strangers: Jane Austen's 'Multiculturalism.'" *Persuasions*, 19 (1997), 130–143.

Brown, Ivor. *Jane Austen and Her World*. London: Lutterworth Press, 1966.

Brown, Julia Prewitt. *Jane Austen's Novels: Social Change and Literary Form*. Cambridge, Massachusetts: Harvard University Press, 1979.

Brown, Lloyd W. *Bits of Ivory: Narrative Techniques in Jane Austen's Fiction*. Baton Rouge: Louisiana State University Press, 1973.

Brunström, Conrad. *William Cowper: Religion, Satire, Society*. Lewisburg: Bucknell University Press, 2004.

Buchan, William. *Domestic Medicine*. London, November 10, 1785. "Domestic Medicine, Chapter XVIII, Of Consumption." www.americanrevolution.org/medicine.html

Burns, Robert. *Poems and Songs*. Project Gutenberg.www.gutenberg.org/files/1279/1279-h/1279-h.htm

Bush, Douglas. *Jane Austen*. New York: Macmillan, 1975.

"Butler." *Wikipedia*.

Butler, Marilyn. *Jane Austen and the War of Ideas*. Oxford: Clarendon Press, 1975, 1987.

Cain, Del. "A Subject Guide to the Le Faye Edition of Jane Austen's Letters." Molland's Circulating Library. 2002. www.mollands.net/etexts/ltrindex/index.html

"Camberwell." *Wikipedia*.

The Cambridge Companion to Jane Austen. Eds. Edward Copeland and Juliet McMaster. Cambridge: Cambridge University Press, 1997.

The Cambridge Edition of the Works of Jane Austen: Later Manuscripts, Volume 8. Eds. Janet Todd and Linda Bree. New York: Cambridge University Press, 2008. Hereafter *CUPLM*.

Campbell, Thomas. *The Complete Poetical Works*. Ed. J. Logie Robertson. New York: Haskell House, 1907, 1968.

Cecil, Lord David. Foreword. *Jane Austen's "Sir Charles Grandison."* Ed. Brian C. Southam. Oxford: Clarendon Press, 1980.

_____. *A Portrait of Jane Austen*. London: Constable, 1978.

Chapman, R.W. *Jane Austen: Facts and Problems*. Oxford: Clarendon Press, 1948.

Cobbett, Alice. *Somehow Lengthened: A Development of* Sanditon. London: Ernest Benn, 1932. A continuation.

Collins, Irene. *Jane Austen and the Clergy*. London: The Hambledon Press, 1993.

Collins, Paul. "The Chamber-Horsemen of the Apocalpse." *Weekend Stubble*. February 2007. weekendstubble.blogspot.com/2007_02_01_archive.html

A Companion to Jane Austen Studies. Eds. Laura Cooner Lambdin and Robert Thomas Lamdin. Westport, Connecticut: Greenwood Press, 2000.

A Concordance to the Works of Jane Austen. Eds. Peter L. De Rose and Sterling W. McGuire. New York: Garland, 1982.

Cope, Sir Zachary. "Jane Austen's Last Illness." *British Medical Journal* (July 19, 1964), 182. www.orchard-gate.com/bmj.htm

Copeland, Edward. "*Sanditon* and 'my Aunt': Jane Austen and the National Debt." *Persuasions*, 19 (1997), 117–129.

_____. "Money." *Jane Austen in Context. The Cambridge Edition of the Works of Jane Austen*, Volume 9. Ed. Janet Todd. New York: Cambridge University Press, 2007. Pages 317–326.

Cowper, William. *Poetical Works*. Ed. H.S. Milford. London: Oxford University Press, 1967.

Craik, W[endy].A. *Jane Austen in Her Time*. London: Nelson, 1969.

Curry, Mary Jane. "A New Kind of Pastoral: Anti-Development Satire in *Sanditon*." *Persuasions*, 19 (1997), 167–176.

"Denham Family Crest and Name History." House of Names. www.houseofnames.com/xq/asp.fc/qx/denham-family-crest.htm

Deresiewicz, William. *Jane Austen and the Romantic Poets*. New York: Columbia University Press, 2004.

Devlin, D.D. *Jane Austen and Education*. London: Macmillan, 1975.

Douglas, Starr. "Martha Gunn: Fishwife & Queen of the Dippers." <u>www.</u> <u>sussex</u> women.org.uk.

Duckworth, Alistair M. *The Improvement of the Estate: A Study of Jane Austen's Novels*. Baltimore: The Johns Hopkins University Press, 1994.

Eden, D.J. *Sanditon*. London: Minerva Press, 2002. A continuation.

Erickson, Lee. "The Economy of Novel Reading: Jane Austen and the Circulating Library." *Studies in English Literature*, 30, 4 (Autumn 1990), 573–590.

Favret, Mary A. "Free and Happy: Jane Austen in America." *Janeites: Austen's Disciples and Devotees*. Ed. Deidre Lynch. Princeton, New Jersey: Princeton University Press, 2000. Pages 166–187.

Fergus, Jan. *Jane Austen: A Literary Life*. London: Macmillan, 1991.

Ferguson, Moira. *Colonialism and Gender Relations from Mary Wollstonecraft to Jamaica Kincaid: East Caribbean Connections*. New York: Columbia University Press, 1993.

Fetter'd or Free? British Woman Novelists, 1670–1815. Eds. Mary Anne Schofield and Cecilia Macheski. Athens, Ohio: Ohio University Press, 1986.

Firkins, O.W. *Jane Austen*. New York: Russell & Russell, 1920, 1965.

Flowers of Literature; FOR 1801 & 1802: OR CHARACTERISTIC SKETCHES OF HUMAN NATURE AND MODERN MANNERS. To which is added, A General View of Literature during that period. With Notes, Historical, Critical and Explanatory. By the Rev. F. Prevost, and F. Blagdon, Esq. (British Library, 12355. d.23). Published 1803.

Floyer, Sir John. *Psychrolousia or, The History of Cold Bathing: Both Ancient and Modern.* Also Dr. Edward Baynard, *Hot and Cold Baths.* London: William Innys, 1715. books.google.com/books?id=rgAAAAAAQA AJ&dq=psychrolousia&printsec=frontcover&source=bl&ots=1i50 HA2lO2&sig=sKlSBBSej7bHJStYODVrZTsa41g&hl=en&ei=AS b_StH3OJDYsgPvuvWdCg&sa=X&oi=book_result&ct=result&res num=1&ved=0CAgQ6AEwAA#v=onepage&q=&f=false

Ford, Susan Allen. "The Romance of Business and the Business of Romance: The Circulating Library and Novel-Reading in *Sanditon.*" *Persuasions,* 19 (1997), 177–186.

Forster, E[dward].M[organ]. "Jane Austen (The Six Novels, *Sanditon,* The Letters)." *The Nation and the Athenaeum,* 36 (March 21, 1925); reprinted in *Abinger Harvest.* London: Edward Arnold & Co., 1936. Pages 148–152.

Frantz, Sarah. "Jane Austen's Heroes and the Great Masculine Renunciation. (Miscellany)." *Persuasions,* 25 (2003), 165–175. A review with excerpts of a chapter, "Social Pessimism and the Self: Mackenzie and Graves," from Clive T. Probyn's book, below.

"French Doors." *Home Improvement.* homeimprovement.lovetoknow.com/ French_Doors

Fullerton, Susannah. "'We shall… call it Waterloo Crescent': Jane Austen's Art of Naming." *Persuasions,* 19 (1997), 103–116.

Galperin, William H. "Austen's Earliest Readers and the Rise of the Janeites." *Janeites: Austen's Disciples and Devotees.* Ed. Deidre Lynch. Princeton, New Jersey: Princeton University Press, 2000. Pages 87–114.

_____. *The Historical Austen.* Philadelphia: University of Pennsylvania Press, 2003.

Gard, Roger. *Jane Austen's Novels: The Art of Clarity.* New Haven: Yale University Press, 1992.

Gilson, David. *A Bibliography of Jane Austen.* Oxford: Clarendon Press, 1982, reprinted with corrections 1985.

_____. "Editions and Publishing History." *The Jane Austen Companion*. Ed. J. David Grey. New York: Macmillan, 1986. Pages 135–139.

_____. Introduction. Arthur M. Axelrad. *Jane Austen Caught in the Act of Greatness: A Diplomatic Transcription and Analysis of the Two Manuscript Chapters of* Persuasion *and the Manuscript of* Sanditon. Bloomington, Indiana: 1stBooks Library, 2003.

"Greatcoat." *Wikipedia*.

Halperin, John. "Jane Austen's Anti-Romantic Fragment: Some Notes on *Sanditon.*" *Tulsa Studies in Women's Literature*, 2, 2 (Autumn, 1983), 183–191.

_____. *The Life of Jane Austen*. Baltimore, Maryland: The Johns Hopkins University Press, 1984.

Hampson, John. *The English at Table*. London: Collins, 1946.

Handley, Graham. *Jane Austen*. New York: St. Martin's Press, 1992.

Hardwick, Michael. *A Guide to Jane Austen*. New York: Charles Scribner's Sons, 1973.

Harris, Jocelyn. *A Revolution Almost Beyond Expression: Jane Austen's* Persuasion. Newark: University of Delaware Press, 2007.

Harvey, Sir Paul. *The Oxford Companion to English Literature*. Third Edition. Oxford: The Clarendon Press, 1946, 1953.

"Hay Making." *UK Agriculture*. www.ukagriculture.com/crops/hay_making.cfm

Hill, Reginald. "Jane Austen: A Voyage of Discovery." *Persuasions*, 19 (1997), 77–92.

_____. *The Price of Butcher's Meat*. (UK title: *A Cure for All Diseases*.) New York: Harper Collins, 2008. A continuation.

Hindle, Wilfrid. *The Morning Post, 1772–1937: Portrait of a Newspaper*. Westport, Connecticut: Greenwood Press, 1937, 1974.

"The History of Tea." *Teacher Vision.* www.teachervision.fen.com/asia/ resource/10364.html?detoured=1

"The History of Women's Hats." *Vintage Fashion Guild.* www. vintagefashionguild.org/content/view/604/55/

Honan, Park. *Jane Austen: Her Life.* New York: Fawcett Columbine, 1987.

"The Honourable Society of Gray's Inn." www.graysinn.info/index. php?option=com_content&task=section&id=1&Itemid=659

Hopkinson, David. "Completions." *The Jane Austen Companion.* Ed. J. David Grey. New York: Macmillan, 1986. Pages 72–76.

Howell, Sarah. *The Seaside.* London: Cassell & Collier Macmillan, 1974.

Huey, Peggy. "Jane Austen's *Sanditon.*" *A Companion to Jane Austen Studies.* Eds. Laura Cooner Lambdin and Robert Thomas Lamdin. Westport, Conn.: Greenwood Press, 2000. Pages 253–258.

Jane Austen and Discourses of Feminism. Ed. Devoney Looser. New York: St. Martin's Press, 1995.

"Jane Austen." *BBC America Shop.* www.bbcamericashop.com/boutiques/ jane-austen.html

The Jane Austen Companion. Ed. J. David Grey. New York: Macmillan, 1986.

Jane Austen: The Critical Heritage. Ed. Brian C. Southam. Volume 1, 1811– 1870. New York: Routledge & Kegan Paul, 1968. Revised Edition, 1986.

Jane Austen: The Critical Heritage. Ed. Brian C. Southam. Volume 2, 1870– 1940. New York: Routledge & Kegan Paul, 1987.

Jane Austen: New Perspectives, Ed. Janet Todd. New York: Holmes & Meier, 1983.

Jane Austen in Context. The Cambridge Edition of the Works of Jane Austen, Volume 9. Ed. Janet Todd. New York: Cambridge University Press, 2007.

"Jane Austen's Letters: Facts and Fictions." The Free Library by Farlex. www.thefreelibrary.com/Jane+Austen's+Letters:+facts+and+fictions.-a0147792429

Jane Austen's Manuscript Letters in Facsimile. Ed. Jo Modert. Carbondale: Southern Illinois University Press, 1990.

Jane Austen Today. Ed. Joel Weinsheimer. Athens, Georgia: The University of Georgia Press, 1975.

Jarvis, William. *Jane Austen and Religion.* Stonesfield Witney, Oxon: The Stonesfield Press, 1996.

Jenkins, Elizabeth. *Jane Austen.* New York: Grosset & Dunlap, 1949.

Jenkyns, Richard. *A Fine Brush on Ivory: An Appreciation of Jane Austen.* Oxford: Oxford University Press, 2004.

Johnson, Claudia L. *Jane Austen: Women, Politics, and the Novel.* Chicago: University of Chicago Press, 1988.

Johnson, Paul. "Jane Austen, Coleridge and Geopolitics." *The Jane Austen Society* (delivered at AGM, Chawton, Saturday, July 20, 1996). Report for 1996. Pages 50–60.

Johnson, R. Brimley. *Jane Austen.* London: Sheed & Ward, 1927.

Jones, Amanda. "Brighton." Jane Austen Society of Australia. July 19, 2003. www.jasa.net.au/seaside/Brighton.htm

_____."Jane Austen and Sport." *Sensibilities*, December 2000. A paper delivered to the Jane Austen Society of Australia June meeting. www.jasa.net.au/sensextdc00.htm

Jordan, Elaine. "Jane Austen Goes to the Seaside: *Sanditon*, English Identity and the 'West Indian' Schoolgirl." *The Postcolonial Jane Austen.* Eds. You-me Park and Rajeswari Sunder Rajan. London: Routledge, 2000. Pages 29–55.

Keith, Rhonda. "Jane Austen and Shakespeare." *Tulsa Studies In Women's Literature*, 2, 1 (Spring 1983), 99.

Keller, James R. "Austen's *Northanger Abbey*: A Bibliographic Study." *A Companion to Jane Austen Studies*. Eds. Laura Cooner Lambdin and Robert Thomas Lamdin. Westport, Connecticut: Greenwood Press, 2000. Pages 131–143.

Kirkham, Margaret. *Jane Austen, Feminism and Fiction*. New York: Methuen, 1983, 1986.

"KM History." Kent Online, The *Kent Messenger* Group Website. 2008. www.kentonline.co.uk/km/history/

Knox-Shaw, Peter. *Jane Austen and the Enlightenment*. New York: Cambridge University Press, 2004.

Kuwahara, Kuldip Kaur. "*Sanditon*, Empire, and the Sea: Circles of Influence, Wheels of Power." *Persuasions*, 19 (1997), 144–148.

"Lace." *New Advent Catholic Encyclopedia*. www.newadvent.org/cathen/08729b.htm

Lamont, Claire. "Domestic Architecture." *Jane Austen in Context. The Cambridge Edition of the Works of Jane Austen*, Volume 9. Ed. Janet Todd. New York: Cambridge University Press, 2007. Pages 225–233.

Lane, Maggie. *Jane Austen's England*. London: Robert Hale, 1986.

Laski, Marghanita. *Jane Austen*. London: Thames and Hudson, 1969, 1975.

Lauber, John. *Jane Austen*. New York: Twayne Publishers, 1993.

"Laudanum, and Its Many Uses." *The Victorian Era*. March 2, 2008. 19thcentury.wordpress.com/2008/03/02/laudanum/

Laudermilk, Sharon H., and Teresa L. Hamlin. *The Regency Companion*. New York: Garland, 1989.

Lauste, L.W. MD, FRCS. "Dr. Richard Russell 1687–1759." *Proceedings of the Royal Society of Medicine*, 67, 5 (May 1974), 327–330. www.pubmedcentral.nih.gov/articlerender.fcgi?artid=1645547

Leavis, Queenie Dorothy (Roth). "A Critical Theory of Jane Austen's Writings," *Scrutiny* X, 1 (June 1941), 61–87; "A Critical Theory of Jane Austen's Writings (II): 'Lady Susan' into 'Mansfield Park,'" *Scrutiny* X, 2 (October 1941), 114–142; "A Critical Theory of Jane Austen's Writings (II): 'Lady Susan' into 'Mansfield Park,'" *Scrutiny* X, 3 (January 1942), 272–294; "A Critical Theory of Jane Austen's Writings (III): The Letters," *Scrutiny* XII, 2 (Spring 1944), 104–119.

Le Faye, Deirdre. *A Family Record*. Cambridge: Cambridge University Press, 1989. Revised and enlarged issue of William Austen-Leigh and Richard Arthur Austen-Leigh, *Jane Austen: Her Life and Letters, a Family Record*.

_____. "Great Girls." Correspondence, January 5, 2010.

_____. *Jane Austen: The World of Her Novels*. London: Frances Lincoln, Ltd., 2002.

_____. "Letters." *Jane Austen in Context. The Cambridge Edition of the Works of Jane Austen*, Volume 9. Ed. Janet Todd. New York: Cambridge University Press, 2007. Pages 33–40.

_____. "Sanditon: Jane Austen's Manuscript and Her Niece's Continuation." *The Review of English Studies*, New Series, 38, 149 (February 1987), 56-61.

Lefroy, Anna Austen. *Jane Austen's* Sanditon: *A Continuation by her Niece*. Transcribed, edited, and with an introduction by Mary Gaither Marshall. Chicago: The Chiron Press, 1983. My copy is number 228 of 500. An unfinished continuation.

_____. "Reminiscences of Aunt Jane." In *Jane Austen's* Sanditon, Pages 155–176.

Liddell, Robert. *The Novels of Jane Austen*. London: Longmans, 1963.

"Limehouse." *Online Encylopædia Britannica*.

List of characters in *Sanditon*. Republic of Pemberley site. www.pemberley.com/bin/regency/janames/janames.cgi?category=Sanditon

Litz, A. Walton. "'A Development of Self': Character and Personality in Jane Austen's Fiction." *Jane Austen's Achievement.* Ed. Juliet McMaster. London: Macmillan, 1976.

Lock, F.P. Review of *Sanditon: An Unfinished Novel,* Reproduced in Facsimile from the Manuscript. With an Introduction by B.C. Southam. 1975. *The Yearbook of English Studies,* 7 (1977), 278–279.

Lyall, Sutherland. *Dream Cottages: From Cottage Ornée to Stockbroker Tudor, Two Hundred Years of the Cult of the Vernacular.* London: Robert Hale, Ltd., 1988.

Lynch, Deidre, ed. *Janeites: Austen's Disciples and Devotees.* Princeton, New Jersey: Princeton University Press, 2000.

MacDonagh, Oliver. *Jane Austen: Real and Imagined Worlds.* New Haven, Connecticut: Yale University Press, 1991.

"The Man of Feeling." *Wikipedia.*

Mandal. A[nthony].A. "Making Austen Mad: Benjamin Crosby and the Non-Publication of *Susan.*" *The Review of English Studies,* 57, 231 (2006): 507–525.

Marsden, Christopher. *The English at the Seaside.* London: Collins, 1947.

Marshall, Mary Gaither. "Jane Austen's Legacy: Anna Austen Lefroy's Manuscript of *Sanditon.*" *Persuasions,* 19 (1997), 226–228.

"Martha Gunn." www.womenofbrighton.co.uk/marthagunn.htm (For "1776–1815" read "1726–1815")

McMaster, Juliet. "Education." *The Jane Austen Companion.* Ed. J. David Grey. New York: Macmillan, 1986. Pages 140–142.

_____."The Watchers of *Sanditon.*" *Persuasions,* 19 (1997), 149–159.

Measham, Donald. *Jane Austen Out of the Blue.* Morrisville, North Carolina: Lulu.com, 2006. A continuation.

Miller, Angela L. "Nature's Transformations: The Meaning of the Picnic Theme in Nineteenth-Century American Art." *Winterthur Portfolio,* 24, 2/3 (Summer–Autumn 1989), 113–138.

Miller, D.A. *Narrative and Its Discontents: Problems of Closure in the Traditional Novel.* Princeton: Princeton University Press, 1981.

"Money & Coins." *English Weights & Measures.* home.clara.net/brianp/money.html

Montgomery, James. *The Poetical Works.* London: Frederick Warne and Co., 1880?

Moody, Ellen. "An Attempt at a Calendar and a List of the Letters in *Sanditon.*" www.jimandellen.org/austen/sanditon.calendar.html

_____. "Oxford's *Northanger Abbey, Lady Susan, The Watsons* and *Sanditon.*" *Media Reviews: Jane Austen's Works.* The Jane Austen Centre. www.janeausten.co.uk/magazine/page.ihtml?pid=738&step=4

_____. *Sanditon,* Ch. 4: "One loves to look at an old friend..." Online commentary, April 7, 1998. lists.mcgill.ca/scripts/wa.exe?A2=ind9804a&L=austen-l&P=23714

_____. "The Sands of Time." *Jane Austen's Work: Jane Austen's Books and Characters.* The Jane Austen Centre. www.janeausten.co.uk/magazine/page.ihtml?pid=187&step=4

Mudrick, Marvin. *Jane Austen: Irony as Defense and Discovery.* Princeton, New Jersey: Princeton University Press, 1952.

Mukherjee, Meenakshi. *Jane Austen.* London: Macmillan, 1991.

Mullen, John. "Psychology." *Jane Austen in Context. The Cambridge Edition of the Works of Jane Austen,* Volume 9. Ed. Janet Todd. New York: Cambridge University Press, 2007. Pages 377–386.

Nigro, Jeffrey A. "Estimating Lace and Muslin: Dress and Fashion in Jane Austen and Her World." *Persuasions* 23 (2001), 50–62.

Nouveau Dictionnaire Étymologique et Historique. Paris: Librairie Larousse, 1971.

Olsen, Kirstin. *All Things Austen: An Encyclopedia of Austen's World.* Westport, Connecticut: Greenwood Press, 2005.

"On the Tea Table." With beautiful illustrations of tables and serving pieces. www.georgianindex.net/Tea/ttable.html

Page, Norman. *The Language of Jane Austen*. Oxford: Basil Blackwell, 1972.

Park, You-me, and Rajeswari Sunder Rajan, Eds. *The Postcolonial Jane Austen*. London: Routledge, 2000.

"A Passion for Hot Chocolate." The Jane Austen Centre. *Regency Recipes: Beverages.* www.janeausten.co.uk/magazine/index. ihtml?pid=144&step=4.

Peacock, Thomas Love. *Headlong Hall and Nightmare Abbey*. London: Macmillan and Co., Ltd., 1927. Introduction by George Saintsbury.

_____. *Headlong Hall. The Works of Thomas Love Peacock*, Volume One. The Halliford Edition of the Works of Thomas Love Peacock. Eds. H.F.B. Brett-Smith and C.E. Jones. New York: AMS Press, 1967.

Penglase, Joanna. "'The poor girls & their teeth!' a Visit to the Dentist." www.jasa.net.au/london/dentist.htm

Phillipps, Kenneth C. *Jane Austen's English*. London: Andre Deutsch, 1970.

Pilcher, Donald. *The Regency Style 1800 to 1830*. London: B.T. Batsford, 1947.

Pinion, F(rank).B. *A Jane Austen Companion*. London: Macmillan, 1973.

"Poetic Pain: The Life of William Cowper." The Jane Austen Centre, Online Magazine: *Biographies: Authors, Artists and Vagrants.* www.janeausten. co.uk/magazine/page.ihtml?pid=414&step=4

Pool, Daniel. *What Jane Austen Ate and Charles Dickens Knew*. New York: Simon & Schuster, 1993.

Poplawski, Paul. *A Jane Austen Encyclopedia*. Westport, Connecticut: Greenwood Press, 1998.

"Post Chaise." *Britannica Online Encyclopedia.* www.britannica.com/ EBchecked/topic/472040/post-chaise

Power, Ted. "Dr. Richard Russell, MD, FRS." www.btinternet.com/~ted. power/rp0208.html

Priestley, J.B. *The Prince of Pleasure and His Regency 1811–20*. London: Sphere Books, 1969.

Probyn, Clive T. *English Fiction of the Eighteenth Century 1700–1789*. Essex: Longman, 1987.

Quaintance, Richard. "Salutes and Satire in Jane Austen's Characters' Sense of 'Nature.'" *Persuasions*, 19 (1997), 219–225.

Rawlence, Guy. *Jane Austen*. London: Duckworth, 1934.

Ray, Joan Klingel. *Jane Austen for Dummies*. Hoboken, New Jersey: Wiley, 2006.

Redmond, Luanne Bethke. "Discussion of Lady Denham's fortune in *Sanditon*." Email exchange June/July 2008.

_____. "Land, Law and Love." *Persuasions*, 11 (1989), 46–52.

Rees, Joan. *Jane Austen: Woman and Writer*. New York: St. Martin's Press, 1976.

"The Regency Period Glossary." *JaneAusten.org.* www.janeausten.org/glossary.asp

Rhydderch, David. *Jane Austen: Her Life and Art*. London: Jonathan Cape, 1932.

"Robert Burns." *Wikipedia.*

Robert Burns: The Critical Heritage. Ed. Donald A. Low. London and Boston: Routledge & Kegan Paul, 1974.

Sabor, Peter, and Kathleen James-Cavan. "Anna Lefroy's Continuation of *Sanditon*: Point and Counterpoint." *Persuasions*, 19 (1997), 229–243.

Sacco, Teran Lee. *A Transcription and Analysis of Jane Austen's Last Work, Sanditon*. Lewiston, New York: The Edwin Mellen Press, 1995. A diplomatic transcription of B.C. Southam's facsimile of *Sanditon*.

Sachs, Marilyn. "Jane Austen and Chicken Soup." *Persuasions*, 19 (1997), 244–248.

Sales, Roger. *Jane Austen and Representations of Regency England.* New York: Routledge, 1994.

Salih, Sara. "The Silence of Miss Lambe: *Sanditon* and the Fictions of 'Race' in the Abolition Era." *Eighteenth Century Fiction,* 18, 3 (2006), 329–353. muse.jhu.edu/journals/eighteenth_century_fiction/v018/18.3salih.html

"Samphire." *Wikipedia.*

"Sanditon." *Wikipedia.*

Schapera, I(saac). *Kinship Terminology in Jane Austen's Novels.* London: Royal Anthropological Institute of Great Britain and Ireland, Occasional Paper No. 33, 1977.

Scott, Peter James Malcolm. *Jane Austen: A Reassessment.* Totowa, New Jersey: Barnes & Noble Books, 1982.

Selwyn, David. "Consumer Goods." *Jane Austen in Context. The Cambridge Edition of the Works of Jane Austen,* Volume 9. Ed. Janet Todd. New York: Cambridge University Press, 2007. Pages 215–224.

—————————. *Jane Austen and Leisure.* London: The Hambledon Press, 1999.

"1795–1820 in Fashion." *Wikipedia.* en.wikipedia.org/wiki/1795–1820_in_fashion

Shapard, David M. *The Annotated* Pride and Prejudice. New York: Anchor Books, 2004.

Shapiro, Juliette. *A Completion of* Sanditon: *Jane Austen's Unfinished Novel.* College Station, Texas: Virtual Bookworm, 2003. A continuation.

The Shell Guide to Britain. Ed. Geoffrey Boumphrey. New York: E.P. Dutton, 1969.

Shields, Carol. *Jane Austen.* New York: Viking Penguin, 2001.

Smith, D.J. *Discovering Horse Drawn Carriages.* Aylesbury: Shire Publications, 1974.

Smith, Sherwood. Conversation. December 25, 2009.

Smith, Sydney. *Selected Letters.* Ed. Nowell C. Smith. Oxford: Oxford University Press, 1981.

Smithers, David Waldron. *Jane Austen in Kent.* Westerham, Kent: Hurtwood Publications, 1981.

Smollett, Tobias. *The Expedition of Humphry Clinker.* 1771. www.gasl.org/refbib/Smollett__Humphry_Clinker.pdf

Southam, Brian C. *Jane Austen's Literary Manuscripts: A Study of the Novelist's Development through the Surviving Papers.* London: Oxford University Press, 1964.

_____. "Sanditon." *The Jane Austen Companion.* Ed. J. David Grey. New York: Macmillan, 1986. Pages 369–373.

_____. "The Seventh Novel." *Jane Austen's Achievement.* Ed. Juliet McMaster. London: Macmillan, 1976. Pages 1–26.

Spence, Jon. *Becoming Jane Austen.* London and New York: Hambledon and London, 2003.

Stokes, Myra. *The Language of Jane Austen.* London: Macmillan Press, 1991.

Surr, Thomas Skinner. *The Magic of Wealth.* London: G. Cadell and W. Davies, 1815. Three volumes. University of Minnesota Library.

Sutherland, Eileen. "'A little sea-bathing would set me up forever': The History and Development of the English Seaside Resorts." *Persuasions,* 19 (1997), 60–76.

Sutherland, Kathryn. "Chronology of Composition and Publication." *Jane Austen in Context. The Cambridge Edition of the Works of Jane Austen,* Volume 9. Ed. Janet Todd. New York: Cambridge University Press, 2007. Pages 12–22.

Tanner, Tony. *Jane Austen.* London: Macmillan, 1986.

Tave, Stuart M. *Some Words of Jane Austen.* Chicago: University of Chicago Press, 1973.

Taylor, Irene. "Afterword: Jane Austen Looks Ahead." *Fetter'd or Free? British Women Novelists, 1670–1815.* Eds. Mary Anne Schofield and Cecilia Macheski. Athens: Ohio University Press, 1986. Pages 426–433.

Tompkins, Joyce Marjorie Sanxter. *The Popular Novel in England, 1770–1800.* London: Constable & Company, Ltd., 1932.

"Tonbridge." *Wikipedia.*

"Tonbridge History." "Jane Austen's Tonbridge Relations." www.tonbridgehistory.org.uk/people/the-austens.htm

Tucker, George Holbert. *A Goodly Heritage: A History of Jane Austen's Family.* Manchester: Carcanet New Press, 1983.

_____. *Jane Austen: The Woman. Some Biographical Insights.* New York: St. Martin's Press, 1994.

Tucker, Susie I. *Protean Shape: A Study in Eighteenth-Century Vocabulary and Style.* London: The Athlone Press, 1967.

_____. Review of Norman Page, *The Language of Jane Austen.* Oxford: Blackwell, 1972. *The Review of English Studies,* New Series, 24, 95 (August 1973), 359–361.

Tuite, Clara. "Decadent Austen Entails: Forster, James, Firbank, and the 'Queer Taste' of *Sanditon* (comp. 1817, publ. 1925)." *Janeites: Austen's Disciples and Devotees.* Ed. Deidre Lynch. Princeton, New Jersey: Princeton University Press, 2000. Pages 115–139.

Vic. "Seaside Fashion, Regency Style." *Jane Austen's World* (August 14, 2009) janeaustensworld.wordpress.com/2009/08/14/seaside-fashion-regency-style-2/

Vic (Ms. Place). "Tea in the Regency Era." *Jane Austen's World* (December 9, 2007). janeaustensworld.wordpress.com/2007/12/09/tea-in-the-regency-era/

The Victorian Literary Studies Archive Hyper-Concordance. victorian.lang.nagoya-u.ac.jp/concordance/austen/

Viveash, Chris. "Sydney Smith, Jane Austen, and Henry Tilney. (Miscellany)." *Persuasions*, 24 (2002), 251–255.

Waldemar, Linda. Review, *Sanditon*, by Jane Austen and Another Lady. November 5, 1997. www.austenfans.com/Jane-Austen-Sequels/Sanditon.html

Watney, Marylian. *The Elegant Carriage*. London: J.A. Allen, 1961, Revised Edition, 1979.

_____. *Royal Cavalcade*. London: J.A. Allen, 1987.

"The Wealth of Nations." *Wikipedia*. en.wikipedia.org/wiki/The_Wealth_ ofNations

Whalley, Thomas Sedg(e)wick. *Journals and Correspondence*. Volume 2. London: Richard Bentley, 1863. books.google.com/books?id=FD8OAAAAIAAJ&printsec=frontcove r&source=gbs_navlinks_s#v=onepage&q=&f=false

White, K.G. "Jane Austen and Addison's Disease: an Unconvincing Diagnosis." *Med Humanities* 2009. mh.bmj.com/content/35/2/98

White, Laura Mooneyham. "Jane Austen and the Marriage Plot: Questions of Persistence." *Jane Austen and Discourses of Feminism*. Ed. Devoney Looser. New York: St. Martin's Press, 1995. Pages 71–86.

Wiesenfarth, Joseph. *The Errand of Form: An Assay of Jane Austen's Art*. New York: Fordham University Press, 1967.

Wilks. Brian. *Jane Austen*. London: Hamlyn, 1978.

Williams, Michael. *Jane Austen: Six Novels and Their Methods*. London: Macmillan, 1986.

Wiltshire, John. *Jane Austen and the Body: "The Picture of Health."* Cambridge: Cambridge University Press, 1992.

_____. "Sickness and Silliness in *Sanditon*." *Persuasions*, 19 (1997), 93–102.

Wood, Tim. *The Georgians*. Bristol: Paperbird, 1991.

Woodforde, The Reverend James. *The Diary of a Country Parson*. Ed. John Beresford. Five volumes. Oxford: Clarendon Press, 1924–1931.

Lightning Source UK Ltd.
Milton Keynes UK
UKHW011444010221
378052UK00001B/28